"JEWEL. YOU ARE SEER-BORN. IT IS TIME THAT YOU UNDERSTAND WHAT THAT MEANS."

The mists were giving way to flat plains.

"I will tell you. If the seer-born choose to do so, they could see the past of a man almost as clearly as they could see the shadows he cast. The future is a place of possibility; the past is fixed. The road between the two is often connected, and once the path is found, it can be followed. The Oracle invited you to walk upon older roads than could be found in even the Stone Deepings. Walk them, Jewel, and in the end, I will be able to hide nothing."

She felt cold. Looked down at the hands that had slowly fallen to her sides, and saw, cupped in them, a round, glowing orb. She blinked; her hands were empty.

But the mist had given way in a sudden gust of wind, pulled like curtains to either side.

Beneath her, extending for as far as she could see, lay a sea of tents. She saw horses, haltered, impatient; saw men, some with spears, some with swords.

"Where are we?"

"We are, if I guess correctly, at the border of the Terrean of Raverra. And this is some part of the army the young kai Leonne faces."

Avandar caught her hand in his. He began to walk toward the body of the army. . . .

**The Finest in Fantasy from
MICHELLE WEST:**

THE SUN SWORD:
THE BROKEN CROWN (Book One)
THE UNCROWNED KING (Book Two)
THE SHINING COURT (Book Three)
SEA OF SORROWS (Book Four)
THE RIVEN SHIELD (Book Five)
THE SUN SWORD (Book Six)
(available January 2004)

THE SACRED HUNT:
HUNTER'S OATH (Book One)
HUNTER'S DEATH (Book Two)

THE
RIVEN SHIELD

The Sun Sword: Book Five

Michelle West

DAW BOOKS, INC.

DONALD A. WOLLHEIM, FOUNDER

375 Hudson Street, New York, NY 10014

ELIZABETH R. WOLLHEIM
SHEILA E. GILBERT
PUBLISHERS

http://www.dawbooks.com

First Printing, July 2003
1 2 3 4 5 6 7 8 9

DAW TRADEMARK REGISTERED
U.S. PAT. OFF. AND FOREIGN COUNTRIES
—MARCA REGISTRADA.
HECHO EN U.S.A.

PRINTED IN THE U.S.A.

*This is for Terry Pearson,
who should know why.*

ACKNOWLEDGMENTS

As always, I owe Sheila Gilbert a debt for her patience and her understanding. Debra Euler, called DAW's Valkyrie by Tanya Huff, provided timely reminders and her particular brand of encouragement. Alis Rasmussen read the early chapters of this book when I despaired of it *being* a book, and as always provided insight and advice. Graydon Saunders also provided a different kind of insight, meant for a later work, which did help for this one.

And Thomas, Daniel, and Ross patiently gave up their time while I wrote, complained, tore out my hair, and wrote more.

Author's Note

I know that I told a great many of you that I was working on the *last* book of *The Sun Sword*—and this was completely true.

A bit about how I work. I don't have a formal outline, or rather, I have several, and none of them are binding; they change with time. I approach my novels as if they were a collection of people I grow, with time, to know, and the motivations of those people change everything, time and again.

I have *never* been good at determining the length of a given story. This has led to much good-natured humor at my expense, and because it's deserved, I accept it.

So . . . I *was* working on the last book of *The Sun Sword*. Family matters brought the book to a screeching halt in January of 2002, as they often do. But we recovered, and the book recovered, and I continued to write it. At the worldcon in San Jose, I was still telling people that this was the last book.

But about a month after I returned home, I realized that I was actually on page 1700 of the manuscript, and by best guess—see above re: me and length—it was going to come in at 2000 pages. So I phoned the DAW offices, and reached Sean Fodera, the rights manager (the wonderful thing about the DAW offices is that you never quite know *who* you're going to reach, but it's always a pleasure, regardless), and I said, "Sean, I think this is going to go a bit on the long side." He laughed and said, "So what else is new?" And after several minutes of ribbing, which I won't recap here, he got down to business and asked, "How long is long?"

And I said, "Ummm, at least 2000 manuscript pages." (Writers are not, thank god, paid for conversation).

All laughter vanished at that point, and he said, "Now you have a problem. You'd better talk to Sheila."

So I did, and at length, and it was decided that instead of attempting to hack 600 pages out of the book, we would split it.

Which is a good thing, given that I'm now at nearly 2100 pages, and although the end *is* definitely in sight, it's not there yet.

I want to apologize to all of my readers for this. I didn't intend to mislead anyone, and I didn't intend to disappoint; to shorten the book would have been to carve out whole characters, and at this point in the story, it seemed to serve no one's purpose. *The Sun Sword* is almost finished, and it will *definitely* be the concluding volume; I hope that you don't find *The Riven Shield*, the first half of that longer work, a disappointment because it's not quite the end.

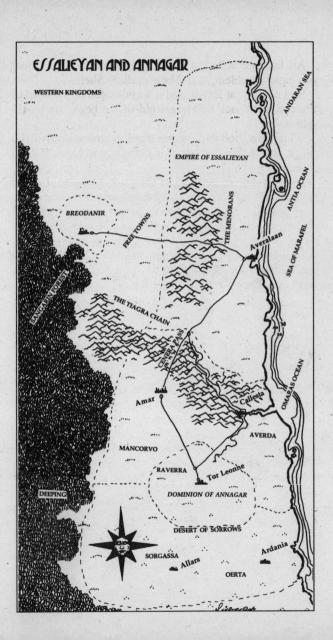

Annagarian Ranks

Tyr'agar	Ruler of the Dominion
Tyr'agnate	Ruler of one of the five Terreans of the Dominion
Tyr	The *Tyr'agar* or one of the four *Tyr'agnate*
Tyran	Personal bodyguard (oathguard) of a *Tyr*
Tor'agar	A noble in service to a *Tyr*
Tor'agnate	A noble in service to a *Tor'agar;* least of noble ranks
Tor	A *Tor'agar* or *Tor'agnate*
Toran	Personal bodyguard (oathguard) of a *Tor*
Ser	A clansman
Serra	The primary wife and legitimate daughters of a clansman
kai	The holder or first in line to the clan title
par	The brother of the first in line; the direct son of the title holder

Dramatis Personae

ESSALIEYAN

AVANTARI (The Palace)
The Royals
> *King Reymalyn:* The Justice-born King
> *King Cormalyn:* The Wisdom-born King
> *Princess Mirialyn ACormaris:* Daughter of Queen Marieyan and King Cormalyn

The Astari
> *Duvari:* The Lord of the Compact; leader of the Astari, the protectors of the Kings
> *Devon ATerafin:* Member of the Astari and of House Terafin
> *Gregori ATerafin:* The second of the Astari to take the Terafin oath

The Hostages
> *Serra marlena en'Leonne:* Valedan's mother; born a slave but granted honorific "Serra" because her son has been recognized and claimed as legitimate
> *Ser Kyro di'Lorenza (Sorgassa):* The oldest of the hostages

Imperial Army
> *The Eagle:* **Commander Bruce Allen**—commands the First Army
> *The Hawk:* **Commander Berriliya**—commands the Second Army
> *The Kestrel:* **Commander Kalakar**—commands the Third Army and the Ospreys

THE TEN

KALAKAR
Ellora: The Kalakar
Verrus Korama: Her closest friend and adjutant
Verrus Vernon Loris: Friend and counselor
The Ospreys
Primus Duarte: Leader
Alexis: (Sentrus or Decarus)
Auralis: (Sentrus or Decarus)
Fiara: (Sentrus)
Cook: (Sentrus)
Sanderton: (Decarus)
Kiriel di'Ashaf

BERRILIYA
Devran: The Berriliya

TERAFIN
Amarais Handernesse ATerafin: The Terafin
Morretz: Her domicis
Jewel Markess ATerafin: Part of her House Council; also seer-born; her den are:
>*Finch*
>*Teller*
>*Angel:* He is not ATerafin
>*Carver*
>*Arann:* House Guard
>*Jester*
>*Daine:* Healer-born
>*Ellerson:* He serves the den as domicis
Avandar Gallais: Also known as Viandaran; he is Jewel's domicis
The Winter King: Great stag, taken from the Stone Deepings
Lord Celleriant of the Green Deepings: Compelled by Arianne to serve Jewel for his failure, he is Arianni
Ariel: Young child given Jewel by Lord Isladar for her protection
Rymark ATerafin: Member of the House Council
Haerrad ATerafin: Member of the House Council

Elonne ATerafin: Member of the House Council
Marrick Tremblant ATerafin: Member of the House Council
Torvan ATerafin: Captain of the Chosen

THE ORDER OF KNOWLEDGE
Meralonne APhaniel: Member of the Council of the Magi; first circle mage
Sigurne Mellifas: Member of the Council of the Magi; first circle mage
Gyrrick: One of Meralonne's warrior mages; seconded by the army

SENNIEL COLLEGE
Solran Marten: Bardmaster of Senniel College
Kallandras: Master Bard of Senniel College

ANNAGAR

THE CLANS

LEONNE: Ruling clan of the Dominion of Annagar
Ser Valedan kai di'Leonne (Raverra): The heir to the Dominion
Markaso kai di'Leonne: The assassinated Tyr'agar, Valedan's father
Serra Diora en'Leonne: Also *Serra Diora di'Marano*
Serra Diora's harem wives
Faida en'Leonne: Oathwife to Diora; dead
Ruatha en'Leonne: Oathwife to Diora; dead
Dierdre en'Leonne: Oathwife to Diora; dead

In Service to Leonne
Ser Baredan di'Navarre: Former General of the Third Army, under Valedan's father
Ser Anton di'Guivera: Foremost Swordmaster of the Dominion; twice winner of the Kings' Crown
Ser Andaro di'Corsarro: Tyran; the only Tyran who serves Valedan kai di'Leonne
Ser Laonis di'Caveras: Healer-born; he has left his home in the North to travel with Valedan
Aidan a'Cooper: Standard-bearer or mascot; young boy

CALLESTA: Ruling clan of the Terrean of Averda

Ser Ramiro kai di'Callesta: The Tyr

Serra Amara en'Callesta: Wife to the Tyr

Eliana en'Callesta: Concubine to the Tyr

Aliane en'Callesta: Concubine to the Tyr

Maria en'Callesta: Concubine to the Tyr

Sara en'Callesta: Concubine to the Tyr

Deana en'Callesta: Concubine to the Tyr

Ser Fillipo par di'Callesta: Brother to the Tyr'agnate of Averda; Captain of his Tyran

Ser Carelo kai di'Callesta: The heir to Callesta, Ramiro's oldest son; dead

Ser Alfredo par di'Callesta: Youngest son of Ramiro, and now his heir

Ser Karro di Callesta: Tyran; half brother (concubine's son); the oldest of the Tyran

Ser Miko di Callesta: Tyran; half brother (concubine's son)

GARRARDI: Ruling clan of the Terrean of Oerta

Eduardo kai di' Garrardi: The Tyr'agnate of the Terrean of Oerta

LAMBERTO: Ruling clan of the Terrean of Mancorvo

Ser Mareo kai di'Lamberto: The Tyr'agnate of Mancorvo

Ser Fredero par di'Lamberto: Younger brother to the Tyr'agnate; left the clan in order to become the kai el'Sol, the leader of the Radann

Serra Alina di'Lamberto: Once given as hostage to the Imperial Court in Essalieyan, she now advises *Ser Valedan kai di'Leonne* and travels with his forces

Serra Donna en'Lamberto: Mareo's Serra

Ser Galen kai di'Lamberto: The kai (former par)

Ser Andreas kai di'Lamberto: The dead kai

Renaldo: Tyran; sent to Lamberto by the former kai el'Sol

Marano:

Ser Adano kai di'Marano: Tor'agar to *Mareo kai di'Lamberto*

Ser Sendari par di'Marano: His brother; Widan; also called *Ser Sendari di'Sendari,* the founding name of a new clan

Serra Fiona en'Marano: Sendari's wife

Ser Artano: Sendari's oldest son

Serra Diora di'Marano: Sendari's only child by his first wife

Serra Teresa di'Marano: Sister to Adano and Sendari; companion to Yollana of the Havalla Voyani, aunt to the Serra Diora

Clemente

Ser Alessandro kai di'Clemente: The Tor'agar; his Tyr is Ser Mareo

Ser Janos kai di'Clemente: The son of Ser Alessandro's dead brother, and the heir

Serra Celina en'Clemente: Wife to Ser Alessandro

Ser Reymos: Toran to Ser Alessandro

Ser Adelos: Toran to Ser Alessandro

Manelo

Ser Amando kai di'Manelo: The Tor'agnate

Ser Franko kai di'Manelo: The former kai; killed in combat after being accused of attempted murder by the kai el'Sol

Darran di'Sambali: Village clansman, almost killed by Ser Franko

Talia en'Sambali: His wife

LORENZA: Ruling clan of the Terrean of Sorgassa

Ser Jarrani kai di'Lorenza: The Tyr'agnate of Sorgassa

Ser Hectore kai di'Lorenza: The kai, heir to Sorgassa

Ser Alef par di'Lorenza: Hectore's younger brother

Serra Maria en'Lorenza: Ser Hectore's wife

THE SWORD OF KNOWLEDGE

Ser Cortano di'Alexes: The Sword's Edge; the ruler of the Widan

Ser Sendari di'Marano: Widan

Ser Mikalis di'Arretta: Widan

THE RADANN

Radann Fredero kai el'Sol: The former leader of the Radann;

died in the Lake of the Tor Leonne, drawing the Sun
Sword

Jevri el'Sol: His loyal servitor; he also serves Lamberto after
the death of the kai el'Sol

Radann Peder kai el'Sol: The man who now leads the
Radann

Radann Samiel par el'Sol: Youngest of the Hand of God

Radann Marakas par el'Sol: Contemporary of Fredero;
healer-born

Radann Samadar par el'Sol: The oldest of the par el'Sol

Radann Jordan el'Sol: A servitor who is a faithful follower
of the ways of Fredero within the Radann

Radann Paolo el'Sol: Another of Fredero's servitors

Radann Santos el'Sol: The leader of the Radann in the city
of Sarel

Radann Fiero el'Sol: The leader of the Radann in the city of
Callesta, and therefore the most senior Radann in the Terrean of Averda

THE VOYANI

Arkosa

Evallen of the Arkosa Voyani: The former Matriarch
Margret of the Arkosa Voyani: The current Matriarch
Elena Tamaraan: Margret's heir, Daughter to Arkosa
Stavos: Travels with Yollana and the Serra Diora

Havalla

Yollana of the Havalla Voyani: Matriarch of the Havallans
Nadia: Her oldest daugher, and Daughter to the Havallans
Varya: Yollana's younger daughter

THE SHINING COURT

The Lord of the Shining Court: *Allasakar*

THE FIST
Lord Assarak
Lord Alcrax

Lord Ishavriel
Lord Etridian
Lord Nugratz

THE COURT
The Kialli
Lord Isladar
Lord Telakar
Anduvin The Smith

The Humans
Anya a'Cooper: Powerful mage, serves Ishavriel—sometimes

PROLOGUE

THE wind was a wild taste in her mouth, a thing that kicked at the tongue and the lips with its strangeness.

It carried the embers of a dead fire, wood ash long past the point of burning, in the lengthening shadows of the coming evening. The living fire burned around it, swirling like eddies of brightly colored water. Wrong, wrong. She lifted a hand, rubbing her mouth with the back of it as if the taste would somehow come off. As if she could clean it away.

"Anya," Devlin said. He caught her hand before she could cut her lips against her teeth; she'd been rubbing too hard, without thinking.

Almost, she pulled his fingers back, but as she touched them, she realized that his skin felt the cool, crisp color of blue—and she knew it was happening again. The tears started, and as they ran down her face, they tingled, a jumble of red and exquisite yellow, burning brightly. She heard the wind, held its voice a moment before it slid into something that she did not understand—some thing that made her mouth water, a smell.

"Anya, Anya, Anya." But she could still hear his voice, his precious voice.

The first time it had happened, she'd been terrified. She'd touched a metal plow in the old shed down by Devlin's uncle's farm, and instead of feeling cool, humped metal, she'd touched *green*. A year ago. A little more.

Then, in the wake of that confusion, pain.

It had passed with sleep and the dawn's light, and she'd said nothing to anyone. Not then. And not a month later, when it happened again. Not five months after that, when it happened once or twice a week, always something un- usual—a smell where a sound should have been, a color in- stead of a sensation, a noise, some pealing of bell or muted susurration when she looked at what should have been cornflower blue.

Not even when the sunlight began to shout in a voice she understood; when the shadows whispered or sang; when food felt like bark or steel shavings, the taste wrong.

No; she hadn't spoken at all until the pain was too harsh to ignore—because when she couldn't ignore it, no one else could either. Devlin noticed first. He always noticed things.

"Anya."

But it was bad this time. When had it gotten so bad? Tears blurred the lines of his face, and she brushed them away—just as harshly—so she could see it clearly. She needed to see him clearly.

He knew what she was thinking, too. Always did. He was Devlin and she was Anya, and they belonged together.

"It's the pain again."

She bit her lip and nodded, and the tears blurred his face again—but it didn't matter, because his arms formed a brace around her body, drawing her in, holding her close— and that close to his face, she couldn't focus anyway.

"Anya, they're coming too close together, these pains. I'm worried, I'm worried for you, little Ann—maybe we should go back."

"No!" She pulled back a moment, and when he wouldn't let her go, buried herself more deeply into his chest. "No, I won't go back. You heard what they were going to do. They were going to send me away with that—with that man!"

"Aye, away. I know it." He held her, rocking her against

the pain. "But that man—he wasn't an ordinary man. Maybe he was a—"

"He was a wizard," she said, her voice a tight scrape of sound struggling free of clenched teeth. "And he'd done his poking and prodding." She buried the words again, as the pain came. Bit his shirt, which helped. Heard his grunt, and knew that she'd bitten more than shirt—but Devlin never complained about anything. He was steady. "They were going to send me away. Without you."

"Anya—"

"Dev—" she bit her lip until it bled, as she'd done many, many times these last few weeks. A wonder it hadn't scarred. A wonder. "Don't you love me?"

Her voice sounded small, even to her own ears, and he answered with words and without, speaking and rocking her, letting her know by motion and presence that he loved her more than anyone else possibly could.

Her parents had called for the wizard. Called him all the way from the city of the Twin Kings in the Eastern Empire. Never mind that they were free towners, and damn proud of it. One priestess' mumbled words and they'd scattered like chickens when faced with a fox.

They were going to give her away.

Anya, love, smart *chickens do scatter when faced with a fox.*

And leave their young behind 'em? No—not even chickens do that. We'll go to the—to the Western Kingdoms. We can make a life together there. Find a farm, a place we can make our own. She hadn't told her parents, and he hadn't told his; they'd packed in bits and pieces over a hurried day and a night. And then, before Anya could be packed up and sent off to the East, they'd slid out of the confines of their parents' houses and headed out into the world to decide their own fate.

Oh, the pain, the pain was terrible. She felt her stomach shudder, and knew that her knees had collapsed, although the ground didn't rush up to meet her. The priestess had said the pain wouldn't stop until she spoke with the mage-born. The priestess had said—

Not even the healer-born can help with this pain, Anya, if you could afford their touch. And all the while, her eyes were round and dark with pity, as if Anya were a lame horse.

She bit her lip, or thought she must have; blood welled up in her mouth as if it were the only drink she was to be allowed. She choked on it, on something thick and chewy, and then she felt something hard between her teeth. Something her teeth could cling to.

She had never been so afraid of fire in her life; she knew it was burning her, burning her to ash.

Devlin!

I'm here; I'm here, Annie. I'm not going anywhere without you. I'm here.

And it helped, to hear his words, even if they sounded as if he'd spoken them underwater.

There wasn't anyone she loved so much in the world as she loved Devlin. He was tall, and handsome, and his hair was like copper, brushed and straight; his eyes were a deep blue that sometimes edged into gray when she least expected it, like the shadowed secrets of a free town dusk. He wasn't the miller's son, with his wandering hands and his sour breath; he wasn't the weaver's son, who wanted to leave his mark on all the young women of the village, taking what he could without giving anything much in return.

Every girl in the fields had had an eye for Devlin a'Smith, and he—he had had eyes for Anya a'Cooper. Oh, not all at once, and even when he knew that she wanted him, he'd kept his distance because he thought she was just a child. But she was more than a child, and she'd proved it in time. Just this past year. After she'd seen her fifteenth birthday, although by the priestess' reckoning, she'd been a woman since she was just shy of fourteen.

Devlin was nineteen. Almost twenty. Broad shouldered, and learning a real trade. And he was the best man in the village, even her mother said so—excepting, of course, her father, although Anya privately thought that between Devlin and her father there wasn't much comparison.

She'd been so happy, even when the pain had started. Even when it had come more and more often, until it seemed to always be there, she could ignore it because Devlin loved *her*. It was when it got sharp and *hot* that she'd finally gone to a priestess. And the priestess had spoken with her at length, and then risen with a worried look, a creased sort of face with thin lips.

She'd given Anya herbs, in a bitter brew, that helped with the pain for a short while—but only a short while, and in truth, not very much.

The priestess had spoken with her mother and father, and they had come home tired and gray, her mother fussing in that sharp-tongued way that mothers fuss when they're worried and everyone else is going to worry just as much, or else, and her father going silent to his work, casting a troubled glance over his shoulder a time or two, hushing the rest of his children while watching them with that same terrible worry that he now watched Anya. As if she was a hailstorm and they were the rest of the crop.

And then, weeks later, *he* came, like the doom out of an old story, walking into her town while the sun was high and the sky was clear. He cast a long shadow, but Devlin sensibly pointed out that it was because he was tall—and he *was* tall, the tallest man she'd ever seen. His hair was white as snow in winter, and longer than any sensible free towner's, and his eyes were gray and cool and hard, very much like metal. His hands were unblemished, and his skin fair, and his clothing—well, his clothing, her mother said, was probably worth more than a cow.

He'd told them he'd walked, but Anya didn't believe it; the dust of the road had a way of marking a man, and no man—noble-born or common as clay—escaped it. But this one had.

I've come from the Order of Knowledge, at the behest of

the church of the Mother. He was polite and distant when he spoke to anyone, even Anya, but she knew when she saw him that he was the end of her life.

He came, and although her parents were allowed to listen to him—more, she thought, for their comfort than her own—he did not acknowledge their presence. Hers, he did; he treated her with—with careful respect. He spoke at length. To her, in his quiet voice.

And that night, that night she made her desperate plans to flee. Went to Devlin, to whom she would have been married by the end of her seventeenth year, and told him that she must leave with him, on the following eve, or she would never see him again. It was, after all, the truth.

Ah, the pain, the *fire*.

What she hadn't told Devlin, and what she was afraid he was beginning to guess, was what the mage had said: she was mage-born, and coming into her power far too quickly, and if she didn't come with him, she stood not only to lose that power—which she didn't much care about anyway—but quite probably her life as well. That was exactly how he'd worded it. Quite probably.

If she hadn't been so afraid of losing Devlin, she might have gone with the mage. But the mage had made it plain: there was only room for the mage-born where she was going, which meant no Devlin. And if she'd told Devlin, if she'd told him what that white-haired stranger had said, that she might die—he'd have betrayed her; he'd've sent her with the mage. For her own good.

Devlin was the only thing she wanted. Had been the only thing she had *ever* wanted.

They'd put up their little tents; the sun's red gleam was cut by those tents into precise shapes as it lowered itself down the horizon behind their small encampment. The light would fade quickly, and when the last of its color had bled into blues so deep they were almost black, the demons would be allowed to feed.

They were feeding now, at an uncomfortable distance, the muffled intensity of the young girl's pain a hint of the sustenance that they had been forced, by dint of the Summoning, to forgo. The Hells, they feared, were lost to them—and if they had ever known another realm, it was buried in the memory of a flesh much different than the flesh the world had surrendered to their return.

Thus it was with the kin: They tended the gardens and the monuments of the Hells with a keen and loving hand. But in a time beyond the memory of all but the most powerful, they had been born to the earth, to the old earth, and the world remembered their names and their spirits. A cunning mage could stumble across those names, and if he was willing to make a bargain of blood and time with the old world, he could force the demon to return to the land of human life and vice; the world itself closed round the kin in a shape, a physical form at once natural and foreign to the Summoned creature.

They wore such shapes now: things of ebony and silver, bodies long and dark with slender claws, long fingers.

Two weeks; two weeks and more, they had watched this girl and this boy. Lord Ishavriel himself came frequently, to take their reports, to cast his spells, and to *listen*. But today, finally, the watching stopped.

"Kill the girl as you please," he told his two servitors, "but do not harm the boy."

Ishavriel-kevar smiled thinly, but Algratz did not; he studied his lord's expression. "What would you have us do with the boy?"

"Frighten him," their lord replied, but carefully. Algratz thought him ill-pleased by the tenor of the question. Or perhaps by the interruption. "Before you take the girl, you *must* force him to desert her. Break his spirit; offer him a choice between his life and hers. It must be clear, to him, and to the girl, what his choice was." He paused a moment, to give his words weight, and then he looked back at the tents framed by sinking sunlight.

Ishavriel-kevar laughed and nodded, straining eagerly as the sun's light ceased its dance upon the windswept waters of the lake.

But Algratz asked. "Why?"

"Because," Ishavriel replied, "I so order." His voice lost all trace of warmth, and there had been little enough of it, and that all carnal. "Or do you challenge me, here?"

"No, Lord Ishavriel."

"Good." His gaze, wrapped in a face that appeared almost human, was the color of the setting sun. "The boy is mine," he said, relenting slightly. "After he has fled, *I* will hunt him."

Ishavriel-kevar nodded, impatient to be gone. They would share the girl and leave the boy to him. It made sense.

Still, Algratz began his approach through the tall grass and the low shrubbery more cautiously than his companion. "Think, Kevar," he said, granting the demon the use of free name. "The Lord has forbidden all hunting of humans until the gathering and the Summoning is complete."

"And *our* lord has given us permission."

"If our lord angers *the* Lord, who do you think our lord will offer as compensation for the crime?"

But Ishavriel-kevar was beyond caring, and as the shadow circle their feet traced brought them closer and closer to the small, rough tent, Algratz well understood why: *she* was there. Her pain was lessening, which was unfortunate. But the pain that she felt now would be nothing compared to what the kin might inflict. To what *he* might, were she trembling in his hands.

It had been such a long time.

Such a long time, to be forbidden the hunting and the reaving. He glanced over his shoulder and saw that Lord Ishavriel waited, impassive, where they had left him; he intended to witness the event. To intervene, Algratz thought, if his servants failed him.

As he stepped forward, the crickets fell silent; the night

animals—and there were not a few—froze or fled. A careful human, in lands as dense with the old earth's life as the forested stretch between the small mortal demesnes, could trace the path of his approach by the silence it engendered—for such silences as these were loud and unnatural.

But the girl's pain was guttering, and the boy was involved with it, almost as much as they were; there would be no detection.

No escape.

He was wary, but as he approached, as the sound of the girl's breath grew as loud to his ear as her ebbing pain, he saw Ishavriel-kevar dart forward, off the path, black hands outstretched, claws ready to cut a swath through the tent's side.

He knew that Lord Ishavriel planned something; knew further that the risk he took—the breaking of *the* Lord's law—was a risk only if there were witnesses, coconspirators, and that witnesses were often disposed of when the work was done. He could not think of a single reason why Ishavriel needed either Algratz or Ishavriel-kevar; a simple girl and a simple boy could have easily been disposed of by one of the *Kialli* with no one the wiser.

Nature intervened: Algratz, of the two, was the more powerful demon, and he *could not* let Ishavriel-kevar take first what was his by right of power.

Faster, sleeker, and more complete in his arc, he landed a foot ahead of the slightly slower demon—and when he cut through the rough, oiled cloth of the tent, the fabric provided so little resistance the tent barely shivered when half its side fell away.

"Welcome," he said, in a voice made guttural by anticipation and desire, "to Hell."

There was a moment of terrified silence; he savored it, stretching it out for as long as he could. She broke it, and her scream was gratifying, an echo of the Abyss. He would have savored the scream just as deeply as the silence, but

Ishavriel-kevar intervened, stepping into the breached wall and grabbing the boy.

The boy kicked and twisted in his grasp—just as a soul might writhe, with just as much success. "Devlin a'Smith," Ishavriel-kevar said, and the boy slumped in a sick shock that even souls did not display. With his free hand, Ishavriel-kevar tore the tent from its moorings, uprooting and scattering its pegs in a single motion.

She disappeared a moment in its folds—but only a moment; Algratz spoke a word and the tent unfurled, exposing her. She was white, white as starlight and the face of the dark moon.

He caught her in his hands at once; marveled at the feel of her flesh, at the fact of it, that something this weak and thin and yielding had managed to survive so long.

Almost casually, he rid her of her clothing, slicing it clear from throat-hem to skirt's edge, as if it were alive in its own right, and he an executioner. He heard her lovely whimper; she had lost her voice in fear, but her fear itself carried everything that he needed to hear.

At his side, he heard the unmistakable sound of flesh being split, a small tear, a slow one. It had a cadence and rhythm of its own, and when the boy screamed in terror, and in agony, and in anticipation, the two sounds blended, melody and harmony.

She did not hear it, he thought; she was concerned with her own fate, her own plight. When she opened her bruised lips, a single word escaped them. "DEVLIN!" All the sweet fear in the name was her own, it was of her, for her. He could almost taste it; could taste it. It had been so *long*.

She kicked at him, abrading her heels against his skin; he bore her down into the tall grass, all the while the boy's name filling his ears and her lungs. And then he laughed, louder than she screamed, a deep, rich sound that hinted at the eternity of the Abyss for a mortal whose soul was, pitiably, far from making the Choice. Ah, well. He did not have an eternity.

He had her life, for as long as it lasted, and then, beyond that, three days in which to bind her soul and hold it.

But first, Lord Ishavriel's command.

"Ishavriel-kevar!" The pitch of his voice was unnaturally loud. "Will you waste your time with the boy when we have what we came for?"

"Devlin!" He silenced her a moment with his lips, and when he drew back, hers were reddened with blood; she choked as he touched her gently. As gently as he knew how. Her voice was gone again, gone to silence and the stillness of breath held by a person who has—almost—forgotten that she needs to breathe to survive.

Algratz caressed her with the sharp edge of claws that did not quite draw blood. Footsteps accompanied the movement of his hands against the stillness of her flesh. He recognized them at once: The heavy, stalking tread of Ishavriel-kevar, and the fleet-footed, grass-tearing scramble of a terrified, half-crazed mortal. But she did not, he thought; she did not know who was coming.

He lowered himself over her, and then, as the tall grass parted and the shadow of Ishavriel-kevar was lent substance by the moon, he smiled. A moment, he waited, until he saw the widening of her eyes, and then he whispered four guttural words.

Run for your life.

The sound of the fleeing boy's ragged breath and uneven steps was taken by the lake and the air and the wind and made louder, made final.

"Devlin! DEVLIN!"

His name echoed, unanswered. Lake water lapped at it, eating away at its edges until even the name was gone.

She was alone. With them.

He entered her then, as the realization did, because this was the first of her fears, and he intended to visit them all.

Devlin.

They hurt her. The one, and then the other, great, terrible

shadows that shone with the harsh light of new silver, of silver that has never known time. What she had kept from the miller's brutal son, what she had offered shyly at first, and then insistently, to Devlin, they took, and in the taking, made her realize that she had never had anything to fear from the miller's son.

Devlin.

They hurt her, and then they left her a moment, like garbage, in an unclean, bleeding heap. She lifted her head and saw the tent, like her dress, spread and torn across the goldenrod and tall grass, white in the poor light, a revenant. She tried to stand, bunching her knees beneath her limp body and pushing her weight up; throwing her hands out to stop her body in motion from returning groundward too heavily.

The tears were on her cheeks, and they were water, and they *burned.*

Why? *Why?*

"Devlin."

It angered Algratz; angered and confounded him. He was not *Kialli*, but he was a free creature, inasmuch as any of the kin could be, who served the Lord of the Hells. He understood pain; no one of the kin did not. Even the imps— even the lesser, squeaking gnats of the outer regions—had it bred into their brittle, tiny bones.

But the pain he inflicted here did not touch the girl as deeply or as viscerally as the pain that the boy caused by his flight.

Is this what you hoped to gain? he thought, as the silver curves of his claws sliced his own palm in reflexive anger. It would be Lord Ishavriel's game—to give and to take with the same gesture. *Is this why you ordered us to let the boy flee?*

She had not, he noticed, even made the attempt to flee. No, wait; she rose. He had so hoped to make her last for hours, for days; he surrendered that hope now. He had no doubt that he could make her surrender everything, but all of the lovely subtlety, all of the pain that might be caused without lethal damage—that was lost to him.

Angry, and hungry, he stalked forward as she lurched to her feet. If there was no subtlety, there was still victor and a victim, and that at least was something. A scrap. From Ishavriel's dominion.

She heard him and she turned at once, lurching, overbalanced.

She stumbled out of his way, evading his grip, and shredded the skin of her hand on the hand of his companion; the shock was bracing in its clarity, its unexpectedness.

She seemed almost confused, and stepped back, bleeding, naked, her whole hand clutching her wounded one, as if she would be allowed, in the end, to keep either.

"What—what do you want?"

They, neither of them, chose to answer, sensing that their silence was worse; in the silence, she might fashion the words she most dreaded, and say them, over and over.

She drew back, and her eyes were white and wide; almost gratifying. Almost enough.

But when Algratz finally touched her, scudding along the underside of her skin with the very tip of his fingers, when she finally screamed, the pain was still distinct.

"Devlin!"

She heard the footsteps with a wild hope, a crazed and terrified hope; the words on her lips were a rush of giddiness, of forgiveness, of anger—that he could *leave* her, but it might be all right somehow if he could just save her now and tell her *why*—

But even in the moon's terrible light, so white and harsh and brilliant, her vision could not contort the moving blur into Devlin's shape; it was too tall and too fast.

And it carried, of all things, a sword.

The creature peeling the skin from her arm froze stiffly

as the sword passed through its body, starting from the crook of its ebony neck and ending at the joint of its hip. She thought it unharmed, for it seemed to turn—

But that was night illusion; the shadows gave lie to the movement and the body fell, at once, into distinct pieces. The grass burned where it landed; the air burned.

The other creature turned, jumped, leaped into the air; he cried out in anger, his voice harsh and metallic. But the man with the sword—and he was a man—only laughed as the creature turned and fled.

Fled.

She stood alone by the lakeside, the insects waking to the warmth of her body and the promise of her blood. He bowed, his bow so perfect he reminded her, in the single motion, of the silver-haired mage. The mage who was the end of her world.

She couldn't see for tears. "And w–what do you want, then?"

He sheathed his sword and bowed again, turning his glance to the blackened patch of earth that would not support life for decades. It was all that remained of the demon's corpse. With great care, he unfastened the golden clips of the chain that held his cloak's collar together. He raised it, slowly, gently, and then, folding it carefully, placed it upon the ground at his feet.

As if she were a hungry, wild animal, he backed away, every movement slow and deliberate. She knew it, of course; she'd seen Devlin do it a hundred times. She had even done it herself.

Devlin.

Her knees collapsed when she took a step forward. She rose; the man had not moved. Scrambling, dirt in the cuts and the scrapes of her hand, she reached for his cloak and wrapped it as tightly around her body as she ever had a blanket after a terrible nightmare.

"Anya," her unknown companion said, speaking for the first time.

She looked up at the sound of her name.

"Come, child. This is not the place for you. I have killed one of the kin, but the other will return."

She shook her head, mute in the face of his words.

"Child," he said again, his voice not unkind. "There is no safety in anything but strength." His gaze was as much a measure of her as Emily a'Martin had ever made when dressing her for church.

Devlin.

"You should not have trusted a boy," he said, as if he could hear her thoughts. She would learn, later, that he could do exactly that.

"And why should I trust you?" she demanded, with the thick layer of his soft, heavy cloak as her armor and her shield. The grass grew tall as her hips this time of year, and the goldenrod and milkweed taller still.

His smile was cold as moonlight, as cold as silver; as cold, she thought, as the claws of the creature he had killed. "Because, Anya, I *have* power. What do you desire? If you wish to return to your home, I will take you there."

Devlin. She looked up at him, and the tears started, a thin, terrible train down the bruised mask of her face. "Where are you going?"

"I? To my home, little Anya." He held out a hand, and it seemed natural to her, as she met the absolute black of his eyes, that she should take it, and be comforted. "And if you wish it, you will find safety and warmth there."

"And who are—who are you?"

"I? I am Lord Ishavriel."

She did not think to ask him what the creatures were. Did not think to ask him why they had come for her. Did not think to ask why he had been there, sword in hand, in the middle of a stretch of land between the free towns and the Western Kingdoms. There was only one question that burned at her, that burned more terribly than the pain that had, in the end, driven her from the free town of her birth.

And she could not ask it, and because she did not have the release of speaking it aloud, it consumed her.

Devlin, how could you leave me to die?

"Never trust a human, Anya a'Cooper," Lord Ishavriel said. "For they want what they want so ephemerally, so pitiably. A human knows fear, and only fear; fear guides him, not oath or honor." The moon faded slowly as he spoke. His voice was soft now, almost distant.

"I am Lord Ishavriel," he told her softly. "And I fear nothing."

He caught her in his arms as she fell, and brought her up and up to the center of his broad chest, cradling her as if she were a babe in arms, and a small one at that.

The wind was a wild taste in her mouth. Ashes. Fire. Salt.

When the demons came hunting him, he was ready.

Not to fight; scant hours had passed, and he was no closer to home—or a weapon—than he'd been when they'd first come upon him. But the flight had broken something in Devlin a'Smith, and it was only hours later, stumbling with exhaustion into the hard crook between two large rocks on the side of a hill's shelf, that he could even acknowledge it.

He was a coward.

Everything else that he'd ever believed about himself had been stripped away like the flesh of his finger; he was just as cowardly as the weaver's weasel of a son.

Aie, even that was a lie.

He was worse. The weaver's flaxen-haired boy had never once promised to love and cherish and protect. Had never, in words and in more than words, told a girl as trusting as Anya that he would be willing to—

that he would die for—

He was too exhausted to be sick; he'd been sick several times already, and none of them had helped; bile had scoured his throat and stung his lips and offered no relief.

There was nothing I could do! He *knew* it for truth.

Ah, but it cut, it cut because what he knew and what he believed didn't quite meet. The words were a hollow, brittle shield behind which he could hide from the eyes of any man—

Any man save himself.

Oh, he tried; he still tried. For just a few minutes longer. *No, it's not true—I couldn't have saved her. All I could have done was die.* His death would have served no purpose.

No purpose but this: it would prove that he was what he had always promised himself he would be. Brave. True. Honest.

He could hear her screaming his name every time he stopped to rest. Could hear the terror in it, and then, worse, the terrible, terrible loss that came with, came from, betrayal.

It ate at him, devoured him from within. But he could no more cast it off than he could the sunlight; he lived with it, as he could.

When he saw the ebon shapes in the pale afternoon light, he was giddy with a terrible relief, although his breath quickened and his heart raced and his body desired to betray him.

As it had already done once.

It had killed him.

But he had not accepted his death; there were stories like that, of bodies whose soul had already deserted them, and which had to be laid to rest. Just so.

He could accept it now. He had no strength—and no desire—to flee. Swallowing, he saw the sunlight glisten off the sinews of their muscles, off the silver of their claws; only their eyes seemed to drink the light in, absorbing it, consuming it. They were the world; the trees lost color, and the goldenrod and the milkweed and the brilliant blue of forget-me-nots that were, that remained, the flower of Anya's choice.

And as he watched them, dazed, the sun bearing witness to this final act in the play begun an eternity and a night past, he thought that they were, in the strangest of ways, so terribly, terribly beautiful. That they were strong, that they were whole, that they moved with effortless, perfect grace, perfect strength.

He wanted to close his eyes, but they held him, hypnotized, and he told himself, as the distance between the demons and the rocks grew smaller and smaller, that they were really only a doorway.

A doorway, after all, to the Halls of Mandaros, wherein he might meet his Anya. Might meet her, and beg her forgiveness and—and ask her, as he never had, as she *always* asked him:

Do you still love me?

When the lightning fell from the clear blue sky without even the clouds to presage its coming, he blinked. It was a flash of incandescent light, a thing without thunder; it was almost beyond his comprehension. Almost.

But it was not beyond the comprehension of the creatures who promised him, with the death they brought, reunion. For they were the field of his vision, and they were what the lightning's fork sought.

Could death scream?

He learned the answer that late afternoon, watching, the rocks hard at his back, rough beneath his thighs, his calves. He cried out, as they cried out, and he could not have said whether the cry was one of denial or terror or relief; his heart froze as their shadows did, as they turned to look up, and around, seeking an enemy.

Was it an act of Cartanis? Did the Lord of Just War ride, so late, to his rescue?

A moment's hope, and then it was gone, as much ash as wood fed to the fires. Cartanis was a warrior's god, not a coward's god; he would not raise a finger in aid of a man who had abandoned his responsibility and broken his vow. No god would.

But then?

Lightning, forked, blue and gold and white. Crackling with an intensity that broke the darkness. And the darkness, in this open day, walked on two legs.

"THERE!" One of the creatures cried, and he turned—turned away from Devlin. A hollowness filled the young man, a hallowing emptiness. He opened his lips and swallowed air, choking on it as if it were water, or a very, very strong draught. His senses returned to him: He could taste the blood in his mouth, smell it on his clothes, and more besides: sweat, fear. He tried to stand. Legs that had carried him this far locked; they would carry him no farther this day.

"The boy!" The other creature cried. "Kill him!"

Ah, death.

But as he waited, as the death came long-clawed and sudden, he saw the lightning for the third time. This time it was no tentative flash: it was a thing that caught. And held. And burned. He could not look; the white was so bright and the pain of the creature so visceral he had to bring his hands up to his eyes—and then, to his ears. But nothing took the smell out of his nostrils; it clung there, burning flesh.

Burning flesh, as if the demons were, and could be, only flesh. In the end, there was silence and when the silence had reigned for long, for long enough, he opened his eyes.

The shadows still waited, but they were no longer shiny, nor graceful, nor new; they were not black, but blue, a deep blue of the kind that only the evening sky sees. He followed their folds up, and up, aware that his gaze had started at the ground only when it finally met hers: violet eyes in a pale, careworn face. She held out a hand.

"Devlin a'Smith," she said softly.

He could not speak. The world returned to him slowly, and the life. He stood, took a teetering step, scraped his hand against the gray-red of rock stained with blood; his blood; that was the shadow he cast. His hand ached terribly.

She saw it, and her brow furrowed, but she moved slowly, as if afraid to startle him. He did not step away as she raised her other hand, and started once when she spoke in a language that was not language. He might have pulled back then, but she moved quickly, encircling his wrist with her hand.

"So," she said to herself, "this is how it was." And before he could ask her what she meant, he saw fire start in her hand; a fire that was white. He closed his eyes.

And screamed as she seared his flesh and bone away.

He clutched his hand, stepping into the rocks again as he sought to protect it—and himself—from his savior. She spoke, but the pain still held so much of his attention the words were a tickle in his ear. He would wonder, later, if the words themselves had been significant.

A moment passed; he stared down at his finger. No blood, no exposed bone, remained; the finger was puckered with an ugly red scar, but it was whole. A neater job than any save the Mother's priestess might have done.

But the Mother's priestess would not cause so much pain in the healing; the pain of the cure lingered, and would, for as long as the pain of the cause, an echo; a twin.

"Who—who are you?" And then, as a wild hope seized him, he added, "Anya—did you save Anya, too?"

Her smile was graven in stone, cold and bitter; had he not been looking at her eyes, he would not have seen the flicker of pain in them. "I do not choose, Devlin, who I will save or who I will leave to death."

The hope left him in a rush, and he collapsed.

"You cannot stay here. Lord Ishavriel will know, soon, that his servitors have failed; he will send others, and they will be . . . less easily disposed of."

"Who is Lord Ishavriel?"

"I have already said enough, Devlin."

"He's a demon?"

"He is more than just 'a' demon. Come. If we debate theology for another hour, we will both perish. These creatures were blood-bound; even at this distance, he will feel their deaths." She offered him a ringed hand; he took it.

"Who are you?"

"I? Call me Evayne." She paused, and her violet eyes narrowed as she looked momentarily groundward. "Evayne a'Nolan," she said, as if the saying of the name was costly.

"You're an Imperial?"

"I'm a free towner. I was."

He relaxed at that; it made her smile again. The smile was not a comforting, or a comfortable, expression. "How do you know who I am?"

"Ask me that in ten years; perhaps in ten years I can answer." Her smiled was bitter and brief. "Or perhaps in twenty. Or perhaps never."

"Where—where are we going?"

"Would you go to your home, Devlin?"

He started to nod and his head froze, and he became aware, fully, that he had lost more than Anya, and more than himself, on this afternoon: he had lost all else, all family. He could not return to them with this crime on his head. He could not face them.

But he had no money, and no gear; everything had been left at the campsite. "No."

Her cloak lifted; later, he would remember that she had not touched it at all, but at the time it seemed natural, a throwing off of guises. Nothing about this woman was natural. Beneath the cloak she had three things. The first was a pack. The second was a bedroll. And the third—the third was a sword. Its scabbard was almost unadorned; it was black and long, with a silver tip and a silver mouth. But in its center there was a large, clear stone that caught the light and held it brilliantly. He wasn't a jeweler, but he thought— he thought it might be real.

"Is it—"

"It's not a magical sword, if that's what you're asking," she replied, with just a hint of wryness. "But if you will make a life for yourself, there is a life waiting. Have you not heard, Devlin? The Empire is at war."

"War?"

"The free towns obviously don't feel the Southerners at their borders."

"With the South?"

"With the Dominion, yes. The war started a year ago; I fear that it may continue for at least another. These are the games that men play, who desire power.

"You'll see what war means, Devlin. Don't forget the cost of it." She paused, and set the pack and the bedroll down at his feet. The sword, she lifted in two hands. "This sword's maker was a man torn by his own past and his desire for vengeance. I believe that you will understand him, or you would have, had you met. Take it."

He hesitated, and then nodded. It was easier to obey her than it was to think—to think about what he was, now.

The blade was bound to its scabbard; he cut the strings that held it, and then, effortlessly, he drew the sword.

He hefted it, swinging it lightly to and fro, in ever faster arcs. As the son of the village smith, he knew weapons, for his father had come from the Empire itself, with a weapon-smith's knowledge of arms—and in the free towns, arms were valued, especially in the warm seasons when Imperial bandits thought to take a small "unprotected" town's merchants.

This sword was light for all its weight and heft; it turned easily in his hand; its balance was fine. Lifting it to the light, he studied its edge. It was so perfect, he thought it had never seen a forge's test, never mind battle.

This was a sword his father would have killed for.

His father.

The momentary wonder was guttered.

"Devlin. Come."

She turned and began to walk, and it seemed that her gait was slow and awkward. He followed at once, and offered her an arm—a gesture as natural to him as breath.

She did not take it. "We have little time, and you must be away, although the gem upon the sword will protect you from his sight unless he himself is close." And she climbed up the hill, strong and spry for all that she walked slowly.

There, waiting impatiently in grasses too summer-hard to be good eating, was a horse. It was brown and slender—no plow horse or cart horse this—and its sides still heaved, as if it had just been run, and hard.

"Take these," she said softly. "The Imperial army is looking for men, for good men."

"Then they won't take me."

"They'll take you," she answered quietly. "The war is growing bitter, and they need the men. You come with a horse, a fine one, and a sword that's finer still. Here," she added, "take this. Buy yourself a rank, if you'll find a House that will let you." Her face was pale. "I know that I'm sending you to the wolves, boy—but learn to be a wolf. It's all you have now."

As if she knew. As if she knew his crime.

He mounted the horse awkwardly, and she paled. "Devlin—you *do* know how to ride, don't you?"

"Some," he answered curtly, because it was the truth. But it wasn't much of a truth; he'd ridden rarely, and more often in wagon and cart than on horseback. He turned the horse around. Turned it back.

And then he glanced over his shoulder to say something, to offer this stranger thanks.

She was looking at her hand—at the rings on her hand—with some curiosity. There were four; she touched them, one at a time, and then when she came to the last, a ruby of red fire and brilliance even at the distance that separated them, she pulled it hard. It did not budge. He might have offered to help, but he knew her now as sorcerer, and he wasn't a fool.

Just a coward.

"In time," she said, although he didn't understand why. "It is not yet your time." Before he could speak, she lifted a hand. "Never thank me, Devlin. It is . . . hard on me." She smiled; it was a bleak expression, a bitter one. He might have spoken in spite of her request, but she took a step forward, and there was suddenly no one to speak *to*.

The horse shuddered once, and Devlin began to ease it into a walk.

But he did not go east, not yet; he went west. To face the truth, and to face himself.

The lake, in the summer day, was alive with the glitter of dragonfly wings, the buzz of insects, the flight of birds large and small. As he approached, he could see the flat, torn square that had once been the tent that he and Anya had shared. Beside it, like so much refuse, the bedroll she'd been torn out of; it was whole.

He saw ash in the sandy pit they'd made for their fire, saw the black soot of burned wood against stone. His hands were heavy on the reins, his breath tight. Minutes passed; the sun rested upon dark hair, heating it, as if in judgment. The horse—the unnamed, too fine horse—was restive beneath him, almost anxious, as if he, too, knew what had been done here. Devlin urged him forward, and the horse went. Barely.

If he owned the horse, truly, Devlin thought, sliding out of the saddle, the horse was going to have to understand who was master, and who mount. But not now. Not now.

He took a deep breath and began to search the grass. For her. The blade saw its first use, against tall stalks of green-gray; white tufts flew in the wayward breeze as he cut loose pods of milkweed. Here and there, birds flew up, chattering in fear or frustration, brown wings spread to catch the wind, to use it. They were, all these things, clouds that he moved through.

He had to find her body.

We have little time, and you must be away.

His search grew more frantic as the sun rose. He had left her to die—but he could not leave her to rot. The Mother's arms had not yet been opened to receive this most precious of her daughters, and he would do this last thing for her because he had failed in every other way.

But search as he might, this last act of penitence was to be denied him. The grass yielded nothing.

He was a coward, he thought bitterly, to the end, because he mounted the horse that the stranger had left him instead of pursuing his search into the lake, and the woods surrounding it, as if the search itself were all that mattered.

No.

He still wanted *life*. Had he ever told her that his life had no meaning without her? He wondered, and it hurt him.

This, then, was the burden he carried with him from these lands that no man owned: A death and a life.

And he would ride to war, carrying such a burden, and he would ride from war, carrying it, and earn his rank, and accept his decorations, all the while carrying it so naturally and so completely that none but he might be aware of its nature.

They might call him brave, who couldn't see how much he had to prove. They might even call him honorable, who did not see just how deep, and how dark, the stains upon his hands could be.

CHAPTER ONE

20th of Misteral, 427 AA
The Shining Palace

A NYA decided there should be rabbits.

This realization came upon her while she stood at the height of the palace wing that housed the human Court. While they huddled inside, in their draping cloaks of flat, shiny fur, she stood just beyond the balcony that opened, wind, snow, or sun, into the Northern Wastes, the flat of her feet against the raw stone of a dragon's swooping neck. That dragon hunched, wings arched, just past the stone rails of the wide, deep balcony, looking down its serpentine nose across the startling white of the morning snow above—and beyond—the City, as if in mid-breath.

The stone was cold and rough beneath the pads of her feet; she couldn't decide whether or not she liked the feeling. But even given that indecision she *knew* this was not the way dragon skin should feel. She knew the old stories; dragons should have *scales*.

And those scales should be larger than a man's arm, and smooth. Definitely smooth. This old stone thing looked more like a giant worm with wings and teeth.

She hesitated a moment.

Since she had moved the throne, Lord Ishavriel had been in a bad mood. And although he never raised his voice, and never tried to hurt her, she didn't *like* it when he was angry.

But she did have her throne, now. She could sit in it

whenever she wanted, and listen to the colors that glimmered along the shadowed floors, like dangerous old friends, their voices unmuted, their brightness undimmed. She could taste their shades through the tips of her fingers—although admittedly that was rare—and sometimes, when she was very tired, she could speak with them.

She spoke to them now, but they were distant.

But that was shadow, and she could think about that anytime. Today she had remembered rabbits.

She usually hated memory. It was all bad. It took her back to the ugly times, before she had been taught just how special, how powerful, she was. She had considered making a spell that would stop her from remembering anything, ever—but Lord Ishavriel had told her it was a Bad Idea, and she had decided to trust him.

And the rabbits proved that he was right.

Today, she had been taken back to a time when colors were something she could see with eyes alone; they had no taste, no voice, no sensation. She could hear conversation as if spoken words had no smells; could touch soft fabrics, hard wood, cold metals, as if they, as they had once been, were once again devoid of taste.

And when that happened, she treasured the memory and did everything in her power to preserve it.

Everything.

She was Anya a'Cooper. There was a lot she could do. But the stone against her bare feet was really starting to bother her, it was just so *wrong*.

Across the grounds of the Shining Palace, from the heights of its towers to the depths of its hidden recesses, its cavernous dungeons, those creatures—human or kin—with a sensitivity to magic, lifted their heads in perfect unison, as if struck by the same blow, no matter how many walls, how much physical distance, separated them.

It had become thus since the Lord's ceremony; the investiture of His power into the flawed but inarguably powerful madwoman had not perturbed her in the slightest—but it had had the effect of deepening the range of her careless, whimsical magery.

Had they not had to endure the results, and the resultant hazards, of the blending of immortal and mortal power, there were men within the walls of the Shining Palace who would have found the entire experiment fascinating. Those men now flinched; they were closest to the balcony upon which Anya had chosen to stand.

Closest to the roar that crushed conversation, stilled movement, filled silence from one end of the Shining Palace to the other.

The wall that was flimsy protection from the Northern cold cracked like thin ice and fell away from the line of the brilliant blue sky.

Against it, for those who cared to look, stood the mad, mad mage, conversing with an angry dragon, a creature of stone and glittering scale.

Anya, the dragon said, its voice rich with the heavy scent of newly turned earth, its words a deep, deep blue. She could feel each syllable crawling across the backs of her hands as they furled around air that was suddenly cold; there was *magic* here. The sensations were always sharpest in the presence of magic.

She withdrew her own power without thinking, and the soles of her feet, protected until then—because she *liked* bare feet—from the bitter cold, now shrieked in protest. She could hear their voice like the rush of a thousand sibilant whispers.

She didn't like it when her feet spoke.

But the dragon roared again, distracting her from her pain.

"But they look so much better!" she shouted. "Everyone knows *real* dragons have scales!"

Thus did the Lord of Night converse with the most powerful, and the least sane, of his many servants, and it must have amused him to do so, for although the outcome of such an argument could never be in doubt, the fact that it existed at all said much.

20th of Misteral, 427 AA
The Terafin Manse

The moon was bright, the air still, the starlight lessened by the presence of thin clouds that huddled, shroudlike, before its silvered face.

A man stood alone beneath the delicate light of the Averalaan night. The sea's breaking rumble was a constant rhythm, the heartbeat of the High City; it could be heard in the distance because so many other sounds were absent: the movement of people, their breath broken by laughter or the harsh, sharp bark of angry syllables; the clipped, steady pace of the horses that drew carriages and coaches from manse to manse along the Isle; the heavy tread of the Kings' Swords as they patrolled the High City with a vigilance not found in the Old City.

True, those sounds were of necessity distant even during the height of day, but he had become aware of them.

Had found it necessary to become aware of them; Amarais, named before her rise to power Handernesse, and then Handernesse ATerafin, had become as silent as stone. Yes, stone, Morretz thought bleakly, avoiding the other comparison that was so colloquial and inelegant.

The Terafin was careful, during the hours of day, to tend her House and the affairs of her House as if nothing troubled her. As if she had had no warning of her impending death; as if death itself was the distant eventuality it would be for the rest of her House. But in the evenings she allowed the full weight of that knowledge to descend upon her, and shrouded by it, protected by it, she sought the solace of the Terafin Shrine—although judging by her expression, both before and after, it was meager solace indeed.

He waited. He found it increasingly difficult to wait at a distance, although he had always waited here, at the edge of this path, for the lord he had chosen to serve so many years ago. That service now counted for more than half of his life.

Amarais.

She would die. She had accepted it with a peculiar, angry grace that Morretz himself had failed to achieve. He hid it; he hid it well. But his days were absorbed by the question of her survival; his mornings—when he had ascertained for himself that a simple thing like the morning meal would not kill her—began, and often ended, with Devon ATerafin.

Devon, who understood the routines of assassination better than any other member of the House, up to and probably including the man—or woman—who would in the end successfully employ them against The Terafin. He had to. He served the Lord of the Compact as a member of his Astari, and he protected the Twin Kings.

The Terafin had not, of course, specifically told Morretz to keep his peace—and his silence—in this affair.

Nor should she have had to. In all things, Morretz of the Guild of the Domicis was her loyal servant. Hers, not House Terafin's. He had spent the better part of a decade using the two—The Terafin, House Terafin—as synonyms. That was gone; what remained was a bitter, simmering resentment, for it was the latter that would destroy the former, and she would offer herself up to it with a willing, terrible grace.

The privilege of power.

He was surprised when she returned to him early, for he had sat this vigil night after night for almost a month, and he knew the hour of its ending almost as intimately as he did the minute of its commencing.

"Morretz," she said quietly.

He bowed, waiting until she stepped off the path before he spoke. Or intending to wait. But she stood, her feet to one side of the line that divided the tended stone walk from the inner recess of the garden, awaiting his acknowledgment.

"Terafin," he said at last. He looked up, the grace of the movement marred by the hesitance, subtle and deep, with which he met her gaze.

She was standing in the shadows between the contained light of two glass lamps, and as he lifted his chin, she smiled. It was a weary expression, which did not alarm him, but it was also unusually gentle, which did. "Terafin—"

She lifted a hand. "I am not yet finished for the evening, but before I am, I must ask a favor."

He waited.

Her smile lessened, ebbing from the familiar terrain of her face as if it were tide. "Please summon the men and women who serve Jewel ATerafin."

"Summon them?"

"Yes. I will meet them here."

"Terafin—"

"Don't ask," she said quietly.

He bowed, but he did not move. They both knew that the only time men and women were summoned to this place was to give their oaths of service to the House, and even then, it was rare for any but the Chosen to be so called. "Did the House demand their presence?"

"No."

He looked at her face; she had chosen to stand where the shadows—in a garden where light was scattered in artful abundance—were strongest. Funny, that.

"What will you do?" she asked him, as the silence stretched.

He chose—as he rarely chose—to misunderstand her. "My pardon, Terafin, I will fetch the den."

But she raised a hand before he could retreat, and the movement, as subtle as command could be to one who understood it, held him fast. "Morretz, when your service here is ended, what will you do?"

He could not speak, although he understood that he could serve her best at this moment by offering her the words she asked for. *And what of me?* he thought, bitter now, the words so foreign they were almost another language. *What of my needs?*

It was so wrong.

And yet, beneath the weight of hers, beneath the years of the service he had willingly undertaken, his needs had been met. Until now.

She had always accepted his silences before. But he knew that she must want companionship very badly, for she did not choose to do so now.

"Will you return to the Guild? Will you teach? Will you return to the home that you have never once spoken of in your years in my service? Or will you choose to take another master? There are few who would not value your service, given what you have built here."

"Terafin." The familiar syllables smoothed the anger out of his voice, although it was there, it was suddenly present. He wondered if she understood how deeply she had just insulted him, and decided that she was Amarais; she *must*, and she had chosen to do so deliberately.

"I will never seek another Master, no matter what the outcome of this current situation is. I am done with power. I am done with the hopes—" He stopped, then, seeing, for a moment, not the glorious evening gardens of House Terafin, but the enclosed classrooms of the Guild of the Domicis.

I will serve a lord I admire.

That had been the right answer; it was the right answer now. But no one had asked him—not himself, especially not himself—what he would do when that service ended. He had made it his life, having found a lord he admired and respected, to serve her, strengthen her, provide her with the support she required that she might meet the goals she held aloft for his quiet inspection.

She was silent as he returned to the present. But he did

not think the silence would last; it had a curious unfinished quality to it that spoke of the hovering presence of unshed words.

"Amarais."

"Morretz."

"I . . . cannot speak of your death."

He thought that would silence her, for she herself had never once spoken of it. It had become impossible not to know that she expected it, but he had waited, in a strained silence he had thought—until this moment—was devoid of hope.

He knew, now, that he had accomplished only the unenviable task of lying to himself. He had had hope, and she meant, this eve, to deprive him of even that.

"If you accepted it, Morretz, you would speak of it. You would speak of it because you would know—as *I* know, and I have accepted—that my death may mean the end of all that *we* have built together. The heir that I chose is gone; the South has taken her. The war—a war that is larger in every way than my House, but only slightly—has devoured her energy, her time, her attention.

"You would speak of it because you would desire a plan, some course of action, that would protect what we value more than we value life."

"Seers have been wrong in the past."

"Perhaps; I will not argue with you. It is not of the past that we speak, it is of the future, and of the future, there is little doubt. What she saw, she saw; in its fashion, it will come to pass."

As if she wielded the sword of Terafin, her words were sharp and terrible. He lifted a hand. They passed through it.

"You are astute, Terafin. I cannot accept what you accept."

"If acceptance is beyond you, can you find it in yourself to forgo anger? I have no intention of walking easily to death; it will come from a quarter that I cannot now foresee. I abjure no responsibility; anything that I *can* prevent

will be prevented." Her smile was the wolf's smile, lean
and powerful. "Let them work for my death. Let them out-
maneuver me, outthink me, outplay me." But the smile was
a ghost; it passed. "Accept that there are things I cannot
do."

And here was the crux of the matter. Here, at last. This
woman, this slender, beautiful woman—yes, beautiful,
more now than as an unformed, grave youth—was *The Terafin.* She had never failed at anything she had set her mind
to—not even when that thing was the governing of the most
powerful House in the Empire. Against odds far greater
than this, she had won her seat, had survived the House War
that had decimated the ranks of the House Guards, divided
all.

*Fight this! Fight it, you can only be killed if you choose
to surrender!*

As if she could hear the words he could not say, she
glanced away.

"Tell me that you are not tired, Amarais. Tell me."

She was silent a moment. At last, she said, "Bring the
den."

He wanted to shout at her then; wanted to grab her by the
arms and shake her, as if by doing so he could force her to
feel what he now felt, measure for measure. *You are Amarais, you are the woman I chose to give my life to. You have
failed at nothing in your life, will you surrender now?*

But he was domicis; and if what he had undertaken with
such profound hope so many years ago had become an almost unbearable burden, he bore it still.

He bowed stiffly and offered her his silent obedience.

Finch woke.

There was no light in her room, but she wasn't Jay; she
found the darkness of the sleeping House peaceful. Whatever fears clung to her from the past that had shaped them
both found its hold diminished, not strengthened, when the
lights dimmed and faded. Had nights in the twenty-fifth

holding been bad? Yes. But the days had been worse, for Finch. At night there were shadows, places made of moonlight and starlight in which someone slender and quiet could hide. Day forgave little.

She therefore needed no Avandar to stand by the foot of her bed, light in hand or cupped palm, as guardian against nightmares that might follow the waning of the day; indeed, had she been offered such a sentry, she would have found it hard to sleep, for she desired the simple stillness of a completely private place; she found in it a freedom from the responsibilities of the waking day.

Teller envied her for that; it was in the darkness that he, like Jay, lay awake, thinking with precision and clarity, about everything that had gone—or could go—wrong, and an hour might pass while he lay, immobile, waiting for something as elusive as sleep.

Not Finch. Covers tucked to chin—the one night foible she shared with almost every one of her den-kin—she could listen to the quiet sounds of the House.

Those noises differed from season to season, and she had grown to know them all, in the quiet and safety of this building, this gift from a merciful god. A merciful god, and Jay.

Jay.

Even in safety, there were barbs.

The House Guards were on patrol.

She heard them, heavy steps almost in unison, in the doors beyond the wing. Since Alea's death, guards such as these—perhaps these; at this time of night, she was uncertain who patrolled—had crossed one end of the manse to the other, in groups of no less than eight; Torvan himself saw to the composition of these small squads to assure that the loyalty of these men was, if not unquestioned, then at least not uniform.

They all serve The Terafin, she'd said, naïve then and no doubt naïve now.

Yes, he'd said, voice soft, gaze on a spot she couldn't see clearly, no matter how close it seemed to be. *But they know that an heir has to be chosen, and they know—all of them— that they've never been Chosen, not by the reigning Terafin. If they choose to support one of the contenders for the title, if they choose wisely, they're in at the ground, and they have a chance at promotion they'd never see here.*

You think they'd—they'd attack her?

The Terafin? No. Never. But each other? They owe no loyalty to any other lord.

Well, she'd asked. Funny, how little comfort answers offered.

The month of Misteral was often heavy with rain, damp and cool compared to the rest of the year. This month was slightly different; rain threatened to fall, but the clouds that carried it were shunted to one side of the city—or the other—by the gusts of salt-laden wind. Nevertheless, sailing merchants that came to make their reports, and take their rest, at House Terafin, could be heard cursing the weather with seasonal fervor.

They drank, Finch thought, nose wrinkling, too much. But when they weren't falling down drunk, or unpleasantly drunk, they had the best stories to tell; tales of lands far to the South, to the North, or—almost impossible to believe— to the East, beyond the ocean that stretched across the horizon without break.

Often in Misteral, Corvil, and Henden—Corvil was worst—they spent time in the city, bound to land; they visited their families, their Lords and their bankers, and they allowed themselves to be wheedled out of a good story. Finch, small for her size and gentle in manner, had become inordinately good at wheedling.

But this Misteral the merchant voices of House Terafin were notably strained or silent; the merchants stayed away from the manse unless they were drunk or commanded to do otherwise. She didn't blame them. If she'd had a choice, she'd've been anywhere else.

But Kalliaris had already frowned, fickle goddess.

Finch missed the merchants' voices the most; they could often be heard late into the night, mingled with the songs of hapless young bards who'd been dragged into the gardens or the halls. Merchants often did that, in *any* House, finding the open space, the acoustical heights, of the stately, fixed buildings irresistible in comparison to the vessels that were their true kingdoms.

No song, tonight. Or rather, no harp, no lute, no raised voice.

She heard owl cries instead; hunting songs, primitive and plain. Too primitive for the tended and controlled gardens, the clipped hedges, the flowers arranged into whimsical, well-ordered patterns that hinted at wilderness without ever being touched by it. She had learned the names of basic edible weeds and plants as a child in the twenty-fifth holding, and none of those graced the gardens. She had never learned the names of the plants, although she knew the tree names: oak and ash, yew and rood. She couldn't always tell which tree and which name coincided, but had learned to gloss over ignorance on the rare occasions she was forced to entertain someone who wished to walk the gardens.

And she found comfort in those nameless trees at night; they housed the wild birds, their sleeping children still wary of the hands and the intentions of men. Did it matter that some of those birds were birds of prey?

It had, once.

Now, they were simply what they were.

She listened as she lay in bed, palms curled round the edge of blanket, thinking: *I never hear the mice.*

Morbidly, she wondered if mice screamed when they were caught by the birds whose cries and calls she did hear.

Jay, she thought. *Are we still mice? After all this time, do you think we've really learned how to be anything else? Come home, damn it. Come home.*

But Jay was a continent away.

And Finch was here.

Thinking about mice. Finding an absurd comfort in the

fact that these small furred creatures—and the red kits, the dwarf rabbits—inconvenient in every possible way to the House and annoying to the gardener if they chose to nest in the wrong places (and they did), persisted; they existed no matter how well coiffed and tended the natural world around them became. Lived, no matter how hunted they were by the birds whose cry she could hear, when their own dying voices were silent, always silent.

Perhaps because she needed that reminder now, she lay awake longer than she usually did. She couldn't say why, but she wasn't surprised when she heard the knock at the door, even though she wasn't consciously aware of the sound of anyone in the hall beyond it. Not consciously.

She knew it was Ellerson.

Funny, that he could be here for so little time and have already worked his way down into an awareness that owed more to instinct than intellect.

She rose quickly, shedding both blanket and reverie, and opened the door; the hinges had time to squeak a faint protest.

He carried no light; the wall sconces did that for him. Jewel had ordered them set with magestones—and once the rest of the den had gotten over the *cost,* they accepted this daily evidence of magery as easily as they accepted all her other orders.

She blinked; light from the hall reached her eyes, wakening vision, returning the sense that the world was possessed of and by color.

"You had best dress," he told her quietly, his voice the essence of gravity.

"Dress well or dress?" she asked, but without much hope.

"The Terafin has sent for you."

She heard another creak down the hall; saw Teller's slender face peer out from the gap between door and frame. "Finch?"

She nodded. "There's trouble. Get dressed. Dress well."

"It is not necessary to assume there's trouble, as you call it," Ellerson told her, his minute frown as familiar as the tone of his voice, the stiff line of his shoulder.

"At this time of night? This is trouble. Teller, get the others, too."

"All of them?"

"All of them. But don't bother arguing with Angel about his clothing."

"What about Arann?"

"Him, too."

"But he's got patrol in two hours."

"Him too."

Teller nodded. His head disappeared and reappeared so quickly Finch wondered if he'd even bothered to change out of his clothing before going to bed.

"Ellerson?" he said, looking past her.

Ellerson nodded.

"Do you know what's wrong?"

"I am domicis," the old man replied.

"Why is she doing this to us?" Finch demanded, between clenched teeth. Her jaw was sore with it—it was an expression she'd learned, over the years, from watching Jay.

"ATerafin—"

"Someone's going to notice this. If we report to her in the day, when everyone else does, they can take note of it, but they can't prove anything significant has happened. But *this*—Kalliaris must have been frowning for weeks. Doesn't she know that they're all watching us?"

He didn't ask her who "they" were. Didn't need to. Instead he said, "You are not the only people being watched." The tone of his voice was critical enough that it would have stemmed the flow of words if those words hadn't been riding on so much fear.

"No—we're the only *insignificant* people being watched." She hadn't meant to sound so bitter; she almost never did. Shame warred with fear, and fear won. "Gods, this is so easy for *them*. They've got money, they've got ex-

perience, they've got friends in all the right places—
they've even got the House Guards all carved up between
them, and she isn't dead yet! They've got everything."

"Finch," Ellerson said, reaching out to touch her shoulder.

She looked up at him, eyes wide, the difference in their
height startling to her. Had she shrunk?

"ATerafin," he added, when he was certain of her atten-
tion. "Do you truly believe you are without your support?
Captain Torvan of the Chosen visits only one of the Terafin
House Council on a regular basis."

"Jay," she said at last. "But Jay's not here."

His grim silence was reproof enough. She was silent for
a moment. But when she spoke, her voice was level. "I'm
sorry," she said quietly. "You're right of course. But I—"

His hand, where it rested on her shoulder, tightened a
moment. She met his eyes.

Was surprised to see his smile. "No one who has responsibilities that they take seriously is completely without fear.
No one. But I have never met a man—or a woman—who
can meet those responsibilities well when fear rules them.
Jewel ATerafin trusted—and trusts—you. If you cannot
trust your own judgment in this, trust hers.

"Or mine, if it is of value. I admit that I was hesitant to
return here. I am retired. I have . . . enjoyed my retirement
immensely. But having begun, I remember what being a
domicis means to me, and I am honored to serve your den."

"And how long will you stay? How long this time?"

"I will stay," he told her gently, "until I am no longer
needed. Come. The others are waiting."

She looked up then. Everyone—except for Carver—was
standing, silent, in the wake of his words. She wondered
how much they'd heard. Carver joined them, struggling to
get his elbows free of the neck of a shirt he was too lazy to
unbutton.

"Ellerson?"

"Yes?"

"Who delivered the message?"

And a familiar figure stepped out of shadows that Finch *knew* weren't natural. Jay had paid a lot of money to see to that.

"Morretz?"

He stared at her a moment, as if appraising her, but his expression gave none of the result of that appraisal away.

"I did, ATerafin. I understand your fear. I understand your caution. I am here to make certain that—inasmuch as it can be—your passage to the shrine remains undetected by any of the would-be rulers of this House."

They had talked to Morretz. To Torvan. To Arrendas. They had spoken with Devon, and with Gabriel; they had become, in all things, Jay's substitutes. They had learned, clumsily, but with a determination that desperation underscored, to navigate the byways of the powerful, dancing carefully along the edge of the increasing hostilities between the four men and women who desired what only the den knew Jay already had—the legitimacy of The Terafin's choice.

Those hostilities had left the injured, the broken, and occasionally the dead, as evidence of what happened when too much ambition met with too much ambition. Had it been up to Finch, not a one of the four would now have the Terafin name behind them.

But The Terafin did not condescend to notice what could not be ignored. It hurt Finch, inexplicably, to see that, to accept it for what it was.

She shook herself.

Since they had understood the full meaning of Jewel ATerafin's vision, since they had realized that The Terafin was to die before Jay's return, they had not spoken with The Terafin. They had listened to her, when she had come to tell them of the demon attack in the Common; they had listened to her again, when she had finally decided that the personal investigation—the sifting through rubble, the tending to the injured—would be brought to a close. But they had not been required to speak; had not been required to meet her gaze and acknowledge their understanding.

Until tonight.

It was funny.

Finch was easily the smallest, physically, of Jay's den. How a bunch of grown men could huddle *behind* her wasn't clear—but they were all trying exactly that, with the single exception of Teller. If Finch had loved him before Jay left—and she had, she always had—she had never understood why he was obviously the most valued member of the den. It had stung, sometimes; still did, when she was feeling low enough to pick at it.

But she understood it now. Silent, he was still present, and when she reached the shrine of Terafin and hesitated a moment at the rounding curve of low, stone steps, he smiled at her briefly, squeezed her hand, and stepped forward.

The sound of his step against smoky, marbled stone brought her back to herself; she looked up, past his back—he'd left room for her at his side—to see the woman who waited for them.

The woman who ruled them all.

There was light, in this place. It perched in torches against the pillars that supported the domed ceiling. Someone had thought to fashion those torches into the shapes of birds, works of brass whose wings, from tip to tip, were polished and gleaming beneath the fires they carried. No magestones here; no even light; one of the groundskeepers or the gardeners must have carried oil, glass, and cloth when they came to this place; someone must have brought stools and ladders, rags; someone must have taken the time to light these lamps, and to gutter them, and to clean the residue of their burning from the backs of the creatures that held them.

And not just once, but over and over, each act deliberate and ephemeral.

Although she had always liked magestones, it seemed fitting that such effort and laborious care be offered here, beneath this simple dome, yet above the grass that surrounded the flat, rising steps. What time could not take from the stones mages made, it would take from the lamps, from the oil, from the labor of men—and the labor of men would again be called. And if the men who performed this maintenance were different, the fire didn't care.

"ATerafin," The Terafin said.

Finch nodded quietly; her nervousness deserted her as she cast one last glance at the natural fire that flickered in ordinary lamps.

She climbed the steps to join Teller, who waited for her in silence. When The Terafin did not speak, Finch turned and gestured wordlessly for the others to follow; only Angel lingered upon the path enclosed on either side by lamp, grass, pillar.

"Angel never accepted the House name," The Terafin said softly. There was a hint of question in the words.

"No. And he blackened Carver's eye when Carver did." Realization of whom she was speaking to followed—rather than preceded—the words; her tongue stuck to the roof of her mouth for just a moment.

But The Terafin's response was an unguarded smile. "He didn't wish to compromise his integrity by swearing an oath to serve the House when his loyalty was simply to one of its members?"

"Something like that."

"And if she ruled the House?"

Teller stiffened; Finch caught the sudden lack of movement—startling even though Teller was not the most animated of people—with the small part of her attention that wasn't focused on The Terafin.

Ellerson, she thought, *why aren't you here?* She wasn't up to a protracted conversation with arguably the most powerful woman in the Empire. Or at least not a politic, intelligent one.

Teller came to her rescue.

"If she ruled the House, he wouldn't need to accept the name; she already owns everything he's willing to give away. Angel's never been one for empty gestures."

"No," The Terafin replied. "And the rest of you?"

He shrugged, although his expression was completely serious. "For the rest of us, it wasn't empty. Jay wanted the name, and because she wanted it, we wanted it. Except for Angel. And Arann," he added, almost grudgingly.

"Arann." She found him easily on the crowded flat of the floor that encircled the altar by which she stood. Her expression shifted, a subtle motion of lines, a narrowing of eyes, a compression of lips. She nodded slightly as she met his eyes, and he came—albeit awkwardly—toward her.

He did what they had failed to do; knelt before her feet, bowed his head.

Finch was suddenly aware of the sword that hung by his side—had to be; it scraped against the surface of marbled stone like fingers against board. No one else wore one. Carver and Angel had taken lessons, but the weaponsmaster Jay had sent them *all* to had chosen instead to focus on the skills he felt they did have: long daggers, short daggers, thrown weapons.

But Arann had joined the House Guards almost right from the start. Jay had hated it. Had been proud of it, and had hated it.

And he knew. Funny, it had hardly bothered him at all when she'd been here. But Finch knew him well enough; he'd gone to his knees tonight, but it was the first time in years that old split loyalties chafed at him.

The Terafin knew it as well.

She'd known Arann for a handful of years as a polite, but respectful half-stranger, but she could also see what Finch, who was almost blood-kin, could see—and no less clearly. That, Finch thought without rancor, was why she was The Terafin.

Arann rose as The Terafin gestured.

"Well," she said, "are you hers or are you mine?"

He was not a wordsmith.

But he was not a coward either; the fear of being forced, after so many years, to choose was more terrible than the event itself. He squared his shoulders, shedding weight in the process.

"Both."

"Is that a suitable reply?"

"It's the only one I have, Terafin."

"I . . . see." The woman who ruled stepped back; her hands touched the pale, cold surface of stone as if she might draw strength from the Terafin altar. It cut across the heart of the shrine, forgotten by the den until the moment she chose to remind them of its existence by this simple gesture.

"You both serve the House," he continued, for if she touched the altar with the flat of her palms, she did not look away.

"I rule the House," she said, the words cool.

"You serve the House best *by* ruling it. And Jay served the House best by serving *you.*"

"And how will she serve the House when I am dead?"

Arann didn't flinch. Finch did. And because she did, she missed the expression on his face.

"By ruling it," he said quietly. "By ruling it because in the end you've left her no other choice."

"I?"

"You know who seeks power. You've seen them. You've seen what they're willing to do to gain it. But—"

"It is not easy to remove the powerful from their positions. I would weaken Terafin immeasurably if I were to attempt such an extraction."

"You weaken it," he said, "by your willingness to leave that task to others."

"Do I?" She turned away. Gazed into the night sky in the distance, broken by the outline of the grand, the glorious, House. "Arann, how many of the four who now desire the title will survive the struggle to gain it?"

His silence was her answer; it was an honest silence. She waited, gaze still upon her home, her life's work. And then she turned her back upon it, to look once again at the handful of men and women who were Jay's.

"I believe that two will not survive. Two will. And those two—whoever they are—will lend their strength and their expertise to the House."

"While they circle like vultures."

"No. They will accept their defeat. They play the edges of a game that could easily destroy what they desire. The Kings have turned a blind eye toward the struggles of the House—of any of the Houses—when there is a question of succession. Such small wars serve their purpose in a fashion. While such ambition is turned toward one of The Ten, it cannot be turned toward the Thrones."

"Only the god-born rule the Empire."

"Indeed, that is true. Now. But remember your history; before the god-born, who ruled?"

It was Teller who said, quietly, "The Blood Barons."

Henden cast its long, long shadow. Even the mention of the demon kin was somehow less threatening than the mention of the men who had made the Empire their battleground for so long that all of its traditions and festivals still spoke of the scars.

"B–but—But that was before the god-born. The Twin Kings can't be unseated now."

Her smile was bitter. "Why do you say that, Arann?"

"Because—they're the children of *gods*."

"They are not, except by cunning and the consensus of the ruled, more powerful than the magi. They are not more powerful than the talent-born. On a whim, the former bardmaster of Senniel College could have forced them to dance to any tune she desired to call. They are not, as the scions of gods, among the most powerful of their kind and—in case it has escaped your notice, and it probably has—they pay for the immortal blood that burns in their veins; their lives are measured in shortened years.

"And you forget, god-born or no, had the first of the Twin Kings not been the children of Veralaan, had they not possessed the blood of the 'rightful' ruler of these lands, they would have received no aid; The Ten would not have joined them in their crusade. The Ten were not god-born," she added softly, "but they believed, then, that blood mattered more than achievement. Or that it was part of achievement; I confess that I do not understand the niceties of those ancient beliefs, having benefited in a fashion from their demise." Her smile was brief and plain.

"You expect much, Arann, from the god-born; they are, after all, mortal. But I digress; The Ten serve a purpose in many, many ways. The ambitious and the powerful are drawn to the Houses like moths to flame. Some achieve greatness within their confines; others achieve merely death. The Kings reign above, and beneath us the rest of the Empire unfolds. We are suspended in a manner of our choosing. We take a risk; we bear the cost."

"But not alone," Teller told her quietly.

She raised a brow. She had not addressed Teller directly.

"You called us; we came. Jay's never called us here, and she comes all the time."

"You are perceptive; I expect no less. Do you know who you will be, if you survive this war, Teller ATerafin?"

His smile was slight. "Teller ATerafin." And sweet.

"Of that, I have no doubt," The Terafin replied. Her voice deepened a moment, her expression shifting in the light as she turned again. "Survive," she whispered. "Haerrad saw clearly when he came to you."

Teller nodded.

"When I was younger—much, much younger—I felt that friends were a weakness. Had I the choice, I would have gathered men like Duvari around me, and no others."

Duvari, Lord of the Compact, was perhaps the coldest man Finch had ever met. He had come, on a handful of occasions, to speak with The Terafin—or Jay—and everything about him made her want to flinch. Or run.

She would really have to learn how to school her expression.

"Yes, I understand, Finch. But a man like Duvari is very, very hard to kill. Of all the men in the Empire, if I could choose one who would survive the world's end, the coming of the second Hells, the return of the Firstborn—it would be Duvari."

"Only the good die young," Finch muttered.

"Perhaps. It doesn't matter; he picks his cause and he never wavers. It was important to me that my compatriots not die. Important that their deaths in no way be laid at my feet." Her arms bent; her hands supported her weight. "It's been so long, I had forgotten how visceral that desire could be."

Finch knew, then. "Until Alea," she whispered.

"Until Alea." The Terafin bowed her head. "Alea was the closest thing to a child the lord of a House is generally permitted. I was fond of her—and I am fond of few. But I was proud of her as well; she was worthy of respect.

"Morretz will never forgive me," she added quietly. "In my youth, I would have sought vengeance; I would have offered death for her death; I would have destroyed even the House I valued in order to achieve that end, and have peace.

"But I am not young, not as I was then. The things that burn me merely scar; they light no spark; they fan no useful flame. And peace is not to be gained by a simple death. Or a complicated one."

"Why will Morretz—"

Teller shook his head, sharply, and Finch shut up. It was as close to command as Teller got.

"I have asked you here for a reason," The Terafin said. She drew breath, gained height; the line of her shoulders straightened.

"You want our oaths."

"Yes."

"You want more than our oaths."

"Yes."

"We don't have a lot more to give you."

"Teller ATerafin," The Terafin said, bowing slightly, "I would never ask you to join the Chosen; you are a foot too short, and several inches too slender. But you have the temperament, if not the build. Finch, likewise." She looked away again. And then back. "Arann," she said, speaking to the only member of the den who had chosen to pledge allegiance to her House, and therefore indirectly, to her.

"Terafin."

For the first time that evening—and Finch would remember this for the rest of her life, no matter how short or how long that might be—The Terafin pulled aside the great cloak she wore. The cloak itself was fine, but weathered, and it sat too low on her shoulders, too close to the ground. Finch might have paid more attention to it, but it was a simple curtain over an unexpected window, and what lay beyond the window held all of her attention the moment she glimpsed it.

The scabbard.

The sword.

Justice.

She raised her hands to her mouth.

"Who do you serve, Arann ATerafin?"

He was, Finch thought, white as the altar at his lord's back. But he must have had some color left, because he got even paler when the sword left its sheath.

He knelt. Raised his face to meet her unyielding gaze.

"You," he said, so softly that Finch wasn't certain she'd heard it.

"Good. And do you trust me, Arann?"

"Yes." Louder.

"Will you trust my words above the words of all others?"

"Yes."

"Will you know which words are mine when all words come to you clothed in deceit and lies?"

He was silent. Finch wasn't surprised; she would have

been. He lowered his face a moment, to look at the ground between her feet.

"To be one of the Chosen is not to be a mindless servant, not to be a fine swordsman; it is not a simple act of loyalty, although perhaps to the eyes of outsiders, loyalty defines the Chosen. You must know *me*, must understand *me*, must decide for yourself when an order you are told is from me is nonetheless not mine. Do you understand? You must, with loyalty and knowledge as a guide, be true in ways that I cannot foresee when I ask you to make this oath and accept the weight of this responsibility.

"Not all who are asked accept. And many of the men and women—Alayra, for one, and Arrendas—asked for three days grace in which to consider what I have just said. But forgive me; I do not have three days to give you. You must decide, as I have, on this eve."

He raised his face again. "Do you trust me, Terafin?"

The corner of her lips turned up slightly in a grudging smile. "A fair question."

"Do you believe that I am capable of what you've asked?"

"A second fair question. Why do you ask?"

"The timing," he said.

The Terafin's brow rose; the smile left her lips. She nodded slowly.

"You want me among the Chosen."

"Yes."

"Because of Jay."

"I would not weaken the Chosen," she told him, her voice cool. "You are loyal to me if you stand among them. You make your vow, and take your rank, from my hands and mine alone."

"Tell me why," Arann said. "Tell us."

She touched his forehead with the tip of her blade. Her hand was absolutely steady; it had to be. Finch could tell, by the sudden stillness of Arann's face, that there was no distance between skin and steel.

"Jewel ATerafin came to the House at a time that might be considered inauspicious by a lesser lord." No humility at all in the words—but Finch didn't mind; they were true. "And proved her value and her worth to my House from the day she arrived.

"Her worth was never in question; yours—all of yours—was. I knew that she took responsibility for you, and I admired that in a girl of her age and her background; I was willing to take you on to observe how she handled the transition from poverty to power.

"But I was impressed. From the streets of the twenty-fifth holding, with very little guidance, she chose her companions, and she chose well. I will leave out the peccadilloes of the two young men; they are beneath regard, but they do not invalidate their worth.

"In time, I offered the den the House name." The Terafin smiled. But she did not lower the sword; it rested between them, like the caress of an executioner. "I did not offer it for Jewel's sake. I did not offer it as a reward for her service.

"You earned what you now bear. But you, Arann, were slightly different.

"I believed then, and I believe now, that had you not been dying when Jewel first arrived at the gates of the manse, had Jewel not bargained so harshly for your life, and had your life not required such drastic intervention to save, you would not now stand among the House Guard; you would cleave to your den.

"But you did receive injuries that would have proved fatal, and Alowan did, indeed, call you back from the foothills—or the bridge—that leads to Mandaros' Halls. I believe that Alowan has so often been forced to heal me that his impression of me shaded yours; you saw not what the den saw, but what Alowan did. And does."

Arann did not move, for the sword still had not wavered.

I never realized The Terafin was so strong, Finch thought, knowing that she would have cut his face from forehead to nose tip about two sentences in because the sword was so damn heavy.

"What Alowan sees in me, he sees in Jewel ATerafin. What she desires for herself, and for this House, is tainted to some degree by the life that formed her—but it is also informed by the life she has built. She has never—and I believe she never will—stoop to assassination to achieve her ends.

"And I will not criticize the limitations that she places upon herself; in some ways it is by the limitations we choose to labor under that we are best judged."

It was Teller who interrupted her. Or rather, Teller who spoke when she fell silent.

"Terafin," he said, with more respect than he usually put into a name.

She shifted her gaze, but nothing else.

"You haven't answered his question. You haven't told us why."

"Do you need to hear it? Very well. If I die here before Jewel returns, the chance of her taking what *is* hers by right of succession is almost none. The Kings will not interfere if she does not petition them, and even if she does petition them, even if she carries some document, some pale piece of evidence of the truth of her words, they will be . . . loath to interfere. She may hold enough influence to sway them, but that will destroy the House. Even if she arrives in time, if there is no support in place—and placed there by *my* command—it will unravel.

"And I do not believe that Jewel would take the risk of opening the House up to the inspection—and far, far worse—the dictate of the Kings."

"But the Kings are—"

"The Kings rule the Empire. *We* rule the House."

Finch shut up.

"If she has, as her support, members of significance in the House and its affairs, if she has among her supporters, one or both of the captains of my Chosen, if she has council members, no matter how junior, the matter of the succession will not be so swiftly decided."

"I therefore wish to confer upon you, her strongest and her most loyal supporters, those titles that your experience will bear." She seemed to lose strength, then; her shoulders seemed to bow, at last, to some inevitable pressure, some invisible hand.

"Gabriel is my right-kin, but he may be sorely tried in this, for his blood-son is among the contenders. I am not completely certain what he will choose to do if I am no longer his lord.

"Arann," she said quietly, "the sword is heavy. Choose."

He nodded; the tip of the blade scored his forehead. "As you have chosen," he said quietly. "I so choose." He held out his hand, and she laid the edge of the blade against it.

No one was surprised who could see the blood well up in his cupped palm.

She lowered the blade, but she did not sheathe it.

Instead she waited until he had gained his feet.

"Teller," she said, "I would have both you and Finch join the House Council."

Just like that.

"The—*the* House Council?" Finch knew she was sputtering. She looked up, and at the edge of the garden path, she could see Ellerson waiting alongside Morretz. She almost raised both of her hands in a wild frenzy.

"We can't give you an answer tonight," Teller said.

Finch let him speak for her. She didn't have words to speak for herself.

"Ah. You misunderstand me, Teller. What I asked of Arann cannot be commanded. It has been thus with The Terafin and the Chosen since the founding of the line. But what I ask of you and Finch is not in any way a request." She paused. "I understand your reservations. Believe that they are not as strong as mine. But you *will* join the next meeting of the Council when it convenes in three days, and you will be introduced there."

"But—but—"

"Take Jester as your aide; you are allowed four, with pay. Take Carver and Angel as two of your guards, if you can have them present themselves decently. Speak to Torvan about the rest." She bowed her head.

"I am . . . sorry . . . to place this burden upon you now. But Healer Levec spoke to Alowan, and Alowan spoke to me; we are certain that Jewel will return from the South.

"She will never be the leader of a den in the twenty-fifth holding again. She understood that before she left. Understand that you will never again be a den in the twenty-fifth holding. You will be the foundation upon which this House survives.

"I can afford to spare you nothing. And having decided, I must ask one further favor." She turned to Arann, Arann of the Chosen. "Arann," she said gravely, "draw your blade."

"I—"

"Draw it."

He had never witnessed the induction of the Chosen before, but even so, he knew that there was something amiss. He hesitated a moment, and then rose, hand still bleeding, and drew his blade. "I won't cut you," she said without thinking. "It is part of the ceremony, but it will wait until the ceremony."

"Then why did you cut him?"

She turned her gaze to Finch. "I have my reasons." It was as close to *shut up* as The Terafin ever got.

"Give me your sword, ATerafin."

Again he hesitated.

As if he knew what she was about to do.

CHAPTER TWO

ELLERSON knew many things, but the things that came to him through the mixture of experience, familiarity and observation were often the most poignant.

He knew, for instance, as he stood beneath the moon's full light, that his sole companion had never been allowed to attend The Terafin at the shrine of Terafin. Morretz did not feel compelled to impart this information and Ellerson did not ask for it; it came to him in the line of shoulder and chin, the widening and narrowing of eyes, the compression of lips and the stillness, the absolutely stillness of arms, weighted by fists, as they rested at Morretz's sides.

This man had been his student so long ago memory had worn the sharper edges away from the experience. What remained, for so many years, had been pride.

That pride was now replaced; it had been shunted forcefully to one side by a bitter, bitter regret. "Morretz," he said quietly, for this was possibly the only opportunity he would have to speak so freely; they were men indentured by their word to the service of masters who required both vigilance and presence, and if Ellerson might be willing to leave the side of his den—yes, after all these years, his—to offer counsel or guidance to Morretz, he was certain that Morretz would never again willingly leave the side of The Terafin to seek it.

Morretz did not look away. But he nodded.

"There is a place for you," the older man said quietly, "within the Guild of the Domicis. You have served only one master, and that master is a master of note. You have seen much, and that experience—"

Morretz lifted a hand, although his attention seemed absorbed by the conversation—if it were that, between a woman of The Terafin's station and that of Jewel's den— unfolding in the distance.

Ellerson knew well that a domicis did not require the ability to hear in order to follow a conversation, but he did require clear vision, an unimpeded line of sight. The distance, and the night sky, denied Morretz that. But he did not look away.

Ellerson did. He studied the profile of this former student, the line of his nose, the rise of his chin, the slight furrowing of brow that had probably become a permanent landmark in the vistas of his expression. And he surrendered with grace.

"Teller told me," he said quietly.

Morretz frowned. "Told you?"

Ellerson did not reply, willing to let the conversation go if Morretz was unwilling to share its weight.

But Morretz closed his eyes a moment; it was as much a turning away from his duties as he would now allow himself.

He will be devoured, Ellerson thought. *He will be devoured and he will allow himself nothing.*

"Teller ATerafin is the heart of Jewel ATerafin's den," Morretz said quietly. "He sees much, and he usually hoards knowledge unless it is necessary that another know it. I am . . . grateful that you chose to return."

"Not, I am certain, as grateful as they are."

That teased a smile from the corner of Morretz's lips; a twitch of motion. But the smile itself never reached the rest of his face.

"What do you desire now?" Ellerson asked him, softly.

"What I have always desired," was the quiet reply. "To serve *her.* To help her attain what she envisions."

"And if you cannot have that, what?"

"What else is there? I have trained for nothing else. Remove that from me and I have nothing to offer."

Ellerson knew it was futile, but he tried. "The guild values you enough that what you offer would be accepted without reservation."

"Ellerson, you know as well as I that there are perhaps a handful of teachers within the hall of the domicis who chose to serve a single lord. And of those, not one lost their lord to war or violence."

Ellerson nodded, although he knew that Morretz would not see the simple acknowledgment. "What will you do?"

Morretz offered a bitter laugh as response. But words followed it, awkward and hesitant. "That is the second time tonight I've been asked that question. What do you *think* I will do, Ellerson?"

"Will you seek vengeance for what you cannot prevent?"

Morretz shrugged.

Ellerson stared at the line of his shoulders, seeing in them something strong enough to bear any burden.

Any burden but this one.

"Morretz."

"Will you lecture me now, Ellerson? You of all people? Will you tell me the guild's rules, and attempt to force upon me the morals and the ethics that—"

"That keep the domicis themselves beyond the reach of assassins? Think, Morretz, and think carefully, before you choose that path. You serve her, and you serve her well. Join the war in such an obvious fashion *after* the term of your contract has ended, and you endanger any who serves in a like position. The domicis have always been neutral after the death of a lord."

"They have always aped neutrality. It is not the same."

"The pretense is not optional, Morretz."

"And if I choose a path of violence? If I choose a path of retribution?"

"You will be disbarred," Ellerson replied evenly, the words sharp and painful on the tongue, but bland and neutral to the ear. "You will be disbarred instead of being honored."

Morretz laughed. "There is nothing worse that you can do?"

"No. Nothing."

Silence.

A long pause was broken in the distance by Arann. He approached The Terafin and knelt at her feet.

Morretz tensed. Tensed and then slumped; his chin lowered by slow degree, as if the weight of his head had gradually become too much to bear. "Ellerson," he said quietly. Helplessly. "Did you ever lose a master?"

"Yes. But my vow and my desire was not yours, and if it affected me, it did not affect me in this fashion. I did not know in advance that I would lose my masters. I did not know that my greatest vigilance would amount to nothing. And I did not—understand this—choose to bind my life so inextricably with the life of another."

"Did you desire no vengeance?"

"Truthfully? No. But I am not the man you should seek."

"Who is?"

"Would you seek him, if I were to give you his name? Would you leave her side for long enough to seek counsel and guidance? Could you, and be certain that your absence was not somehow the catalyst that led to the death you see as inevitable?"

Each word made Morretz flinch.

The older man flinched as well. But once. He had chosen to interfere, and he did so now with economy and quiet determination. It was hard, to care. It made one vulnerable to pain. Not even age and experience could shield him.

Across the cultivated path, between the standing lamps with their orbs of protected fire, their halos cast by colored magestones, the breeze swept across grass and flower bed.

It carried the sound of steel against steel. Both men watched as The Terafin drew her sword. She drew it, held it. The kneeling man did not flinch or hesitate, although she brushed his forehead with its point.

"I . . . would seek him . . . if it were possible. There are times when she will not . . . have me present."

"Morretz," Ellerson said quietly, "everything you have been to her has come out of what you are: domicis, of the Guild of the Domicis.

"Do you think she desires your disgrace? Do you think she does not know what you face? Do you think she does not fear for you? She understands that the end of her life is the end of yours in some fashion, and if I am any judge of character, that knowledge weighs upon her heavily. Do not disgrace yourself in her memory; do not burden her with that."

The younger man's lids shut tight; lashes compressed into a dark line that would have been lost to sight but for the particularly bright silver of moonlight. "She will be dead; it will not trouble her."

"No?"

He might have answered. Had he, he would have answered honestly, and the dialogue might have opened up an avenue of discussion that would have saved him much pain at a later date.

But the kneeling Arann now rose, and the tableau shifted and changed in such a way that Ellerson's eyes were also drawn, his gaze held.

The only member of Jewel's den to serve as House Guard drew his sword in the presence of his chosen lord. The Terafin transferred the blade she held to her left hand, and held out her right, palm up, its emptiness illuminated with startling clarity by the flickering fires that circumnavigated the underside of the dome.

Morretz watched.

Watched as she held out the Sword of Terafin.

Arann took a step back, and although the distance was enough to make words difficult to glean from the motion of lips, it was not so great that shock—and fear—were easily hidden.

But she did not shrink or flinch. She had chosen. What she offered was not a request, although Ellerson would not have been surprised had she cloaked her command in the niceties of polite speech.

Hands trembling, Arann fell to one knee.

The Terafin did not move until he rose again. Rose and accepted the sword that she offered him. He held it before him, as if it were a serpent, or worse.

She stood, her bearing as regal as the bearing of any King Morretz had ever watched. All motion was his, and it was stiff, raw, fearful. For a moment.

But her resolve carried the short distance between herself and Arann, and after a moment, he stilled.

Only when he sheathed the sword did Morretz grunt in pain.

Ellerson looked away.

After they were gone, she was alone.

And although she was old enough to know that "alone" and "lonely" were not synonyms, she felt the isolation sharply nonetheless. Her hands were empty. She had sheathed the sword that Arann had carried to the shrine, and its weight, against the length of her thigh, her left hip, felt wrong.

She would get used to it, of course. But of all the steps she had taken to ensure the survival of the House that she had built, it was the most painful. Symbols? She understood their value.

Amarais closed her eyes.

He came to her.

She was aware of his presence, although until he spoke he made no sound at all.

"Terafin," she said softly.

"Terafin," he replied.

She turned, the hem of her skirts brushing stone, the

soles of her shoes rubbing its surface. His touched nothing. What face, she thought, her hand dropping to the hilt of her sword, what face would he wear?

She was unprepared to see Morretz.

She almost told him to leave, but something about his eyes invoked silence. He waited until she groped her way through that silence to say something entirely different.

"Do you disapprove?"

"Of the Sword?"

She nodded.

"No, Terafin. It is a sword, and if it has history, it is that history which makes it valuable. You have chosen." He smiled. "There is not another leader of this House that has passed that blade on before his death."

"Of all the things I possess that might add verity and strength to a claim, it is the only one I can do without."

"Indeed."

She lapsed into silence.

He waited.

"Can you see the future?" she asked him. "Can you see who will—who must—rule Terafin?"

"No more than you, Terafin. But I, too, have made my choice, and it is hard to rule the House Terafin without my blessing."

"Is it impossible?"

His pause was shorter than either of hers had been, but it bore greater weight. An answer.

"Will she return?"

"If word reaches her, she will."

"Will she return in time?"

Again, he chose shelter in silence.

She walked, slowly, toward the stairs that circled the shrine; the night was dark, the air chill. It was cold, even for the season; she gathered her cloak about her shoulders in hands that trembled.

"Will you not ask the first question that came to you when you saw me this eve?"

"No."

To her surprise, he chuckled. She turned, then; he stood between her and the altar upon which she had, literally and figuratively, offered everything she had ever desired or owned.

"Shall I answer it before you flee?"

That stung; she was not a child, to be prodded by her elders, no matter who that elder might be. She stopped, her foot an inch away from the edge of the dais.

But she had no desire to see the Terafin ancestor take Morretz's face and make it his own; she had felt less qualms when he had come to her as a dark, gray mirror—a harbinger of the doom she struggled daily to accept.

And to reject.

"I do not want the House to devour him," she said coldly.

"And you have decided this only now?"

"It has been some months in coming, but . . . I have decided, yes."

"It is a pity then," the voice, not Morretz's voice, drifted closer. "The decision is—among the many that you have made—one of the few that is not yours."

She did turn then. "Not mine? Perhaps. But it is even less yours. He is not—"

"ATerafin?"

"ATerafin. He is not ATerafin. He has never been ATerafin. He would never disgrace his guild by taking the name, although would he—would he, I would have given it to him years ago."

"When?"

"Does it matter?"

"Perhaps. Perhaps not. You are correct—he would not have taken the name. If you offered it now, he would refuse. But name or no, he has served me well."

"He has served *me*," she snapped, for a moment losing the fine control and bearing which marked her position.

"Yes," the Terafin spirit replied.

She lapsed into silence and anger. The anger was terrible.

"Do not let it consume you," the spirit said, and she cursed him.

"Does it matter? Anger, sorrow, hatred, fear—in the end they make no difference; my fate, such as it is, is here, or—" she lifted an arm and pointed to the manse—"there, where my enemies watch. I chose them," she added, "all but a handful."

"Yes, and you chose wisely; no House is built without men of ambition. Those that survive this will strengthen the House."

"If I had my way, none would survive."

"The Sword is named *Justice*," he said softly, "but you cannot simply give it away. Or give it to another for safe-keeping."

She turned then. Said nothing at all.

The expression upon the face of the Terafin spirit was not an expression that had ever graced Morretz.

"Amarais," he said softly, "be wary. Now is the time that the danger is greatest."

"To me? Or to you?"

He did not answer that question. Instead, he said, "Morretz will never return to the Guild of the Domicis."

She lifted a hand, palm out, a command.

But he was already beyond her.

"He made his choice, years ago, and it was no less binding a choice than yours. He will falter if you falter; that is all.

"Be kind, as you can."

"He has never asked for kindness."

"Ah," the spirit replied quietly. "I did not necessarily speak of him."

She started to speak, and then thought better of it as steps—heavy, but not so heavy that they were unpleasant, approached this last of her strongholds, this private retreat.

"I am . . . trying . . . in my fashion. To be kind to him."

"By summoning what remains of Jewel's den? By delivering the Sword of Terafin into their keeping? By speaking of nothing that concerns your fate where it might trouble him?

"If these are acts of kindness, Amarais, I am troubled."

"Oh?"

"It would appear, to me, that you do not understand your domicis at all, after he has offered—and you have accepted—a life of service."

The footsteps were real. Corporeal.

She started to speak, but he had turned to face those steps; he stepped forward, becoming one with the night sky that was visible from beneath domed ceiling, captured light.

Framed by his vanishing form was the man whose appearance he had harbored.

Morretz.

They stared at each other. Morretz did not venture down the path to the shrine, but he was unarguably present. He did not speak.

She lifted her hands to the edges of her cloak, drawing it across her shoulders. It was Winter in Averalaan, or what passed for Winter, and it was both dry for the season, and cool. But she knew the weather as well as anyone who had lived upon the Isle for years; if the chill worsened, it would not become so terrible that it would invite the Northern snows.

She drew her shoulders back; let her hands drop to her sides where they rested, unnaturally heavy.

She had thought to remain silent, but the words of the Terafin ancestor remained in his absence. She said, without thought, "this is the last Winter."

As if words were permission, Morretz, who was not of Terafin, rose to the dais by climbing the steps that led to his lord. "The last Winter," he repeated.

She looked up, and up again, to meet his eyes; she was not a short woman, and she had always known that he was not a short man—but she seldom felt the difference in their height so keenly.

He said, simply, "The Sword, Amarais."

And she tried to answer, but the words were lost; she managed a shrug, no more. The shrug was awkward; it dislodged the line of the too-large cloak she wore. The cloak that had a history that came from a time before House Terafin, before her rule here, when comfort had been easier to ask for, easier to accept.

Handernesse. Her grandfather's house. Her grandfather's cloak, and he dead these many years.

Morretz stepped naturally toward her, his hand finding the lining of the cloak, the seams of worn and faded cloth, and righting them, gentling their fall from her shoulder.

But his hands did not leave her shoulders. She could not see his face, and that made it easier.

Amarais Handernesse ATerafin closed her eyes and in the space hallowed by vow and history, dropped her hand to the hilt of a foreign blade and began to weep.

CHAPTER THREE

21st of Misteral, 427 AA
Sea of Sorrows

H E HAD a debt to pay.
There was only one way to pay it. Marakas par el'Sol faced the desert in grim silence.

The Sea of Sorrows could not be crossed by Northern boat; it was a haze of heat, and the waves that formed in the sand were laid there by wind, baked by sun, hardened by the lack of water.

He had seen them for days, crossing each ridge, riding each slope, his gaze traveling to the South, although often the East or West called him. To the North, he did not look; it contained only the shadows of Raverra, the Terrean in which the Tor Leonne lay, contested and shadowed.

He carried his water with him, and he drank sparingly; the skins were not so heavy that they would hold him long if he chose to be careless. His desert craft could lead him to succulents and night flowering plants, but even in these there was no guarantee. Only a madman made such a trek.

And perhaps he was mad. He had only himself as judge; he could ask no other's opinion. Marakas par el'Sol undertook this journey in isolation. It suited him.

After the death of his wife and his son, he had found little comfort in company. But not none. He carried *Verragar,* and he understood its true nature; the blade brought him purpose, and purpose brought him a measure of peace.

When he had first come North to the Tor Leonne he had
thought that death alone would grant him that.

He paused a moment, breaking the hard ground to mark
it. It was easy to walk in circles; the heat made a man unwary. His shadow was long, but it grew shorter as he
worked; a warning. A sign.

But the breaking did not lend him shelter; not from the
heat, and not from his memories.

Love had scarred him; failure to preserve what he had
loved had driven him from the Terrean of Oerta to the
Radann. He had thought that no one could understand the
depth of the pain he had felt then—arrogance, surely. He
had, with age, come to understand that all men bore scars,
all men suffered loss.

The sun, in the desert scrub of the Terrean of Raverra,
was rising and he would have to seek shelter soon. But from
memory there was no certain shelter.

"You are Marakas el'Sol."

He nodded. Time, now, to bow and accept his choice. He
glanced at the ground, his gaze sliding away from the
weathered visage of a man who was not much older than
he: the kai el'Sol. The man who ruled the Radann.

"Among the Radann you will have no other name."

He nodded again. There was little else he could do, and
words—among men—were used sparingly.

It was the words he missed most. Amelia had chattered
from dawn until dusk, and often past that into the Lady's
time. When their son grasped the use of language—with a
glee that encompassed the whole of his chubby little
body—she would let her own words blend with his as if
words were music, emotion, truth. The silence of their absence had never abated.

But the man who questioned him did not seem interested
in silence, and Marakas understood that among the Lord's
men, power ruled.

Still, he had waited.

"Did your family accept this?"

The Radann kai el'Sol had not smiled when he posed the question. If he had, it might have gone unanswered.

"If I still had a family, I would not be here."

"Ah." Fredero kai el'Sol had offered a moment of silence. And then he surprised Marakas, for the first time. But not for the last. "My family did not approve. When I became the kai el'Sol, I had hoped it would mollify them. But my father merely considered it proof of all that my family had lost by my choice." His smile was wry. "My brother wished me well, although in truth he understood my choice no better than my father." The kai el'Sol rose. "But I think you do, Marakas."

Marakas stared blankly at the kai el'Sol.

"Come, walk with me."

They walked, and to the surprise of the less experienced of the Radann, they walked beneath the open sky.

Only Jevri el'Sol accompanied them, although by title and rank, the kai el'Sol was accustomed to the presence of armed servitors; indeed, they were as much a part of his regalia as the sword he carried and the sun he bore, ascendant, across his chest.

Still, on this day, he dismissed them, and they went without demur, leaving only the old man behind. Jevri el'Sol was Fredero's man. Although he carried the name, and the symbol, of the Lord, his carriage and bearing spoke of the finest of seraf training.

But he was no seraf; no seraf could serve the Lord.

Fredero spoke first. And his words stayed with Marakas as if they were personal epiphany. "What power exists without honor?"

Marakas was silent. Not because the question demanded thought, although if a question had been asked this day that did, it was that one, but rather because the kai el'Sol's voice had taken its edge, revealing it. Marakas had not come to the Radann to die, and although he had told himself a hundred times, a thousand, that death was preferable to this

searing half-life, this empty existence, he was weak enough
to cling to life. His shame.

But the kai el'Sol asked no idle question; he turned once
to meet Marakas' gaze, and his own gaze was a command.

The sun was high, the bright face of the Lord that
Marakas hated. Before he could stop himself, Marakas said
bitterly, "Does the Lord concern himself with honor?"

The kai el'Sol stopped. Jevri's breath, drawn once and
held, was the only sound that followed Marakas' question.

Marakas el'Sol knew a moment of despair, and then he,
too, revealed his edge; he turned to the kai el'Sol. "You
know why I came."

"I believe that I understand it, yes. But I wish to hear it
before I judge you."

"Is not judgment, beneath the Lord's gaze, meted out by
combat, by victory, or by loss?"

"Perhaps. Do you challenge me, Marakas?"

"Not you."

"Oh? I am the first of the Lord's servants. I am the man
who upholds his law."

"You are Lambertan," Marakas replied evenly.

"No man retains family ties who comes to the Radann.
Was this not made clear to you when your oath was accepted?"

"My oath was accepted by men," was the reply. "By
men."

"It is not the men who accepted the oath, but the man
who offered it, that concerns me. Why did you join the
Radann?"

"Justice," he whispered. "I desire justice."

"Justice." Fredero drew breath and began to walk again.

"Lamberto is known for its honor. If you seek to sever
family ties, if you seek to deny family loyalty, I have no
choice but to believe you. But you were born, bred, raised
by Lambertans. Do you seek to tell me that Lamberto no
longer rules your actions?"

"Am I only Lambertan?"

"No."

"Then, no, I seek no such refuge. You have not answered my question."

"Power without honor is what the bandits wield. It is what slavers own. It is what criminals demonstrate, when they buy swords and wield them against those who are helpless. The Lord bears witness. The Lord does not judge. They survive, at his whim, because they *can*." He should not have started, because once begun, the words had a force, a desire, a life of their own; he no longer controlled them. "What honor is there in the slaughter of the helpless? What honor is there in the destruction of the innocent? Surely, if victory is all that the Lord requires—and it seems that it is, indeed, all that he *does* require—then the Lord that we serve is no different from the Lord of Night?"

"Indeed. If your supposition were correct, there would be no difference."

"And how is it not correct?"

Fredero was silent. He lifted a hand, and his servant, who appeared on the brink of words—and anger—withdrew. "Your wife, your son, they were not killed by violence."

"No."

"And yet you resent the Lord for their deaths."

"I was called away by the Tor'agnate my family serves. Because of *his* chosen violence. A plague swept the villages in which my family lived while he was campaigning at the edge of a Torrean not his own. Because I was not there, they perished. And I would not have left them. Understand this. I would not have left them, had I the power to refuse the command given without causing their deaths."

The kai el'Sol nodded bleakly. "Surely," he said softly, "You would have perished in that plague."

Marakas had never confused Lambertan honor with stupidity. He understood, by the question Fredero offered, that the kai el'Sol knew of his gift. "No," he said softly. "I would not have perished." He looked away. "But had I been a man of *power*, they would not have perished either, be-

cause I would never have been commanded to leave. I did
not understand that. Not then. The hoarding and gathering
of power," he added bitterly, "had only been of peripheral
concern."

"Do not claim to understand it now." The stern voice
held some hint of the Lord's fire—the first hint. "If you had
power, Marakas, what would you do with it?"

"What does any man do with power? I would live my life
free of the dictates of others. I would choose the course my
life would take."

"Indeed. Your dead are gone now. And it is of the living
I speak. If I give you power, if I teach you its use, what will
you do with it? The Lord is beyond the justice you seek; believe that. Only the men who serve him, or are served by
him, however poorly, remain in your path."

"I—" He fell silent, the sun in the cloudless sky upon his
upturned brow.

"You were not a student of power, not an acolyte of its
use. I understand that. I was the second son of the Tyr'agnate of Mancorvo, and as such, could not avoid the lessons
you did. I learned.

"For instance, did you know that predictability is considered a weakness? That adherence to stricture—of any
sort—a weakness as well?"

"Men must be free to maneuver," Marakas replied, his
voice as flat as the Mancorvan plains.

"Indeed. And so I learned that the enemies of Lamberto
must indeed be incompetent fools if they could not unseat
my father."

Marakas was surprised into laughter.

Fredero smiled.

"Of the many things I have heard said of the kai Lamberto, that is not one. He has never been called a fool."

"Not never," Fredero replied serenely. "But infrequently.
He does not take well to personal insult."

"And what kai does?"

"As you say." The smile left his face. "Come. There is a

small stone garden in the west courtyard; the shadows cast by sunlight at this time of day are most pleasant there."

23rd of Misteral 427 AA
Sea of Sorrows

The shadows cast by sunlight in the flatlands of Raverra were not so pleasant. Only those plants that could exist without the easy grace of the Lady's bounty grew upon the plains, and the ground was often harsh and dry beneath them. But it was not broken yet; it was not sand. Look carefully, and one could see where wagons had cracked the surface of the dry earth, and in numbers.

He built his shelter here, thinking about the past.

Three days passed.

When Jevri el'Sol came to his rooms, Marakas had been surprised to see him. "Your ma—the kai el'Sol has a message for me?"

The mistake, were Jevri of rank within the Radann, would have been fatal; Jevri was not. Born into slavery and released from it solely to follow the kai el'Sol into the ranks of the Radann, he was the consummate servant. He was also proof that Lambertan dignity extended from the highest to the lowest of its subjects, for once freed, Jevri was not compelled, and could not be forced, to such service. To others, perhaps, but that was not the point. He served.

"He wishes your presence," Jevri said gravely.

"Where?"

"I will lead you."

Marakas bowed. Among the Radann, weapons were not forbidden. The Lord did not expect his servants to strip themselves of the proof of their prowess. But Marakas carried a poor man's sword, and knew it; he therefore often left it behind. It was unarmed that he walked behind the armed Jevri el'Sol.

Jevri's backward glance said much. But so, too, did his frown. He was not, Marakas thought, seraf any longer. He had mistaken the older man. No seraf of worth would have said so much by glance alone. And certainly no seraf, worthy or no, would have then paused when he felt glance alone did not convey what was necessary to find words in its place.

"Marakas el'Sol," he said evenly, "I wish you to understand what the kai el'Sol would never insult you by putting into words. The Lord's men," he added, "often forbear to speak where speaking would solve much.

"I have served Fredero for many years, and before him, I served his family. You were never born seraf; you will never be seraf. Were I given my freedom, I would have served willingly in the same capacity, and subject to the same laws, as I have lived."

"You are free."

Jevri shrugged. "In slavery, I have known freedom that men who are free have never known. Fredero is, as his father, a man who understands the value of honor, of duty, of loyalty. But that can be said of many.

"He understands more. Why do you think the Lambertans are honored?"

"For precisely those reasons."

"No. They are honored because they hold power."

"But—"

"And they consider that power a duty. For if they can cleave to those things they hold as *truth*, and still be honored, honorable men, they serve as an example that it is *possible* to do so. Fredero chose the Radann because he admires the Lord and he despairs at what is done in the Lord's name. He became kai—at some personal expense—because he hoped to impose those beliefs upon the men who carry the Lord's symbol and do the Lord's work."

"And what is the Lord's work?" Marakas asked bitterly. "I have walked among the corpses that are left at the end of a day in service to the principles the Lord holds dear. I have

tended the injured, the dying; I have returned broken the
men who came with youth and weapons under the service
of flags and commanders who cared little for their loss. I
have carried the news of their loss to their wives and their
sons, and in those cases where the families were too poor,
or too base, to uphold the responsibilities of the dead, I
have seen women and children sold into slavery because
they are not beloved of the Lord.

"What is there, in this *work*, to admire?"

"Nothing at all," Jevri said gravely, and with just the hint
of a nod. "But let me ask a different question. If you were
to change this, how would you start? By destroying the
Radann? By burning their temples? By the acts of a war
which would repeat, in an endless cycle, that which you
have justly decried?"

Marakas stared at this seraf, this man who continued to
serve.

"Is that the reason that you joined the Radann?"

"That," Marakas looked away, "and one other. I desired
freedom from the dictates of the Tor'agnate, and service to
the Lord was the one way in which I might find it. I have
no wife, no children," he added, "to hinder me."

"And you intend to take no other."

"No. I have already failed the only woman I cared to
offer my name."

Jevri nodded. He walked, and Marakas followed, but the
lesson was not yet finished. "I ask you to observe the kai
el'Sol. He will invite you to travel in his company; it is an
honor that you may, perhaps, be worthy of. Accept that invitation."

"An invitation offered by a man of power is seldom open
to refusal."

"Do not insult us," Jevri said curtly.

Marakas had the grace to feel shame. But he also felt curiosity, and something else that he did not care to name, and
when he at last met the kai el'Sol, he forgot both. For Jevri
el'Sol did not lead him to the kai's austere rooms; did not

take him to the gardens or the platforms that the kai's position made his by right. He led him instead from the splendor of the ancient stone building into the grounds of the Tor Leonne proper, through the winding paths of tall trees that offered the illusion of privacy.

The light was upon the Lady's Lake, and in the distance, the wavering reflection of the palace of the Tyr stretched out, and out again, broken by floating lilies and the movement of summer insects. Gold leaf caught light, warming it; the rays of the sun, embroidered upon a field of azure, flew in the winds.

Amelia would have been reduced to the silence of awe and wonder, but their son would have known no such dignity. He felt her presence, for the first time in years, at the side of this solemn man, and it cut him deeply.

So deeply that he did not, at first, recognize the standing stones, the carved statuary, that Jevri led him to. There were open bowls at the feet of that stone monument, hidden from view by the low-lying leaves and petals of delicate flowers. But they were full, these bowls, and tended by birds with no necks, who wisely took flight at the passing shadows of men.

"I will leave you now," Jevri said quietly.

Marakas nodded.

Because men did not come, in daylight, to this place, they did not gather here. Certainly not the Radann; this was the Lady's shrine.

But it was here, in the hollows of the carefully tended shrine, that Marakas el'Sol met Fredero kai el'Sol.

He did not see him at first, for he had not made peace with the Lady, and not since the rites that the deaths of his family demanded had he sought her shrine. He came as stranger to this place; he carried no water, no wine; brought no incense, and no candles. But he had girded himself with no weapon either, and he stared a long time at the words that time, wind, and sun had not defaced upon the standing stones.

A man did not bow at the Lady's shrine when the Lord's face was turned upon him; such obeisance, if offered, was offered when night had fallen and night thoughts were allowed their reign. He therefore felt no need to bend at knee, to bow head. But the compulsion—hated, cursed—coiled within him, demanding stillness, silence.

"Marakas," the kai el'Sol said, and Marakas turned.

To this man, he could bow should he so choose. But although he recognized the crest of the sun ascendant upon his chest, he offered nothing.

"To the Lady," Fredero said, "that which is the Lady's."

"In her time."

"In her time."

They stood, separated by shadows and foliage and the questions which, unbidden, remained unasked.

"Make peace with the Lady, if you can. Such peace is a thing that the Lord cannot take from you."

"The Lady failed them," Marakas replied, the bitterness of years undiminished. "I served her, as any with her gifts might serve, and in return, she failed *me*."

"Ah." The kai el'Sol rose, and rising, made Marakas aware of the fact that he had offered what no man was required to offer. "So."

"You summoned me."

"Yes."

"How may I serve?"

"You may not. Not yet. Where I go, there must be no fury, no hatred, no anger such as the anger that sustains you. I have watched you, this past year, and I have waited. I will wait longer, if that is necessary. But I wish you to be whole. What would your wife desire, were she beside you now? Think on it. The sun will fall, soon; the Lady's time will begin. Wait here."

Marakas had no desire to obey this command.

"And think. She chose you, and you her, for a reason. Would your wife have desired you to turn your back upon the gifts that you possess? Did she not, time and again, counsel you to offer comfort and aid to those who were less fortunate than she?"

Marakas felt his eyes grow round and wide. "Did you know my wife?"

"No."

"Then how—"

"You could have made much, much more of your talent than you did. You could have been a richer man, a more powerful one. You could have owned houses, serafs, and a place in the court of any man you chose to serve.

"But you came to the Radann. I believe that nothing happens without reason, even the bitter death of a loved one. And I believe that had your wife been a different woman, you would have had all of those things, in abundance—and I would not now have you. Forgive her for her absence. Forgive her for your failure." He turned and began to walk away.

Marakas did not call him back.

But something did; he turned, the robes of his office catching light and containing it. "I will come to you in the dusk, and I will ask of you a favor at that time."

In the evening light, Marakas par el'Sol awoke. He could not say why; no sound greeted him when he sat up in the confines of his poor tent. Such a tent as this had not been his home for some time, but he was Radann; he was not trapped by the finery that rank bestowed.

He could not stand in the small tent, but felt no loss of dignity when required to crawl through its narrow length to push aside its flap.

The Lady's face was bright in the night sky. There were clouds, thin as fine, Northern lace, that obscured the paler of the stars, but she was undimmed. Silver light shone. Without hesitation, he reached for his dagger and his wineskin. He broke dirt with the tip and the flat of unsheathed steel, making the most primitive of bowls by dint of his effort. Into these, he dripped water with care, and wine with abandon. She would understand.

The Sea of Sorrows was before him, and not even the most fanatic of her followers denied themselves water here.

On that day, too many years ago, he had made his peace with the Lady.

Funny, that he should think of Fredero during the Lady's time. It was Amelia who most often came back to him; Amelia and the ghost of a son whose smile was so bright, whose joy was so infectious, they could only continue to exist encased in memory.

But they stood in shadows this eve; it was the kai el'Sol whose spirit the Lady invoked.

And as he had done on that first day, Marakas par el'Sol bowed to the will of the kai el'Sol, and followed where he led.

Fredero could not have become the kai el'Sol without dint of will, display of force, cunning, guile; he could not have held that position without prudent exercise of the same. Although the par el'Sol did not speak, words could be coaxed from those who served them, and Marakas had, with a diligence that he had shown little of since his induction into the ranks of the Radann, coaxed those words, those tales, from any who could be moved to speak.

He built a story, a picture, a painting in progress, of the man who led the Radann. And when he was certain of facts—and facts were sifted for with the care of a man who has lost a diamond among grains of rice—he went at last to the one man who, he was certain, knew Fredero kai el'Sol better than anyone.

And during this time, Jevri el'Sol was available. He had not found it odd, then, although in retrospect he should have.

"Marakas," Jevri said, bowing. His rooms were sparsely furnished; mats lay between the narrow stretch of walls, and upon those mats, a hard roll, and a low table. That low table now bore the weight of his plain, fine sword, and in a low, flat dish, a young lily.

"The kai el'Sol," Marakas said, kneeling as Jevri gestured toward the table. The older man rose, and from a corner of the room, in a small cupboard, retrieved two fine ceramic cups and a flask of sweet water.

He poured, with a grace and elegance that was absent from the rest of his movements—the remaining elements of his tenure as seraf to a high clan. "Yes?"

"Is it true that he survived three attempts upon his life as par el'Sol?"

"Inasmuch as men who serve the Lord would stoop to such measures, yes, it is true."

"And true as well that he defeated Caranos par el'Sol for possession of *Verragar?*"

"Yes. I see that you have been . . . busy."

Marakas had the grace to color.

"But is it of these events that you have come to speak?"

"Yes."

"Ah. There are others. Before he rose to the rank of par el'Sol, there were also difficulties. Men consider the name Lamberto to be a challenge, or perhaps a judgment. He was almost embroiled in a delicate trap involving his brother, and he avoided it with care." The old man lifted his cup and waited.

Marakas joined him, guest to his host. He drank first.

"But surely you would expect no less from one who has become the kai el'Sol." There was a slight pause. "Ties of blood are ties of honor that demand loyalty; abjure those, and the most base of behavior manifests itself. The Radann are not brothers; they are equals in the eyes of the Lord."

"And the Lord's laws."

"Indeed."

"There are other stories."

"There will always be other stories."

"It is . . . the other stories that have brought me here."

"Ah." Jevri set the cup aside, his eyes piercing and clear as the water it contained.

"Is it true that one of the Radann in the Tor Leonne fathered a child?"

"Many have."

"And are the laws of the Lord not clear?"

"They are clear."

"But the man was not executed."

"No."

"At the will of the kai el'Sol."

"Indeed."

Marakas was silent; he lifted the water; he drank. It slid down his throat as if it were air. "The kai dismissed him from the ranks of the Radann."

"Yes."

"And he sent him to Mancorvo, to his brother's house."

"You have delved deeply. Yes. With the woman and the child. His brother met him, spoke with him, and judged him worthy of employ. He serves the Lambertan clan."

"In what capacity?"

Jevri's eyes narrowed. "I dislike wasted words. You must know of this, or you would not ask."

"I know of what is said, but many things are said. I want the truth."

"Truth is difficult. The man serves as Tyran to the Tyr'agnate."

"Even though he is an oathbreaker."

"Even so."

"And Lambertan honor?"

"The kai el'Sol sat in judgment. He considered the man's youth, his crime, and his honesty."

"What honesty?"

"He was young," Jevri said quietly. "And the woman came to him for protection in the village to which he had been sent. She, too, was young, and fierce in the way the young are. Saving her life was a bond that the young Radann could not break; he understood that in his absence there would be no protection for her, for she had lost her brothers to skirmishes with the bandits that season.

"He therefore took it upon himself to bring her here. And here . . . things unfolded as they often have.

"A different man would have dismissed her. A different man would have understood the threat she posed. And when . . . things developed . . . a different man might have had her killed; if not, he would have disavowed the child of that union; it was not a son."

Marakas bowed his head. Against the word of a Radann, the word of a disgraced, kinless girl would count for nothing.

"But this man?"

"He came to the kai el'Sol. He came in fear, but with dignity, and he confessed his crime against the Lord, and against the Radann." The old man's eyes seemed to cloud as they gazed past Marakas. "Fredero heard all that the young man had to say, and then he dismissed the Hand of God, and spoke to the man alone.

"He said, 'Not all men serve the Lord best by joining the ranks of the Radann. And not all men learn the unsuitability of that life with grace or with honor. What you have done, you cannot do in service to the Lord, for the men of the Lord must be seen to be men who favor no family, and who own no ties greater than the oaths they have taken to the Lord.

"I remember that man," Jevri continued softly. "I remember that he stood, alone, shoulders bowed, face pale. Of the Radann, it was only the kai el'Sol that he feared, although any of the others could also have been his death. And I would say that it was not fear of death that moved him then. He admired Fredero."

"You admire Fredero."

"Yes.

"Fredero asked him why he had not chosen to hide the woman, and the child. Why he had not disposed of them;

they were poor and without family, and their absence would have been beneath notice.

"The young man's reply was simple enough. 'They have no one,' he said. 'And they trust me. I have already betrayed your trust, and in the end, betraying theirs would not regain it.'

" 'I might never have known.'

" 'No,' he said. 'But I would know.'

"Fredero looked at the man then, looked long, and said, 'You have not betrayed my trust, Renaldo.' "

Marakas closed his eyes.

" 'You may serve the Lord yet. I will send Jevri el'Sol as your guide and your companion; heed him. He will take you to Mancorvo, and in Mancorvo, you will be granted an audience with the Tyr'agnate. Accept it. Tell him only what you have told me. I believe that he will find use for you in Amar.'

" 'What use?' the young man asked. 'I have done nothing with my life but learn the use of this.' And he touched the hilt of his sword.

"Fredero simply smiled. That was all."

But it was enough. Marakas set the cup aside. "I do not understand the kai el'Sol, but when he leaves the Tor Leonne ten days hence, I will travel with him."

"If I am not mistaken, Marakas el'Sol, you will travel a long road at his behest, and by his side."

24th of Misteral, 427 AA
Sea of Sorrows

Are you ever mistaken, Jevri el'Sol? Were you ever mistaken in your youth? Marakas wondered what had become of Jevri, although he could guess: The sword of the Radann kai el'Sol had gone missing after Fredero's death. Peder had not given the order to search for the sword; nor had he given orders to search for the missing Jevri.

And that said much.

I did not intend to walk this road without him. I am not sure I know how.

What sleep he had taken had been poor, but sleep was often poor in the desert. What warmth the sun did not grant, the Lady denied him as well, and he was no longer a supple youth; he was stiff with the receding chill of her gaze. Days, he counted.

Still, he walked. The evening's chill lessened as the sun began its ascent, the temperature shifting like grains of sand, like a Northern clock. Marakas was dressed for this trek. He drew hood down; drew cloth across his dry lips, and continued.

Lady, he thought, *give me guidance. I have destroyed one of your daughters in our war against your enemy. Demand your due, and I will pay it.*

Marakas par el'Sol could not have served Fredero kai el'Sol without understanding obligation and debt. But it was hard to pay debt when one could not find the debtor. He walked.

Rape was not an uncommon activity among the men of Annagar. For this reason, women with any family at all were never seen alone; they were accompanied by seraf, cerdan, fathers, brothers, or cousins. These women did not interest the kai el'Sol. But upon the roads they traveled, other women did: the elderly, the infirm, and the women who had no family to protect them.

Fredero did not raise his sword often, but when he raised it, it seldom fell unblooded.

Marakas discovered that the kai el'Sol was known. His cloak and his robes fell across the low villages like a tent, and time and again people came to him, seeking the protection they offered.

The first time a young woman had darted between the shoulders of men who had gathered to speak with the Radann kai el'Sol, Marakas had been surprised. That surprise had not lessened when the woman—past girlhood, but barely, her skin dark with sun, her eyes dark with much else—had thrown herself at his feet, grasping his hem in shaking hands.

The Radann who accompanied Fredero had not removed the girl; they had drawn themselves up to their full heights, dropped their hands to the hilts of their swords, and waited.

He had wondered why. But only that once.

In ones and twos, bending at knee and covering the exposed ground with their exposed backs, the serafs of the village surrounded the Radann, their hands flat against dirt in the most submissive of postures. Old women, old men; the children were scattered or gathered and hidden by roof or hill or field. Of these, only one sought to raise his face; he was old in the way that strong men suddenly are when struck by loss.

Marakas turned his attention to the girl again.

Four men had come seeking her.

They were, not to his surprise, finely dressed; they were younger than the kai el'Sol, but older than the girl. The villagers, who had made no move to hinder the girl, now cringed to either side to grant passage to the men who pursued her.

Those men stopped just short of the kai el'Sol; to do otherwise would have insulted the symbol—the full symbol— of the sun ascendant. Not even the Tyr'agnati would dare such an insult without cause.

The kai el'Sol gazed upon them without comment for a full minute, and then he bent to the girl, whose hair now streamed down her shoulders and neck, obscuring her face, and trembling, as she trembled, like a dark rain.

"Child," he said, his voice remote and forbidding, "who are you?"

She did not look up. And she did not release his hem. But she did not refuse his question. "Talia," she whispered, her voice so broken Marakas could not be certain that he had heard the name correctly. "Talia en'Sambali."

"Talia en'Sambali," he said quietly, "where is your husband?"

She did not speak for a moment, but not even Marakas could mistake her silence for anything other than terror. The kai el'Sol waited. And waited.

Marakas knelt. He knew that the robes of his office would suffer for this lack of dignity, for not one of the Radann had shifted, and they were each more experienced than he. But at that moment, such dignity had seemed a paltry thing. He touched her shoulder. She flinched. But she did not draw back; the hem of the kai el'Sol's robe twisted in her shaking hands as she shrank away.

"Child," he said, touching her shoulder gently. It surprised him, this gentleness; he had thought it scoured from him by the deaths of his family. "You must answer the kai el'Sol. But answer without fear."

She raised her face slowly until it was at a level with the kai's knee. "He is—"

"He is dead," one of the finely dressed men said coolly. "She is widowed, and her family does not speak for her here."

"Ah." Fredero looked at the young man. His face was slender, handsome, his beard trimmed and tended. "Who then speaks?"

"I am kai to the Tor'agnate."

"The Tor'agnate?"

The man's brows rose a fraction. "The Tor'agnate Amando di'Manelo."

"Ah. And he serves the Tor'agar Gerrardo di'Verrens."

The man nodded.

"Who in turn owes loyalty to the Tyr'agnate Mareo di'Lamberto, if I am not mistaken."

"You are correct, kai el'Sol. This girl is a villager in my father's lands. She is without husband."

One of the scattered villagers made a sound. A low sound, like a grunt of pain.

Fredero turned to him. "You know her husband?"

The hesitation was profound. Marakas understood it well; the kai el'Sol did not appear to.

"Speak," the Radann Jordan el'Sol said, breaking his silence without motion. "The kai el'Sol is a man with many responsibilities. Do not waste his time."

"He was not—was not dead—this morning."

"And now?"

"If the kai di'Manelo vouchsafes his death, it must be so." The words were broken.

"I see." Fredero turned to the young man. "When did this death take place?" It was only barely a question.

The kai did not answer. And the girl, who should have known better, now raised her head fully. The sun's light traveled down the necklace of red marks around her throat, and lingered on the soiled, common clothing she wore.

"They killed him," she whispered. "He is just beyond the south fields, among the trees that serve as protection against the wind."

Marakas rose. To the old man who had spoken, he said, "Do you know the place of which she speaks?"

The old man nodded.

"Take me there. *Now.*"

He felt a moment's pity for the man; the son of the Tor'agnate glanced at him coldly, and the glance was a command. But the old man, eyes cast groundward in humility and fear, did not appear to see that glance. When Marakas approached him, he turned, wordless, and walked away from the village center.

Marakas heard the kai el'Sol's command; no one followed them. When the village center was beyond them, the old man began to run, forgetting the Radann who trailed behind him like shadow. If the sun had added lines to his face, and the wind had broken the straightness of his back, it had not robbed him of agility; Marakas found it difficult to match his pace.

They crossed the field; the stalks of wheat were high, and the corn, green, was still as tall as a young man. The furrows between rows were not wide enough to grant two grown men easy passage; stalks fell as they passed, a punctuation to the story of their movement.

Other stories were written here; stalks trampled and crushed by the hooves of larger beasts. As they cleared the tall growth of the field, as they passed into the wilderness that farming had not banished, they came to the line of trees. Marakas had spent his youth in the land of Oerta; Mancorvo, with its abundance of life, its long stretches of rivers and lakes, was still a miracle to him.

But in that land, or in these, men with power still left their mark. They found the young man against the trunk of a tree. He had been wounded by swords, and his farmer's cotton had absorbed blood without staunching its flow.

The old man cried out, wordless, and fell at once to his knees by the young man's side.

"I told him," the old man said. "I told him, not her, not that one. I told him not to marry that girl." There were tears upon his cheeks; they caught no light, for the trees provided shade from the harshness of the Lord's glare. "It is no boon to desire a beautiful girl," he added, although Marakas knew it well. "And no boon to have that desire returned."

But Marakas had also fallen to the ground beside the young man, and the life of the Radann, the desire for vengeance against the perfidy of the Lord, slipped past him, falling away as if it were a poorly fastened mask. An iron mask, a mask with no obvious weakness. He learned much, that day.

He touched the man's face—if someone quite so young could be called a man—and then turned and barked at the older one.

"Bring water," he said. "Bring fever root. Bring arsal, if you have it, and if you do not, for the love of your son, *find* it."

The old man was motionless for a second, but only that long; he turned and Marakas heard the crashing of fallen stalks as the old man receded into the distance.

He was left alone.

Into the silence, he offered his only hesitation, but the hesitation was profound. He had touched the boy's face, and he knew—as no one else would have known it—that the spirit had not yet fled the body. He also understood what the cost of holding that spirit here would be; the winds that were howling in his ears had nothing to do with the gentle breezes of the Mancorvan plains.

You did not come to the Lord to heal, he told himself angrily. *You did not come to the Lord to offer what you promised Amelia you would never offer again.*

How many promises, made to his wife, had he broken?

He withdrew his hands. Stared at them.

Amelia . . .

A small bird flew down from the tree's height. It was brown, plain, clearly a female; its chirping was an agitated cluck and whistle.

He touched the boy again, wondering, as the bird continued to worry at him—from a safe distance—if this were a sign. How could it be? In daylight, here, the symbol of the Lord upon his breast, who would dare give a sign such as this?

But that question was to go unanswered.

He knew what the cost of this healing would be, and he feared it, as he had always feared it, but he welcomed it as well. He reached for a name, and he found it as if it were his own; his own, he released.

Darran, he said. *Darran di'Sambali.*

The injuries the body had suffered were profound. He had thought the spirit well on its way. But the boy answered. A warrior, he thought; a warrior to the end, be his weapons the simple implements of the field.

He felt fear, rage, helplessness as Darran di'Sambali struggled against his enemy: Death. The death that would remove from his new, his beloved wife, the only protection he could afford her.

Was it so different a fear, so different a rage, than his own? No. It *was* his own.

He had called men back from the winds before, and the winds had hollowed him, reducing him to emptiness, loneliness, a terrible gnawing need. But the need of this man was so strong it swept him up, carrying him, rejecting all weakness.

Where is she? Where is Talia?

The voice was wild, terrible.

His own.

He struggled against it, and because this was not his first healing, because he had developed the ability to retreat—if only a little—he answered.

She is safe. She has claimed the protection of the—of the clan Lamberto, and her claim has been accepted.

The voice stilled.

But she needs you, Darran. She needs your silence, and your strength. You were wounded. You survived. Be still now, and you will do more.

He felt the wounds closing.

They were many.

And as they closed, he felt other things; the depth of a longing that he had thought lost forever, with youth, with Amelia. He saw Talia, not as a terrified girl, but as a wild wood spirit, a creature feral and frightened, who might be approached with care, with quiet motion, with soft words. He saw her ferocity, her loyalty, and more, much more; he would have spared them both the intimacy of this knowledge, but to withdraw was still death.

And he wanted this personal affirmation of life, this reason for living, this profound sense of belonging.

He knew that Darran would understand why, for he knew that Amelia, and his son, the boy she had insisted bear his name, would be no less revealed, that his longing, and his sense of bitter failure, no less horrifying; that Darran would forever be scarred by the Radann's loss.

They clung, in the warmth of the healing trance, until someone dared to touch them.

He heard, from a great distance, a voice he knew well, and did not recognize.

"Marakas el'Sol, you have done enough. Come away."

He opened his lips to refuse, but sound was beyond him; the kai el'Sol was a force that could not be denied. Not by a man who had offered him his oath.

Two cries broke the silence, and it was hard to tell which man had uttered which; they were one sound of denial.

"It appears," the kai el'Sol said, "the reports of this man's death were exaggerated."

Marakas opened his eyes. His hands were shaking. He reached for Darran, but caught, instead, the fabric of the kai el'Sol's robes, the embroidered gold of the sun ascendant, its rays spreading in all directions.

"You are brave," the kai el'Sol said quietly, "and foolish beyond belief. Remain here until you are composed. I am grateful for what you have chosen to do here, but you are Radann; the weakness which holds you now must pass unseen. I will take the young man to the village; there is work to be done. If you can join us, join us; if you cannot, do not worry. Nothing that has happened here has happened in vain."

Marakas looked past the golden sun to the kai's face; he shuttered his eyes against the brightness of the Lord's symbol. Lord's man, he thought, and for the first time in his life—perhaps because he was weakened—he understood what those words meant.

They were alone, the kai el'Sol, Darran di'Sambali, and Marakas. Not even the old man from the village had been allowed to attend them.

For the sake of the Radann. And for the sake, Marakas realized, of those who might witness what could not in safety be witnessed. He knew, then, that he could trust this kai el'-Sol with far more than just his life.

Darran cried out as the kai el'Sol lifted him. But Darran

was no Radann; what weakness he chose to show disgraced none but he.

"Darran!" Marakas shouted. "She thinks you dead, and she is waiting. Whose needs have precedence?"

And although he was not a well-learned boy, he understood every word Marakas spoke; they were almost one man, for a time, for a little while longer.

They left Marakas and began to make their way to the village center; he watched the field bend and sway as they moved through it. They had not yet traversed its length before he, healer-born and weak as a girl, found the strength to compose himself, to rise, and to follow. The part of his mind that was healer-born, trained to both the power and the terrible vulnerability of that gift, thought it best to linger, but the part of his mind that held the memories, the desires, and the fears of a much younger man, had to *know* that she had found safety.

Or perhaps that was not true.

Perhaps it was Marakas himself who needed to know this. Because without safety, the depleting, exhausting, revealing work of this day meant nothing. Less than nothing. What was hope, after all, but another way of torturing a man? Had he not, with hope, returned through villages made funereal by the passage of disease, looking for his wife, his son?

He found strength. He walked quickly. And stopped when he reached the village center.

For Fredero kai el'Sol had drawn his sword. *Balagar* burned as if steel could be the heart and essence of fire. There were almost no villagers in sight; few were willing to bear witness to the unfolding of events when those events involved the naked blade, and men of rank and power. Marakas understood their absence well; he did not even consider it cowardice, although among the high clans it would have been dismissed as such. Marakas was not born to the high clans, just the free ones; he was an indifferent swordsman—at best—and he had abjured use of blade where the simple expedient of hiding in safety would do.

And all of these things, all of them, were part of an old life, a different life. The crest upon his chest had never felt so *alive* as it did this day, and it demanded its due.

The Radann had drawn swords as well. They caught sunlight, reflecting it, scattering it.

In their midst, the young girl stood, straight and tall, her left eye bruising now, her lips thick with the weight of ungentle hands. But her eyes were clear, her shoulders straight, her back unbowed; she was achingly, piercingly beautiful, and he would have given his life, in a frenzied instant, if it would have saved her any sorrow, any misery.

Ah, Darran, he thought. For he stood, husband to her, and proud of it, terrified of it, hallowed by it, at her side, his clothing wet and sticky with unstaunched blood, his face pale, his lips set. His arm was across her shoulders, and he drew strength from the contact. Enough, in Marakas' certain opinion, to be able to remain standing.

The man who had claimed to be the kai of the Tor'agnate di'Manelo had drawn his blade as well; so had his men. They were not, in Marakas' opinion, Toran—or if they were, they did not deserve their rank. They had an easy confidence about them that spoke of youth and familiarity with the privileges of power—but not with the responsibilities. There were some lessons which one did not survive the learning, or the teaching, of.

He witnessed them now.

"This man," the kai el'Sol said evenly, "is *not* dead, as you can see. This woman is therefore claimed, and protected, by a family."

"An oversight," the kai di'Manelo said quietly. He had not taken a step forward; he was younger than Fredero, but not so young that he overestimated the effects of age upon the kai el'Sol's sword.

"Attempted murder is seldom considered oversight."

"Murder?" The kai di'Manelo's eyes narrowed. "There

must be some misunderstanding, Radann kai el'Sol." He
bowed, but he did not lessen his grip upon the haft of his
curved blade. "We came upon him in this condition, and his
wife, believing she had been widowed, was grieving. She
was distraught; she mistook our concern for something less
seemly. There must have been a bandit attack."

"The bandits are thin at this time of year; the harvest has
not yet proved so poor that men must kill for food."

"Then perhaps it was the Voyani. They come at will, and
they take what they can, like the carrion creatures they are.
Ask him what occurred," the young man added. "I am certain that he will explain the misunderstanding."

The kai el'Sol turned. "The Lord is witness here," he
said. "I call upon him to be judge as well. What was done
was done beneath the open sky; the Lord sees all. Understand, Ser Darran kai di'Sambali, before you reply, that I
am the first of the Lord's servants. What he witnesses, I
witness.

"What happened in the south fields?"

"Think carefully," the kai di'Manelo said.

"Indeed," the kai el'Sol said, nodding gravely.

In his youth, Marakas would have known a horror at
being trapped, like a pawn, in the game of two powerful
men. But Darran knew no fear this day, and Marakas, a
giddy elation. Not hope, but something more substantial.

"The kai di'Manelo demanded the right to my wife. I refused him. She had no desire to accept his offer, and had
she—"

She tensed beneath the curve of his arm and his eyes in-
voluntarily traced the side of her face. His hand tightened,
his expression, for a moment, was youth defined.

"I said no."

"And?"

"He ordered his men to kill me. He said a widow with no
family had no business tending farm without escort; that
she was simply inviting her own . . ." His wife reached up
and caught the hand that trembled against her shoulder. She

said nothing; now that her husband was at her side, it was not her place to speak. But Marakas knew that the gesture was an offer of strength, comfort, and pride, and that Darran would draw from it all of these things.

He felt Amelia's absence more viscerally than he had for two years.

"Enough," the kai el'Sol said, but not unkindly.

"Will you take the word of this . . . this village worker . . . over the kai of the Tor' agnate?"

"He is not seraf," the kai el'Sol replied, "and his words have the advantage of containing truth."

"He lies."

"Does he?"

"Beneath the open sky, I swear it. He lies."

"Then you will have the opportunity to prove your claim," Fredero told him quietly. "By right of combat; by test of sword."

The smile on the young man's face was thin, sharp, and dangerous.

It vanished when Fredero continued. "But as it is I who am judge, and I who have accused you, however mildly, of lying, it is I who you will face." He did not turn, but the Radann Paolo now sheathed his sword and joined the kai el'Sol. "Tell the villagers to gather. Tell them to gather and bear witness."

Paolo bowed.

"Kai di'Manelo, we will convene again in the village center, when the Lord has passed the height. Choose your Toran; choose the man who will guard and second you. Marakas," Fredero added, "will you be my Sol'dan?"

26th of Misteral, 427 AA
Sea of Sorrows

The Radann Marakas par el'Sol now paused in his solitary voyage. The dawn had come; dusk slipped past as the min-

utes changed the color and the texture of the light that filled
the sky. The Lord, he thought, had come, and the Lord
would soon reign.

He had not yet eaten. Water had passed his lips, wetting
his throat, but he felt no desire for food. He therefore chose
to continue the reverie of his journey, step by step, a balm
against the day's growing heat.

Sol'dan.

"What does it mean, Jevri?"

Jevri el'Sol brought water, food, and shade to the
younger Radann. "It means many things," he said, as he unrolled the bamboo mats upon ground he had carefully flattened with the balls of his feet.

"Do not . . . serve me." Marakas spoke carefully. He had
come to respect this man, and the fact that he had once been
owned disquieted him. In the Radann, there was freedom.
That, at least, proved true.

"I serve merely myself," the old Radann replied, voice
serene, eyes cast toward the food that he was arranging so
artfully. He frowned, shifted the balls of rice perhaps an
inch or two, and nodded. "If you choose to join me, I will
be honored, but I do not require company."

"But this—"

"This?"

"This service . . . it is . . ."

"Unseemly?"

Marakas shook his head. "It seems so much more than
the Lord demands. Only a seraf . . ."

"Yes." Jevri el'Sol gave no sign of offense. "Only one
raised as a seraf in the High Courts. You must have lived on
the plains," he added, "among the free clansmen. The
Courts would consider such work as this beneath notice, beneath contempt."

"You are free of the . . . duties . . . of the High Court."

"Indeed. And of that contempt."

"Then why bother at all?"

"I find comfort in it. It gives me something to do with my hands—other than wring them, or fight." He met Marakas' gaze, and to Marakas' surprise, a smile tugged at the corner of lips and eyes; humor. He had not expected to find it, not here.

"We all find comfort in the rituals of our childhood, and food, our manner of taking sustenance, is among the earliest of our learned rituals, our pleasures and our hungers. I do not like to eat as if I were a wild creature, or worse, a boorish cerdan.

"I was raised to serve. It was not clear, not immediately, what form that service would take, and I was watched carefully and tested for many things. I was not a large boy; I did not grow into my size; I was therefore not considered suitable for the kai Lamberto. But I had an eye for arrangement—flowers, food, fabric—that led me, in the end, to the service of the Serra. In the harem, all life starts, all paths begin.

"I watched Fredero as a child. I watch him now. And he does not deny me the simple pleasures of a life lived with order, with decorum, with simplicity. He does, however, deny me the right to impose that life on any of the Radann save himself." Jevri el'Sol smiled again. "But I am stubborn. I educate those who are able to learn.

"And that, of course, is not what you asked me."

Marakas was bewildered.

"You wear your heart upon your face," Jevri said, with mild disapproval. "It is a habit you would do best to lose. Masks are your only freedom, Radann el'Sol; learn to wear them with grace and subtlety. The Lady will offer you what privacy you choose to take; the Lady's Festival will offer you more. Use these wisely.

"Very well. You have asked what Sol'dan is, and I should not be surprised. You have been with the Radann for a very brief time."

"I have been with the Radann for the better part of a year. And I have learned how to wield a sword, that is all."

"Be grateful. When I joined, I was taught how to better wield a broom; the Lord suffers no slaves to serve him, but the cleaning must still be done. I digress.

"A year is a short time, the better part of a year, even shorter. When you have lived this life for a decade, when you have lived it for two, come to me and tell me how long you've been at it."

"You have not been here for nearly that long."

"I see that Fredero has chosen to trust you. No, I have not. But experience is an able teacher. If it were not, you would sit at some other man's knees and offer him your questions.

"There are no Tyran among the Radann. No Toran. No cerdan, no serafs. There is the Hand of God, and among the men who comprise that Hand, only one is kai. The four who remain are par. We are men, after all; we have need of our brothers."

Marakas met the older man's eyes and held them, thinking them darker than he remembered, and brighter. The Lady was in them; he had learned the signs among his travels in service to the Voyani.

And this man knew, as Marakas did, that kinship counted for nothing among serafs. Not in the Lord's eyes.

He said, stiffly, a rebuke to the fates that were absent from this conversation, "It is said we are equal in the eyes of God."

"It is said. But it is not believed, even among the men who serve that Lord. We make our allies, we make our enemies, we fight our battles. We choose—on rare occasions—to trust, to take the risk of trusting. There is no blood to bind us, no blood to tie us or hinder us. We are men."

"And yet you serve."

"Yes." He was silent for a moment. "But it was my choice, if any man can be said to have choice in this life, beneath the gaze of this Lord. All choices of import, in the end, have been out of my hands.

"But perhaps they are of import because of the lack of choice, the struggle; those things that are easily within our grasp are not things we prize." He shrugged; his shoulders dipped and lifted, as if he were sloughing weight.

"What is a Sol'dan?"

"Sol'dan. It is an honor, but it is not a rank. It is not a title. You cannot claim it as a symbol of power, and if I judge correctly, there is a risk of death or injury if you choose to accept. But it is tangible."

"Is it service?"

"It is, in a fashion. But it is different. Is 'brother' a form of service? No. But to be one brings the responsibilities and duties all families know.

"Agree to stand as his Sol'dan, and you agree to serve as only Tyran serve their Tyrs; you agree to defend his cause as if he were your brother. He has chosen challenge beneath the open sky; you must accept that, and abide by the rules of the governance of men. But should the man so challenged seek to gain by treachery what he cannot gain by the grace of the Lord, you are given leave to intervene."

"That is . . . that is all?"

Jevri el'Sol stopped speaking. His hands fell into his lap as he straightened his shoulders. "Yes," he said quietly. "But you are young, Radann. If you can ask that, you are young."

CHAPTER FOUR

27th of Misteral, 427 AA
Sea of Sorrows

AT THE height of day, Marakas par el'Sol once again built his shelter. He laid *Verragar* by his side and removed the mask that protected his face from the winds that swept out of the desert, carrying with it sand, heat, the story of a thousand deaths. The desert was fierce this day.

An omen.

He could see where horses had passed before him; their tracks were not shadowed by the heavy ridges of wheels in the dry ground. Alesso di'Marente's men, and in number. He wondered when they had passed; how long it would be before they passed this way again. The patrol was overlarge to be perfunctory, and that was disquieting; of all places that one watched for danger, the Sea was not one.

Or perhaps it was not a danger that armies could be threatened by, had they the sense to remain beyond its grasp. Marakas had taken precautions when traversing the shores of the Sea of Sorrows, but they had been perfunctory; had there been battle, or death, within miles, he would have known it by the movement of carrion birds. The sky was bereft of their shadows. Even they chose to shelter when the sun was high.

And the sun was at its height, its glory a radiant death that disturbed the air, distorted the vision, transformed what was left of unwary sight. The Lord's dominion was undisputed; if men served him, they served with the full knowledge of his ascendance.

Men did not make oaths of note to women; the oaths that were offered women were private. No wooden medallions bore the marks of raised and lowered sword; no blood was shed. Even in marriage, the oaths a *man* made were made to his wife's fathers and brothers.

So Marakas had been brought to the desert by an oath that he had not made.

Evallen of Arkosa had died a terrible death, and the wind's voice was her voice; he could not escape it. For he alone had known her as the Matriarch of her kin, the mother of her people, and it grieved him to deprive a whole people of the woman whose guidance was crucial at a time of such darkness.

Thus, the power of the Matriarch.

Thus, the power of Fredero kai el'Sol.

Marakas was not a young man. He had not been young when the Radann had accepted his service. But he had been a different man. The winds had etched lines in his face, and in the fires of his enemy, he had been reborn, come new into the world with a sword, hairless as an infant.

He had seen only one enemy. It was a blessing unlooked for, to possess such perfect clarity of vision; to be free of the conflicts and the conscience of any imperative other than that war.

But the weeks had curbed and clouded that vision; as each day passed, he felt the weight of humanity, with its incumbent frailty, return. He accepted it.

With it came memory.

The kai di'Manelo and his men met Fredero kai el'Sol at the heart of the village. The villagers had been instructed to bear witness, and the command of such men as these could never safely be ignored, but although they were present, they were ill at ease. Words had been offered, between one kai and another; words had been sent on the back of the swiftest horse present.

But those words would not reach their destination before judgment was made.

Darran di'Sambali and his wife, now adorned with a veil that hid her face from the open view of sun and man, were pushed forward by the oldest of the women present; they stood beneath a hastily constructed canopy. Marakas desired nothing more than to object; from prior experience, he knew that Darran should be resting as far away from the man who had healed him as it was possible to be.

But the kai el'Sol had spoken.

Jevri attended them, boy and girl; Jevri made clear—to the wife, not the husband—that the boy's welfare and sanity depended upon her ability to keep him still. Jevri was wise, and although Marakas had acknowledged that fact from the first day they had met, he found it a surprise and a blessing to be so often reacquainted with the knowledge.

As for himself, he was given leave to draw his sword.

Jevri's expression, when the metal cleared the scabbard, was as dire a criticism as the finely-mannered servitor was capable of offering. "If it were not for the gravity of the situation, Radann, I would insist that you use mine. But it must be your sword."

Marakas nodded, shamed for the first time by the quality of the blade itself. "Will it be enough?"

"It is not by the blade that you will be judged. It is by your actions. And you will weather that judgment. You have chosen."

"I . . . do not know, Jevri. I know only that I—that I wish to see Fredero kai el'Sol's vision of justice."

"It is not as witness that you stand," Jevri replied quietly. "That robe . . . that crest . . . did you embroider it yourself?"

Marakas' frown was a quick thing, there and gone like the flash of light in summer storm. "I was not taught the arts of embroidery," he replied stiffly.

"No," the old man answered, "of course not. Forgive me; it is not a skill taught to free men." The frown deepened as he added, "As the evidence shows. Go now; he is waiting."

As if, Marakas thought, he never doubted what my decision would be.

He turned again to Jevri. "He understands my gift," he said softly. "Does he seek to use it?"

"What man would not seek to use the shield that is offered him? He is no fool; of course he seeks to use it. But think on this while you stand beneath the open sky: He takes little that is offered, for he understands the burden of debt. If he receives a service from you, he must be prepared to offer in return a service of no lesser merit."

"He is kai el'Sol. I am merely Radann."

"For now, Marakas. For now."

"I have no ambition."

"You have," the old man said, "but it is not an ambition that lesser men would understand. He is waiting."

Marakas swallowed. Nodded, and bowed gravely. The sword was heavier in his hands than he had thought possible; if he were called upon to wield the blade this day, if lives depended on it, they would be lost.

But he set his lips, straightened his shoulders, lifted his chin, and strode forward.

Fredero acknowledged his presence—his decision—with the simplest of nods. "Kai di'Manelo." He bowed.

The kai di'Manelo returned that bow, gracefully, fluidly. They were, Marakas realized, of a kind; men raised to the privilege and grace of the High Court; men to whom hunger was no enemy, to whom drought was a stranger. At their word, a village such as this could be consumed in flame, destroyed by sword.

They exchanged no pleasantries. They bowed again, and when they rose, their blades readied, they seemed kin, to Marakas' eye. He could not imagine that such a combat could end in anything but the mildest of injury. He could not imagine that the so-called crime this lordling had com-

mitted could in truth be considered a crime; after all, who
was the injured man? Who had heard of the clan Sambali?
Who cared for the fate of a beautiful peasant, a girl one step
from seraf, if women were ever truly born free?

He cared.

He had cared when Amelia lived, for she had been like
this girl. He had cared fiercely, with a panicked, quickening
pride, when his son had been pulled from her arms and
given over to his, and had let his displeasure in this change
of arrangements be known.

But he had learned that the Lord did not care, and he had
never forgotten the brutality of that lesson.

And so he watched, almost numb, as if the events unfolding were a courtly dance, a simple maneuver, a political exercise.

And when the young kai di'Manelo paid for his excesses
with his life—at the single, quick stroke of the kai el'Sol's
blade, he felt—surely he felt—what every villager present
must have felt: shock. Fear. A terrible certainty that someone would pay for that death.

But beneath that, for he was aware that much of that
emotion, much of that certainty, was Darran di'Sambali's,
he felt something within him break.

The kai el'Sol wiped his blade, sheathed his sword, and
turned to the slack-jawed men who had not had time to
ready their weapons. "I will wait," he said evenly, "upon
the Tor'agnate. We will raise tents in the South field—with
the permission of the clan Sambali—and when he arrives,
please offer him our apologies for the humility of our lodg-
ings—but send him to us."

A man's son is his son.

Marakas, his own lost as a child just able to walk, had
barely begun to understand what motivated men to allow
sons whose criminality was certain to live; he did not, however, expect that the Tor'agnate would accept this turn of
events with grace.

And why should he? This village was his, and within his territories, and had the girl not been married, his kai might have lifted her from servitude in the fields beneath the damaging gaze of the Lord, the withering voice of the wind, and placed her within the confines of his harem, as concubine.

The fact that she was married might have been of note had she been the wife of a man of rank, or a man whose merchant ties gave him the less impeccable credentials of wealth, but Darran was clearly neither; he was one step from seraf.

And for these, the kai di'Manelo had died.

The Radann had lifted the dead man's body with care, and with much honor; they had lifted his unblooded blade and arranged it studiously beneath the kai's crossed and bloodied arms, and they had traversed the village and returned with funereal poles across which they might drape white fabric. This would be the last resting place of the kai di'Manelo.

Of the men who had served the kai so poorly, only one had chosen to stand his ground; only one had remained by the side of the fallen. He was a young man, his face slender, his eyes large, dark. When the Radann approached the body, he had drawn sword a moment, but he had not lifted that sword against them.

The kai el'Sol's expression was as dark as this stranger's eyes, but older, wiser. He said nothing, but he lingered, waiting for the man to speak.

Nor was his wait in vain.

"Kai el'Sol," the young man said, surprising Marakas with the depth of his bow.

The kai el'Sol said, simply, "Ser Alessandro." He turned to Marakas, and added, "Radann Marakas el'Sol, may I present Ser Alessandro par di'Clemente."

Marakas bowed stiffly. He did not—at that time—recognize the clan. But the fact that Fredero did, and more, recognized the man, said something.

"There will be a price to pay," Ser Alessandro said, gazing down upon the body of the kai di'Manelo. "For this day's work, there will be a price."

"Did you think to tell him that, before he embarked upon it?" Fredero asked.

"Very clever, kai el'Sol. I do not judge. I do not threaten. I merely observe. He was impulsive. He was—as many men are—attracted to beauty. He was powerful, in a fashion, competent with a sword, deadly when it was necessary." He knelt by the man he spoke so softly of. Very gently, he brushed strands of dark hair from a face that death had made noble. The Radann had chosen to close eyes left wide by the surprise of a death unforeseen at the start of an ordinary, unremarkable day. He did not touch them.

Instead, he reached for the sword held below the awkward repose of crossed arms. The kai el'Sol did not see fit to stop him; Marakas therefore said nothing.

But he was surprised when Ser Alessandro rolled back his sleeve until he had exposed his arm from wrist to elbow. Shocked when the par Clemente laid his arm against the blade's edge, its outer curve, and, tightening fist, drawing sharp breath, cut himself. The blade was a fine one; sharp and true; the wound itself would only sting after the blood began to flow. Ser Alessandro waited until blood pooled visibly in the runnels along the sword's edge; it didn't take long. The cut was deep.

Radann Paolo el'Sol offered him a long, pale cloth. As that cloth passed from sun-darkened hands to pale ones, Paolo also bowed; there was nothing in the gesture that spoke of falsity. Alessandro raised his head, for he still knelt and he had to look up to meet the Radann's dark eyes. Something passed, wordless, between them before he chose to tend to the wound. He asked for no aid, and Marakas knew that he was warrior born; he would ask for none. Accept none.

Marakas looked to Fredero, but the kai el'Sol was watching the stranger closely, his expression impenetrable. At last, stiffly, he said, "You honor the kai Manelo."

Ser Alessandro did not reply, although he chose to speak. "If I am not mistaken, kai el'Sol, there is thunder within the cloudless sky."

Fredero nodded, although Marakas could hear nothing.

"What would you have done, kai el'Sol, if the Tor'agnate had arrived before the Lord's test?"

"What do you think, Ser Alessandro?"

Alessandro smiled, but it was a thin smile. "I think you are Lambertan, kai el'Sol."

"So is the Tyr'agnate."

"Indeed." He had finished binding the wound tightly, and now drew his sleeve across his arm. He had been careful, his cut had been exact, precise. No blood had fallen from blade to sleeve, and if the bandages had been bound tightly enough, none would be immediately obvious for perhaps an hour.

"They come," Ser Alessandro said, rising. "And as you seem to persist in valuing those who barely value themselves, I must make haste to greet them outside of the village. I will bring them, kai el'Sol."

The kai el'Sol said nothing, but he watched Ser Alessandro leave, and Marakas noted that, in the entire time they had been within sword's reach, Fredero kai el'Sol had not once taken his hand from the hilt of his blade.

When he was gone, Fredero said quietly, "There are some lessons that must be learned time and again. There are some that need only be learned once." He raised his hand to his eyes, as if sheltering vision from the glare of the sun over the moving sheen of emerald and gold that comprised the field of the Sambali youth.

"Perhaps, kai el'Sol. But in my experience, in villages such as these, the truth is slanted. We say there are men who learn quickly and easily, and men who are only capable of remembering their own names because they hear them shouted so often."

Fredero's smile was slight. "True enough. And which of these are you, Radann?"

"I? I am a man who learns quickly."

Fredero raised a brow.

"It is truth. I learn so quickly, in fact, that I find myself in the position, often, of being forced to relearn, reexamine, reinterpret. Today is one of those days." He lifted his hands; found to his surprise that they shook and trembled—and that he was willing to expose this weakness to the kai el'-Sol, and to the Lord *he* served. "I thought never to heal again. I thought to abjure what I could not use to save those to whom my greatest duty lay." He bowed. "Had you asked, I would have vowed it; I would have offered you my life as proof of the truth of that vow.

"And yet, today, because of a stranger's wife, a young girl with a pretty face, I have healed. I walked in the darkness, and the light that I see, now that I have returned, is not the light of the sun I left behind." He lowered his hands. "I am Sol'dan," he said quietly. "I understand that you will bring justice to the Dominion, with the Radann in your service, in the name of the Lord."

"Does that concern you?"

He could have pretended to misunderstand the question; he was tempted. "No. I would not have given you the same answer had you asked me that question yesterday.

"I do not care for the Lord. I understand that many a man, driven by perfect nobility, finds clarity, and purity, in a life led as a warrior, but I am not one of those. The Lord is concerned with men of power; you are a man of power. Let me be beneath his notice, beneath either his contempt or his benediction, while you stand in his glare without flinching. You are the shield, kai el'Sol, and I am a man who can make the riven shield whole, time and again, without question, without conflict."

"There will come a day, Radann Marakas el'Sol, when

you will find the safe side of such a shield no longer suits your purpose."

"I am no longer certain that I have a purpose."

Fredero's frown was subtle, but it altered the lines of his face. He offered Marakas his silence, and when he chose to break it, he spoke as if Marakas had not. "And when that day comes, I will be waiting."

"For what?"

"An ally. A man who can also be a shield; who can bear the scrutiny of the Lord without once stepping away from the road I have chosen. I do not fear the Lord. I serve him. I desire power, and all power I have gained, both before I joined the Radann, and after, was at the expense of others who sought the same.

"You have already learned how costly it is to be bereft of power."

Marakas closed his eyes.

"You will come in time to understand how costly it is to *have* power. But without it—without it, Radann—how can we force our will upon others?"

Fredero added quietly, as he looked down at the carefully arranged corpse upon the white sheets, "This is only one death, Healer. There will be others. Many, many others."

Marakas was silent.

"Justice, in these lands, is a sword. A sword." His hand touched the hilt of *Balagar* as if the gesture were a benediction. "And what, in the end, can we say of swords? Does the Lord make them? Does he temper them? Is it his eye that inspects the ores, his hands that make first the one sword that will be so hard it is brittle, and the other, that will withstand the ravages of water and blood so completely that it cannot hold an edge? No. With almost no exceptions, a sword is made by men, wielded by men. Only men."

"You wear *Balagar*," Marakas said quietly.

Fredero's glance fell to the scabbard that housed the second most famous blade in the Dominion. "And yet, wield it or no, in the end, it is *I* who decide what it kills, and when, and why; it is thus with all swords, be they famous or unknown. And by our choices, we who wield these weapons, we are judged."

"By who?"

"By who?"

"Who judges the kai el'Sol?"

Fredero's smile was weary. "A fair question, Radann. A fair question. In the Dominion, it is said that in the end, there is no judgment. The winds take us all; we are trapped in the howl of its voice, and the eternity of its caprice.

"And perhaps that is even true; I cannot say. But if *this* is to be our only life, should it not be a life in which honor is valued, and justice is preserved? Aye, ask. Who judges the kai el'Sol? I have taken power—and I will keep it—for the purpose of imposing my will, my desire, and my vision upon others."

He knelt then, beside the dead kai Manelo, and placed his hand against the curved skin of his closed eyes.

Jevri, silent until that moment, spoke. "The kai el'Sol will face the harshest of all judges, and the least forgiving," the former seraf to the clan Lamberto said. "He himself."

So many words.

Words were a measure of time, their absence a measure of distance. Fredero was silent. The only words he would speak again would be spoken in memories such as these; there would be no new wisdom, no guidance.

Marakas par el'Sol placed his hand on the hilt of the sword that hung—as no other had before it—so comfortably by his side. *Verragar* was guide, ally, protector—but in spite of that fact, Marakas admitted privately what many of the Radann seemed incapable of realizing: A sword was not a man.

Fredero, he thought quietly. *I have allies. I have a worthy weapon. I have a cause that will define the Dominion— and more—forever. What is this shadow?*

But he knew. There had always been a difference between allies and friends.

He continued to walk. The sun began to creep upward, inch by inch, a slow return of warmth and color to the desert landscape.

Memory was a funny thing. Of his rise from the ranks of the Radann, he cared to remember little, and events remained shadowy; where light fell upon them at all, it was moon's light, some brightness cast by the memories of the man he had chosen to follow. In the contrasting harshness of day, they were almost pleasant, but drained of color, as much else was: the sand, the flats, the scrub. Even his arms were now dusted, and his robes gray with the weight of fine grains. He sat in the lee of his tent, and only when water touched cracked lips did he close his eyes.

"I will not serve Peder. If he is responsible for your death—"

The kai el'Sol lifted a hand. "Enough. He is not an assassin. He is a man. He cannot be 'responsible' as you so quaintly put it, for *my* death. To speak in such a fashion does not insult him, par el'Sol. It insults me."

Jevri glanced up from his place at a workbench that spread from one end of the room to the other, its flat, continuous surface broken only by bolts of fabric, containers that held crystal beads, pearls, small decorations of raw silk and linen that were meant to be the minimalist's abstraction of flowers.

The bench was not usually used for storage in this fashion, but the breadth of the tables over which Jevri el'Sol ruled were covered in ivory silks. Marakas had never understood Jevri's devotion to the craft of dressmaking. He tolerated it because Fredero tolerated it, but he found nothing in it to admire.

And yet, acknowledging that, he found Jevri at work to be a compelling figure; his hands did not shake; his gaze did not waver; he did not seem to draw a bead or a pearl, a spray of lace or a small gemstone, that did not conform to a larger working that unfolded, beyond Marakas' ability to follow, beneath his hands.

"But you tolerate him."

"He is a capable man," Fredero replied dispassionately. "And he is canny in ways that you—or I—are not."

Marakas was silent. He had known Fredero for many years, and although he had often observed Fredero in session with those who intended to succeed him, he had seldom seen the mask he now wore when such Radann were absent; it pained him. *Will you play at politics with me, Fredero? Will you hide the truth?*

"Kai el'Sol," Jevri said, his hands continuing their dance of needle, of thread, "Explain it."

"Jevri—"

"But, if you would be merciful, be brief. I have much to do here, and I am in need of the assistance denied me by this conversation."

Fredero's brows rose; Marakas was not certain that the expression, transformed for a moment by shock, would not descend into anger. But anger did not follow.

"He is canny," Fredero said quietly, "but that is a talent either you—when you are cautious—or I, possess. He is capable with a sword. He has danced with the fire. He is ambitious. All of these are traits that the par el'Sol must possess." He lifted a hand to forestall Marakas. "Agree that you are the exception, Marakas, or there is little point in continuing to force Jevri's aged hands to work alone."

Marakas bowed.

"You cannot treat with the enemy. What you desire is not a thing they could understand, and if they do not understand it, they will not work with you."

"He did not begin—"

"Enough." Fredero's expression was hard. Distant. "What is of concern is what exists *now*. He is a capable liar. And that, in the end, is what we need at this time. The time may come—*will* come—when that is not the case, and at that time, you have my leave to judge him, and to find him wanting, if that is your perception."

"And of honor?"

"Marakas."

"What of all that we have struggled for? You speak as if you have already lost, Fredero."

At that, the kai el'Sol looked up, and the anger that he had not bestowed upon Jevri, he now granted the par el'Sol. Anger was as rare as distance. Marakas held his ground because the Radann did *not* step back in the face of hostility, but for the first time in many years, such steadiness took effort.

"Understand, par el'Sol," he said, in the chilliest of voices, "that Peder par el'Sol came to me. I understand your fear, and I remind you that such fear is unacceptable in a Radann of your stature. Was he plotting against me? Of course. But he *is* Radann. He serves the Lord of Day."

Speaking seemed to bleed the anger out of his tone, although the corners of his lips were drawn tight. "We no longer fight the same war, and the war that we fight is a war that we *must* win. Lose it, and all of our past victories mean nothing."

"All battles are battles we must win," Marakas replied quietly. "They have been so for many years."

Jevri, working in silence, lifted a brow. "Well, Fredero?"

"Enough. Enough, both of you." He lifted a hand. "Remember your stories. Do I speak of defeat? No. But in any war, victory has many guises."

And in this conflict?

Fredero had won a battle, and had left the war in the hands of the par el'Sol.

Significant, then, that although Peder had immediately adorned himself with a title and the vestments that the High Court best understood, he had not taken up *Balagar.*

Marakas was tired. He understood the nature of the war

that drove them all, forcing them to cooperate in ways that no one—except perhaps Fredero himself—could have foreseen. But the desert sun was high, and the road that he traveled seemed interminably long and empty.

He did not pray.

He had been Radann for long enough that he understood the futility of that action. But had he understood it less well, had he been the younger self that he barely remembered—if he remembered himself truly at all—he might have.

Instead, as men do, he turned the whining edge from his thoughts, blunting them; he gathered his anger instead, honing it, and demanded some acknowledgment from the Lord of the Sun.

The Radann served, but they served not as Tyran, not as cerdan; their Lord stood robed in a harsh light that destroyed the sight of those who dared to gaze upon his glory in an attempt to discern his desire, to extract his commands. Such service demanded, in its turn, men who could speak in the Lord's name, and with the Lord's voice, for the lesser among the Radann desired some sense that they served more than the capricious voice of the wind.

Those men, guided by the kai el'Sol, served faithfully and with devotion from the moment they arrived at temples across the Dominion. They almost always brought swords; they almost never brought anything else of value, although the scions of the High Clans, those few, like Fredero—who were wed to privilege and power—often gifted the temple of their initiation with gold, or wheat, or rice.

Fredero had come with nothing but his name.

The Radann knew, when he arrived at their doors, that his father desired them to turn him aside. And his father, the Tyr'agnate, was Lambertan; he held much sway among the Radann.

Jevri had told him this much, but not more.

The rest, Marakas had been forced to forage for, as wild animals forage for food when the lands are dry. Such foraging had been poor.

He knew, of course, that the Radann had not rejected the par di'Lamberto. But the reasons, given the pressure—and the threatened displeasure—of the Tyr'agnate, were less clear. He suspected that had the decision been left solely in the Hand of the Lord, Fredero would have returned to his family; the par el'Sol and the kai el'Sol were born to, and of, the High Courts.

All, thought Marakas, save himself.

Men like he, though, might rise in the unnamed ranks that guided the temples in the cities ruled by the Tors; they might, with luck and skill, become part of those temples that graced the capitals in which the Tyr'agnati made their homes.

And men like himself, seeing the younger son of the Lambertan Tyr upon their steps, be he naked and swordless, would understand what the coming of that bloodline might mean to the worship of the Lord. What, then, could the Tyr'agnate offer that would convince them to return this son home?

Not gold.

Not men.

Not threats.

Fredero par di'Lamberto forswore his name, his clan, and entered the harsh exile of the Lord's service. Men followed him. Men served him.

Aye, even now, even in death, he commanded the loyalty of men.

Marakas turned his face skyward, risking white light.

Fredero was never defeated. He served you, and he was never defeated. Surely, surely had his will not expressed the hidden truth of yours, he would have failed against men like Peder years ago.

In the North it is said that in the Dominion of Annagar, we make our gods in our own image.

It was blasphemy; he did not care. What was blasphemy to the Lord, if the man who uttered it could defend himself against those who took offense at the words? *If it is true,*

*then the only god that I wish to serve is the god Fredero par
di'Lamberto envisaged when he came to the Radann to
serve. Can you be that god, Lord?*

Can you be worthy of Fredero kai el'Sol?

He knew that the Lord did not listen to demands; no more
did he listen to pleas or the wayward wishes of the young
or the desperate. Who better to know it, having watched the
fires of the Sun Sword destroy Fredero, eating away the
heart first?

Yet he found himself raising a sword that had left its
sheath so effortlessly, and so lightly, he was as unaware of
the motion as he was of drawn breath. It was the sunlight
that spoke in the silence, glinting against the flat of the
blade with a brightness the Lord himself did not possess in
the desert sky.

Marakas closed his eyes, turning his head slightly as if at
a blow.

And as he did, he saw it: a second flashing gleam of light,
thin and long, curved against the vision like the arc of a
Southern sword. He stumbled; had any other man reported
this flash, this lingering glint of light, Marakas would have
gently touched his brow, his hand, any exposed flesh, seeking for traces of sun madness.

He stumbled. His vision blurred.

He was born to the South. He expected no mercy; no dialogue with the Lord, no sign.

In times of duress, it was the unexpected that had the
power to cut, to bind, to wound; it was the unexpected that
had the ability to touch, to move. He stood, silent, his sword
falling, tip to ground, as he stared, as understanding came.

A river.

A river in the Sea of Sorrows.

A river that, in the height of moon's light, in the cool of
desert night, he might have missed at this distance.

He knelt, knees to sand; knelt, forehead to sand, closing
his eyes against the heat of the ground. Against the waste of
water that could mean death in the desert.

Fredero, he thought. *Kai el'Sol.*

Men did not pray; not to the Lord; not to the Lady. Therefore, Marakas par el'Sol, who had given the first half of his life in service to the one, and the second half in service to the other, did not pray.

He rose instead.

He felt the heat of the Lord's gaze, and he knew that if he lingered too long, the fires would consume him as certainly as they had consumed the kai el'Sol. But light trailed the length of his face from eyes to jaw as he walked; he did not lift a hand to wipe his face clean. In the desert, water and blood were one and the same. He offered his life cleanly, as if all things unessential had once again been scoured from him by fire, leaving only the truth in its wake.

28th of Misteral, 427 AA
Tor Arkosa

The Serra Diora stood at the height of the Sen adept's tower. The winds were warm and dry; they pulled at the folds of her robes, chafed at her veils. Only her hands were exposed as she laid them, palm down, against stone that was smooth as Northern glass, hard as diamond.

No one came here.

No one but the Serra and the Matriarch. To these two, the wards of the Sen adepts posed no threat, offered no resistance; they had walked in the shadows of the ghosts of women so long dead not even dust remained.

But memory did. And memory had yielded what Voyani lore could not: the words and the signs by which they might pass through the great doors of the adept's tower unharmed. The Serra turned her face a moment to see the surface of the orb at the tower's height. She could hear its whisper, but even her gift did not lay bare the words that whisper carried, no matter how long, or how hard, she listened.

Diora.

Ona Teresa.

Are you well?

I am . . . well.

The Matriarch of Arkosa seeks you.

Diora did not reply. Instead she looked back to the City
that slumbered in a terrible silence beneath her feet. The
Voyani were few; the Tor Arkosa was large. They had chosen to take refuge in what might once have been a place that
served as home to wealthy travelers, and they huddled
there, planning a future that they had never truly considered
a reality.

They had come home.

Na'dio?

She raised a hand to the hollow of her throat. The Heart
of Arkosa no longer beat within it; she had shed that burden, and Margret of Arkosa now carried it, as was both her
right and her duty.

Tell her that I am in the tower.

Her gaze slid past the City to the walls that kept the
desert at bay. The waters that the earth had revealed now
flowed beneath those walls and through the heart of the
City itself, and on the banks of the river, flashes of green,
new and pale, told their own tale.

She was almost ready.

And because she was, she waited.

Without flight, there was only one way to reach these
heights.

The tower of the Sen adepts would, Diora was certain,
buy the loyalty of any member of the Sword of Knowledge
that Margret cared to approach. Any save one.

Ser Cortano di'Alexes. The Sword's Edge.

How long? How long would this city remain hidden?

Her gaze roamed the breadth of its streets, the heights of
its towers, pausing to trace the glittering length of the river
that now ran through it, a silk ribbon that reflected the light
as if it were steel. Not long, she thought. Not long at all.

She ran her hand across the glass-smooth edge of stone

and then turned her back upon the open sky, the cloudless sun. She wore desert robes, and had she been upon the ground, Ramdan would have attended her with shade, with silent shadow, offering her the protection that was both his duty and his right. Who else might stand, unaccused and unattacked, by her side? He was one of the few things the heights deprived her of that she could be said to miss. But she knew that Margret did not—could never—understand what his presence meant; it was one of several small walls that would come between them for the rest of their lives.

There would be others, if they lived long enough to discover them all.

She lifted her head and gazed upon the white, pulsing surface of the giant sphere that stood at the heart of the tower. She knew it as one of seven such spheres; the others, spread across standing towers as old as this one, pulsed and moved as if alive, each unique, each with a sigil and a sign that warded it against the interference of outsiders. The heart of each was a different color; she could make them out only when she stood here, in the lee of the sphere, and she was careful not to notice too much. She would be gone from this place in too short a time, and any knowledge that she bore with her was a weapon in the wrong man's hand.

The spheres had protected the Tor Arkosa for the entirety of its long slumber; she wondered if they had been meant to endure beyond that; if, for eternity, they would defy the will of gods. She was of the South; she did not pray. Did not ask for mercy. Did not reveal, by that plea, her hope. The Lord was at his height.

But she did turn when she heard the unmistakable sound of curtains being drawn in midair. No silk curtains, these, no heavy linen, no beaten cotton; they were fine, like beaded glass that had caught the light of a dying sun and trapped it in links as strong as any chain shirt—like armor that could not be pierced or breached except in this fashion: by parting.

The Serra Diora bowed her head, and only her head; it

was the only acceptable gesture of respect that she could offer the Matriarch of Arkosa. Kneeling had been forbidden.

You are not a slave here.

I am not a slave, Margret.

I am not a clansman. If I have power . . . it is not a power that demands obeisance. Not from you. Never from you. You were . . . my sister. If we were free to choose our kin, you would bear the blood of Arkosa. You bore its heart. She had paused and looked away. *Bear it. Understand it. Do not offer me what you would offer any other ruler.*

When she looked up, she met the weary gaze of the Matriarch of Arkosa. "Margret."

"You spend too much time here."

"It is peaceful."

Margret's snort was short and loud. That something so graceless could be so eloquent said much of the Voyani.

Diora walked, slowly, toward the tower's North edge. She saw her shadow lengthen and change as she passed before the orb; a piercing chill struck her, but she did not change her gait. This was the desert. She was a Serra of the High Courts.

Margret took no such trouble to hide weakness or her distaste for this unnatural cold; she cursed loudly and forcefully, in two different languages. "I hate it here."

"I know." She did not ask why the Matriarch had sought her; she knew. Placing one hand firmly upon the tower battlements, she lifted the other, pointing.

They stood, side by side, in silence, watching the progress of a distant stranger, and seeing, in the steps he took, the end of their own journey together.

The Serra Diora had thought to be done, forever, with farewells. But the desert had offered her one more chance to say good-bye to something she had grown to care for, and she did not relish the opportunity.

Margret brought the lip of her hood down, to better shield her eyes from the sun's glare. "Who is he?"

The Serra Diora could have said that the distance between the solitary stranger and the tower's height was too great for certainty; it was. But she bowed her head instead.

"Diora?"

"I believe . . . that he is a man who owes Arkosa a great debt. And he has come to pay it."

Margret stiffened. She had none of Diora's subtlety, and that lack was her strength. Everything could be read in the language of form, of posture, of expression that tightened lip and narrowed eye. Diora knew this; she did not look. "He will be here within three hours."

"On foot?"

The Serra hesitated just a moment, and then said, "Mark his speed. Mark the length of his stride. If the desert has diminished him, he has changed greatly since . . . last I saw him."

Margret did turn. "When?"

"When?"

"When did you last see him?"

"On the day the kai el'Sol drew the Sun Sword."

"Margret."

The Matriarch of Arkosa did not turn at the sound of the voice; she knew it well enough, by now. She did, however, acknowledge her name with a curt nod.

Yollana of the Havalla Voyani drew close; her shadow was short and awkward. She had not yet regained full use of her legs. "You will let her go," the older woman said.

Margret started to speak, and stopped. "I am the Matriarch here," she said at last, but it sounded petulant, even to her own ears.

"Even so," Yollana said quietly. "I am sorry to disturb you, but you have a visitor."

"The kai el'Sol? He will not be here for some hours yet."

"Not the kai el'Sol," Yollana said, and something about the unusual control in her voice at last pulled Margret around.

"You," she said. It was all she could think of *to* say.

Standing like shadow—unnatural, unwelcome—in the lee of Yollana's more natural form, stood the mysterious Evayne. A younger Margret would have been paralyzed by sudden anger. But she had in truth left the *Voyanne*; she was instead weary.

"What have you come to take from us this time?" she asked.

The woman seemed to flinch. But she did not ask what Margret meant; instead she drew the hood from her face. "Margret of the Arkosa Voyani," she said quietly, "I have come with information."

"You always come with information," she said bitterly, before she could stop herself. "What will it cost us?"

"Some part of your ancient magic," was the unexpected reply.

"What ancient magic?"

"In the towers of the Sen adepts were many things that were crafted by mages whose knowledge has since been lost. I will not speak of the act itself; you know what the cost was."

"I do," she said, stilling. "But you? How do you know?"

Evayne a'Nolan did not reply. She was younger than Margret remembered, and the smooth lines of her face could not be illusion. Her eyes were dark, and her expression was not the cold expression that Margret knew. Who was she, who could change everything so easily? She almost asked. But asking was a sign of weakness.

"The Serra Diora di'Marano must leave the Tor Arkosa, and she will miss it."

Margret's turn for silence, and the Voyani did not love silence. "What of it?" she said, to break it.

"She will carry with her what she brought to the desert, and she will carry it into lands that will be . . . hostile. It is a gift, and it is a duty; I would have that duty made easier."

"You speak of the Sun Sword."

"Yes."

Margret turned to Yollana. "Matriarch," she said curtly, and Yollana surprised her by bowing. She left slowly, but she did not look back.

"I cannot offer you a sheath, although you will find many within the towers. Not one of them could contain the Sword without dimming it; it is not in the nature of their magic. But there are also veils and cloaks, blankets and boxes, things that were touched by makers long dead. Among these, you will find something in which the whole of the Sword might be placed."

"What am I to look for?"

"A box, I think. Something about this size, this width, this length." She placed her hands as she spoke; it was a very small box.

"It cannot contain a Sword."

"It can contain more," Evayne replied, "but not the living."

"And if I do as you ask, how then can this box be used?"

"She must blood it to make it hers," Evayne replied.

"She doesn't much like bleeding."

"She is the Flower of the Dominion; she has done much worse. Go to the West tower. The wards there will allow you entry. On the third floor, in the North room, you will find what you seek."

The Radann Marakas par el'Sol saw the City in the distance, and sight of it caused him to falter for the first time that day. He lost a step; lost motion; settled into a stillness so profound he could not disturb it by breath. All of his wisdom, accumulated over the years at such expense, had not prepared him for this, and he wondered—although as one born to healing, he also knew—if he were affected by the Lord's glare.

Still, if he faltered, he did not fall; if he stumbled, he did not lose his footing. He had come to pay a blood debt, his debt alone, and he knew for a moment the exquisite grace of an honor that knew no bounds. He bowed his head. He touched the hilt of *Verragar* and the sword seemed to sing a moment in the curve of his exposed palm.

He walked.

He stopped twice for water, and each time he did, he looked up quickly, to see if the City had vanished like the ripples of a distant mirage. He had walked the desert in his time, and he knew that it offered visions to men almost as often as it offered death.

But the City did not waver.

And the Radann did not waver. They drew closer together by dint of his will, until at last he reached the outer wall. Stone—if it were stone, it was so smooth and so unblemished—rose skyward in a perfect stretch that ended in unmanned curtain walls.

The gates were open. Beyond them, towers rose at heights undreamed of even in the Tor Leonne, for the lay of the land was flat from edge to edge. But the river that he had followed as guide and path led beneath that city, and before it, arrayed in silence, he saw men.

They were few, and in the end, as was so seldom the case, they were inconsequential; it was the women who waited that counted; the women who held power. He knew them by height, at first, for of the four present, none were tall.

Of the four, one stood, hands gripping the curved knobs of canes, and one stood by her side, in the lengthening shadows cast by the walls themselves. It was cool, in this shade. One woman stood, hands on hips, and at her side, still as the stone walls themselves, another, the smallest of the four.

They wore the masks and the hoods of desert travelers, as did he.

He did not kneel, but after a moment, he reached up and shed both mask and hood, revealing his face for their inspection.

"Well met, par el'Sol." The foremost of the women

reached up and likewise pulled hood and mask from her face.

He bowed his head. "Matriarch." The word was a whisper. "Matriarch of Arkosa."

"Aye," she replied, coolly, "I am that, now." He thought she would say more, for her expression was sharp as knife's edge, curtained by strands of fallen hair.

But he spoke first, forestalling the accusation in her eyes. "I have come," he said, kneeling for the first time, "to discharge the debt I owe the Arkosa Voyani."

It was the oldest of the women who spoke next. She, too, shed mask, although her hood still framed the wild gray of her hair. "Radann," she said, a glimmer of a bitter smile twisting the corners of her lips. "You were always a strange one. Will you kneel before mere women?"

"There is no love lost, no love owed, between the Voyani and the Radann, but there has always been respect."

She snorted. It was graceless, a sign of her power. Only the Voyani women could be so careless. He said nothing, waiting. Recognizing—as perhaps few of the Radann would—Yollana of the Havalla Voyani.

"What debt does a man of power in the Dominion claim to owe its women?" Margret of the Arkosa Voyani asked. Her lips were thin, her nose thin; she wore her age as all women did who toiled beneath the open sky.

"A debt of blood," he replied, feeling the weight of his body against the folded bend of his knees. He adjusted *Verragar*'s length across his bent lap. "A debt of honor."

"So." Margret's frown deepened. "Do you understand what it is that you offer?"

He nodded.

"And to who?"

Nodded again. The line of his shoulders straightened, as if he was shedding the weight of a great burden.

Life could be that, could seldom be less than that, in the

Dominion. He waited, in the calm that comes with surrender.

"What you have seen today you must not speak of to any who does not bear the name and the blood of Arkosa."

He nodded.

"Swear it."

And stiffened. Marakas par el'Sol was a man of his word; he was accustomed to the respect that reputation demanded.

She waited.

"What oath would you have me swear?" he asked at last, when it became clear that she would not speak.

"Blood oath."

It was almost an insult. Almost. But a simple insult did not absolve him of the part he had played in the death of Evallen of Arkosa. He reached for the hilt of *Verragar,* and drew her from her scabbard.

She was blue lightning, a flash of steel and old magic, as she came, unhoused, from her sheath.

Yollana of the Havalla Voyani cursed and lifted a hand; her cane was caught by the woman who stood at her side before it could strike ground.

Behind them, a large man drew his own sword, and Margret barked a single word. The man did not sheathe his sword, but he did not advance. Marakas noted that the Matriarch had not even glanced over her shoulder; she was certain of her people.

Marakas par el'Sol drew the edge of his blade across his palm. He had done so perhaps a handful of times in his life, and this stroke would create a new scar, a new line to be read by the ceaseless eye of Voyani fortune-tellers in the shadowed hovels of their secret life upon the open road.

"By blood," he said softly. "I swear to preserve the secrets of Arkosa. Beneath the open sky."

"Beneath the open sky," Margret replied. "I accept your oath. You will wait here. Tor Arkosa will never be home to the Radann; it will never house the clans. It is of, and for, the Arkosa Voyani.

"But we share a common enemy, a common danger. Evallen of Arkosa chose to journey by your side for her own reasons, and she paid the price that in the end we will all pay if we fail or falter.

"You owe a debt to Arkosa. You owe a debt to *me*."

He nodded. The blood ran from his injured palm to the sparse greenery that was, in itself, a miracle in this place.

"Pay it. Accompany these women, these three, to the Terrean of Averda."

"Averda?"

She turned, then, to the woman who stood so perfectly still by her side. In a much different tone of voice, she said, "Are you ready?"

And this smallest of women raised her hands delicately, deliberately, and pulled the mask from her perfect, pale face.

Eyes wide, dark, unblinking, she met the stare of the Radann par el'Sol.

He bowed his head again, deeply, thinking: *Fredero*. Unlooked for, unexpected, the Flower of the Dominion blossomed in the heart of the Sea of Sorrows. "Serra," he whispered. Seeing not the desert robes, but the pale, white dress of the Lord's Consort, golden hem lost beneath the waters of the Tor Leonne, hands cupped beneath the weight of the Sun Sword.

If a sword had a heart as fierce as hers, it would never break; it would never lose its edge.

"Radann."

The Serra turned to the Matriarch of Arkosa. "Yes," she said, straightening her shoulders. "Bring me only the burden that I must bear, and I will bear it."

The Matriarch of Arkosa hesitated; it was the first sign of vulnerability she had shown since he had arrived at the gates of a city he knew now must be the end of the *Voyanne*. The Voyani did not speak of the *Voyanne* to strangers, but

Marakas par el'Sol was born with a healer's gift, and he had offered that gift in their service.

He knew what such an ending must mean.

"Stavos," the Matriarch said.

The man who had drawn sword now nodded.

"Tell them. Tell the strangers that it is time to leave. Have them gather what they will take upon the open road."

The large man bowed and nodded, vanishing through the wide gates into the streets of the city. Marakas did not strain to see where those streets took him; he had offered his blood as vow, and he desired to carry as few secrets as he could from this place.

"Wait here," the Matriarch said. "We will return within two hours. When you leave us, travel as guide and guardian. Protect the Serra Diora. See her safely to the man she seeks, and all debt between Marakas par el'Sol and the Arkosa Voyani will be discharged in full." Her brows gathered, and her expression darkened; he knew that she would offer him threat for failure if he allowed it.

"Choose another quest," he replied, before she could frame the next sentence. "For the task you have set is a task that I would undertake of my own volition."

Margret's smile was cold. "Your own volition? It is said that the Radann serve the man who styles himself the Tyr'-agar. Do you claim to serve a different master?"

"I serve the only master the Radann have ever served," he replied coldly, exposing the steel of his own words. "And the Radann serve the Lord of Day."

"They have served another master in their history."

Anger deprived him of words.

But the Serra Diora gently lifted a hand and touched the Matriarch's sleeve. "Matriarch," she said, bending knee without brushing ground.

She met the Serra's eyes and her expression shifted.

It surprised Marakas. Of the Arkosans, Margret was known for the ferocity of her contempt for the clansmen. Or so she had been when Evallen had been Matriarch.

"My apologies," the Matriarch said stiffly. "In our history, many great men—and women—have served . . . unwisely. It is not history which is of concern; it is our future, the choices we make now, which are.

"But I set you no other task. You are counted among the wise. Or so Evallen thought. You were counted among the merciful. I do not ask you to simply raise sword like a hired guard; I do not ask you to serve as cerdan. I ask you to serve—inasmuch as your oaths allow—as Tyran to the Serra Diora *en'Leonne*. I ask you to do whatever must be done, and whatever can be done, within your power, to deliver her to the side of the man who claims the bloodline of the clan Leonne.

"And I ask you to see that she is—always—treated with the deference that her rank demands. See the man who lays claim to the Tor and the Lake; to the crown and the Sword. Judge him."

"And if he is found unworthy?"

Margret drew a deep breath. "Then return her to the Tor Arkosa."

"Matriarch," the Serra said again.

But this time, the Matriarch did not deign to meet her gaze.

CHAPTER FIVE

B UT how is worth in a man judged?

3rd of Corvil, 427 AA
Callesta, Terrean of Averda

Steel voice.

Sun like lightning flash from ground to clear sky.

Steel song, broken by little harmonies: Breath. Sweat. Movement.

All watch.

Who judges?

"Again."

Valedan kai di'Leonne lifted sword; brought it, dull edge to chest, tip to forehead, edge out.

Andaro di'Corsarro mirrored the motion; there was a man's length between them, no more, and it was measured by cast shadow.

Valedan moved first, moved slowly, bringing the blade to the sheath by his side. Against Andaro, he had no clear advantage. He watched.

Andaro nodded, the movement economical and controlled; he drew his blade up to shoulder height, extending his free arm.

Shadows here.

Beyond these men, deprived of motion, stood the Ospreys, deprived of colors. They were not—would never be—dress guards. Duarte AKalakar was aware that as Tyran, they failed on several fronts. But it was a proud failure, a Northern failure.

Alexis, dressed in the shirt and pants of the Kalakar House Guard, had drawn her hands to hips; her palms hovered above the pommel of a sheathed dagger. Beside her, restive, Auralis mimed the motion, but his blade was longer, heavier, straight where the Southern swords curved in a deadly crescent. His blade, as Duarte's, was double-edged. And, as his Captain's, sheathed.

Beside him, and one step back, stood Kiriel di'Ashaf. Her dark hair was bound in a single braid; her eyes, dark, were unblinking. Of the Ospreys, she was the only one who could stand at attention while Ser Anton played at war; the only one whose gaze never wavered, whose attention was drawn and held, in its entirety, by a combat they had all seen, day in and day out.

There was one significant difference on this warm afternoon. The Tyr'agnate of Averda stood opposite them, his Tyran by his side. And in front of him, brooding, radiating the heat of an anger that had not yet worked its way into words or actions, his son. Alfredo. The new kai.

Kiriel had grown used to the heat. Used to sweat. Used to combat whose purpose was not death.

Duarte told himself this again and again, willing himself to believe what did not seem credible. She had changed in the days since they had left Averalaan. He was not certain when he had first noticed the change; it was subtle. But it was there.

He knew it, because he was no longer comfortable turning his back upon her. Oh, he did it; he forced himself to do it. Forced himself to feign a nonchalance that, day by day, was ebbing. *Kiriel,* he thought. He said nothing.

Instead, he focused his gaze upon the back of the youngest member of Valedan's entourage. Aidan, born in the streets of the hundred holdings, the son of a near-crippled wheelright. His hair was white now, with sun, and his skin much darker than it should have been; he burned too easily beneath the gaze of the so-called Lord.

He should not have been here at all.

"I will not take him," Valedan kai di'Leonne said.

"He is almost of an age," Ser Anton replied with gravity. "He can carry either drum or banner; he can be horn-bearer or shield-bearer; he can serve you as the most junior of your footmen."

"He is a child, Ser Anton. He was well-pleased at your offer to teach him and school him; he will not expect more."

"He is almost thirteen years of age, Tyr'agar." The clipped use of his title was—almost—disrespectful. But the Ospreys were lounging in the distance against any flat surface; they did not affect to hear the brewing argument, although he was certain Alexis at least had her opinions, and she seldom kept them to herself.

"I would like him to reach thirteen," Valedan snapped back. He reined his tone in; the words themselves; he did not regret. Ser Andaro di'Corsarro, often distant when Ser Anton was present, joined the Ospreys; this was not an argument that he could afford to hear.

"No more than I," Ser Anton replied coolly. "But I've listened to your Ospreys—"

"They are no longer Ospreys."

"They will always be that, to the men of the South."

Silence, but it wouldn't last. Valedan touched the hilt of his sword restively. The sun was high, and he was too exposed.

"Aidan nearly gave his life to preserve yours," Ser Anton said at last.

The heart of their argument, and he had exposed it first. But Valedan knew a moment of frustration, for he perceived that to Ser Anton, it was not a weakness.

"You do him no favor," Ser Anton said, when Valedan

did not tender a reply. "If you wish him to survive, he must learn."

"Learn what? How to kill?"

"That, and more."

"We do not arm children."

"He is *not* a child. Your life is proof of that. He served as only Tyran would serve: he was completely yours."

"Ser Anton—"

"Honor his courage and his choice, kai Leonne. Accept that his life is not entirely in your hands."

Valedan was silent.

"You are in the North, Valedan."

"I know."

"But you must be *of* the South. No Tyr—or Tor—would deny him his request."

"Aidan is not of the South."

"No. But he is tempered steel. I say again: He has proved himself."

"He—"

"He was not struck down by accident; he chose. Would you dishonor his choice?"

"No. By leaving him here, I intend to honor it."

A dark brow rose then. Ser Anton bowed his head. Valedan thought—for a moment—that he had won this bladeless duel.

He should have known better; he never bested Ser Anton in a fight.

"You are afraid," Ser Anton said, "of war."

"I am willing to die to achieve our ends."

"It is not the same thing, kai Leonne. You are afraid to see the cost of battle written upon the things you value or treasure." He lifted his head, his eagle's profile burnished now by the full day's light. "Take him."

"I—"

"Take him; he will remind you, in the end, of *why* you fight."

"I do not need reminders."

"All men do," Ser Anton said. His hands joined behind his broad back; he stood a moment, the very statue of contemplation. A warrior's pose. "Even I, in the end, have benefited from the reminder, although I came to understand it almost too late."

The words were devoid of heat. Had they been sparring, it would have been as if Ser Anton had put up his sword, exposing his chest to Valedan's blade.

It was never something that Valedan found comfort in.

But against the history that bound these men, Ser Anton and Valedan kai di'Leonne, the younger lost all words. He felt a bitterness cloud the sun's light, and he was young enough not to be graceful in his surrender.

"If I choose to accede to your request—"

"It is not my request, kai Leonne."

"*If* I do so, you will surrender to me something of like value."

Ser Anton's brow rose, but he did not speak; he waited. He was damnably good at waiting.

"You have said that in the South you will no longer be my master."

"You must be seen to have *no* master, and no equal."

Valedan shrugged. It was a forced gesture, and it was a hollow one; he could not have felt nonchalance had he bent the whole of his will toward it.

"You will continue to train me. You will continue to teach."

Ser Anton said nothing.

"That was not a request, Ser Anton."

The swordmaster's frown was slight; more felt than seen. But it was a powerful presence. Valedan weathered it.

"Tyr'agar," the swordmaster said, bowing.

Valedan knew what he was thinking, then. And he smiled. "You intend to hamper yourself in my training, to better elevate me in the eyes of those who watch."

Ser Anton did not reply, but the reply was wasted breath;

his only options were denial or agreement, and he clearly favored neither.

Valedan was bitter, and Valedan was content: as a swordmaster, Ser Anton di'Guivera was a purist. Intent, when there were no blades and no flaws in their wielding, would in the end find scant purchase against the unquestionable integrity of his chosen craft.

It was all he had.

Steel song.
Short. Loud.
The boy at the edge of the circle—the invisible circle, a thing made of witnesses and not a thing etched in powdered grass—heard it all; the strike and the clash, the rich harmonics of a tuneless, timeless melody. His reddened, peeling face was still, and his lips, still as well. It was almost the only time that Aidan knew how to *be quiet*.

Ser Anton turned for just a moment, and the oldest of Valedan's servants met the gaze of the youngest; they exchanged the briefest of nods before the swordmaster lifted a hand. "Enough."

The two sparring men froze in place.

Ser Anton di'Guivera turned to the Tyr'agnate.

The Tyr'agnate nodded, but his gaze did not leave the kai Leonne. The breeze moved the grasses of the Averdan hills, turning the trees into an ocean of sound, a muted, constant whisper. It spoke to them quietly.

The Ospreys, however, lacked the skills to translate what it said. Auralis rolled his eyes. And Duarte knew that he should not have noticed the open expression of boredom, because he should not have been looking at his men. He grimaced, forcing his gaze back to the men that mattered.

The kai Leonne sheathed his sword and executed a perfect bow. Ser Andaro's was less perfect to Duarte's admittedly untrained eye, and the sword that slid into sheath slid less silently. It was subtle; it was artifice. Duarte knew; he had seen Andaro and Valedan spar a hundred times. Ser

Andaro was as graceful, as silent, as perfect in the language of the Court of Swords, as Valedan himself.

But by the little imperfections, he granted perfection to his liege lord.

He did not do so in the circle itself, but he was Ser Anton's student, in spite of their estrangement. What Valedan received in their drills, he earned.

If any of the Southerners noticed, they did not betray that knowledge. They waited for Valedan to leave the grounds that had been designated for this test. For when he did, he became again the Tyr'agar presumptive; the man for whom they would fight and die.

Now, he was part of Ser Anton di'Guivera's life's work; a testament to his art. This was the true test of a master. For in the end, the student, by dint of time and skill, might surpass him on his way to becoming both rival and legacy.

There was fire in both of these men, Northern and Southern, but it was like fire wielded by man; it burned, and it scarred, but it remained, visibly, in control.

Ser Anton nodded. It was a brusque, wordless gesture.

Ramiro di'Callesta nodded as well. The nod was a fraction deeper; an acknowledgment of his appreciation for the drill itself. His Tyran bowed.

But his son did not.

"Kai Leonne," Alfredo said, lifting both chin and shoulders in an attempt to gain height, "you fight well. If it pleases you, I would be honored to test my sword against . . . yours."

All of the watching men froze.

Valedan's sword was sheathed. "Kai Callesta," he said, bowing deeply to Alfredo.

Alfredo was not yet a man, but more than a boy; a few years older than Aidan, but a head taller. His shoulders were broad, but he had yet to fill them; he was lean in the way that the youthful are.

And angry.

Duarte tensed.

His eyes skirted the gathered men, and came to rest at last upon Ramiro kai di'Callesta. The Tyr'agnate's face was completely still, his expression like steel.

There was a risk here. Introduced by the Averdan heir, it waited for Valedan, a Southern trap. A man did not fight with children.

A man did not refuse a challenge if it was offered.

And what Alfredo kai di'Callesta had offered was just short of challenge. Had his words been a shade less graceful, had his sentiments been given leave to surface beyond the sullen rage trapped in his expression, Valedan would have had no room to maneuver.

Nor would the Tyr'agnate.

"Alfredo," Ramiro said softly. "The kai Leonne has agreed to ride with the Tyran after we have taken our midday meal. Join us." It was not a request.

Alfredo did not acknowledge his father's words.

Ser Valedan kai di'Leonne did. "Tyr'agnate." He bowed. "If it is acceptable, I, too, am curious, and I would grant your kai his request."

The General Baredan di'Navarre stepped between the open ranks of the Callestan Tyran. Silent and still until that moment, he drew closer to his lord. But he did not speak.

"We will be allies," Valedan continued, "your kai and I. When I gain the Tor Leonne, he will be second only to his father. I am from the North." He said it firmly and without hesitation. "His . . . curiosity . . . is not unfounded."

"He has seen you in action, kai Leonne."

"Does a man learn to fight by simple observation? Does he take the measure of his ally at a distance?"

Ramiro raised a dark brow. "You and I have crossed swords," he said at last. He moved slightly; sunlight glinted off the golden sun embroidered across his surcoat. "I have taken your measure; you have satisfied me."

"I mean no offense, Tyr'agnate." Valedan shifted slightly, drawing himself up to his full height. Funny, that; he was only a handful of years older than the kai Callesta, but he knew how to carry those years to advantage. Duarte wondered where he had learned that particular skill, if it was learned at all. "And I take no offense. Alfredo is blood to the man whose sword I now wield."

Alfredo stiffened.

And Duarte understood, then.

"Let me prove, if it is possible, that I mean no disservice to the memory of that man. Let me prove that I am worthy of the honor I have been offered in the wielding of that blade."

It was said. It was *well* said.

"Ser Anton."

"Tyr'agar." Ser Anton stressed each syllable.

"Do us the honor of overseeing the match."

Ser Anton nodded. "To first blood."

"To first blood."

Watching Andaro and Valedan circle and strike held passing interest for the Ospreys. Watching Alfredo di'-Callesta unsheathe his blade riveted them.

"Is he insane?" Fiara hissed.

Duarte's backward glance had the force of a blow; she stilled instantly.

Ser Andaro di'Corsarro hesitated for a fraction of an instant before taking his place at the side of Ser Anton di'Guivera. His hand was on his sword.

The Callestan Tyran stayed their ground. Ramiro di'-Callesta stepped back, closing their ranks. He nodded.

Valedan placed hand upon hilt, bending into his knees. Duarte recognized the stance; was surprised by it. In his estimation, the kai Callesta was no match for either of Ser Anton's students—but Valedan's sword form was the one he chose when Andaro had hit his stride. It was his most defensive offense.

The Callestans must surely be aware of that fact; they had watched him often. So had Alfredo. But Alfredo saw with anger's eyes, and with anger's judgment.

Still, he was Ramiro di'Callesta's son. He fell back, shifting his stance. Both hands took the sword hilt; he held it before him as if it were a weightless pole.

Ser Anton di'Guivera lifted a hand. "Begin."

Neither man moved.

Duarte had some patience with this silent assessment; the Ospreys had none. That they watched in silence was a testament to his temper, not theirs.

He had seen combat last twenty minutes; he had seen it end in one. Andaro and Valedan knew each other's measure fully; they understood, before they started, what they faced.

He was curious. This stillness, this waiting, had been slow to come to Valedan; even in the Kings' Challenge, he had not shown this patient intensity. But those were Northern games, in the end; in the South all games led to death.

First blood.

When Ser Alfredo moved at last, everyone drew just enough breath that they could continue to hold it. The boy was fast. But Valedan was fast as well.

Swords clashed, inches of steel running across each other as Valedan deflected the ferocity of the younger man's first strike.

For a moment, Duarte watched, eyes narrowed, assessing the situation. The politics of the Sword were both old and new to him, but across cultures, there was a difference. In the South, everything was scrutinized with a care and a deliberation that seemed so calculating to Northern observers. What Valedan did here would be defining. Duarte searched only for the definition that the combat would give rise to.

Alfredo was good for his age. Agile, light on his feet, deceptively strong. But he was not, in the opinion of the Kalakar Captain, Valedan's equal. Not yet, although with time and dedication, perhaps he would be. Valedan was not without mercy; he had shown that, time and again, in the North.

He could throw the combat—at some risk. In the North,

he could do so cleanly. But in the North, this type of combat did not carry the same weight.

They drew apart.

Valedan's sword was now in play; it had left the sheath, and it would not return. Alfredo charged again, swinging his blade in an arc perpendicular to the ground. He let out a loud, harsh cry as blade met blade; the force of the blow drove Valedan back. Alfredo pressed him, using force and speed, seeking a decisive, early victory.

In silence, Valedan denied him.

They parted again. This time, Alfredo was cautious.

He had twice attacked, with no visible effect; he was wise enough to know that he could not outlast the kai Leonne. Stamina and youth were twinned in this circle.

A third time, Alfredo swung, leaning into his knees, back straight, arms extended.

Valedan moved then, stepping in perfect time with the swing, cutting the distance between them to less than a sword's length. He caught Alfredo's sword an inch above the hilt, twisting his own blade beneath it, grunting with the sudden strength he exerted.

Alfredo's blade left his hands, and it flew in a heavy arc toward the Southern observers.

Ser Fillipo leaped in front of the Tyr'agnate in that instant, his blade unsheathed. But Ramiro himself did not move to deflect it as it traveled. He trusted his Tyran.

The sword, with no hand behind it, clanged off Fillipo's exposed blade and fell to earth.

Alfredo leaped back, raising his hands as Valedan raised his sword.

It hovered a moment between them before he lowered it.

"First blood," the Tyr'agnate said quietly.

Ser Valedan kai di'Leonne stepped back. He glanced to Ser Anton.

"To first blood," Ser Anton concurred.

But Valedan did not raise his blade. Instead, he met the

steady gaze of Alfredo di'Callesta. "With any other sword but this one," he said at last.

Alfredo's brows rose slightly.

"It is a Callestan blade," Valedan continued. "And it *is* yours. If you seek blood, you will have it; there are enemies—in number—that must be faced and defeated in the war to come.

"But a Callestan blade should not be raised against a Callestan blade, except in a test of strength; unless you demand it, kai Callesta, it should not be used to draw Callestan blood.

"I meant you no dishonor when I asked permission to wield this blade. I only meant to honor the fallen."

Their eyes clashed, as their blades had, and as their blades, it was Alfredo's in the end that glanced away.

"Alfredo," the Tyr'agnate said quietly, in a tone of voice that made it clear that the word was a command.

Both men turned to look at the man who ruled Averda.

He was completely still. "First blood," he said again.

Alfredo met his father's gaze more easily than he had met the kai Leonne's. Ramiro di'Callesta was the undisputed ruler of the Terrean.

Alfredo did not hesitate. Stepping forward, he reached out and gripped the end of his fallen brother's sword.

Valedan had the time—and the reflexes necessary—to pull the blade clear; he did not.

The kai Callesta gripped the blade. Blood seeped up between the tight fingers curled around edged steel. It welled there slowly until its weight drew it toward the crushed grass. There, red against green, the end of the challenge was signaled.

"First blood," Ser Anton said quietly. "Ser Valedan, the match is yours."

Valedan nodded. But he bowed to Alfredo. The boy's grip relaxed. His blood was bright and wet against the sash that Valedan wore after he wiped the blade clean.

Duarte AKalakar studied the faces of the men who had watched the short combat from beginning to end.

He could not tell, from the complete lack of expression on their Southern features, what Valedan had won this day. But one thing was clear.

Ser Alfredo kai di'Callesta was a young man who should be very grateful that the Callestan Tyr had no other sons behind him.

"You have," Ser Anton di'Guivera said quietly, "A strong son, Tyr'agnate."

Ramiro kai di'Callesta said nothing.

"He is blessed by the Lord."

And how is worth in a man judged?

3rd of Corvil, 427 AA
Terrean of Raverra

Although Marente was not among the richest of the clans, it was among the oldest; if Alesso had not spent his life in the idle and frivolous luxury that the dead kai Leonne had imported from the North, he had spent enough of it in its presence.

He knew the cost of silk, of gold, of glass—especially glass, that pane of artifice that kept the world at bay. He understood that there was a beauty in the garish designs and workmanship that the Northerners so prized; understood— with a much clearer precision—just how much of the Southern gold had, through merchants from the Terrean of Averda, left the Tor Leonne.

He valued none of these. It was not his desire to impress the Northerners by the conceit of wealth, although he did desire to leave upon them a lasting impression.

Here, in the building his cerdan had constructed, the maps around him like the pieces of a great mosaic, were the things he valued. He dropped his hand to the hilt of his sword and stood a moment in perfect repose, gazing upon the whole of the Terrean of Averda.

As if it were, line by line, a dense, irregular poem, he studied it, absorbing it whole. He knew the roads, knew the rivers, knew the valleys. He knew where the cities lay, and where the villages—those villages that provided food and sustenance in abundance—were most vulnerable.

What the maps could not tell him was more subtle. He could be certain that Ramiro di'Callesta was housed in Callesta itself, grieving over the death of his son. But he could not be certain of where the last of the Leonnes was now encamped.

The armies of the North had moved, and in numbers greater than either he or Sendari had expected. If his spies were correct, they had brought with them the three Generals who had experience in the terrain of Averda: the flight. The Eagle, the Hawk, the Kestrel.

Thirteen years had passed since he had last been called upon to take arms against these Commanders; against Commander Bruce Allen, Commander Devran Berriliya, and Commander Ellora AKalakar. The kai Leonne had been a fool; he had completely discounted the third division, the division over which the Kestrel presided, simply because it had been led by a woman.

What harm can a woman do, on the field? What loyalty can a woman command, among men?

With respect, Tyr'agar, the Demon Kings do not grant control of their armies to fools and those with an inability to lead.

How can she lead? There must be another upon whom she relies.

The Tyr's overly heavy face was a permanent part of the geography of Ser Alesso's memory. In just the same way that he read maps, read the stuttering chaos of the movement of whole armies across the landscape, he read that expression. He had chosen to retreat, while retreat was a possibility.

But Ramiro di'Callesta, Tyr'agnate of the Terrean in which their armies were housed, said what Alesso, at his vastly inferior rank, could not in safety say.

She commands the Black Ospreys. They report to her. And, Tyr'agar, she will not forsake them; she values them overmuch. Perhaps there is weakness in that.

The Tyr'agar had not chosen to respond to the edge in that observation. But he had not chosen to heed the advice in it either. He had been—and had died—a self-indulgent fool.

It was not a mistake that Alesso would make.

The field was now his.

He rose. The doors to the room slid open just enough to allow a man's face to peer in. The man, a seraf, pressed his forehead to the ground and left it there.

"Speak."

"The Sword's Edge has arrived."

"See him in."

The doors slid shut. He listened; heard the fall of a single set of steps. When the door slid open again, it opened wide; the seraf stayed upon the other side of the screen. Ser Cortano di'Alexes entered the room. When the Widan had fully crossed the threshold, the seraf saw that the doors slid quietly, and completely, shut.

Only then did Alesso begin to speak.

"Ser Cortano."

"Tyr'agar." Cortano's bow was brief, but it was not perfunctory.

"Ser Sendari?"

"He is occupied at the moment, but will return with word when he receives it."

"Good enough. Have you carried word?"

"From the North?"

"From our allies."

Cortano's gaze was like light on water. His eyes, a pale blue, were unblinking; like Northern glass, they offered the illusion of access without its fact. "Lord Ishavriel sends word."

"Word?"

"He has been delayed, but will arrive within the week."

Alesso glanced at the man who ruled the Widan—if such a group of men could be said to be ruled. "The Sword of Knowledge?"

"Those that I deem a liability have been deployed as messengers. They are crafting the tubes that we will require to send word among the Generals."

Alesso grimaced. Cortano's words were a veiled criticism. He had not yet chosen the men who would take command of the armies. Ser Jarrani kai di'Lorenza, Tyr'agnate of Sorgassa, and possibly the shrewdest of his allies, had a younger son. That son, Alef par di'Sorgassa, he wished to have at the head of the first army. Alesso had considered this carefully; Alef was quiet, and completely loyal to his brother. He was also competent.

But this, this was *his* war.

He walked, putting the table, with its detailed map, between them. Bending, he said, "Will they be of use to me?"

"The Widan?"

"The *Kialli*."

"Ah."

The silence was a Southern silence; movement broke it, but words had to be gathered, and offered, with care.

"Lord Ishavriel will arrive in person?"

Cortano nodded.

"Does he intend to remain with the army?"

"To the best of my knowledge. He is prized among the *Kialli* for his ability in war."

"And his followers?"

"For the moment, the Lord's Fist has agreed to your request. They will send only those who can pass themselves off as men."

Alesso nodded. He moved a pin across the map. "Here,"

he said. "The valleys narrow; if we are to gain the advantage of the terrain, there are three places we must avoid."

Cortano nodded again.

"There will be some difficulty with the *Kialli*."

Cortano's smile was brief. In its fashion, heavy with irony at the understatement, it was also genuine.

"Have you ever seen one ride?"

"Never."

"Nor I. But I have been horsed once or twice when they chose to show themselves, and even I had some difficulty controlling my mount.

"We cannot afford to take them with the cavalry."

"No."

Alesso moved another pin across the map. "Nor can we afford to have them reveal themselves."

"No."

"Have you thought upon the role you wish them to perform?"

"I? No. But I am not a General."

"Well said. I have."

"Then I should warn you, Alesso, that there has been some rumor in the Shining Court about the deployment of . . . His forces."

"What warning?"

"There is some chance that Anya will be on the field."

Alesso, were he less cautious, would have spit. "On our field?" he asked at last.

"By Lord Ishavriel's side."

The silence stretched; the map lay beneath him, and he saw it shift as he looked: Anya a'Cooper was mad. Powerful, yes, but her power could not be trusted; could barely be contained. If containment was a word that applied here. He struggled a moment with anger.

Into that silent emotion, Cortano spoke again. "If they risk her here, they require her power."

"To what end?"

"They wish to win this war, Tyr'agar. To destroy the Commanders will deal a blow to the North."

"Ah, yes. They fear the North." It was a bitter statement. The South did not seem to be of concern. He would teach them the error of this assumption. "Cortano," he said quietly.

"Tyr'agar."

"I wish a small delegation to be deployed. I have received a letter, carried by a clansman of some standing; he awaits my reply."

"Ah."

"It is from Ser Amando kai di'Manelo."

Cortano frowned. "He serves the Tor'agar of Vellens, does he not?"

"He does."

"His Torrean is deep within the boundaries of Mancorvo."

"Indeed."

"What does he wish, and what does he offer?"

"He offers his allegiance, Sword's Edge."

Cortano said nothing.

"And I wish to reward that offer. I would send *Kialli* among my delegates; let them travel to the Torrean that Manelo now holds. If he can be of aid to us, let us use what he offers."

"You will court war with Lamberto."

Ser Alesso di'Alesso smiled thinly. "Perhaps. But I think not. In the end, with some loss, the kai Lamberto will not stand by the side of the Callestan Tyr; too much has happened between them, and the Callestan Tyr now travels in the shadow of the Northerners."

Cortano bowed. The hatred that Ser Mareo kai di'Lamberto bore the Northerners was legendary.

"Do not discount the threat he poses," Alesso said softly, guessing at what Cortano did not say out loud. "The subversion of the Leonne Tyran was . . . distasteful to him, and if he desires vengeance, he is not a fool. He would not surrender the whole of Mancorvo in order to achieve it."

"And how will you then send word?"

Alesso par di'Marente's ghost haunted the plains fifty miles from the intersection of the disputed Mancorvan-Averdan border.

Sendari met him as he traveled, horsed now—on a beast that Alesso himself had chosen and given, in public, to his most trusted adviser. He met him when his shadow passed over the trampled grass; met him when his horse cantered through the wide stretches between rows of tenting and the wooden structures that serafs had spent the better part of a month constructing and perfecting.

He heard his laugh, saw the edge of his smile, saw the glint in the eyes of a perfectly still face; he saw him, horsed, and on foot, *Terra Fuerre* by his side, in the colors of Marente, a minor clan of the High Court. He saw him, not in the men who, little better than cerdan, had been gathered from the villages of the Terrean of Raverra, but in the men who commanded them; in their youth and the vibrancy of their quest for victory.

Dark hair, dark eyes, strong jaw, broad shoulders that had filled out in the strength of early manhood—that had been Alesso.

Of himself, Ser Sendari par di'Marano saw little. His home had not been on these fields, and his name had not been made upon them. His battles had been personal, his losses inflicted not by the harsh and sudden stroke of a sword or the pointed haft of a spear, but by the simple expedience of living a life in the Dominion of Annagar.

Of loving those whose lives had touched his.

When Alesso had last ridden to war as a promising commander of note, he had ridden under the banner of the kai Leonne. But his men had looked not to the Tyr; they had looked to Ser Alesso. And it was Ser Alesso di'Marente who had managed to salvage a retreat from a rout, saving face and lives in the process, and becoming worthy of the title General.

The years were gone. Twelve, almost thirteen. Ser Sendari now wore the rubied sword that told the ignorant he had passed the hidden tests demanded of the Widan; his edge was the hidden power, the will, of the Sword of Knowledge.

But he would never be the striking figure that Alesso had cut then; he would never have that breadth of shoulder, that wild determination, that terrible grace of cunning that had given Alesso the Tor Leonne.

In his youth he had bitterly resented that fact.

Now, he was above it; unlike the ghost of the young Alesso di'Marente, his own youth did not haunt him. Nor did his dead.

But the living were treacherous.

He could not escape them.

Narro, great black beast with braided mane and braided tail, was restive. Sendari had given him leave to gallop three miles past the Northernmost edge of the encampment. But three miles for a horse of Narro's quality was the beginning of a run, not the end of it; he was restive. The robes of a Widan fell across his flanks as he tossed chunks of grass-laden dirt to and fro.

"Wait," he told the horse, pulling at the reins.

Narro accepted the command with ill grace. Sendari shrugged. There were none here to bear witness to his inability to exert perfect control over the beast, and the witness that would come would not judge him for the weakness.

The sun had risen; he judged time by the fall of shadows. There were other ways of judging it, but this way served him best; he had developed, over the long month, an instinctive acceptance of the rhythm of day.

He missed his wives. Many of the Tors who had gathered upon the plain had brought a wife or a concubine with them; those who had not had taken, from the Raverran vil-

lages, the companionship they required. Sendari found no
comfort in the arms and the words of strangers, and beauty
spoke not to his heart, but to something too cerebral to be
easily comforted.

That part of him was Widan.

And the Widan's knees tightened around the girth of his
horse as he heard the distant sounds of travel. There were
men upon the road.

He nudged his horse forward; had to fight to hold him
back. This meeting was not a meeting that he relished.

He saw the standard first; it was lifted by the hands of a
man he did not recognize from this distance. Unfurled,
heavy enough to withstand the ferocity of wind, it caught
sunlight and scattered it. Six rays above the full face of the
rising sun.

Adano kai di'Marano had come.

Behind the standard, four men traveled abreast, their
horses cantering in a unison that spoke of the quality of
their riders. Those riders wore the half sun, with six distinct
rays; it marked them as Toran. Behind them followed another group of four, and behind them, two men rode
abreast. Sendari counted them; eight, two, eight.

He waited; the distance between the riders and Narro
lessened. Narro's neck rose; his nostrils flared. Sendari
straightened his shoulders; ran one hand through his
Widan's beard. Adano would know, if he saw the gesture,
what it meant; the Widan was nervous.

Only when the standard-bearer stopped did Sendari dismount. Upon horseback, the differences between himself
and his kai were pronounced. Sendari wore a sword gracelessly; it fit him as well as any sword ever had. It was accoutrement, afterthought, a part of the uniform that spoke
of coming war.

But it was not his weapon.

The ranks of the Toran broke as the two men in their center edged their horses forward.

They wore Marano colors: emerald and night blue beneath the hooded visage of white hunting bird. Beneath its flight, the sun, the rising sun.

He waited. Their horses slowed.

The older of the two dismounted. His stride was long, his steps quick.

"Sendari!"

Sendari par di'Marano bowed; the bow was perfect, inflected with genuine respect. When he rose, he stood ten feet from the kai Marano: his brother, Adano, the Tor'agar.

The sun had not aged him; the wind had not bowed him. He smiled, nodding at the glint of ruby and gold that divided their achievements.

"Adano."

"Par Marano," his brother said, extending his arms.

The embrace was brief. This much Sendari expected.

It was formal. This . . . he had not. And although Adano had chosen to travel with his eldest son—which was, in disputed terrain, an open gesture of trust—he did not summon his kai to his side.

Compared to other cuts, other losses, this was shallow, but it stung nonetheless. The human capacity for pain, it seemed, was endless and subtle.

Sendari stepped back and bowed, rising to the sight of Adano's almost expressionless face.

"We . . . have had word . . . that Ser Alesso has massed his armies on the Northern front of Raverra."

Sendari nodded. "It is true."

"No word was sent to the Tyr'agnate."

"No word was received from him," Sendari replied, slipping with effort into the smooth neutrality of the High Court. "We do not trespass on the Terrean of Mancorvo; nor do we seek to feed or house our forces upon its soil. As such, word was not deemed necessary."

"Indeed."

"No word was received from the Tor'agar."

"There are some words that serafs cannot be entrusted to

deliver," Adano replied. He hesitated, and then added, "I sent word to you."

"I am not the Tyr'agar."

"No. You are par di'Marano."

"And Widan."

"Indeed. Adviser to Ser Alesso."

Sendari nodded.

"And of the Serra Teresa?"

"I have not seen her since the Festival of the Moon."

"Others have?"

"Perhaps. No one in the Tor Leonne."

"Did you send her from the Tor?"

"I?" Bitter word. "The Serra Teresa answers to the kai Marano, when she chooses to answer at all. I thought, perhaps, you had summoned her North."

"In the North, at the moment, she would be of value to me. But no. I did not summon her." He drew his hands behind his back, clasping them there. "Sendari—"

"Kai Marano?"

"Is she dead?"

"Not by my hand."

"Forgive me. I had to ask."

"What is there to forgive? There was little love between us."

"But not none. She is Marano."

"Not none," Sendari replied. He met his brother's gaze. Held it. "But it is not of the Serra Teresa that we meet to speak."

"As you say."

"The Tyr'agnate?"

"The Serra Donna en'Lamberto received a letter," his brother replied. "Or so she said to one of my wives."

"And its contents?" Sendari's hand rose to his beard; Adano smiled in spite of the formality of his stance.

"It was a letter written to a Serra, by a Serra."

"Ah. And your wife?"

"She is well. She has hope that we will be spared the rigors of war in the future."

Sendari was weary.

Adano knew it; he wore the same lack of ease.

"You know the Tyr'agnate better than I," Sendari said quietly, hands idly brushing the strands of his beard. "You have served him well since ascending to our father's rank.

"What do you think he will do in the coming conflict?"

"It depends on the actions of Ser Alesso. The taking of the Tor Leonne occurred with no warning—none, at least, to the Lambertans. Mareo di'Lamberto is a man bound by honor, but he is not blinded by it. He is aware that Oerta and Sorgassa have fielded armies in service to Ser Alesso. That did not come without negotiation."

"Ser Mareo kai di'Lamberto would never have condoned what occurred."

"And you expect him to do so now?"

"I expect nothing."

"Ah."

Ser Adano bowed. "Understand," he said, his tone a match for his brother's, "that I have sworn an oath to Lamberto."

"Indeed. As Tor'agar you could do little else."

"He is a man worthy of such an oath, Sendari."

"And Alesso *di'Alesso* is not?"

Adano met his brother's eyes. "Sendari." He raised a hand.

Sendari subsided.

"I am the kai," Adano told his brother. "I have, as I can, aided you. I sent Teresa to the Tor at your request. I sent information about the events in Mancorvo as it was politic. I will *not* order you not to serve Ser Alesso. No man who fought in the war almost thirteen years ago would.

"But I will not be forsworn." His gaze was now unwavering. "Mareo di'Lamberto was neutral to your cause."

"Neutrality was prudent."

"Yes. And Mareo di'Lamberto is prudent. But it was not merely a matter of prudence. Now he is torn."

"He owes no loyalty to the clan Leonne."

"None. And when the last member of that clan comes at the head of the Northern armies, he owes less than none."

"The Northern armies have moved, and in number. They are almost certainly amassing—if they have not already done so—within the borders of Averda."

"In what numbers?"

"We believe they have traveled with not less than twenty-five thousand men."

Adano's silence was gratifying. It did not, however, last.

"Mancorvo and Averda were not meant to survive the new Tyr's rule under their current rulers."

Sendari offered no reply; there was none that could be offered without insult.

Adano's lips thinned. His smile held no mirth whatsoever. "Rethink that strategy."

"The strategy is not mine."

"No. But Alesso values your counsel."

"And Mareo di'Lamberto values yours, does he not?"

"Yes. But he values it less than he values his clan. Less," he added, "than he valued his brother. When Ser Alesso can draw and wield the Sun Sword, the Tyr'agnate will offer his oath and his services."

"And until then?"

"I . . . believe that he will not move against you."

"That is all that we desire at the moment."

"Will you withdraw your troops?"

"They are not mine to withdraw."

"They are amassed between the border of Averda and Mancorvo. It seems—to those with no information to counter it—that Alesso has not yet decided which Terrean he seeks to invade."

"In the end, Brother, he will invade only what he is not offered. He is the Lord's man."

"Which Lord, Sendari?"

Ah, it was out in the open. Sendari did not hesitate. "The Lord of Day."

"Then the Lord will judge."

Sendari bowed. He reached into the folds of his robes, and pulled from it two things. A letter, in a coded tube, and an oath medallion.

Its wood had been broken by the edge of a sword's single strike. "This is the mark of *Terra Fuerre*," he said, his fingers brushing the rough runnel. "Tell the kai Lamberto that we will avenge what Mareo di'Lamberto himself could not avenge."

Adano took both scroll and medallion.

"If Ser Alesso chose to travel, he might bear word himself."

"He is," Sendari said, composed now, "occupied."

"And Lamberto," Adano replied, "is not."

That drew a smile from Sendari.

"Did you write the letter?"

"I? No."

"But you know its contents."

"Indeed."

"I will carry it for you." The Tor'agar Adano kai di'-Marano turned to leave. Without looking back, he said, "Do not offer me safety, Brother. If, in the end, the man who styles himself Tyr'agar sees reason to invade, I will fight and fall with my liege lord." He took another step, and then spoke again, the words drifting in the breeze of the plains.

"And if, in the end, this comes to pass, I will acknowledge that you are Sendari *di'Sendari*; you are a clan in your own right."

If he had been a younger man—if he had been his younger self—Sendari would have spoken, then. But the enormity of the acknowledged gift was daunting, and he retreated, as men do, into silence, losing the moment.

28th of Misteral, 427 AA
Terrean of Averda

Commander Bruce Allen surveyed the mouth of the straits.
There were boats moored among the docks that his soldiers
had spent a week constructing; there was not a Southern
ship among them. The trees that lined the river did so at a
distance; those that had had the misfortune to grow where
the army built its encampments had been cleared.

In another four days, the last of the ships would arrive,
and their cargo—men and supplies—would be left upon
these wooden docks, their reflections broken by the rush of
moving water. Nothing was still in the South.

He shook his head. Nothing stayed still in the North either. Turning to the younger man who waited ten yards
away, he gestured.

The man turned instantly and began to cover the distance
between them; the light of the medallion of the Order of
Knowledge was a brief, bright flash as he moved.

Commander Allen had worked with his share of magi in
the past, and he could count on one hand the times that he
had not found it frustrating. They were not military men;
when inducted into the army for fieldwork, they responded
as Members of the Order of Knowledge and not as soldiers
in the Kings' armies. They could be obdurate men, and
when they felt that they dealt with inferior intellects—
which, in the case of most magi, was almost always—they
were curt when they tendered what they felt was due obedience.

Gyrrick of the Order was therefore a surprise to him; a
man who seemed to understand the chain of command, at
least as far as it extended between himself and the Commanders he served. He spoke little, and when he chose to
speak, he tendered replies that were brief and to the point
without bordering on rudeness.

It should have been comforting.

Commander Allen found it mildly disturbing. And that

made him smile ruefully. He let the smile linger as the man reached his side.

"Member Gyrrick."

Gyrrick bowed. "Commander Allen."

"I wish a message to be delivered to Commander Berriliya."

Gyrrick nodded. His eyes, rather than closing, became glassy; his face lost all expression. The Commander waited.

"Commander Berriliya is present," Gyrrick said, speaking as if speech itself were foreign to him. "The Member Aldraed asks me to tell you that he has spent much effort purifying drinking water for the three vessels today; the communication—unless of course it is urgent—should be brief."

"Tell him that his warning is appreciated. I merely wish to know where the ships are."

"They have reached the Ocean of Omaras. They are on schedule. The weather is calm at the moment."

"Good. Tell the Commander that we will expect him in four days. We have received word from Callesta, and we are expected to travel there in haste."

"Commander Berriliya wishes to know if we will travel by land or by water."

Commander Allen gazed at the turbulence of the river in the distant west. "By land," he said at last. "The horses have had enough of the water."

"Commander Berriliya asks if Captain Duarte AKalakar has sent word from Callesta."

"Only that."

Gyrrick's eyes snapped shut.

But he had not finished speaking. "Member Aldraed has one message to add."

"What message?"

"Meralonne APhaniel of the Council of the Magi will be joining us directly."

"When?"

The younger man's eyes snapped open, his lids jerking

up in a curl of dark lash. He turned swiftly, his face shedding neutrality and stiffness. He did not waste words; they were unnecessary.

Commander Allen could hear the sudden cry of his men; could hear the clang of swords hastily leaving their sheathes in the encampment below the riverbank. He leaped from the peaceful lee of water's edge, his voice raised in command.

Damn these mages, he thought. He heard the arc of an arrow's flight. Saw it as it paused in midair, trembled a moment, and fell, deprived of momentum.

No others joined it.

In the middle of the clearing that housed the command center, arms folded, hair streaming loose down his back, stood the Member of the Council of the Magi. He raised a pale brow as Bruce Allen strode between the armed men who served as his personal guard.

"At ease."

Simonson had already brought the men to order; he had not, however, given them orders to sheathe their swords. "Commander Allen," he said, drawing his arm up and across his chest in the sharpest of salutes. It was, strictly speaking, unnecessary—but it was also his way of reminding the magi who ruled here.

"Member APhaniel."

"Commander Allen."

"We received very little warning of your arrival."

"Ah." He lifted his shoulder in a shrug that was in itself an act of monumental arrogance. This, this was what the army was accustomed to dealing with when they traveled with the magi. "I see that things have changed little in twelve years."

"Very little. Why are you here?"

"I was sent," he replied, "at the behest of the Kings." He gestured; a scroll materialized in the air between them. "In light of the present difficulties, my expertise was considered of value to the army."

Commander Allen nodded brusquely; Simonson plucked the missive out of the air without any visible hesitation. He placed it carefully—and quickly—into Commander Allen's upturned palm and stepped to the side.

The Commander nodded. "Join me," he said curtly.

The tent was large. It housed a desk, chairs, and a large table. The table was covered with maps. They were not Northern in manufacture; they were Southern, a gift of the Callestan Tyr.

As such, they were considered to be incomplete. Commander Allen had his own men—those who were skilled in surveys—in the field gathering information; what they brought him would determine how incomplete the maps were.

Simonson entered the tent; the men who had been selected as the Commander's personal guard cast shadows against the fabric. They did not, however, enter.

Bruce Allen broke the seal upon the scroll. He unrolled it, and noted that it contained not one, but two, pieces of paper. The second, seal broken, was of more relevance than the first; the first was a simple confirmation—if it were needed—of the magi's claim to legitimacy.

We regret to inform you that Jewel ATerafin is unavailable at this present time. When she has returned to the House Terafin, she will be sent in haste—at the expense of House Terafin—to any location deemed safe and accessible.

It was signed by The Terafin.

He looked up.

Member APhaniel waited.

"Where is she?"

"I am not a member of the Terafin House Council," the mage replied coolly. "And she is not a member of the Order of Knowledge."

"She was given leave to travel?"

"As she is not a member of the Kings' army, or the Astari, she is not considered to be under the direct command of the Kings."

"She was to be seconded to the army."

"Indeed, that is my understanding. It was not, apparently, the understanding of House Terafin."

The Commander raised a brow; he spoke after a pause. Those who knew him would understand the significance of such a pause.

Clearly, the mage was not among them.

"Has she been seen since the attack on the Common?"

"I am privy to exactly the information contained in the letter you now carry." Before the Commander could speak again, the mage lifted a slender hand. "However, I am also privy to rumor, if that suffices."

"Speak."

"She is alive."

"That is not of significant value if she is not here."

"It is not of value to the army, no. Let me assure you that if her whereabouts were known, she would be with you now. If they become known, I have been authorized to . . . retrieve her."

"And your researches have not given you the ability to discern her location?" It was a bitter comment.

"We are not seers," the magi replied, with just a trace of arrogance. "Nor are we bloodhounds. We cannot be set to hunt. She is alive, and if I am not mistaken, you will see her before the war is finished."

"And this information?"

"A . . . hunch, Commander Allen."

Commander Allen was accustomed to the magi; he did not grind his teeth. Barely. "Where does rumor place her?"

"With the Voyani," the magi replied.

"And they?"

"They are not easily found, when they wish otherwise. But they wander these lands; they claim no home."

Commander Allen nodded curtly. He had heard of—and even encountered—some few of these wanderers in his previous journey into the Dominion.

It had not been pleasant.

CHAPTER SIX

1st of Corvil 427 AA
Sea of Sorrows

THERE was life along the riverbank.

In and of itself, it was not remarkable. Jewel was no botanist; she could not name the plants that grew, roots near their only source of water, in vibrant, pale greens, in dark, deep emeralds. In Averalaan, she would have passed over them without noticing them, for they reminded her of the weeds that grew up between the stones on the old roads, wedging themselves between gate and grass; that grew, unwanted, and in a way that advertised neglect in the hundred holdings.

But in the desert, the plants were proof—if it were needed—that water was life; water, as the Voyani said quietly, was blood. For good measure the older women would add, when speaking to children, that blood *would* be spilled if their horseplay spilled water. It was said with mock gravity, but Jewel knew the tone well; none of the children had been careless near the desert's edge.

She missed them, in its heart, but children did not travel in the Sea of Sorrows unless death threatened them otherwise. Having survived the trek, she knew why. She wondered where they were.

She trod carefully when she approached the water itself, afraid to crush these small miracles, these new births. She noticed their leaves, small and squat; their stems, thin and supple as they leaned toward the moving river.

If she knew how to listen, she thought she might hear the plants whisper or speak as they nodded and bowed like a congregation of children.

But she did not know how to listen; only how to observe. In the brilliant hue of setting sun, she watched.

Kallandras of Senniel College walked the river's bank in silence, but not in isolation. Celleriant of the Green Deepings, Celleriant of the Court of the Winter Queen, walked beside him. He moved without apparent effort, his steps light and graceful; he disturbed nothing as he passed over it. Every so often he would bend, his knees brushing sand and dirt, his fingers caressing the upturned face of a pale flower, a leaf's bud, a delicate stem. He would speak, then. But even when she could hear his voice, his words were like a song; she could understand none of them.

If Kallandras was likewise encumbered by ignorance, it did not show. He would tilt his head to one side, listening, and on occasion, he too spoke.

Those words were private words; they made no sound. She envied the person who did hear them.

Was surprised at the strength of that envy.

By her side, warm shadow, and tall, stood the stag. He left her only to drink from the waters that rushed past, and he did not stay long in that water.

Yollana of the Havalla Voyani and the Serra Teresa were likewise inseparable. Stavos attended them in almost perfect silence, for they seldom acknowledged his presence. He had left wife and Matriarch behind, but if he yearned for either, it did not show; he walked with quiet purpose.

The man who had identified himself as Radann—which was, as far as Jewel could tell, a priest of some sort—often walked alone. But like the stag to Jewel, he did not stray far from the side of the Serra Diora. Neither did her seraf.

Seraf.

Jewel knew that in the Empire, he would have been

called a slave; knew, too, that in the Empire, she would have despised the Serra for retaining him. Knowledge and emotions tangled briefly, and as was so often the case, emotion won; this was not a man who seemed chained and bowed by the servitude that his country considered his only recourse. Although he seldom spoke, his attention was focused, tuned, honed; *she* was his craft; she was his life's purpose. In the relative prosperity of the Empire, the concept of a willing, proud slave would have been anathema, an intellectual puzzle at best.

Jewel was far from home.

And the only person that she had brought with her was as silent as this seraf.

But he was not her shadow. He walked alone. Ate alone. Slept alone. He was never far from her side, but he was never too close; she could look at him and see profile, the proud line of brow, the strong nose, the unmoving jaw, a statue's repose.

Something warm and wet brushed the nape of her neck. She turned to meet the large, unblinking eyes of a creature that had once been—in a lost season—the Winter King.

"What?"

He nudged her arm gently. Only when he did so did she realize that she had been reflexively rubbing her sleeve, running its rough, heavy fabric against skin broken by the mark on her arm. It was flat; she could not feel it. Nor could she see it. But she knew its shape better than she knew the shape of her hands, her legs, her feet, the parts of her body that she could almost always see. Red, red S, livid like burned flesh, broken in the middle of each of its outer curves by a silver V and a gold one. She stopped at once, letting her arm fall loosely to her side.

The stag nudged her arm again.

"Let it be," she whispered.

You are worried.

The sound of his voice was warm and deep. She remembered, dimly, that she had once found these words vaguely threatening, but all that remained of that feeling was memory.

"I'm always worried. If it's not one thing, it's another."

She heard the dry chuckle of an older man. *You are worried about Viandaran.*

"Avandar."

As you wish.

"You read too much into gestures."

You read too superficially.

Her shrug was economical.

Speak to him.

She said, by way of reply, "I think Marakas is about to call it a night."

But the stag nudged her again, drawing tines across her brow. They were sharper than she remembered, a reminder—if she needed one—that he was not the hunted, here.

You are worried, Jewel.

"I told you—"

And because of your gift, you cannot afford to ignore what you feel.

She hesitated for another moment. "You were like him, when you were . . ."

When I was a man?

Her nod was brief. *Yes.*

I was like him, yes. But unlike; even at the height of my power, when I could see no threat to my dominion, I acknowledged the power of the Warlord.

She hated that word. "It's easier to forget that. About you."

You have no desire to remember it. And I have little reason to remind you. But again, he stroked her forehead with his lower tines.

She withdrew then. But she also surrendered. "I would. I'd speak to him if I could think of anything to say."

*   *   *

Avandar had come too soon from the mountains, and he yearned for them, although he knew the passage into the Stone Deepings had destroyed much of the bindings that kept them safe from the old paths, the hidden ways.

He might have returned, but he was held fast by a binding he had made in haste. It had been centuries, more, since he had last chosen to cast such a spell, and leave such a mark, and after it, too, had failed, the disappointment had scoured him of desire. He had not thought to be tempted by mortality again.

And had he guessed that the time would come when he would be, he would never have guessed that it would be for someone as simple, as reckless, as Jewel ATerafin.

She was no fool. Had she been, they would never have met. But had she been competent, had she been—as all of his wives had been, in a painful and distant past—truly powerful, he might never have been summoned from the halls of the Domicis to serve her.

The service rankled.

The past, invoked by the dormant Tor Arkosa, had opened its doors and windows, beckoning. Not a single one of the Voyani could claim the kinship with that unearthed City that he could, should he so choose; not a single one of these diminished, neglected descendants could conceive of what that City had been—and could still be—when it was ruled by a man who understood how to take and wield power.

They were broken, shadows, crippled mortals whose only link to the past lay in a name and a measured span of years. They could not understand what had passed before them, and even if they did, he was certain that they would not seek to attain it again.

And why should they?

In their mediocrity and their fear they had almost outlasted the ancient powers that had guided their ancestors; one or two of the ancient weapons, crafted in the forges of the Deepings, were theirs to command—but they understood these weapons so poorly.

It was their war.

It was theirs, but he had walked the perimeter of the Tor Arkosa, and he had heard, in its ascension, the ancient voice of the slumbering earth. He had seen the ghosts of his own dead, and he was forced to acknowledge the fact that he had not—could never—join them.

Lord Celleriant of the Green Deepings cast a slender shadow in the slow progress of dusk. The mount of the Winter Queen cast a man's shadow, if one knew how to look; for Avandar, such knowledge required no effort. The knowledge that Lord Ishavriel walked across these sands had hardly moved him.

But the existence of Telakar in the wastelands spoke to him in a way that he could not deny. He desired power, now.

And he desired peace.

He stood between these two, and thought of the mountain stronghold in which he had often sought refuge.

ATerafin.

He lifted his arm. Lifted it, letting the folds of his simple shirt drift elbow-ward at the behest of gravity. She was his; he had placed his mark upon her in an attempt to save her life. She had reacted as she so often did: In haste, in anger, and in ignorance.

But this binding, unlike the previous one, was unique. He might have explained it, had his waking in the mountain vastness been untroubled and unencumbered. He might have explained it later, but her vision, hobbled by lack of training, by lack of exposure to the path of the Firstborn, was cutting nonetheless, and he had retreated from the unexpected vulnerability left him by her sight.

If he had wondered, in the distant past, about the power of the seer-born, he wondered no longer; his only hope of maintaining his own control lay in her profound inexperience.

Lifting his arm, he gazed at the skin between wrist and
elbow. Nestled there, gleaming like the edge of a narrow
blade, was the sigil of the Warlord.

In the long years of his adulthood—childhood was a territory that had long deserted him, and not even the memories of its passage remained—he had only chosen to bear
such a mark once; it had almost killed him.

Death should be a gift; it was denied him. He had
searched many years for it, and each time, it had eluded
him. But he felt a different desire now, and it was hard to
turn away from it.

He let his arm drop to his side. Night was falling.

He needed no protection from the elements, and he was
capable of sustaining himself in the absence of food and
water, although it was costly.

But he had learned, with time, that sleep was a necessity.
For three days now, he had avoided it.

But it was coming. This evening, he would sleep.

And in dreams, he had little defense against her.

Jewel stood upon the flat of a grassy hilltop. Her boots
were wet with dew, her feet cool. She wore her own clothing—the thin Northern cottons that she favored when the
humidity in Averalaan had become at least as uncomfortable as sweat. Her arms were bare. Her head was covered,
although her hair—curling ferociously in the damp air—
constantly pushed the covering askew.

Finch gently prodded her about hairpins and braids;
Jewel hated both because she couldn't keep track of where
she'd put the former, and the latter, besides being a bit of a
fuss, made her feel like a twelve year old.

She turned to say as much, but Finch wasn't there. Nor
was Teller.

Instead, she saw Avandar, robed as domicis, his expression vaguely disapproving, his arms by his sides. He looked
so *normal,* she had a sudden urge to hug him, to cling to

him, as if by clinging she could force him to retain this shape.

"Knowledge," he said, the word itself a condescension, "is power. How many times must I repeat this?"

"As many times," she replied, "as you want, if it makes you happy."

"You cannot be a power and dwell in ignorance."

"I don't want to be a power."

"It is far too late for that, Jewel. Far too late. You have made your vows." He lifted an arm, pointing, and she followed the gesture, her gaze dragged by the imperative of dreaming.

The mists that were often so heavy in the city began to clear, and she realized that the hilltop was not to be a refuge. She was not in Averalaan.

"Where are we?"

"At the heart of your gift," he told her, almost gently.

She *knew* it was true.

"Avandar."

He looked down. "Yes?"

"Why are you here?"

"I will always be here. But that is not your question."

Rolling her eyes, she spoke again. "Why are you *here,* in my dream?"

"I . . . do not know. But, yes. I am . . . myself."

"Where are we?"

The lift of his brow was a gift, although she knew she had annoyed him. "Did I not give you the maps of this terrain?"

". . . No."

"Ah." He lifted a brow. She was a terrible liar, which was why she so seldom tried to lie. "Let the mist roll away, and you will have your answer."

She watched; the sun was creeping up along the eastern edge of an obscure horizon. "Avandar. I—the City—"

He lifted a hand. "I have never asked you about your past."

"I've never hidden it."

"No?" His hand brushed her shoulder; she felt his palm against the curve of her exposed skin. As if it were fire, she leaped back, lifting both hands, palm out. Denial.

She knew—*knew*—that her control was precarious here; that she could take a step backward into a landscape that had ceased to exist years ago. There were places she never wanted to see again; she held her ground.

"Does your past never anger you?"

She said nothing.

"Does the lack of justice in your early life never give you pause? Have you never wondered if justice was a concept that only those in power could enforce—or reject?"

"Whatever happened in the past is there—in the past. I am not ashamed of my life. I am not ashamed of what I did in order to survive it."

"Good. Let it go, Jewel."

"I'm not the one bringing it up."

He smiled. She hated it.

"You could answer your own questions, if you so chose."

"How?"

"You are seer-born. And the Oracle acknowledged your gift; you are not without power. The seers were prized at the height of man's rule. Why do you think they were valued?"

She shrugged. "Because with a lot of work, you could get answers about the future."

"Indeed. With some work. But the future is a murky place, full of possibilities, probabilities, foolish hopes. What you see does not always come to pass. Try again."

"Avandar."

He raised a brow.

"I'm not a sixteen-year-old girl any more. I'm responsible for one third of the trade routes owned by House Terafin. I—"

"You are the heir to the seat, yes. But Valedan kai di'Leonne is heir to an entire kingdom."

"No one treats him like a child."

"It is my supposition, from our limited exposure, that he frequently fails to act like one. But he is a good comparison, because in the end, if he is to succeed to the throne, he will wage a war in the Dominion the like of which has not been seen in generations.

"He understands this. Accepts it."

The mists were giving way to flat, clear plains. Jewel had expected to see trees, for some reason; had expected to see forest, roads, rivers. The hill was high.

But what the mist suggested, its absence denied.

"I will tell you. If the seer-born chose to do so, they could see the past of a man almost as clearly as they could see the shadows he cast. The future is a place of possibility; the past is fixed. The road between the two is often connected, and once the path is found, it can be followed.

"The Oracle invited you to walk upon older roads than could be found in even the Stone Deepings. Walk them, Jewel, and in the end, I will be able to hide nothing."

She felt cold. Looked down at the hands that had slowly fallen to her sides, and saw, cupped in them, a round, glowing orb. Inside its wall of curved glass, mist was in motion, a constant dance.

She blinked; her hands were empty.

But the mists of the morning had given way in a sudden gust of wind, pulled like curtains to either side.

Beneath her, extending for as far as she could see—and she was no fool, she looked—lay a sea of tents, gray upon gray except where a banner stood upon a fixed pole. She saw horses, haltered, impatient; saw men, some with spears, some with swords.

"Where—where are we?"

"We are, if I guess correctly, at the border of the Terrean of Raverra. And this, this is some part of the army the young kai Leonne faces." He held out a hand. She stared at it, but he did not withdraw it.

She shook her head.

"Jewel. You are seer-born. It is time that you understand

what that means. Come." He caught her hand in his, and she was surprised at the difference in the size of their palms. For just a moment, she relaxed, hand clinging to his as if he were someone she could trust.

He began to walk toward the body of the army.

"No," she whispered. She would have said more, but she heard her own voice, and she knew that she *was* a child, younger even than the child he accused her of being. He led her toward the tents. What had seemed so large grew larger still; the army was *huge*.

But they passed through it as if it were the illusion, the mist, the vision, and they were real. He paused a moment every few steps, contemplating the forces gathered.

"Ah," he said. "Come."

She did not withdraw her hand.

The ground beneath their feet was trampled; what had grown there before the men had chosen to lay down their camp was flat now; soil, moist and soft, showed through layers of wild flora. She saw the curved imprints of heavier feet; horses had passed here, in number.

"That," he said, pointing, "Is the banner of Eduardo kai di'Garrardi, the Tyr'agnate of Oerta. He is present. I do not see the banner of Lorenza; the men gathered here represent the forces of Raverra and Oerta."

He began to walk again, but this time she pulled against his hand "Not there," she whispered.

"No?"

She shook her head. He frowned, but he hesitated.

"Can't you see it?"

Gathering in the heart of this tent city was a darkness that spoke of storm. But it was a wild storm, dense and heavy; she could not look through it, could not see around its edges.

"We can't go there," she said abruptly.

What had been a comfort was now her only leverage; she pulled at his hand, gaining weight and substance; true dream or no, dreams had a way of shifting.

To her surprise, he smiled.

Yes, he told her, his lips motionless. *Yes. They have a way of shifting. Use it, and you begin to understand what you can do. You have been born to a blind world; see, Jewel. That is your gift.*

She turned her gaze upon him, losing sight of shadow and army. He was blurred now, indistinct, but he grew taller as she watched.

She stood, only her chin lifting as she followed the widening and shifting of Avandar's eyes. They were dark, the eyes she had known for over a decade, but the heart of them was a terrible, burning gold.

She had seen the god-born before, at a distance; the Mother's daughter; the sons of Cormaris and Reymaris; Kiriel, whose golden light was limned in shadow. This was different. Terrible.

Like, very like, the sands of the Sea of Sorrows.

She wanted to weep.

"No," she told him, "that is only part of my gift. Of whatever it is that you call it. The rest is *me*. I am Jewel. I'm Jay. I'm—"

"You are," another voice said, "far from your home."

She lost sight of Avandar as she spun.

Where the armies had stood upon the trampled field, there now stood a single man.

He knelt upon the blackened ground left in the wake of the fires. Later, she would wonder what had caused those fires; now, she accepted what the dream offered her. The buildings around him were broken ruins, the stone as black as the ground except where walls had cracked, revealing what lay beneath the surface.

They were bleeding, she thought.

She reached out to touch them.

"I wouldn't, if I were you," the man on the ground said. "There is always a danger when you heal the injured."

He looked up as her fingers brushed the sharp edges offered by sheered rock.

And bled.

She felt the pain; it was wrong. Everything about it was wrong,

Jewel! Avandar's voice. She could see him nowhere, but she turned; his voice was more felt than heard.

The man upon the ground straightened the curve of his bent back, his rounded shoulders. As he did, she saw that his arms were shaking; they were pressed tightly, not to his chest—for he was a slender man—but rather around some-one's back. A spill of dark hair mingled with his injured arm; blood from a gash across his forehead still wept, adorning the girl he held.

For just a moment, Jewel thought the child was dead, but she stirred, lifting her head along the line of his exposed chest. She moved slowly, carefully, minimally.

"This is irony," the man said, and Jewel suddenly knew where she had heard his voice. She froze. Wondered why it had taken so long for recognition to come.

"Viandaran," he said, lips thinning.

Jewel turned, then. To her back, like standing shadow, the man who was domicis—and could *never* be domicis—now stood. He held her hand. She could not remember when he took it, but she clung.

"I . . . do not . . . recognize you," Avandar said quietly.

"Perhaps not. Recognition was never a concern of mine. Yours, perhaps; when the gods walked the world, there was not a creature upon it who had not heard of the Warlord."

"It is not a title I use."

"It is not a title, Viandaran. It is a simple statement."

Avandar's hand was torn from hers. She had time to cry out, but not time enough to tighten her grip against its loss.

She did not need to look to know that he was gone. Which was good; her gaze was no longer fluid; it had come to rest upon the face of Lord Isladar of the Shining Court.

"This is no dream," she whispered.

"It is a dream. But it is your dream, Jewel ATerafin. What you see, I cannot see; what you see, I will not interpret."

She took a step, but wasn't certain whether it was forward or back until she saw that he was closer.

Kiriel, she thought. "I see the child you hold."

His eyes widened slightly, although his expression did not otherwise change. "It is a pity that I tried—so unsuccessfully—to kill you."

"It wasn't because of the Sight."

He lifted the arch of a blackened brow; blood shifted its fall. "No. But I will take care in the future, when we next meet. I should have known that Viandaran would never suffer allies of middling power."

"Why are you here?"

He bent his head above the head of the child, obscuring her.

Jewel should have been afraid for the girl; in some way, she was. But she knew that he meant her no harm. As if he could hear what she felt, he lifted his head again.

"Ariel."

The child shook hers in denial, pressing her face so far into him Jewel thought she would disappear. He winced, and she realized that the blood across his chest hadn't fallen from shoulder or forehead; he was wounded.

"Yes. I am . . . injured."

"And the girl?"

"Her name is Ariel. She is . . . whole."

Jewel took another step.

She knelt an arm's length from the girl's back, aware as she did that she was now within his grasp.

Aware that she was not in danger, not yet.

"You are predictable, ATerafin."

She lifted her chin. "So?"

"And defiant." His smile was gentle. His eyes were cold. "Never put yourself at the mercy of a *Kialli* lord. Do you understand?"

She said, without thinking, "Kiriel did." The moment the words left her lips she stilled; she knew they were true, and knew that in time she would know how. But that time was not now.

In the silence, he put the warmth of his smile out. "She was put at the mercy of one; it is not the same. Do not be confident of Kiriel's intentions. She will hold the world in her hand, and she will remember that her power comes not from the Isle, but from the Wastes."

The child in his arms whimpered, and he stilled. When he spoke, the edge of *Kialli* voice was once again hidden.

"Viandaran is your guide, and he is your protector. I would advise you to choose another, if you have the choice."

"Oh?"

"Everyone that the Warlord has ever cared for has died."

"Everyone does," she said, flippant although his words disturbed her.

"True. But they die unusually badly, and in my experience the process is profoundly more amusing than the result.

"No," he added, "the child cannot understand me. She does not speak Weston. It is by tone alone that she measures my intent. Or yours."

"Ariel," he told her quietly, speaking in a language that sounded like Weston to Jewel, "the others are coming. They hunt me now, and I must elude them by taking a path that . . . you cannot travel."

The child tightened her grip. He reached up and pried her fingers—with ease—from their perch around his neck. "What did I tell you?" he said, but he spoke so gently Jewel felt herself listening almost as eagerly as the child did.

She sniveled. "No fear."

"More."

"Show no fear."

He nodded.

"She doesn't need to show it," Jewel snapped, angry at the compulsion that he *must* be employing. "You're demons. You can smell it a mile away."

"And how do you know this?" Soft, soft question. He lifted a hand and touched the side of her cheek before she could react. Or withdraw.

He smiled. "I will give you this information. It will mean nothing to you. But take it to Kiriel and she will understand its import. Tell her that Ishavriel and Etridian have left the North; tell her that Assarak will join them.

"Tell her that when the battle is joined, Ishavriel intends to bring Anya to the field."

"Why are you telling me this?"

"Ah, an intelligent question. I fear that I must leave you to puzzle over it. The Lord's Fist has been . . . distracted . . . by events within the Court; they cannot afford to risk the wrath of their Lord by remaining distracted.

"I will send you this child."

"*What?*"

"I will send her to you." His smile was thin.

"Why?"

"Another question I have no inclination to answer." He rose; his legs seemed frail enough that they would not support his weight. But they did.

He pulled the child from the protection of his chest, cradling her a moment in his arms. And then, after a pause that would—in any other man—have been a hesitation, he bent and pressed his lips gently against her brow.

"Take what you will from this," he said softly. "But . . ."

"But?"

He shook his head. "You are predictable," he said again. "I could tell you that she hosted the body of a demon that could shed her form at any time, and because she is small and obviously weak, you would take that risk; you would suffer her to live where she might, at any time, have access to you." He set the child down.

"I would know her," Jewel replied coldly. "I would trust myself to know when—and if—something changed."

"And if she were still there, beneath *Kialli* control, Jewel ATerafin, would you allow yourself her kill?" His smile was as cold as her voice had been, but his tone was soft, gentle. Jewel knew this was not for her benefit. "That is what is predictable about you. You have not yet grown bereft of hope. You are not a practical person."

"You . . . know nothing about me."

"No? I know that you sheltered Kiriel. And I know that you know what she is."

"She is one of mine."

"Ah." His eyes, narrowed, were almost entirely black. Jewel did not step back. Would have, but the child was there, and Jewel knew that if she wasn't speaking, she was listening. Not to words; the words wouldn't mean much; they had been speaking in Weston. But tone told enough of a story.

Lord Isladar was aware of this. "She is Jewel ATerafin," he told the girl gently. "She is from the North. But she will know how to speak, and she will defend you."

The child turned to face her. Her skin was darker than most Northern skin, darker than Jewel's; her hair was dark as well—and straight, or it would have been had it not carried the weight of so much debris. She was bird thin, the way young children are, and her chin was a little too pointed; wherever she'd been, food hadn't been abundant.

But it was none of those things that were her weapons. Her eyes, much larger in a child's face than they would have been in an adult's, were wide with fear. With loss.

Above her, Lord Isladar watched, daring Jewel to gainsay him. Daring her to be unpredictable.

Jewel was already kneeling; the dream had shifted her and she had let it, absorbed by what she could—and could not—see.

The child's hair was a thicket; dust and blood and shards of stone were twisted in knotted strands. Her left cheek was swollen, her lip was bleeding, her arms—the forearms that were exposed to light—were scraped and raw. But the blood across the front of her small gown was clearly not her own.

She was crying.

Jewel looked up to meet the eyes of Lord Isladar.

And then she looked beyond his shoulder.

In the ruins, a fire had started to burn; a fire that needed no wood, no oil, no air. She could see it, contained in the eyes of two who now approached the *Kialli* lord's turned back.

Without thinking, she lunged forward, grabbed the girl; she was almost weightless.

Blue light flew out in thin, sharp strands, the edge of a hundred blades; a thousand.

Lord Isladar turned his back upon Jewel and the child. *"Go."*

It was her dream. Hers.

But she ran.

The first thing she felt was fingers on her shoulders in the darkness. She cried out, wordless, her hand already moving in the shallow depths of the tent.

No one touched her when she slept. No one.

She kicked off silk, rolling, her hands reaching for the dagger that lay by her side.

Jewel.

In two syllables, she gained fifteen years; she was able to force herself to be still. "Avandar."

"I apologize for the intrusion. But—"

Gathering the silks she had thrown off, she sat up, the curve of her knees beneath her chin. "What—what is it? Why are you here?"

"I had to wake you."

"Why?"

The tent's flap opened; light from the clear desert sky filtered in, lending gray, dark and pale, to the interior.

"Wait." The air was cold. She saw her breath as it hung for a moment in the stillness.

He stopped. Turned; she could not see his face, although the moonlight made his outline clear.

"You were there."

He was silent.

"In my dream. You were *there*."

His nod was minimal. It would have been easy to miss, but she watched him as if he were the only thing in the tent. "I owe you an . . . apology. What you saw was no artifact of dream."

"The armies?"

"The shadows. The armies were simple vision." His chin dropped, the movement slow and deliberate. "We needed that information."

"And you woke me because?"

"Don't play the fool."

"I'm not. I want the information."

"You have it. I was thrown out of the dreaming—and not by you."

Because I don't have the skill. She didn't say it; Avandar was forever lecturing her on her ability to belabor the obvious. "Fair enough." She smiled thinly. "I've been terrified by dreams, but I've never been hurt by them."

"It's not pain that concerns me."

"No, of course not."

She could almost hear Avandar grinding his teeth; it was strangely comforting. "You are vulnerable in the dreaming state," he said quietly, "because you are not used to guarding against intrusion."

"People don't usually invade my dreams."

"I will give you the benefit of the doubt although you haven't earned it. I will assume that this ignorance is genuine."

Comforting.

He stood. She saw, in the folded loose fist, the magestone that he carried; light, for nightmares. She was not home, but she missed it viscerally. "In the Empire," he told her, "dreams are significant."

"Some dreams."

"Indeed. Some dreams."

"I . . ."

"Yes?"

She nodded.

"Do you think those are accidental, Jewel?"

"I haven't really thought about them much."

"No. You wouldn't. Think now."

It didn't take much time. "No."

"Good. Where do you think they come from?"

"Avandar—I have no idea. If you do, and you want me to know, tell me."

He laughed. It was an unexpected sound; deep and lingering. "In my youth, they were the gift—or the curse—of the gods, if there is any differentiating between the two; they were wyrds placed upon the unwary."

"And now?"

"Now?" The laughter ceased. "I do not know. The gods are beyond us; they cannot easily interfere in our affairs."

Neither named the god who could; they were silent for a moment. It was cold in the tent; the silks, skewed, had been exposed to night air. Jewel envied Avandar his ability to rise above the weather as if it were an Imperial fashion trend.

"With skill, and some knowledge of the dreamer, those who were powerful could visit the dreaming; could touch the edges of those who sleep unguarded.

"What did you see, Jewel?"

"An old . . . acquaintance. Of Kiriel's."

She heard his brief curse, although it was as minimal as his nod had been, and far less deliberate.

"Did you speak with this acquaintance?"

"Some."

"Jewel."

"Yes, I spoke with him."

"Who was he?"

"Lord Isladar. Of the Shining Court."

"The lord who tried to kill you in Averalaan."

"And failed. Yes."

"What did you tell him?"

"Nothing important."

"What did he tell you?"

"Nothing important. Avandar—"

He caught her wrist. Silk curtained down the side of her leg. "ATerafin, this is not a game."

His hand was warm. She shed it. And rose. "Avandar."

"ATerafin?"

"My clothing. The outer robe. I need it."

She could not see his face, but she felt a brief, and fierce, impatience. Light flared in the tent, trapped in the curve of palm that had curled into fist; his fingers, above the light, were a pale, pale red.

She grabbed the clothing he held out, and donned it, freeing her feet from the bedding that was entwined round her ankles. She struggled with her boots.

When she rose, she rose swiftly. He knelt at the sole exit, eyes dark, face illuminated in such a way that it seemed more shadow and hollow than flesh.

Their eyes met.

She looked away first. She grabbed the sleeping silks, winding them tightly around her shoulder, like a Northerner preparing for an early, deadly snow.

Avandar's brow rose a fraction; she could see this because he had moved out of the tent entrance.

She crawled out as well, gaining her feet clumsily. The river's voice, never silent, seemed unnaturally loud in the quiet chill of desert evening.

Unerring, she headed toward the river, aware of his presence as shadow, a thing cast by light.

The stag joined her, steps light and almost silent in the silvered landscape of night. The Lady's light, she thought, and then wondered why. The South exerted its influence here, where the North was as distant as dream.

In the North, there would have been snow.

It didn't happen often, but snow in Averalaan was death.

Death informed her first memory of Teller, his loss an echo of all of her own. She saw him clearly as she walked,

a continent between them, huddled in the snow, crouched
like an animal that is incapable of hunting to sustain itself
in a landscape of wolves and indifference. He'd been so
small for his age, so skinny, so utterly terrified; she had approached him with a caution born entirely of her certainty
that aggression would startle him, cause him to run. Had
approached, hand extended, eyes unblinking, with the over-
whelming desire to protect.

That had defined her, in her early years.

It defined her now.

She admitted it as the night, in clarity, resolved itself.

She walked with purpose; the stag fell in beside her, and
Avandar walked slightly to the left. No one spoke; there
wasn't any need for words, and the squabbles that had
plagued her den in the streets of the twenty-fifth holding
were beneath the companions she had now.

She missed it.

At a bend in the river, she found what she had known she
would find: a child, in the moonlight, shivering at the touch
of desert cold, the absolute absence of warmth.

The girl looked up when they were close enough to make
noise. Her head bobbed from side to side, her eyes wide;
she got to her feet, exposed her chest to the night air.

Her clothing was pale, but in the moonlight, Jewel could
see patches of black. Dreams.

She lifted both of her hands, one to either side; a command. They stopped moving, stag and man, and Jewel
thought she could sense, in their silence, a mild unease.
This was territory that they had seldom traversed, these
two, who could admit without regret all that they had done
in the service of gathering their own power.

She continued on foot, bridging the gap that divided her
and the girl.

She stopped ten feet away.

She was predictable. Predictable enough, it seemed, that
Lord Isladar had chosen to leave the child here, bereft of the
clothing that would allow her to survive undetected until

morning. Jewel wondered if he had consciously made that decision; if he had decided that the child needed the pathos of utter helplessness in order to influence her decision. No answer came to the silent question; no hint of gift by which she could better understand the creature who was, without a doubt, her enemy.

All that he had left was this child.

Why?

And did it matter?

The girl's arms had come up; she cradled them across her body as she stared at Jewel.

Jewel dropped slowly to one knee, her hands before her, palms exposed to the bite of the cold and the child's inspection.

"Ariel," she said, in Torra.

The child nodded, as if the name were a question, as if it were something that she only barely had the right to use.

"Lord Isladar sent you to me."

The child nodded again.

There were so many questions Jewel wanted to ask. Instead, she said, "It's cold out. I'm not—I'm not like he is. Come; our camp is a mile to the East, and we should return."

The child nodded again, but she did not move.

Jewel rose slowly.

The girl watched as she approached.

Watched as she took the silks from around her shoulder and held them out. "Ariel, please. Come here."

Wordless, the girl obeyed.

Jewel wrapped silk around her shoulder, around her slender frame. Then she lifted her right hand.

The stag came in the silence.

As Jewel had done, he knelt, his slender legs bearing the whole of his weight. Jewel lifted the child a little too high; she had overestimated her weight.

She placed her upon the stag's back, and then took her

place behind her, wrapping arms around her to keep her steady.

"Are you ready?" she whispered into the child's ear.

The girl nodded.

"Me, too."

The stag rose, bearing their weight without effort.

She heard the girl's breath catch, and she smiled. "He won't let you fall off," she told her. "*I* won't let you fall off."

The stag turned toward the camp.

Only when he had turned toward the East did he speak. *Jewel, who is she?*

CHAPTER SEVEN

5th of Corvil, 427 AA
City of Amar, Terrean of Mancorvo

SER Mareo kai di'Lamberto was surrounded by his Tyran. When he walked within the confines of his domis, they attended him; it was both their honor and their right.

He walked now, but did not linger; his steps were quick and forceful. He came from the walls; his cerdan were stationed both at the base and at their heights, and they gazed out upon the vast plains of the Terrean. The city was old; beyond the walls, serafs tilled and farmed the soil, and beyond them, horses ran; he treasured both, but he knew that they would find no protection within Amar unless he wished to forgo the late planting.

War was in the air. The face of the Lord was bright and without mercy.

The armies of the North were gathered East of the borders that separated Mancorvo from Averda. And the armies of the traitorous General, Alesso di'Marente, were gathered to the South. He knew that they must meet, these two armies; what he could not yet be certain of was where.

Those men that could be spared, he had summoned, and they had begun to arrive in number. The granaries were full, but would not remain so.

He had no intention of allowing Mancorvo to be turned into a battlefield.

The Tyran parted when they reached the gates, and he strode between their perfect ranks, shorn of expression.

Ser Adano kai di'Marano waited, Toran at a respectful distance. His horse was, to Mareo's eye, nearly exhausted.

And a man of Adano's caliber did not push his horse to ground without cause.

The Tor'agar bowed; the Tyr'agnate returned that bow. The Court was in the nuance of those gestures.

"My pardon, Tyr'agnate," Ser Adano said, speaking with the formal precision of a man raised to power. "I have come on a simple errand, and I did not mean to disturb you."

"The visit of a liege is never a disturbance, Ser Adano. I bid your men enter my city."

The Tor'agar bowed again, and when he rose, his men bowed. "We are grateful for the hospitality you offer," Ser Adano said. He reached into his sash, and took from it the harbinger of war: a small tube, edged with the stylized runes of a war-message. They met perfectly; it was not clear to the Tyr'agnate's eye where the break in the tube was.

But it had not been breached.

Possibly could not be, if it came from the General Alesso di'Marente.

"You did not speak with the General," Ser Mareo said, clutching the tube in his sword hand.

"No."

"And his armies?"

"I did not think it wise to cross the border," Adano replied. "But I have received word that the kai Lorenza and the kai Garrardi have joined the General's forces in Raverra."

"The kai Garrardi?"

Ser Adano's face was a careful composition, an artful one. Ser Mareo kai di'Lamberto did not envy him. But he did not distrust him either, although perhaps this was not entirely wise.

"His forces were last to arrive, if our information was correct. But he arrived with numbers."

The Tyr'agnate nodded quietly. "So. It is Raverra, Sorgassa, and Oerta."

And in the North, he thought, although he did not speak, Mancorvo and Averda. The two Terreans to suffer loss of land in the previous war. He was not a fool; he knew that the presence of Oerta and Sorgassa upon that field implied much, for the gathering of an army was not a casual task.

"Ser Adano," he said quietly, "I will retire for the moment. My serafs will attend you; please remain in Amar for the next few days."

Adano bowed again, and then smiled. "Our horses thank you, Tyr'agnate."

He dismissed his Tyran when he approached the harem. They were accustomed to this; they left only two men at the closed door that led to the most sheltered quarters in the domis. On all sides, halls and rooms formed a boundary which could not be easily crossed; the Lord's light came to the women of the harem through the open gardens and courtyards the harem boasted. If the domis itself were ever breached by enemy forces, the last place they would reach would be the harem—and if they did, it would signal the end of the clan Lamberto and its ancient rule.

Not all domis were constructed in this fashion, and perhaps, at the dawn of the clan's preeminence, the inner chambers and courtyards were used differently. No one living, however, remembered that day, and history had conveniently forgotten this single element; the present was all that existed.

And the present contained the Serra Donna en'Lamberto and her wives. Ser Mareo kai di'Lamberto had sons and daughters who still dwelled within the harem walls, and he was quietly proud of them; they were a source of strength and amusement, a source of chaotic beauty and unparalleled noise. Two, Marianna and Karina, had been born to

the same wife on the same day, the youngest of his kin.
They were now four years of age.

But as he walked the halls, he did not hear their voices,
and he felt a pang of disappointment. He could not, of
course, ask after them; not when a missive of war awaited
his attention. It was not what men did, in the Dominion.

Yet Donna, Na'donna, knew; she often had the children
with her when he arrived, and let them play for some small
time before dismissing them. Two days ago, Marianna had
insisted that she was strong enough to carry his sword, and
he had shamelessly indulged her by allowing her to make
the attempt. He had not, however, unsheathed the blade—
which was not to her liking, although in the end the scabbard had bruised both her feet when she dropped it.

This is why women are not given swords, he told her,
with mock severity. That truth was in the words as well
would become evident with time; already Karina had begun
to develop a keen interest in the saris and the jewelry that
adorned his wives. But Marianna was stubborn and willful.

With effort—and it was an effort—he could pretend that
he saw no similarities to another young girl, another willful, indulged, and sharp-tongued woman.

Certainly his daughter was lovelier than his serpent of a
sister.

He shook himself; neither daughter nor sister was present; only his Serra waited, seated before a low, flat table,
the flowers in her hair still wet from the vessels that had,
moments ago, contained them, the water cups empty and
evenly placed upon the flat, wooden surface.

She offered him a graceful bow as he entered the room,
and he accepted the obeisance simply because he loved the
shape of her back and the effortless way she exposed it.

She rose without leave or permission. He met her eyes
and noticed that lines were worn into the corners, and shadows into the hollows. Not age, not exactly, but care.

But her smile was genuine, made warmer by the open affection and pride with which she now graced him. She

lifted an arm, trailing silk, and caught the long, long stem of an artisan's water vessel; it was too slender, too perfectly proportioned, to be called a jug.

He nodded and she poured sweet water. Lifting his cup, she held it out in both hands, almost bowing again as she offered it to him.

He took it quickly, and settled himself into the cushions which lay at the table's base.

She waited. There was no obvious anxiety in her silence; just peace. It was a blessed peace, and he was old enough now to desire little else. War should have to wait, he thought.

But he set the cup upon the table and placed beside it the tube that Ser Adano kai di'Marano had traveled in such haste to deliver.

She saw it.

"My eyes," she said quietly, "are not what they once were, my husband. Who sends word?"

He allowed her both the lie and the curiosity.

"The General Alesso di'Marente," he replied. He did not grant Ser Alesso either the use of the title he claimed as his own, or the use of the clan name; they were not—yet—earned.

And they would not be, until the disposition of both Mancorvo and Averda were decided.

She was neutral now, carefully concealing all hope and all fear.

He understood, as he watched her, why the children were absent; if he desired to show no weakness in front of this woman, she desired, in equal measure, to leave the world of their brief childhood undisturbed. He loved her, then.

But he had always loved her, clansman's daughter.

"I have not read it," he said, when the silence gradually grew loud.

She started to rise, but he lifted a hand, and she sank back onto her knees.

"No, Na'donna. This is your world, not mine; I am honored that you have welcomed me, time and again, across the boundaries that define it. I would not bring war into the harem, but war is coming, and you already know this. Have you had any other letters?"

She shook her head, but there was a marked hesitation in the reply that made his eyes narrow. "Na'donna?"

"A message," she said at last, and with great reluctance. "But it was not confined to brush and parchment; it was delivered, instead, in person."

"Where?"

"To your domis," she said.

"Na'donna—"

She said, "It is not yet the Lady's time, Mareo. And there are things I fear to speak of while the Lord reigns. Leave it, I beg you; in a few hours, you will have the whole of the answer I can give you—if indeed I can tender a reply at all."

He said, after a pause, "The Havallans."

And her brows rose a fraction. She could be startled, like any wild creature, and here in the harem's heart, it showed. Her eyes widened before she could school her face, and when she offered him expression again, it was in the form of a rueful smile.

She nodded.

"Did you call for them, Na'donna?"

"How could I? No one commands the Voyani."

"So it is said. No one but their Matriarch. Yet the Voyani come, and often, and they treat with the women of the clans in secrecy. I allow them in Amar, although it is not to the liking of the Radann."

"They are women," she replied, "and in Mancorvo, they do little damage."

"They ask you for secrecy," he replied gravely. "What worse damage can they do but separate a husband from his wife, even in this mean a fashion?" He caught her hands in his; he had not yet touched the water. Hers clutched his tightly, as if by so doing, she might keep him at last from the General's letter, from the General's war.

He pulled his hands away, and she let them go, but she bowed her head as she did. Love and pain, pain and love; they were almost twinned in the Dominion. For the first time, he wondered what love meant in the North, where women led armies and ruled powerful clans.

He lifted the tube, and placing his hands on either side of what he assumed to be the break, he cracked it open.

The parchment was long, and the hand in which it was written was no woman's hand. It was fine and court-trained; the bold brush strokes of a man. He knew, then, that Alesso di'Marente had chosen, at last, to leave the delicate negotiations of the writing of Serras.

And she, seeing this, knew it as well.

She whispered a name.

He heard it, but it was not until he had read the first few lines that the syllables penetrated the writing and he recognized the name of his kai—his dead kai. Andreas.

Pain. And love. And in the wake of these two, rising from cold slumber, anger.

"It is—it is the General?"

He laughed. The sound was short and harsh. "No other," he said. "And he is bold indeed."

"How so, my husband?"

"He acknowledges that he may have misplayed his hand in his dealings with Lamberto."

"He . . . says . . . that?"

" 'Tyr'agnate, your presence was missed at the Festival of the Sun, and the grace and beauty of your wife, missed likewise at the Festival of the Moon. Of all men in the Dominion who might find offense in the manner of the kai Leonne's death, none are more worthy than you. It was a calculated risk on my part, and the handling of it was less wise than it might have been.

" 'I regret your absence. I will not excuse my choices; they have been laid bare. But the kai Leonne was not—

could not be—a man worthy of your service. If I have not been so, I endeavor now to correct that error in judgment.' " He looked up to study the lines of his wife's face, clear as writing to one who knew her well.

She waited, however, denying him expression. She was capable of it, although her vulnerability was also genuine. A mystery.

You are the Lord's man. And you are a man of honor. Honor, perhaps, has been absent upon this field, and I would do much to return to it; I am not so foolish as to think that the Dominion will stand, ruled by men of lesser ability and lesser worth.

I have acted in haste; that is the way of the sword. But the High Courts are not ruled by sword alone, as I have come to understand at leisure.

As you are no doubt aware, the Northern armies have again chosen to cross the borders of the Dominion. Where once they were repulsed with what force we could muster, the Terreans no longer stand together. The Tyr'agnate, Ser Ramiro kai di'Callesta, has invited our ancient enemies in.

You may have surmised that the armies of Lorenza and Garrardi did not come to me blindly; they serve their Tyrs, and their Tyrs serve their own interests. Some of that interest lies in the lands of Mancorvo.

The Serra Donna en'Lamberto did the first clumsy thing that she had done in many months; she spilled the water that she had, in the silence, attempted to pour. It pooled upon the surface of the table like a stain or an accusation, but he barely noticed it himself.

Ser Mareo kai di'Lamberto was a man of the High Courts; the contents of this letter, shorn of the nuance and the subtlety of that Court, were as unexpected as an assassin's blade; they cut deeply, robbing him of like words.

It is an interest that I cultivated.

And cut again: The geography of the known world was shifting beneath his feet, and Ser Mareo kai di'Lamberto, as all Lambertans, was a man whose feet were firmly planted upon the ground.

You will no doubt have surmised this.

Lesser men may equate honor with stupidity, but I have seen you upon the field, Tyr'agnate, and if in my youth I might have made the same mistake, I have learned—at cost—the error of that assumption.

The lands to the North of Raverra have always been the most fertile of our lands; they are also the lands which have been most vulnerable to Northern attack. You, better than any, know the cost of that vulnerability.

I have considered all options with care, and I have come to this conclusion: Ser Ramiro kai di'Callesta, and his clan, must pay the price of their treachery. Were I not the Tyr'-agar, they would still pay: they have given to the North what men have died to prevent, and for less reason.

Averda itself cannot be governed by a man who would turn against the clans, and the lands of Averda are therefore forfeit.

It matters little that Ser Ramiro hides behind the Leonne name. He brings a Northerner with a Southern face and a tenuous claim to a dead clan at the head of Northern armies; how will a pawn of the Demon Kings serve the Dominion? Could you pledge allegiance to a boy who bears such a strong Northern taint?

I gamble, now; I assume that your answer is no.

And therefore I offer this: The lands to the West of Mancorvo are yours, if you can take and hold them against the Callestans. I have reason to believe that you can; past history supports this.

The lands that were to be claimed by the Tyrs will be offered solely from Averdan soil. In this fashion, all may benefit from the defense of Annagar.

I do not ask for your answer immediately. I understand that my own haste has brought me to this position, and if I am a man who is prone to error, I am seldom accused of making the same mistake twice.

Consider what I ask. If you cannot, at this time, bring yourself to join your forces with mine, I ask simply that you hold the borders against the Northern foe. They will be hemmed in on all sides, with no clear advantage.

Ser Mareo kai di'Lamberto did not look up until he had read the letter three times. The sun had not set, but he felt the nighttime wind through the distant screens. "My apologies, Serra Donna," he said, "for bringing this war to your harem." He made to rise; she caught his elbow.

They stood, thus bound by her delicate touch.

"Mareo," she said quietly.

Something in her tone was not right—but the whole of the letter was a shock to the conservative Tyr; he said nothing for a time, meeting her eyes.

"So," he said at last. "He has admitted all."

"No," she said, surprising him. "Not all." She rose, and walked past him, past the table, to the closed screen that opened, at last, upon the room they shared.

There, stark upon a simple stand, stood the sheathed and silent *Balagar.*

"Your brother's sword," she said softly.

He nodded.

"You want to trust Ser Alesso."

He did not answer her; she knew him well. "Na'donna, speak. Tell me what you think."

"I think that this is war," she replied, an evasion. "And war is not the province of Serras."

He bowed his head. He did not touch *Balagar.*

"But I think, as well, that Ser Fredero died because he wished to strike out at Ser Alesso."

"Yes."

"I spent little time with your par," she continued, failing to meet his gaze. "But enough to know that he was not a foolish man. Speak to Jevri, Mareo."

"Can you not—"

"No. He is Radann, not seraf. I am Serra." She walked past him, evading his grasp. "It is day, Tyr'agnate."

"Tyr'agnate, Na'donna? Why so formal? Have I angered you?"

"Calculating man," she said, a hint of amusement and affection in her voice. Only a hint; something lay within the words that was stronger.

Na'donna was afraid.

"War has come to the harem," she said. "But not with your letter. Not with the arrival of Ser Adano."

He was still, now. Although Ser Alesso's letter was not forgotten, he found that he could set it aside. He waited.

"It is too bright," she continued, "to speak of these things."

"The Lord does not rule the harem."

"Aye, no. Nor our hearts," she added. "But it is not the Lady's time." She drew breath, held it, and slowly lowered her shoulders. "The Havallans came to the domis," she said at last.

"The Voyani?"

She nodded. "Not Yollana. But her daughters."

"Why?"

She lifted her head as well. "To speak of war," she told him quietly. "And to speak of the future. One of the two— I do not know which, so please, do not ask—has lifted the veil and gazed."

"What did she speak of, Na'donna?"

"They will leave our lands," she replied.

"The Voyani?"

"Yes. The Havallans. The Arkosans have already forsaken Averda."

"So. Even they."

"No. Not because of the war. Not because of the Northerners; they care little for such things."

"Then why?"

"They would not say."

"You did not ask."

"It is said that it is unwise to know the business of the Voyani. More so, Tyr'agnate, for the men of the clans than their Serras."

"Why did they come, Na'donna?"

"To speak," she told him quietly, "of the Lord of Night. Of the Lord of Night and his kin."

8th of Corvil, 427 AA
City of Callesta, Terrean of Averda

Kiriel di'Ashaf stood in the moonlight on the height of the plateau.

In Callesta—the only city in the Terrean to be named after its founding family—the manor of the Tyr'agnate stood at the height of the city, surrounded by gates that were cleverly placed behind standing trees, bushes, sculptures. The sculptures themselves were larger than life; they did not resemble people except in the fanciful light of day, when sun lit their stone features, their marble countenances. In the evening, serafs walked the length of the Callestan estates, and placed fire in the hands of these carved garden denizens, and that fire, red and orange, lent them menace and an air of threat.

Valedan had chosen to accept the Tyr's offer of hospitality while he awaited the arrival of the Commanders; two days had passed. During that time, some attempt had been made to integrate the Ospreys with the cerdan and Tyran that served Callesta.

In Auralis AKalakar's admittedly subjective opinion, it had not been a disaster; the Ospreys had acquitted themselves as well as anyone—even Duarte—could have expected. But they were not dress guards, and the exacting standards held up by the Tyran were particularly trying. The heat did not bother the Callestans; the endless repetition of Ser Anton's training seemed to hold an equally endless fascination for them. They spoke only when spoken to, and seemed content to follow the minimal orders they received.

The Ospreys tried.

But in the end, they served best in two capacities. The first was by Valedan's side. He had Ser Andaro as Tyran, but had chosen no others; the Ospreys—or whatever it was they were calling themselves at any given moment—had proved themselves worthy of their place at his side by their defeat of numerous would-be assassins in the distant North. Demon assassins.

Unfortunately, there had been no similar attempts in the South with which to shore themselves up.

So they served in a secondary capacity as well: They guarded the perimeter of the Callestan holdings in key areas, although Duarte had elected to use them only in the evening, when the differences in their uniform and, more particularly, in their gender, would be less easily noted.

Valedan, however, had declined to remove the women from active duty.

It bought him respect from the Ospreys; they were suspicious enough to smell politics a mile away, and Auralis had won a tidy sum of money when laying wagers among the more cynical Ospreys about the length of time the women would be allowed to be useful once they had crossed the border.

Not that Auralis wasn't cynical; he was simply more competent at being so. Kiriel was part of the heart of Valedan's defense; would-be Tyr or no, she could not simply be set aside at the whim of Annie sensibility. Alexis, maybe—although Duarte would suffer for it later. Fiara, maybe. Any of the others, certainly. But not Kiriel.

And Valedan was not generally of a mind to make glaring exceptions to the few rules he set.

But he was politic enough that, when staying within the heart of the Callestan manor—if such an open, foreign building could be called that—he did not put the women on rotation within the halls themselves.

Kiriel, therefore, was here, beneath the night sky, the city of Callesta growing still and dark through the slender bars of the fence.

In the light shed by fire in cupped, stone palms, she cast the occasional shadow; it flickered with wind, as if it were living, and separate, from her.

She, too, had grown still.

In and of itself, this was not particularly disturbing; she was on duty; there weren't a lot of other places she should have been. But Auralis, at a distance of not more than twenty feet—twenty very boring feet—found his attention caught by her, held.

"Kiriel?"

She turned to look at him, and the hairs on the back of his neck rose. His hand was on the hilt of his sword before he realized it had moved.

Her brow rose slightly, and then her eyes widened.

"Auralis?"

He nodded. Forced his hand down.

"I can see you."

Something about the way she said the words made them significant. "What do you mean?"

"I can see . . . you. The way I used to see."

He didn't ask any more questions. He knew what she meant.

But instead of backing away, he walked closer; close enough that he was aware of her slightest move; the rise and fall of breath, the slight turn of her head, the way her lips quirked up in a dangerous, edgy smile.

"Does it matter?" he asked, with a shrug. No nonchalance, not here; she wasn't an idiot.

She looked nonplussed.

"Does it matter," he said again, "what you see, whether you see it?"

Her eyes were an odd color in the fire's dim light. "Doesn't it matter to you?"

He stared at her for a long time. "No."

"Why not?"

There was a sharpness to her genuine curiosity; an expectation of pain.

He shrugged. "Can you change what you see?"

"Change it?"

"Sure. Change it. Can you make it something it's not?"

"No. I can tell you what it is."

"So what. I can tell you what it is. Maybe your vision upset someone back wherever it was you used to live, but maybe they were stupid. I know what I am, Kiriel."

"And you're proud of it."

He laughed.

It was Kiriel who took a step back.

"Are you proud of what you are?" he responded, half snarling.

"I don't . . . know what I am."

"You can't see yourself the way you see me?"

She shook her head; her hair curled around her shoulders as if it were alive.

"Then how in the Hells can you trust what you see in anyone else? Have you ever thought that maybe it's all just a mirror?"

She stared at him for a long time, and as she did, Auralis watched her eyes change color. It was slow, deceptive; a trick of the light and heat she had moved away from.

But his hands relaxed as he watched.

"Maybe you'll be lucky," he said softly. "Maybe you'll never know what you're capable of. Maybe you'll never have to live with it."

The Serra Alina was given a room adjacent to the rooms Valedan occupied. It was far smaller than the rooms she had occupied when she had lived in her brother's harem, but in every other respect, it was a Southern room. The hanging across the doors was weighted; no wrinkle, no fold, marred its blue background, its brilliant sun, each ray embroidered in such a way that no one seeing it could mistake it for any rank but Ramiro's. It fell like steel, like an ordinance. Mats were laid against the floor; upon them a low table that had been decorated with fruit, twin fans, a spray of small, white blossoms which hung like silent bells toward the east.

She looked at them critically, but all commentary was silent.

To the West, a set of sliding doors, paper opaque but thin enough to suggest external light, lay. Beyond them a seraf crouched in the stillness of born servitude. All of her form-ative years had been spent with such living shadows. But they felt strange to her now.

And why should they? Servants in number had attended the Southern hostages in the Arannan Halls. They had come from the South, as gifts from the families that had been forced to surrender their kin; at the border, they had been granted their freedom in a land that made no more sense to them than the language it claimed as its own. It was a for-mality; she had known it; they had known it. Only serafs of worth had ever been given leave to attend the families of the ruling Tyr'agnati.

But formality or no, over the decade subtle changes had been wrought; they had been slow in coming, slow to take root. For the most part, they had been beneath notice; the former serafs served, as perfectly and obediently, as they had always served.

But there was a difference.

She acknowledged it now.

How could there not be? In the North, no death waited disobedience. More: no hunting parties went in search of those serafs who disappeared. If they chose to serve—and all but a handful did—they *chose*.

But in the North, Mirialyn ACormaris was among the Kings' most trusted advisers, and when difficulty arose, it was the Princess who often mounted horse and rode through the streets of Averalaan, attended by soldiers, but clearly in command.

In the North, it was Mirialyn who had given Valedan his

earliest martial lessons, first with sword and then with bow. In the North, the Queens slept with their husband's fathers, and were revered for doing so. And in the North, the golden-eyed ruled the Isles.

Anyone who had met them, these men who would have been exposed at birth across the South, discovered the first of many lies: for no one, seeing them, could believe them to be demonic. And no one, hearing them, could fail to believe that they carried the blood of the gods in their veins, for they commanded more than simple attention, and they saw truths, in a glance, that were so deeply buried they might well have been dead.

The Serras were slow to adapt to these new surroundings; they had children they hoped to return to their home in the Dominion, and they feared that the contamination of the North would forever separate them from the people they were born to preside over.

All save the Serra Alina di'Lamberto. Considered too difficult to be a dutiful Serra—and therefore no asset to the clan Lamberto—she had never been offered as wife to any of the men who might have been of suitable rank; she had never left the confines of her father's, and later her brother's, harem. She had attended her mother, and after the death of her father, had also attended the Serra Donna en'-Lamberto, Mareo's very proper, very dutiful wife. If they had been friends, it would have been easier, but Alina was sharp of tongue within the harem's confines—too sharp to be a comfortable companion to the Serra.

Her brother had sent her, as insult, to the court of the Northern Kings, and in that court, she had found a freedom that she, unlike the serafs, had not been promised when she had crossed the border, that invisible line between trees and rock that somehow bore the ideology of nations.

She had thought to feel at home in the South.

Proof, if it were needed, that one's knowledge of oneself did not keep step with one's life.

The sun was setting. She faced the prospect of sleep as if

it were an executioner, for in the dark, the clean, spare lines
of the table and its decorations, the color of the hanging, the
squares of paper in the screen door, could not distract her
from the sight of the dead assassins; the men who had killed
Ser Ramiro kai di'Callesta's oldest son.

She knew those men.

Even in death, she knew them. They were older; they
wore their years with far less grace than she bore her own—
but they were unmistakably her brother's men.

Mareo, she thought, clenching hands.

The hanging shifted in place, folds of cloth gathering
shadow and reflecting light as it rose. She forced her hands
to open and knelt carefully, placing them palms down in the
silk of her lap.

Valedan kai di'Leonne entered the room. She lowered
her head to the ground; felt the spill of her hair on either
side of her face. From this posture, her back curved, her
hands hidden, she listened.

He approached; she heard no other footsteps but his.

"Alina."

She rose when she was certain that no one else had accompanied him.

He was staring at her. "I . . . am sorry. It must be very difficult for you here."

It was not what she had expected to hear; not in the
South. Not from a man. She waited.

"Must I give you permission to speak?"

She nodded.

He closed his eyes, and the line of his shoulders shifted
subtly. "Then speak. Speak freely."

"Valedan, what have I taught you of the South?" She cast
a glance toward the closed screen doors, and spoke quietly.
He followed her glance; acknowledged the still form of the
seraf who knelt without, waiting a signal—any signal—that
his presence was required.

"That there is no freedom of speech."

She was silent.

He approached; humbled her by kneeling, by diminishing the distance between them.

Waited for her, as if he knew the question she longed to ask.

He was young; he was too young to be wise. But when she met his gaze, she knew that that was exactly what he waited for. "Kai Leonne." Formality rested in the syllables of that title; a formality that put a physical distance between them.

He ignored it.

"Serra Alina."

"Why?"

"Why?" He waited, and when he realized that she would not continue, he offered her mercy, of a kind. "Why did I make my vow to the Tyr'agnate of Callesta?"

She nodded. "You asked me to identify the . . . assassins. You know that I recognized them."

He nodded.

"Perhaps you came to the North too young. Perhaps you spent time observing the High Court of the Isles; spent too much time in the company of those who share a family name without blood to bind their loyalty and their service."

"The Ten," he agreed.

"The Ten would not rule here. Could not. Their existence is . . . anathema . . . to the South. They leave their families, they disavow their history, they break ties with the parents who bore them, nurtured them, raised them; they leave brothers without a backward glance to join the Houses that rule at a distance.

"But you know this. I have said as much. Mirialyn ACormaris has certainly said more."

He nodded quietly.

"Ramiro di'Callesta will make no peace with my brother. Perhaps you cannot understand this; you are young; you have fathered no children. His *kai* is dead. His voice is the wind's voice now, and it will drive him. Why did you not leave the dead in peace? Why did you ask me to identify the fallen?

"If you had not—if you had not asked a Lamberto to identify Lambertans—you might have been able to play the political game; Ramiro di'Callesta, of all the Tyr'agnati, is the man most known for his pragmatism. Had you said that the dead wore the clothing of the Lambertan Tyr solely for the purpose of preventing any concord, he may have chosen—in public—to believe you. To at least *allow* for the possibility.

"But through *me,* you have denied him that option."

"I believed that that option was . . . not an option," he said, after a pause, his face smooth as Northern glass, but far less clear. "I believed that the dead were, as they appeared, Lambertan."

"More reason not to summon me. The word of a woman, even a Serra of the high clans, is little valued in the South."

He shook his head. "It is valued by me," he said quietly, reaching for her hand. She did not withdraw. "And it is valued, clearly, by Ramiro di'Callesta; his wife is no adornment, no silent, obedient shadow. I asked you to identify the fallen because I had to know."

"And now you know."

He smiled. "Yes. Now I know."

The smile was gentle; she found it, of all things, infuriating. How very Northern of her.

"I know," he continued, his hand upon hers, his palm warm, "that Mareo di'Lamberto would not stoop to this particular form of assassination."

She lifted her head sharply, gracelessly. "Did you not understand what I said? Did you not understand what I acknowledged? Those *were* his men. I knew them."

"I understand that those were his men," Valedan said gently. "But that was not what I needed. It was you. You are of the South; you choose which expression to offer those who observe you. And the expression you offered there was unguarded; you were shocked."

She raised a dark brow. The use of the word "shock" was harsh, but it was accurate. That he used it not as criticism, but as simple fact did little to still the sense of humiliation she felt; she had been in the presence of . . . her brother's enemies. Her smile was brief; bitter. Family it seemed, complicated and full of its own special rage, was something that could neither be denied or avoided.

"You are the judge of character I best trust, Serra Alina. If you have chosen to hide behind the curtained wall of the Southern Serras, it does nothing to change this fact. I know there was little affection between you and a brother who could use you so poorly in his rage at the North—but lack of affection and lack of understanding are not the same.

"You *knew* that your brother would never do such a thing. To be faced with proof of such an act was beyond your ability to imagine. Faced with it, you reacted.

"And it is that reaction that guided me."

She reached up with her left hand; caught his, held it. "Do you understand what you are saying?"

"I hope so." His smile deepened, but it was gentle; there was none of the edge she herself might have displayed. "Your brother is not a man known for his ability to lie."

She laughed, and her laugh was bitter. "Indeed, he is known for the opposite."

"Ask him, then. Ask him for the truth."

"And if he denies it? Ramiro will not accept the denial."

"No, not without proof. But I know it, as you must know it. Your brother did not kill Carelo. And if not your brother, then who? Who would benefit by his death?"

He lifted his head then, and gazed to the South. "I believe that this was meant to forever divide the Northern Terreans." He rose, freeing his hand.

"And neither Lamberto nor Callesta will benefit from that division. Not now."

"Valedan—"

"I need you with me," he told her, the smile bleeding from his face. "I need your advice. I need your wisdom and your knowledge. I understand that you are concerned with my status among the Annagarians; be concerned, if it is wise—but find some way to give me what I require.

"And trust that I will find some way to give you what you require."

"A Serra requires—"

"Hush, Alina."

She nodded then, bowing her head to ground in a very real gesture of respect. She heard his steps as he retreated; heard the rustle of cloth as he entered his rooms. Wondered how the Serra Amara would react when she heard of his words.

She had no doubt whatever that the seraf who waited outside her doors would bear them to his mistress.

"It is possible," Ramiro di'Callesta said, his face devoid of emotion.

The Serra Amara knelt in the center of her rooms. In the heart of the harem, in the privacy between man and wife, such a gesture was seldom required; she used it to advantage.

"Baredan di'Navarre escaped assassination by magical artifice," he continued. "He hid his true form; Ser Alesso di Marente buried a wooden doll, thinking it the General."

She said nothing at all.

"Amara."

The word was a command. As only a proper wife could, she heeded its warning, rising. She met his eyes, her own unblinking and dark.

They had held that darkness, undiminished, since his return. He wondered if she would ever smile again, and he felt the loss of that warmth as keenly as any injury that had ever been inflicted upon him. He would have approached her; but she had made a wall of posture, and he knew better than to breach it.

He stood; she knelt, her back rigid.

"It is possible," he said again. "Amara. Please."

She had not looked away; she had not looked at him.

A lesser man might have been angry.

But a lesser man would never have known how to value this woman, this wife.

"I have never gone to war without you."

She was silent; he thought that she would remain silent. "I have never ridden to war." The words were stiff. Formal. "It is men who fight battles. It is men who seek glory."

"Men who die?" he asked her gently. He placed his hands behind his back and stayed his ground. The Serra Amara had always been one of the strongest people he knew; she was also, in her fashion, among the most delicate.

She did not cry.

It pained him.

"Men who die," she whispered.

"Women die in war as well."

"As do serafs. It is not of their deaths that tales are written; not for their deaths that poets find words."

"No?" He looked away; looked at the flowers that she had arranged, with her own hands. They were white, the blossoms; white, with ribbons of blue and gold. She would mourn forever if he allowed it.

"We traveled from the North with Ser Anton di'Guivera. There is not a man—or a boy—in the Dominion who does not know the tale of his dead: His Serra, his son. I have seen him. What poets make of his life is true."

Gently rebuked, she bowed her head.

"Amara," he said, daring to approach her, but still careful to touch nothing, "do you think I feel no loss?"

She looked up. "You have the war. I have . . . an empty harem."

"You have a son," he replied. "We have a son."

"And will he be sacrificed as well?"

"No."

"Will you keep him from battle?"

"Battle is everywhere."

"Even in the heart of Callesta."

"Even so." He moved closer. "Carelo was my kai."

"He was my child."

"Will you allow his loss to divide us?" He was not a particularly gentle man, although until he had traveled with the
kai Leonne, he had never clearly understood this. Strange
that; the boy was so young. "Will you allow our mutual
grief to be used in a way that nothing else could be?"

"You have your other wives."

It was a blow.

He understood what lay beneath the words; willed himself not to respond with the heat of the momentary fury he
felt. "Amara, I have taken no wife that you have not chosen. They are mine, yes, but they are yours first. If I desired
them—and I am a man—I have treated them as if they were
what they appear to be: delicate, ephemeral.

"You are the only woman—the only person—that I have
ever treated as an equal."

She hesitated a moment, and he felt a brief hope, but the
light flickered and dimmed as if it were a seraf's candle in
a strong wind.

"What would you have me say? I am here. You are here.
And the body of my son lies beneath Callesta for the sake
of this war."

He closed his eyes. "Very well, Amara. Very well." He
rose. "I will retire. On the morrow, the Northern Commanders arrive."

The doors opened as he approached them, gliding
smoothly in wooden tracks, the seraf responsible for their
movement almost invisible, as any wise person would be.

Ellora hated the South.

From the moment she set foot upon this foreign soil,
memory stirred, and memory was unkind. She was not
Devran; not Bruce; although she was by nature an expert at
the game of war, she counted the losses personally. The
men and women who had followed her here would fight

and die. No matter what she did, she could not prevent it, and she was pragmatic enough to accept it as truth.

Years of peace had not gentled her, but it had given her the opportunity to indulge the ferocity of her pride and her affection. The Kalakar House Guard would be winnowed by this war; many would face the mirror of life and death for the first time.

And for what? The sake of a boy who claimed rulership of the Dominion of Annagar?

No. *Be fair.*

She had seen the demons in the Hall of the Kings. She understood that this was a battle that the North could not afford to lose—and such a battle was best fought on foreign soil.

But she had seen whole villages razed, the people in them slaughtered like cattle by their own. The South was a land of death.

She wondered how well Valedan understood this. Having spoken with him briefly, having observed him at a distance, judging him and finding a grudging respect for his raw ability, she wasn't certain.

Her horse was restive. She let him destroy the undergrowth in a prancing circle, shifting her weight in silence; it was her way of apologizing for the sea voyage. In all other aspects, he was the perfect mount; intelligent, inquisitive, and obedient by turns. But he had the sea legs of a sick cat. He was going to be put out with her for a few more days yet, and when he was put out, he was an impressive sight; he was not a small horse.

The Berriliya favored black; it was a stately color. And although it pained her to admit that Devran was not a vain man, he was pragmatic; he knew that his rank demanded attention. He was careful to preserve distance, to preserve the illusion of infallibility; House Berriliya—and its small cadre of House Guards—was to be represented by a man who understood the value of a regal, severe bearing.

But her horse, Merrin, was a shade of brown gold; his

mane was dark, his tail dark, and his flashings white. He
had good ears, a good, solid build, but his eyes were considered too small to be, strictly speaking, beautiful.

He was, nonetheless, beautiful.

Verrus Korama AKalakar kept a respectful distance from
that beauty. His own horse was a gray mare, perhaps a hand
shorter than Merrin, and infinitely more docile. Her eyes
were the size of a child's gathered fist, her lashes long, her
mane perfectly plaited; she accepted sea squalor and confinement with the same steady bearing that her master did.

"Ellora," he said, when Merrin had paused for a moment
to survey what was left of the ground, "we're ready."

She nodded.

Korama paused, his silence a search for words, not an
end to them.

"Duarte will be there."

She nodded again. Merrin began his mincing step, and
she wondered, briefly, if it was always to be the wild things
that she loved best.

Callesta was large.

It lay across the width of the valley like a declaration,
and the Commanders paused at the height of the sloped
track to gaze upon it, reading between the lines of buildings, fields, walls.

Ellora's men were restless.

More than a decade ago they had approached Averda,
seeking entrance into the city. They had never reached it, although they had come close enough to end a war; to drive
men whose venue for conflict was political to the tables and
halls where their power resided.

Vernon Loris had not chosen to accompany The Kalakar,
and she had refrained from making an order of the offer. He
stayed with her troops, overseeing the logistic machine that
kept her army fed and sheltered in a way that did not demand more than the terrain would bear.

If the war was long, that would change.

She urged Merrin down the slope, pushing past the men who were, in theory, there to protect her. They were used to this; only Sentrus Brotherton dared to argue the point, and he did so with the pained expression of a man who knew that the argument had never been his to win.

Ellora led her men.

Such an action was the source of many of her conflicts with Devran. Although she was clearly in no danger, his preference was to present a united front to the troops; to exercise caution, and to allow men to perform the duties for which they had been handpicked.

Certainly, for House Berriliya this approach was acceptable. Men adapted to almost any circumstance, and those men he chose to personally serve him wore this signal honor with a gravity that spoke of distance and respect for the rank they served.

Ellora AKalakar had created the Ospreys, coming between them and the gallows and fashioning, out of the men she had saved, a unit under the care of Captain Duarte. Ellora AKalakar earned affection by offering it; earned respect by offering it, especially when it was unlooked for.

Devran's men were drawn from the sons of the patriciate. His Verruses came from families only slightly less significant than The Ten; they responded as nobles respond to most situations. The hierarchy of the army was preserved both on and off the field.

Korama was the only Verrus that came from such a family.

But he was, of the men who served, the one she most trusted. He was not interested in power; he was interested in *her* power.

She turned when his horse's nose crossed the line of her peripheral vision. "Stranger things have happened, haven't they?"

He smiled. "Some. We always vowed that we would bring the army to Callesta."

"And you always told me to be careful of rash oaths."
She laughed. "Especially my own."

"You're looking forward to this."

"To some of it. I want to see that man's wife." There was
no mistaking whom she meant by "that man." In the Empire, it was rare for the Inheritors of the House Seats to
marry. Commander Allen, when he stepped off the field,
had had no such limitations, no scrutiny of his personal life.
On the field, he chose to deprive himself of companions,
and it was just as well; Sioban was no soldier.

Korama wondered, briefly, if they would see her on the
field. As the bardmaster of Senniel College, her life had
been contained, confined by the responsibilities of the Col-
legium's many students, and the responsibilities laid upon
any bardmaster by the Kings. Upon retirement, she had
only the responsibilities she chose.

But retired or no, very few were the men—or women—
who could tell her what to do. Or what not to do.

"What are you thinking, Korama?"

He shook his head. "Wives."

"Wives?"

"You want to see his wives, if I'm not mistaken."

"Wives, then."

"Why?"

"Because he's not a man who tolerates mediocrity where
he has the choice."

Korama nodded quietly, as he did all else. "But if confronted with a mediocrity that he doesn't have the choice
of, he accepts it. He doesn't have your style," Korama
added, "but I've watched his Tyran. They serve *him*."

"They've made their oaths," she replied.

"So did I."

Her gaze was sharper; he offered her his profile.

"I didn't demand your life," Ellora said at last.

"No. But if you hadn't been certain that that was what I
was offering, you wouldn't have accepted it. Rough speech
or fine, words are easy."

She laughed. "Tell that to the Ospreys." And then she stopped, the strange joy at approaching the open gates of Callesta diminished.

"Ellora—"

She lifted a hand. Swatted the words away as if they were insects.

"Words are easy to say," he told her softly, "and sometimes the saying is easier than the accepting. No one else thinks of Duarte's men as anything other than what they were. They were the only unit under your command that came together in the South. In a sense, they were born here; this is their home."

Every aspect of life in the South was a calculated risk.

In the fields, beneath the glare of sun, in a race against weather and the shortness of the season; in the kitchens and dressing rooms of the Court, in a race against the expectations of the High Clans and their need for seemingly effortless perfection; in the taking of a wife, in the bearing of a child; in all of these things, risk.

In halls very much like this one, in the grace of Southern stone, southern screens, open courtyards in which graceful ponds and tall trees hid the egress of men, the Serra Alina di'Lamberto had learned this lesson, first from her mother—while her mother lived—and then from the serafs and the wives of her brother, the kai Lamberto.

She had learned to stand, in silence, a beautiful accoutrement to an otherwise empty room; she had learned to arrange the flowers and the food brought by serafs with an eye to every detail, every droop of leaf, every fallen petal. She had learned to play the samisen, although in truth she hated the instrument because she had never managed to play it well enough to please her own ear; had learned to choose sari fabrics, in texture and color, by which the wealth of her father, and then her brother, might be advertised in a fashion that was considered both seemly and modest. She had learned to sit perfectly still in a room where men spoke and ate and drank; had learned to listen to the tones of their voices when their words were just a few feet beyond her hearing.

She had learned to plan, had learned to improvise—as only a Southern Serra might—had learned how to speak to the men whose duty it was to protect her reputation and her person; had learned how to read the women's language, and how to lift brush, wet with the darkest of inks, to write it. She had learned to read poetry, to read philosophy, to read the letters of the Court, first to her father and then to her brother until he found a wife who might better serve that function.

And she had learned, as only a Serra might learn, to distinguish friend from foe; to spot, at a distance, a man who might become a worthy ally, or an obedient vassal. That had been her mother's gift to a sharp-tongued, sharp-eyed daughter.

Had she been indulged?

Yes. By her father. By her grandfather.

But by her brother?

Ah, the old arguments rankled. She had left them behind when she had been traded to the North. She had never thought to return here, and she had therefore taken no care to make certain they had died.

Your son was killed by war, Mareo. He died the Lord's death.

My kai was killed by the Northerners.

Your kai was killed by his own choice. He was one of hundreds of men.

They killed him.

They killed him because the Tyr'agar is a fool.

Alina, the Serra Donna had said, her voice gentle, her expression as gracious as grief and fear allowed.

He was not even considered worthy of ransom, her brother had continued.

Ransom happens after surrender. She had known there

would be a cost for the words. Had known it, but had been unable to contain them.

He was your blood!

He was my nephew, she snapped, her own voice breaking beneath the thin veneer of control. *He was my nephew, and I raised him; I stood by his side at his first trial; I held his hand when he took his first step. I sat, idle, while you trained him to be the perfect vessel for Lambertan honor.*

Be silent!

No! I was silent. I was silent, and now he is silent, and he will never have a chance to speak for himself. He died because he wanted to prove himself worthy of you!

It had not been Mareo who had intervened; it had been the Serra Donna. For the first time—for the only time—she had raised her hand.

At a remove of years, Alina could still feel the stinging rebuke of her open palm.

Horrified at what had been said, horrified at what she had done, the Serra Donna had risen, stiffly, had bowed with complete poise at her husband's feet, and had retreated.

And less than one month later, the Serra Alina had been sent to the North.

Of all memories of the South, the day of her departure had been the clearest. She shed no tears, of course. Instead, as a dutiful daughter might, she had knelt upon the flat mats of her brother's outer rooms, hands palm down a few inches above the bend in her knees. She had worn white and blue that day—not only because the death of a kai demanded mourning, but because she did mourn.

He was not even considered worth ransoming.

Have you shed a tear for the men his decision led to death? Have you paused to weep or berate your enemy for his lack of consideration in the deaths of those who had no choice at all?

Ugly words.

All hers.

But ugly or no, there was a twisted, strange liberty to be found in the folds of truth.

As she waited for the palanquin to be equipped, the serafs to be chosen, the bolts of silks to be loaded into the wagons below, she repeated those words, again and again, in the silence behind closed lips.

And during this terrible ferocity of litany, the doors slid open.

She had turned to tell the seraf to leave, and had found herself face-to-face with the Serra Donna en'Lamberto, knees bent to the wooden slats of the exterior halls, hands upon the rounded lips of sliding door, face framed by its warm panels.

The Serra Alina began to rise.

The Serra Donna rose swiftly instead, closing the doors at her back.

"So," Alina said. "He cannot find the grace to say good-bye; he sends you in his stead."

She was careless now with her words—although she had been accused of such carelessness in the past, it was never with such truth.

The Serra Donna had never been so careless; not with words. But she had expected the Serra Alina's reaction, and barely flinched when Alina raised her hand to her cheek—accusation and reminder.

Such an accusation might have made a lesser woman wither, but although Donna was in all aspects the perfect, dutiful wife, she was no weakling. She met the Serra Alina's bold stare, and after a moment, surprised her by nodding.

Had Alina's anger been so easily stilled, she might never have left for the North. With far less grace than the Serra Donna had shown, she said, "Why have you come?"

"To tell you what you know he cannot tell you."

"That he has decided that I am the perfect insult to offer the Northern victors? Have no worries on that account,

Serra Donna. I was present for each of his discussions on this very subject; I am aware of his feelings."

The Serra Donna's gaze had darkened.

"Are you?" she said coolly.

Alina had spoken in anger, but confronted with anger, she fell silent. "Not, clearly, as aware as you are. You are his wife. I am only his unmarriageable sister."

Serra Donna rose stiffly. "It is not because you are his sister that you are . . . where you are. You are harsh, Alina, and your temper is unbecoming."

"For a woman?"

"For," Donna replied, "A Lambertan. Of all of his kin, only you can invoke such anger. And it is your choice."

"It is as much his choice, is it not? I am merely a Serra; he is the Tyr'agnate."

The Serra Donna bowed stiffly, without kneeling. She opened the screen doors and would have stepped lightly between them.

But Alina said, "Na'donna, wait."

The stiff shoulders of her brother's wife relaxed. She turned, her hand against the soft panes of the closed screen. "Na'ali," she said quietly. "He is not an evil man."

"I know," Alina replied bitterly. "He is an honorable man."

"He—regrets—what he has done."

"And he has told you so?"

"You know him; it is an admission that he could not make."

Alina said nothing.

"I chose the silks that are to be sent with you; I've sent brushes and inks as well as gold. I do not believe that you will be treated poorly in the Northern court." She paused. "You were wrong," she whispered.

"Wrong?"

"They killed his son."

"Na'donna—"

The Serra's head rose in a snap of motion; her eyes were

red. Surprise stilled Alina's voice; surprise humbled her and
sent her in search of different words.

"He was your son, too."

"Yes. But—"

"What happened on the field? Mareo will speak to no one
of it."

"He was not there. But—"

"But?"

"Word traveled. Be as gentle with him as you can in your
thoughts, in exile. Please. For me."

"What word?" She was still Alina, still sharp and hard-
edged. But she was perhaps much like her brother; she was
not immune to the pleas of his wives, where orders failed to
move her.

"They demanded the kai's surrender."

"I know."

"No. You don't. The cerdan, the Tyran—they were present when the demand arrived. The Northerners sent word to
the Lambertan General."

"The *General?*"

Donna nodded. "The letter said, in substance, that they
would cease all hostility. If . . ."

"Lady's blood."

"If the General was willing to surrender the kai into their
custody."

For the first time since she had heard of the death of her
nephew, Alina's eyes were also heavy with tears. She held
them back.

"They demanded *his* surrender."

Alina closed her eyes. "Just his?"

"His."

"And his men?"

"They would not countenance it. Who, of the Lambertan
men, could have done so with any honor at all? Had they
demanded the surrender of the General, he would have offered it, and gladly, in return for the promise of safety for
his men and the kai. It would have destroyed him person-

ally. It would have destroyed his ability to lead our men in the future. But he would have done it."

"But he could not give them the kai." There was no criticism at all in the words. "Na'donna—"

"They killed my son," the Serra whispered.

This time, this time Alina said nothing at all. She rose instead, leaving the very empty pretense of servility behind. Crossing the room blindly she wrapped her arms around the Serra Donna's shoulders.

In that fashion, in silence, she offered the Serra Donna her promise to forgive—as it was possible—her brother for his anger and his crime.

She remembered this clearly. The years had not dimmed the conversation. But they had explained it.

The kai, by Northern standards, was not considered to be of age. No boys led Northern armies; no boys led Northern units. The kai Lamberto, heir to the vast Terrean of Mancorvo, was not considered adult; he was not considered the person in authority upon the field.

The Northerners had therefore chosen to send their word—their perfunctory word—to the man they felt was in charge.

Ah.

She bowed her head. They had expected a surrender. They were not so bloodthirsty that they had expected to be forced to slaughter any man who would not flee.

But what man would, when the future of the Terrean had been entrusted to them?

For this, for this misunderstanding, her nephew had died, and her brother had been permanently scarred, enraged, embittered.

It was in the past, but the past formed the root of the present, as birth informed life.

And her life? She bowed her head to the ground again, waiting. Waiting in this foreign hall, in the stronghold of her brother's enemies.

Enemies that he had made because the Callestans had chosen to treat the war as another form of politics; had opened up their borders to trade and treaties; had forgiven the North for its trespass, its act of willful murder.

A seraf paused in the hall before her. He fell to the ground, his posture matching hers in both grace and suppleness.

"Serra," he said gravely, "the Serra Amara en'Callesta will speak with you now. Please accompany me."

The Serra Alina was no fool. She expected anger.

And because she expected it, she had chosen to dress in the most demure of fashions. Her hair fell straight across her shoulders, unadorned by combs or flowers; her sari was white, her sash blue. These had been bought at some expense, but she had felt expense necessary; she was certain that the Serra would know when she had obtained these things, and from who.

The Serra Amara had chosen to forsake the veils of mourning, although the colors were in evidence everywhere; in the flowers upon the low table, in the hangings upon the wall, in the rugs upon the ground on which she knelt.

Her expression was forbidding in its utter perfection. She was not a young woman, but she conceded nothing to age; her posture was perfect, the line of her neck long and unbowed, the stretch of her shoulders straight as the steel of a Northern blade.

When she smiled, the smile did not reach her eyes, but she did not frown, did not glare, did not express her rage in any way that would embarrass a Serra of her stature.

"Serra Alina," she said, nodding graciously. "To what do I owe the honor of your presence?"

The Serra Alina's bow was not perfunctory; it was short of—just short of—servility. She knelt; she rounded the curve of her back, exposing it in its entirety to the woman whose harem she had entered, acknowledging in full measure the power that Serra held.

The power of Callesta.

"Forgive me," she said, "for intruding upon you at this time." She held the bow. Held it in the lengthening silence the Serra Amara offered in return.

Silence was the Callestan weapon here. It offered insult. Not even a seraf would have been kept waiting in such a posture for the length of time that it took the Serra Amara to gather words.

But the Serra Alina expected no more. Indeed, she was surprised that she had been granted entry here at all, and she was willing to suffer the loss of personal dignity in exchange for that permission.

Valedan needed this woman.

The seraf rose. Alina saw his shadow across the floor, heard the light pad of his bare feet as they passed her. The screens slid open and shut so quickly had he not been a seraf of the High Court she would have wondered if he had had the time to leave.

Only when he was gone did the Serra Amara speak.

"Have you come," she said softly, "to plead your brother's innocence?"

Alina did not rise. She waited in a humbling silence.

"Have you come to offer me assurances that, feeling as he did, the kai Leonne's words were offered in honor?"

Again, she offered silence in return for the smoothly spoken words.

At length, the Serra Amara offered her first concession. "Rise, Serra. There is no need to humble yourself; you are an honored guest."

Alina rose. Her hands were in her lap, her shoulders curved slightly toward the floor; in all ways she assumed the supplicant posture. She had no doubt that this would displease the Serra Amara. But she negotiated the fine edge between displeasure and anger with the finesse of a woman who had observed the interactions of the court for the whole of her life.

"I have come to do neither of these things," she said softly. "Both my kai and my lord are full capable of speaking for themselves; they are men; they play a man's game."

"Ah. And the Serra Alina di'Lamberto?"

"I am not a man. I am only barely acknowledged a Serra by my brother, and you must know that I have never been considered worthy enough to be offered as wife to any of my brother's valued lieges."

"I know as well that you were the coddled grandchild and child of two Tyr'agnati who had no desire to lose you; they were selfish men; they gave, to your brother, a sister who was too wise and too old to be of value in so simple a marriage."

Serra Alina looked up and met the eyes of the wife of the Callestan Tyr. It was not what the Serra Amara had expected, and her own eyes widened slightly.

"Is that what is said?" Alina asked softly, although she did not otherwise change the line of her shoulders, the subtle slump of her spine.

If she had expected the Serra Amara to look away, she was to be disappointed. Brown eyes met brown and held them over the light of flickering lamp, the array of mourning flowers and cloth, the scant decoration of table.

Serra Amara the Gentle.

Serra Alina di'Lamberto.

They were almost of an age. They were both capable of a deep and abiding anger; Alina saw that now, clearly. She nodded.

"Many things are said of the Serra Alina," the Serra Amara said, cautious now.

"And many of the Serra Amara."

"Ah, yes. Serra Amara the Gentle."

"You have never been called a viper in the court of the Lambertan Tyr."

This drew a smile, almost unwilling, from the lips of the

Callestan Serra. "Nor have you, in *this* court." The smile dimmed. "It is the Lady's time," she added quietly. She rose.

This surprised Alina.

When the Serra Amara offered her hand, she accepted it, and rose as well. Together they left this chamber, this outer room of politics and meeting. "The Lady is restless this eve."

"And the ladies, it seems," the Serra Amara replied. "I . . . did not expect your arrival here."

"And you accepted it with the grace due your station," Alina replied softly.

"With less grace," the Serra Amara said. "Come. I would visit the Lady's shrine. Be my company."

With her own hands, she slid open the screens that led to the outer courtyard. The screens shook slightly as they parted.

If she had surprised the Serra Amara, the Serra was not to be outmaneuvered; Alina had expected to fence with words, to use them to both reveal and hide her purpose here. But the Lady's shrine was an invitation, a shadow gift, that she had not expected.

She had not visited such a shrine in over a decade.

It humbled her.

"I did not expect your arrival here," the Serra Amara continued, when they had reached the shrine, had knelt, side by side before it; had bowed their heads in the evening's colors, becoming for a moment one with them. "But I had warning."

"Of course."

The Callestan Serra reached into the folds of her sari and drew from it folded pieces of paper. "You must forgive me the scant light," she said softly, handing them to the Serra Alina.

Her hands shook.

Alina noted this, and took what was offered, opening it

to a familiar script. Women's writing. Her brother's wife. She read the letter carefully.

"Is it genuine, Serra Alina? Does it come from the pen of your kai's Serra?"

Alina read it again. It was the carefully crafted plea of a woman who has lost her son, and who asks that her husband's rage and desolation be overlooked by those who can.

She nodded quietly. "It . . . is her writing."

"The script?"

"And the words. Serra Donna en'Lamberto *is* my brother's wife; the woman he chose to spend his life with, to have his sons with." She smiled almost fondly. "She was called gentle, in the Court of Amar."

"Can it be read another way, given the death of my son?"

Alina did not turn to gaze upon the Serra's face; she had no need to. The slight turning of the edge of her voice said everything. But she had been asked the question, and in the Lady's presence, she answered it. "No."

"Would she—"

"If, as you suspect, my brother's hand is in this act, I will swear by the Lady's mercy and the Lady's judgment that the Serra Donna en'Lamberto knew nothing of the crime." She placed the letter in her lap, beneath her flat palms. "She would never have countenanced it," she added softly.

"And the Serra Alina?"

"I am no fool," Alina replied coolly. "I understand what is at stake."

"And that, Serra?"

This time, Alina did lift her head, did turn.

The Serra Amara's gaze was full upon her.

"You know, as well as I, that if Callesta and Lamberto fail to come to an accommodation, we will not win this war."

"Do I?"

"It has been said that the Tyr'agnate of Callesta knows the value of his wife."

"Much is said of men and their wives."

"Indeed. And had I not met you, Serra Amara, I might

have discounted what is said. But you are . . . no fool. And
I have watched the Tyr'agnate in the streets of the Empire;
I have watched him in the folds of the Imperial Court. I
have seen him handle his Tyran, and his par, as he pledges
allegiance to a boy whose measure he has taken only in
judgment.

"He is no fool, and he trusts you. You have met the
Tyr'agnate of Mancorvo."

"On one or two occasions."

"And of him?"

"He is a man bound by convention."

"Indeed. Bound by Lambertan sensibility. It is possible—barely, and only just—that he might have considered
the death of your kai the balance by which he would be
willing to serve at your side in this war."

"They were his men."

"Yes."

"His Tyran."

"Yes."

"You believed that his hand was behind this act."

Alina's gaze was upon the columns that bound the Lady's
shrine. "I did. Who else could give commands to the Tyran?"

She nodded. "It is so with my husband's men."

"Your husband's Tyran are also his blood. He is the only
man in the Dominion who has made, of his par, an oathguard. I have often admired the courage of that decision."

"And the wisdom?"

"Ah. The wisdom was only evident when they met in the Imperial Court. Ser Fillipo is cunning, and not without ambition."

They were silent a moment, and then the Serra Amara
said softly, "and now?"

"Now?"

"Now you believe that this assassination was not done at
the behest of your brother?"

"I believe that it is a possibility. And yes, Serra, I have
the desire to believe it that makes the belief itself suspect.
You have no such desire. How do you see it?"

The Serra Amara's brow lifted. "You are bold, Serra Alina."

"It was always considered one of my failings."

"Ah."

"I did not lie to you. I did not come to persuade you of the possibility of my brother's innocence. He will do that, or fail in that, when next you meet, if you afford him the opportunity. But I will tell you now that he will not stoop to lie. His is a game of politics that very few men are given the chance to play. He uses honesty and honor as weapons, and because they are his weapons, he is forced to display cunning in their use.

"If he was responsible, you will know."

"You are saying that he will not lie?"

"He will not lie."

"Ah." The Serra bowed. "I . . . thank you, Serra Alina. And now I admit my own curiosity. Why did you choose to seek audience with me this eve? If not for your brother's sake, if not for the sake of the man you have chosen to accompany?"

"It is for Valedan kai di'Leonne's sake that I chose to come, but I do not speak for him. We have had no speech, formal or informal, no strategies by which he wished me to approach this meeting. He is not aware that I am here, and I am uncertain that he would understand my presence if it were to be revealed to him."

"Is he, then, so very Northern?"

Ah. Now, she must tread with care.

But care and timidity were only synonyms for those without bold hearts.

"He speaks to both the South and the North," Alina said quietly. "Had you asked me that question at any other place, I would have said he was very Southern."

The Serra Amara's smile was both slight and genuine as she acknowledged the Serra's oblique compliment.

"But he chooses which part of his heritage to honor and which to reject, and although he asks my advice, he will not always take it."

"Will he take some of it?"

"Indeed, and value that which he takes."

"He will be a good husband."

Alina hesitated a moment, although the hesitation was not visible. And then she, too, smiled. "He proposed to me," she said softly.

The Serra's brows rose at least an inch. "To you?"

Serra Alina nodded.

"You refused."

"How could I do otherwise? If he wins this war, the wife he requires will be . . . a different wife. A younger wife." She bowed her head a moment.

"You are Lambertan," the Serra Amara said, speaking the clan's name for the first time in weeks without rancor. "And you are, of course, correct." She gazed at the columns which formed the confines of the Lady's shrine; at the darkening sky. "Did you love your nephew, Serra Alina?"

"How could I do otherwise? He was raised in the harem that was my home." She closed her eyes. "I have no sons, and I am no fool; I will have none. None but Mareo's. I would have given anything of value I had to save him. But what does a woman have of value in a war?"

The words were bitter.

But they were Serra Amara's words, her thoughts, on this eve. They sat, the divide between genders greater, for this moment, than the divide between bloodlines.

"What would you have of me, Serra Alina? You have answered all my questions; I have none left."

"I would have you answer mine, Serra."

"Then ask."

"The kai Leonne is no longer content to come to the harem, to my chambers within the confines of the harem, when he seeks advice."

"Ah."

"No, it is not what you think. He . . . he has ordered me to be available."

"You are."

"Upon the field."

The words robbed the Serra Amara of hers; she was silent. At last, she said, "Does he truly not understand what this means?"

"He understands that Ramiro di'Callesta values your advice. He understands that the kai Lamberto values his wife."

"In their proper context."

"Yes. But he values the appearance of context less than he values the advice. Understand, Serra Amara, that this was not a request. Any request of this nature that he has made, however obliquely, I have refused. He believes that he understands the cost he will incur, and feels that the cost of such an appearance is less of a difficulty than my absence."

"He does not understand the South."

"Indeed."

The Serra Amara was again silent. Even in the privacy of this garden she was not alone; the hour of the night excused her frankness, but only to a point. She could not openly criticize the man to whom her husband owed allegiance, although that man clearly deserved such a criticism. Alina knew this, and waited.

"Will he avenge my son's death?"

"Yes."

"And if what you believe is true is not, in fact, true?"

"He will kill my brother."

"You are certain of this."

"I am certain that he will try."

"He is young."

"Indeed. And the young make our greatest heroes with cause, with reason."

"Then I will aid you."

Serra Alina waited.

"Bring your clothing and your personal items to my quarters. Bring them publicly. Make your display of obeisance, if you are determined to serve this man in the fashion he desires."

"And?"

"I will take you into my harem. I will . . . open my doors, and its heart, to your use."

"I am Lambertan."

"You are merely a woman," the Serra said, with another of her slim smiles. "As am I."

"And I?"

"You will do what you intend; you will take up Northern dress, Northern clothing, Northern armor. You will braid your hair in the fashion of the North, expose your skin, stand with arms by your sides in the company of other such Northerners. You will be an object of scorn and derision and curiosity, as they are—but you will be a part of their foreign life.

"You will not be the Serra Alina di'Lamberto to any who does not already know of your existence and your value to the young kai Leonne."

The Serra Alina bowed low, her forehead touched the soft moss on the stones at the foot of the shrine. Resting there, absorbing their cool in the stillness of this perfect evening.

Then she lifted her head.

"My brother," she said softly, "the Tyr'agnate of Mancorvo, did not choose the war he fought thirteen years ago. He did not choose the battle in which his kai died, untested, and alone. He did not choose the moment of retreat and the moment of surrender.

"But there was choice in the venue and the turn of the battle."

"And my husband chose this battle?"

"To his credit, and his honor, yes. Knowing perhaps less than we knew, or perhaps more. He chose to preserve the life of Baredan di'Navarre."

The Serra Amara said, softly, "You *are* a dangerous person."

"Our fates are bound; Lambertan, Callestan, Leonne. And I believe that more is at stake in this war than the simple disposition of a few miles of land; more will be gained—or lost—than a title, a Dominion."

"Women have never had a place in war."

"And they have always had it." Alina bowed again. "This war will mark us, and remake us. Those," she added softly, "whom it does not kill." She rose.

"Alina."

"Serra Amara?"

"In the morning, I will see the world once more in the light of the Lord's gaze."

"And I. But seeing it in the darkness of the Lady's will grant me the insight and the courage I require to continue in the face of the Lord."

The Serra Amara rose as well.

"I will return in the morning with my possessions, my cerdan, my attendants."

"You have no serafs here?"

"I came from the North. No, I have no serafs."

"Take two of mine."

"I would not take them onto the field."

"Take them. They will—as you must suspect—be my eyes and my ears. But they will also be a gift to the kai Leonne from the sorrowing wife of the Callestan Tyr, and they will attend his needs with the unquestioned perfection of grace and movement expected by the High Courts."

"There are few upon the field who could appreciate that perfection; I, among them, but I will be encumbered by the guise I am forced to adopt."

"Baredan di'Navarre will be present. My husband. His Tyran. There will be others. If, in the end, the kai Leonne is to be victorious, there will be others, and they will be far less inclined to overlook his flaws than we."

Alina knew what Valedan would say; knew it, and knew as well that she would accept what the Serra Amara offered.

He hated slavery.

He wished to own no one.

Perhaps, she thought, as she nodded in genuine gratitude, you might change this world, Valedan. Perhaps you might bring some of the North into the heart of the South. But all things take time, and if you are not to wage war forever against the men whose support and respect you *must* have, you will bow, in this. You will learn to bend.

CHAPTER EIGHT

JEWEL had missed the Arkosan children when the caravan had left them at the desert's edge. They were a source of noise and life, a little well of chaos, a sturdy innocence that spoke of the future, the future's promise.

But the child she had taken from the river's edge, at the coldest hour of desert night, was unlike those children: she spoke, instead, of the loss and the suffering that war engendered. It was not a reminder that Jewel desired.

"Ariel."

The girl looked up, mute, her injured hand hidden in the folds of a shirt that was, oh, four sizes too big. The child reminded her of Finch, of Finch on the day she had been found in the twenty-fifth holding. Silent, small, injured, it had taken her time to find her voice.

How much time, Jewel thought, do we have? She smiled, but the girl was cautious. As Finch had been cautious.

Ariel slept only in the presence of Jewel ATerafin, and then, only when Jewel herself was awake. She spoke very, very little, and again, she would speak only when Jewel was alone; if Jewel had any hope of hearing what the girl had to say, she was forced to dismiss Avandar and Celleriant. The bard's voice was soothing enough to lull the child's natural suspicion, but it took two days of quiet riding before she did not view the stag with fear's eyes.

What have you seen, child? she wanted to ask, and Avandar almost demanded that she do so, but he knew her well enough to know that this would merely be grounds for fruitless argument, and he did not press her.

The child liked Stavos—and who wouldn't?—when she saw him. She did not sleep in his presence, but she did allow him to accompany her on those occasions when Jewel was deep in conversation with her companions.

As now. The colorful baritone of his voice carried a great distance, suggesting the rumbling amusement of the earth itself—if earth as dry and barren as this could ever uphold such an analogy. Enough, Jewel. Pay attention.

"The dream itself was an accurate guide," Avandar was saying in a curt, brusque voice.

The Radann par el'Sol—a title of note in the Dominion, as the Serra Diora had quietly and firmly pointed out—nodded. But the nod was a gesture of punctuation; it granted nothing but the certainty that you had his attention.

"ATerafin?" the Radann said, when she failed to fill the silence.

Jewel raised a brow. "You're asking me?"

"It was your vision, was it not?"

She shrugged. "It was. But Avandar is my domicis."

"What is this domicis?"

"It's a . . . a servant. Sort of. More than that. But not a House Guard, or anything like. It means . . ." She struggled to find a word that had nothing at all in common with seraf. Shrugged and gave up. "I trust him."

Marakas raised a dark brow. It was a thin brow; Jewel thought he must usually go completely clean-shaven, for his hair and his face were graced by what could only generously be called shadow. "Do you?"

"With my life."

"A fair answer."

She waited for him to point out that the value of life in the South and the value of life in the North were different entities, and she waited with less patience and grace than she usually did—which is to say, none at all. But in the week that they had traveled together, he had gleaned enough of her personality to understand the futility of such an observation; he remained silent.

"I am not always . . . cogent . . . when I wake, " she said quietly. It was an effort to speak slowly to the Radann, but her Torra was not of a class that was good enough for him, and she did not wish to reveal her inferiority; she therefore chose to speak Weston, which he understood, albeit with some difficulty.

Understand, Avandar said, *that this is a compliment. He is unusual for any man who holds power in the South; he is not oblique in his curiosity or in the way he pays his respects to you.*

And this is a compliment because?

Women have, in theory, no power.

Jewel gazed at the hidden face of the Serra, and she shook her head. *So much for theory.*

Dismiss it, Avandar said, *as coldly when you see the practice behind that theory.*

The Radann's Weston was stilted; it was clearly learned for use in the environment of a Court that had some exposure to foreigners, but not a lot. It was left to the Serra Diora to translate.

"It is upon waking that these dreams are usually transcribed, and it is the waking witness—my domicis in this case—who is considered the first, and therefore the most reliable, source of information. What he tells you of my dreams—especially when I am present—is truth. All of the truth," she added, with a trace of bitterness, "that the dreams themselves can be said to contain.

"If you wish proof of their truth, simply continue as you have been traveling."

The Radann turned the slightest of gazes upon the waiting Serra, who sat with such demure and perfect grace it was hard to believe that she would offer the sole opinion he valued. Hard until one saw the minute nod she offered, the tipping of her fan beneath a jaw barely exposed to something as trivial as the sun's light.

"Then we cannot journey as we intended."

Hard to bite her tongue. Hard to contain her sarcasm. But Jewel had learned, with real effort, to do both in her sojourn as a reluctant member of the Terafin House Council; she kept her peace.

"There is another danger," Kallandras said quietly, into the stillness of this simple gesture.

He had their attention immediately, this strange man with his pale golden roots lengthening beneath a dye that had given him the appearance of a Southern native. "In your vision, only two of the armies had gathered; the third had yet to arrive."

Jewel nodded.

"Sorgassa was not yet present."

"Not according to Avandar. I confess that I studied the banners and the regalia of the South for a short period of time; I did not recognize which were missing."

She felt, rather than heard, Avandar's derisive snort.

Don't start, she snapped.

I would not dream of belittling you in front of those whose respect you require, he replied, sardonically. And truthfully.

"If the army has not yet arrived beneath the banner of Lorenza, there is a chance we may meet them on the road."

A subtle shift in the lines of the Radann's shoulders caught Jewel's attention.

"Serra," he said softly. Urgently. She shook her head.

"The armies that you saw gathered—where were they?"

Jewel looked to Avandar.

Avandar did not roll his eyes; did not frown; did not otherwise make his annoyance at her ignorance obvious. But it was clear to Jewel's many years of experience that he expected her to recognize the geography of the terrain she had passed through at his behest in the dreaming.

"They are gathered upon the Northern border of Raverra."

Marakas nodded. "As expected."

"They are gathered equidistant between the Terreans of Mancorvo and Averda; to an inobservant eye, it would not be clear which road they intend to take when they at last choose to move."

"It has been a few days; are you certain they are not already upon the road?"

"I am certain of nothing except for their disposition on the night the ATerafin ventured into her dream."

The Radann nodded. Rose. "We are not so small a party that we will not be noticed by scouting—or raiding—parties, if any are searching for us."

It was Kallandras who spoke next. "Consider the possibility that the army gathered where it did along the border with that eventuality in mind."

"Pardon?"

"Of the duties the Serra Diora in her wisdom assumed, one is anathema to the General di'Marente. He cannot know for certain in which direction she decided to travel. But if he believes that she has traveled to one Terrean over the other, he may move in that direction first.

"She has, besides herself, something that holds an incalculable value in the coming war. If he can claim it before she conveys it to its rightful owner, he has struck a blow, in the South, that the armies of the North will be unable to overcome.

"The kai Leonne has, as his only claim to the Tor and the waters of the Lake, the bloodline of the Leonnes. And his only proof of that is in the Serra's hands."

"In the Dominion, stranger," the Radann said quietly, "that claim is paramount."

"It would be," Kallandras countered, his hands upon the still strings of his careworn lute. "Save for the disaster of the last war, it would be. But the Lord of Day favors no bloodline blindly. What the General Alesso di'Marente has chosen to build for himself, he has built with the approbation of at least two of the Terreans. Were it not for the General's brilliance, the General's ability to engender both loyalty and confidence in the men who served him, the losses to the North in the ill-advised war the previous Tyr'agar chose to prosecute would have been severe."

"Severe or not, it was still a loss."

"Indeed. And it was a loss incurred because of the incompetence of the Tyr'agar." He lifted the neck of his lute in the curve of his palm, settling it in his lap. A warning, perhaps. "I mean no disrespect," he added quietly. "But we face what we face. It is best to accept that if we are to triumph here."

"And what is triumph, here?"

"We seek shadow, subterfuge, the ability to hide in the open. It is the Voyani way," Kallandras replied swiftly. "Like it or no, man of the Lord, it is that road that we must travel if we are to arrive in safety in the Terrean of our choice."

"And that is the crux of the matter," Avandar continued smoothly. "Which Terrean, Radann par el'Sol? Which Terrean will be friendliest to our cause?"

"Averda, certainly," Marakas replied. "But it is for that reason that I believe the armies will move upon Averda."

Celleriant rose suddenly; his blade, completely silent, now shone in the clearing in which they had gathered.

Kallandras was on his feet in an instant, and if lute could be wielded as weapon, it, too, was readied.

The Arianni lord's pale brow rose, and a smile lifted the corner of his lips. "Even you, bard, might best be advised to select a different weapon."

"We choose the weapon at hand," Kallandras replied, but his smile was rueful. "What draws your attention?"

"I am not certain. But . . . there is something unpleasant in the air. It will be night soon. I feel that there is a risk here."

The stag had risen as well.

Jewel called him wordlessly, and he came.

Lady, he said. *Lord Celleriant speaks truly. I believe that we—he and I—have heard the sounds of a hunt being called.*

Whose hunt?

Not the White Lady's, he replied.

"Mancorvo," the Radann par el'Sol said quietly.

They looked toward him. He was not in command of the expedition; no one was. But he had been given the choice.

Yollana, silent until now, also rose; the Serra Teresa was her cane and her crutch. She lifted her aged hands and made the symbol of the circle across the sandy stretch of Voyani desert robes. "Mancorvo," she said, nodding. She turned her unblinking gaze upon the Radann. "If the sun is not in my eyes, Radann par el'Sol, it is in Mancorvo, in the end, that you will discharge the greatest of your debts."

"I am the keeper of those debts," he replied coolly. "I will decide when—and if—they are discharged."

"Indeed." Yollana slumped against the strength of the deceptively graceful arm that held hers. "But before then, I fear we will all be tested. The Lord of Night is at work here. If the armies of the General Marente are not aware of our work in the desert, *He* will be, and he will seek to prevent its completion.

"Come. If we are to start in the morning, we must take what rest the desert offers."

Marakas turned to look at the river that rushed past them, its steady whisper the only noise the silent desert now offered them. "The desert has offered many surprises to even a man such as myself," he said at last. "Let us do as the Havallan Matriarch commands.

"And in the morning, let us take the winding road into Mancorvo."

Stavos brought the child to Jewel's tent the moment the awkward circle opened. The fire that had sustained its heart was a meager thing, for there was little in the way of wood

in these parts. But Yollana had insisted upon setting two
sticks into the hard sand, and she had lit them with care, allowing no other hands to touch them. They smoldered,
trailing dark smoke.

The Voyani heartfire burned down in the odd clearing.

"Two more," she said quietly to the Serra Teresa. "Two
more, and we will be vulnerable. It is not to my liking."

The Serra Teresa di'Marano lifted her head, tilting it a
moment to one side. "We are vulnerable," she said softly.
"It is only our words that are hidden, and words have little
value to the dead.

"But . . . I heard the roar of the desert storm, Matriarch,
and against it, we emerged."

"You speak of the Northern bard." No question there; a
lift of gray brow, a sharp look, but no question.

"Yes. Kallandras." Her smile was brief, but genuine. "He
has been a shadow in our lives, as have the Voyani—and it
is all the proof I need that the Lord of Night does not rule
the whole of the darkness." The smile dimmed, the gaze
sharpened; the whole of Teresa's face shifted subtly in the
silver light.

Yollana's frown added wrinkles and creases to the lines
of a face scoured by wind and exposure to sunlight. "Your
hearing is better than mine, Na'tere."

"But not, I think, better than those that serve Jewel ATerafin. If you have charms or wards, if you must let blood, do
it now."

Yollana grimaced. "They will pay," she said almost ab-
sently. "For the use of my legs. They will pay."

She looked toward Jewel's tent.

The younger woman had stiffened, rising. Her right hand
sought the belt beneath the folds of her robes; her left, the
child's shoulder. The child.

The great, tined beast moved in silence, coming to stand
by the ATerafin's side. She bent on one knee. Spoke to the
child, her voice soft enough that no words carried the dis-

tance between them. Then she lifted the child as the stag bent its antlered head. The girl was utterly silent.

Jewel turned to the man who now stood, back toward her, facing the expanse of the desert's coming night.

"Avandar," she said.

"ATerafin?"

"There are no wolves in the desert, are there?"

"None at all."

She swore.

"So," Yollana said. "It begins."

"It continues," Teresa said, correcting her. "Come. I intend to survive to see its end, no matter how long that may be in arriving." She held out a hand, and Yollana gripped it firmly.

Their scent filled the air. Their warmth left its trail across the still night: If they were capable of hiding, they had chosen to do otherwise. Costly mistake.

The kinlord smiled. The leader of the hunters rose on two legs and walked toward him, breaking the sand with the force of curved claws. He could, when he so chose, make his tread invisible—but it took effort, and it cut his speed.

The kinlord had seen no need for such a precaution; what life there was in the desert was not sentient enough to carry a warning to the men whose knowledge the Lord of the Shining Court deemed dangerous.

He had scoffed when the possibility of danger from mortals had first arisen, but he had not yet seen the shadow of the Tor Arkosa in the dimming brilliance of night sky when he had been given his orders.

Yet he had seen it now, and it had stirred its bitter memories; he could still feel the spells which contained and protected it. Not for such a kinlord as he was the breaking of that spell, not for one such as he, the entry into that City. He could admit this now, in silence; it cost him nothing.

The hunter waited his word, aware of the difference in power between them; the kinlord was cautious. "Yes," he

said softly, aware that he was not the only kinlord abroad.
Others were hunting, and in terrain in which caution was
forced upon them by the mortals who crowded this realm.

The Voyani had proved themselves a danger.

One City had risen. One line had returned to the desert.
The Lord of the Shining Court desired there to be no others.

"Now."

Avandar did not speak.

Even in the privacy of thought, he was notably absent.
But Jewel could feel what was not put into words, and she
listened.

During the reign of man, such hunts as these were not in-
frequent; they were not unknown. Men did not travel in the
desert unless they were prepared for battle, and such battles
had proved a testing ground, a way of culling the weak and
the unwary.

No such test was necessary now.

She felt his annoyance war with a sense of dark amusement; he had walked the length and breadth of the hidden
byways that served as roads to those who had the power to
navigate them. He had walked in company, and he had
walked in isolation, and in either case, the kin had chosen
to avoid any encounter that involved him.

Clearly, then, they did not understand what they faced.

The stag lifted antlered head, casting a shadow in the
moonlight that was too long, and too strange, to suit his
form.

The moonlight, he said, hearing what she did not say, *is
the Lady's. This is my form,* he added, *but it is not my truth.*

Are you fearless?

I would be.

If?

If not for your command, Lady.

*Obviously not the one in which I told you to call me
something else.*

He snorted. Ariel sat on his back, her hands bunched around folds of his thick fur. She looked at Jewel, and only at Jewel; the stag remained standing in such a way that the child could clearly see her.

The child, he said quietly, *is mortal.*

So is Kallandras.

He speaks with power's voice; the child does not speak. She is not even graced with a hint of gift.

No?

You know this.

And she did. She had not known it until this moment.

Then why?

I do not know. But she is under no spell; the only protection offered her here is offered willingly, by you.

Jewel nodded.

In another time I would ask you why.

I know. And in another place I would hate you for asking. We are what we are. She needs me.

Only because you need to be needed.

You sound like Avandar.

He laughed. His eyes, round and luminous, opened fully upon her. *Do you disdain him so much because he does not need you?*

Pardon?

An idle question Lady. It passes time.

I don't . . . disdain him.

No?

The first of the kin crested the distant horizon. In the chill of night, the wavering lines of heat were distant memory; everything was clear for miles.

Jewel glanced at the child; the child met her gaze, steady and silent.

"Ariel."

She nodded.

"You've seen these before."

She nodded again.

"He will not let you fall, no matter what happens. If you

lose sight of me, he will protect you, and when it is safe, he will bring you back."

She nodded again, her silence unnerving.

"Lady?" Celleriant's voice, clear as bard's song, cold as night.

"Lord Celleriant?"

"Will you allow us the privilege?"

As if it were a game.

She nodded before she thought to ask who "us" referred to.

Had her answer as Kallandras of Senniel College joined him in the moonlight, his weapons gleaming with a strange light that she knew was not dependent on the height of moon, the lack of cloud.

Another creature joined the first, and another; Jewel counted five in all. They were of a height and not even the night sky could grant them the illusion of mortality. They were as large as the stag, and they moved with a deadly, supple grace that belied, in every possible way, their size, the awkward build of their fore and hind legs. Sand seemed to shroud their feet in a cloud that was always a few yards behind them.

They *moved*.

The Serra Diora and the Radann par el'Sol came to stand at her side.

"Where are the others?"

"Coming," Yollana said brusquely.

Stavos joined them; Serra Teresa, lending weight and strength to the older woman, joined them as well.

The Radann par el'Sol drew his sword and Jewel flinched; it burned the vision with its pale, blue fire.

Across the plain, the demons saw its light; they stopped a moment, then rose on two legs. Their song was a cry of recognition.

"Serra," the Radann said coldly.

But the Serra Diora did not cower. Instead, to Jewel's

surprise, she smiled. "I believe," she said softly, "that you move too slowly."

He raised a brow. Turned his back upon her and gazed out at the two who now stood ten yards ahead.

"I ask, as a favor, that you put up your sword," she continued, her voice as demure and soft as a Serra of her rank's could be—and as steely, as cool, beneath that facade.

"There is a danger here," he said softly.

"The danger that is perceived is the danger that we might face—we, the Matriarch, the Northerner, and her ward." Silent as shadow, Ramdan stood behind her, his hands by his sides, sleep and weariness shorn from his face by the demands of his duties: her presence. "It is for us that concern was shown.

"Watch," she said, speaking not as Serra, but as a denizen of the Lady's Night.

"But—"

"Watch and listen. The wind is speaking."

He raised a brow. Frowned. "Do you trust the voice of the wind, Serra?"

"The wind," she said serenely, "has only one voice, this eve."

Lord Celleriant drew his sword. Summoned his shield.

He gazed at Kallandras, and at the weapons he held. "You have courage," he said softly. "In the heat of our last battle, I did not notice what you wielded."

"They are mine."

"For the moment." His gaze was a mixture of appraisal and approval. But it held more than that; his eyes were alight with an excitement that he seldom showed. "I will take the leader," he said, "if that is agreeable."

Kallandras smiled. "Among my brethren," he replied softly, "the honor of the kill was merely the honor of being summoned to serve. I fear I will be an unsatisfactory competitor if you hope to count kills."

Celleriant laughed, and his voice was a cascade of music,

a wild echo of the song that Kallandras had heard for the whole of his adult life. "You are so very different," he said at last.

Kallandras smiled as well, the expression graceful and easy. "I am. I am no longer a youth. I fear I am not your match in speed."

"Haste makes a poor warrior."

"Indeed." He leaped, then, his legs straight, toes pointed groundward. The light of the ring upon his hand flared white in the darkness, captured essence of starlight, cold and perfect. He did not touch the ground again.

But he heard his companion's delighted laugh as the wind swept him across the stretch of their chosen battlefield toward their chosen foes. Here, at this moment, there were only three things that mattered: a brother, life, and death.

In the light of the wind's vision, he could see clearly what he faced: five demons. They strode now upon two legs, but their forearms were curved groundward as if by gravity. Closer inspection revealed the reason for that drift: their hands were stubs from which long blades protruded, chittering against each other. Their faces were long, their jaws slender; they smiled with the gleaming, sharp fangs of predators.

He offered them no quarter, no greeting.

Celleriant did. "Turn back," he said, "and we will forgive you your presumption."

His voice was low and deep, a sonorous call to battle. He knew, before he spoke, what the answer would be; delighted in it, extending it by the simple grace of conversation.

They roared. There was, in the cadence of their outrage, the trappings of language, but it was a foreign language, a thing unlearned in his years of study in the labyrinth of Melesnea, or the halls of Senniel. Kallandras understood it by the grace of his gift, for he was born to understand.

They were *fast*.

But he was deliberate; quick enough to slide sideways, to

avoid the whistle of hands that bristled with edges and weight. He had taken injuries in his aerial battle with the Serpent of the storm; they hampered him.

But he had learned to fight in almost any condition; he adjusted the rhythm of his movements, minimizing them; he allowed the wind to alleviate the weaknesses injury determined.

When he struck, he struck quickly; blood flowed as an arm fell, severed at the joint.

Jewel watched. "Avandar?"

He nodded, his eyes upon the field and the battle that she had chosen to grant the most reluctant of her followers.

"There's another one," she told him softly.

He raised a brow. "Where?"

"Beyond the swell of the dune. Toward the east."

"You see him?"

"I see . . . something . . . that extends from the demons."

"Good. Shall I?"

She hesitated a fraction of a second, and then nodded, watching him.

Jewel.

Seeing in him something out of a dream that she had entered without choice, and had not yet fully wakened from. Do I, she thought, guarding the question from his hearing, fear you because you don't need anything from me?

No.

So much for privacy.

His smile was dark; she realized as she gazed at the curve of his lips that he was standing just a little too close to her.

You fear what you cannot control. In me. In yourself. I will return. He bowed, the motion as sardonic as the smile.

You fear, he added, as he turned his back upon her and began his trek across sand so cold it might as well have been the ice of the Northern Wastes, *what* you *need.*

I don't need anything.

You need to eat, to sleep, to breathe. You need what mortals need.

She didn't ask him what he meant. Told herself it was because she didn't want to distract him from the battle he was about to enter.

Didn't believe it for a minute.

There was a lyrical grace to the dance of the wind; to the sweep of two blades in the arms of a man trained to music's subtlety. There was a spare elegance to the economy of his motion, the precision of his chosen strike, his chosen retreat.

There was beauty of a different kind entirely in his companion's wild charge, the sweep of his blade, the grandeur of his gestures. The length of his pale, pale hair swept out and back like the edges of a finely weighed cloak; no mortal man would have been allowed such a dangerous vanity.

But Lord Celleriant was clearly no mortal, and his beauty did not seem to be tainted by anything as petty as vanity; it was a part of him, a part of what made him compelling.

Audience to this, they watched, they bore witness, and they felt, as they did, the weight of hope as it settled around them, precious burden.

They counted, silent, as the demons fell before wind and blade and wild magic.

The Lady's Night was a strength, a secret place, a dreamscape unlike any other. They welcomed it, shivering, unable to dispel the cold and unwilling to find the blankets and the robes that might do so; they would miss some step of this dance, some part of the gift of its magic.

It was over so quickly.

Lord Celleriant lifted his blade, twisted it, sheathed it in the air before his heart center. "Brother," he said softly, extending a hand.

Kallandras reached for it, and the gem about his finger

dulled as he let gravity claim him. He smiled. "We are three for two," he said gravely.

A pale brow rose. The lord of the Green Deepings laughed. "A poor competitor? Your words are too pretty and too serious, bard, when they are not wrapped in song." He laughed again, releasing the hand he held. "Three indeed, and in your favor. But there will be other battles."

"Yes," Kallandras replied gravely. "Other battles, and with a less . . . obliging . . . audience. We will lose lives before we set our swords down."

The Arianni lord raised a silver brow. "Not each other's."

Not each other's. Kallandras closed his eyes briefly. "No," he said softly. "But neither of us are Moorelas. There are lives, in this war, that will count for more than either of ours if we are to have victory.

"And we might not know, now or ever, which lives those will be."

"I had almost forgotten," Lord Celleriant said, "that you are mortal."

"I . . . had almost forgotten as well." He bowed. "But that is the nature of mortality; if we are to fight, to face death, to live, we forget what awaits us at its end."

Lord Celleriant lifted his eyes; they were burning in the deep of the night sky. But he said nothing; all of his denial was in the ferocity of that simple gaze.

It was too soon; too soon to notice such a fierceness.

And yet.

Kallandras, master bard of Senniel College, born to the South and raised by the brotherhood of the Lady's darkest visage, turned to face the men and women who had become his responsibility. But it was not to them that he spoke.

"I have seen Viandaran," he said quietly, speaking in a voice that would not carry, no matter how close his companions were. "More, I have heard his voice.

"Do not wish that upon me, brother."

Arianni lords did not spit.

Therefore, Lord Celleriant was still. Ferocity fell into lines of genuine anger. "Do not lie to me."

Kallandras was rarely surprised; he was surprised now. "Lie?"

The Arianni lord who had ridden, mounted, in the Winter Host reached out gently with his left hand, and brushed the strands of Kallandras' hair aside, revealing the lobe of his ear. Although it could not be seen by mortal eyes, Kallandras knew what Celleriant saw: the Lady's mark. The mark of the *Kovaschaii*.

"The brotherhood has served the Lady for as long as I have served mine. Do not think I am ignorant of what that mark means," the lord of the Green Deepings said coldly.

"It means—"

"To you, Kallatin, forsworn. Do not tell me not to wish Viandaran's life upon you; I *know* what waits you."

Kallandras bowed his head, and his shoulders, the perfect line of his graceful posture, slumped. And straightened. "It is many years away," he said at last. "And although this will surprise you, those years do not feel as short to those of us who are confined by them as it must to those who live above them and beyond their grasp.

"Many things can happen in that short span."

Lord Celleriant said nothing.

When they returned, Stavos and Ramdan were already taking the tents down.

Kallandras turned to Jewel and raised a pale brow.

"Avandar," she said curtly.

"What of him?"

"He . . . arrived too late. Whoever held the leash of the demons you killed fled."

He listened a moment to the wind, but the wind was silent. Then he nodded and set to work on his own tent.

In the heart of the desert, beneath the surface of the cold earth, he listened, bore witness, waited.

He heard the claws of the kin scar the surface above as they passed over his chosen resting place; heard the words they spoke to their lord before they joined battle.

He heard the words the kinlord chose to speak after they had traveled beyond his hearing. A moment drifted past; in earth time, it was over so quickly it was almost impossible to absorb the whole of what had occurred.

But if earth had not been his strength, it had not been among his weaknesses; of the *Kialli*, he had been one of the few who had invoked its power with ease. It raged against his touch here, in the heart of lands that had once known the breadth and depth of life seen nowhere but in the Green Deepings; it had raged against him in the bitter stretch of the Northern Wastes.

But he had called it nonetheless, choosing his time and his place to reacquaint himself with its confines, its crushing presence, its slow, slow life. Wild earth. Not ally, now, but not—never quite—slave.

Take the water, snare the fire, demand the movement of air. But the earth? It could be done. Ishavriel had done it, time and again, expending a vast outlay of power in order to exert, to prove, his mastery. That was the way of the Hells.

But the way of the *Kialli*, the way of the chosen servants of Allasakar, before the Sundering, had been different, and it was that path that Lord Isladar had sought. Earth. It would never love him. Perhaps once, and in the bitter darkness beneath its surface, that once gave him pause for regret, for a pain akin to loss.

But if it did not love him, it knew his voice. *Taint,* it whispered, in its rumble, its treacherous crush of stone and dirt, of root, of ancient waterways.

Yes, he replied calmly. *It is a taint I bear, and no cleansing will expunge it. I am sorry. I have paid.*

The earth's anger was slight, this eve.

He paid it its due.

Spoke to it of old glory; of the trees that had once

reached the heavens, of the flowers that had nestled in the still, hidden ponds, of whole lives lived in the plants whose roots depended upon the soil for nourishment.

Not for Isladar the anger of rejection, the satisfaction of that momentary pain; his was the long path, the patient path. He had, over the course of decades, forced the earth to remember his voice.

His voice.

It knew him, and it chose, for now, to tolerate his presence. And so he watched, and waited, and learned.

The demons were dead. The kinlord had returned to the Northern Wastes. He would make his report to Etridian, and he would wait instruction—or punishment for his failure— at that lord's whim.

No one would return to the Shining City to make such a report to the Lord Isladar. Anduvin's sword had weakened him. Kiriel's blood had weakened him. He had been unable to completely obscure the marks under which he now labored.

And sensing his weakness, the Lord's Fist had chosen to remove him. It caused no resentment, no anger, and no surprise; he had lived by the side of the Lord of the Hells for long enough. He knew the laws of the Hells, and he—as they—abided by them: Power ruled.

But he smiled as he thought it.

The vision of the Lord's Fist was so remarkably narrow; the definition of power so completely predictable. Had it not been for the child, there would have been no risk at all.

But the child had been present, in the Tower that had become a symbol of all things despised and hated. He should have left her. She had no power, no gift, no role to play; victim to Anya a'Cooper's insanity, she was an afterthought, kin to grass crushed by the hooves of cavalry.

He should have let her die there.

Instead, he had come South, and in the South he would reside until he had seen the outcome of the battle for the Dominion.

Ariel. It was not the name she had been born to; she had
been unwilling to part with that, and he had chosen to gift
her with another. She was like, and unlike, Kiriel. She was
devoid of the strength that came naturally to Kiriel; could
not withstand cold, would be scorched to death by fire. She
had no easy joy, no bright curiosity, no heated, bitter fury;
she had no cruelty. She was almost a flicker of life, robed
in form—but behind her fear, she waited. If he was patient,
she would shed it; he had been certain of that.

And patience was his defining strength.

The mortal woman, Jewel ATerafin, was no less predictable than the Lord's Fist; no less manipulable. To him.
To the kinlords, she would be a mystery, for it was clear that
she possessed some degree of power—and if, as it appeared, she counted the Warlord among her servants, that
degree must be vast.

He smiled.

The meaning of power among mortals was delicate; it
shifted and changed, impurities arising in the stretch of
short years that caused it to be examined and defined over
and over again.

She would preserve the child until the day of his return.
Of that he was certain.

And what then?

He closed his eyes, and the earth closed its eyes; he
rested in the darkness of death.

And then, across the miles that separated them, he felt a
sudden shift in the landscape, a sharp, bitter pain.

His brow lifted in surprise, and although he could not
speak, he turned to the North. To the North, to the Terrean
of Averda, where she now resided, her companions so distant they were invisible to him.

Kiriel.

He smiled softly.

CHAPTER NINE

FINCH cringed as she stared at the flickering lamp. Although she was a member of House Terafin and, at that, a member of some standing, she had never forgotten the years she had spent in the streets of the twenty-fifth holding. Jay had occasionally found candles, and, preserved for either emergency or celebration, they would burn in the small rooms the den had squeezed into a lifetime ago. They had been luxuries; fire had been meant for warmth or food. The den had faced whole seasons where both were in jeopardy.

But frugality was no longer an acceptable choice; she had work for days in piles that had once been small and neat. At the moment, her concentration—such as it was—was absorbed by a simple letter. Letters always confounded her; they consigned her words to a type of permanence over which she had no control once the letter left her hands, and the act of composition made clear to her the poverty of her own expression. She struggled with each sentence, hating the powerful.

There was a gentle knock at the door, and because it had been preceded by silence, she knew it was Teller or Ellerson on the other side. She rose quietly, accepting any excuse to set quill aside, and opened the door.

She was surprised to see Devon ATerafin in the shadowed halls. "Devon?"

"Finch," he said, bowing, the gesture completely unnecessary. "May I?"

She moved out of the way instantly.

"My apologies for disturbing you."

She shook her head, gazing ruefully at her work. "To be honest, I'm sort of looking for any excuse not to have to work. Uh, any excuse that doesn't involve death, dismemberment, or more work."

He laughed. The sound was rich and deep, entirely out of place in the confines of her chosen office. She did not entertain people. Not here.

"Now," he said, stepping into the room, "You sound like a member of the Imperial Trade Commission. You've grown into your rank."

At the mention of rank, her shoulders slumped. "I'll never grow into my rank," she told him.

"If you wait for the magical moment at which you feel that all work is inconsequential, and all labor is easy, you'll wait a long time. In House Terafin, the work itself is a sign of the confidence of its governing body."

She cringed. "You heard."

His hesitation was visible, and of all reactions, the most telling. "Yes," he said at last, "I have. You and Teller are to join the Terafin House Council when it convenes on the morrow."

She bit her lip. "If you've heard, everyone's heard." And was rewarded by the startling lift of a dark brow.

"Perhaps. I was informed by The Terafin."

"W–why? She told us that we were to tell no one but our guards—well, and each other—until we arrive at the Council meeting itself."

His silence was unsettling.

"What else has she told you?"

Supple shrug of shoulder. Telling shrug.

"You know."

"Yes," he told her quietly. "I know. But . . ."

"But?"

"It was Jewel who chose to inform me. The Terafin's wishes have not yet been made known."

"When? When did she tell you?"

"Before she left."

Finch bit her lip. It was a habit that she had worked very hard to lose, and although she had had some success, it returned at awkward moments.

"You know we're being watched."

"Of course."

"Then you know that everyone will know you've come to visit."

He nodded again. "But you are not the only member of the House that I have visited this eve; I have spoken to all of the House Council."

"Why?"

"Does it matter?"

"Yes."

He laughed again. "You are not politic yet. Very well. There are matters of import to the House which might affect the Kings."

The night grew colder. "He sent you?"

"Not per se. But I am here with Duvari's consent, yes."

"Why?"

He hesitated for another moment. "This issue is unlikely to be raised in the open, and it is of import that it remain hidden."

She nodded.

"The Terafin's mage discovered a demon among the House staff."

Her eyes rounded, her lips fell open. "But—but he said that things were in order. Before he left. For the South."

"Please do not take this the wrong way, but we're aware of what was said. Understand that this is not the first time that a demon has been found in The Terafin's presence."

"I . . . know." She closed her eyes. All of her darkest

memories were waking in the face of the man who stood before her.

"Indeed," he said softly. "You, and your den, know a great deal about the kin."

"No. We don't. We just—"

"You know enough. Do you understand the significance of its presence here?"

She shook her head.

"Think a moment."

Think. She bit her lip again, kneading it between her teeth. "You think that the kin are involved in the . . . succession race."

"Very good."

"But that means—"

"Yes. It does." He walked across the room and took the chair closest to the desk, sitting in it. Seated, he robbed himself of the advantage of height—but not by much; Finch had never been tall. Would never be tall. The legacy of an early life in the hundred holdings.

"The kin attempted to kill The Terafin years ago. They attempted to kill Jewel ATerafin months ago. It is possible—just—that the latter attempt was solely of relevance to the war in the South; the demons came to the Hall of the Kings when the Kings themselves presided over The Ten in regard to the question of the hostages. But the former attempt stands on its own."

She nodded.

"It is considered possible that the attempts were unrelated, but we believe that they were part of a larger war. It is for that reason—and that alone—that the armies were sent to the South."

Finch nodded again. She understood what the significance of loss in that war meant: She had lived through the Henden of the demon voices, and she would never, ever forget it.

"It is not in the interests of the Kings to play favorites among the candidates a House fosters for its succession," he told her quietly. "Nor is it in the interests of the Empire. How much of the history of The Ten do you know?"

She shrugged. "As much as anyone does."

"Tell me."

"The Lady Veralaan was the sole surviving child of the ruler of the Empire. Her brothers had killed each other, somehow, and her father was dead. The Blood Barons thought to gain her hand in marriage, and with it, the Empire. But her father had given her into the keeping of the Mother, and in the halls of the temple, she had been trained as a priestess. So she knew what that marriage would mean for the people who weren't born to power."

"Go on."

"She prayed. She asked for help. And the Mother interceded, summoning her into the Between, where she met the Lords of Wisdom and Justice. Time passes differently there, and she stayed with them. In the Between, the Twin Kings were born to Veralaan, the heir to the Imperial throne."

"Indeed."

"Although she was gone a few days—or a few months, the story isn't always the same here—when she returned, the sons she bore were of age. They were presented to the assemblage of the patriarchs, the scions of the Blood Barons. She abdicated her throne to her sons."

He nodded.

"The Blood Barons weren't really thrilled. But the people were. Veralaan's sons, Cormalyn and Reymalyn the first, made it clear that they were willing to wage a war for control of the Empire which was theirs by right of birth. They traveled the Empire, and survived many attempts on their lives, seeking the support of the nobility in their war. In the end, ten of the most powerful of the families who governed the Empire chose to lend them their support. The Ten," she added softly, "who rule now. They came from the West, and the East, from the North and the South, and they came bearing arms, at the head of small armies, to lay their swords at the feet of the god-born.

"The Kings accepted their pledges of allegiance."

He nodded, his eyes never leaving her face. He didn't seem to blink at all; his eyes were luminescent in lamplight, in darkness.

"We celebrate those vows every year," she told him quietly.

"Indeed. In Henden, in the darkness, and in Veral, in the Spring. But understand that the offer of The Ten was not so simple an offer as the High Days make it out to be in story; that if it involved nobility of purpose—and it must have—it also involved the brokering of power.

"The Kings accepted conditions to the rule of The Ten when it accepted their pledges. The Ten were to be first among equals in the new world; they were to have their seats of power within the grounds of *Avantari*; they were to be left to their own devices in 'internal affairs.' In essence, the Kings were to allow them rule of their own. The laws that bind the Ten and the laws that bind the rest of the Empire are somewhat different.

"It is not, as you might guess, to Duvari's liking."

"Nothing is."

He smiled. She had forgotten, until then, how handsome he was. Finch, like Jay, distrusted handsome men. "The oaths that were made to The Ten were binding. They are recorded, even if they are not examined often. In a House War, the Kings' hands are tied by those pledges; they will not intervene unless the war itself is of such a magnitude that it encompasses those who are not allied with the Houses."

She nodded.

"If The Terafin chooses to kill you," he said evenly, "and you are incapable of defending yourself, the law will not intervene on your behalf."

She nodded again.

"And if a member of the House chooses the same course," he continued, "the same law applies."

"But—"

"There is no but."

"But—"

He smiled. "There is a reason that the death of Alea, among others, was not reported to the magisterial guards."

"But there have been cases, in House history, where members of the House have been turned over to the magisterians. Uh, the magisterial guards, I mean."

"Indeed. On all occasions in which the crime committed has been committed outside of the jurisprudence of the House. If a House member murders an outsider, or commits an act of treason, the House member forgoes the protection of the House. This, too, is written in the covenant between The Ten and the Kings. But in cases in which the wrongdoing is entirely internal, justice is an internal affair.

"The Terafin, in order to ask for Royal intervention, would have to cede to the Kings what has never been ceded in the History of the House: her sovereignty. I understand that you grew up within the warrens of the hundred holdings; that the force of law does not therefore seem sacrosanct to you. You have lived with the limitations of men, not the rule of the law, for the whole of your life. But the theory of your life in the holdings and your life here are different."

"Does it matter? It's all just words."

"It matters," he said softly. "We believe that the first would-be assassin did not intend to make the death of The Terafin obvious; that he in fact intended the opposite: To replace her, to assume her form and her role."

"If that had happened, the Kings would—"

"The Kings," he said softly, "would rely solely upon the Astari."

"The Astari? I . . . I don't understand."

"I know," he told her gently. "It is why I came this eve. I thought it might be preferable to a visit from Duvari."

She nodded.

"Had the control of the House devolved in such a fashion, the Kings would rely upon Duvari and the men and women who serve him. They would rely upon shadows, Finch; upon a war waged in those shadows. In order to move openly against the House itself, they would have required proof of a type that would be hard to obtain, if not impossible, without the direct consent of the other Nine."

"But surely The Nine—"

"No. That is what you must see, and see clearly. The Nine would know, when approached by the Kings, that by granting them this tacit permission they would be endangering their own power in the future. Even if the House itself were aligned with the worst of our enemies, they would turn a blind eye until it was impossible to do otherwise. If the City itself were under siege, if the armies of the enemy were at the gates, the Kings would have their full cooperation.

"But until then, they would insist that the matter reside within the power of the Houses, by the laws written at the beginning of the Kings' reign, centuries ago."

She absorbed this quietly. After a moment, she said, "But if the Astari moved against the House, The Nine would know."

"Indeed. They would know. But unless they were forced to acknowledge it, by some clumsiness on our part or some threat on the part of the creature who ruled Terafin in human guise, they would turn a blind eye. They understand the necessity of such a delicate operation.

"It is clear that our enemies have some understanding of this condition. Clear, at least to Duvari, that they intend to manipulate such conditions to their full extent."

"But why our House?"

"Why indeed?"

"You don't think it's only House Terafin."

He said nothing. She realized that he would continue to say nothing.

"Devon, why are you telling me this?"

"Because I think it is something that you have failed to understand."

"Why is it necessary that I understand it?"

"You are a member of the House Council," he replied grimly.

"You don't approve."

"The choice was not mine to make. And although it may seem strange to you, Finch, under other circumstances, I would do more than approve. I have some understanding of the den, and I trust it entirely. You have been tested in ways that most people—with luck—will never be tested, and you have passed those tests, and survived."

"But it's not 'other circumstances.' "

"No," he conceded.

"And in these ones?"

"I think she risks your lives needlessly."

Finch grimaced. It was a prettified version of what she herself thought. "We have to trust her," she said quietly.

"Yes. You do. But it is not lack of faith in The Terafin that prompts my visit. While she presides over Terafin, there is no question of her loyalty."

"It's the others."

"It is, as you put it so quaintly, the others."

"Does Duvari trust Jewel?"

Devon considered his words with care. Finch, who had learned only late in the game to do the same, envied him his poise. "Duvari considers the attack upon Jewel ATerafin to have been a genuine attempt upon her life."

"What does that mean?"

"It means," he said, giving up, "that he trusts her because our enemies clearly want her out of the way."

"You told him."

Devon did not reply, not directly. But he continued to speak. "He is willing to support her rule, if it comes to that."

"The others?"

"Are being investigated. Understand that that investigation is hampered; it does not, in theory, exist."

Finch nodded, because she did understand it.

"Understand that we, too, watch."

"Watch?"

"The others," he said quietly. "And the den."

"I won't spy for you, if Jay won't."

He nodded. "I know." Rose. "And I would not ask it. Not directly."

"Indirectly?"

"Indirectly, I ask that when you take your guards with you to the House Council meetings, you accept one of my choosing."

"The House Guards are chosen by The Terafin."

"Yes," he said softly, "and no. She will accede to your wishes if they are clearly stated; she has done so with each member of the House Council. This is not House Kalakar; the House Guards are not, by virtue of their position, accorded the House name. They earn it, or they fail to earn it."

"Does she know you're here?"

"What do you think, Finch?"

Finch grimaced. "She knows."

"Very good."

"Who is this guard?"

"An associate of mine."

The words were met by silence. She absorbed them, turned them over, understood that, unlike the letters she struggled with, they would never be consigned to anything as permanent as paper. "I'd have to meet him. Or her."

"Of course." He walked to the door and swung it open silently.

"Gregori," he said.

"Devon—"

"ATerafin?"

"I meant—later. I mean—"

A man stepped into the room. He was dressed in Terafin House colors, but his movements were subtly wrong for a House Guard. His hair was dark, his eyes dark, his face slender. He bowed as Devon closed the door behind him.

"Finch ATerafin," Devon said gravely, "I would like to

introduce you to Gregori ATerafin, the newest member of the Terafin House Guards."

Finch looked up; she had to. He was tall. Taller than Devon. "Are you Astari?" she asked him bluntly.

One of his brows rose; he looked at Devon, and Devon nodded.

"I serve the Kings," the stranger replied, his voice slightly higher than Devon's. "And I serve the House."

"You can't serve both."

"No? You serve the House, and you serve Jewel ATerafin."

"In case you've failed to notice, she *is* Terafin, so it's a stupid example. And anyway, Jewel ATerafin would never do anything to harm the future of the House."

He smiled. "Perhaps. You think I would, ATerafin?"

"I—"

"Think carefully before you answer," Devon told her. "If the House Guards are not always chosen directly by The Terafin, the members of the House are."

Gregori *ATerafin*. ATerafin, same as Finch. She knew what she'd done to earn it. Wondered what he had. Remembered the woman who ruled the House. "I . . . I guess not."

Gregori's smile was sardonic. "I have never made a vow with intent to break it. What I have offered The Terafin, she has accepted."

Finch hesitated. "I don't know," she said at last, speaking to Devon. "Jay makes all the decisions."

"Jewel is not here," Devon told her quietly, his hand upon the edge of the open door. "You are. She trusts you; think about what has been said here, and decide."

It was late.

Sleep eluded her only because she held it at bay with lamplight and company. That company watched her quietly, his hands behind his back, his shoulders an exquisitely perfect line.

"Well?" She prodded the edge of her desk with her left toe; her shoes were somewhere under the bed.

"It is not a decision I can make for you," Ellerson replied. "What is your own feeling in the matter?"

"I don't like it."

"Then refuse."

She shrugged, restless. "I don't want to make Duvari angry. Or suspicious."

"You are unlikely to make him angry," Ellerson replied. "And he is already suspicious. Nothing you can do, short of joining the Astari, will allay those suspicions; they are at the heart of his chosen vocation."

She nodded. "What would you do if you were me?"

He smiled. "I am not you, Finch ATerafin. I am merely domicis, and matters of such a political nature are not a part of my duties. Why do you dislike the idea?"

"I don't know. I'm not sure I like him."

"Ah. And if it were Devon ATerafin who offered his services, would you accept them?"

She thought about this, or tried; she was very, very tired. "Yes."

"Because?"

"I know him."

"Do you?"

Thought about this. After a moment, she shook her head. "Ellerson?"

"Yes?"

"What do you think is going to happen?"

He was silent.

"I want to know."

"I think you already know."

"Okay, I want to hear it."

He sighed. "I think," he said quietly, "that it is likely that The Terafin will die. As she is aware of this, she has gone to some length to protect what she values in the House she has built. You are all that remains of that protection at the moment; you, the den, and your absent leader.

"If the Astari cannot protect you when such protection is required, I cannot think of anyone who can."

"Jay," Finch replied.

"Jewel," Ellerson told her gently, "is not here. It is to be hoped that whatever holds her in the South will release her in time."

In time. Finch closed her eyes. "Is it always like this?" she asked him, in the darkness behind her lids.

"It is often like this," he replied. "Come, ATerafin. It is late. You have a meeting with the House Council in the morning. I have taken the liberty of choosing your clothing."

She nodded. But she wasn't allowed to sleep yet. There was one more duty to attend to.

Captain Torvan ATerafin waited in the kitchen.

Finch joined him there. Although the operations of the den had been moved over the last few weeks into the heart of the rooms she occupied, there were some things that were best done where they had always been done.

The table was bare; the lamp was the only source of light in the room. Windows were shuttered, but moonlight appeared through the cracks of wooden slats, half turned to allow its entry.

Of all of the House Guards, it was Torvan she most trusted. Torvan ATerafin, one of the Terafin's Chosen, had been the first man to show them mercy when they had stood outside of the gates of the manse. Had it not been for his intervention, for his instinctive trust, Arann would be dead. Jay had never forgotten the debt.

Nor had any member of her den.

He looked up as she entered the room, and waited in silence while she made herself comfortable. Or tried.

His smile was gentle. "ATerafin," he said, the formality of the word eased by its warmth.

"Angel and Carver are going to join the House Guard," she told him.

He nodded. "We were given that much warning."

"They'll attend us at tomorrow's meeting."

"Jester?"

"I think the quartermaster thinks he's too short," she replied.

Torvan laughed. "He is too short to be suitably attired on short notice, yes."

"Is there anyone else we should take? We're allowed four guards."

"Have you any you wish to second?"

"You."

His smile faded. "I am honored by the request," he said gently, "but it is not a request that I am capable of fulfilling."

"But—"

"The Chosen serve The Terafin. I cannot serve you in that capacity, although I assure you I will be present."

"But we're taking Arann."

He nodded. "I am . . . aware of that."

"He's been Chosen."

Torvan nodded quietly. "He has. And among the Captains, this is known. The Terafin knows it as well. But the House itself has not been apprised of this fact."

She snorted. "And you think the others won't know?"

"I believe that if they care to do so, they can find the information; she has been discreet, no more. But his presence by your side will raise no brows. He is already considered to be one of Jewel's people."

She had expected as much, but had to ask. "Have you met Gregori ATerafin?"

He was silent. After a moment, he said, "Why do you ask?"

"He has . . . offered . . . to serve in the capacity of House Guard."

"Ah."

"Torvan?"

"It is not my position to advise you, ATerafin; you are a

member of the House Council, and, as such, are deemed
worthy of ruling."

She snorted. "Enough. Enough already."

His smile was genuine, although it was worn with care.
"I have met Gregori ATerafin. I did not realize the capacity
he would choose to serve in, but having met him, I approve."

"You trust him?"

"That is not entirely what I said," he told her gravely,
reaching for the lamp. "It's late, Finch." He lifted the light;
it swayed in the crook of his palm. "Sleep, if you can."

"That is just what I was about to tell her," another voice
said.

Ellerson. Finch lowered her head to the surface of the
kitchen table, and then she rose.

9th of Corvil, 427 AA
Terafin Manse, Averalaan Aramarelas

"A demon?" Teller said, as he adjusted the buttoned shirt
that Ellerson had laid out for his use. It fit perfectly; there
was nothing at all that needed adjustment. The colors, a
deep blue with gold edges and a pale green insignia, were
adorned by a crest in House colors.

Finch, fussing with her own dress, nodded.

"What's being done?"

She shrugged. "I don't know."

"You didn't ask."

"No, I didn't ask."

Teller shook his head. His hair had been tended by Ellerson, but he was unused to such care, and ran his fingers
through it, leaving furrows that refused to fall back into
place.

"I'm sorry. It was late, and I wasn't really thinking. I
didn't expect to see Devon," she added, trying to keep the
defensive tone from her words. It was a dismal attempt.

The knock on the door was firm.

Finch answered it; saw Ellerson on the other side. He looked as perfect as he always did. But to her great surprise, so did Carver and Angel. And Angel looked pretty darned unhappy about the transformation. His hair, his one vanity, had left its awkward spiral; it had been pulled back from the angular lines of his face and knotted, warrior style. Strands had escaped, but they were few; Ellerson had done his work well.

Carver's dark hair had been parted in the center, and pulled back over his face; Finch couldn't remember the last time she'd been able to clearly see both of his eyes. The long, silver scar that adorned his jaw was plainly visible.

"What," Angel snarled, "are you staring at?"

"What do you think?"

He snorted.

Carver and Angel wore armor; chain shirts, with surcoats that clearly marked them as men who served House Terafin. They wore heavy boots, heavy gloves, and swords.

The swords themselves were a weighty, awkward decoration; it was the daggers that rested in sheaths on those belts that were their true strength. Only Arann, of the den, had spent enough time training with a sword to be any good at it at all, and the weaponsmaster had made clear that he thought Arann's size and strength were responsible for his ability with the weapon; he had come late to its use.

"Where's Arann?"

"Outside, waiting."

She nodded.

"There's another guy with him."

Nodded again. "We needed four guards."

"Technically," Ellerson said, with the faintest hint of disapproval, "you are allowed *eight*. And your math, ATerafin, is up to a simple act of multiplication."

"We'll find the other four later. Right now, I don't think we need strangers. Or more strangers."

He bowed stiffly, the gesture a mild rebuke.

She ignored him. "Do we look okay?"

"You look like court fops," Carver said cheerfully.

"And you look like House Guards," she snapped back.

"Before this degrades further," Ellerson told them severely, "I would like to point out the time. You have ten minutes longer than is strictly necessary to reach the Council Hall."

She looked at Teller. He said, "I thought we could bring Jester with us."

She nodded. "He's your whatever it's called?"

"He serves as adviser," Ellerson said, with just the barest hint of frustration. "He would commonly be called an aide."

She nodded. "All right. Let's go." *Before we lose our nerve, get conveniently lost, and miss the meeting entirely.*

She took the lead; Teller fell in beside her. Ellerson, the domicis who guarded the wing, walked four feet behind. As domicis, his presence was expected, if not required, and Finch had no intention of leaving him behind. She had to work hard not to glance back to make sure he was following.

But she did the work.

The halls of the manse had been this forbidding on only one other occasion: the day that the den had first arrived and been ushered through the gates. On that day, as this, she had noticed the stretch of marble and carpet that could have covered the whole of a city block; the grand hall, the hall from which all else could be found if one knew where to look. Above her head, in sconces that shone with the work of a small army of servants, were lights; they were lit, their flames steady and low as befit the hour of the day. Great windows adorned the walls, and light flooded in, glinting off gold, off silver, off the hanging crystals that caught and scattered its pale, bright beams.

Paintings and tapestries, their colors untouched by years of exposure to light, heat, and the humidity of the Summer months, marked their progress; mirrors as tall as the ceiling reflected it; alcoves, with small fountains and smooth, stone benches, caught and held the sound of their passing feet.

Money, she'd thought, when she first walked these halls. The other thoughts—of how she might palm something that she could take back to the holdings to sell—were not absent; they returned, as a memory of who she had been on that day, on that daunting walk. Of who she was, on this one. She felt no different until she thought it; wondered if age truly made anyone feel different.

Yet now, she thought of power.

What was it? How was it defined? Not strictly by birth, although The Terafin had been born to the patriciate. Not by money, for the merchants who crowded these halls during the months when the storms swept the harbor with abandon, had that in plenty. Not intelligence, for the Order of Knowledge was not the primary Order in the High City; that accolade—if it was one—belonged to the Guild of Makers, and it was jealously guarded.

Cunning?

Not even that.

Desire, maybe. Ambition.

She took a deep breath. Her steps had slowed; she knew this because Teller reached out for her arm, his own, clothed in too-fine cloth extended and bent. She met his eyes, his dark eyes, and wondered if he thought what she thought in this place. But she took his arm gratefully. It helped.

The hall had never seemed so long.

Not even on the day that the grand foyer had been destroyed by the creatures that worshiped the Lord of Darkness. Then, terror had given her feet wings. Then, Jay had been at their head, in charge of everything they did.

Was it so much easier to follow?

She closed her eyes. Felt the pressure of Teller's hand.

What had The Terafin felt, when she had first walked this hall, on the way to this chamber?

Powerful? She had certainly been that. But she had car-

ried the title of Council Member, same as Finch, or Teller.
Same as Jay.

Was she ambitious? She would have had to be. She had
fought a House War, won it, forgiven or destroyed her enemies. She had taken the seat.

She would have had to be cunning. Intelligent. Subtle.
She would have had to understand the whole of the dance
that the powerful performed, in all its variations. She would
have had to work, to make ties, to bind the Chosen.

And what had it gotten her?

Finch opened her eyes. The hall's vastness filled her vision, but for just a moment, she saw beyond it.

What was The Terafin's power?

Responsibility. Duty. Fear. Command.

Jay, she thought, *I don't belong here.*

And she heard Jay's voice, across a very long distance,
telling her to shut her mouth. *You understand duty. You understand responsibility. You sure as Hells understand fear.
You can do this. I'm counting on you.*

Power.

Why did people want it so badly?

She looked at Teller, and he smiled his quiet, wordless
smile, encouraging her. Thinking of her.

And the answer came to her, in the curve of those familiar lips.

They wanted it so that other people couldn't abuse it.

Yes, she thought, for the first time, the halls shortening as
she walked them, as they led her to her destination. *I can do
this. For Jay. For us. For The Terafin.*

The guards at the door were good; they didn't raise an
eyebrow when the den stopped in front of them. The den
was known to the House Guards; known to the House servants, known to the people who ruled and the people who
served. Although it was true that birth had no place in
House Terafin, it was also true that high birth helped; it

gave prospective members the opportunity to learn, to gain the skills the House valued.

But people still loved a story, and Finch was aware that Jay and the den were a part of that story: they were the street urchins who were determined to Make Good. Whatever that meant. Rags to riches. She knew, because Carver still spent way too much time among the women in the servants' quarters, that the House quietly cheered them on; that they did what they could to make life easier and less bewildering.

She started to bow, thought better of it, thought better of it again, and stood there, in front of the two armed men. Teller took up the slack; he nodded gracefully at the guards.

"Roger," he said. "Albrecht."

They did not so much as smile, although the older man, Albrecht, nodded in return. He stepped aside, catching the door's great handle in a gloved fist.

It opened, and she stared into the home of the Terafin Council.

The hall possessed two tiers of seats to the North and the South; to the West and East were windows of such complexity and color the tapestries in the long hall were put to shame.

And between the seats and the windows, was the grand table, its chairs as tall and fine as any throne old stories boasted.

The Terafin sat at its head, in a chair that was slightly taller than the others, slightly wider, its arms trimmed in gold and a deep burgundy, its back, hidden by hers, in the crest of the House. She looked up as they entered, lifting her gaze from a small pile of papers that rested beneath her hand.

"ATerafin," she said, nodding regally. "ATerafin. Please join us."

Join us.

Finch drew a deep breath and looked beyond the woman who ruled the House. The only woman, the only person, in

one of these seats that she trusted. But that wouldn't be true
for long; Teller would take a seat, and she trusted him:
Three, she thought. Three of us.

Gabriel ATerafin had the seat to the Terafin's right; the
seat to her left was occupied by Elonne ATerafin.

Elonne, coiffed and elegant, had chosen a deceptively
simple gown, one that fell off her left shoulder in an unin-
terrupted drape of fine silk. Her hair was pulled back and
up; it lent a severity to her features that suggested the power
and wisdom of experience without actually condescending
to notice age. A pale brow rose and fell over the slight
widening of blue eyes; if she was surprised, and Finch
thought she was, she did not otherwise show it.

Instead she smiled and nodded, much as The Terafin had
done.

Marrick's smile was much less guarded. He rose. "Well,"
he said, his voice jolly, his face creased in lines of welcome,
"I'm happy to see that youth has finally been allowed to
grace these tables. Welcome, welcome, youngsters, to the
nefarious halls of the Terafin Council, where plots great and
small are hatched." He laughed; there was nothing forced
about the sound of his voice.

Finch's first impulse was to like him. It had been her first
impulse when she had accepted his invitation to lunch a
month past. He had none of the perfection of appearance
that defined the other three; he was slightly overweight, and
his beard was shot through with white. His hair looked like
iron, his eyes were dark; he seemed like a favored uncle, a
harmless man who might take children upon the flat of his
lap and tell them outrageous stories.

But she had seen him in other guises; had seen the smile
fall away from his face in those moments when he thought
no one observed him.

Haerrad took no such pains; he was as grim and dour as
ever; his face was frozen in lines of disapproval. Of the
four, he was the easiest to dislike.

And she did. In fact, of the four, he was the only one that

she hated. Because of Haerrad, Teller had been confined to the healerie for weeks, a display of power, a threat offered to Jay in the hope that threat alone would buy her loyalty. As if.

Her eyes skirted his face. She wondered what Teller felt.

Rymark was last to react, but he was also the most flamboyant; he rose, leaving the confines of the chair that was his by right. Bowing deeply, he said, "Welcome, ATerafin, ATerafin, to the Council of the House."

He lifted his head and looked up, his eyes catching Finch's as she studied him. She felt her cheeks warm; she didn't like the way his gaze swept across hers. Predator. She had met men very like him in the holdings; too pretty, too powerful. She nodded in silence.

There were two chairs, side by side, that were empty; they were between Elonne and Marrick.

She walked toward the first. Ellerson was at her elbow in an instant, pulling the chair out for her. It was a good thing, too; she could tell, by the way it dragged against the carpet, that it was heavy, that it would be an unseemly struggle for her just to move it.

He waited until she was seated, and then aided Teller in a similar fashion. But he did not speak. He was a man who knew his place, and worse, knew theirs.

She didn't want to disappoint him.

When they were both seated, The Terafin looked up.

"May I introduce the newest members of the House Council," she said quietly. "Finch ATerafin and Teller ATerafin." She turned to Morretz, who waited behind her chair, just as Ellerson was waiting behind theirs. He bowed and left her side, and Finch could sense his reluctance from where she was seated.

He came to stand between them, and took from his robes two things. These he placed before them on the perfect sheen of the wooden table. Gold caught the light, reflecting it, held in the shape of two rings.

"What exactly," Haerrad said bluntly, "will the duties of the new members be?"

Finch picked up the ring in a shaking hand as he spoke, hesitated for just a moment, and then slid it upon her finger. It fit perfectly, no surprise there. But it was heavy and cold.

The Terafin's pause was significant; she held it as she gazed around the table. Haerrad did not withdraw his words, but he did not make the mistake of adding to them.

"They will," The Terafin said at length, "oversee the merchant lines in the Menorans and to the South."

"The merchant lines in the South have been severely lessened, of late."

"Indeed."

"If I am not mistaken," Rymark said smoothly, "those lines are currently overseen by Jewel ATerafin."

"The services of Jewel ATerafin have been seconded by the Kings," The Terafin replied serenely. "When she returns, an evaluation of her progress will be in order."

"Given the current state of affairs, Terafin, was it wise to accede to the wishes of the Kings in this regard?"

"No motion was put forward in Council about such a placement," Haerrad added.

"No motion was put forward; her disposition is not a matter for the Council to decide. She was offered a choice, and she made her decision; she waited upon my leave before she accepted her assignment. Or is more now required, Haerrad? Shall we decide that the private activities of each member of the Council bear public scrutiny—and equally public accountability?"

"The gifts she has acknowledged in her tenure in the House must surely be considered one of the House advantages, and as all advantages that accrue to the House, one not to be squandered."

Finch was almost shocked.

But The Terafin did no more than raise a brow. "I consider the talents of all Terafin to be of such value," she replied. "Jewel is not the only talent-born member to preside on the House Council. Would you fetter Rymark ATerafin in such a fashion?"

Rymark's smile was grudgingly offered. "House Member Haerrad means no disrespect, Terafin, when he points out that a mage—of any talent—is far less a rarity than one who is seer-born."

"Perhaps. But such a talent cannot be owned; it can be valued; it can be cultivated. In some cases, it can be directed." She lifted her hand. "The meeting is now in session. I have reports in hand about the progress of the armies in the South; they are sketchy, but they will do."

She passed the papers to Morretz.

"For the duration of the war, Meralonne APhaniel has also been seconded by the Kings; we have therefore sought the services of another member of the magi."

There was some whispering among the members of the House Council and the shadows who served as their advisers. The Terafin rose.

"I am certain that that member requires little introduction, but for the sake of formality, such an introduction will take place." She walked to the doors, and Finch failed to recognize the significance of this action until the doors themselves were opened.

Standing, framed by their open width, was a diminutive woman who carried age as if it were wisdom's mantle.

"I am honored to present Sigurne Mellifas to the Terafin House Council."

CHAPTER TEN

9th of Corvil, 427 AA
Callesta, Terrean of Averda

"I DON'T like it."

Valedan raised a brow. The Captain of his guards—the man he had, with effort, ceased to identify as an Osprey—had forsaken the customary stiffness of the South in the enclosure of the large tent, and with it, the cautious use of words, the tone that clearly—and properly—conveyed disapproval. Ser Andaro di'Corsarro did not find this as amusing as the lord he had pledged his life to did, but *he* was determined to bring dignity to the proceedings in spite of the unsuitable behavior of his companions; he said nothing. Loudly.

Ser Anton di'Guivera, whose roots were among the insignificant clans, although his fame far exceeded those of nobler birth, was under no such compulsion. "I must agree with the Captain."

He did not turn his head to the side, and his gaze did not condescend to travel the distance between himself and the newest member of the Northern retinue.

"Your objections are noted. Serra Alina?"

She wore the leather armor that the smaller women favored, and over it, a surcoat with a distinctly bland emblem across its heart center; at a distance, it would pass for the crest of the Kalakar House Guards. Valedan was aware that he would meet The Kalakar again, and soon; he had no desire to presume upon her authority, and she had not given leave to Duarte to recruit South of the border. The Serra's hands were gloved; her feet, heavy in the leather boots the Northerners wore. Of all the things that she suffered, it was the boots that seemed most cumbersome, for they changed the fall of her step as she walked. Her hair was bound in a nondescript braid, shorn of ornamentation; her face would be exposed to the sun's light.

She stepped forward, toward the table across which maps lay like dead butterflies. It was clear that she was not comfortable in this room; she hesitated before the table's height and gazed at it with a critical eye.

Valedan thought, if she had been allowed, it would now bear some decorations; not flowers, for they would by their presence indicate a delicacy and a poetry that had no place in a war room, but perhaps by stone or wooden carving, or better, the two-tiered sword stand, evocative in its emptiness. A leader's symbol.

"I am not . . . familiar . . . with the language of cartographers."

Valedan shrugged. "It is not for your ability to read what is written here that I desire your presence."

Ser Anton's jaw tightened.

"Ser Valedan," Duarte said, "none of the members of the—of your guard—are decorative. They serve a function. If another assassination is attempted—"

He lifted a hand. "I am willing to see her here in the saris more suited to her station."

What Ser Anton had been about to say was lost.

"The choice of attire is not mine," he continued. "It is entirely her own. If you take issue with it, you must speak with the Serra Alina. And let me remind you, Captain, that long before the Ospreys were assigned to me, the Serra Alina saved my life with the use of a single dagger."

The Serra Alina's brows rose a fraction; her eyes widened and then resumed their normal shape. A warning. A warning he understood. In the South, she was a Serra; he a ruling lord. In the South, should she choose to serve him, or he to suffer her service, he must not imply that her will had precedence over his.

He felt a touch of Ser Anton's frustration, although he was aware that it was for entirely different reasons. He placed both palms on the edge of the table and let them support his weight as he pretended to read the lines of a map that he had almost memorized, he saw it so often.

"Belay that," he said at last. "She serves in the capacity of a Northern adviser. There is no place in the South for the role she has been forced—at my command—to assume. Understand, Captain, that she *graces* your unit with her presence; that she serves a purpose that is only marginally less imperative than yours. There are many forms of conflict. Upon the field, or before it, there are no finer men than the men who now serve under me.

"But I have been raised in the North; I have been deprived of the harem that is mine by right. The Tyr'agnati of Callesta and Lamberto are not likewise encumbered; they speak through their wives, their sisters, their serafs.

"I will speak in such a fashion through the Serra Alina."

"They do not bring their wives to the battlefield," Ser Anton said curtly.

Valedan's smile was brief. "They have no need; they have their years of history as a guide, as guidance, in matters in which a wife—or a Serra—might be consulted."

"You take a risk," Ser Anton replied, cool now, his antagonism securing Ser Andaro's grudging support.

"Always."

The swordmaster nodded. "She must not be present when you are introduced to the kai Lamberto."

Valedan said nothing at all.

He waited; after a moment, the tent's flap lifted and the General Baredan di'Navarre entered. He paused a moment at the table, lifted his head, and stared at the Serra Alina di'Lamberto. Then he shifted his gaze, took in the expressions of the men who now stood around her, and chose to remain silent.

Ramiro di'Callesta followed. He bowed as he entered into the presence of the Tyr'agar, and when he rose, he smiled. "I have had word," he said. "The flight has arrived in Callesta."

He did not spare a glance for the Serra, and by this lack of reaction, Valedan knew that he was well-informed.

"Your presence is requested, Tyr'agar."

Valedan nodded.

The care with which the Northern Commanders were treated was not lost on them. From the moment they arrived at the city gates, they were escorted by no less a man than the captain of the Tyran: Ser Fillipo par di'Callesta. The men who accompanied him likewise wore the miniature crest of the sun rising, its rays a declaration of the oath they had collectively and individually sworn.

He met them on horseback, and did them the honor of dismounting; did them the further grace of offering them a bow that would have been reserved for the Tyr'agnate himself had he been present.

The Tyran were a heartbeat behind their leader, but when they dismounted, they offered bows that were no less perfect. As dress guards, they were exceptional.

As warriors, there were none finer.

Commander Allen, however, noted that they wore the blue of a dark midnight, the white of mourning, in a sash across their chests; their horses were likewise adorned. Someone had died; someone of import. He closed his eyes a moment. Opened them, reaching for a memory that was over a decade old.

"The Tyr'agnate of Averda waits you in the citadel," Ser Fillipo said quietly in flawless Weston.

Commander Allen nodded. As they had done, he dismounted; it was as much a signal to the Northern guards as Ser Fillipo's gesture had been to the Southern; they fol-

lowed his lead in a taut silence, their movements far less
graceful than their allies'.

"A moment," Commander Allen said.

Ser Fillipo nodded, holding the reins of his pale horse.

The man who had won the war for the Empire years ago
now walked to his saddlebags; he drew from them a sash
that was like, and unlike, the sash the Callestans wore. Devran and Ellora watched him without comment as he draped
the sash across his left shoulder and hooked it once around
his waist; it bore the crest of the crowns across a white
background; the sword and the rod on either side emblazoned in gold. The sash was edged in a thick, weighted
black.

Ser Fillipo raised a brow; the two Commanders who
were legend for their rivalry gazed a moment at each other
and then found similar sashes in their saddlebags; they
donned these.

"Your pardon, Ser Fillipo," Commander Allen said
gravely.

Ser Fillipo bowed. "No pardon is necessary," he said
softly. "I have spent time in the North, and I recognize the
colors of Imperial mourning; you honor our fallen."

The Tyran whispered among themselves until they felt
their captain's gaze; they fell silent at once.

Thus accoutred, the three Commanders entered the city
of Callesta. The streets were not empty; they were lined
with the men and the women whose lives were defined by
their service within the walls. There was curiosity upon the
faces of these witnesses to the procession, but it was not
their curiosity that drew the attention; it was the colors they
wore: Blue and white. Not so fine as the colors that graced
the Tyran, they were nonetheless a clear indication that the
city itself was in mourning.

Not an auspicious beginning, but a fitting one.

He bowed his head a moment; by war's end, there would
be three colors on the field, and off it: black, white and
blue.

He had ridden through Imperial villages similar to this at the start of the border war thirteen years past, and although the deep and somber shades of blue had been absent, black was there in abundance; black of fabric, black of hanging, black of bowed head, of bruised face, of eyes made hollow by food's lack, sleep's lack, and worse, the loss of the things which defined a full life.

He had chosen to parade the best of his troops—hand-picked among the divisions—through those towns for two reasons; the first to offer comfort to the bereaved, to offer the promise, in silence, of the Kings' Justice, and second, to make certain, to make absolutely certain, that his men understood the human face of a war that would leave many more villages in smoldering ruins before an end was called to the hostilities which defined the shape of two nations.

But more, he had done so to remind himself.

"These people," he had said, "had no choice in the battle; they cannot make decisions that affect the fate of nations, but they suffer the cost of the decisions undertaken—by us, by our Kings, by our enemies. You want justice. Good. Justice has defined the Empire of Essalieyan since the founding of Averalaan.

"But Wisdom has tempered that Justice; call upon that Wisdom when we cross the border. Call upon it when we take the villages of the Averdan valleys; call upon it when you see the old and the weak, the women, the children, and the young men who, like ours, have lost all but their desire for vengeance. *You* are the Kings' representatives here. *You* bear the burden of their name, and their honor, upon the field. The standards that you see are ours, but they embody more than the men at your side, than the fight for survival.

"Very few of the men and the women who people the villages of the Dominion are free. Very few have a choice in how they live or how they die. Remember this for as long as you can. Hold on to it.

"Understand why you are here."

He drew breath, and that breath drew him back across the

decade, confronting him with his own words, his own resolve.

We are killers, he thought, his right hand upon the pommel of his sword, his left upon the reins of his mount. *But
we are not monsters; we are not murderers. The name we
make for ourselves will be defined by our actions here. Let
us carry that name with pride.*

Devran stood to his left, gazing upon the whole of the
city of Callesta, inscrutable and silent.

Ellora walked to his right, her hand upon the reins of her
mount; she did not seek the solace of a weapon. Not for her
the prettified speeches; not for her the tame instruction. She
paused, shortening the grip on her horse.

A second later, a child appeared between the ranks of the
gathered Callestans, his eyes too large for his face, his
cheeks widened by a smile that had clearly been indulged.
He slipped past the hands that reached for his chubby arms,
his fat, round shoulders, and ran toward the legs and limbs
of the passing soldiery.

Ellora caught him, with the hand that every other man
present now gripped their weapon, kneeling to bring her
face closer to his. Her hair was pale, her skin pale, her eyes
light; she wore armor and crest and the scars of previous
battles with equal grace. There was no braid at her back, no
adornments in her hair, no silks, no cotton saris; she wore
white, black, and the colors of the House she ruled.

But she laughed, and her voice was clearly no man's
voice; it was loud, it was foreign.

The child's brows rose.

In accented Torra, she said, "Well, you're a brave boy,
aren't you?"

He hesitated for just a moment, and then, having made
his decision, smiled. "Brave," he said, nodding. "Brave
boy."

"Kalakar." Devran's voice was as cold as any weather
Averda ever saw.

She ignored him.

Yes, it started; it started now, in this place, this foreign city. The Callestan Tyran continued to walk for another ten yards before they realized that the gap between them and the Northerners had widened; they stopped, turning, their beasts turning with them in idle curiosity.

Ser Fillipo, at the head of these men, was not immediately visible, but the Tyran themselves hesitated. They wore helms, but their visors were raised, and their expressions were clear; they were surprised.

Worried.

So, too, was the child's grandfather. The child's grandmother. His mother and father, if they were there, did not break the stretch of the white-and-blue line that was both barrier and honor guard.

The elderly woman fell at once to her knees in the open street; she was so close to the hooves of the horse that had it been moving briskly, she might have risked being trampled. Her forehead struck the dirt, remaining there as if fastened.

Her husband—Commander Allen assumed it must be the husband—likewise abased himself, but he did so at the feet of The Kalakar, and his lined, dark hands, instead of residing in the hidden fold of his lap, now reached for the child she held.

"Brave boy you have," Ellora told the man, her voice a Decarus' voice, loud and booming.

The man's face rose, his eyes wide; Commander Allen could almost see the reflection of this Northern aberration, this monstrous woman, in them. She lifted the child, releasing her horse to do so.

"Horse," the boy said.

"My horse."

"My horse."

Without hesitation, she placed him high upon the saddle, speaking in Weston to the horse that bore her upon the field. To the horse, she spoke calmly and softly, her voice more feminine that it would be anywhere else. She was rewarded by the child's hesitant smile, and after a moment, the pounding kick of his small, bare feet. The horse would not feel it; the child's weight was too slight.

She let him sit astride the stallion's back for five minutes, and then she lifted him again. He reached for the pommel of the saddle, but Ellora was far faster; she disentangled his fingers, smiled, and whispered something that evaded Allen's hearing.

Then she set him down.

His grandfather hesitated for a fraction of a second, watching this woman, the fear in his face almost wrenching.

Ellora looked down upon him. "You have a brave boy," she said again, and again her voice could be heard for a mile on this windless day; a mile in any direction.

"And he," she added, "brave kin. This is not the last time he will sit upon horseback."

Bending, then, she caught the old man's outstretched hands and lifted him. When he had gained his feet, she helped his wife to rise.

"Your future," she said, struggling for the words. "Your future, here." All of the Torra she was familiar with was military in nature, but she had no fear of sounding the fool.

Ser Fillipo par di'Callesta had come, horseless, through the ranks of his Tyran; he stood not twenty feet away, his hands behind his back, his expression completely unreadable.

The old man bent down, grabbed his grandchild, waiting until his wife had extricated her hand from the pale, foreign hand of this Northern woman. And then he turned to look at the par Callesta, his face almost as pale as Ellora's, and with a good deal more cause.

But Ser Fillipo par di'Callesta merely nodded, his expression slowly easing into a smile that was, if slight, completely genuine.

"Well met, Decasto," he said. "Your grandson is brave indeed to risk being surrounded by three such men—and women—as these; they are the Northern birds of prey. Be grateful that they have not yet begun their ascent; be grateful that they have chosen prey that is wiser and more canny than he."

The old man swallowed. "Par di'Callesta," he said, his voice breaking with both age and emotion. The child squirmed; the old man's grip was tight.

"Aye, I have returned; I have come from the Northern Empire, the Northern Isle. And I have discovered, in my sojourn there, that there is no truth behind the tales of Northern women who devour their children whole."

The Tyran at the par di'Callesta's back now smiled as well, broadly, and with some affection.

"But don't give the boy a sword just yet; he is likely to use it where it is unwise." He nodded genially, and turned to face The Kalakar.

"Decasto wishes to apologize for the intrusion of his kin. If you take no offense, Commander, I will dismiss them without censure."

She laughed, speaking now in the comfortable confines of Weston. "The Kalakar wishes to beg your forgiveness for this indulgence. In armor and mounted, it is seldom that I see children; if the children themselves are not too timid to keep their distance, the parents are."

And then her smile changed, subtle now, her eyes narrowing slightly. "We all need reminders of why it is that we do what we do, par Callesta. We all require something for which to fight; tell your man—Decasto?—that although the women of the North wear armor and wield swords, we understand, better than any, where the future of a nation lies. Tell him," she added, easing the command out of words that were not quite request, "that he has given me such a reminder this day."

She turned to the old man, and Commander Allen winced as he braced himself for more of her clumsy Annagarian. "We fight," she said—and those two words came easily— "and die," these two as well, "for our young."

The old man hesitated.

Commander Allen thought he knew where the boy had acquired his boldness, for the woman was white as the buildings that lined the road. "You have children, S–Serra?"

"Of my own?" She let a shadow cross her face; there was theater in the expression, although the regret itself was genuine. Thus did Ellora use vulnerability as bridge. "No. I was never so blessed.

"But for that reason, I understand that children *are* a blessing, and I swear to you that, as we can, we will spare your son—all of your sons, and all of your daughters— from the swords and the fires of any who would challenge the right of Callestan rule in Averda."

She reached out and touched the boy's cheeks.

"Horse?" he said, reaching for her. His grandfather caught hands that seemed to have multiplied in their frenzied grab, stilling them.

"When you are older," she told him. She turned to Commander Allen and bowed briskly. "Commander. My apologies for detaining the men."

Commander Allen raised a brow, "Your Torra is greatly improved."

"Thank you, Bruce."

"Greatly improved in the course of five minutes."

She laughed. Caught the reins of her steady beast, her right hand swinging freely by her side as she began to walk, once again, toward the building upon the height of the gentle slope.

Behind her, behind the body of the Northern guards, the Northern soldiery, the denizens of the city of Callesta were already moving from a whisper to an excited blur of language so intense that Commander Allen quickly lost the single words to the stream.

Devran of the House Berriliya rolled his eyes. He did not argue with her; not here, and not in the open, with so many Southerners as witness; the Imperial Flight had always presented a unified front. But the spark of an argument, old as the current Imperial border, had kindled in earnest.

*   *   *

Ser Fillipo par di'Callesta had spent more than a decade as a "guest" in the Arannan Halls in *Avantari*, the palace of Kings. But he had seldom come in contact with The Kalakar. He regretted it now.

For he could clearly hear the words that passed beyond them in a widening circle, and he knew that within two days, the entire city would be speaking of the pale-haired, scarred, Northern woman, a woman considered by the South to be an abomination in every possible way; knew that the word abomination, the word monster, was already softening and changing as it passed from mouth to ear, mouth to ear.

How monstrous could a woman be, who could show such affection to the child of strangers? How abominable could she be, when she had sworn to use her sword, her army, in defense of their children?

Even he was not immune to the effect of an interruption that would have been unthinkable, inconceivable, had the procession been composed solely of men.

He had wondered why Ramiro had seen fit to deprive himself of all but a handful of the Tyran in order to form such an escort; had wondered—albeit briefly—if he considered the flight so much of a threat. He saw clearly now. A man was defined by his ability upon the field of battle, but in the High Courts, such a field could exist in any place that two men of power stood.

They had met, here, for the first time, and without raising a sword, the woman known as the Kestrel had made her mark.

Had she traveled with lesser men, had she been given to the escort of simple cerdan, she would by that action have become the authority; by placing the Captain of the Tyran in the position of authority over their guests, no matter how subtle that authority was, Ramiro made her gesture subordinate to Callesta.

Women were canny. Ser Fillipo had learned this early in life, and he had never forgotten it, but he had somehow expected less of this woman who had chosen sword over harem's heart; the life of a soldier over the life of a wife. Clearly, Ramiro had labored under no such misconception.

He thought, with some regret, of his own wife; she had remained in *Avantari*, in the halls of the hostages, with the children. She had not asked to accompany him, and he had deemed it wise to leave them there in safety. He missed her.

But of the Callestan wives, she was the dove. He had chosen her because she least reminded him of his mother; she was unlike his brother's wife, for she had none of the Serra Amara's cutting grace, her ready wit, her piercing gaze; she had none of the wisdom, the understanding of the ways of the powerful. She was his oasis; she was the place that he retreated to when he required peace.

And there was to be no peace here.

In truth, Ser Fillipo had not been unhappy in the court of the Twin Kings. He had not, from the moment he was first ushered into their presence, feared them as demons; he had not feared for his safety at any time in Averalaan save the last one, when the hostages faced a certain death.

When a boy he had never considered a man had made a choice, taken a stand, and saved them all.

He wondered if Ramiro understood the depth of the debt owed to the kai Leonne by the Captain of the Callestan Tyran; he could not imagine that his brother, who saw clearly in all else, did not see clearly in this.

Was I tainted by my time in the North, brother? Was I softened by it? He reached down to touch the hilt of his sword.

How soft could the North be, when it could produce women of the caliber of The Kalakar? He smiled again, let his hand fall from his side. He had no fear of the Northerners; he could hear his mother's honeyed edge as she berated him for his foolishness, his naïveté. Yes, he missed his wife.

But this, this was Callesta, his home.

And this stranger had made herself at home here, with the careful choice of a few strategically broken words.

The Serra Amara en'Callesta had been busy.

Her serafs, the finest in Averda, worked with the diligence and the faithfulness of an army, transforming the whole of the Callestan citadel into a thing of sparse beauty. In the gardens, they tended the flowers and trees that best showed the beauty of the season; the season itself cooperated. She had chosen the colors; the blues and the whites of the flower beds a conscious gift to the memory of her son, the first of the fallen.

But into the blues and the whites crept gold and red, and the leaves of the trees themselves were emerald, jade, and ivory; life defied death, even here. Grass, the most deceptive of all plant life, had been shorn to its essential soft roots, and the serafs watered it and cut it as if it were the mane of the Tyr'agnate's finest stallion.

They were content to do so; it was the first thing that the Serra Amara had demanded of them since she had come to gaze upon the body of the kai Callesta. If her orders were at times contradictory, they were nonetheless recognizably the words of a woman who had once again chosen to enter the world.

The city came to life, waking slowly into this new and unimagined world: The Northern Commanders had come to pay their respects to the Tyr'agnate of Callesta, in the heart of the lands Callestans had held for over two centuries. And even if they were barbarians, even if the grace and the subtlety of her artistry were to be lost upon them, it would be there; the lack would come from them, and not from the family of the Tyr'agnate.

The serafs knew when the Commanders first entered the city. They knew when they were within a mile of the palace gates. Word was sent from one seraf to the other, traveling by wing, by wind, by foot, and it passed at last into the

keeping of the Serra Amara en'Callesta, in the harem's
heart.

Her wives tended her hair, helped to place in it combs of
gold and jade; they tended her face, her hands, her feet, and
also helped drape the finest of silks across her body. They
did not speak to reassure her; they knew her well. But they
offered her reassurance nonetheless, and perhaps some
envy.

She had long desired a chance to meet with these men,
this woman; it had been a fond and foolish desire, one that
she had never thought to realize.

These men, this woman, had bested the Tyr'agar. They
had won a war which, had they desired it, could have continued for decades, destroying the Terreans of Averda and
Mancorvo. But instead, for the price of land across the
Northern passes, they had chosen to withdraw their armies,
content with the simple cessation of hostility.

She had sat, with her husband, examining the costs of the
war to both sides, and it was her husband's guess that the
Empire could afford to continue their battle with an ease
that would have eluded the Terrean in less than two years.

If the Lambertans were too foolish to realize this, that
was their concern; she was Callestan. She understood.

And she was a child of the Dominion; to the victors respect accrued, and it was a respect she felt without rancor
or fear. The Lord had watched. The Lord had judged.

"Serra Amara," Navello kep'Callesta said, from behind
the opaque screen doors that hid the harem from the outer
world. "They will be upon the plateau in the quarter hour."

She rose at once, and her wives fell away in a quiet circle.

Maria smiled. "You look perfect, Na'amara."

Eliana en'Callesta, the youngest and the most beautiful
of her wives, merely smiled at Maria. "She *is* perfect."

"Enough, enough from all of you," Amara said, with
mock severity. "I am needed now. But I promise that I will

remember each word and each Northern gesture, and I will return to the harem this eve to share what I have learned."

Maria's laughter was high and soft, musical in her joy. She did not clap her hands; she was of an age where such affectation would seem strange. But the gesture was present in her stillness, in the accentuated lines at the corner of eyes that had once been the envy of every woman present. "Will she be there, Na'amara?"

"The Northern General?"

Eliana nodded.

"Yes. She is upon the road as we speak."

"Will she look like a man?"

"In any way that is significant, she *is* a man. Think of her that way, and she will not be so hard to understand."

Eliana nodded. She hesitated for only a moment, and then threw her arms carefully around the Serra's shoulders.

Amara returned the embrace, and stood a moment, her forehead touching the forehead of a woman who was closer to her than her own daughters had ever been. "I will be safe," she said quietly.

"It is not for your safety that I fear," Eliana replied, her voice a whisper. She caught Amara's hands tightly in her own.

Maria lifted the veil. "Will you wear it?"

Amara's smile dimmed. She gazed at it, white gauze edged in the darkest of blue, and glittering with crystal, with pearl, with bead.

They watched her in silence. As so often was the case, the difficult questions were left to Maria.

Would she? She wore blue now, blue and white in all its variations. She had worn nothing but these colors since she had gazed upon the face of death, of her first real loss.

"Yes," she replied.

The sparkle left the eyes of her oldest wife; left the step of her youngest.

"I have been unkind," she said softly, as she reached for

the length of the veil. "To you, of all people, who deserve so much more."

"You have been no such thing," Maria said, valiant now, her smile once again creasing the lines of her face.

"No?"

"Na'mari," Eliana said quietly, "let her speak the truth. She *has* been unkind."

Maria looked scandalized.

Sara looked away; she had been silent the whole of the afternoon.

"Na'sara?"

"Eliana is right," Sara said, gazing at the floor. "You have been so distant, Amara. You have gone so far away we have been worried that you might never return." She lifted her face. Slender, aquiline, that face was striking in its composition; she was not classically beautiful, had never been that. But the beauty that she did possess would never age or weather. "He was your son, but he was our son as well, all save Eliana, who might have been his sister if you had ever left them alone for more than a minute."

Eliana blushed.

"He has suffered enough," she continued.

"Who?"

"Our husband."

"Na'sara," Maria snapped. "Enough."

"No, not enough. It needs to be said."

"It does not need to be said at this moment."

"But it does." Sara turned to Amara, who stood rigid in the center of the room.

Amara said, cool now, her hands trembling beneath the veil, "I have not forbidden you our husband."

"No. You have not. But who among us has ever been able to offer him comfort? We offer him pleasure, or amusement; we offer him indulgence. He has never needed anything else, and for your sake, for love of you, we have been honored to give what little he will accept.

"But he *needs* you. You are his Serra. And Amara?"

"Na'sara?"

"You need him."

"Sara," Maria said, an edge in her voice. "Enough."

"And Alfredo needs both of you. Do not make him choose; he is angry enough, and he is at an age where his anger is a danger to him. All of our sons are with him," she added softly. "All of our sons have faced the loss of their brother. Amara, please."

Amara looked at the veil in her hands.

Sara, at last, fell silent.

"Na'sara."

She raised her head, and the defiance in her features crumbled completely.

"Take this," Amara said gently. She held out the veil.

The Serra Amara had chosen the venue at which dinner was to be served. She had opened the wall through which the moon's light could be clearly seen among the rushes and the lilies in the large pond at the garden's heart. The sun shed light and color as it fell; she had chosen the hour as well, and the serafs had busied themselves with the glass globes in which light lay trapped.

It was fire's light; although the garden itself was home to the magical artifice of a light that did not fade, dim, or flicker, it was not to her liking; such a light was costly in its fashion, a symbol of the power of unnatural men. As a child, she had loved it; as a woman, she abjured it. Everything had a beginning and an ending.

Ser Ramiro di'Callesta saw this clearly as he approached the gardens at the side of the kai Leonne. Valedan's return to the city had taken longer than either man had intended, and they carried the reason for that tardiness behind the silence of closed lips.

Word had come.

He would deliver it when the Commanders joined them. Baredan di'Navarre had excused himself from the recep-

tion with obvious reluctance. "Offer my regrets," he said,
bowing deeply, "to your lovely Serra."

"I fear that any regret I offer will be met with less welcome than you hope," the Tyr'agnate replied, with an open
grimace, a gesture of the confidence he felt in the third of
the dead Tyr's Generals.

It had come as a surprise to the General, who raised a
brow in askance.

Ramiro's smile was thin. "She has lost her son," he said
quietly.

Baredan's grimace was reward enough. "Aye," he said.
"She is a woman who feels strongly all that she chooses to
feel. But I envy you, kai Callesta. She will survive this; she
will grow stronger."

"Tell her that," Ramiro replied, "and she will either love
you as kin or revile you for your lack of feeling. Or both."

The General laughed openly. "I have met at least one of
your wives," he said, as the laughter receded, "and if the
Serra chose that wife, she cannot be harsh. Is she not called
the Gentle?"

"Indeed, she is."

"Then you are blessed, kai Callesta."

"Blessed?"

"A real man has, from his wife, all facets, all truth; the
best, and the worst, that she has to offer beneath the open
sky. Had you been less of a man, she would be less of a
woman; her grief would remain trapped behind the walls of
her face, her anger hidden in the artifice of grace and seeming."

Ramiro's smile was genuine; he was pleased. "See to
your men," he said softly. "Take word; we will join you as
soon as we may safely take our leave."

"And the Northern armies?"

"I fear they will join you as well." He gazed at the gardens, his shoulders lifting. In a scant few days, his wife had
accomplished much. He turned to the General and offered
him a deep bow.

Valedan nodded, his expression intense. He was young; the word of war had disturbed him, and he did not trouble himself to hide his concern. The gardens would be lost upon him; a pity.

Baredan left them.

Ser Miko met them as they approached the gates.

"The Commanders?"

"They arrived safely." His bow was deep and perfect. "Ser Anton and Ser Andaro have been summoned."

"Captain Duarte?"

"He waits within," the Tyran replied. "With the Serra Amara." He paused. "And the Serra Alina di'Lamberto."

"Ah. Good. Kai Leonne?"

Valedan nodded again. His gaze passed between the trees whose branches had been so expertly pruned, passed over the flower beds that had been rearranged, the grass that had been cut back, the stones that had been moved into such a pleasing and peaceful array.

When his eyes found what he sought, he relaxed; the Ospreys were present.

You trust them, he thought, surprised. Ramiro had taken their measure in the Northern capital, and having done so, he viewed them as a necessity, no more. They owed loyalty to each other; they swore no oaths to Leonne.

The North has left its mark on you, kai Leonne. Hide it well. But he said nothing. His Tyran were present.

The doors opened before them. Serafs cast shadows in the sun's light, long and thin. Ramiro removed his boots, exchanging them for the simplicity of bare feet. Valedan, without hesitation, did the same. He walked with unconscious grace, adjusting the weight of his step until it fell in near silence, his stride matching his host's. They were almost of a height, but Valedan had not yet attained his full growth.

Tyr'agar Markaso kai di'Leonne had passed through the city of Callesta during the disaster of a war that had left its mark upon the two Northern Terreans. He had walked this hall, in a regal silence, surveying all that lay within it as if it already belonged to him.

He had offered the graces of the High Court, had bowed low before the Serra Amara, had taken refuge in her gardens and her hall; he had spoken, discreetly, with her wives, assessing them, judging the man who owned them by their appearance. He had smiled at the young kai Callesta, the oldest of Ramiro's many sons.

"What will you do with the rest?" he had asked, speaking carelessly, casually, about the sons of Ramiro's concubines.

Ramiro could see, over the distance of years, the sudden stillness in his Serra's face.

The question had not been addressed to her directly; no man of the Tyr'agar's station would have lowered himself to do so. But it had been said in her hearing, and she, servile in posture, but stiff as sword, had waited upon her husband's words.

As his wives had waited—the wives who had born him those sons.

"They all bear the blood of Callesta," he had said, cool to the question.

"The blood, yes. But only one among them has the right to bear the sword. What of the others?"

"They will all bear swords," he replied, "in the service of Callesta. They will be brothers, oathbound and trusted, to the kai they will serve."

The Tyr'agar had raised a dark brow. "I see," he said softly. "Is that wise?"

"My Tyran all bear the blood of Callesta; all save a handful who have proved themselves in other ways. Judge them, kai Leonne, if it pleases you."

The Tyr'agar had shrugged and passed on, but Ramiro had lingered a moment to meet the eyes of his wife. His wives.

There was a bitter pleasure afforded him in the method of the Tyr'agar's demise, although he had never given it voice.

He looked now at the son, the one remaining son of his Serra.

He could not imagine that Valedan would ask so cruel a question. Could not imagine that it would bear asking. He was young.

And he, already as tall as the father, was infinitely more gifted. He had shown this to the Serra; had shown it to the Tyran who always graced the Tyr'agnate's presence. Had shown it in the arena of the Demon Kings, when he had forced, from the lips of Ser Anton's finest student, an acknowledgment of the truth of his title.

Ser Anton served him. Ser Andaro served him. Were it not for Valedan, a death would decide the silent war between those two. Yet they worked together, for Valedan's sake, and if Ramiro was any judge, it was a harsh alliance.

Markaso kai di'Leonne had not been a man who knew mercy. Ramiro himself was not noted for that singular grace; it was considered a weakness among the men of the Dominion.

And Valedan kai di'Leonne chose to uphold it, again and again, as a strength.

Almost impossible to believe that the father and the son were of the same blood.

And that was the heart of the matter. It was almost impossible. There would be one test of its truth, and only one, and if Valedan, in ignorance, failed that test, the war was over. Callesta and Lamberto would be thrown to the Southern Tyr, Alesso di'Marente.

All of life was a gamble. All gambles presented the possibility of loss. He accepted it with equanimity.

"Tyr'agnate?"

He looked up. Smiled slightly, as if at an older son. His own, dead now, a ghost in these halls. "My pardon, Tyr'agar. I remember the last time a kai Leonne . . . graced these halls."

Valedan's face was as serious as youth can be. "You did not admire my father."

He trusted this boy. "No."

Valedan nodded. "Did anyone?"

It was not the question Ramiro expected. He laughed. The serafs who lined the hall unobtrusively jumped at once to nervous attention.

"You do not remember him well, if you can ask that question. He would have been respected had he won his ill-advised war. Had he chosen to heed his Generals, there was some chance that the war itself would have ended in a way that would have saved face, and land." He bowed. "I mean no insult to your line."

"Such as it is," the boy Tyr said, with a grave smile. "I take no offense. I have asked for your opinion because I desire it; if I desired pretty, empty words, I would ask elsewhere."

"Have a care, kai Leonne."

"Do I offend?"

"No. But you take too much on faith; you trust too easily. It is a Northern habit, and one that you would do well without."

"Will you war against me?"

"Who can say? I cannot conceive of the circumstances in which such a war might be necessary, but fate and circumstance are seldom clear in the light of the sun."

The fading sun.

He picked up his pace; Valedan followed, his steps perfect, a complement to the Tyr'agnate's. At his side, the scabbard of the kai's sword swung; they had shared blood, he and this boy. They had bound their fates together. "We will have apologies to make for our appearance," he added, as the sliding doors of the hall approached.

Valedan frowned.

"We wear the regalia of war, and even if that regalia is clean and prettified, even if it is suitable for public appearance, it is not . . . always suited . . . to the table of a Serra."

Valedan nodded, understanding then. It was a reminder

of death, of a son's death. "Will she forgive us if we are late?"

"She will forgive nothing, if it suits her," her husband replied. "And we have matters to attend to that require just such dress." He paused at the edge of the doors, and serafs bowed, head to ground, in total subservience. He nodded, and they slid the doors wide.

Ramiro preceded Valedan into the hall.

He took in the table, low and Southern; it had been many months since he had sat in such a fashion. Cushions were placed upon the floor in a cascade of colors meant to soothe—and catch—the weary eye; the table was sparsely decorated with flowers.

Each of them, lily and ivory spray, were white, their petals opened to suggest life, the height of the bloom. Black lacquered bowls with gold edges lay evenly spaced across the table above flat mats of similar shade; Amara had chosen well.

As always.

He looked up; the room was empty.

"It appears we are not so late as all that," he said quietly. "We are the first to arrive."

"Not so, my husband," the Serra Amara said.

From the recessed hanging in the West wall, she entered the room, drawn by the sound of his voice, by the fall of his steps.

She was tall for a woman, and tonight she had chosen to accept that height, to accentuate it. She wore silks, deep, deep blues, gold falling among its folds like an afterthought, a subtle adornment. Around her wrists she wore white ivory, and in her hair, ivory and gold; she had chosen the colors of mourning, even here, where guests of import were expected.

But she wore no veil, nothing to hide the lines of her face from the world. Her expression was remote, serene; she was the hostess, the Serra of the hall.

She was his wife.

How much did he trust the kai Leonne? He paused, held in place by the sight of her exposed cheeks, her dark eyes, her dark hair that only now showed the traces of age through its length.

How much did he care?

He walked across the hall, leaving this most honored of guests in his wake; nor did he fail to notice that Valedan's step had fallen completely silent.

He reached her, and stopped a full ten feet from her straight shoulders, the chin she turned slightly up to meet his eyes.

"Na'amara," he whispered,

She hesitated; he could see that indecision play with the lines of her expression, transforming it.

As if this were the heart of the harem, the Tyr'agnate of Callesta bowed. He did not fall to his knees, although had he been certain of privacy, he would have.

As it was, he risked much; he closed the distance between them and reached out to take her hands, his own falling from the hilt of his sword for the first time since word of the Southern armies had arrived in the encampment.

She took his hands.

Hers were shaking.

"I have always wanted to meet the Northern Commanders," she said, serene now, the woman that he had claimed years ago. "And I thank you for the grace of the opportunity."

"Amara."

"Ramiro," she said, gentle now, "your guest is waiting. Would you keep him?"

"I would keep him waiting for the rest of the evening, if you allowed it."

"And let my preparations go to waste? And lose the single opportunity a woman of my station will ever have to meet the men and women who will decide the fate—and the boundaries—of my Terrean?"

But she smiled, wearily, tiredly, letting him see, letting him finally see, what lay beneath anger, loss, accusation.

The future. His life.

Holding her hands as if they were anchors, he bowed to her, bowed fully. Exposed all to the man whose respect and whose fear would define his later life, if the war was won.

She understood what he offered her, then.

Her eyes widened, and then they shifted; he thought she might cry.

But she was his Serra, the pride of his harem, the partner he had chosen to hide in the secrecy of his private life. She shed no tears.

"Tyr'agar," she said softly, "I bid you welcome to my humble hall."

Valedan kai di'Leonne bowed low. "There is not a hall so humble that it would not be graced by your presence or the presence of your husband. You honor me, Serra Amara, and in the future, I will repay that honor in kind."

When the serafs came to the rooms set aside for the use of the Northern Commanders, Ellora was ready. Of course, she'd been ready for about an hour, and had taken to pacing the perfect surface of flat wood with the heavy tread of dress boots. Unlike the serafs, many of whom were women, she had brought no dresses, no skirts, no hint of feminine clothing upon her travels; she had dress jacket, dress pants, dress shirt—the standard kit for an officer of importance in the Kings' army.

She had been offered—with no hesitation whatsoever— the aid of the serafs who seemed to haunt this place like quiet ghosts, and had refused that offer, with just as much hesitance. She was certain she saw some relief in the faces of these serafs, although it was hard to tell; culture tended to throw up a hundred subtle walls to understanding.

Her rooms were adjacent to The Berriliya's and Commander Allen's, but there were no doors adjoining them; no easy way to gain access to the two sides of their triad. She understood that this was because of the odd conservatism that informed the whole of Southern attitudes toward their women, but she found it cumbersome and annoying nonetheless. Upon the battlefield, such nonsense had no place, and here, in the citadel of Callesta, the battlefield was foremost in her thoughts.

A knock at the door alerted her to the presence of Verrus Korama. She swept out of the sliding doors before they were fully open, and narrowly avoided tripping over the flat of a perfectly exposed back in her haste.

Korama winced. "Kalakar," he said, bowing studiously. He had always been a graceful man, but that grace was in evidence in this place in a way that it was not in her own.

"The others?"

"Are waiting."

"Good. I'm starving."

He laughed. "You're always starving."

"A fact, clearly, that spies have neglected to feed to our hosts."

"You are not of a rank where hunger has ever been a threat," he replied, with just a hint of reproof in his perfect words. He did not offer her his arm; he waited until the seraf upon the ground felt it safe to rise.

They followed the girl's silent movements; she was to lead them to the dining hall.

"Is the Tyr'agar present?"

She nodded, abjuring speech. Ellora suspected this was due to the fact that she could speak no Weston at all; she could answer the question because she recognized the mangled pronunciation of Valedan's title. It was a significant title in the Dominion.

Be honest, Ellora; it was a significant title in the North as well; for a lesser title, fifty thousand men would not have weathered sea and storm and the hazards of encampments in a land that was not designed around the movement of a large body of men.

Perhaps that was unfair.

The Commanders had gone to some lengths to hide the details of the logistics behind the movement of their armies; they had no reason to suspect that Ramiro di'Callesta was not equally canny, equally reluctant to expose information when it was not critical to do so.

The halls were not as tall as the halls of The Ten; they were poor indeed in comparison to the stone grandeur of *Avantari*. In the Tor Leonne, stone was in fashion; in the Northern Terrean, wood was the building material of choice. The floors, the walls, the multiple doors with their opaque screens, were all of perfectly oiled wood, and the ceilings, much lower than those to which Ellora had unconsciously become accustomed, were as dark, their beams unmarred and unknotted. There were no obvious hangings, no grand mirrors, no great glass windows; in their place, a flower, a vessel, a stand that contained water bowls or great brass bells, inverted upon cushions.

But here and there, doors had been rolled back upon their grooved resting places; the night, in its falling splendor, had been exposed for the eye to see. The lack of windows brought the sound of nature into the halls with a keen immediacy lacking in the Northern structures of Ellora's home, and she paused a moment, reflectively, as she gazed out upon the spare vista of the Callestan gardens; their simple standing stones, the movement of slow fountains, the hidden pathways that led into the night.

The seraf waited every time she paused, as if attuned to her movement and her mood.

Not even Ellora's servants were as skilled as this. She found her ability to accept and admire such a trait disturbing, and forced herself to concentrate on the simple task of walking without pause to their destination.

When they reached the last set of doors, she noted that words had been carved in the wood above them; they were Torra, but old Torra; the ability to glean meaning from their spare strokes was beyond her.

Korama, however, was not saddled by such ignorance. He stopped at the doors, and knelt, bowing before them.

The seraf smiled for the first time, and spoke softly to The Kalakar's adjutant.

His reply, grave and sober, passed just beneath the range of Ellora's hearing, a sign of her advancing years. She didn't need to hear them to understand that he had offered a gesture of respect that was at home in the Dominion. She waited a moment, and then bent stiff knees, mimicking his stance, his sobriety.

It did not particularly suit her, but nothing about this country did.

She rose when he rose, and found that the doors had silently opened before them, revealing the subservience of their posture.

She looked up, gaining her feet with markedly less grace than her adjutant.

Seated about a low, flat Southern table, were men whom she recognized and a woman she did not.

It was the woman that held her attention, for her eyes were keen and sharp, and they seemed to be fixed upon Ellora with an intensity that belied simple curiosity.

Women had no power in their own right in the Dominion. Any schooling at all in the affairs of the South made that clear as the cathedral's dolorous bells. But power was subtle, in any country—in any House—and she knew that in the case of this woman, power was present.

Having gained her feet, she let her gaze wander.

Ramiro di'Callesta was seated to the right of the Serra, which would make her his wife.

To the left, a young man with a grim expression that almost robbed his face of its likeness to the woman. Son, she thought, and about as interested in an awkward dinner engagement as any Northern patris would be. No, there was more to his expression than sullen boredom; there was a very real resentment there.

She filed it away, but she did not forget it.

To the left of this boy was Valedan, the kai Leonne, the man for whom the course of the war had been planned. He nodded gravely when their eyes met, but he did not speak.

And to Valedan's left, knees obscured by the flat of an exquisitely spare table, Duarte AKalakar. She lifted her hand, ran three fingers through the pale strands of her hair.

He placed two fingers flat upon the table's surface. But she noticed the hesitation, subtle and short, before he made that gesture. That stung, but she was old enough not to be surprised that it did.

Ser Anton di'Guivera was seated to the left of Duarte AKalakar; to his left, Fillipo par di'Callesta. Baredan di'-Navarre was not present. Perhaps he had not yet arrived.

As she entered the room, she heard the sound of heavy feet at her back; they seemed unnaturally loud, even clumsy, in the stillness of this place, but she recognized them: Devran and Bruce had also arrived.

Devran had chosen to bring his adjutant. Bruce had, characteristically, come alone.

Ramiro waited until Commander Allen had entered the room, and then he unfolded, gaining his feet preternaturally quickly. Ellora saw the hilt of his sword against the mats upon which the table rested. Wondered if he always dined with sword close to hand, or if he did so in honor of his guests.

The Northern Commanders had chosen to forgo the company of their obvious weapons; in the Kings' Hall, when The Ten gathered to dine, weapons were by custom forbidden. Not so, it seemed, in the stretch of this spare room.

Ellora took the seat beside the par Callesta; she smiled as he nodded, finding her knees uncomfortable beneath the rest of her weight. She was not a small woman, but she took care not to slouch. Bruce took the seat to her left, placing himself—as he so often did—between herself and Devran. As if the Southerners were not the ones who threatened the meal's peace.

"Please," the Serra Amara said, speaking only after her

husband had resumed his seat, "forgive me for the state you find our city in."

"If you feel a need to apologize for the state of *this* city," Ellora replied, "I live in terror of the day you choose to grace ours with your presence." She smiled as she spoke, her Torra heavy with Northern accent, Northern liberty.

The Serra Amara inclined her head gracefully; Ellora suspected that she did little that was not graceful. But her eyes were sharp and clear, and her expression did nothing to dull the edge of intelligence that glinted there.

"You wear black and white," the Serra said, after a pause filled by the movement of the silent serafs who would bring dinner, course by course, in pretty lacquered boxes, trays, dishes.

"We do." It was Ellora, again, who replied. "They are the colors of mourning in the Empire."

"You suffered a loss upon the road?"

This was a test. Ellora had always been a quick study, although she abhorred unannounced tests. "The roads in the Terrean have been well guarded," she said, careful now, her attention split between the box before her and the woman across the table.

She hadn't lied to Korama; she *was* hungry.

But she hadn't risen to the rank of The Kalakar without learning a little patience.

"We suffered a loss." She raised her face fully, then, and met the woman's unblinking stare. "Yours."

She saw, out of the corner of her eye, the movement of Duarte's fingers against the tabletop. But she did not give his silent words her full attention; the Serra commanded that.

She had wanted to meet this wife of Callesta.

"Are we not allies?"

CHAPTER ELEVEN

FOR a moment, the Serra Amara regretted the lack of her veil; it was her shield, her wall, her defense. The moment passed. She met the pale eyes of this woman in men's clothing, with her forward stare, her blunt way of speaking. Her features lacked any delicacy. In the South, she would have been a monstrosity—or a seraf whose only worth was measured in toil in the fields.

But she was more than that, much more.

Do you speak of my loss?

Yes. Clearly, yes. "It is not my place to choose the allies of my clan," she said softly. But she did not look to her husband; she found herself fascinated by the scarred geography of this woman's face, and she had no desire to miss the nuance of expression across it. Ramiro would forgive her this lapse; there were none to witness it save the most trusted of his kin and the Northerners themselves.

"I ask your pardon, Serra," the barbarian woman said, bowing, if such an awkward slouch could be called a bow. "I am of the North; our customs differ."

"They differ, yes. But in the North, warriors are still valued, are they not?"

"They are not so highly prized."

"What is prized then, in your Northern City?"

"Food," the foreign Commander replied, with a smile that was far too wide. "And wine. Song. Art, artistry, the molding of words into phrases that invoke images of beauty. Magery, healing, drama. The Makers. The Kings."

"In the South, these things are of value, but they are not separate from the way of the warrior."

"In the North, I fear, the soldier's life is less poetic, more mundane. Only a few, a very few, make an art of such a task."

The Serra Amara could see that the eyes of the Commander who sat between the woman and the silent man were unblinking, intent, as he watched the side of this stranger's face.

Commander Ellora AKalakar spoke slowly, her accent poor, her words deliberate; she chose them with care. With more care the Serra suddenly realized, than she would have swung sword in the middle of a combat that would end in death. There was only one way to measure failure in such a combat.

But this, this life and this death, were subtle, slow, strange. *I have misjudged you,* Amara thought, watching. Listening. *You are not so bold or foolish as you would like to appear.*

"Is not your Kings' Challenge the pinnacle of achievement among your young men?"

The woman who was called The Kalakar almost answered. But although the words hovered on the edge of her lips, they did not emerge. She looked across the table, to the kai Leonne. Instinct.

"The Tyr'agar has participated in the Kings' Challenge; I confess that I have not. I could not answer your question as truthfully as he."

Again, Serra Amara knew a moment of surprise. Deft, she thought; deftly done. She had extended herself too far, and the Commander had taken advantage of the question, parrying it, turning it in a direction that could prove awkward.

"Ser Anton di'Guivera, honored guest, has done so twice," she countered. "And perhaps it is to he that the question should have been posed. Forgive me, Commander."

"Ser Anton is entirely of the South," the Commander replied. "And his view on the Challenge is entirely Southern. It would have to be; he is the only man to have won the crown two years in a row.

"No, it is the Tyr'agar whose view on the matter might prove the most enlightening."

Amara allowed herself a glance at her husband. His expression was serene; composed. He had gone to the North, had witnessed the Challenge. Whatever reply was to be tendered, he did not fear it; did not fear that the question, so artfully deflected, so artfully returned to, would offer offense.

Valedan was quiet for a moment. "To the young," he said at last, "and to those who feel they have something to prove, winning the crown in the Kings' Challenge is, as you suggest, the pinnacle of success." His smile was disarming, and far too young for his title; it suited his face. Amara knew a moment of fear then. "I speak from experience. I would not have entered the Challenge had I not felt I had something to prove."

She glanced again at her husband's face, and this time his reaction was—to her—telling. But his expression did not falter. His hands remained in the fold of his lap. She almost told the kai Leonne that such a display of vulnerability was foolish, dangerous. Almost.

And she felt a terrible blur of emotion. This man was *not* her son, but by his gesture—no matter what motivated it, he shared blood with her husband.

Unaware of this turmoil, Valedan kai di'Leonne continued. "But the men who gain the crown are not revered. They are . . . celebrated. They are feted, for a year. They pass into obscurity unless they make their mark in some other fashion." He glanced a moment at the perfectly still face of Ser Anton di'Guivera.

Amara's curiosity was intense. She said nothing.

"Perhaps," the boy added, with just a hint of self-deprecation, "I speak thus because I . . . did not win that

crown. But I will say that it is, in the end, a game. This," he
added quietly, "is real."

"The kai Leonne suffers from unnatural modesty," Ser
Anton said quietly. "He did not take the crown because he
chose to accept a Southern Challenge. The rules of the
Kings' Challenge are Northern; the blood that is shed is not
shed in pursuit of death. To accept a . . . different challenge . . . is to disqualify yourself from the tournament.

"Even when I participated, in my . . . younger years . . .
it was thus. It is not a game of death, although in odd circumstances, death may occur. It is my belief that, had he
chosen to withhold his sword, to deny the challenge offered
him, he might have taken the crown."

"Whose Challenge did he accept?"

Ser Anton smiled quietly. "Mine."

She was absolutely still. Her grief had robbed her of the
presence, the intelligence, of the Tyr'agnate of Callesta;
had it not, she might have been apprised of this strange turn
of events before the meal.

She glanced again at her husband.

Saw the barest flicker of a smile cross his lips and fade.

"It was," Ramiro di'Callesta told his wife, "truly enlightening."

Had they been in private, she might have shown him her
displeasure; she might even have raised voice, certainly
brow, at the lack of information his words contained.

Had it been so long?

Had she truly been so far from him?

As if he knew what she was feeling—and he was
Ramiro; he must—he continued to speak. "There was another presence upon the field; an ancient presence." Gravity informed his expression, lent weight to his words. "In
sun's light, the shadow of the Lord's enemy.

"The kai Leonne, in full sight of the delegation from the
South, defeated that presence; injured, he then accepted the
challenge offered by Ser Anton di'Guivera."

But they both stand, she wanted to say. *They both live.*

"He won, Serra. He won the challenge that he accepted. And he chose . . . to accept Ser Anton's pledge of allegiance in return for the grace of sparing his life."

There was more. She heard it in the spaces between his spare words. But she accepted ignorance as the cost of her terrible anger, her terrible grief, and she bowed her head.

"Then truly we are honored by his presence."

"We are," Ser Anton said. "I have served other men, in my time; I have never served another that I considered to be so worthy." His words were devoid of the falsity of flattery; he spoke them surely, quietly, as if their truth was self-evident.

Ser Valedan kai di'Leonne looked . . . uncomfortable.

She liked him, then, in a way that she had not when he had taken up her dead son's sword.

Ser Anton di'Guivera was, in truth, his man. She had heard the rumors, of course. But it had been almost impossible to lend them credence until this moment. She gazed at the impassive face of the Dominion's living legend; saw the lines sun and wind had carved there deepen for a moment. Understood that he was not a political creature, although he understood politics well enough; he had offered to serve.

He served.

She felt a fierce envy. "Commander Kalakar?"

"Serra."

"Did you witness this battle?"

"I did."

A terrible envy. "I envy you," she said, choosing the starkness of truth as a means of disavowing the weakness.

"Do not envy me, Serra Amara. It is not the only battle I have seen; indeed, it is one of the few that has not scarred me. I am not, I realize, a pretty woman—even by Imperial standards; I live a soldier's life. It is my duty, and my responsibility, to lead to their deaths men whose wives, mothers, and children lie waiting in the illusion of safety.

"My duty to deliver to them the first word of their loss. Do not envy me."

She should not have spoken. She knew it. As a Serra of the High Courts, the choice was entirely hers; she could not impulsively speak her mind whenever a stray thought entered it. She was Serra to the Tyr'agnate of Averda. His wife.

His first wife.

"Should I not? For you will be at the side of the fallen; you will hear their last words, offer them their last comfort, ease them in their passage. And I? I will sit. And wait. And know that nothing I am capable of doing will prevent a single death."

She felt her husband's hand take hers beneath the thin protection of the table's flat top. She did not meet the gaze that she knew was waiting. She had no desire to look away.

The barbarian met her eyes, held them across her untouched, cooling meal. After a moment, she nodded her head. "It is always hard to be helpless," she said gravely. "I envy you your composure and your peace, and perhaps I do so unfairly."

She did not laugh. She did not cry. She was the Serra Amara. But she desired both composure and peace, for she had none. They had died with her son.

What she had was the empty shell of either; the appearance, the seeming. And it was wasted, upon these foreigners. Her own people would have understood the cost of such perfect control; they would have seen beneath it, acknowledging the mask in respect and admiration for precisely what it was, no more.

She lifted her hands, freeing herself from her husband's gentle warning. That he had had to offer warning at all must have been a severe disappointment to him. With a smile— a perfect smile, a Serra's smile—she clapped her hands twice.

Serafs filled the silence with their graceful movements. Water was brought. Wine. Delicate, dark bowls. Everything was perfect.

Empty.

"Serra Amara," the kai Leonne said.

She met his gaze. "Tyr'agar?" And bowed as low as she could gracefully bow, encumbered by the dinner posture.

"You honor us with your presence at this difficult time. Please, remain while we discuss what must be discussed."

Ramiro's head lifted slightly. She saw his expression shift, his lips tighten. But he said nothing.

"You, your wives, your city, will pay the price for our presence here. You have already begun what will certainly continue. You have shown your people, by your example, how loss can be borne. Understand, then, how that loss might unfold. "

"Tyr'agar," the Tyr'agnate said. "Is this entirely wise?"

Words, Amara knew, that he would *never* have offered the father to this strange, this vulnerable, this *likable* son.

Ser Valedan did not reply directly. Instead, he turned to Duarte AKalakar. Duarte rose. "With your permission, Tyr'agnate, I would like to . . . secure the perimeter of the room."

The hesitation between the question and the response was marked, exaggerated. Amara was almost shocked.

But the Northerners did not seem to notice it; neither did the kai Leonne.

Yet she could not believe that a boy so schooled in manners, in grace, could be, in the end, a scion of the North. He must understand how great her husband's reluctance was.

"You may."

Duarte AKalakar bowed. He rose quickly, and with an ease that spoke of practice. "The serafs?"

Ramiro turned to his wife. "Dismiss them."

She nodded. Clapped once. They left the room as gracefully as they had entered it, but perhaps more quickly.

Duarte AKalakar then rose and walked the length of each of the four walls in the room. "This door," he said, to the Tyr'agnate, gesturing at the open wall that let the gardens and the moonlight in. "May I close it?"

"If it is necessary, of course."

He nodded. He was no seraf; he struggled with the doors as he drew them across the grooves that held them in place. Then he bent. Touched the floor. Gestured.

Magery, she thought. Widan's art.

Here, in Callesta. Her mouth was dry. She regretted the absence of her husband's hands, but she did not reach for them; it was not her place.

Only when Duarte AKalakar resumed his seat beside the Tyr'agar did the younger man speak.

"You may have noted the absence of General Baredan di'Navarre," the kai Leonne said quietly. He did not speak to her; he did not speak past her. She realized that he intended to speak openly of matters of warfare while she was *in* the room.

She had desired this. Why should she suddenly be so fearful?

The Commander who sat to The Kalakar's left lifted his head slightly; his gaze was sharp enough to cut. He nodded. "His absence was noted."

"We received word this afternoon."

"The armies."

"Indeed. The armies of the pretender are on the move."

The village was burning.

The thatched roofs of the small cottages that had been home to the serafs who toiled in the Averdan fields collapsed slowly beneath the weight of flame. Some death could not be avoided; Alesso di'Alesso watched as the soldiery swept down the rough dirt road, destroying it beneath the weight of hundreds of shod hooves.

There had been little resistance offered. The serafs were not the Lord's; they screamed, they cried, they begged for their lives. If they had weapons, they had chosen to forgo them, hoping for mercy.

And in a fashion, mercy had been granted. Less than a quarter of the villagers had died. The clansmen who oversaw the fields themselves perished in the first few minutes of the attack, of course; they expected no more. Their swords, he broke, and their bodies he offered to the fire.

But he did not fire the fields. He did not destroy the granaries. They were of value to his army. The serafs themselves were accustomed to the vagaries of war; they would serve one master just as well as they had served another.

At his side, Ser Eduardo kai di'Garrardi watched, his face lit by distant fire, the green of his eyes robbed of their color. Night had almost fallen.

He had come late to the field, but he had come at the head of the armies that he had so grudgingly promised. He spoke seldom; spent little time in the company of the man to whom the armies owed their allegiance.

A certain reminder that allegiances, like winds, could carry scouring sands.

She was between them, of course; although they were mounted, armored and armed, although they traversed the length of the fields upon which they would remake the Dominion, her presence fell like shadow cast by the burning village homes.

Serra Diora di'Marano.

Flower of the Dominion.

"Where is she, Alesso?"

"I do not know."

"Widan, is this true? Is this the truth?"

Sendari, gaze hooded, expression completely neutral, had bowed. Bowed far, far too low. Eduardo had spoken the words in a room graced by the significant, the powerful: by the Tyr'agnate of Sorgassa, Ser Jarrani kai di'Lorenza, his son and heir, Hectore, his par, Alef; by the Sword's Edge, Widan Cortano di'Alexes, and his closest advisers; by Peder kai el'Sol, the leader of the Radann who had become significant as allies, and significant as enemies. Only the delegates from the Shining Court were absent, and their absence was equally significant.

An accusation.

Alesso's hand had lingered at the hilt of *Terra Fuerre*. He had almost drawn her.

But Sendari had chosen, instead, to grace the accusation with a reply. "It is true. When the Lady rode from the Lake, the serafs fled in panic; the cerdan—and the Tyran—situated themselves outside of the buildings in which the women were housed.

"When they returned, she was gone, although her absence was not noted immediately; very few were the men granted access to the harem in which the Serra was guarded."

He paused, then, unfolding from the bow that was far too low to be necessary between the Tyr'agnate and the man who was acknowledged to be the Tyr'agar's most trusted adviser.

That much, Sendari offered Alesso for the smooth course of war. It was far too much for Alesso's liking.

"There was," Peder kai el'Sol said, into Eduardo's thin silence, "the disappearance of something of far more value to the Tor Leonne." Of far more importance, his tone said, than a mere daughter, a woman.

Eduardo's lips compressed into a line as thin as a blade's edge. But Peder wore the open symbol of the ascendant sun, the regalia of the Radann at Court. And Peder kai el'-Sol, as Eduardo knew—as they all must know—was only barely an ally to the Tyr'agar; he was no friend.

Eduardo did not therefore seek to antagonize a man whose friendship he might later require. He said nothing.

"The Sun Sword," the kai el'Sol said quietly, "has also vanished."

Eduardo had been silent. The silence of anger and the silence of political surprise held two different shades of emotion, and the kai Garrardi had not the grace to blend them to his advantage. "When?" was the single sharp word he offered.

"We are not certain. After the night of the Festival Moon, there was much to do in the City; the swords of the Radann

were occupied in its cleansing. The care of the Sun Sword
has been diminished of late." He did not add, although
every man present could, that this was due to lack of a
wielder. "We care for the swords that we use," he added
softly, his hand falling to the hilt of the sheathed sword
Saval. "And they have been used much of late."

He bowed to the Tyr'agar. "The loss of the Sun Sword,
is, measure for measure, the loss of the Tor. But another
blade has been absent these many months." He placed his
hands upon his lap and lowered his head a moment.

Alesso waited. He knew.

"*Balagar,* the sword that is mine by right, vanished
shortly after the death of Fredero el'Sol. The Radann have
been searching for it—with discretion," he added, making
his meaning plain. "And we believe we have discovered
where it lies."

He rose. "With your permission, Tyr'agar, I would ride
with the armies to the Northern border of Raverra."

Alesso nodded quietly.

"When we regain *Balagar,* the Hand of God will again be
complete; I will elevate another to the rank of par el'Sol.
There is much work," he added softly. "And there will be
more. It is best to have all of the Lord's weapons in play."

Ser Jarrani kai di'Lorenza inclined his head. "I had wondered," he said softly.

"We were much occupied," Peder kai el'Sol replied. "But
this war is the Tyr'agar's war."

"And not the Radann's?"

"We serve the Lord of Day." His hand fell to the hilt of
his sword, leaving his lap. It rested there comfortably; there
was no threat offered or implied by the movement.

Alesso wondered, idly, whether or not the change in posture was deliberate; he was a judge of men, and understood
their moods well. Peder kai el'Sol had done much to rise to
the rank he now held; the loss of *Balagar* was not the formality that the loss of the Sun Sword had been.

"Where is *Balagar*?" he asked, the question deceptive in its mildness.

Peder kai el'Sol said, simply, "Mancorvo."

"And the Sun Sword?" Eduardo added coldly.

"We have searched," was the cool reply. "But our arts are not Voyani arts. We do not know where it is."

"And if you did?"

"If we did, Tyr'agnate, that information would now be in the hands of the man who claims the Tor." The Tor Leonne. But he did not speak the full name.

Thus rebuked, Eduardo's silence grew weighty.

They watched, the men who would be his allies. Waited.

Ser Eduardo kai di'Garrardi rose.

"I will take my leave," he said softly. "I will return to Oerta."

"And the armies?"

"The armies were promised. But so, too, was the Flower of the Dominion."

A dangerous game.

"Find her." It was not a request.

Alesso's shrug was smooth and supple; it masked his anger. "We have been searching," he replied. "But the night of the Festival Moon, this year, has made the search . . . difficult. The gates were riven to the East and the West. Clansmen, Voyani, and seraf alike chose to flee the Tor."

He did not say why; it was not necessary.

They had been in the Tor when the ancient Hunt was sounded; had seen its beginning.

Only Alesso and Sendari had witnessed its end. Neither man understood what they had witnessed, although the Widan toiled, even now, to gain some glimmer of comprehension.

"We have ascertained that the Serra Diora di'Marano did not travel to the Northern Terreans—and had she, had she made any attempt to cross those borders, we *would* know.

"She has passed either to the South, or remains well

within Raverra. Either that," he added, "or she was destroyed in the rush upon the gates."

Eduardo's eyes were dark and narrow. "You had best
hope that that is not the case."

"No body has been found," Ser Sendari said, speaking in
the stead of the Tyr'agar. "Although it is a possibility, we
do not lend it credence."

"I will fulfill my oath," the Tyr'agnate of Oerta said, rising, "when all oaths are fulfilled."

After he had left the room, Ser Jarrani kai di'Lorenza
rose. "Tyr'agar," he said, according Alesso di'Alesso the
full measure of a respect that continued to elude the kai
Garrardi. "He is a danger."

Alesso nodded.

"The Serra Diora?"

"I have no need to lie, Ser Jarrani. She has not passed to
the North."

"Did she take the Sun Sword with her?"

Alesso lifted a dark brow. It had been a long—and a trying—morn. "That is our belief, yes."

"She was not seen."

"No."

The kai Lorenza cursed a moment. "She will head to the
North."

Alesso nodded. "It is what I would do, in her position."

That he said as much plainly said much indeed. But the
men in this room had all underestimated the Serra; they
would never do so again. They accorded her a measure of
respect, in privacy and silence, that women were seldom
accorded. She was, against all odds, a worthy foe.

"She will take the sword to the Leonne seraf?"

He nodded again. "The Sun Sword can serve in only one
fashion in this war. She—if she is indeed the thief—must
mean to deliver it into his hands."

"And where will she travel, Tyr'agar? Mancorvo?
Averda?"

"She might find a home in the former, with the kai of her clan."

"Widan?"

Sendari stirred. Nodded, his fingers stressing the length of his beard. "I concur. Ser Adano would grant her harbor. Should she reach him."

"It is not Marano that concerns me."

"No?"

"It is Lamberto. Has Mareo sent no word?"

"His Serra has written to a number of the Serras within the High Court; they speak of the affairs of women, and bemoan the coming winds of war."

"And in this wifely prattle, there is no hint of the direction in which he will place his loyalties?"

"None at all. But the Serra Donna en'Lamberto took pains to remind the Serras with whom she has corresponded of the . . . cost of the last war to the clan Lamberto." He paused again. "These letters were written weeks ago; what will come in future, we cannot say."

"He is no fool," Alesso said quietly.

"Aye, damn him," Jarrani replied, with the first real hint of humor.

"He knows, by now, that both Lorenza and Garrardi have committed themselves to the shadows of war."

"Does he know that Lorenza has been offered some part of the rulership of the Terrean over which he presides?"

"Only a fool would not suspect it." Ser Alesso di'Alesso's face was a cold mask. "But there is land to be had in Averda, if the Leonne seraf is indeed there; if Lamberto joins our war, we might content ourselves with the entirety of Averda."

"Ah." Silence, and then, "Will he stand with Callesta?"

Alesso shrugged. "Our allies have taken some pains to ensure that if he was willing, Callesta will not be."

"What pains?"

"The deepening of their hostilities," Alesso replied, his voice completely neutral. He, too, rose. "Gentlemen. The

Northern armies have amassed, and they will move into Averda if they are not already a presence there.

"Therefore, although we will encamp in such a way to . . . encourage the cooperation of the Tyr'agnate of Mancorvo, it would be prudent to move the armies that will gather across the Averdan border in haste."

"Will they gather?"

Alesso frowned. In the silence he heard the ghost of a song. The Serra Diora di'Marano.

"I believe that the kai Garrardi will, in the end, choose to honor his vows."

A portion of the lands of Averda had been offered to the clan Garrardi, as cement for their necessary alliance. This village was within that redrawn border.

A pity.

"Tyr'agnate?"

Eduardo nodded coldly. "Rumors of the organizational skill of the Callestan Tyr were not exaggerated." Sword's Blood was restive. The Marente horsemen did not ride mares; they rode stallions or geldings as befit men of their station. But not all of the horsemen had chosen as wisely, and the mares presented their difficulties.

Garrardi held the reins of Sword's Blood in gloved hands; those hands, if one knew how to look, were shaking with effort.

"Indeed. Nor are the rumors of his military skill."

"You fought under him in the Imperial-Dominion war."

"I fought . . . at his side."

"This village?"

"It is within the boundaries of the lands granted the clan Garrardi," Alesso replied smoothly. "The disposition of the village is therefore left to your discretion."

This was a formality, but it was a necessary one.

"With your leave, Tyr'agar, I will assign one of my men to oversee the operations of the village."

"Of course."

He was silent a moment; the Tyr'agnate rode his horse in a tight circle beyond the waft of black smoke.

The Serra Diora had not been found.

The Tyr'agnate had arrived three days late, and if those three days proved costly, Alesso vowed that Oerta would pay the price.

But he had, in the end, arrived.

Therefore, Alesso did him the honor of treating him with the respect that was his due; he offered him the first of the taken lands in the name of their strained alliance.

But as he did, old words traveled on the wind that held smoke and the growing silence: He had sacrificed a village in order to purchase Sword's Blood; how many would he sacrifice, in the end, in order to secure the Serra Diora?

"Our apologies," Commander Allen said stiffly.

The table that he had graced, a scant hour past, with his presence now seemed a confinement, the jess which prevented his flight.

"Apologies?"

"We had hoped to contain the first stages of the war to the South of Averda, in Raverra."

The Callestan Tyr shrugged, a model of restraint. "To be expected," he said coolly. "Without Lamberto, without Mancorvo, it was at best a theoretical hope. Your troops?"

"Encamped along the Moonstone River."

"Supplies?"

"Housed by the river's mouth. We have taken the liberty of setting up a supply train between the Omaras and the delta."

The Kalakar leaned into the tabletop, placing both of her large hands against it. She was no more at home here than Commander Allen. "Word has been sent to Mancorvo?"

The silence was cold.

Valedan kai di'Leonne raised a hand, providing the room's only motion. "No word," he said quietly, "has been sent."

The Serra Amara lifted her face as the three Commanders absorbed the whole of his words. She hesitated a moment. Valedan had never seen such a hesitation from her; it was profound.

"Word," she said at last, "has been sent."

The Kalakar turned quickly.

As did the Tyr'agnate.

She had the grace to flush; the color added a youth to her expression that Valedan had never seen there.

"My apologies," she said, her voice very low. "My apologies, Tyr'agnate, for my presumption."

But if Valedan was any judge of expression, none were necessary; the Callestan Tyr was surprised, but it was a surprise that held no anger. "Serra Amara," he said gently.

"We do not often speak of such things as if they were significant," she added, dissembling. "Men decide the course of war; women watch as it unfolds. And any word sent, meager and insignificant though it might be, was sent merely to the Serra Donna en'Lamberto."

"The Serra Donna is the Tyr'agnate's wife?" The Kalakar asked.

"She is his Serra, yes."

"When?" It was Commander Allen who spoke.

"Two days ago. Before the Commanders set foot within Callesta."

Valedan glanced at the Serra Alina di'Lamberto. She was as still as the Callestan Tyr, but her silence was one that encompassed motion, movement; she gazed at the tabletop, the lacquered box that no seraf had been summoned to remove, as if her glance was weighted and immovable.

"How was word sent?" the Commander continued.

She did not answer. After a moment, it became clear that she would not.

He did not frown; he did not raise his voice. But he posed, instead, a different question. "When will it reach her? When it will reach the Mancorvan court?"

She looked to her husband; her husband smiled. The

smile, his first, held both warmth and a hint of playful malice. "I am afraid," he said gravely, speaking to her, although the whole of the room waited, "that I am unable to answer that question.

"It is said that the conversations of Serras are beneath the interest of Tyrs. And that such conversation, such correspondence, is much like the wind; impossible to stop, impossible to command. In truth, Commander Allen, I do not know.

"If she chose to send word by horseman, it will be days yet before that word arrives, and the message would have to be carried across a border whose roads are well guarded. If the messenger was wise, and chose to forgo the open road for the wilderness of forest, days would be added to the transit. If the messenger was unwise, or unallied, such subterfuge would be unnecessary."

"So it might be a week, or more, before that message was in Lambertan hands?"

"If it were delivered in such a fashion, yes."

"And if it were delivered in another way?"

"Ah," he said. He nodded regally to the bowed head of his unveiled wife. "If indeed it were delivered in a different fashion, it might rest in her hands now."

"Magery?"

The Tyr frowned. "Magery is not so common in Averda as it is in the Imperial capital."

There was silence, heavy with the unsaid.

To Valedan's surprise, it was the Serra Alina who broke it, although she did not otherwise look up. "You do not understand, Commander, the subtleties that are a necessity in the Dominion."

He took no offense at the words, or seemed to take none. He nodded.

"Believe that the kai Lamberto is no fool."

"It is a wise belief," Ser Ramiro added distantly.

"If he is not . . . the hand . . . behind the assassination of the Tyr'agnate's oldest son, he will not have been apprised of the death," the Serra Alina di'Lamberto said, speaking for the first time. Speaking in a way that Serra Amara could not, married and bound by duty to uphold her husband's dignity.

"And unapprised," the Serra Alina continued, as if speaking to favored children, "he might commit an unforgivable transgression in the negotiations that would otherwise be deemed a necessity between the two clans. Understand, as well, that the words of Serras are not binding; they are, as the Serra Amara has said, women's words, with all of the weight that implies.

"But where men of power must treat, they tread cautiously. As women are free to say what must be said, they may speak through their wives of things that men would otherwise be above saying. Before they can meet—surrounded by their lieges, their Tyran, their courtiers—which is a Northern word," she added, "that has no true counterpart in the South—there is much that must be discussed.

"Serras, therefore, play some small role in those early discussions; they speak with all the freedom women indentured to their husbands can have.

"If the Serra Amara chose to begin such a discussion, we must be grateful for her wisdom."

The Kalakar snorted. "Indeed," she said, her impatience almost an insult. "But if what you say is true, shouldn't the Tyr'agnate be apprised of the letter's contents?"

Serra Amara did not reply, which seemed reply enough.

But Serra Alina continued to speak. "The Tyr'agnate may be apprised of the contents of the letter, although I find it doubtful. It is a letter, no more, between women whose sole distinction—in the eyes of the clansmen—are their husbands. The letter that the Serra Donna replies with, should she choose to reply, has more weight. Her reply forms the beginning of any negotiation that might be entered upon.

"But if she makes no reply, no insult is offered."

Valedan noticed that the Serra Amara was now staring, subtly, at the Serra Alina.

"Understand," Alina said, after a long pause, "that you are speaking of a man whose oldest son was killed by the Northern armies."

"It was war," The Kalakar replied, with an ease that no woman—North or South—should have spoken.

"Spoken," Alina said, "as a member of The Ten. Spoken as a Lord who has no understanding of the visceral nature of blood ties."

The Kalakar raised a brow.

As did Valedan. But Valedan smiled as the shock of the words dissipated. This woman, this was the woman he had grown up listening to. This was the companion of the Princess Royale, Mirialyn ACormaris.

He had never thought to see that woman in the dining hall of the Tyr'agnate.

"You do not understand the significance of the Serra Amara's gesture," Alina continued, speaking now as she would have spoken to Valedan when he had been particularly obtuse. "You do not understand her gift."

"Gift?" The Kalakar's word was not sharp, but her reaction made clear the truth behind Alina's accusation.

"It is generally acknowledged that the Lambertans are the hand behind the kai Callesta's death."

The Kalakar nodded, her expression now hooded. "I see."

She had not. Perhaps, Valedan thought, she better understood.

Until she spoke. "It was unfortunate. It *is* a tragedy. But surely Mareo di'Lamberto—"

"The Tyr'agnate," Alina said smoothly.

"The Tyr'agnate of Mancorvo," The Kalakar continued, aware of the correction, "can see that the survival of his clan, and his Terrean, depends upon his ability to forge an alliance with—"

"With the men who murdered his son?"

The Kalakar stopped. Her gaze narrowed.

"In war, there are acts of murder. The death of the Lambertan kai was not considered one of them. He was out-numbered, outmaneuvered; his Generals chose to secure the death of their forces for reasons that are not clear to us, even now."

"You do not understand the Dominion," Serra Alina replied, in a voice as cold as any she had used upon Valedan when his ignorance had been particularly galling.

"We understood it well enough to win its war," the Commander countered.

But Commander Allen lifted a hand. "Ellora," he said quietly. "Please."

She subsided.

The Serra Alina, in silence, did not.

Commander Allen turned his gaze upon the woman who had been one of the Imperial hostages, in a terrain vastly different than the political one she now occupied. "Serra Alina," he said gravely, inclining his head, "you speak truth. We do not understand the Dominion. We understand that the enmity of the Lambertans has never faded. We do not understand why, and it has not been of concern to us to do so, until now.

"Forgive our ignorance, and lessen it, if that is your desire."

"There are two deaths," Serra Alina said, after a long pause, "that will decide the course of any possible negotiations. The first is the death of the kai Lamberto, the second, the death of the kai Callesta.

"Whole clans have willingly perished before they sought mercy from, or alliance with, the men who murdered those of their bloodline. Among Lambertans, that truth will be harsher than it might be among any other clan of the High Courts." She raised her face, her hawkish thin profile gaining the beauty that ferocity had always lent it.

"Ser Andreas, the kai Lamberto, was much like his father; a Lambertan son."

"He was, what, thirteen? Fourteen?"

"Ellora," Commander Allen said, and this time Valedan was certain The Kalakar would remain silent.

"He was fourteen," Serra Alina replied. "Fourteen is not considered unworthy of note in the Dominion. The Imperial laws govern the age of manhood; in the Dominion, there is no universal law. The Tyr'agnate saw fit to grant his eldest son command of an army upon the field. By his grant, he acknowledged that his son had come of age.

"But he did more, by such an acknowledgment; he surrendered to the field a boy that he valued more than he valued himself. By example, he offered his lieges proof that he was willing to meet, measure for measure, the sacrifices that he asked of them, in the name of the Tyr'agar."

"They chose his death," The Kalakar Commander said quietly. "He was offered his life; he chose to forgo that offer."

Alina *laughed*. She laughed, and it was a bitter, harsh sound.

"Had you offered *him* his life, in exchange for his surrender and the surrender of his men, that might have been true."

Her gaze at last broke from the tabletop, from the dinner that she had not touched. Her head came up, her chin sharp, her cheeks flushed.

Serra Amara was shocked.

She had heard laughter in her life; certainly from the wives she had chosen to grace her harem. But not one of them would be capable of this harsh sound, this grating accusation.

She would have said, had any asked, that such a sound was beneath the Serra Alina di'Lamberto. It was a Northern sound. No, worse, it was a man's laugh.

And a woman's duty was to ease the harshness of a room full of men; to offer those sounds—laughter, where appropriate, speech where not—that would bring peace and harmony. There were only three women in the room: The

Kalakar, who by the roughness of her speech and the sheer folly of her ignorance, must be discounted, the Serra Amara, and the Serra Alina.

Has the North so scoured you of grace, Serra?

She turned to her husband; saw that his expression was entirely hidden behind the stiff mask of his face.

She knew what her duty was, then.

Knew it. "Serra Alina?"

The Serra turned at once, obedient, to face her.

"Did they not make the offer *to* the kai Lamberto?"

"Ah. No, Serra Amara, they did not."

Amara almost closed her eyes. Almost. But it was a weakness, with her: she had to see, to know, to hoard the naked truth that she was certain she would not witness again.

"He was a boy," The Kalakar said quietly. "And it was clear, from the campaign, that it was not a boy's hand behind the commands that controlled that army."

"They delivered their offer to the General who stood by the kai Lamberto's side. They offered the General the safety of internment, in return for the kai's surrender."

Nothing that had been said this evening was as grave a shock to the Serra Amara as the Serra Alina's words.

"But—but—"

Serra Alina nodded bitterly.

Serra Amara turned to the barbarous woman of the North. "Had you demanded the *General's* surrender, in return for the safety of the kai Callesta, it would have been difficult, for the Northerners have no way of sealing their oath.

"But *that* would have been possible. Surely you must understand that no General could have acceded to the demands you did make?"

Ramiro's hand touched hers. She felt it as a sudden warmth and a sudden pressure.

"We understand it now," Commander Allen said quietly. He bowed, both to the Serra Amara and to the Serra Alina.

"And if there existed some method of changing the past, we would undo the damage we did, in ignorance, more than a decade past. Your ways are not our ways, Serra."

But Serra Amara's gaze was captured by the Serra Alina's face.

She had never understood the Mancorvan hatred of the North until this moment.

How can you sit by the side of that boy, she thought, clenching her husband's hand—the hand that had been offered in command and in warning. *How can you sit across from these . . . these barbarians? How can you work with them when they murdered your nephew?*

As if she could hear what had not been said, the Serra Alina spoke to the Serra Amara.

"The mercy of the North," she said softly, "has often been mistaken for weakness." She closed her eyes a moment. "I have spent twelve years in the Northern court. I have spoken to the Kings who rule it; I have conversed with their children. I have spoken to the men who serve it in capacity of war; who serve it in capacity of peace. I have seen . . . much . . . there to admire.

"But it was bitterly, bitterly galling to understand, in the end, that Ser Andreas died for the folly of their ignorance. They did not intend his death, Serra Amara. I know it. I understand it. But . . . I have returned to the Dominion, and the knowledge rests uneasily now that I am . . . home."

She bowed her head. "It is not a mistake that Valedan kai di'Leonne would make. Would ever have made."

As much an explanation as a woman could offer in such a terrible room as this.

"And you," Commander Allen said, into the moment's silence, "Serra Amara. What would you cede to your son's assassins, if indeed the Lambertans *are* the hand behind his death?"

She was shocked. He turned to her, spoke *to* her. It was a

question not even the bold would ask of her husband, the answer was so obvious. The question was an insult.

And yet, the man who asked it meant no insult; his expression was clear of malice, and free also of the mask of neutrality that served Generals in good stead. She turned to look at her husband; met his gaze. She knew how to read the subtle lines of his face, the careful neutrality of his expression.

But this eve, he offered nothing.

"It is not my place," she said quietly. "It is not my decision."

He seemed to accept this.

But he did not speak again, and the silence grew awkward. She had wanted the company of these people; she realized her mistake now. They demanded the intimacy of the harem without even understanding the demands they made. They were shorn of grace, these men, this woman.

"We did not kill the kai Lamberto," she said at last. "And we will not pay the price of his death, if that is a part of their negotiations."

"Not even if the price we pay for the lack of those negotiations is the death of the rest of your clan?"

She was shocked again.

Silence reigned, but briefly, and when it was broken, it was broken by the kai Leonne. She would remember this.

"Commander Allen, enough." He raised a hand; there was, in his tone, a gentleness that did not belie the command beneath the words. "There are some prices that *cannot* be paid."

Commander Allen was, indeed, silent, but his gaze crossed the table like the sudden plummet of an Eagle in flight. She thought of their names, of their Northern names, and understood them completely.

"Do you not remember the Mother's judgment?"

Commander Allen said dryly, "The Mother judges many things. Of which judgment do you speak, Tyr'agar?"

"The story of Olivia and her children."

"Ah."

Serra Alina bent slightly across the table; she whispered a few words that did not travel the distance, and Valedan kai di'Leonne nodded.

"It is a Northern tale," he said quietly, nodding gravely to the Serra Amara. "And it is long enough that I will handle its telling poorly. I will say this: She had a son and a daughter. In the South, the tale might better be told if she had two sons. But . . . it is a Northern tale.

"A son and a daughter, and she loved them both. They were young. Her bloodline was found guilty of treason against the Baron of Estrican—one of the Blood Barons who ruled before the founding of the Empire. But because she was his kin, if distant, he decided against the destruction of her family.

"He desired that she remember the cost of her crime, however, and told her that she might choose among her children: one would live, and one would die."

"She loved her children. It was her greatest weakness."

He said nothing for a moment. Serra Amara watched his face carefully. "The rest of the tale, kai Leonne?"

"She could not choose; they were young, but not so young that they did not understand what she had been offered. They were terrified, but as children do, they both believed that they were best loved, and that in the end, their mother would choose to spare them.

"And she knew it, of course. She would have fled with her children, would have taken the Mother's oath, and forced it upon them. But the Baron was canny, and he understood her weakness well. He did not trust her.

"And he was wise. She accepted his offer, accepted his poison, and in the end, she told her children that the Halls of Mandaros awaited them all, and that she would never send them, alone, to the Lord of Judgment, although she told them he greatly loved children."

Serra Amara said, simply, "She killed herself, and her children."

"Indeed."

"And what is the point of this tale, kai Leonne?" A bold question. The Serra Amara, stripped of gentleness.

"The Mother came to her daughters in the lands of Estrican, after her brother, Mandaros, had told her this tale. And in the lands of Estrican, while the Baron ruled, no healing was done. His crops failed. His children were left to suffer the ravages of plague and illness without her aid or her blessing."

"Surely he did not allow this slight to go unpunished."

"Indeed," Valedan said gravely, "he did not. The Mother's temples, within Estrican, were pillaged and burned—but he had little satisfaction in that burning, for they were left almost empty; the sons and daughters who served the Mother hid themselves among the villages and the towns that he claimed.

"And the Barons on either side of Estrican understood the weight of this judgment, and they offered no similar insult to her, and in time, when the Baron of Estrican was overthrown, his sons rebuilt the Mother's temples, and did all that was in their power to placate her great anger."

"Ah," she said softly. "This Mother, this Northern goddess . . . she is not like the Lady."

"No. She is not. But she understands well the parent's heart, and she will not see it blasphemed."

Commander Allen coughed into the cup of his palm.

"Commander Allen?"

"The parable is, of course, a parable of value—but it is not analogous. The kai Callesta is regrettably already dead, and his mother had no hand in the manner of his departure."

"It *is* analogous," Valedan replied quietly, "in the Dominion. Do not ask her that question, Commander Allen. Do not ask it again."

"As you command, Tyr'agar. But I wish to point out that during the reign of the Blood Barons, it would have been acceptable to the Mother had he merely had all three put to death."

"Indeed."

"And in the end, it is the results that concern us."

"The ends justifying the means?"

"In the end, the dead are dead. It is to prevent more death that we have come."

Valedan's smile was a rare one: it was cold.

But the Serra Alina di'Lamberto looked across to the Serra Amara en'Callesta. "Do you understand, Serra Amara?"

Serra Amara bowed.

This boy, this man, this kai Leonne with his Northern fable, was a man that even she would be willing to serve.

She turned to her husband. "We have already lost the towns along the border."

He nodded quietly. "We have had no word, but our forces were there in no strength."

"How great is the loss?"

"That remains," he said softly, "to be seen. Alesso di'-Marente is shrewd. He will not destroy the villages he has taken; he will use them to feed his armies unless he is forced to retreat. Retreat means that we will lose the villages entirely; he will raze them as he passes back toward Raverra. But if he holds true to form, he will attempt to fight his decisive battle before his army reaches the foot of the valleys."

"Will he not attempt to take the valleys?"

"If he can, of course." Ramiro's smile was thin as blade's edge. "But taking the valleys will require him to move through the Northern armies. Commander Allen?"

"The armies are ready," the Commander said quietly. "They can begin to move on the morrow."

"Send word, then. We will join them on the plains, if they can hold the forces of Marente upon it." He lifted his head. "Tyr'agar?" he said quietly.

Valedan nodded. "You know Raverra and Averda better than I; I will follow your lead in this."

CHAPTER TWELVE

9th of Corvil, 427 AA
Terrean of Averda

"WAKE."
   From a great distance, a single word. She understood it, but everything about it was unfamiliar. The voice. The cadence. The word itself, prefaced by nothing; no snort of irritation, no edgy amusement, no gruff annoyance.

No warmth.

She saw darkness. Into night, the single word came again, unchanged. She listened and heard it: foreign, strange, unfamiliar. No voice of hers.

She was used to waking in sunlight; to sleeping in sunlight; used to waking in dusk or at the edge of dawn; used to waking in the dead of full moon. If there was a rhythm that punctuated her life, it was the lack of routine. The only demands were those of the open road; the weather in the Terreans, the season, the possible conflicts brought to the Voyani—or carried by them—and the clansmen.

She was accustomed to shedding sleep the way waterfowl shed water. But this sleep was heavy, and it lingered in her limbs, like the edge of sickness.

"Daughter of Arkosa, *wake*."

Ah, a change in tenor.

Anger. Fear. Something that hovered on the edge that separated them.

She woke.

Saw starlight, saw the moon's face, slipping by sliver of gray into nadir; woman's face, veil falling. The stars were her stars. The air was warm.

Elena struggled to sit.

She felt something between her lips, her swollen lips; water trickled from the corners of her mouth before she remembered that water was precious. She curved those lips, tightening them around the mouth of a waterskin.

Her hands were shaking; she forced them to rise, lifting them as if they were weights. They worked against her until she lost moonlight and looked at the person who held that water.

He held her gaze for long enough to be certain that it no longer wandered, and then he waited until she took the burden he carried.

Had she not been so thirsty, she would have refused to swallow.

He rose. She was not comfortable with the sudden difference in their height, but she could not stand; her legs were weak.

The robes that had been graced by blood, rent by sword, were now whole. "Elena Tamaraan," he said quietly. "Where are we?"

It was not what she had expected to hear. If indeed she had expected Lord Telakar to speak at all.

The Lady was gracious this eve; Elena's vision, better than Margret's in the night sky, was not so good as Adam's; she could see the lines of the creature's face, but they were softened by shadow. She knew that he could see her clearly.

She drank in silence.

"Elena," he said again. "I asked a question."

She nodded. "I heard you."

And dropped the waterskin as his hand struck her face. It was a brief gesture, and no hint of its violence marred his perfect posture when she turned to face him again, her eyes stinging from the pain of the contact.

"You are no longer among your kin," he said softly.

"Learn to speak with grace, if you choose to speak at all."
His lips turned up in a smile. "You no longer carry a
weapon. If I am not mistaken, you shed it in the desert."

Her hands stilled.

"Now. Where are we?"

She could see trees in the darkness; the moon had risen
above their tops; the forest was sparse.

But the stars were familiar. Stars.

She was alive. By the Lady's grace, alive. And any gift
the Lady offered was to be treated with respect, with fear,
with caution.

But she accepted that gift; with life came possibility.

So she looked. She studied the stars. She listened.

And in listening, she felt the cold of the desert night, although she now knew that the desert was far, far away.

It was absolutely silent. She heard her own breath; heard
the rustle of her shirt against the trailing folds of desert
wear. Heard the wind's voice in the distant branches.

But that was all; there was no other sound in the clearing.
No insect song, no cricket dance; no movement of light carried on the back of night flies. There was no hunting cry; no
owl voice, no padding through the undergrowth that spoke
of waking predator.

"It's too quiet," she said, without looking at him.

"It is quiet, yes." He moved in the silence, part of it.

"Is this—" *Speak with grace.* "Are you responsible for
the silence? Is it like the heartfire?"

"I do not know what the heartfire is," he replied. "But I
am responsible for the silence."

Some changing current beneath the surface of his words
made her look up.

"It is . . . interesting. It appears that life, no matter how
little sentience it possesses, is aware of my presence. Of
what that presence entails."

She said nothing.

"It is unfortunate as well. It appears that I am never to re-

turn to the forests of my youth upon this dwindling plane.
The silence follows me."

Something about his words. She frowned. "Are you not
alive?"

He lifted a hand; it made a shadow against the moon's
face. "Alive? No, Elena Tamaraan. I am not alive."

His voice. The Voyani almost never spoke softly; their
voices, like their skin, were cracked and harsh. Before she
could consider the wisdom of her words, she said, "Were
you ever?"

He turned to her then, and knelt. Kneeling, he was taller
than she; she reached his shoulders, if that. Felt dwarfed by
his presence. Threatened by it, and Elena was no girl. But
he did not raise hand again.

"Why do you ask?"

Had he been Voyani, her answer would have been
couched in flippant nonchalance. She bit back that reply.
When you traveled the *Voyanne,* you learned how to keep a
safe distance when distance was necessary.

Here, now, she doubted it was possible.

"I don't know. If . . . someone else . . . had said what you
just said, I'd probably ask them if they were a ghost."

His smile was silver. Too long, too thin.

"Ah. But?"

But I don't want you to hit me again. "You aren't a ghost
of mine."

"Indeed."

"Too solid, for one. Too cold."

"Cold?"

She laughed; it was a forced sound, and it died quickly.
"We don't trust anything that's too hot or too cold. Either
one is a desert in the making."

"We."

"The Arkosans." She paused. Her feet were finally waking, and they ached beneath the weight of her legs. She
wanted to rise; was afraid that he'd forbid it. She lived with
the discomfort. "The Voyani."

He shrugged. "Your trust is not of concern."

"No." She returned the shrug with care, watching his hand. It was still raised against the moonlight's fall, dark and still; the trees knew more motion than he did.

Hells, statues probably did.

"But your description is of interest."

She was not born to the clans; she made no mask of her face. Expression moved across it with quickness and ease.

"Mortals have changed much, diminished much, with the passage of time. But we were often described as a cold people. I understand what was meant by it in the past; what do you mean by it now?"

She stared at him as if he were mad.

Saw his hand shift slightly as it hovered in the air.

"I . . . don't know. I don't have the words for it. I've never really thought about it before." Although his expression was absent, she struggled to find words now. "Distant. Remote. Merciless."

"Ah."

"And heat?"

"Too quick to anger. Too quick to do anything, really."

"Passionate?"

She shrugged again. "Maybe."

"Among my kin, I was not considered cold."

"No. But among their kin, neither are the clansmen of the High Courts."

"There is a difference," he said softly. "Among their kin, the clansmen of your High Courts have trust. Among my kin, it was always considered an entirely mortal conceit." He rose. "Where are we?"

"The Terrean of Averda."

"Is that what these lands are now called?"

She nodded. "What—what were they called before?"

"Before you were born? I don't know. But when I walked these lands last, they were wild places. The earth woke here. The valleys were not so low, not so silent. They are silent now."

They were. She swallowed air, and struggled to gain her feet, hoping they would hold her. "No," she said quietly. "They aren't."

"You have nothing to compare them against."

"I have. I've walked these valleys by day and by night; I've passed through the villages that they hold; I've spoken with the people who tend the lands."

"They are," he said coolly, "little better than cattle; if they speak, they speak in voices that not even the wind chooses to heed." He waited until her legs stopped shaking, watching her in a darkness she was certain did not inconvenience him. "You yourself have said as much, Elena."

She shrugged. "Maybe."

"Maybe? Do the Voyani now claim to be shepherds? Do they claim some touching concern for the welfare of those outside of their boundaries?"

"What boundaries?"

"Arkosa."

"I don't speak for all of the Voyani. I don't speak for the Arkosa Voyani. I speak for Elena. For me. If you want authority, go back to Margret."

"Margret?"

"The Matriarch."

"Is that a family name? Margret?"

"It's a name." She shrugged.

He laughed. "Sen Margret," he said quietly, "was the founder of your wandering clan."

She thought about correcting his use of the word clan, and decided against it. It wasn't hard to curb the words.

"Who was Sen Margret?"

"Do you honestly not know?"

"Lord Telakar," she said, struggling to keep her voice as even—as respectful—as possible, "maybe you have all the time in the world. I don't. I don't ask a question like that if I already know the answer."

He was perfectly still for a long moment; Elena thought he would slap her again, and she braced herself.

But instead he said, "Fair enough. Sen Margret was an adept of the Sanctum." He waited. After a moment, he shook his head. "You have lost your history," he told her.

"Maybe. Maybe it's no longer ours. Maybe we only live long enough to make history, not to remember it."

He laughed. "Why did you seek to save me from the City?"

The moon was bright. "I don't know. Why did you interfere with the other demon?"

"Ah. I *do* know," he replied. "But I do not think that this is the time to discuss it. Nor the place. Come, Elena." He began to walk.

"Where?"

"Where?"

"Where are you going?"

"We," he replied, "are going to pay a visit."

A visit? She closed her eyes. "Lord Telakar?"

"Yes?"

"Why did you bring me here?"

He was silent. After a moment, he said, "By that, do you mean to ask what I intend to do with you?"

"To me."

"For the moment, nothing. You are mortal, you are of these lands. Over the rise of that ridge, there is a city. It is not large; it is not—in any way I once understood the word—a city of note. It is flat, its buildings of stone and dead wood; people huddle behind its walls as if they think to find safety there."

He shook his head. "But there is no safety in such a poverty of power. Can you feel it, from here?"

"Feel what?"

"The city."

"No."

"No. Nor can I. It did not draw my attention in the way the old Cities once did. But it is there, and if I am not mistaken, it is the city in which the man who claims to rule now resides."

"You mean Callesta?"

He shrugged. "We will travel there."

"On foot?"

"Unless you wish to travel in another fashion, yes."

"How did we get here?"

"There is a reason, Elena Tamaraan, that you remember nothing of that passage."

"How—how long has it been?"

He shrugged again. "Days. Weeks, perhaps."

There was no road beneath her feet; she had no way to judge the distance.

She said, "If we're in Averda, we can find my people."

"They are in this Terrean?"

She nodded. "Most of them."

"And you wish to take me to them?"

Silence, then.

He laughed. "Come."

He walked for hours.

Hours, as the passage of the moon shifted, and shifted again, changing the face of the sky.

She was used to walking. Although she was Margret's cousin, the daughter of the Matriarch's sister, she disliked the closed walls of the wagons, and where possible, she avoided them. Especially in Averda.

But her legs were shaky; her feet, stiff. His pace was even; he did not deign to notice the geography of Averda as it passed beneath his feet. Did not seem to be inconvenienced in any way by the fall of the ground, or its rise.

She stumbled.

Felt his frown.

"We will not arrive in the city before dawn if you walk at this pace."

Struggled to keep up.

He stopped. "You are so frail," he said at last. "In the time when the Cities of Man held the heartlands, you would have perished."

She was hungry, tired. Hot. He approached her, and she stopped herself from flinching.

"Come," he said again, and before she could speak, he lifted her in the cradle of his arms. As if she were a child.

"I can walk."

"Yes. But I cannot wait."

"Then leave me here."

He smiled. "Elena, you are safe."

She laughed. She could not keep the hysteria out of the sound, and she hated herself for it. "How can I be safe, with you? Don't you know what you are?"

"Oh, yes, I know." He crested the ridge and stopped for a moment.

She could see the lights of the city of Callesta in the distance.

"Do you know what you are?"

"Elena," she whispered. "Elena of the Arkosa Voyani."

"That is barely a name," he replied.

She said nothing.

Felt his chest beneath her cheek as if it were the cool low winds that swept down from the mountains.

"Is my cousin safe?"

"Your cousin? Ah, the Matriarch. Yes. Inasmuch as she resides within Tor Arkosa, she is safe. Only upon the Isle of the god-born would she be safer. I do not understand how the City came to rise; I would never have been trusted with such information." His smile deepened. "Nor, it seems, would you, and you are of that City."

"My other cousin?"

"Who?"

"Nicu."

He frowned. Closed his eyes. Eyes closed, he looked almost human. "I do not know," he said quietly. "Why do you ask?"

"I want to know."

"Is he not the man who stood at the side of Lord

Ishavriel? Is he not the man who intended to deliver Arkosa into the hands of her ancient enemies?"

She said nothing.

He laughed. "Were you another person, Elena Tamaraan—or were I—I would do you the grace of pretending to believe that you asked out of a desire for either justice or vengeance."

Lies came easily to her lips, but they did not pass them. "He's family," she said at last.

"And that is so important?"

"It's all we have, on the *Voyanne.*"

"It is all you *had.* But if I am not mistaken, Elena of Arkosa, it cannot be all that remains if you are to claim what was stewarded for you by the wild earth."

She was quiet for a long time.

"Telakar?"

"Yes?"

"What is a demon?" Her voice was hushed.

"A name, not unlike the name Elena."

"What do you call yourself?"

"Among the kinlords, we are rarely required to call ourselves anything. What are you told about demons?"

"They serve the Lord of Night."

"Ah."

"We don't."

"No, you don't."

She was *so* tired. "Why did you challenge Lord Ishavriel? Aren't you on the same side?"

He laughed. "You are quaint, a child. Not one of the kinlords serves any master but himself and his own interests."

"But the Lord of Night—"

"And we are all interested in our own survival."

"Does he know you're here?"

Silence. Then, "You are a very clever child." But he did not answer the question.

She woke again at the gates of Callesta.

Had anyone told her that she would have slept, she would

have cursed them for a liar. But she did not remember the passage from the ridge to the walls. Could not remember the exact moment when she had given up on wakefulness, retreating into the luxury of a sleep that depended upon another person's arms, another's motion.

But she remembered the last thing she'd heard: his description of the trees in the far, far North, in a land that she had rarely heard of and never visited.

"Elena."

She struggled; he set her down.

"I have need of you here. There are guards at the gates, and for the moment, I am content not to kill them. They will not allow me to pass without questioning, and I am not so well versed in the etiquette of these lands that that questioning would go smoothly."

I am content not to kill them.

"I . . ."

"Elena."

It was night. The Lady's face was clear and bright. Elena met her silver gaze beneath a sky that went on forever. "Have the skies changed?" she asked him softly.

"Perhaps. It has been an hour. Two."

"Since . . . the last time you walked these lands."

"Ah. Yes, they have changed. But not so much that they are not recognizable."

Lady's face. She hesitated. There were, as he said, guards at the gates, and she knew that they would soon draw swords.

"Why are we here?"

He did not reply. He watched her.

She whispered something softly.

He heard it anyway. "A dangerous vow."

We will live as free men, and we will fight as free men; not for power, nor for love, will we again serve the Lord of Night.

She drew her shoulders back, lifting her chin. Not for power, not for love.

But for fear? For fear's sake?

Not for fear. Lady, not for fear.

"We should have come in the Lord's time," she told him quietly.

"We are here now."

"I won't help you."

He shrugged. "You do not aid me, Elena," he said gravely. The sound of steel leaving sheath punctuated the quiet sentence. "You aid them. If you do not choose to obey me, it is of little concern. As I said, this city is remarkable for its poverty, its powerlessness. I am content not to kill.

"But only barely. Decide. But be aware that it is not your life that is at risk."

The life, she thought, of clansmen. Of cerdan.

Not for the lives of men such as these would she be forsworn.

There were two men. They wore the symmetrical lines of neatly kept beards; clansmen, both. Free.

One man carried a lamp with him, and he raised it. Light lined the exposed folds of her desert robes; shadows darkened its valleys. She was aware of both because she looked down, to her feet, to the path beneath it.

Steel was much brighter when it caught light; there was nothing pleasant about that light's glint. She had no weapon to draw in return.

"The gates of Callesta are closed," the older of the two men said.

She nodded, silent, and then shrugged her arms and her shoulders free of the robes. Beneath them, she wore the colorful clothing of the open road.

The cerdan's brows rose. He said a single word to the man who waited, lamp in hand.

She heard it.

"Yes," she said, speaking slowly and reluctantly. "Voyani. I am of Arkosa."

"You . . . wear desert robes."

"Yes." But not for long. They were conspicuous, these

heavy folds of clothing that had served Arkosa for generations. Margret had once worn this robe. Elena, remembering this, removed it, folded it with care and handed it to Telakar.

As if he were, in truth, Arkosan.

Beneath the desert garb, she looked like a wanderer. The dyes of the clothing that she had literally owned for years had faded with exposure to sun, to sand, to wind; it marked her.

"You travel alone?" the older man asked.

"Not alone," she replied. "My cousin travels with me, and he is known for his prowess with blade. But he will not draw it here, at the gates of Callesta."

The man nodded.

He stood seconds away from his death, unaware of it, his sword steady but not—yet—raised in a way that offered obvious threat.

She heard the guardhouse doors open; saw two men join the two who had come to speak. Four. Four men, now. She had entered through the gates of Callesta before. During harvest season they were always open, and the guardhouse itself was laid bare to the inspection of those who passed by.

But the planting had only barely begun across the Terrean; harvest was months away. Months of sun, months of rain, months of careful tending. And between that time and this one, the guardhouse was emptied.

The men—the younger men—were often called to the fields by their families, to oversee the work that would, in the end, feed Callesta.

"We heard rumor," the oldest man said.

"Rumor?"

"That the Voyani Matriarchs were being hunted by the man who styles himself Tyr'agar."

No, she thought. *No, I will not do this.*

But the thought was curiously detached.

"Rumors seldom contain that much truth." She lifted a hand. "But what you have heard *is* true."

"And you have come with word?"

"I have," she replied gravely. She hesitated again. The High Clans had little love of—or use for—the Voyani of *any* family. But the low clans often traded with the Arkosans for salves and potions, charms and wards, and the hint of the future that awaited them. The low clans, she thought, with a trace of bitterness, and the women.

And the High Clans did not guard city gates.

Two more joined the men who had first come. Six. Six now. She looked at them in the lamp's flicker, and wondered if six such men could kill Lord Telakar. He had been injured in his fight with the other demon. Surely that injury might count in their favor.

Moonlight. Lamplight.

Lady.

"Are there Arkosans gathered within the walls?" Her voice. Traitor's voice.

"None that we know of."

Which meant simply that none had come with the caravans that marked the Voyani. It was more or less the answer she had expected; the Arkosans seldom came to Callesta. This close to the Tyr'agnate, the clans showed their disdain and their suspicion openly.

"Elena," Lord Telakar said quietly.

The lamplight shifted as the cerdan who held it lifted it, drawing Telakar out of anonymity and shadow.

"Forgive us," he said, "for the hour of our arrival. But we desire an audience with the Tyr'agnate of Averda."

The cerdan's brows rose. Elena's did not, through sheer dint of will.

"We have word," he continued, speaking for Arkosa in a soft, even voice, "that we believe will be of value. And we come with an offer."

"An offer?"

"The man who styles himself Tyr'agar has proved himself no friend to the Voyani. Of any family."

"He's proved himself no friend to Callesta," the cerdan replied cautiously. "But the Voyani are known for their inability to choose sides in a war."

"The Arkosan Voyani," Elena replied, taking the conversation out of Lord Telakar's hands, "will fight a war when a war is declared against us."

The words were so *wrong*. She'd thought she'd been afraid before; she knew now that she was mistaken. "I cannot claim to speak for any other family," she added, and the words were steady, calm, another woman's words. "But I am of Arkosa.

"Grant us entry, or deny us entry; our time passes quickly and we are expected elsewhere."

"Entry such as you have requested," the cerdan said gravely, "is not so simple a matter. We must ask you to wait here."

She turned. Telakar stepped forward.

"We will wait," he said.

Dinner had not, in the Serra Amara's considered opinion, been a success; the food itself had been eaten as if it were simple sustenance, and the Commanders had given the meal short shrift. They spoke in the Northern tongue, their words passing above her meager comprehension as if it were thunder or lightning; the storm's voice.

She was grateful. She understood Weston; could read it almost as well as a native. But such reading demanded time, and the Commanders left little of that.

She gazed at her husband's face; he was absorbed in their conversation, and occasionally chose to join it, offering a scant word or two in return for the many they sent his way.

His words, she understood. She wondered if that understanding were an artifact of the years they had spent together in the harem's heart; wondered if Ramiro could speak any language that would not, in the end, sound familiar.

The Serra Alina did not choose to speak at all; her gaze remained fixed upon the table, upon the hands of the men who commanded the Northern armies. She had withdrawn into the posture, pleasing and utterly devoid of motion, that the Serras adopted when they were forced to keep company with men of power.

Amara was intimately acquainted with such posture, such grace; it was almost the one that she had chosen. But she could not keep her gaze upon the table, upon her hands; she wanted to see the faces of the men who would decide much of the course of the war.

Wanted to know, in the end, if the boy who claimed the Tor Leonne—and all that that implied—was merely a puppet in their eyes. Or if he was more.

Because the clan Callesta would suffer for the presence of Northern troops in the Terrean. It was already said, in any Terrean but this one, that Ramiro had sold all sense of Southern honor for the simple expedient of Northern coin.

It stung, of course; such accusations, baseless and empty, still did their damage.

And how much greater would that damage be if they were true?

Kai Leonne, she thought, studying his face with unseemly intensity.

Perhaps because of this, she failed to notice the sudden silence that descended upon the men—and the woman—who spoke so freely in their foreign tongue.

Duarte AKalakar had lifted a single hand, and dropped it gracelessly upon the flat of the table.

The kai Leonne turned, in silence, toward him; Amara lost sight of his face for a moment.

"Someone is standing outside of the doors."

"Standing?" Valedan asked.

"Yes."

She did not ask how he knew this. Instead, she turned toward the doors he indicated. The screens were opaque, but they were not so solid that they denied the passage of light. Caught in the large, wide squares made by crossing beams of wood, she saw a shadow against them.

Fillipo rose swiftly. He did not draw blade; did not move in haste or in obvious alarm.

The Northerners did not rise with him. They had not chosen to bring weapons into the hall itself. She wondered if they now regretted this choice.

Fillipo was no seraf. The doors beneath his hands were not noiseless as they slid in the tracks that moored them; nor did he open them fully.

Amara could not see who waited beyond them, but she saw the back of her husband's most trusted Tyran relax. Relax and then stiffen. He spoke; she heard the cadence of words shorn of content.

He slid the doors shut and turned back to the table.

"Tyr'agnate," he said, executing a formal bow.

Ramiro frowned.

"Apologies, Tyr'agnate. I gave explicit orders that you were not to be disturbed."

"Ah."

Fillipo's severity eased a moment; a smile passed between brothers. "But you are served by the finest of the Tyran in the Dominion. A matter that requires your personal attention has arisen."

He rose.

Amara almost rose with him, but there was, about Fillipo, nothing that spoke of immediate danger. She clapped her hands, and noise must have once again passed through the doors and the thin, opaque walls, for her serafs returned their life and grace to the hall.

Ramiro and Fillipo conversed very briefly; she saw her husband's nod.

"Commander Allen, Commander Berriliya, Commander Kalakar. I offer my apologies, and request your indulgence."

"Of course," Commander Allen said quietly.

"Tyr'agar?"

Valedan looked up.

"I believe that this matter is one that would be of interest to you. If it pleases you, I would be honored by your attendance."

Ser Fillipo par di'Callesta led the way to the stables; the horses—four—were already saddled, their bridles in the hands of cerdan.

Valedan looked at Ramiro, and the Callestan Tyr smiled. "My par," he said, with grave affection, "might have been in the North these twelve years, but he knows me better than any man in Callesta."

Ser Andaro di'Corsarro stepped forward, between Valedan and the cerdan; he took the reins of his horse, and the horse that Valedan had been given by Baredan in the Northern capital.

"We travel in haste," Ramiro said quietly.

It took Valedan a moment to understand why. But he was enough Alina's student that he did. Valedan, with little time to prepare, had only Ser Andaro in attendance. Ser Andaro, his first Tyran, and the only member of his retinue to swear the binding oath.

"Your Tyran?"

"I require one, and one only," Ramiro replied. But his gaze, as it slid deftly across Valedan's, was appraising.

He mounted.

Ser Andaro said quietly, "He honors you. Ser Fillipo clearly guessed that the Tyr'agnate would ask you to attend this meeting—whatever it presages—and he had four horses prepared. The Callestan Tyran are ready for any contingency; he would be well within his rights to take eight, or more, with him.

"But you could not summon an equal number of men on scant notice. You will be his liege lord when the war is won;

he takes care not to emphasize his power in the face of our lack."

He mounted.

"Ser Anton often said that of the four Tyr'agnati, Ramiro di'Callesta was the most dangerous."

"You concur?"

Ser Andaro nodded. "Now, yes. He is a subtle man."

Valedan said nothing. But he noticed that this was the first time since the Kings' Challenge that Ser Andaro had chosen to speak Ser Anton's name unencumbered by anger or loss.

They rode through the streets of Callesta.

Valedan was familiar with the chosen route, although it took him a few miles to realize this; he had traveled it only by daylight. Moonlight changed the face of the City.

In the North, night was held at bay by magelights. Not so, Callesta; the heights held power, but the streets were home to serafs and the poorest of clansmen. Sleep, when the planting season was at its height, was a necessity. There were, no doubt, the Southern equivalent of taverns nestled within the city's heart, but they had remained purely theoretical; not even the Ospreys ventured into the streets of the city to relax in the fashion for which they were famed.

In the absence of manmade light, the moon reigned.

There were no people upon the roads; the hooves of shod horses seemed the night's only language, its only expression.

They reached the gates quickly.

The guardhouse was lit from within, and as horses approached, bobbing lights came out to meet them.

Ser Fillipo reined his horse in, dismounting.

Ser Andaro dismounted easily.

Valedan waited.

The cerdan approached the Callestan Tyr, set the lamp upon the ground, and bowed. "Tyr'agnate," he said.

"Ser Callas."

"We have two visitors outside of the gates."

"So I have been informed."

"They wished to speak to you, and only to you."

"That is . . . unusual."

The cerdan rose. "It is the Lady's time," he replied.

"Ah. I have been informed that they claim to represent the Arkosan Voyani."

The man nodded.

"Have you been able to verify the truth of their claim?"

"No, Tyr'agnate. But we have taken the liberty of sending for one who can."

"Good. She has not arrived?"

"Not yet."

"Then," he replied, turning to Valedan, "with your permission, Tyr'agar, we will wait."

"It seems prudent," Valedan replied.

The man at the gates was not so finely mannered as the Tyran who served Ramiro; his brows rose as Valedan's title took root; his eyes widened, reflecting the lamplight at his feet.

It grew closer as he fell at once to his knees, bowing in the open street.

No one spoke.

Valedan waited for a moment, and then realized that no one would. "Ser Callas," he said quietly, "please, rise. It is, as you said, the Lady's time, and her light is both pleasant and scant. In the Lord's time, I am certain that the crest I bear would be visible."

The man did not move.

Valedan glanced at Ramiro; the Callestan Tyr merely waited.

This was a test.

With Alina by his side, Valedan might not have been aware of this fact; he felt her absence keenly. He turned to look at Ser Andaro, for the movement of his Tyran's horse caught his attention; it wasn't hard.

"Ser Callas," Valedan said, "rise." It was easy to put strength into the three words.

The cerdan obeyed the command as if it had come from the Tyr'agnate; he rose. But again, his lack of training in the High Courts showed; his eyes were too wide.

The title Valedan desired, the title for which this war would be fought—was being fought, even now—was heavier this eve than it had been since he had first chosen to take it in the Halls of the Northern Kings.

For it came to him, as he stared at the Callestan cerdan, that Ser Callas had indeed committed a crime. He had failed to pay the required respect to a man whose power and title were so far above his own in importance, Valedan might as well have been a god.

And it was not as a god that he had come.

Not as a god that he desired power.

Why, then?

He had taken the title, had laid claim to the bloodline, for only one reason: to save the lives of the hostages in *Avantari,* the palace of Kings. There, surrounded by the Northerners who had marked his life in every possible way, he had done his thinking, his planning, had made his choice. Had felt the weight of it keenly.

But in the North, such a lapse as Ser Callas had committed was not worthy of notice. It was certainly not worthy of death.

Ramiro's silence granted Valedan power; the power to choose, and to judge. He almost threw it away, because he desired no such power.

But he had come this far with the guidance of Serra Alina di'Lamberto, and she had been the most adept of teachers, the harshest of masters. He understood, as he sat astride his great horse, that he did, in fact, desire such power. He called himself the Tyr'agar.

And in the South, the power that he abhorred and the power that he was willing to die for were so intertwined he could not easily dismiss the one without damaging the other.

"Ser Callas."

"Tyr'agar." The man would have fallen to the ground again, but Valedan—the Tyr'agar—had bid him rise.

"I am not Markaso kai di'Leonne. I bear the Leonne blood, and I serve the Leonne clan—but I serve it in a fashion of my own choosing, as every Tyr has done before me." He took a breath now, committed. "Markaso kai di'Leonne once bid the Terrean of Averda to fight a war that was ill-considered and costly.

"I am aware of the cost; I am aware that it was borne upon the shoulders, and by the bloodlines, of clans such as yours. You bow. It is a social grace, a gesture of respect. I accept it. That you offered your obeisance to the Tyr'agnate before me, I also acknowledge.

"But it is the gestures that I will never personally see which will define you. You carry a sword by your side. Had the visitors at the gate meant harm to Callesta, had they drawn sword or offered threat, you would have used that sword in defense of the city in which I am honored to reside.

"I might never have witnessed such an act, but it is *that* act, that willingness to serve and to sacrifice, that I value. I am aware that it will be granted me, time and again, by all of the men who are bound to serve the Tyr'agnate Ramiro kai di'Callesta.

"And I will not squander it lightly."

"Ser Callas," Ramiro di'Callesta said, his voice cool.

With no relief at all, the cerdan now turned to the Tyr of Averda.

"You have been honored by the Tyr'agar, and by receiving such honor, you honor Callesta."

The lines of the man's shoulders shifted slightly. In the North, they would have sagged with open relief.

"However," the Tyr'agnate said, "I do not wish to . . . expose . . . the kai Leonne to such blatant disrespect from the rest of the men who serve you. Inform them that we have arrived."

"Tyr'agnate," Ser Callas said. He lifted the lamp and walked quickly to the guardhouse.

Only when he had passed beyond their hearing did Ramiro di'Callesta turn.

"Well said, kai Leonne."

Valedan returned that gaze quietly. "Tyr'agnate, a question."

"Ask."

"Had I chosen to take offense at the order in which our titles were acknowledged, what would you have done?"

"I would have allowed Ser Fillipo to take the man's head and offer it to you for his crime."

Valedan did not doubt him. He chose his next words with care, skirting the sudden anger that weighted them. "You could not expect him to recognize me."

"No."

"What would his death have accomplished?"

"The cerdan at the gates would never again make such an obvious mistake. In the South, they learn quickly from the errors of others; if Ser Callas could not serve in one way, he would serve in another."

Valedan was speechless.

Carefully, deliberately, speechless.

But Ser Andaro, who now stood by his side, his reins in hand, his horse as still as any horse of his size and temperament could be, spoke.

"His inability to recognize your crest and your title does not reflect poorly upon Ser Callas, Tyr'agar. It reflects poorly upon the Tyr'agnate. By such omissions, the Tyrs freely offer slights to one another that they could not—without war or bloodshed—otherwise offer."

"Had it been deliberate, I might have accepted his head."

Nothing in Ser Andaro's quiet gaze spoke of belief.

"But word will now travel," the Leonne Tyran continued. "Among the cerdan who serve in this capacity, your name will be known. And your words, your words will be known as well. They will grow in the telling, they will change. But they will carry the seed of a truth that must be felt: You bear the Leonne blood, but you are not your father's son."

"And in truth," Ramiro di'Callesta said, "because it is the Lady's time, I will say this: Ser Callas is not of the High Court, but he has served me well in the capacity for which he was chosen. Had I been forced to surrender his head to you, I would have done so with regret; I would not have destroyed the rest of his family, and in time, I would have ceded to his son the position he now holds."

"Let me speak as well with the Lady's voice," Valedan replied.

Ramiro waited.

"I desire no such gestures. I seek to take no offense. It is not by the death of men such as these that I wish to prove my worthiness to rule."

"I am aware of this, kai Leonne. If I were not, I would not have requested the honor of your presence on such short notice."

Valedan was weary. And because he was weary, he spoke freely, aware that it could be costly. Aware that, when Serra Alina discovered it, it would be.

"I am weary of this testing."

"You consider the respect due the rank you desire a game, Tyr'agar?"

"No. But this—this is a game."

"Ah. No. I will speak freely, although perhaps that word does not have the same resonance in the South that it does in the Halls of *Avantari*. You are not my son; your instruction is not in my hands. But you have bound your blood to mine, and I grant you this much.

"You desire to rule in the South, and in the South, such title *must* command respect. It must be a matter of life and death. If you do not desire to be the cause of such careless death, there are ways to avoid it. And one of the accepted ways is not to simply ignore insult when it is offered—even when it is offered in ignorance.

"Make yourself known, kai Leonne. I will put at your disposal the necessary funds with which to do so. Take serafs. Hire cerdan. The building of your Tyran will of necessity be something you must approach with caution, but at the moment, the only guards that attend you are not guards conversant with the ways of the South. If you wish to spare men like Ser Callas, you must become a man that such men will know on sight. You must carry yourself as if death is a matter of whim—your whim.

"I will treat you as if you are that man, kai Leonne. Others will not; they will seek advantage if they feel that there is weakness to be exploited." He lifted a hand. "You are not weak. I do not accuse you of weakness, although my words seem harsh to your Tyran."

Ser Andaro's face was completely impassive.

"But others will mark any hesitation that you give them. If it is suspected that you care for men such as these, they will use them against you. Make yourself a man above that suspicion." He bowed, and then, with care, he dismounted.

The sudden difference in their height was not lost on Valedan.

"There are many ways in which a war can be lost," Ramiro said, with no rancor. "And I believe that I have witnessed most of them."

"Had one of my men offered such an offense, would I be expected to offer his head to you?"

Ramiro did not condescend to answer the question; the reply was obvious.

"You are not in the North, kai Leonne. And if you are successful here, you will never again call *Avantari* home. I admit that when I traveled with Baredan di'Navarre, I expected very little. I understood his desire; he is, in all ways but the oath itself, Tyran, and honored to be so.

"But you distinguished yourself in ways that I had not anticipated in my sojourn in the Northern capital."

Ser Andaro bowed to the Tyr'agnate.

Ramiro's nod was cool. But the moon was at its height; after a pause, he continued. "I will be surprised if Eneric, the man who won the Kings' Challenge, is not upon the field of battle. I will be surprised if the men who serve your banner in cause of war in *my* name, do not in the end, serve your banner because of yours."

Valedan, mounted, noted that Ser Andaro now watched the Tyr'agnate like a hawk.

"Ser Fillipo," he continued, "is my par; the captain of my oathguards. Scour the Dominion and you will not find his equal. But I will tell you what he will not say himself, even if asked in the full blush of the Lady's Night: He serves you."

"Ramiro—" Fillipo began.

The Tyr'agnate raised a hand casually, and the words died.

"Ser Kyro serves you. He is a man cast in the Lambertan mold. Even Ser Miko, second of my Tyran, has become proud of the war we fight in your name."

"It is a war," Valedan said with dignity, "that Averda *must* win if Callesta is to survive. You have . . . honored me. But in doing so, you say little of your people, little of what you have offered them.

"You would have offered me Ser Callas' head."

"Indeed."

"But you have already stated that you would not have asked us to travel in haste, to join you at the gates, had you guessed that such an offer would be necessary."

"True as well. It would have been a disappointment to me. But I have lived beneath the Lord's gaze for all of my life; I accept disappointment when I choose to take that risk. Had you taken his head, it is the last thing Callestan that you would have been willingly ceded, the politics of necessity aside. Are you aware that the Serra Amara holds you in high regard?"

Valedan said nothing.

"She is canny, and she is cautious; far more cautious than either I or my brother. She is a Serra; she will accept with grace any order that I choose to give her. She understood, before we left, that I would seek the last of the clan Leonne, and that I would bring him to the South, in order to protect Averdan interests.

"But she did not expect to like you. Did not expect to feel any respect at all for you, however grudging. She remembers well the last time a kai Leonne walked within Callestan lands.

"I am a man who holds his wives in some esteem, and although it is unwise, I will admit that I have been impressed by your ability, your wordless, guileless ability, to draw from the Serra what even I have almost failed to obtain.

"And perhaps it is because of this that I offer you the instruction that she herself would offer were she ever to be placed in the enviable position of being the woman to whom you turned for advice. Fillipo," he added, with a rare smile, "you may speak."

Fillipo grimaced. "The Tyr'agnate is far too kind," he said with a wry smile. "Scour the Dominion and you will find men who match my worth. I am not a humble man; you will not find many. But you will find none that are Ramiro's equal. And I begin to think, under moonlight, on the day that we have received word that war has begun in earnest, that were we to scour the Dominion, kai Leonne, we would not find another man that was yours.

"Without your intervention, I would not be here, to fight this war at my kai's side. That," he said, wolfish now, "would be his loss." The grin faded. "But without your intervention, my wives, my sons, my daughter, would also be lost to the howl of the winds. You have spent much time in the company of the Princess Royale; you must understand the Kings at least as well as any of the other hostages. You must know that you risked your own death at their hands when you refused their first offer of clemency.

"But what I do not think you fully understand is the debt that we, as survivors, have accrued. Any of us."

"The Kings are not known for their lack of mercy."

"Indeed. Our deaths would have been private, swift, merciful. But the Justice-born King demands his due. Or do you think that he would have held his hand? If the Northern gods are not the gods of the South, they are gods in their fashion, and they demand their due."

Valedan nodded quietly. "Ser Fillipo?"

"Kai Leonne."

"Had Ramiro di'Callesta ordered you to take that man's head, would you have hesitated?"

"No."

"And had I ordered you to withhold your sword, what would you have done?"

Ramiro chuckled. "You are clever, kai Leonne. Fillipo, answer the question."

Beneath that humor, steel. Genial, affectionate steel.

"He is my Tyr," Fillipo said gravely. "And as oathguard, I am bound to him by laws that supersede all other loyalties." The words were stiff. True.

But they were not the last words that Ser Fillipo offered Valedan. "You are not my son," he said gravely, echoing the kai Callesta's words. "But I will offer you advice, as my brother has sought to do. If you are ever to find yourself in such a situation, do not deliver your orders to Tyran. You would serve only to insult the Tyran in question.

"Deliver those orders, instead, to the Tyr'agnate himself."

Ramiro laughed out loud.

Valedan looked between them.

Ser Andaro said gravely, "Such an order, bluntly given, would be obeyed by any man who did not desire your death. And the Tyr'agnate of Callesta has proved himself, this eve, to be a trusted ally."

Valedan could almost hear Alina's sharp words in the distance. "You honor me," he said quietly.

"Indeed. But the time for such honor has almost passed. Listen."

Hooves thundered in the distance of the dark Callestan streets.

Ser Callas came out of the guardhouse at once. He moved quickly, his stride as wide as stride could be that was not an all-out run.

He met the horses in the distance, using the pull of his bobbing lamp to catch their eyes. Valedan could hear his voice, but could not make out the individual words; he didn't need to. He could guess at some of what was said. Could almost hear his title carried by the caprice of the night's breeze.

The horses slowed to a walk.

There were four; upon the backs of three, made dark by the night sky and the silver moon, were men armed and armored. On the back of the fourth, two figures.

Ser Callas led them to the waiting men, and he bowed, first to the Tyr'agar, and second to the Tyr'agnate. "Tyr'agar, Tyr'agnate," he said quietly, "she has arrived."

"Good. Bring her into the light."

Valedan waited as the last of the horses walked forward, its reins in Ser Callas' hand. The cerdan who rode the horse became obvious in the light of the lamp; he all but carried a woman across the back of his mount. Her legs dangled freely to either side of the beast; freely and stiffly. She was not used to riding.

Valedan chose that moment to dismount.

Ser Ramiro approached the horse with caution.

"Aliera," he said quietly, removing his riding gloves in the scant light. He offered the woman in the evening robes his hand. "My apologies for the harshness of this summons. You were not harmed?"

The words themselves were pleasant enough. But Valedan heard them clearly: There was danger in each syl-

lable should her answer be the wrong one. None of it was
for her.

"Harmed? No. The summons itself was not, of course, to
be denied—but no one lifted hand; no sword left sheath."

"Good."

"Tyr'agnate," the hooded woman said. "I did not expect
to see you here, not at this hour." She accepted the hand he
offered, and left the back of the horse with a grace that her
posture upon it had not suggested she possessed. When
both of her feet were upon the ground, she fell at once into
the full subservient posture that Valedan had seen Alina assume so often.

"My apologies," she said, in the softest, the most pleasantly musical, of voices. "I did not ask for the time to dress
myself appropriately. No one thought to inform me that you
might be present."

"No matter how you choose to dress yourself, you could
never be accused of impropriety."

She lifted her face. The lamp's glow was soft in the
evening light, but not so soft that it could completely disguise the lines in her face, the pale edges of hair that had
once been black as night. "Is that Ser Fillipo I see? By your
side?"

Fillipo looked, for just an instant, ten years—twenty—
younger than he was. "It is, Aliera."

"Then our enemies have much to fear, much indeed, if
the two Callestan brothers stand once again side by side."

Ramiro smiled. "It has been far too long, Aliera."

"You have been busy, of late. Or so I am told by your
lovely wife."

"She is, as usual, correct. I have been busy. But sometimes the rigors of duty are eased by the grace of the familiar and the trusted. Aliera en'Callesta, it is my privilege to
introduce you to Ser Valedan kai di'Leonne."

Her expression, perfect in spite of—or perhaps because
of—the lines that spoke of age, shifted; her lips widened in

a smile that seemed, to Valedan's eye, to be entirely genuine.

He bowed. She was en'Callesta, but she was far too old
to be wife to the Callestan Tyr—and had she been, she
would not have been summoned in haste in such a fashion.

"Aliera en'Callesta was the youngest of my father's
wives," Ser Ramiro said. "I asked her to attend my Serra
after my father's death; the Serra Amara herself enjoined
me in my pleas."

Her smile deepened. "You must not speak so openly of
things that are said in the harem, Ser Ramiro, lest you be
judged to be too fond of that harem." But she bowed her
head to ground as she turned to Valedan. "Tyr'agar," she
said gravely. "Please, accept my apologies for the terrible
disarray you see. The Tyr'agnate honors me greatly by offering me the name of his clan, but in truth, I am no longer
wife; I am no longer a part of the harem. It has been many,
many years since I was required to perform the rituals and
the observances of the High Court, and I will not have the
worth of the Callestan wives judged by so humble an appearance as the one I now present.

"I lead a simple life within the confines of the city
Callesta, and Ser Ramiro has been far too kind; I want for
nothing. His serafs attend my simple needs with grace and
care."

"She is, and will always be, my father's wife," Ramiro
said quietly.

Valedan understood what that meant: she was one of the
many mothers that the kai and the par Callesta had had during their enclosure within the harem itself.

"You honor us with your presence," he told her, meaning
the words.

Her smile did not falter, but for just a moment, her eyes
seemed as bright and sharp as new steel. "The honor is entirely mine. I believe that I will petition the Serra Amara for
some small part of her time, if she herself is not absorbed
whole by the task you have set yourself, Tyr'agnate.

"But it is not to speak of the foolish desires of the elderly that I was summoned."

"It should have been," the Tyr'agnate said, and there was no doubting the authenticity of his affection. "But alas, no. You are the only woman present in the city of Callesta that I could call upon, Aliera. I trust your judgment, and it is both that trust and that judgment that I require.

"Ser Callas."

"Tyr'agnate."

"Please escort us through the guardhouse. I wish to see those who have requested an audience."

"Tyr'agnate."

CHAPTER THIRTEEN

HOURS seemed to have passed since the cerdan bid them wait; too many hours. The moon's face had grown brighter, larger; it hung low in the sky, as if approaching, at last, this most wayward of daughters.

The packed dirt beneath Elena's feet had given way slowly to the weight of her boots, the repetitive cadence of her steps. She walked the rim of a circle, deepening its edge. Wondering what it enclosed.

But when the guardhouse door opened, she stopped her instinctive pacing and took a step back. Had her answer.

Men entered the moonlight, as if gracing the Lady's dwelling; they were sleek with metal, drawn sword, and the soft orange glow of lamps. Those lamps now numbered four; they were carried upon the stiff backs of wooden poles.

Twelve men entered the small clearing in front of the gates. Had it been possible to flee, Elena might have. But she knew that Lord Telakar would not join her in her flight. She drew breath; held it. Her knees locked.

She did not recognize the men—any of the men—who now watched her, swords drawn, faces expressionless. But she recognized the crest that two men bore. The full face of the sun rising, with eight distinct rays, and the half sun, with eight rays. The Tyr'agnate. And his Tyran.

Evallen of the Arkosa Voyani would have recognized the man; Elena was certain of it. But neither Margret nor Elena had ever had cause to meet him—at least not in Elena's memory; cause or desire.

Without thinking she took a step back. Another.

Lord Telakar's hand rose; it landed upon her shoulder. A warning. Or a threat.

The Tyr'agnate stepped forward. He turned to the young man at his side. "With your permission?"

The young man nodded.

It confused Elena, and confusion—in company such as this—was close kin to fear. The Voyani did not meet with clansmen. Not like this. Not even under the cover of the Lady's Night.

Lady, she thought, *guide me. Guide me, Lady.*

The Tyr'agnate stepped to one side. Behind him, in the center of the four lamps, stood a woman in night robes. She lifted her hands and drew the hood from her hair, settling it with unconscious grace upon her shoulders.

And then she smiled. "Elena," she said softly.

No. No, not this, not here. *Lady,* she thought, bitterly aware that she had lost the right to bespeak the goddess.

"You recognize this woman?" The Tyr'agnate said quietly.

The older woman nodded. "Although it has been almost a year since last we met, I recognize her well." She stepped past the Tyr'agnate; past the circle of light, the circle of silent swords.

But her feet stopped just shy of the circle walked into ground, the circle of dirt.

"Elena," she said again. "How fares Tamara?"

"My—my mother is well," Elena replied. Her throat was dry, too dry for Averda. She had swallowed the desert air.

"And the Matriarch? Her daughter?"

Too damn dry. "Margret of the Arkosa Voyani is Matriarch now."

Aliera en'Callesta crossed her heart center with the flutter of deliberate, delicate gesture. Even in horror, she was delicate.

"Aliera," the Tyr'agnate said, "can this woman speak for the Arkosa Voyani?"

No. No. No.

Aliera turned to the Tyr'agnate. "She can," she replied quietly. "For if I am not mistaken, she is now daughter to the Matriarch; she is heir to the line."

The Tyr'agnate nodded. Turning, he bowed.

He bowed to Elena, daughter of Tamara. "I am Ser Ramiro kai di'Callesta," he told her gravely. "And I am honored that you have chosen to travel to the city of Callesta. Few of the Voyani do, and of those who have chosen to speak with me, you are the only one who has asked for me directly.

"This is a poor welcome," he added quietly. "And it is perhaps not the right place in which to speak. If you will trust me, I offer you the hospitality of Callesta. It is, I assure you, far less threatening than the hospitality of the Tor Leonne."

A smile touched his lips; it was as cold as the blade his Tyran held.

She hesitated.

Into that hesitation, he poured more words. "And this," he told her, meeting and holding her gaze, "is the true heir to the Leonne bloodline; the man who is meant to wield the Sun Sword."

She froze.

"Ser Valedan kai di'Leonne."

She almost told them then. But Lord Telakar's hand was cold; cold as desert night.

She offered the Tyr'agar presumptive the most proper, the most careful, of Voyani bows.

His brow rose slightly, and then he smiled; he returned what she offered. As if, Elena thought, he was used to women who did not place knees and forehead against the ground at the mention of his title.

He was young. Older than Adam, but not, she thought, by much. He was slender with youth, and his face was pale, his skin smooth. His eyes were wide and dark, night in miniature. Lady's Night.

She said weakly, "We bear word."

"Come, cousin," Telakar said. "Let us not keep the Tyr'agnate waiting."

They opened the gate. It was unnecessary; both Elena and Telakar could easily follow the cerdan back through the guardhouse, leaving the gates themselves untroubled. But such opening of gates, between the man who ruled the Terrean in daylight, and the woman who was heir to the night of its wild roads, was a symbol.

A symbol, as well, the offer of horse.

Elena accepted. She was no clansman, but she knew the beasts of the field, and of the open road. She was not the Matriarch, but she was of the bloodline; there was not a beast of burden that she could not, in the end, bend to her will.

And yet, as she approached, the horse reared up, up again, on two legs; his hooves fell hard, creating crescents in the dirt.

Telakar. She knew that the horse would not bear one such as he.

"My cousin," she said quietly, "does not ride."

The Tyr'agnate nodded. "And you?"

"I do."

If the cerdan disapproved, they were silent; they offered her the respect, measure for measure, that their Tyr offered.

She approached the horse again, her voice soft, low, steady. She spoke in the old tongue, the wild tongue, the Voyani tongue. It came to her naturally, easily; she held out her hands and the cerdan who had—just—managed to calm the horse reluctantly slid the reins into them.

Women, she thought, did not ride in the Dominion.

But she was Voyani.

She brought the reins low, brought the horse to face her. Saw the foam flecks around his muzzle. Telakar had chosen prudence; he had withdrawn the hand from her shoulder, and then, as the clansmen came with the horse, had even withdrawn the night shadows he cast; she could see him if she turned to look over her shoulder, but she could also ignore his presence.

Tell them, she thought. *Tell them, Elena. There are enough of them now. The Tyr is famous for his sword skill. Tell them.*

But she hesitated.

When she spoke at all, Elena Tamaraan was known for the quickness of her tongue; it was second only to the quickness of her temper. Many, many were the Arkosan faces that bore the imprint of her palm, her instant anger; many were the Arkosan eyes that had witnessed the tears that followed, as clansmen and women accepted the furious apology that she could not—quite—put into the grace of words.

Therefore it might have come as a surprise to many of them to find that she was aware of her words. That in some fashion, as they rushed past her grasp, conveyed by an emotion that defied control, she watched them, listened to them, weighed them.

As a child, she had been cousin to the Matriarch's daughter. As an adolescent, she had proved that she had more—much more—than that simple, tenuous claim: she could see, as the Voyani Matriarchs so often could, some hint of the future that waited, lurking around the bend in the twisted path of the *Voyanne*.

It had not started with dreams, as it often did.

It had not started with images, with the bright, sudden flare of event that transported *now* into *later* as she stood transfixed by the fraying colors at its edges.

No; it had started with words.

Margret had said, *You're just growing up. Stop worrying so much; you sound like an Ona.*

If Evallen had said as much, Elena would have listened. But Evallen said nothing. The shadows of her gaze had shifted and changed with time, sharpening, deepening.

Elena knew that she was watched, and would be, until the Matriarch died.

Because Margret had failed to show the hints of such an early gift. And because, in the end, the Matriarchs did what was best for all of Arkosa. Not just their daughters, their own kin.

She wondered if the dead watched; wondered if there was truth to the belief that the Matriarchs who served the Lady's interests might reside by her side in the comfort of the night sky, rather than in the folds of the howling winds. *Evallen.*

A name.

A word.

The gift had come in words. Later—much later—she would have the rest: the dreams and the bright, clear visions that seemed to come on like desert mirage in the glare of the waking day. But it had started with words. She let them come, and after they had fallen out of her mouth in a tumble, one after the other, she would suddenly sense the truth inherent in them. Or the lie.

She was younger; she would practice her gift on the most trivial of games: the fates of the affairs of the heart that have such terrible intensity in the years of early womanhood. *Giavanno will fall in love with me.* Or *Giavanno will leave Elisa.* Or *Giavanno will one day understand just how big a fool he is.*

She had been so young, then; so very young. Love had encompassed the whole of her ability to dream; the whole of her desire.

No, not love; something sweeter and far more destructive. Ah, and to remember that here, the rough strands of mane between her fingers.

Foolish or no, she had learned the truth of her terrible gift when the Lady had chosen to lift the veil and give her a glimpse of the desolation of the future: Giavanno would never fall in love with her, no matter how much she tried to please him, how much of herself she was willing to offer.

He would, big, stupid oaf, never leave Elisa. And he already understood how big of a fool he was, had been, would be; but he would not regret his love for Elisa, no matter who else offered him the whole of their heart.

She whispered into the peaked ears of the waiting beast in the singsong voice of freedom and binding that was used by the Voyani women. She knew that the clansmen watched; knew that when the horse stilled at her command, she would hear their voices, their muted surprise, even their disgust, the revulsion they felt.

She didn't care.

She had measured the truth of her silent words, their import so much greater than those earlier, girlish incantations, the pleas that she now found embarrassing, and she had found them wanting.

If she warned them at all, these arrogant clansmen, these trusting idiots, they would die. It shouldn't have mattered.

But the time for making a stand, and an expensive one at that, had passed. A handful of cerdan could, of necessity, be easily replaced.

But the Tyr'agnate of Averda? She glanced at him as the horse began to move; his eyes were full upon her face.

Margret, she thought, suddenly glad that she would not be required to speak for some minutes. *Forgive me.*

The Tyr'agnate of the Terrean of Averda was, of necessity, a man who appreciated subtlety; who strove to achieve it, and who understood it when it was presented to him. His birth to the High Clans had not, however, granted him access to the low clans; the low clans had been observed at a distance.

It was a distance that he had gone to some lengths to lessen, to the amusement of his father and the very cool horror of his mother.

In the end, he had told them both gravely, *it is upon the backs of men such as these that my Terrean will rise—or fall. If I do not understand how men such as these are bought and sold—*

They are not serafs. Na'miro, his mother had interjected.

They are not, he replied, acceding, with a great patience that he did not feel, to the nicety of the grace that an obedient son owed the woman who birthed him in the heart of the chambers she ruled. *It was a figure of speech.*

Indeed. And a low figure, at that. She had turned to her husband, then, falling artfully to knees that age had stiffened. *You see, my husband? You see what he brings into these chambers? He spoke without thought.*

Your mother, in this, is correct. If it amuses you—or better, strengthens you—seek the lowborn. Learn how to motivate them; how to manipulate them; learn how to elevate them. Or crush them utterly.

It is certain, in your life, that you will be forced to all of these actions before the winds scour you.

But while you are learning these things, Ser Ramiro, the name a pointed counter to the Serra's use of the harem name, the child's name, *you will* also *learn that while the appearance of speaking without thought—the appearance of the fecklessness or the naïveté of youth—is of value, the substance behind it is not.*

Do not speak without thought. Among the lowborn, among the highborn, among foreigners that you cannot imagine, at this stage in your training, you will stand beside. Never speak without thinking.

There will always be witnesses.

His father, a man not prone to giving advice, had offered him—that day—the most valuable advice he was ever to offer. It had surprised Ramiro, years later, to hear just such advice travel from the lips of a peer to the ears of wayward youth. It had seemed so singularly profound, so terribly important, given with the full weight of the Tyr'agnate's voice.

Memory.

He smiled. He had learned, with time, that the lowborn

clung to many of the ideals that the High Court sheered away. That they did, as he had been cautioned against, speak freely and with little thought. It made the presence of the highborn particularly difficult, for the words of the foolish were always an avenue to death, should the powerful desire some scant excuse.

He had not, however, offered those clansmen his father's words. Instead, as efficiently as he had done much else in the tumult of that youth, he had attempted to have them teach him *more*.

It was to be his only real failure.

For he had desired some knowledge of the more intimate workings of the Voyani—Arkosa, Havalla, it didn't particularly matter which—and although the lower clansmen were willing to trust his stranger's guise in matters of drink and money, they fell silent when he asked them of the Voyani.

"It's women's work," they would mutter, into their cups or sleeves. He had, of course, a ruler's means to compel obedience, but the words themselves would not give what he desired: egress into the Voyani world.

And so, of the peoples who made their living across the vast plains, the ones he could not quite fathom were the Voyani.

But something, Ramiro thought, was wrong.

The woman was terrified. She was not as wild and ineffectual as many of the Voyani were wont to be; she hid the fear behind a seemly mask. Could her terror be ascribed entirely to his presence?

He could not be certain.

He glanced at her; was certain she was aware of the inspection. She was, if he was any judge of character, accustomed to speaking freely. Was probably accustomed to obedience, if the Serra Aliera en'Callesta was correct in her surmise.

The Matriarch's Daughter. Here, in the heart of Callesta.

The city unfolded in the darkness of a historic night.

*   *   *

Elena hesitated when the streets began to climb; hesitated again when they reached the flat plateau beyond which—by decree in all such cities of her acquaintance—they were forbidden any further height.

Both times, she had chanced to look up—if chance were something deliberate, and cruel—to see Lord Telakar, striding in raiment of moon and shadow across the winding road. He seemed a thing out of place, the essential wildness that lay at the heart of a desert tunnel, or the heart of a forest's fire, when sticks of standing deadwood indiscriminately consumed everything in its path.

What do you want? she thought, and realized—belated, and stupid—that she had never once asked this. Not of him, of course; she couldn't trust any answer he'd give her, and she was smart enough—barely—not to want to anger him. But she hadn't asked it *this* way, in words that she could shape and test beneath the tight line of closed lips.

Why?

Because she'd just woken up.

Because she'd been carried from the densest growth in the valleys to the height of the Callestan plateau. Because, even in slapping her, openhanded, his eyes intent, he made her feel not like victim, but like Voyani child. Voyani child in dangerous territory, where a misstep is death.

She'd struck children in her time. Wasn't proud of it; wasn't ashamed. When there *was* time for patience, patience was used. But she knew the difference.

She took a deep breath. Horse scent filled her nostrils, the insides of her mouth; strands of mane tangled in the rounds of her palms, the stiff curve of her fingers. Night in Callesta held none of the death that night in the Sea of Sorrows did by the simple expedient of existing.

Instead, it held the death offered by intrigue, the death that always surrounded men of power. Her gaze brushed the length of Telakar's face.

Are you alive?

No. Elena Tamaraan. I am not alive.

Alive or not, he was beautiful. She hadn't seen it in the desert. Wondered why she saw it now. He reminded her of the man who followed in the wake of Jewel ATerafin; the long-haired, pale-skinned lordling who defied desert sun, desert heat, and desert cold with the same nonchalance.

Yet she knew that that lord would have answered her question—had he condescended to speak with anyone save Jewel ATerafin or the Northern bard—very differently.

And so, she began.

You will kill the Tyr'agnate of Callesta.

Silence.

You will kill the kai Leonne boy who would be Tyr'agar.

Again, silence.

You intend no harm by your presence here.

The words drifted, hollow and tinny, in the silence she had forced upon them. She knew this was a lie.

And she knew that the gift that she did possess, the gift she was possessed by, did not stoop to answer direct questions.

She shook her head. Once more. Once more.

You will carry information to the demons that will cause the death of the Tyr'agnate or the Tyr'agar.

Again, silence.

Silence was better than the hollowness of lie, but it was less pleasant than the stabbing viscerality of truth.

She had her own instinct to go by; all that was left her. That and the certainty that he did intend someone harm by the journey he had chosen to undertake.

She stood in as Matriarch here. She would be identified as Arkosan. The Serra Aliera en'Callesta—the retired wife, the honored friend of the Arkosans in this city, and the woman to whom such rumors of war and the wayward behavior of the worst of the clansmen were sent, in Evallen's youth—had marked her as clearly as a woman could be, and still retain any power in a city ruled by clansmen.

All cities were.

Had been.

Margret.

Therefore anything that came out of the meeting to which they traveled would rightly be laid at the feet of the Arkosan Voyani.

The only way that Margret could distance herself from any tragedy or betrayal that occurred would be to disavow Elena Tamaraan; to choose another Daughter from among her younger kin.

And such a betrayal was only answered in one fashion, among the Voyani of *any* clan.

Not that, Elena thought. *Not that; poor Margret. Not my death, too.*

And knew, the moment she thought it, that Nicu was indeed dead.

She sucked in air at exactly the wrong time; it was too dry and it scoured her throat, some tendril of malicious wind, of wayward breeze. She choked, losing her grip a moment on the mane of the horse; her knees locked in place and held her steady.

Nicu was dead.

Margret had killed him.

Aie, and where was she? Where was Elena, the only person who could truly understand what such a loss, such a death, *must* mean?

Here, at the side of a demon, the words *Arkosan Voyani* spread before her like a lie.

She rode.

They gained the plateau before Elena could think upon how she might extricate herself from her situation. Gained it before she could be certain to keep some room between Lord Telakar and herself. Only the horse guaranteed his distance; he traveled in front of the palanquin and behind the main body of horsemen; the Tyr'agar, the Tyr'agnate, and their two Tyran.

She wondered bitterly what the gatekeepers had said in their message to the Tyr; never in her life had she heard of two such important men traveling in such negligible numbers. Did not have long enough to wonder.

The Tyr'agnate himself came to stand by her side, dismounting with the ease of long practice. He paused for just a moment, and then he offered her a hand; it was gloved, but open; he carried no dagger, no other weapon.

The Tyran at his side stood, hand on sword hilt, in a posture with which Elena was much more familiar.

She hesitated, wondering if accepting his help was an act of weakness. *Think, idiot. Women don't ride.* Of course it would be construed as an act of weakness. But such an offer, to a rider, would also be construed as insult, and it was clear from the way he stood that he intended none.

She was practical. She had tired, the horse was large, and her legs were shaking; she accepted his hand. Did her best to make sure that her dismount was not as clumsy and awkward as it should have been—or as it would have been without his support.

He said nothing, however. He allowed her to gain her feet and then stepped back, dropping his hand to his sword side, all hint of the gesture gone in that instant.

The boy Tyr dismounted, as did his man. The cerdan who had carried palanquin through the dark city streets deposited it with care and then retreated, retracing their steps back to the gatehouse. She wondered how long it would take those men to fall back into the boredom of nights punctuated by cricket, hunting bird, and starlight.

When Aliera en'Callesta had emerged from the palanquin, their party was complete; the Tyr'agnate bid them enter doors—the main doors—that had been drawn wide for just such purpose. The grounds of Callesta lay before them, a sea of shadowed trees, of captured light in transparent globes, of the flutter of insects drawn to fires that could not, by presence of glass, consume them. Elena paused for a moment, and drew a sharp breath.

Too audible; she knew it.

She saw the Tyr'agnate look down, a ight smile turning

the corners of his lips skyward. "It is possible," he said
gravely, "that you will encounter the Serra to whom responsibility for these gardens belongs. No doubt you will
be more schooled in expression at that time; in my limited
experience with the Voyani, it is women who command
their attention and their caution.

"Do not think poorly of me, however, if I recount your
first expression upon seeing what she has labored over
these past weeks."

She smiled. For just a moment, the smile was genuine.
Although the Tyr'agnate's words were inflected in the man-
ner of the High Courts, the meaning behind them was clear:
He loved his wife, and he wished her to be honored.

It surprised Elena. She had not expected it, although in
truth, she had not thought much about it at all.

"If I had time," she said quietly, "and she considered my
presence an honor, I would honor her gardens for the full
three days before I took my leave. They must be beautiful
beneath the Lord's gaze."

He nodded. "The face they wear is very different in the
day, but, yes, I find them beautiful."

He turned and set off down the path; she followed, aware
that Telakar had joined her.

"He is not a fool," Telakar said quietly.

"He couldn't be. He is Tyr'agnate."

"And none of the five Tyrs are fools?"

"Not one. Well, perhaps Garrardi—if rumor is to be believed."

"But not this one?"

She was irritable; it was almost comfortable to be so.
"No. Not this one; not the one who rules Mancorvo, and not
the one who will rule the Terrean of Raverra."

"These three?"

"They are the fertile lands. They are the richest. It is seldom that people starve here; seldom that they suffer from
the lack of rain, the lack of water in the riverbeds."

"It makes them soft."

She shrugged. "We'll see."

"Ah, yes. The armies will clash here."

She said nothing.

Was trying to think of something to say when the world changed.

Swords were drawn beneath the night sky; the stillness of the garden was broken by the teetering dance of glass globes, and the bleeding flicker of spilled light as those globes fell groundward and shattered, scattering glass among the foliage, and wounding the leaves and the grass over which they passed.

She was afraid; sharply, deeply afraid.

She had no weapon to draw. The dagger was gone. She wondered if it would ever be replaced, or if it—like so much else that had *been* her life, had been replaced by the sharp edges of ice that hid in the shadows of the Lord of Night.

"Ramiro! Run!"

"Tyr'agar—behind me!"

Those two voices, haunting, distinct, an overlay of syllables that didn't match, and urgency that did, were clear as birdsong in the morning valleys. Clear, and welcome. They drew swords, and although the lights in the garden had wobbled, some falling and some finding their balance, there was enough to lend an orange-yellow glow to the flats of their blades, the height of their cheekbones, the line of their foreheads.

She was certain death waited in the approaching shadows, the approaching swords; she felt the shadow as keenly as she had in the stark, stark brilliance of the open desert, when she had stood between Lord Telakar and Lord Ishavriel.

She was shocked when the Tyr'agar's voice rang out, clean as steel.

"Hold!"

Everyone froze.

Everyone but Telakar. He closed the distance of a careful, casual walk in the instant of stillness the Tyr'agar's voice created, placing his hands gently on both of her shoulders and holding her forward like a shield.

The Tyr'agnate stepped into the line of Elena's peripheral vision. His brother stepped in front of him, lifting his arm in warning: Stand back.

She saw a ripple of annoyance spread across the Tyr'agnate's neutral expression. In this, without his direct order to the contrary, the Tyran was correct.

He gave no such order.

Nor did he draw his sword; instead, he waited. She wondered why; could not believe that he could face a threat without arming himself; there were very, very few of his men in the garden. Two, she thought. Two more.

But the Tyr'agar snapped out the order that caused his Tyran to step to the side; the Tyr'agar drew his blade.

There were men on the garden paths that led from darkness into this well of traveled light. No; four men. Two women.

Women. With swords. They were scarred; the oldest was darkened by sun. She stood like a Voyani Matriarch, or at least a Matriarch's Daughter, and if it were not for one simple detail, Elena would have assumed that that's what she was—Matriarch's Daughter. But the detail was large. Armor.

She turned to stare at the Tyr of Callesta, her jaw slack. *Northerners. Here.*

"Decarus," the kai Leonne said, speaking to a tall man with hair the color of bronze as he stepped onto the path hidden by the fronds of leaves and the shadows of night. "Decarus," he said again, nodding to the older woman. She could not catch the rest of his words; they were spoken too quickly, and they were not spoken in Trade, the universal tongue that had been cobbled together by the men who crossed borders in search of new ways to enrich themselves.

It was frustrating, to be trapped in this ignorance. Elena knew the traders' tongue at least as well as she knew her mother tongue. She knew some of the tongue of the old thieves in the Tor Leonne as well.

But the Northern words she understood were not up to the fluency of the Tyr'agar.

What did she know about this boy? This boy whose claim to legitimacy must come from the strength of Ramiro di'Callesta? Nothing. Nothing that the Arkosans did not know: the rumors of the Sun Sword. Not even the Voyani could fail to be moved by the story of the kai el'Sol's death.

And she knew that this boy would face that death, and fail if the Sword did not know his blood. It was enough.

"What are you doing here?" Valedan did not raise his voice. Perhaps because he had spent his life around a mother who did nothing except raise hers. Had he, the entire city of Callesta would have heard the words that he wisely chose to speak in Weston.

Alexis said nothing. But she turned her hawkish profile— as if it were a dagger, and at that, a thrown one—toward Auralis AKalakar. She had lowered her sword, but she had not sheathed it, a fact not lost upon Valedan.

He *knew* why they were there; knew why they had walked with such thundering, clumsy steps through the Serra Amara's night gardens, shattering glass and light as if to mark their trail. He had seen just such certainty of motion in the Arannan Halls, in another life, in *Averalaan Aramarelas.*

What he did not see was the demon that they were hunting.

And here, in the foreign city of Callesta, surrounded by the people they had once slaughtered, they could *not* run freely.

Auralis stared straight ahead; his gaze, unlike Alexis', did not waver.

And because Auralis was no dress guard, because his

gaze was so deliberately fixed, Valedan knew that he was
protecting someone. Auralis protected no one. That was a
truth that the Ospreys acknowledged, and took some pride
in.

But it was a broken truth, a half-truth, a thing in the
process of being rewritten or unmade. Valedan, keen-eyed
and silent, had watched the progress of the unpredicted, unpredictable friendship that had grown between Auralis and
the Osprey's almost-outcast, and he turned immediately to
meet the gaze of Kiriel di'Ashaf.

And took a step back, the first.

"Kiriel," he said softly, in a voice that was heavy with respect. With caution.

Her eyes were golden. It was the only thing about her
face that suggested light; the pale white of her skin seemed
a thing of death; the length of her hair had escaped from the
workaday braid that bound it, and it spread, unfurling like
great wings, terrible wings, across the night sky.

Stars were lost to it. Vision.

He had seen this woman before, but never like this. Not
even in the Arena of the Kings had he encountered this
darkness, although he had been told, much later, that it had
existed.

He would have taken another step, but he was now
braced for the difficulty. He stood his ground.

Ser Andaro was at his side, blade drawn.

"Kiriel," Valedan said again. "Why are you here?"

She looked at him, and then past him.

"Telakar," she said, her voice as cold as Northern Winter.
As clean.

Lord Telakar looked up. His fingers grew thin and long;
Elena felt them as claws against the mesh of Voyani cotton,
around the curve of collarbone and the thin skin that covered it.

The girl stepped forward.

The Tyr'agar said a single word. "Kiriel."

Her name, Elena thought. She heard each of three syllables as if they were spoken beneath the domed ceilings of the Merchant Court in the Tor Leonne; they passed through her as if she were insignificant, out of place.

In comparison, the voice of the man who had spoken seemed thin, youthful, foolish.

But the girl hesitated, lowering her blade.

"Kiriel," the Tyr'agar said again.

Her skin was as pale as the skin of women harem-born and confined; her hair was darker than Lady's Night, her eyes wide and large, her cheekbones high. She might have been lovely.

She was not.

"Telakar," Elena whispered, "who is she?"

"If you are very unlucky," Lord Telakar replied, "you will have an answer to that question." He shook her, as if by doing so, he could shake free any further stupidity.

"She knows," Elena told him.

He chuckled. It was not the sound Elena expected. She could not have summoned mirth in this cold night, in the face of this unknown woman.

Kiriei stepped forward.

The Tyr'agar lifted a hand.

Interesting, to watch her hesitation, the muddle of her changing expression.

"Kiriel. Do you recognize this man?"

"Yes."

"Is his presence the reason you have destroyed some part of the garden in your haste to arrive?"

He was speaking in Torra now. Elena wondered why.

"Yes."

"Is he *Kialli*?"

The hesitation was profound.

Answer enough. But the question was repeated.

"Yes."

"Is he bound? Is he contained? Does the woman he travels with hold his name?"

"No."

Elena closed her eyes.

Cacophony.

Not a single sword remained in its sheath. Voices were raised in alarm, some in Torra, and some in the Imperial tongue. Men moved, forming walls that were far too sparse to keep Telakar from his goal.

Whatever that was.

He did not move.

He did not lift hands from her shoulders, and she knew that if she attempted to evade them, he would draw blood. *Knew* it.

"My apologies," Lord Telakar said, in a voice that was preternaturally loud.

Everyone froze in that instant; everyone except the pale, dark girl. She stepped forward, unhindered a moment by the command of a petty Tyr. No light glinted off her blade; Elena could see it as moving shadow. Slowly moving.

"Why are you here?" she asked. Desert night, in the words.

Elena could not see Telakar's face. She wanted to. In just that moment, she wanted to—because she knew that he would be judged by his expression; knew that she faced the same death, the same judgment. She could not turn.

"Do you mean to ask if Lord Isladar sent me?"

The girl froze. Her eyes narrowed. Golden light fled, and it was the only light in her.

"Did he?"

"No. No, Kiriel, daughter of—"

"I am called di'Ashaf now." Her blade rose.

Elena's breath stopped. Without intent, without plan, she retreated in the only direction available: Telakar's chest.

He laughed. "You see well, for an ignorant mortal. But you are safe. For now. Very well," he continued. "Kiriel di'Ashaf. I was sent to the South."

"Ordered?"

"Only the Lord may command me, and not without cost. As you should well know, now."

Again, the sword drifted up. "And?"

"He is concerned with greater issues than a single *Kialli* lord."

"He is unaware of your presence here."

"Indeed."

"And Isladar?"

"He is unaware, as well. And if I am not mistaken, he will continue to be unaware. Some rumor has come from the Shining City."

"What rumor?"

"It appears that he has . . . fled the towers. And in haste. He took injury, but the source of that injury was unclear. The Lord's Fist sensed the weakness. They used it."

"You lie."

Telakar was very, very still. The sudden absence of all motion was remarkable. Frightening. But after a moment, he spoke. "We all do." His voice was as close to neutrality as Elena had yet heard; stripped of amusement, of almost all shadow. Not mortal, but close. "I have not returned to the North to ascertain the truth of those rumors. Nor," he added softly, "is that my intent."

"You cannot evade the Lord," Kiriel replied.

"I can, and for some time yet. But not in the Northern Wastes."

"And you choose to abandon them?"

"You have forgotten," he replied quietly. "My tenure was seldom in the North. I came for the ceremonies that required my presence. I came," he added coolly, "as we all did, to witness the investiture. That last time, I chose to stay, but the North is not my home.

"You, of all the inhabitants of the Shining City, should well understand that; did you not make a similar choice? Are you not here, among *these?*"

A man who had until now been a tall, broad statue,

stepped forward in that instant, edging past the woman to whom Telakar spoke with such care.

His blade was bright as he swung it.

It clattered off hers. "Auralis."

"Kiriel, he talks too much." The words were almost a hiss. As if, Elena thought, this man sought to protect Kiriel. Which was odd; he didn't have the look of a fool about him. More the look of a killer. His sword, deflected with ease— with impossible ease, given the difference in their size— fell slowly, slowly groundward in the lee of shadows cast by lamps they had not managed to dislodge.

Kiriel nodded. "He does." She did not consider this stranger, this pale-haired Northerner, a threat; her eyes had not left Telakar's face. "I have never heard him speak so much."

The man she had called Auralis glanced at her profile; it was all she offered him.

Her gaze shifted. Elena met it squarely, without flinching. Realized that she was actually, of the two, the taller.

"I am Kiriel di'Ashaf," she said. "You?"

"Elena Tamaraan."

"Tamaraan—you are Voyani?"

"Arkosan."

For the first time since the strangers had come crashing through the Serra's garden, the Tyr'agnate of Callesta spoke. "She is the second most powerful woman in the clan Arkosa." His voice was the coldest thing Elena had heard this eve. "If indeed she is what she claims to be."

"She is mortal," Kiriel told him quietly. "If that is what you meant. I was told that the Voyani served the Lady, and not the Lord. Certainly not the Lord of Night."

"You were told the truth," Elena said, struggling not to sound as defensive, as pathetic, as she felt.

"You keep odd company."

Elena smiled almost bitterly. "We are not always fortunate enough to choose the company we keep."

Kiriel nodded. "Telakar," she said, without preamble, "release her."

His grip tightened. It drew blood. She saw the crimson spill down the rise of her breast; it was dark enough that it looked like the spread of shadow. Warm shadow.

The pain followed.

Kiriel's sword rose.

"She is my guest. Tyr'agnate," Telakar turned to the man who ruled the Terrean. "Forgive this subterfuge. I was concerned about your ability to sense the kin; had I known who you keep as . . . guard? . . . here, I would have been less so."

"Telakar," Kiriel said again, her voice fuller now, louder. "Release the woman."

Blood again, from her right shoulder this time. Spreading, absorbed by cloth. Elena was glad that she had lost her voice; she did not want to belittle Arkosa by screaming or crying. Or whimpering. The moon was sharp now, the light of it clear.

"I will release her in one way, and one way alone. You may take some joy from her corpse, but if you continue to press this, Kiriel *di'Ashaf,* it is the only thing you will have of her."

"You cannot fight and hold her."

"Indeed. If you force me to draw blade, I will kill her first. You have your mortals to play with, Kiriel. This one is *mine.*"

Kiriel did not blink. At all. She continued to meet Elena's gaze, although it was to Telakar that she spoke. "You will kill her, and you will perish. Is that why you chose to come?"

"Oh, no, little Kiriel. Make no mistake. I did not intend to be so revealed in this diminished place, but I intended to deliver warning, in a fashion."

"And that?"

"I fear that it is less relevant. Release me, and I will take my leave."

"I do not hold you."

Telakar was silent.

"Kiriel," the Tyr'agar said quietly. "The Ospreys come. What would you have them do?"

She raised a brow, and the shadows dissipated. Moonlight, silver, remained across the fine porcelain of her skin. "He is *Kialli*," she said softly, "and of necessity, no friend of ours."

But the boy Tyr frowned. "I have seen you approach the kin before. You have never once hesitated. You have never once chosen to speak where attack was possible."

"The *Kialli* have never held so obvious a hostage." She turned to Valedan as an equal, her gaze intent. "Is the woman important?"

"She is important."

"And her loss?"

He shook his head.

"You take too many risks," she said calmly.

"And you. But this one?"

She turned to face Elena, to face Telakar. "I have not attacked because he did not. Had he desired it, he could have killed you, and ended the war in that instant; we were too far away when I . . . became aware of his presence."

"Perhaps," Telakar said, with an edge of amusement in his voice, "I did not recognize his import."

She did not grace him with a reply. "It is what our enemies would have demanded, Tyr'agar. Your death. And perhaps the Tyr'agnate's."

Ramiro di'Callesta stepped forward. "What warning," he said softly, "would it suit your purpose to give?" He spoke to the *Kialli* lord.

"I came with information," he replied quietly. "First: The Tor Arkosa has risen in the Sea of Sorrows."

Elena cried out in denial. She was bleeding now; the two wounds that were obvious were beneath notice; the third consumed her. "You cannot speak of that!"

Telakar laughed. "It may have escaped your notice, Elena Tamaraan, but you are not in a position to dictate."

"I thank you for your information, but I confess that its meaning is not plain," Ramiro kai di'Callesta said.

Telakar stilled. After a long pause, he said softly, "You are so diminished, and the greater part of your history has been buried more effectively than the Cities of Man. Very well, Tyr'agnate. It is a refuge of great power, a place which the *Kialli* cannot, without temerity, approach. There is knowledge there, old magic, old artifacts, that if bartered for, would make your cities a great deal safer from the incursion of the kin."

"I . . . see." He met Elena's gaze; she turned away. She would not answer his questions; not about the Tor Arkosa.

Not even to save her life.

"Second," Telakar continued, "to tell you that there are indeed demon kin within the city of Callesta; there are certainly kin, and kinlords, within the borders of Averda. Averda is a distant concern," he added coolly, "compared to Callesta."

"If that were true, would we not have seen evidence of their presence?" Ramiro kai di'Callesta continued, speaking softly, his gaze intent. As if demons were just another part of the political game that men of power played.

"I expect that you would see evidence, yes, but in time. I had not counted upon the quality of your . . . guards. If the kin are still present, and they are aware of just how much power resides within the walls of your city, they will bide their time."

"There are ways," Elena said, against her will, "to detect those who serve the Lord of Night."

"Oh, indeed. And they are time-consuming, little one. They also depend greatly upon the kin's inability to flee or fight. I had thought," he said quietly, "to offer my services."

"And in return?"

"Amusement," Telakar replied. It was probably the only answer he could tender that would be acceptable to the

Callestan Tyr. Elena saw that, now, in the lines of his face.
She had not recognized him when she had first seen him;
she would never forget him now. She was trapped between
them, Telakar and Ramiro di'Callesta, and given a choice
between the two, she was no longer certain in which direction she would run.

"My own amusement. War does not displease me, but if
the odds are too uneven, it is a short and pathetic affair. I
seek merely to prolong it until it reaches its inevitable conclusion."

"And that?"

"Your defeat, of course."

"Ah."

But he shifted. "Kiriel di'Ashaf," he said at last. "Will
you grant me leave to depart?" He spoke coldly, but the
words were softer than any he had used this eve. Certainly
softer than any he had spoken to Elena.

"The woman?"

"She goes with me."

"And if I grant you leave to remain?"

Telakar stilled. "I do not believe that such leave is yours
to grant."

It wasn't; Elena knew it. Telakar knew it. But Kiriel did
not seem to; she waited, her gaze inches above Elena's. For
the second time that eve, Elena desperately wished she
could see Lord Telakar's face.

"Tyr'agar," Kiriel said quietly. "Tyr'agnate."

She had their attention instantly; the titles she had chosen
to invoke to gain it were of almost no import.

"Kiriel," the Tyr'agar said. The Tyr'agnate, for his part,
was silent.

Into the silence, footsteps came, like the fall of hail. His
guards, she thought. Callestan Tyran. Nor was she mistaken.

"Tyr'agar," Kiriel said again, as if the Tyran were of no
concern.

"You cannot trust him."

"No."

"Will you release him, then?"

"To the Lord of Night and his *Kialli* lords? They can trust him even less than I," she replied. "I believe that his destruction will aid their cause, even if they are unaware of it."

"And you believe him when he says he came to offer warning?"

Her silence was as cold as the Callestan silence. Her eyes were once again upon Lord Telakar's face, her gaze above Elena. "I believe him," she said softly, gaze dropping, eyes once again meeting Elena's. Cold comfort. Elena felt light-headed.

"Why?"

She shook her head.

Auralis, the Northerner, stepped up to her side. Elena had heard the phrase closing ranks before, but it had always had some distant military meaning, had hinted at the neatly ordered posture of their foot soldiers, their legendary discipline and organization. The uniforms that graced the handful of men and women who had arrived at Kiriel di'Ashaf's side were made mockery of by the disparity in their size, but they had done just that: had closed ranks.

"Tyr'agar," Auralis said.

But the woman—the other woman—now lifted a slender hand. "Kiriel," she said softly.

"Decarus."

"The question?"

Kiriel shook her head.

The woman was poised to speak; the Tyr'agar simply nodded.

It was not to the liking of Ramiro di'Callesta. "Where are the kin?" he asked abruptly.

"Tell him," Kiriel said to Telakar.

Elena's shoulders stung. The wounds themselves had been clean; she was certain of it. But what had started as a sharp pain had spread, had become something very like a

burden—one that her shoulders were no longer capable of
supporting. She could feel the beat of her heart to either
side of her bent neck. Her clothing was sticky.

Telakar's words came at a distance.

"Come, come, Kiriel di'Ashaf. Not all of the *Kialli* are
military creatures; some are born merchants. I do not consider myself a creature of war, although war is the crucible
of preference.

"What will you give me in return for that information?"

"The value of the information you offer is not high; I am
here. I found *you*."

"Indeed. And that is curious to me, for I am almost certain that you have failed to find the others, and I can only
guess that that failure has been deliberate. Of your choosing."

Again, again the large man with the sword stepped toward them, toward Telakar, toward his shield. "Kiriel—"

"Auralis, *no*."

This time, Auralis almost snarled. Elena didn't understand what he chose to say; it was fast, Weston, guttural.

"We can hardly be trusted any *less*. Lord Telakar?"

"It appears you have made allies in the short time you
have been absent. I would have thought it impossible, given
how poorly you mingled with the human Court." He
shrugged. "What will you offer?"

Kiriel di'Ashaf was silent. For a moment. And then she
smiled.

Elena swallowed. Closed her eyes. She could not step
back. Could not, she thought, although she did not say it,
stand for much longer. The world was losing color at the
edges of her vision; night was spreading inward from all
sides.

"If the information pleases me," Kiriel replied, "and if it
pleases the two men who rule these lands by mortal law, I
will give you the life of the mortal you hold captive."

"It is not yours to give," he said coldly.

"No, but I fear that you've overestimated her ability to bear casual injury. It is . . . a failing . . . among the kin."

Elena only barely understood the words.

She wondered, briefly, if she would be better off if she could actually *see* the face of the woman who had spoken them, and decided that, better or not, it didn't matter.

The ground was a long way away.

CHAPTER FOURTEEN

KIRIEL di'Ashaf watched the stranger fall as if her injuries and her probable death were beneath concern.

For a moment, they were.

Her vision had shifted again; the fires banking. She could not longer see. She saw Lord Telakar no more clearly than any mortal present could, but she *had* seen him. For a moment, for a handful of moments, she had seen his name as a fire, a nimbus of light, a thing that was woven through him, and *of* him, in a way that it could be of no other. Beauty, in that, beauty and danger, and a terrible, visceral desire. To speak the name, to speak it *well,* was to offer challenge; to win that challenge was to own it.

There were very, very few who could win that challenge; his name was a subtle binding, a thing of power far easier to destroy than subvert.

Her hand was warm; the ring, as she lifted it slightly, luminescent. Luminescent or no, Telakar's gaze was not drawn to it; it was beneath his notice. Whatever she saw when it burned, he could not see. Comfort, there, but it was cold.

When she had first touched the ring, it had almost been beneath her, but the woman from whom it had fallen had shown the only moment of fear that Kiriel had yet seen, and she wore it to invoke that fear. To enjoy it.

She had paid. Small and perfect, it was the only cage she had ever lived in; it had taken her power. It had robbed her of self. She had been frenzied with the terror of being helpless. That frenzy could not sustain itself—or her—and she had moved from it to a terrible frustration as she was exposed, at last, to weakness and mortality: She felt the air's humidity, the sun's heat; she *sweated* and *burned* when she toiled, feckless, beneath it. She had always needed to sleep; she had always needed food. But the strength of those needs dismayed her.

Those, and others.

They had demeaned her.

For a while.

Her hand became fist. Closed. It had been months since she had felt the loss so sharply. She was not the power that she had been when she had dwelled within the Shining City—but her tenure there had taught her that power alone did not give her the ability to defend the things she most valued.

Aie. Loss, and here. What had her answer been?

To value nothing. To value nothing so highly that its loss could cause such a terrible, profound pain.

"Kiriel?" Auralis. Face long, almost gaunt in the evening shadow.

How weak had she become? How weak? Her first impulse had been to *send the Ospreys away*. But why? Without the certainty of her power, she needed the Ospreys. Or whatever it was they were now called.

She looked to Auralis, looked away. The Voyani woman's knees had buckled; were it not for Telakar's hands, she would have crumpled to the ground, struck it with chest and forehead, and lain there, still against the earth.

She wanted to tell Auralis the truth.

She had no idea how she'd been allowed to find Lord Telakar, although in the Shining City, such recognition had been the second nature upon which her life depended. Worse, she believed that he had come—for his own reasons, of course, always those—to deliver warning about the *Kialli*; believed implicitly that they existed, as he said, within the city of Callesta. Believed that he knew where they were to be found.

And worse, worst, *knew* that she would not be able to find them. Before she destroyed Telakar—if, indeed, she could in her weakened state—she wanted the information that he had come, in secrecy, to deliver.

Not for the first time, she cursed herself for her impulsive—or compulsive—behavior. She had, in triumph and joy, revealed herself too soon. Isladar had always—

No, no, no. Not here. Not here.

Valedan stepped toward the fallen woman.

Kiriel lifted a hand; touched the center of his chest. She never touched him; felt the contact as a small shock, although her hand was gloved and his chest, mailed.

"She's dying," he said sharply.

And she nodded. She had, after all, seen mortal death before. She knew the look of it. "Give him no other easy hostage," she said coldly.

"I am not certain that it is as hostage that she is here," he replied.

She shook her head. *Wait.*

And he, Tyr'agar, ruler of this vast, abundant place, nodded.

Lord Telakar frowned. His grip shifted, falling from shoulder to arms as he attempted to lift the Voyani woman to feet that had long since ceased to be able to bear her weight.

"I see that we conversed overlong," he said quietly. "I am afraid, Kiriel di'Ashaf, that this conversation is at an end. Find the kin—or ignore them—as you choose; they are not a threat to you, and they will hardly prove a threat to those you guard. If you are vigilant." His smile was a thing of beauty, all edge and glitter, all teeth. "Of course, if I am not mistaken, you do require sleep. How inelegant."

Her turn; her turn to smile.

He saw it, and the ring, if it denied her all else, did not deny her this. She *smiled.*

And he, lord, kinlord, free as any of the *Kialli* could be, took a step back, shifting his grip upon his chosen burden.

"Before you flee, Lord Telakar, you might attempt what it is now clear you intend to attempt."

He was still; he could afford to be still for only a few moments longer.

"Kai Leonne," she said quietly, "if there is a healer who travels with you, if there is a doctor of note in the Tyr's domicile, summon him."

Lord Telakar growled.

Of all sounds, it was not one she expected. "I will kill them if they touch her."

"No," Kiriel said, the softness of the word a mockery of gentleness. "But you will kill her if they don't."

He hesitated. Laid bare, she reveled in his weakness. And there was more to follow: Lord Telakar touched the stranger's face with the open palm of his hand; he took care not to pierce her skin, although his fingers left their mark. He gestured. Gestured again. The frown that grew upon his face was not so beautiful as his smile had been.

And it was. To Kiriel's eyes, it was.

He knew, of course, but he did not choose to acknowledge it; the whole of his attention was now focused upon this stranger, this dying woman.

His left hand flew back, flew up, his palm cupped night air, moonlight, and shadow. There was a glow about it, a darkness that was beautiful as he was beautiful.

Kiriel waited.

And then, although she could not say why, she forced the smile from her lips. "Lord Telakar," she said coldly.

His hands were in flight. His lips moved. He spoke words that should have held power; they held none. They were words, no more, and in a foreign tongue, a language that Kiriel could not understand.

Valedan moved again, steel shadow, and bright.

"Tyr'agar," she said, remembering herself now. "Tyr'agnate."

"Kiriel, what is happening here?" Valedan's question was devoid of command.

She did not answer, not directly. "Lord Telakar."

The *Kialli* lord's hands stilled. The woman, pale and motionless, made no reply to the conversation of his movement, did not acknowledge the command in it, the insistence of its intensity.

His eyes met Kiriel's over the face of the dying.

"Give her to us, and we will see to her care."

"No."

"Then keep her, and see to her burial." She turned. Timed the turn, the movement of heels against the soft grass, the delicately laid stone, of the Callestan grounds. All around her, in a silence punctuated by breath, the Ospreys waited.

"Kiriel!"

She turned again. "Lord Telakar."

"This woman is of value to her people. And if I understand her people at all, they are now of value to the men you stand among."

She nodded.

"I . . . will allow . . . the interference of your healers."

"Why?"

He weighed silence; weighed the passage of time. "She is mine," he said softly.

"Ashaf was mine," Kiriel replied. "And she was Isladar's. And in the end, death was the only blessing granted her. I will not give this stranger to you. I will not give her over to the three days of containment." She swallowed the harsh night air; it hurt her throat. The words were swollen there; she could not speak.

Telakar was still for a moment. Still, tasting pain, testing aura. She knew it. Braced herself for the cruelty of smile as she found her voice. "I will never again cede mortals to the kin." The words contained a different type of shadow, a different power, than any she had spoken before. They were truth. Her truth, her chosen truth.

"Ah. And why, Daughter of Darkness? You know as well

as any who have lived in the rivers of the Hells what joy lies within such a reaving."

Time. They had no time. Kiriel shook her head; she had seen the edge of a larger truth and she wished to grasp it before it eluded her. It was almost hers. She had only one way of containing it; one way of holding it captive.

She drew the sword.

And the night was bright compared to the flat of its blade, the dark, moving surface of the things written in steel and forged by the Swordsmith. Her name was upon that blade; she saw it for the first time, although the weapon had been hers since she had stood upon the threshold of adulthood.

She drew blood; her own. The blade absorbed it; no evidence was left of the wound in either the mound of her palm or the subtle serrations of its edge.

His eyes widened.

He recognized the blood-binding; he was the only witness that would. He waited while she swore the oath that would, if broken, kill her.

"I will *never* grant it. Never again."

"And the dark communion?"

"I am done with it," she said, spitting the words into the night. Speaking them not to Telakar, but to a kinlord who was all of her history.

And then, of all things, Lord Telakar laughed, drawing the unconscious woman closer to his breast. "You think that I am interested in such paltry games? That I am so starved for the charnel wind and the song of the damned? You think that I would play such a game with her?"

Kiriel's turn to frown. Valedan said something to Ramiro kai di'Callesta, but she lost the muted hush of his words; sensed only movement. Retreat.

"I am not a fool," she told him, her hand upon the hilt of her sword. "Why else, Telakar? What other value have the mortals to the kin?"

He said, simply, "They burn." Just that.

She spoke his name. His true name.

His eyes widened. The name itself was a whisper.

But he did not fight her. Instead, he gave her the whole of his attention, his form shifting subtly, his hold upon the stranger tightening. He bowed his head.

"I have seen the rise of the ancient Cities," he said, speaking now in a tongue that no one but Kiriel might understand. "A gift, a gift unlooked for. They are diminished, these scions of that glory, but they are its heirs. The Cities are whole, Kiriel. They wake slowly, but when they wake, they will be a force to be reckoned with, even by the Lord we must serve."

"He does not know where you are."

"He has not turned his attention toward me," Telakar replied. "But he has turned his attention to you, and you have somehow escaped his grasp."

She shook her head. "What is mortal," she said quietly, "cannot be bound by the mantle that the gods created. It can be killed. It can be tortured. It can be preyed upon by the powerful. But the nature of mortality—"

"Lord Isladar's words."

She almost lost her composure then.

"Ah, Lord Isladar," Telakar said then, "I begin to understand."

She didn't. She didn't, but she had been raised in the Shining Court, and she could not—for the paltry sake of enlightenment—expose the weakness of ignorance to the kneeling lord.

"She is mine," he said again. "Accept that. She is mine, or she is no one's." The edge of his hand gleamed like steel beneath the moon's bright face.

"And if I grant her to you, what will you offer in return? Think quickly, Lord Telakar."

"That is not the way, Kiriel."

"It is, here. It is, now."

"What would you have of me?"

"Be part of *my* court," she told him, speaking before she

could think. "Be part of my court, Lord Telakar; be the first of my lords."

"I will not be bound."

"You are already bound."

"Not by you, mortal. Never by you."

Thought caught up with words. She heard movement at her back.

"Kiriel," Valedan said, speaking in a foreign tongue, an interloper now, and unwelcome. "The healer has come."

She lifted a hand, a call for silence. The Tyran saw her; saw Valedan fall silent. She had injured him by the simple action, and knew it.

"You served Isladar," Kiriel told Telakar, delaying the healer, playing at death's edge.

The kinlord was silent.

"Isladar did not see fit to force that binding upon you. What he risked, I will risk. Isladar could not offer you what I offer now."

"And that?"

"Her life," she said simply. "Her life, and the future of the Cities."

"She is *mine*," he said.

"Yours," she replied, "but not to harvest. Choose, Telakar."

He was silent for a long moment. Silent. And then, at his leisure, he rose, carrying the stranger as if she were weightless.

It hurt. Kiriel herself had been carried in just such a fashion. Had not thought to miss it, here.

He stroked the underside of the woman's chin. Blood followed his fingers, his hands, as ink follows quill across a blank page. He spoke, and this time his words had power enough to raise the hairs on the back of Kiriel's neck.

A binding. A binding such as she had never seen.

"I will serve," he said quietly.

"Who?"

His smile was sharp. "Clever girl. I will serve Kiriel di'Ashaf, the Queen of the Hells."

The healer came. He was a quiet man with a severe face, and when he approached the woman, his hands trembled. He looked to the Tyr'agnate, and saw no escape in the aloofness of his expression.

"You will allow this," Kiriel said quietly.

Telakar met her eyes; his were all of the night. But he nodded bitterly. "There was a time," he told her quietly, "when I could have offered the necessary sustenance to one such as she."

Confession.

Kiriel's brows rose. "Impossible."

"Now, yes." He waited. The man's hands touched the stranger's face and held it, as Telakar had held it, but without drawing blood. "But I was not always . . . as diminished . . . as I appear to have become."

She heard the anger in the words; he revealed that much.

"We knew life," he said softly. "We were your distant kin."

"You were never part of—of—"

"Us?" Mockery there, the edge of it cutting. "Do you number yourself among the cattle, you who were born to—"

"Enough. Enough, Telakar."

"You expose too much." His eyes were lidded now, serpent eyes.

She had no time to frame an answer; there had only ever been one among the *Kialli* who had cared to criticize her for her weaknesses.

In the silence, Auralis moved. When he did, she realized that he had stood by her side, utterly still, his hand upon the hilt of his great sword.

"Kiriel," he said quietly, "we have a problem."

She laughed. "Only one?"

His shrug was most of his answer. "When it's this big, we only need one."

She turned from Telakar then.

Saw the ring of drawn swords held by the Tyran of Callesta; saw the bright blade in the hands of the sole man who served Valedan kai di'Leonne.

Beyond him, the Ospreys stood: Alexis, with two daggers, Fiara with a sword, and Duarte, hands stretched wide, his weapon more subtle and therefore more dangerous. She had not seen Duarte arrive.

Only the Tyrs were motionless.

Telakar's laugh was rich and dark; she felt it run the length of her spine; felt the hair on the back of her neck rise, and with it, anger.

It was the anger she struggled with now.

Struggled with, and won, if victory could be measured in such a complex thing as simple obeisance.

She sank, in front of the Tyran, the Tyr'agnate, and the Ospreys, to her knees. "Tyr'agar," she said.

"I have accepted the rules that govern the Ospreys," he said quietly. "I accept them now. Your past is your past, Kiriel di 'Ashaf."

She lifted her head; met the brown of his unblinking eyes in the bob and sway of lantern light.

"I have lost count of the number of times you have saved my life; I am in your debt, and I acknowledge it in the hearing of the most trusted men of Callesta." He spoke in Torra now, and there was no hesitation, no crack or break, in his voice. Just youth, but the youth was buried beneath the midnight sky.

"But you have named this man our enemy. If you will not destroy him—and it is clear to me, although the tongue you spoke was foreign, that you have reached some understanding, you injure our cause immeasurably."

"Tyr'agar," Auralis began.

Ser Andaro was between the Tyr'agar and the Osprey in that instant.

"Decarus," Duarte said, his word a clipped, cold command. "You will be silent."

He almost always was. Funny, that.

Kiriel did not rise. The hair that had unfolded about her like a shroud or a great pair of wings fell slowly toward her shoulders; her face lost the ice and the white of winter, the paleness of the dead. She lifted it again. "In the Court of the Tyr'agar who was assassinated," she said quietly, "were all men of one thought, one mind? Were their goals so similar?"

Valedan kai di'Leonne lifted his arms; drew them across his chest. "I am not so old that I remember clearly the maneuverings of the High Court of Raverra. Tyr'agnate?"

"I would say that the death of the Tyr'agar Markaso kai di'Leonne is answer enough." Was there a faint hint of amusement in the words?

Kiriel could not be certain.

"Very well, Kiriel. You have your answer."

She bowed her head. "The High Court of Raverra has much in common with the Shining Court."

She heard Auralis' breath; it was heavy, a rush of air. But he did not choose to speak again. She wondered dispassionately if Duarte would kill him otherwise. Was certain that he would try.

"The greater kin vie for power in their own right. They play games, and if the games are not familiar to those of us who fight against them, they are motivated, in the end, by the desire for power.

"The proof of power," she added softly, "being the ability to hold it. Only that."

"And this . . . man?"

"I believe that he has come to offer warning, as he said" she told them all.

"And you would vouch for this belief with your life?"

Silence. And in it, the beginnings of a new respect for the man who would be Tyr.

"Yes."

Telakar said nothing.

"Good. Because nothing less would be acceptable. What warning does he offer?"

"He can lead you to the demons the city of Callesta now harbors."

Valedan kai di'Leonne nodded. He turned to the waiting Tyr'agnate. "Kai Callesta."

Ramiro di'Callesta nodded coldly. "We must join the armies," he said softly. "And we must join them soon. It ill behooves us to allow our enemy to prey upon those we must leave behind." Without turning, he spoke a name. "Ser Fillipo."

"Tyr'agnate." The Captain of the oathguard bowed, sword unsheathed.

"Are there, among the men gathered here, any who are not Tyran?"

"None, Tyr'agnate."

"Good." He turned to his brother. "Wake the Tyran, and only the Tyran. Make clear to them the necessity of silence."

Ser Fillipo bowed.

"Tyr'agar," the Tyr'agnate said, "we will be ready within the hour. If it pleases you, gather those that you trust; what we do must be done in haste."

When the Tyr'agnate was gone, silence went with him.

Duarte contained, by dint of magic, what could not be contained by dint of will.

Words clashed as Auralis and Alexis filled the vacuum of mannered speech with something decidedly less delicate.

Duarte let them. The whole of his attention was focused upon Kiriel di'Ashaf. Not even the creature who stood in the lee of her shadow could command some lesser part of it.

She was young. It was hard to remember, when the power was gathered within her, just how damn young she was. Paradoxically, impossible to forget.

"Are you trying to lose the war for us?"

It was not the question she expected. Her brows furrowed. "I am trying," she said, after a long pause, "to make sure Valedan survives it."

"By openly declaring yourself a member of the Shining Court? By allying yourself—however much it might be necessary—with a *demon?*"

Her frown deepened, and he was almost relieved to see it; it was the frown that spoke of both confusion and contempt—the earliest of the expressions he associated with her oddly delicate features. "He is not my ally," she said evenly.

"No?"

"No. He is my vassal."

Auralis slapped himself in the forehead.

Duarte struggled a moment to find words. "Do not," he said, spacing the words evenly, "repeat that again in my hearing."

She frowned.

"Do not repeat it at all. Ever. Do I make myself clear?"

"Yes."

"Good." He closed his eyes.

"Primus." Valedan spoke quietly. He was the only person in the clearing, besides Kiriel herself, who seemed able to do so.

"We will lose Mareo di'Lamberto," Duarte said coldly. "We will lose him, if word of this evening escapes."

"He is correct," a soft voice said. Soft, perfect in its enunciation, the accent a subtlety of intonation, the pronunciation perfect.

Duarte cringed. Cringed, but without surprise. "Serra Alina," he said, without turning.

"My brother is a cunning man, and a powerful one; he is not, however, always practical." She stood in the cloak of the Ospreys, shorn now of the finery of the Southern Court. When she had arrived was anyone's guess; she moved as quietly as the damned Astari when she chose to do so.

"Serra." Valedan turned to her at once.

"Ramiro di'Callesta understands the risk he takes," she told him without preamble, as if the garments she wore now defined her position; as if she were in truth Northern, the dark sister of the Princess Royale upon the Isle. "And he risks much. But it is his people who will be left without protection if the word of such a creature as this can be believed."

"It is not his word," Valedan said quietly, "by which we have chosen to make this decision."

"Oh?"

"It is hers." He turned to Kiriel di'Ashaf. "Rise," he told her quietly.

She rose as bade, her face smooth as steel.

The creature spoke in a language that defied Duarte's studied comprehension. Kiriel did not acknowledge him at all, and by the lack, Duarte understood that she had made a choice. The choice itself was opaque to him, but for no reason he could think of, it brought some measure of comfort.

Kiriel di'Ashaf nodded briefly to the Serra Alina di'Lamberto, a woman whom she had never conversed with. "I am an Osprey here," she said.

"I had been given to understand that that name no longer existed."

Kiriel's smile was cold; Northern ice was warmer and more forgiving. Duarte did not retreat; he had seen the expression before, and experience gave him the ability to rise above its subtle menace.

He wondered what experience had molded the Serra Alina; she, too, stood still in the face of the dark expression, and her stillness was not a rabbit's stillness; it was the wolf's.

"It is a true name," Kiriel told the Serra. "Call them anything that the Northerners desire, and the fact of the name will not change. They bear it," she added, gesturing briefly toward Auralis, Alexis, Fiara—even Duarte himself. "And I . . . have chosen to bear it as well."

"It is not what you are."

"It is not *all* that I am."

Silence again. Valedan waited between these two women, measuring their silence; matching it with his own.

"And the rest, Kiriel di'Ashaf?"

"I am my mother's daughter," she said.

The creature spoke again, the words sharper, the tone different.

She lifted a hand, as if swatting a mosquito, something that flitted from side to side, seeking purchase and blood. Finding none.

"And these—the people in these lands—were hers."

And then she bowed her head, closed her eyes; her fists tightened. Duarte thought them white beneath the mail of her gloves.

"Kiriel."

She smiled. Turned to Auralis, acknowledging him in a way that she had acknowledged no one else in the broken mass of branches and crushed petals, the bed of glass shards. "I believe I was winning."

His brows rose. "Winning?"

Duarte smiled and shook his head. It eased him. "She was, Auralis."

"The Hells she was."

"Of the six demons that attempted to assassinate the kai Leonne, she's taken four."

"First blood—"

"The rules, I believe, were clear; first blood doesn't seem to faze them—but they pause at the loss of limb. Or life, if they have it."

Auralis spit. Duarte knew, by the sudden twist of his lips, that he had money riding on what Duarte had thought of as an informal contest. Saw by the sudden gleam in Alexis' eyes that he wasn't the only one.

He damned them both genially.

"These Annies," Alexis said, "are *our* Annies. The kin

want to hunt them, they can damn well hunt among their own."

Fiara spit to the side for good measure. "Duarte?"

"Primus," he said curtly.

"Pri-mus Duarte."

"Yes?"

"I'm going to wake the others."

"You might as well. It was getting crowded here anyway." A reminder of death.

He watched her leave, and then listened to her, feet as heavy as horse hooves through the ruins of the path their haste had made. If he was any judge, someone would pay for it; the Serra Amara was not the most forgiving of women, and she had made it clear, in the perfect grace of feminine Southern pride, that these were hers.

The Serra Alina touched Valedan's shoulder; he turned at once.

"The deaths," she told him.

He nodded.

"They must be seen. By the serafs. By the common clansmen. They must understand that what you have brought from the North is death: death for the servants of the Lord of Night. Must understand that you have taken this risk because you value their service, indentured or no.

"If you can accomplish this without killing the men and women we need as witnesses, the presence of your Northern guards will no longer be an accusation of your weakness and your diluted blood; you will not be—in Callesta—the mere scion of the Northern Generals."

"Ah. And the Commanders?"

"Best to leave them," she said quietly. "This hunt, if it is a hunt, must be seen to be yours."

"Ser Andaro?"

Silent, the perfect Tyran, Ser Andaro nodded. "The Serra Alina di'Lamberto is known for her wisdom."

"And the unfortunate sharpness of her tongue," Alina

said coolly. But a smile dimpled her cheek, the lines proof that it was genuine.

"I fear, Serra, that you will be disappointed," Duarte said quietly. "The Ospreys are not theatrical."

"I might have thought so." No veil hid her face, no fan obscured it; she sought no courtly grace beneath the open face of the watching moon. But the grace that she had been born to did not desert her, and the night gentled the lines that the sun, wind, and time had begun to wear in the corner of lips and eyes.

"And now?"

"I have never seen her kneel to you," she said quietly, gazing at Kiriel. "And if she kneels thus, blade bloodied, and triumphant, it is to you that they will look."

Kiriel di'Ashaf, risen, said nothing.

"It is a risk," Valedan said at last. "And the risk is great. But—"

"Tyr' agar."

"Kiriel?"

"I have never met Mareo di'Lamberto. I . . . do not understand . . . the whole of his significance. But I believe that Lord Telakar will have much to say, even beneath the face of the reigning sun, if the Tyr'agnate can be brought to listen. And what is said, he might find of interest."

"He is Mareo," Serra Alina said bitterly.

The Voyani woman was carried into the Callestan domicile. She did not wake, but she stirred; unconsciousness had given way to sleep beneath the hands of the nameless healer. That man was spent; he had dwindled in size and stature, and he had had little of either before he commenced. He did not allow himself to be touched; accepted no offer of support. Nor did he allow himself to touch the woman again; he gloved his hands and waited.

"Telakar."

"Lady."

Kiriel frowned. "It is not the time for games."

"You do not understand, do you?" Telakar's slender hands caressed the woman's brow; strands of her hair, red brown as dried blood, but living, moving in the lift and fall of his fingers, caught light. Caught him. Something in the texture of his voice was familiar. "Games are all we have. Mortals are foolish; if the stakes are high, they cease to acknowledge that what is played is indeed a game.

"Have you become foolish, Kiriel? You are the only student that Lord Isladar has ever chosen to take; I cannot imagine that you have descended into mortal folly. Had you, you would not have survived the Court."

"I do not intend that most of the Court survive me," she told him, blunt now. Angry.

"No. No more do any of the kinlords." He shrugged, bored.

"That was never your game."

"No. It bored me. It bores me now."

"And that brought you here?"

"You are mortal. You will live only briefly, and you will die; you cannot contemplate an eternity of boredom if you can ask that question." Hands stilled; his fingers hovered above the membranes of the woman's closed eyes. Kiriel wondered briefly if he intended to remove them.

"There were, among the *Allasiani*, those who did not choose to follow Allasakar into the Hells."

"Allasiani?"

"Ah. How odd. Lord Isladar has always evinced an interest in history. Perhaps you ended your tenure as student too early. I am not a teacher; I am not his equal."

Kiriel stared at the *Kialli* lord.

"But I have always been fascinated by things mortal."

"All of the *Kialli* are." She could not keep the fury from the words, but her expression was rigid.

"They are fascinated by suffering and death," he said with a bored shrug. "The least of the imps can grant either; it does not speak to power, but to self-indulgence."

Again she stared at him, at his hands upon the face of the sleeping woman, his captive now.

"I will tell you what the *Allasiani* were," he said quietly. "It is a gap in your education that should never have been allowed."

She could have demanded his silence.

But curiosity had always been a failing. Unbidden, she heard Isladar's voice, felt his hands upon her brow, felt the heat of his anger, and beneath it, something she had mistaken, in her foolish youth, as concern. Several times in her childhood, curiosity had almost killed her.

No comfort there. It had failed.

"The servants," he continued quietly, "and the allies of Allasakar."

"That name is not spoken here."

"Indeed, and perhaps that is wise. I forget myself."

She did not believe it. He knew she did not.

"Some among us are called kinlord," he continued, his eyes upon this woman's face, upon the rise and fall of chest made by shallow breath. "And some *Kialli*."

"I . . . understand . . . what *Kiallinan* is."

"Ah. He gifted you, if you understand that much."

"And the other?"

"It is what we *were*," he told her, looking up for the first time. "When we walked this plane. When we knew life, knew birth, and even, in our time, death. You see us as the plane permits us to be seen. Those who are too weak to negotiate with the primal force of the ancient earth bear forms that were never ours: talons, blades, bodies of chitin and bestial faces. Yet among those, some memories still burn.

"I was *Allasiani*. I was counted young. Among my brethren . . . many were lost to the Lord's Hells."

"Not you."

"No. In my youth, I was passionate. Although I was fascinated by the flaws and the imperfections of the short, short lives of the mortals, I loved the Lord. Perhaps you can see what we saw in him then. I do not know; it is lost to me now. Lost in the Hells; in the boiling rivers, the charnel winds, the sensuous cries of the damned." He lowered his face again.

"But when we . . . lived . . . I was among the few who were given stewardship over the mortals who served. Because I was one of the few who could be trusted to winnow their numbers with care."

He lifted his hands.

"It was not an easy task."

She said, cruel now, "You attempted to heal her. Tonight."

He did not deny it.

"Why?"

"Because I am still encumbered by memory," he replied bitterly. "It is not an act . . . that I have attempted since the passage from the Hells; not an act that I have attempted since last I walked these valleys. The desert was no desert then; it was the heart of the power of Man. There, among the mortals, I found one or two of interest; they were seen as my pets; they were seen as creatures of value to me." He shrugged.

She knew, by the shrug, that it was true.

"I learned their art, in a fashion. I learned the workings of the frailty of mortal heart, and lung, and bone, of blood, of the tissue that binds the whole."

She shook her head.

"It is lost," he said quietly. "I should have known. I did not intend to endanger her life. I merely wished to show that it was of little value to me. Things of little value are seldom threatened. I assumed that I could . . . repair . . . the damage done." He stared at his hands, at the hands that were twined in her hair, a binding of her own, unconscious as she was. "But that gift, so bitterly won, is gone."

"Bitterly won?"

He raised a brow. "You ask too many questions," he said without rancor. Or judgment.

He turned to her then, and his eyes were the color of fire. "I have forgotten nothing," he said, and it was a vow.

"You will leave her now."

"Yes." Very slowly, he disentangled his hands.

"She will be safe here."

"You promise safety, Kiriel, when you must sleep, must eat, must breathe?" His laugh was bitter. Unkind.

It made her long for home.

The Tyr'agnate came. He came as kings must come, his armor fine, his sword fine, his helm unblemished by dint of war.

Artifice, that. The Serra Alina understood that though the helm itself was new to battle, the man beneath its confines was not. In the North, in the history of the North, Commanders lay trapped behind their lines of mastery; the faceless and the nameless legions were driven forth before them, to fight and die at a distance that made the individuals insignificant. The map of their deaths, the length of the line their combined bodies made, counted for much, and each man stood as the link in a chain, a mesh, armor of a different caliber.

Thus had Mirialyn taught her in the long, empty halls of *Avantari,* beyond the stretch of the Arannan Halls in which Southern women were expected to be Serras. In grace. In silence.

She had surrendered silence for the sake of the Princess; had surrendered distance, distrust, the caution that comes with a life lived in the High Courts of Lamberto. And in return for that surrender she had taken knowledge.

The knowledge was theory.

The theory was empty now, but she might see it played out for her inspection by night's end; the Ospreys had been summoned.

In the Dominion of Annagar, the Ospreys defined the ferocity and the power of the North. Not even the Callestan Tyr understood how little loved, how little respected, the

Ospreys were by the Imperial army; they, outsiders all, had won from the South the respect that the North had been denied—and had won none of that for themselves in the North, by their ferocity, their brutality, their pragmatism.

They were few. Thirty men and women, dressed in armor that was not nearly as fine as the Callestan Tyr's. They did not stand in lines; they did not stand abreast; they did not master the watchful stillness that informed the Tyran.

Instead, they spoke among themselves, the silence of their language a movement of fingers in air, against shoulder, against chest. Few of the Ospreys wore shields; Cook did, and Sanderton, a scattered number of the men. The shields were defaced; the bird of prey that plunged to earth at their center painted over in the sedate colors of House Kalakar—colors muted by night, even in the lamplight.

They looked to their Captain.

He alone was worthy to serve, and he stood with the grace and attention denied his impatient troop.

Kiriel came last, and by her side, the stranger; the man she had called kinlord. He was tall, the line of his face long and patrician; his eyes were dark, and his hair dark as well. But it was long; unfettered by braid, uncut. Young men might take such a risk when they faced battle, and those men were often carried from the field in pieces.

Not this one.

She did not like him. Wondered if it were the truth of Lambertan blood, come to dull the edge of her perception.

"Serra?"

She turned. Decarus Alexis stood beside her. Not for her the vanity of long hair. It was drawn from her face, forced from her eyes; it exposed the slender line, the narrow nose, of a hawk's face. She lifted a weapon; a long, slender knife too short, and too slight, to be sword. It was not a Northern weapon. It was not raised for use, but as an offering.

In spite of herself, the Serra Alina smiled. She considered the obligation she accrued by accepting this unasked for

gift; considered and dismissed it. She held out a hand, and
the blade was turned, pommel first, toward her.

"I am in your debt," she said softly.

Alexis was no Serra; she snorted and tossed her head,
like the finest of Mareo's stallions. "You're not an Osprey,"
Alexis said quietly, "but if the Ospreys are family, you're
our cousin, our distant kin. We watch out for our own."

A decade ago, in the protected confines of the ferocious
grace of Lamberto, her brother's Tyran would have struck
the woman for the gravity of her offered offense.

Ten years.

How much could a life change, and how deeply, in such
a span of time? "I have nothing to offer in return."

"Maybe not. Maybe not yet. Doesn't matter. You're an
Annie, and you're a Serra—but if you're wearing that
armor, you mean to come with us."

Serra Alina nodded. She tried to add definition to the motion; tried to rob it of the cultured grace, the regal simplicity, that was hers by birth and training. Her mother would
have been shocked; Decarus Alexis didn't notice. All subtlety was lost upon these people; they were like children,
like savage, willful children.

She had loved such creatures, in her time.

And she was determined to expose herself to no such weakness now. "Valedan will travel with you," she said softly.

"Oh, yeah." Her smile turned sly. "And ten gets you one
he's about to tell you to take a hike."

Valedan kai di'Leonne approached the two women. By
his side, supple and wary, Ser Andaro di'Corsarro. Alina
had taken his measure in the weeks of the Kings' Challenge, and she had found much to recommend him. But in
the weeks of travel to the South, and again in the South itself, she had found more: she admired him. She knew that
Mareo would do likewise. Was tired of thinking of what her
brother might—or might not—do.

But she was surprised when a third man joined these two.

Ser Anton di'Guivera. The swordmaster.

She did not fall to her knees, but it was difficult. Valedan himself was informed by the North, and Ser Andaro was his oathsworn servant. But Ser Anton was of the South, and not even Valedan's command could rob her of the certain knowledge that she did him insult by remaining upon her feet.

She squared shoulders: such stance was Valedan's wish, and he, Tyr'agar.

"Serra Alina," Valedan said gravely, "You honor me with your presence this eve. But I am loath to risk you."

"If the demons are within Callesta, there is no safer place for me to be."

That evoked the smile she had intended.

But not from Ser Anton. "You are no doubt trained in the lesser weapons," he said without preamble. "But it is not the lesser that will hold sway here."

She did not speak. Instead, she met Valedan's eyes, and held them for a beat longer than was either safe or polite.

"I have faced these creatures," Ser Anton continued, when it became clear that Valedan would not continue. "I know the danger they represent."

Again, she chose silence. But as a Serra, silence was often prod, often accusation. In grace, of course, and in a sweetness she had never quite mastered, it was a weapon.

"The Serra Alina di'Lamberto," the kai Leonne said quietly, "has experience of these creatures as well. What was said at the Serra Amara's table was no lie."

Ser Anton's expression shifted; it surprised her to see his shock so clearly upon his face, although she knew that to a Northerner the lift of brow would signify little.

Valedan did not acknowledge this lapse. Instead, he continued to meet her gaze. But the words were not meant for her. "Before the Ospreys came to serve me," he said softly. "Before the Kings' Swords were arrayed around me like a Northern shield wall. When all of the other Serras—and many of the clansmen—had the wisdom to flee for their lives, she stayed her ground."

"She is still alive."

"Indeed; she stayed her ground long enough to plant a dagger in the creature's eye. It did not kill the creature, but it slowed him until the Kings' men arrived. Serra Alina, it is not my desire to put you in that position again."

She nodded. And then, in Weston, she said, "But it is my desire to accompany you."

Weston, the language of freedom, where anything might be said, and understood.

In Weston, he replied. "Thank you."

It was not what she had expected to hear, and she knelt before the words, head bowed. Not for the first time did she regret her inability to accept the marriage he had offered. But this time, this time she vowed to allow him no lesser marriage.

Kiriel di'Ashaf came upon them. "We are ready, Tyr'agar."

"Good." He left them then. Joined the side of the Callestan Tyr, by gesture alone giving Kiriel the order to follow.

Alina was surprised, for she recognized the slight dance of hand; it was not Southern, not Northern; it was a thing born of the fields of battle: the language of the Ospreys.

Kiriel bowed.

The Callestan Tyran had grown accustomed to women in the ranks of the Tyragar's personal guard, but they did not welcome the intrusion of the gentle sex. Still, they were not Ospreys; it didn't show.

"Tyr'agnate," Kiriel said without preamble—and without the complicated request for permission that Southern women were required to offer—"we are ready. But I do not believe you will be happy with our destination."

"Any destination within Callesta is unlikely to bring me joy," he said, with just the faintest hint of humor.

She nodded. Turning to Valedan, she said, "We go to the temple of the Radann."

CHAPTER FIFTEEN

A MOMENT of silence.
Ramiro di'Callesta used it as a shield. Stood behind
it, expression impenetrable as he examined the choices laid
out before him. He was aware of the Tyran; aware that they
looked not to the Tyr'agar, nor to the Tyr's unfortunate
choice of guard, but to the Tyr'agnate, the man who em-
bodied Callesta. The decision was his.

Must be his.

"Kiriel." The Serra Alina turned her shoulder toward
him. It was easy to see her as a Northern guard; easy until
she spoke. The nuances of the Southern Court informed the
Weston she chose to speak, marking her, in two ways, as
foreign. Proud woman, he thought her; hawklike. She carried the grace of her lineage, but it was scarred, had always
been scarred, by the ferocity of her temperament and her inability to disguise it.

Yet she had found a place in the harem of his wife, the ir-
reproachable Serra Amara; had made, of an implacable
enemy, something that might—in times of peace—be called
friend. His par, Ser Fillipo, had always admired this particular Lambertan. It was almost easy to understand why.

Kiriel di'Ashaf, shadowed by the creature who had almost killed the Voyani woman, turned to the Serra Alina
di'Lamberto.

"The temple of the Radann is forbidden to the women of
the Dominion," Serra Alina told her. It was so much a
Southern truth that Ramiro kai di'Callesta knew no one else
would think to speak it aloud.

A shrug was Kiriel di'Ashaf's entire response.

"If, indeed, what you seek is within the walls of the temple, we cannot face it there."

The shrug became a frown. He heard the wind's howl in the crease of her thin lips. But she did not speak.

The Serra waited a moment, and when it became clear that Kiriel would not speak, continued. "You, Alexis, Fiara, and certainly myself, must wait upon the Tyrs. It is an offense in the eyes of the Lord for women to set foot within a place consecrated to his use."

"It is not the Lord's time."

"No. But even in the darkest of nights, there are places which are the Lord's; places which bear his light and his commandment. This is one."

"And are there such places for the Lady?"

The Serra's smile was thin. The bitterness that did not—quite—reach her face tainted her voice. "It is said that all of the recesses of a woman's heart belong to her."

Kiriel's silence had none of the quality of the Tyr'agnate's. She bristled as she approached the Tyr'agar. But she did not demean him again; did not snap or snarl as the Ospreys were wont to do among their own.

"Tyr'agar."

"Kiriel."

She hesitated. Ramiro had seen her hesitate in such a fashion many times, and each time was a surprise to him; there was something about her demeanor that such evidence of uncertainty ill-suited.

"The Serra Alina is correct," Ramiro said quietly. He had not meant to say as much, and smiled inwardly. Vulnerability in the young had its appeal, especially when it came unlooked for. His Amara would not have approved.

She turned to him, seeing in his words some hint of the indulgence he should not have felt. But it was not simple indulgence that moved him. He understood this young woman's value. He was canny; he had learned, over the reach of years, to blend his weaknesses and his strengths so that the former might be hidden and the latter valued openly.

"Tyr'agnate," she said, and she bowed. It was a man's bow, and the free fall of hair across her face and shoulders deepened its incongruity.

"Rise," he said softly, realizing that she waited upon his permission to do just that. Canny child; a pity she was so out of place in the South.

"The temple is built upon consecrated ground."

"Indeed."

"But . . . if it contains what we seek . . . has it not already been defiled? If the temple harbors one of the kin, can the presence of . . . mere . . . women be worse?"

Behind her, the Serra Alina nodded in silent approval.

It had been a difficult question to ask; he could see it in the lines of her youthful expression. But she asked it. He had seen her, once, upon the field of the Kings' Challenge. Even at a distance, he had felt, for just a moment, the endless fall of night.

You have a warrior's heart, he thought. *You will do what must be done.*

He understood it well, for it was a truth that they shared; was a truth that had come to define him, wearing away the edges of a wild, impatient youth. In the High Courts, or the low, words were weapons; grace and silence, the dance that hinted at the strength of a blade that was seldom drawn. He had learned these early; they would never leave him.

But upon the field, he had learned other truths.

He had seen his father fall. Had lost his uncle; his cousins; he had seen the messy, intemperate valleys, sodden with rain, dark with the hollows of fire's majesty, and had come to understand that they could not be accurately represented by the flat, spare surfaces of the maps by which decisions were made. Upon such a field, sword, horse, rank—nothing was proof against death.

And upon such a field, men were horsed, armored, armed; they carried swords, spears, and the bows that were so despised by the clans. It would never have occurred to him—to any born Callestan—to take the field with less than his enemy carried.

The field had been defined by her sparse sentence.

Would he deny himself a weapon? He studied her face, and only hers; the creature at her back, the woman by her side, the Osprey who had come, in silence, to stand in her wake, were insubstantial.

The Lord of Day and the Lord of Night were implacable enemies. But the Lord of Day valued, above all, the prowess of warriors. If there had ever been a time in which he had derided the folly of those who had chosen the banner of Allasakar as their rallying point, he repented now; he understood the allure. The risk.

"The sanctity of the temple is not within my jurisdiction," he replied. "But your point is valid. Fillipo. Miko."

They came, his shadows. His power.

"Tyr'agnate."

"Come. We wake the Radann."

The city of Callesta was no stranger to war, although it had been many, many years since the fact of its brutality had been seen within the heart of the Callestan grounds.

There were therefore subtle ways to wake the Radann; to seek audience in the darkness of the Lady's Night. It was seldom done; the men of the Lord were not completely comfortable in their power while the Lady's veiled face rose in the skies, and, as any clansmen, they sought the advantage of home ground unless they were certain to see battle upon it.

Ramiro chose to abjure subtlety.

He waited, arms folded, while the Captain of his oath-guards lifted sword and used the flat of its blade to strike the great brass bells that formed the centerpiece of the temple's hidden grounds. The bell tolled, echoing the strike of steel; tolled again as Miko's sword joined his brother's. No man hearing this could mistake it for anything other than what it was: call to war. Warning of combat to follow.

He waited. The Radann Fiero el'Sol was not a young man, but his servitors were almost the equal of the Tyran. The wind carried the sound of their feet, the distant clatter of steel, the chime of chain link and shield.

The tenor of the bell changed. Ser Fillipo, as the Captain of the Tyran before him, knew how to clap those bells in a way that identified the order behind their call; he did so now. No matter that he had been twelve years from this temple, and these ritual practices; he made no misstep. Miko was a beat behind; off in his practice. He did not see the Tyr'agnate's frown.

The temple doors rolled open; fire, unadorned by glass or the bob of lamp, lit the path as burning torches came into view. Orange light changed the grounds; the light of fire that was contained, but barely.

Radann stepped into the night.

When they saw the Tyr'agnate, they stopped.

He stepped forward, by gesture stilling the Tyran.

In the face of the Lady's Moon, he bowed. "Radann Allanos," he said quietly. "It is urgent that I speak with the Radann Fiero el'Sol."

The dark-haired man bowed. He was ten years Ramiro's junior, and the distance of years put all power in this discourse upon Ramiro's shoulders. As, he thought, with fleeting amusement, it should be.

The temple of the Radann was not, in theory, his, and he was conversant with the laws that governed its existence. But his or no, he was the Tyr'agnate; the symbol of sun rising, eight rays glittering gold in a reflection of hastily gathered light, was in all ways equal to the robes that the Radann Fiero el'Sol would wear when he at last chose to join them.

Allanos bowed. When he rose, he was still for a moment: in the torchlight he could see the length of the Callestan blade. *Bloodhame* had been drawn.

The Radann was pale. Ramiro chose to see this as an artifact of the light.

An act of mercy.

"The Radann Fiero el'Sol will join us," Allanos said. "Are we under attack, Tyr'agnate?"

"We are at war," Ramiro replied smoothly.

Allanos nodded grimly. "Radann Fiero el'Sol has prepared the blessing for the dawn."

"Such a blessing *is* a blessing, but we are not always fortunate enough to choose the hour of its necessity."

"Indeed, that is the Lord's truth." The Radann parted; Radann Allanos gave way with just a hint of relief to the man who controlled the Radann el'Sol in the Terrean of Averda.

If Radann Fiero el'Sol was disturbed by the manner of the Tyr'agnate's chosen summons, his bearing gave no evidence of it. He bowed, his hand upon the hilt of sheathed blade. Without hesitation he stepped across the threshold, giving himself over to the world of the clansmen and the will of the man who ruled them here.

"Radann Fiero el'Sol," the Tyr'agnate said quietly, "I have come with the Tyr'agar and his guards." He bowed to Valedan, the gesture perfect.

The Radann's bow was minutely different as he extended it to the last of the Leonne bloodline.

It was difficult to cede the rest of the negotiation to the untried youth, but Ramiro was capable of such surrender. He stepped aside, wordlessly demanding Valedan's attendance.

Saw the slight lift of dark brow in the otherwise smooth countenance of the Radann. "Tyr'agar."

"Radann Fiero el'Sol."

"How may we serve?"

"With your permission," Valedan said, as smooth in speech as Ramiro had been, his Torra the perfect Torra of the High Court, "I would guard this conversation from ears less friendly to our cause than yours."

"Of course."

"Primus."

Primus Duarte AKalakar lifted arms in a wide, swift circle that reminded Ramiro of a bird's flight. Hunting bird. The Ospreys, he thought, had always been well-named.

While Duarte drew the eye with the grace of his gesture, and confounded the ear with the unpleasant gutturality of his spoken, impenetrable words, Valedan gestured Kiriel forward.

He turned, met her gaze openly; she offered him no pretty bow, no Serra's obeisance, no graceful obedience. Her gaze traveled across the gathered men; her fist clenched. After a moment, she shook her head.

"Thank you, Sentrus. That will be all."

It was not a choice Ramiro di'Callesta would have made, but he had already made his decision, and now abided by it.

"Radann Fiero," Valedan said quietly, "I ask for your judgment."

Fiero's brows rose. What seemed dark in the darkness was lined silver; age, there. The strength of an age that weakness had not yet diminished. Men called it wisdom.

Radann Fiero el'Sol waited.

"The temple of the Radann is forbidden the women of the Dominion," Valedan continued. "The Lord seeks warriors, and the women of the South lift no sword, and join no battle, for his greater glory."

"Indeed."

"But among my men are the warriors of the North. This woman," he continued, acknowledging Kiriel, and by such acknowledgment, forcing the same from the Radann Fiero el'Sol, "lives by the sword she bears. She has fought the servants of the Lord of Night both in darkness and beneath the Lord's gaze, and she has always emerged victorious; if he judges, he judges her as one of his own."

Ramiro closed his eyes. The line of his jaw was stiff as a blade, stiff as Annagarian pride. He did not speak.

"The Lord does not reign in the North," the Radann Al-

lanos el'Sol said, his modulated tone belying the outrage of
stiff words.

"The Lord," Valedan replied quietly, "is not confined by
the borders drawn—and contested—by men. There is not a
one among you who can best her in battle."

"Kai Leonne," Ser Ramiro said. A warning.

One that the kai Leonne chose not to heed.

"She is blessed by the Lord. I have seen it. The Tyran that
now serve the Tyr'agnate have seen it. She has defeated a
darkness that existed, whole, in the light of day."

"She is a woman," Radann Fiero el'Sol replied. Seeing,
now, where the conversation was headed, and not liking it
overmuch.

"She is. But she has more than a warrior's heart." He
bowed. "We have traveled far this eve, and we have received word that the servants of our enemy reside within
Callesta, waiting upon the departure of the Tyr'agnate before they strike at the heart of his lands: the city of Callesta
itself."

"Grim news," Radann Fiero said softly, relenting.

"There is only one place they might reside in safety,"
Valedan continued. "Only one place that is considered
above reproach, and therefore, above suspicion."

Wisdom. Light in the face of the Radann Fiero el'Sol:
fire. Lord's fire. "Impossible."

"That is our hope," Valedan replied. But his tone offered
none.

The Radann turned to his Radann, to his armed servitors.
He gestured; he spoke.

And the Tyr'agnate saw what he had never seen as lord
of Averda: the Fire of the Radann. Light leaped from
Fiero's eyes to the edge of the blade he drew, as if it were
lightning strike in the heart of the storm.

"Yes," the kai Leonne said softly. "Within the temple itself."

Dangerous. Dangerous that; it bordered upon accusation.
Boy Tyr, Ramiro thought, *tread cautiously.*

"We harbor no servants of the Lord of Night."

"Not knowingly; it is not the way of that Lord. But within the temple itself, our enemy is waiting."

The Radann turned toward the open doors, toward the darkness made of night's fall through the crafted glass of the Northern Empire.

"If such a creature has made his abode in this place," Valedan said softly, "is the temple of the Radann not defiled?"

The Radann Fiero el'Sol was curved, Lord's blade. Southern blade. "If such a thing were true, Tyr'agar, yes."

Be careful, kai Leonne.

"Then the Lord has consecrated these grounds in a manner befitting the warriors he chooses to test. *This* is his blessing." Valedan drew blade; it was dull and flat as it met the fires of the Radann, but he held it firmly, raised it without hesitation. The Radann Fiero el'Sol recognized the blade at once: the blade of the heir to Callesta. "We take battle to the only place upon the grounds of Callesta that knows the Lord's sight in the darkness of the Lady's time.

"Will you deny us our warriors?"

"They are women," Fiero said slowly.

"Yes. And the judgment that I wait upon is in the hands of men who know best the Lord's will. Deny them entry, and we will abide by the decision of the Radann."

The moment stretched.

Valedan kai di'Leonne did not move; although he was capable of—could be accused of—being gentle, he was steel now. Behind the respect he offered the Radann was, at last, the edge of a threat that only the Tyr'agar could offer. The Tyr'agar, who wore the sun ascendant, as even Radann Fiero el'Sol could not.

The Radann Fiero el'Sol's eyes fell first and, as they did, gazed at last upon the full splendor of the sun ascendant. "Tyr'agar," he said stiffly. "As you have spoken. Let the Lord judge."

Just that.

Valedan kai di'Leonne offered the Radann el'Sol the lowest of bows he might offer from the distance of his rank.

"Sentrus," he said coldly to Kiriel di'Ashaf. "Find what you seek."

It was a command. And more, for if she was mistaken, it would be costly, and the cost would be borne, in its entirety, by the man who would be Tyr.

Although he had given the command, Kiriel waited.

She understood the subtle play of politics between the powerful; had seen it many times. Kinlords often offered their vassals a chance to earn their deaths, and the deaths were never pleasant.

He waited a moment, and then he nodded. "Follow," he said quietly.

She saw, out of the corner of her eye, the slight incline of Ramiro di'Callesta's head. Was surprised at the momentary pleasure his approval afforded her.

Lord Telakar waited by her side.

"You are . . . interesting," he said, in the tongue of the *Kialli*.

She gave him no answer; Valedan stepped between the open doors and she followed, moving so quickly and gracefully not even Ser Andaro was given the chance to cleave to the side of his lord. She drew her blade carefully, avoiding the theatrical sweep of black steel in the confined space the backs and chests of men made.

"Where, Telakar?" She, too, chose to speak in the *Kialli* tongue.

"Can you not sense it, Kiriel? You are almost upon him now."

She hesitated for only a moment. "If I could sense him, I would have killed you instantly."

"Then perhaps it is not in my interest, Lord, to satisfy your curiosity so quickly."

She shrugged. "You've already exposed your weakness, Telakar. Thwart me, and I will kill her."

"You lack subtlety."

"Yes."

"Very well. But be quick, little one."

She froze. Turned to him, then, the blade wavering in her hand. She almost killed him.

Didn't. "Never call me that," she said softly.

He bowed. Rose, expression remote. He lifted a hand and gestured.

Toward the altar.

Toward the body of the kai Callesta.

Kiriel reached out; touched Valedan's shoulder. He froze. "Kai Leonne," she said, using the familiar title and not the formal one. "It would be best if you . . . waited outside with the Tyr'agnate."

Her only mercy. A mistake; she had little time. Telakar's warning was clear: if the creature escaped, if he made good his return to the Shining City, it would change the face of the war before she was ready.

He would carry news of Lord Telakar to the Shining Court, and if the Lord's will was bent upon Telakar, she had already lost him. Worse, he would know where *she* was.

But the ring upon her hand burned suddenly hot and the colors of the shadowed room darkened and brightened, speaking a language that mortals were never meant to understand.

Valedan's expression was cloaked now in the colors of night; his face was pale. She could see, beneath the thin stretch of skin, the colors by which mortal lives were defined: the brilliance of pale, pale white, the beauty of the grays that defined its edges. No darkness here.

The sight stilled her.

And in that moment, the Tyr'agnate joined them as they stood, crowded now, too many bodies pressed into a small space.

She looked at the older man. Wondered why she had

thought of sparing him this combat, and shook herself free of the desire.

Lifting her blade, she shattered the silence with the strength of her unbound roar.

She could *see*.

For a moment, the ring seemed to fall from her hand; it was luminescent, yes, but slender, a transparent circlet, a harmless adornment.

Not so the blade; it woke at the sound of her cry, quickening in her hands. She could feel its pulse as if it were alive; as if it were an extension of her arm, her flesh and blood.

She had wielded it for all of her adult life, and it had never responded thus.

The creature upon the altar rose at once, caged in dead flesh, his eyes shrunken now by the lack of water and vision, his lips cracked, the hollows of his face containing wells of shadow. Beauty, and in it, the whole of the facade of death.

Those lips stretched out across flat teeth.

She could not see his name. Could not command him; could not draw him out of the body that housed it.

But she had learned the art of combat, the dance of survival, long before she had mastered the pronunciation of The Name; she leaped past Valedan, past Telakar, curling her knees to her chest and trusting the force of momentum to carry her well above the rounded curve of closed helm.

Her blade struck stone, shattering it.

The creature was no longer there.

He hissed through dead lips; she heard the sibilance of its laughter. "Daughter of Darkness," he said, "I thank you for this opportunity."

She twisted, turned toward the flat, broken rasp of his voice, and saw where he had landed: within striking distance of Valedan. The kai Leonne.

She did not cry out a warning; did not express any hint of

the sudden fear that moved her. Here, training held her in a grip that could not be shaken.

Light came to the creature; red light, in twin flashes: the sword of the *Kialli*. And the shield.

He had armed himself, this nameless lord, and she had been slow enough to allow it. Some part of her reveled in the opportunity.

What did it matter, in the end? Valedan was not bound for the Hells; if his body and spirit were sundered, he would go where the dead went, would stand in the Halls of Mandaros, and would wait upon his return.

She saw that clearly.

And more.

Saw the colors of a man she recognized. When the *Kialli* blade circled, it struck the steel of Auralis AKalakar's sword.

The Osprey's blade shattered, as stone had shattered.

But it bought her time. She leaped again as the Radann scattered, and this time the creature did not seek to evade her. Hissing, it turned.

He was slow, she thought; slowed by the form he had taken, by the casement of flesh through which she could so clearly see the shadows that burned. Why did he not relieve himself of the burden and be done? The masquerade was at an end.

Black met red. Thunder came of that brief conversation, lingering in the reaches of the ceiling above. She struck again, and the creature was driven back as it raised shield against her. The shield held.

Power, here. No simple minion had been sent to the heart of Callesta.

But the only fear she felt was for Valedan kai di'Leonne; the only failure she contemplated, the end of his life. None of the battles that she had faced in the Shining Court of her youth had prepared her for this.

And all of them had. She laughed as she deflected the controlled arc of his blade; she had called the shadow and it had come. She held his attention, and all she needed to do was to hold it a few moments longer.

But he stilled as her laughter died, as the wildness left her.

He drew his blade up, the red of its fire the only true light in the cavernous room. His eyes were as dark as hers, the skin he wore as pale. "This is not your battle," he hissed.

"Any battle I choose is mine."

"And you choose this one? Did you not dwell within the heart of the Shining Court, in the towers of the Lord? Did you not choose to take your place by the side of the *Kialli*, in the halls of the Palace?"

"Never by the side," she whispered. "You are not my equal."

His turn to laugh. "Your *equal?* You have walked the plane scant years, and I have ruled in the Hells; not even when I walked this plane as a youth was I so much the child. Do not stand against us, Daughter of Darkness, or you will meet the fate of the mortals."

She left ground as the burning blade whistled cleanly through the air where her chest had been.

"What of it?" she shouted, gripping the haft of sword in both hands as gravity and power forced her down. "I *am* mortal."

"Mortalis," he hissed. "So be it."

She had time to raise the sword before the ground at her feet cracked and splintered, shards of stone as large as her arms driving up and into her feet.

By that act, she knew him.

Lord Telakar watched.

Having spent much of his time upon the plane in the Southern reaches of the continent, he had never had a chance to see Kiriel di'Ashaf in combat.

He was unimpressed.

Isladar, brother, what in this foundling has driven you to make the choices you have made? What in her is wo th the risks you have taken? She was feckless, wild, impulsive—and in the Shining Court, in the Hells, in the lands that had once been the home of the kin when the kin knew the spectrum of life and not its shadowed mockery, these things were death.

She was injured; her power was weaker than it should have been. The stones themselves had broken the underside of her boots, and although he could not see it clearly, the dust of falling rock did not obscure the scent of blood.

She will die here, or die soon.

Dispassionate, he folded his arms across his chest; bore witness to the event that unfolded before him.

Silabras was no youth, no wild kin; his memories were strong. He was unhindered by her anger, and the wildness that drove her broke against the simple surface of his shield. He would take her; none here could prevent it. She had come to master her blade, but she had no shield, and there were none—not even Lord Isladar himself—who could fashion one for her.

But the folly of mortality knew no wisdom; one man tried.

Light, orange and pale, spread before her like a web, its lines a spiral that rose and fell, touching ceiling and broken ground as if to anchor itself. Lord Telakar raised a brow; in the open doors of a building too insignificant to be called a cathedral, one of the mortals stood, arms raised, face still.

He would not have been worthy of the title mage had he walked the streets of the fallen Cities. But in those streets, he would not have had the courage—or the ignorance—to attempt to intervene in the affairs of the powerful.

She found her feet.

He recognized her pain. He was *Kialli*. The winds of the Hells had spoken to him in all of its languages. She labored under its grip as she stood—but she stood; her face showed nothing.

And it hid nothing. Not from Silabras. Not from Telakar.

Silabras smiled. The visage of dead flesh would never

again settle into the lines of peaceful repose; the flat of white teeth cracked and sundered as the truth of what it contained could be contained no longer.

"My only regret," the kinlord said, gazing past the thin, the inconsequential barrier of pathetic magery, "is the lack of a worthy audience. The Lord sought to place you above us, forgetting the laws of the Hells. I will send you there, Kiriel, and when I return, I will find you."

He staggered, his voice breaking on the last syllable. A sword, dull metal, dead steel, protruded from his chest.

Lord Telakar raised his chin. This, this was the first act to capture his attention.

The hand behind the blade released the hilt as Silabras turned. The guise of human hands was discarded as the kinlord extended his reach toward the man who had wounded him.

Was he slower? Hard to tell. Not slow enough, surely, that the human who had chosen to join the intimacy of *Kialli* combat could avoid the reward for his folly.

"Kiriel!" The man shouted, dancing back, the sheets of chain metal shredding at the force of Silabras' blow. "First blood!" The scent of blood was strong; for a moment, Telakar wondered if the man was speaking of his own.

Kiriel shouted something that made as little sense. "Bastard! He was mine!"

And the injured man, the man who stood one side of death, laughed. Laughing, drew *another* blade as Kiriel attacked Silabras, drawing his attention, saving the man's life.

Silabras' blade tore through the orange weaving of the weak mage. But it moved just a shade more slowly than it had; there was power in the weakness that Telakar had failed to correctly assess.

Kiriel roared. The whole of the city must waken to the voice that she used; even Telakar was frozen by it.

Her blade cut a clean arc through air; it was met by the casual lift of Silabras' shield.

The shield sundered.

He saw, then, the signature of the dark blade she held, and he knew that she had been granted a blade made by the hand of Anduvin. Rumor had said as much, but rumor had also said that she had failed the test of its mastery.

The Lord's Fist would be vexed indeed to learn the truth.

Your pardon, Isladar, he thought, letting his hands fall to his sides. *I better understand your weakness now. And why should I not? Is it not kin, in some measure, to my own?*

The injured man circled, wary now, his chain shirt hanging open. He navigated the rise and fall of broken stone as if he were used to fighting upon mountain terrain.

But he was not Kiriel; bleeding or no, she danced from stone tip to flat, her sword trailing shadow. Silabras spared her no further speech.

Nor would Telakar have done so.

He would have said, watching, that the child who had started this combat, and the one who engaged Silabras now, were entirely different, but he did not doubt the truth of his senses: he could see Kiriel, could see the signal truth of her claim to mortality: The soul; the only thing about her that could not, in the end, be destroyed.

But something *had* changed. The shadows were sharper now, and darker, than they had been, and they wove round her like a cloak, like a second skin—something she was only peripherally aware of. Her face was sharp with it, her eyes—her eyes were golden. The only light she cast.

Silabras chose fire because fire was his element.

But in the depths of her power, the fire guttered.

She swung her sword.

The half circle shifted, the blade dipping suddenly, the edge rising.

And the mortal, the injured man, also swung.

He would lose a second sword, this eve.

But in the losing—to Telakar's profound surprise—the remaining pieces of the shield of Silabras were also lost.

Impossible.

Kiriel swung her blade with a cry of triumph as the mortal man stumbled back, the rocks impeding escape, the floor opening up beneath his back.

Silabras parried, the motion circular; her blade glanced off the exposed flat of his as he continued his swing groundward. Groundward toward the foolish mortal who had thought to fight by Kiriel's side.

It struck the steel of Lord Telakar's sword.

Silabras knew a moment of surprise, a moment of anger, of thwarted desire.

And then he knew nothing.

The head rolled free of the body, bouncing against the broken floor as if it were a soft boulder.

It came to rest at the feet of the Tyr'agnate of Callesta, passing between the feet of the Tyran, beneath the reach of their drawn swords. Ramiro had drawn *Bloodhame*, but he had stayed his ground. And because he was of the South, because he was of the High Courts, he could offer the pretense of prudence for his lack of action.

The Northerners would accept this; might even feel some contempt for it. But the Tyran, born to the South, and of it in a way that no transplanted Northerner could ever be, would understand the truth.

Fillipo subtly closed ranks as the silence in the temple became absolute. He turned his face outward, planting his feet to either side of a great crack in the stones of the Lord's haven. Miko joined him to one side, Stevan, to the other. Gazing outward, they offered their Tyr the dignity that he could not afford to lose.

He knelt.

Bloodhame scraped floor, cold hiss of steel unblooded, untried. He had failed his son, not once, but twice.

The face was a dead man's face. It bore little resemblance to the living; less even than it had under the watchful eyes of the Radann and their spells of preservation. The flesh of his lips had been torn from corner to cheek on either side; the eyes were open, empty. But his hair was still bound in a warrior's knot—the only dignity left him.

Ramiro's hands shook.

The Tyran had spared him their knowledge of this; they bore no witness to the weakness itself.

Removing his gloves, he bent down and closed the lids of his kai's eyes.

Men did not pray. Men did not cry. They weathered loss as they weathered wind, sand, sun.

Carelo.

"Tyr'agnate," an unwelcome voice said, its speaker hidden by the backs of his oathguards, the only kin he trusted. "Be wary. The kin—"

"He is gone." Kiriel's voice. Lady's voice.

He gathered his son's head in his hands. Pulled the folds of his cloak across it. Then he rose.

"Par Callesta."

Fillipo nodded; he did not turn.

"Extend my gratitude to the guards of the kai Leonne. I have duties that must be attended."

"Kai Callesta."

The doors of the temple were open; they sat awkwardly astride their great hinges. They would not, he thought distantly, close with ease this eve. It signified nothing. He walked between them, and the night sky wavered in his open eyes. The Radann were not his kin, but they were men of Callesta; they bowed as he passed them, offering him the full measure of their obeisance.

Offering him, by that measure, the privacy he desired; they saw his feet, the sweep of his cloak, the edge of *Bloodhame* and the scabbard in which she no longer rested.

Starlight, moonlight, a hint of nebulous, illuminated cloud: the raiment of the Lady. Everything was silver. The night was cool, the wind gentled into breeze.

He swallowed it, and it almost devoured him.

Almost. But he was the kai Callesta, his father's son, his son's father. He swept out of the temple and across the grounds trampled so thoroughly beneath the feet of clumsy men.

Only when he left the path that marked the temple's bounds did he pause. The darkness behind the lids of his eyes was welcome; a darkness that had nothing to do with the Lord or the Lady; a night of his own choosing.

He shared it with his son, with the memories of his son; rage did not respond to his hollow call.

Instead, he saw the combat; saw the fire of the Lord of Night, so similar in color and texture to the weaker fires of the Radann. He saw the small, slender form of Kiriel di'Ashaf; saw her move as the wind moves; saw the impossible speed that was matched only by the Northern Osprey that served the kai Leonne. The Radann had lifted swords; the Radann had been scattered.

She had laid his son to rest.

He would not forget this debt, but he would not dwell on it. Instead, he looked across the grounds, the flowers now as dark as the trunks of trees, the night leaves; glass lay among them, broken shards a delicate echo of the temple's floor.

He trod carefully, but with purpose.

In the city of Callesta, Ser Ramiro kai di'Callesta was known, with pride, as the Lord's man. His presence commanded the respect of cerdan across the length and breadth of Averda, invoking the glory of old wars, old battles.

But even upon the grounds of his home, he honored what must be honored: the Lady's hour. The Lady's time. Hidden among the trees that trailed blossoms so artfully into the passing stream were the standing stones and the small, stone altar, that could be found upon the grounds of any clansman of wealth. No stones marked the path that led to it; no fire burned at its heart. Any light that was given it was given at the Lady's blessing—and her light, this eve, was bright.

He found the offering bowls in the lee of the altar's southern edge, and he knelt before them, shifting the weight of his cloak to the side and revealing a burden that simple burial would never relieve him of.

There, his knees against the moss by the small stream's edge, he offered the Lady his prayers and his pleas; he begged her indulgence and her forgiveness—but as men do. Silently.

In the first bowl, wine, cooled by the evening and not yet soured. In the second, sweet water, come from the passing stream. And in the third? Nothing. Nothing yet. He lifted *Bloodhame*; on his knees, he found the sword ungainly. But it had been drawn; it demanded its due with the single-minded purpose of steel. Willingly, he drew it across his exposed arm. Blood fell, adorning stone, the one hot, the other cool.

Lady, he thought. *Bless this, my son. He died defending your right to rule the Southern night.*

He reached into the bowls. Wine, water, blood: these were the ablutions by which he cleansed his son of the taint of the Lord of Night.

These, and one other, his head bowed, his son's dead cheek inches from his face.

CHAPTER SIXTEEN

12th of Corvil, 427 AA
Terrean of Mancorvo

THE Serra Donna en'Lamberto took the message that was handed her by the young seraf. He was not a seraf of the domis, but rather of the stables; through his hands passed saddle and rein. And through his hands passed other things.

He bowed, but the bow was awkward; had he been a girl, she might have been moved to correct him in some fashion. Now, however, she held her peace; the letter bore a seal. It was a seal she recognized, although she saw it seldom.

Two letters, she thought, rising only when the screens had been closed upon the clumsy, loud step of the seraf. The one, from the General Alesso di'Marente. The other, from the Serra Amara en'Callesta.

She could not say which of the two harbored the greater danger. But these were women's words, and the edge they contained was blunted. For now.

She did not call her husband. She did not bespeak her wives. She listened a moment for the sound of children; heard them in the distance, and chose to retreat to chambers that might not be so easily breached.

When she closed the screens to the smallest of her chambers, she knelt, and removing the scroll, she broke its seal. Out of habit, she was careful to catch all traces of wax; to leave nothing that might attract the watchful eye as evidence. If women did not war, they played a different game of politics; if what the letter contained was not to her liking, it would go no farther than the brazier in which incense was burned.

Ah, she had *so little* time.

She gazed at the muted shadows of sun through the thinnest of screens, and saw where they fell. Guests of import would arrive soon, and they could not be put off.

Her hands shook.

What do you want, Donna? She asked the question without rancor and without panic. She had asked it a hundred times an hour since the letter from the General had arrived in her harem, borne by the man she best loved in the Dominion.

Her dead son *was* the wind's voice.

But Lamberto was her life. Could she surrender the one without losing the other? Mareo trusted the General's offer, and he was not a man easily lied to. But trusting it, he had yet to make his decision, and because he had not, she could not. *Yes, Na'donna, I believe he will honor the offer he makes in his letter.*

Then why do you hesitate?

Grim-faced, tired, he had turned to her. "The Voyani," he said quietly. "The letter contained truth, yes, but not the whole of the truth."

But enough of it, surely?

"I do not offer you counsel," she had said, which was true; she could not. He had not asked. "But there is no way to avoid war now. All that is left is to choose *which* war we will fight; the cost is ours to bear, regardless."

"And if you could spare the Terrean the hardship entirely, would you forgo the battle?"

She had not answered. Answer enough.

But now, she thought, the edges of other truths might stand revealed. In this letter.

She unrolled it with hands that shook. She could not be perfect while she held it; it was for this reason that she sought solitude. What no one witnessed could be ignored in safety.

Serra Donna en'Lamberto, the letter began. She recognized the script; it was perfect, if perhaps a little too bold.

I received your graceful letter, and I apologize for my delay in response; the gravity of its contents were such that I desired to offer a response in every way as perfect.

But events have conspired to rob me—to rob us both—of time. And where there is little time, there is oft little grace; please accept my humble apologies for the haste with which this is written.

You spoke of your gardens, of your husband, of your city—and it has been long indeed since I have been privileged to see any of these things; I was grateful for the glimpse of your Court. But it is of the last thing that you wrote that I can now speak. The death of your kai.

She stopped reading for a moment, and felt old anger rise, as if it were the first fruit of a bitter planting.

My own kai was killed by assassins shortly after your letter arrived, before my husband returned to Callesta.

And just as quickly, the anger was gone; buried. She felt instead a pang of sorrow, a kindling of sympathy.

I do not know if this brings us any closer to understanding one another; if it does, this understanding has come at too high a price, and I beseech the Lady daily for some sign that I live in the folds of her nightmare. But I have not yet wakened.

I will not insult you now. It was my intent to write a letter that was, like the letters of Serras, graceful, gracious, an attempt to bridge the distance between the two men who have always ruled the North.

But the events have transpired in a way that may prevent this; I write now in haste.

The last of the clan Leonne dwells within Callesta. He has come at the side of Ser Anton di'Guivera; I assume that word of this has reached you, in Amar. I assume that other

*words have reached you as well, but they are a matter for
men; they are a matter of war.*

*What perhaps has failed to reach your ears, is this: the
Serra Alina di'Lamberto also travels with Ser Valedan kai
di'Leonne. She came from the Northern Court; they have
released the hostages there to the keeping of the young kai
Leonne.*

*When the Tyr'agnate returned, he asked to see my son.
And he asked, as well, to see the bodies of the men who
caused his death. This was done, as all things are, at the
command of the Tyr'agnate.*

*What was done at the command of the Tyr'agar was dif-
ferent: he bid your husband's sister come to identify the
assassins.*

And, Serra Donna, she did.

*She identified them as the oathguards of Ser Mareo kai
di'Lamberto: His Tyran.*

*I would not have thought her bold enough to speak with
me after she had done so, but she serves the kai Leonne,
and she came to me. I thought she would attempt to speak
on behalf of the Tyr'agnate—and knowing the freshness of
my loss, and the ferocity of my grief, you can imagine how
I welcomed her, for she came to my harem.*

*But she offered me solace and wisdom, and she offered
me this as well: She said that if I asked Ser Mareo kai
di'Lamberto if his was the hand behind the sword that
killed my son, he would answer truthfully, no matter what
that answer might be.*

*I have never understood your husband. I mean no disre-
spect by this; I have no doubt that you would say the same,
if asked about mine. But lack of understanding and lack of
respect are not the same. We have guarded our borders
against his raiders; you have guarded your borders against
my husband's. Serafs have died, and cerdan, in those skirmishes—it has been a long decade.*

*But I never imagined that I need fear this death from
Lamberto, and had I not witnessed the Serra Alina's reac-*

*tions with my own eyes, I might have been convinced, with
difficulty, that this was not tied with the clan Lamberto.*

*Yet even now, Serra Donna, I am not so certain. The ev-
idence is there.*

*But other evidence is there as well. It is true that our hus-
bands have not been allies since the end of the war, if indeed it can be said to have ended. But it is also true that the
shape of the coming war will define the Dominion for
longer years to come; true as well that the North will fall if
the Tyrs cannot stand together.*

*And true, last of all, that the man who commands the
larger part of the armies of the South has already resorted
to such mean assassination and betrayal in order to gain
his crown, his Tor and the Lady's Lake.*

*So I ask you, now, as a mother bereaved to a mother be-
reaved: Was your husband's hand behind this?*

And if, as I hope, your answer is No, I wait your reply.

Ser Mareo kai di'Lamberto was unamused.

He was not—yet—angry, but the day had been long, and
the wagon that housed the Voyani now resided in his courtyard beneath the open sky. It was not to his liking.

Less to his liking was the absence of his Serra, for *men*
did not treat with the Voyani; they certainly did not treat
with the daughters of their Matriarchs. Too much could be
said—and done—in the presence of such women that
would harm him; they were without grace and respect.

Wives dealt with them, if anyone did.

And given the coming war, wives were of import.

Yet it was not the Serra Donna en'Lamberto who greeted
these most important and undesirable of guests, but rather
one of her wives, and the difference in the rank was not lost
upon the women who waited with fading patience.

Such as patience was, among the wanderers.

For her part, Ramona was gracious and perfect; she offered sweet water and fruit to the women, and also offered
them the excuses of the Serra.

What the women heard there he could not tell; he did not deign to approach the wagons directly, but watched them from the distance of the domis.

It was while watching them that he met his wife.

And when he saw her, the irritation that had moved him was all but forgotten; she was as pale as she might have been had she lost blood. Her hands were shaking, and in them, clutched too tight, he saw parchment.

She knelt before him, and he allowed it; she could not keep her feet with easy grace. But he touched her hair with his hands, gentling the distance between them, the severity of his height.

"The Voyani are here," he said quietly.

"I know it," she said. "And I would meet them, my husband, but . . ."

"Na'donna?"

"But I could not meet them yet; they will see what I have not managed to conceal from even my serafs."

He frowned. "Na'donna, they come to *you*."

She nodded, but she bowed low, hiding her face. Had she worn the veil, she would have been just as distant.

"What do you carry, Na'donna?" he asked, when it became clear that she could not speak.

"A letter," she said, although this much was clear. "It is only a letter. From a Serra."

"You have received many such letters these past months, and not one has robbed you of composure. Can I guess that the letter you carry bears the seal of the Serra Amara en'Callesta?"

She swallowed and nodded. "Forgive me," she said.

"There is nothing to forgive. You wrote to her?"

Again she bowed her head, but this time a blush lent color to her pallor. "I wrote to her," she said, as if admitting something shameful. "When it became clear that—"

But he knelt before her and touched her lips gently with his fingers. "What passes between Serras," he said quietly, "is not the business of their husbands. I trust your discretion, Serra Donna, and I understand that you have *always* been motivated by a desire for peace. I do not disdain it; I did not marry a warrior."

She lifted her face, then, and met his gaze. "This letter," she said, the last syllable trailing, "this one." And she held it out to him.

He did not touch it. Instead he rose, putting distance between her obvious distress and his acknowledgment of it. "It is women's writing," he said quietly. "And I know little of it; it is seldom taught to men."

She nodded. He lied, of course; she allowed it because she had no other choice.

"What does it say that upsets you?"

"The kai Callesta," she said, "the heir."

"What of him?"

"He is dead, Mareo."

Ser Mareo kai di'Lamberto said nothing. He waited.

And she understood by this that he would not wait forever.

"He is dead. Assassinated within Callesta."

"By who?"

"By—by your Tyran."

He turned back to her. "There is more," he said, "more to this accusation. You believe there is truth in it, or you would be angered. You are not angry, Na'donna. Speak."

"The Serra Alina di'Lamberto is within Callesta now," she said, and her voice quavered. "And she saw the bodies of those who were said to have done this thing."

"Alina? *There?*"

"She identified them, Mareo."

"And the Serra Amara?"

"Say what you like about the Callestans; most of it is probably true. But do not say this: that the Serra Amara, for political reasons, would see her son murdered. She would not destroy her own kin to harm yours. No mother would."

He was silent for a time, but at length he spoke. Two names. She recognized them both. Her face was paler, in the fading light; he knew that, should he allow it, she would sit, crouched in what, save for her grace, would be a huddle upon the floor by his feet.

"Where are they, Mareo?"

"In truth? They must be dead, and in Callesta," he replied evenly. "They were my men when Alina left us."

"Why are they not here? Why are they not in Amar?"

"They traveled," he said quietly.

"To what end?"

"I . . . do not know. They came to ask my leave to depart Amar. I granted it; they have asked little of me, these long years."

"And were they—"

His eyes snapped shut, and his hand rose. It was not a threat.

But she found threat in it, and he cursed his temper in perfect silence. "How many?" he asked, at last.

"She does not say. She says only that the dead were identified as your oathguards."

"And more?"

Oh, her hesitation. If anything might wound him, it would be this. He wanted to gather her in his arms. He did not.

"Mareo," she said, defining his sudden turn of mood, "I do not believe that you ordered this death." Clear, without a trace of anger or reproach, the words lent her strength. She clung to them; he allowed it. The belief in them was all he needed to hear.

No, that was untrue; it was what he needed to hear *from* her.

"No one could give orders to those men," he said quietly. "No one but me, or my father before me. They were not young."

She nodded.

"What did she ask of you, Na'donna?"

"She asked me if yours was the hand behind her son's death."

"She does not believe it?"

"She . . . believes it."

"But?"

Serra Donna closed her eyes. "She is a Serra," she said at last. "Mareo—she is not what I am. She is fierce and cunning; she plays a different game."

"But?" he prodded her gently.

"But she desires either peace or alliance; the shadow of the coming war puts our skirmishes to shame. She knows—as I know—the cost the Terreans will bear. Averda lost land in the last war; it will lose everything in this one, without luck and wit."

"She has asked you if we will stand with Callesta?"

The Serra looked scandalized; it was not an act. He would never, he thought, with just a hint of frustrated amusement, understand women. Never.

"She *is* a Serra," his wife said, speaking of her as distant cousin, or half sibling, and not as the wife of his greatest enemy. "She could no more ask that than she could challenge me to a duel beneath the Lord's watchful eye."

"What, then, does she seek?" It was the right question; he knew it the moment she heard it, because the tension in her face eased, and she sat a moment contemplating the words.

"She seeks," she said at last, "to inform us of this turn of events. If you are to meet with the Tyr of Averda, you must know this; you must have time to think on it."

"It is not solely that."

"No. She seeks the truth. She will accept whatever truth you offer," she added. "Because you are Lambertan. She knows that you will not stoop to lie." She spoke these last words with quiet pride.

"So," he said softly.

"Mareo?"

"Yes," he replied. "I am angry."

"She does not mean to insult you."

"No, and I take no offense; I cannot even read what she

has written. Her words were offered to *you,* as Serra to Serra; they have little meaning for me."

She nodded then, and exposed her back to his gaze.

"But I confess, Na'donna, that I was concerned at your absence; the Havallans wait, and they wait with neither grace nor patience. It may be that your delay is a blessing."

"A blessing, my husband?"

"Yes," he said quietly.

She was patient, now. The fear left her slowly, but it did leave. She was in Amar, and in the domis; she was at her husband's feet. Here, of all places, she should know peace.

"Did she say that there were witnesses to the killing?"

"No, my husband." She hesitated, and then added, "But I believe there must have been."

"I believe it as well," he said softly. "Let me ask you a question."

She waited.

"If you were the Serra Amara, and the kai that was dead in such a fashion were our son, you would be angered."

She nodded; it was not a question.

"And if the bodies that were—that must have been—adorned as *my* Tyran were identified by the sister of the man who ruled them, and that sister, no matter how much a serpent she was, was also known as Lambertan, would you then have *any* room for doubt? Would you believe that the assassins were somehow other than they appeared?"

She hesitated, but the hesitation was minute. "No, my husband." She flushed. "I should have considered this before I came to you."

"No," he told her gently. "If you and the Serra Amara have nothing else in common, you are both mothers; if she left room for doubt, she did so for a reason. She is not—as you said—a woman who would sacrifice her son for political gain."

His wife's nod told him that she believed *no* woman capable of such an act, and he loved her for it.

"Does she mention any reason for her doubt?"

She shook her head.

"Then she must have some suspicion, some information that we lack. I ask you to go to the Havallans," he said quietly, "and ask them."

"Ask them what, my husband?"

"Ask them how this might have been done."

12th of Corvil, 427 AA
Terrean of Raverra

Kallandras returned before dawn. Jewel noted his absence because she was awake. Sleep, this last week, had not been kind. The child slept in the confines of her small tent, unperturbed by the whimpering cries that marked the worst of Jewel's nightmares, and Jewel was content to let her sleep; to sneak out of the flaps of the tent into the scant dew of morning. She could not otherwise leave the child; the child found comfort in the presence of no one else. No one but Stavos, and he tended the Matriarch.

But she would sleep when Jewel slept, and this was an improvement; she would ride the great, tined beast as if it were a simple, stupid mule—and at that, a docile one. She would venture a smile at Stavos, from behind the flap of Jewel's desert robes. She would even take food with the Serra Diora, although she never spoke in her presence.

That, at least, was worth a smile: it was clear the girl worshiped the Serra, seeing in her the Flower of the Dominion, the unattainable perfect beauty for which, the Radann par el'Sol said, the Serra Diora was known.

Yesterday, at dinner, she had inched her way to where the Serra sat, legs folded, knees upon an unrolled mat that was meant to protect her from contact with the earth itself. She could not meet the Serra's eyes, but she had at last approached closely enough that she could offer a drooping bouquet of river flowers.

The Serra had taken them quietly, and with such stunning, perfect grace, that Jewel herself felt some of the child's awe.

She had not felt it during their trek into the Sea of Sorrows; had felt none of it at all during the long days when the anger of the Matriarch was as open as the winds that swept the sands from the desert floor. But the absence of the Matriarch had gentled this perfect woman, and the simple, yearning worship of a disfigured child had been met with a quiet, peaceful joy, a radiant smile, that could not be simple facade.

The child had been quick to withdraw her three-fingered hand; to hide it in the folds of clothing too large for her scant frame.

But the Serra Diora caught that hand, held it, speaking in tones so low that no one but Ariel was privileged to hear the words. Then, for the first time since they had left the Tor Arkosa, the Serra had looked up at her faithful shadow, and the man had bowed, departing. He had returned with the samisen, and she had taken it with the same care she had taken the child's bouquet.

She settled the child to one side of her mat, and taking her hands, had placed them upon the strings, drawing some music from their tightened length.

The child's skin was as dark as Voyani skin in comparison to the Serra's, and it was clear that she had come from a family that had no great riches, and no ability to school a daughter in the arts and graces of the courts, low or high. But the differences were invisible to the Serra's eyes—or so it seemed to Jewel—and she gave the child a simple lesson, disguising it in music.

After she had finished, she sang. Ariel was not so emboldened that she chose to join her voice to the Serra's; Jewel wouldn't have either. The disparity between their voices was greater even than the disparity between the shape and color of their hands.

The Serra, as the child, now slept enclosed in the con-

fines of protective tarpaulin. Jewel listened for her; heard
no sound that might indicate wakefulness.

She stretched; the night air was brisk, but it was not the
chilling death of the desert heart. She wondered what day it
was. Realized that had she been at home, she would have
just asked Teller; he paid attention to details like that: passing time, the obligations that waited, like a trap, upon each
of the days of the month.

And the month?

She frowned.

Henden? It was dark enough, cold enough, bleak enough.
But she closed her eyes a moment, forced herself not to be
lazy, and counted the days. Corvil. The middle of Corvil.

"ATerafin."

She looked up. The bard stood beneath a moon's face
partly veiled, but the veil was of moon cycle, not cloud, and
the light cast soft shadow at his feet.

Beyond him, in the distant perimeter of the encampment,
stood Lord Celleriant. His hair was the color of the Lady's
face, his skin the color of the Winter that she had taken him
from, denying him at last the turn of the seasons: the Summer of the Queen's Court.

If he was angered by the loss, it did not show; he stood,
weaponless, a sentinel worthy of The Terafin's best guards.

She shook herself; Kallandras waited in silence, noting
the direction of her stare. He followed it, and the faint hint
of a smile tugged at the corners of his lips.

"He never sleeps, does he?"

"He does not appear to require sleep, no."

"Figures."

The smile deepened.

"The borders?"

And fell. He nodded. "We were delayed," he said quietly.

"We noticed. Did you . . ."

"We had no cause to engage the enemy, no. But it
was . . . close."

"They're at the borders?"

"The army spent time at the border of Raverra." He paused. "They constructed a stockade there, and they patrol the borders twenty miles in either direction; they have taken the roads as well."

She shrugged. That wasn't unexpected. "How many?"

"In the stockade?"

"On the road. Let's assume we can avoid the stockade."

"Perhaps a thousand men."

She whistled. "And the kin?"

"The kin are present. But not, as we feared they might be, in great number. General Alesso di'Marente is a cautious man; the presence of the kin is well disguised." He glanced at Lord Celleriant. "We feel that they are upon the road, rather than within the main body of the army."

"What about the army?"

"It has moved North."

"Averda or Mancorvo?"

"The standard of the General moved into Averda. I do not feel it safe to assume that he has taken the whole of the army with him."

"No?"

"I wouldn't. I would send some part of it into the villages and towns closest to the border of Raverra in either Terrean. If I had not yet declared war against Mancorvo, I would not take Mancorvan villages in the Tyr'agar's name—but the presence of his armies would enforce the respect due the title he has taken."

"How many men?"

"We were unable to ascertain that without moving farther into Mancorvo, and we did not wish to leave you here for the length of time that would require."

She nodded again. "We have a decision to make. I'll wake the Radann; you wake Yollana."

His brow rose. Yollana of the Havalla Voyani was not pleasant when woken at any hour. She reminded Jewel of her long-dead grandmother that way.

*   *   *

As a council of war, it was a strange one, even to Jewel's admittedly unorthodox eye. The old woman, pipe in the crook of thin lips, had set about making a fire, snapping in colorful Torra at any foolish enough to offer her help, and snapping in equally colorful Torra at any lazy enough not to. Judging from Stavos' reaction—a resignation that seemed almost out of character—this was standard behavior for a Matriarch of any line.

The Serra Teresa was, in the end, granted the dubious honor of assisting the Matriarch. Jewel watched them, the younger woman astonishingly graceful given the confines of a desert robe, the older querulous and annoyed. They were odd friends, but they *were* friends. Jewel didn't envy the Serra that burden.

When the fire itself had started to burn, Yollana used some part of its flame to light the packed bowl of her pipe, and sat, legs folded awkwardly before her. The Serra knelt beside her niece, and the Radann Marakas par el'Sol chose to stand.

Ariel, waking alone, had found comfort in Jewel's lap, and sat there in silence, eyes half-closed, stumbling across the boundaries between sleep and wakefulness. Jewel herself sat against the wall of the stag's back, while Avandar stood, arms folded, by their side. He, as the Radann, chose to keep to his feet. Of all gathered, Stavos was the only person who chose to absent himself.

"The business of Havalla," he said quietly, "is not the business of Arkosa." By Yollana's curt nod, she approved— she certainly didn't show it in any other way.

Kallandras knelt by Yollana's side; he was the only man who did not stand.

But he spoke, his words low and measured; he wasted no time. Yollana had made clear how little time the fire would provide them.

When Kallandras had finished, he waited.

Yollana spoke first, the beginning of her sentence colliding with the words of the Radann par el'Sol. It was odd, to

see this grave and serious man struggle to give way to the
woman who was in every way his opposite; Jewel was surprised when he fell silent, and realized by her surprise that
she had come to feel at home in the South, this awkward
place where men ruled simply by the expedient of *being*
men. She wondered what he would make of The Terafin.

"The Leonne boy must be in Averda."

The Radann's brow rose. He did not argue with the fact,
but the form in which she had chosen to describe the rightful Tyr rankled.

"That would be my guess," Kallandras replied gravely.
"And the main body of the army has certainly traveled
there."

"The Tyr'agnati?"

"He has Lorenza and Garrardi."

She removed the pipe from her mouth, spit, and returned
it. "The Radann?"

"Their disposition is less clear."

Marakas nodded.

Yollana, who appeared to pay little attention to the
Radann, swiveled. "With Marente?"

"They travel at the side of the General, yes."

She removed the pipe and spit again, but this time kept
its lip from her own. "Why?"

"It is where the strongest of our enemies will gather.
What other field would you have them choose?" Curt
words. Cold ones.

"The right one. Or have you forgotten your history?"

His head snapped up, pulling the line of his sparsely
grown beard with it.

"Matriarch," the Serra Diora said softly, "not one of us
will forget *our* history. Not here. But let us not be governed
by what has happened; let us be guided by it, instead. What
will happen must be our concern."

If possible, the lines around the Havallan Matriarch's
mouth deepened. But she held her tongue.

Jewel stared at the Serra Diora di'Marano for a moment.

But she had fallen silent; the Radann Marakas par el'Sol began to speak instead.

"The swords granted the servitors of the Lord are our strongest weapons against the servants of the Lord of Night. They warn us of the presence of the enemy, and they are equal to the weapons they summon from the fire's heart. We do not serve the interests of the Lord of Night; we will never serve them again. Offer us another method of detecting the servants of the Lord of Night, Matriarch, and we will gladly dispense with the pretense."

Yollana nodded gruffly; it was as much of a concession as Jewel had seen her offer. Tobacco burned down, acrid, where the smoke of the fire was sweet. She held it in the cupped palms of her hands before she condescended to speak. "We go to Mancorvo."

"I think it wisest," Kallandras said quietly. "The Havallans gather there."

"You know the movement of the Havallans now?" Yollana spoke testily.

"The Voyani call no place home, but in time of war, they gather in the Terreans that are least . . . contested. Havalla has always had ties with Mancorvo. I believe you will find your daughters there."

The old woman snorted. "You offer no comfort, bard."

"No."

She cursed the cold genially, and without much fervor. "We'd best start now."

The Radann par el'Sol had a face smooth as glass. Jewel read nothing in it, but she knew from the line of his shoulders that he was angry. Angry and mindful of the burden of debt. He turned to the Serra Diora.

"Serra?"

"The kin see as well in darkness as they do in light—but according to Kallandras of Senniel, they are few. If it pleases you, Radann par el'Sol, we will travel now. The moon is bright enough to see by."

Yollana snorted. "Not in the Mancorvan forests, it isn't.

And the plains are too open." She gestured to Teresa. "But there are roads the clansmen don't take. Na'tere, lend me your arm. I'll lead."

Jewel rose. "Matriarch," she said quietly. "If you wish, you may ride."

Yollana gazed at the stag; he lifted his head, bent tines toward earth, and waited.

She shook her head. "Not him," she said softly. "Maybe if you had a decent horse—but I'll owe no debt to the horned King."

She does not trust me, Jewel. Do not press her.

I didn't offer out of kindness, Jewel snapped back in silence. *She's too slow.*

Maybe. But she is the Matriarch of her line, and she understands the debt she would incur by accepting your offer.

What debt? You serve me.

Ah. He lifted his face, his dark eyes reflecting a light that did not hang in the night sky, did not burn in the heart of heartfire. *I serve you, yes, but not as Lord Celleriant does. The Winter Queen no longer binds me.*

If that were true, wouldn't you be a man?

I am a man, he replied, just a hint of the arrogance of kings in the tone of unspoken words. *And she is wise. You are almost a child.*

I am not—

Almost. You have already begun to walk a road that will change you, and only your . . . domicis . . . can see clearly where it will lead.

But you carry the child.

Yes. For you. Because if I did not carry her, you would, and although you would find the burden too costly, you would bear it anyway. I have it said before, Jewel ATerafin. You are weak.

Some weaknesses are better than some strengths.

Shall we debate that, here?

She lifted Ariel, struggling to balance bent knees with

child's weight, and succeeding. "Ride," she told the child.
"I'll be behind you."

We can discuss it.

His chuckle was warmer than his tone. *Indeed. We can
discuss it until you are old; I fear you will never be wise.
But in the end, this war will define all truth, and it will
grant victory either to your position or mine. The Lord of
Night is waiting in the farthest reaches of the Northern
Wastes; he feels his power, and he grows confident.*

*And if the Lord of Night rules, if in the end the battle de-
cides the course of the war, you will have your answer.*

And the end will justify the means?

Only if you win. He rose as slowly, as carefully, as Jewel
had, but with infinitely more grace, shouldering the burden
he accepted at her behest. *Ask the timeless one, if she
chooses to visit again. Ask her what she has done in the
name of war; ask her what she would not do for the chance
of victory.*

The chance?

*The chance. There is no certainty, Jewel. You fight a god,
and you have no god behind you.*

We have the Cities.

*You have one—and it is an empty place; armor without
the warrior at its heart, sword without the wielder. Perhaps
if you had the other four . . .*

Four? There are only three other Matriarchs.

Indeed. I have spoken overmuch.

She mounted almost carelessly; he gained his feet before
hers had left the ground.

"We'll ride ahead," Jewel told the Matriarch of Havalla.

Yollana nodded. "Only the gifted will see you. Or the
wise. And it cannot be said that the wise travel with the
armies of Marente."

I wish you would tell me your name.

Ah. Names have power.

You're not a demon. You've said you're a man—what power does a name have?

He laughed. Wind curled round the crown of antlers, broken and snarled in the multifoliate branches; it was not allowed to pass, to offer the worst of night's chill. *If names have no power, what does it matter whether or not you know mine?*

It's a little bit awkward calling you "that big deer."

He said nothing.

The obdurate, condescending silence was familiar. She didn't press him. Instead, she gazed out.

ATerafin. The Havallan Matriarch bids me tell you that you must travel to the West for some miles yet.

She had no way of answering Kallandras, but she passed the message on.

The Winter King—for in the end, demeaned in some fashion by his loss to the Winter Queen, he retained that title in Jewel's mind—nodded.

Jewel, answer a question.

If I can. Not that he answered many of hers.

What is the Voyanne?

The Voyanne? *I don't know. If you asked Yollana, she would say it's what my Oma deserted in order to live in the North, in the Empire.*

She would indeed say that, if you were unwise enough to ask. She would also ask your Oma's name, and her lineage, to better determine whose bloodline you follow. But that is not an answer. Again.

It's—I've never had it explained. It seems to be a way of life. Laws, rules, customs—and wandering. Always the wandering.

The Voyanne, he said quietly, *is more complicated than that; it is not merely a way of life, although perhaps your Oma did not fully apprehend this when she chose to find a home for her family. This Matriarch—this woman—has strong blood.*

What do you mean?

You must ask her. I could tell you, but you are not . . . discreet. And there are secrets that the Voyani will trust with no one. I will not be responsible, indirectly, for your death. He turned, his feet finding purchase in the dark, dark shadows cast by foliage in the moonlight. *But I know this road. My feet know it.*

Is it safe?

No. But no road is. We will trust the Matriarch.

There was no path. None that Jewel could see. But she did not doubt the Queen's consort.

They traveled in silence. Ariel fell asleep, leaning into the curve of Jewel's collarbone. She was warm, and Jewel wanted warmth, but the memories that came with it were bitter. The streets of Averalaan came back to her—the old streets, the streets of the holdings.

Ah.

Ah, what?

You would never have been Matriarch, he said softly, *but I believe that you have some of that talent.*

Memory stung. *What do you mean?*

You have made roads of your own, in a foreign place. If you traveled it again, you would find them.

She said nothing, thinking of how little she desired to find them again. Thinking, as well, that she would never lose them, no matter how hard she tried.

"Matriarch."

Had any other woman chosen to speak, Yollana would have pretended that her hearing was much worse than it actually was; such pretense was one of the few advantages of age.

But the woman who had spoken was the Serra Teresa di'Marano, and her lips were inches away from the older woman's ear. *That* much pretense was beneath Yollana's dignity.

"Serra."

"Where do we travel?"

"Into Mancorvo." The words were smooth, softly spoken; as much of a warning as the older woman ever offered.

The Serra Teresa nodded gravely. But she did not demur. "Lord Celleriant and Kallandras of Senniel have been speaking," she said quietly. "And Kallandras bids me warn you."

"Warn me?" Bitterness seeped into the smoothness, lending it the cracks and fissures of experience. "Warn *me*?"

"It is presumptuous," the Serra said, being entirely too agreeable. Yollana wasn't fooled.

"What do they wish to warn me of?"

The Serra was silent a moment, tilting her head to one side as if listening. Which, of course, she was. "It is the Lord Celleriant's opinion," she said gravely, "that the dead are bound here."

"They seek to frighten me with ghosts?"

"I do not think they seek to frighten; merely to inform."

"Tell them the ghosts are mine," she said coolly. "And the past, as well." After a moment, she added, "And tell them to *shut up*."

The Serra Teresa had never admitted the existence of the gift that Yollana was certain she possessed; she did not admit it now. But she offered no pretty protestation, no insult to the perception of the wisewoman of Havalla. Instead, she said, "How costly will this passage be?"

It was not the question Yollana expected. She stumbled, her legs—legs that would never be right without healer's gift, and healer's invasive touch—giving in to the weakness of cut muscles. "Why do you ask, Serra?"

"I am concerned."

"For yourself."

"Of course. And for my niece."

"Hah. You lie so prettily it's no wonder poets made such fools of themselves in your presence."

"Say rather that I do not choose to speak the whole of the truth, Yollana."

"Why?"

"It is kinder."

She laughed. "I'm not known for kindness."

"No. But it is not beyond your reach."

Yollana shrugged. "What purpose does it serve?"

The Serra said nothing, shifting her grip upon the older woman's arms. The handles of the canes were cold and hard; the old woman's hands were shaking.

"Did you see Evallen die?"

"No. But you know this."

"Did you hear her?"

"No, Yollana."

Yollana stared a moment at the face of the moon. "You didn't choose to listen."

Teresa bowed her head.

"The Lord burns those bold enough to seek to gaze upon his face; the Lady denies us little, choosing fan or veil when she seeks privacy. It is said that the Lady is the more merciful of the two—but you understand the veil, Teresa. You understand the fan." She stumbled; Teresa righted her. There was a rhythm to this motion that had become almost as natural as walking. "Do you understand the choice Evallen made?"

"I understand that she felt it necessary. And seeing the Tor Arkosa, hearing the change in Na'dio, makes it clear that she was not wrong."

"Good. Her price is not my price, not yet. But my price is necessary. I will pay it." She grimaced. "All Matriarchs make their plans. For escape. For return to safe harbor. Some see clearly enough to plan well. Enough. If you will not give my advice to the young man, follow it yourself."

That drew, from the Serra Teresa, the prettiest of smiles. It was not a court smile. There was no veil between them.

"But stay to the road."

"I cannot see it, Yollana."

"No? Let me make it clear." The old woman gestured, and although she was hobbled by injury, there was grandeur in the motion. Command.

"I have traveled this road in secrecy once before," Yollana said quietly. "But there are no secrets now; I think that only Stavos and the child will be unaffected by what we pass across." She shook her head. Her hair was sun-dry, harsh as desert scrub. "Do you see them, Serra?"

The Serra Teresa followed the direction of Yollana's shaking hand.

Against the floor of forest, absorbing the silver light of veiled moon, were the imprints of footsteps.

"No," Yollana said bitterly, "they are not mine. But they were made by my kin, and they have endured against this moment."

"Our enemies?"

"They might see them if they know how to look." She kept her voice flat, forced it to be the uninflected mask that might better protect her from the unspoken gift that lay within the Serra Teresa.

But she thought that the Serra Teresa heard what was there anyway: fear. And not of the demon kin.

An hour passed. Two. Yollana stopped once to gain breath, and the Serra dropped to her knees, her hands against injured calves, massaging warmth and blood into them. She offered no words, for Yollana would accept none, and she had come to understand the Matriarch well enough to offer her the blessing of silence.

The stag returned. In the darkness, Teresa saw that his hooves—hooves that were at once delicate and deadly—stepped among the footprints that Yollana's gesture had invoked; he did not touch them, and did not allow either of his riders to touch the ground they crossed.

As if he did not trust them to step carefully.

Kallandras.

Serra Teresa.

Are we followed?

Celleriant sees nothing.

She nodded. Waited until Yollana made to rise, and rose

as well, becoming crutch and cane, bearing the burden of the Matriarch as carefully as she had borne the burden of any power the High Courts had granted her. In truth, it was much, for she had had the respect of her brothers as a shield, and she had used it at her convenience more than once.

It was gone; she would never shelter behind it again.

In its place, sun, wind, sand; the desert lives of nomads played out against the skin of her hands, her arms. There was a curious freedom in bearing the marks of the elements so openly, but with that freedom, fear. Beauty had not been her only power, but it was the only power that she had been allowed to acknowledge, and live.

She turned to gaze over her shoulder at her niece, stepping carefully, balancing the weight of Yollana with the weight of curiosity. None of her grace had left her; she managed both with care.

Ramdan stood a step behind Diora. He carried no weapon, for as seraf he was allowed none, but although he now bore a burden of years greater than most who served in such an exalted position, he did not waver in his duties. If it was true that the Lady loved serafs, she would honor this man above all others when the winds at last claimed his voice, his solid presence.

Diora herself was silent.

She was Serra, still, and the only effective role she could play in this war, gift notwithstanding, was that one. Serra Diora en'Leonne. Bride of Tyrs.

"What do you mean, they lost her?" Eduardo kai di'Garrardi was an unpleasant shade of red. "Alesso, I warn you—"

Ser Alesso di'Alesso raised his head in silence. It was enough; the threat did not leave Eduardo's lips. "I am aware of her import, both to our alliance and to our enemies. But the report our scouts made was clear enough. She travels in the company of Voyani—which, we cannot be certain; the scouts are poorly informed, and they chose not to engage the enemy in conversation."

"Were it not for the stupidity of your allies, General, the Voyani would not now be so hostile to our role in the Northern Terreans."

"They have never been friendly to the clans."

"No. Indeed. But they have rarely aligned against them either, and if I am not mistaken, they will be so aligned now." He had regained his composure, falling into the cadences of a conversation more suited to his rank. And to Alesso's. "And the Sun Sword?"

"Yes," Alesso said softly. Again, he met the kai Garrardi's glare; they fenced that way, in silence.

"The borders?"

"If she seeks to enter Averda, it will avail her nothing."

"Mancorvo?"

Alesso shrugged. The Widan Sendari di'Sendari had absented himself from the conversation as quickly as he could while still preserving dignity; he had satisfied his curiosity, that was all.

"Our forces are deployed among the border towns, and beyond. The Tor'agnate Ser Amando kai di'Manelo is not unsympathetic to our cause, and he has granted us access to the lands he holds; they will be a base of operations, if such a base becomes necessary. It would be best if that base became necessary only after the fall of Callesta."

Serafs had been forbidden the General's tent, and Alesso missed them sorely. He desired sweet water and a moment's peace, but would not demean himself by such a menial task as the pouring of that water in the presence of the kai di'Garrardi.

"I would ride to join our forces in Mancorvo, if that is acceptable to you."

"A man of your skill is not easily found, kai Garrardi." He invoked the informal title deliberately, adding sincerity to the compliment. "And our armies will be sorely tested in

Averda if intelligence proves true, and the Northern flight is once again upon the field."

Eduardo di'Garrardi inclined his head; black hair caught lamplight. He lifted a hand to his chin, poised there like a statue. But his expression was now remote.

"Let me consider," Alesso said quietly. "I do not wish to lose the Oertan forces to Mancorvo when the war is to be fought in Averda."

"My men are not trained to the hills and the valleys," Eduardo said.

"No. But they will fight under the Oertan banner with the ferocity of the skill the desert edge demands. If you are present. In your absence?"

Eduardo shrugged. "They are my men. I have acknowledged your right to rule; they will not gainsay it. They will not dare to embarrass me."

It was true. All of it. Alesso took care; he composed himself as if thought were required. A dance. "What numbers would you travel with?"

"A hundred men."

"Mounted?"

"Fifty."

The Tyr'agar set his hand upon his sword hilt and rose, unbending at the knee. "I had not considered this possibility. Let me consider it now, with care. I will tender you an answer within the hour."

The kai Garrardi rose as well, and offered Alesso one of the few perfect bows he had ever offered in the privacy of the General's tent, when none were there to witness it. When he left, Alesso knelt once again.

"Let him go."

"Ah. Widan Cortano. You were absent from our meeting."

"Indeed; I thought it wise."

"You thought it wise to avoid gauging the intent of an ally who has proved less than reliable?"

Cortano walked through the open flaps of the tent, raising his hands in a steeple. He bowed, hands locked in that position; it was not a gesture of respect, but rather a gesture of power. Alesso almost shrugged.

"His intent has always been clear." The words were as cool as the passage through the Raverran night. "He is a fool."

"A necessary fool," Alesso replied, speaking as coolly. "If indeed he is one."

"Were he not, he would ride by your side with the Oertan forces; he would assure himself of the disposition of the lands you have granted him in Averda."

"Perhaps he trusts my word, Widan."

A peppered brow rose. Cortano was pale in the lamplight; weariness made him unguarded. The field was a very different court from the palace of the Tor Leonne, and it afforded Alesso a rare glimpse into the men upon whom he depended.

"And were he a fool, he would not now preside over Oerta. He is . . . intemperate. He is driven too openly by his desires. But he has never failed to achieve them, and the lack of that failure marks him as something other than fool."

"There is always a first time."

"Indeed, there is always that."

"You intend to let him go."

Alesso smiled. It was a war smile. "No."

"No?"

"Not yet, Sword's Edge."

"He will be angered."

"He will. But with Garrardi by my side, I am served by three of the five Terreans. If my position is . . . contested . . . I am served by at least two who are not likewise encumbered. Garrardi has held Oerta for generations."

Cortano frowned.

"The kin made clear that there was little battle offered; those who served him perished. He spoke of scant numbers. Five of his hunters were vanquished, and with ease. If the party of the Serra Diora encounters the kai Garrardi, I am

almost certain he will not return in time. No, Cortano. For
the moment, we have need of Eduardo kai di 'Garrardi."

The lines of Cortano's shoulders shifted slightly. Approval there, but it was tainted by exhaustion. "I bring you
word," he said quietly.

The smile dimmed. "Speak plainly."

"I have seldom spoken otherwise."

"Ah."

"Lord Isladar has left the Shining Court."

Alesso reached for the water, and in silence, poured it.
He was not as graceful as a seraf—a matter of choice, of
will. Water sloshed around the rim of his glass, pooling
upon the flat wood of the sitting table. He offered that glass
to Cortano, and the Widan accepted it without comment,
pausing to dry his hands before he drank.

"Why?"

"It seems the Lord's Fist saw reason—or weakness
enough—to dispose of him. They failed in that attempt, but
he did not choose to stay by the Lord's side in order to further wage the war."

"And his whereabouts?"

"Unknown, of course."

Alesso nodded. "Is he a threat?"

Faint lines of irritation marred the expression of the
Sword's Edge. "He is *Kialli*. And of the *Kialli*, he desires
no obvious power, no title, no lands; he demands the respect that anyone would demand in a position of power, but
he enforces it in a manner of his own choosing, and in an
unpredictable way. Of the kinlords, he is the most subtle. Of
course he's a threat."

"To us?"

"If we better understood his desire, if we better understood his game, I would have answered that question
months ago. His departure does not have the appearance of
careful planning; he does not appear to have chosen the
timing of his unfortunate exit."

"Carefully said." Alesso reached for a second glass and, with the same care, poured water.

"I do not believe he intends us harm," the Sword's Edge continued, speaking into a distance of tabletop, his gaze intent. "In his fashion, he has been of aid to us."

"His loss?"

"I do not know. You have seen the Lord's Fist. You have bested them in your skirmishes. But they have never openly attacked you."

Alesso bore scars that might make a lie of that statement; he said nothing.

"But in subtle ways, he stood beside us. I believe, of the *Kialli*, there is none who understand mortals half as well. That understanding is a double-edged blade."

"He has not been destroyed?"

"No."

"You are certain of that?"

"Yes."

Alesso nodded. He did not press the Sword's Edge for the information that was not volunteered.

"Where is Ishavriel, Alesso?"

Alesso frowned. "He is in the encampment."

"No."

And rose, water and the peace of its promise forgotten. His hand was upon his sword, his eyes narrow as its edge. Lord's man.

"When did he depart?"

Cortano shrugged. "A . . . messenger arrived less than an hour ago."

"Kialli?"

"Kin at the least. If kinlord, not a lord I recognize."

"They spoke?"

"They spoke in the tongue of the kin; Ishavriel did not look greatly pleased."

"He spoke to you?"

"No. But he chose to depart the camp."

"His part in the battle is not yet come," Alesso said

coldly. "And any part he might play before the right time will harm us."

"I *am* aware of the difficulty."

"You are certain he is no longer here."

"Oh, indeed."

Alesso waited. This time, his patience was rewarded—but it would have to be; Cortano was no fool. "The Radann kai el'Sol came to me ten minutes ago with that information."

"And the other *Kialli*?"

"They are present."

"Good. Did the Radann kai el'Sol choose to further enlighten you?"

"He believes that Lord Ishavriel has traveled North, in haste. He will not be missed unless someone chooses to enter his tent; he did not leave by the conventional methods the army usually uses. The Radann kai el'Sol apologizes for his inability to provide you with more precise information; the sword he bears has some limitations."

It spoke, of course. It spoke in the storm's voice, and while it spoke, Peder forgot that the sky was clear, the night unfettered by cloud or rain or the sweeping winds that sometimes came South from Raverra. He had expected to maintain his distance from Alesso di'Marente—a man he did not, in privacy, acknowledge as the equal his rank demanded. But to maintain a distance from *Saval* was far, far more difficult; a life spent in the study and practice of the subtle politics of the High Court was no preparation for this silent battle. The sword, the only true symbol of rank that he now desired, burned his hand when he touched hilt; it burned his vision when he drew it, singing of death, of impending battle.

Its rage was contained; its truth barely so.

He drew *Saval* seldom for this reason. The men who served Alesso, the cerdan who marched under his banner, the Tyran who rode above them on the backs of horses that would beggar large towns, were aware of the legends associated with the Lord's Swords; if they could see the light that took the blade's heart and laid it bare, they would understand what it meant.

And worse: he was attuned to *Saval*. Some part of him, Radann now, and purified by the Lord's fire, wanted that revelation. But if he had intended to take the title of Radann kai el'Sol by treachery, it had come to him instead as a gift born of sacrifice and necessity. He was bitterly aware of the kai el'Sol's legacy, of Fredero kai el'Sol's truth: The man who could achieve what was necessary was not Lambertan. The Lambertans were cunning, they were wise, they were cautious in ways too subtle to be seen by those who cast aspersions on their honor as a thing of quaint, rustic Courts. But they were not masters of subterfuge. They did not lie easily. Or well.

What would *Balagar* have demanded of Fredero? Peder took his hand from the sword's hilt, knowing the answer: no less than *Saval* now demanded. But Peder knew how to wait; knew when to bide his time.

Let the armies know of the existence of the *Kialli* before Alesso was prepared, and the *Kialli* might now rule in the Dominion. Rule in subtlety, rule in stolen, human guise. The *Kialli* were not yet weakened by their role in this war.

And until the Sun Sword came into play—if, he thought, the Lady's Moon high in the darkness of sky, her thoughts troubling his, it ever came to pass—they fought with half their strength, perhaps less.

And is the boy Leonne? The heart of Peder's fears. *Is the boy truly the child of the bloodline, or is he the bastard of a discarded concubine, the illegitimate get of a night offered in honor or amusement to an unknown man by Markaso kai di'Leonne?*

No one knew. No one voiced these fears aloud.

Lord Ishavriel, he thought, gazing North into the heart of Averda, its valleys the site of so many massacres and so much death in the previous Imperial-Dominion war. *Where have you gone?*

CHAPTER SEVENTEEN

12th of Corvil, 427 AA
Callesta, Terrean of Averda

"IT WAS my kill," Kiriel said, with some satisfaction.

Auralis parried. "But first blood was mine."

"He hardly bled."

"And if you want that to be true of either of the two of you," Alexis cut in, "I'd suggest you *tone it down.*" She gestured, her hair flying out of her tight braid in the direction of the somber Tyran who now stood around the broken stone of the Radann's temple. Torches had been lit, although they could no longer be set in the wall sconces provided for them; hands caught them, made of their orange and red a floating, uncertain light.

Auralis rolled his eyes. He had the usual cuts and scrapes, which didn't bother him, and a great rent in the center of his chain hauberk, which did. The quartermaster frowned upon unexplained damage to army property, and it had been made clear by Duarte that the explanation might have to be forgone—which meant that Auralis would be responsible for the cost, and the inconvenience, of the armor's repair.

Kiriel had taken less damage—her boots would need replacement, but for the time being she could get by with a simple resoling, depending on the nature of the terrain they were forced to march across and the type of encounters they were to face. In the foothills, they wouldn't last, but Auralis thought it vastly unlikely the fighting would take them to the Menorans; the valleys lay to the South and West, and it was in the valleys that all wars, in the end, must be fought.

He grimaced. He was not a superstitious man; the Tyr'agnate had taken some pains to move battle outside of the forested slope of the valleys in which most of the food of the Terrean was produced. His men had massed, and Alexis let drop the information—strictly forbidden, of course, and probably likely to cost her Decarus if she were discovered—that the Kings' armies already waited just past the delta of the largest inland river in Averda to that end.

"Kiriel?"

She nodded. "But it counts," she added quietly.

He snorted. "Of course it counts."

As if the conversation had not been private—and in the South, it was said no conversations were, Duarte appeared beside them. "Sentrus," he said curtly, speaking to Kiriel. "Decarus," he added, even more curtly, to Auralis.

Auralis, used to Duarte's moods, was surprised by the sharpness of the offered word; surprised and suddenly wary. He knew the tone of voice.

But he had forgotten it, the way a body forgets the reality, and the viscerality, of injury in battle until one is once again enmeshed in a fight for survival.

Kiriel nodded, unperturbed by the subtle change in Duarte's tone. His past—the Averdan valleys, the war in the South—separated them; of her own, she would not speak.

But she turned to the shadows. "Telakar," she said, speaking in a tone almost identical to Duarte's. It surprised Auralis.

The kinlord bowed. And followed.

They did not retreat far; Valedan kai di'Leonne awaited them at the edge of the Radann's path. The Tyr'agnate had not yet returned.

"Primus," the kai Leonne said quietly. "We desire privacy."

Duarte nodded. "The Commanders?"

"They have been summoned. They will join us shortly, but their time is valuable; cast now, and we will wait."

He cast, frowning.

"Is there a problem?"

The question seemed to be absorbed by the spell, the words deflected. But Duarte looked up after a moment had passed, his hands settling into bunched fists at his sides. "There may be."

"And that?"

"If I were to guess, I would say that someone is already listening."

"And the spell?"

"It is not a powerful one," he replied. "With spells of this nature, it is best to expend little power."

"Oh?"

"Power has its signature, and it draws the attention of the powerful, if they are aware and they   e looking for it. What I cast . . . is not a major magic. Ther are those with skills far greater who could breach its barrier with ease."

"With pathetic ease," the kinlord at Kiriel's side offered quietly.

"Telakar?"

He looked at her for a moment, eyes narrow. "I am not a mortal," he said stiffly. "I will not be tested."

She hesitated for just a moment; the hesitation caught their attention, drawing all eyes. And she was aware of the weight of each stare. She had lived her life in the Shining Court, in the presence of the *Kialli* and the kinlords of note; nothing in that life had prepared her for this one. Not even for this war.

Telakar waited.

They all did, but it was his gaze that brought the past back, that defined her in its light.

When the *Kialli* went to war, battle was a thing of light and fire, a dance of ferocity, a movement that ended only in the destruction or subjugation of the combatants. They might bring their servants into play, the blood-bound, the creatures who had chosen slavery over death—but those deaths counted for little.

Here, upon the heights of Callesta, those wars seemed small and distant, and their cost, negligible; in the end, they were simply another expression of the laws of the Hells: Power ruled. There was no regret at the deaths of the weak; the Hells absorbed them, fed on them, sometimes caused them to be reborn in a fashion, weaker by far than they had been, and destined to serve.

She looked at the kai Leonne, a man who had chosen to stand against the forces of the Shining Court in defiance of all advice she had offered—would have offered—when they had first met. And yet, having chosen to join a battle that he half understood, he did not flinch or waver. Nor did he approach it as the *Kialli* did. He was mortal; he was surrounded by mortals, by those who could either seek death or wait for its approach, but could never rise above it.

She had met mortals in the Shining Court. Lady Sariyel, and her lord, the mage; the Imperial humans who kept their visits a secret from the mortal lords they pretended to serve. All of their fighting was done with words, and some little magic; they played games of power without apprehending the cost of those games, and their losses, in the end, were the more profound, for the mortals in the Court, when killed, were often escorted to the Hells, there to be fodder for the entertainment of demons the Lord had not seen fit to return to the plane.

She had cared little for them, had trusted them even less.

There was only one mortal in the Court that she had trusted. Only one. She bowed her head, losing the thread of Duarte's words, his reasoned caution, his mild frustration.

Ashaf. Ashaf kep'Valente. She pronounced the words in the only place she would ever pronounce them: in silence, the privacy of thought. And she waited for the pain they caused, the terrible, burning anger, the truth of *Kiallinan*. Instead, she saw an old woman with soft arms, a softer face, a voice that cracked in the wind and wavered in the cold of

the Northern tower. No weapons girded her; no power set
her apart from the mortals that were said to populate the
lands beyond the Northern Wastes.

Instead, she offered song, cradle song, child's song. She
offered stories of tall grass, and small children, of baking
bread and casting clay in the summer kilns; of stalks of
wheat in fields that the sun made golden. She spoke of
rivers that did not freeze, of water that was offered openly
beneath a warm sky, of the fall of rain.

And she spoke of love.

Not even the mortal Court had been so bold, and so foolish.

Ashaf had paid the price for her weakness.

And in paying, had gone forever beyond Kiriel's reach:
for Kiriel might never join her in the lands it was said the
mortals reached when at last they knew peace.

And yet.

She stood among these men, these women—the Commanders had come upon them silently—and she saw in
them some hint of Ashaf's weakness, although they told no
tales, offered the comfort of no open arms, no folded lap.
She saw them converse; saw them, expressions guarded, as
they teetered upon the edge of a power that no single one of
them could wholly claim, in the end.

They deferred to Valedan. That was his right. But they
did not fear him; they did not plot to overthrow him. In his
turn, he deferred to their knowledge, trusting their experience, and trusting his instinct, balancing carefully between
the two.

No: life in the Shining Court had offered her no preparation for this, this mortal mess.

"Kiriel?"

She shook her head. Decided. "I cannot sense them," she
said quietly.

"Them?"

"The ones who listen."

But decisions were complex, complicated, things done

by halves. She glanced at Lord Telakar to see what he made of the weakness of that confession, aware that his home was the Shining Court, aware that his rules were the laws of the Hells.

She had not bound him. Did not know how. The only binding that lay within her grasp was distinctly mortal: the uneasy alliance that did not quite trust, but could not quite dismiss.

"You found me," he said quietly. "Is your instinct so dulled that those of lesser power escape your attention?"

Old anger bridled at the accusation in his words. Old lessons returned, and with them, the voice of the Lord she *had* trusted, in a different life. His name, she could not say.

"I . . . do not know . . . why I found you," she said at last.

Commander Bruce Allen raised a brow. "Do not know, or are not willing to say?"

It was a fair question. A reasonable one.

But Valedan kai di'Leonne raised a sharp hand, as if it were blade. "She has said that she does not know," he told the Eagle curtly.

The Commander fell silent. As silent as Kiriel, as surprised by the interruption as she had been.

Lord Telakar's eyes wavered an instant, crossing the distance between Kiriel's face and the man she had chosen to serve. "Is he so foolish that he has chosen to trust you?"

"Apparently."

"And you have become so practiced in the *Kialli* arts that you are capable of playing at the game of being trustworthy?"

"No."

Silence. Then, softly, "You have changed, Kiriel. I do not know what to make of it."

"You have not been asked to judge."

"Indeed, no. But judgment is a failing of mine; it is the reason that I am kinlord and not servitor. My name is my own."

She nodded. And then, although she could not say why,

she lifted her hand. Her sword hand. Upon it, in the veiled moonlight, in the orange of the lamps the Commanders—or their adjutants—carried, was the pale, simple band she had taken from the ground at the feet of Evayne.

"What is this?" he asked softly, speaking again in the tongue of the kin.

"A ring," she answered in the same tongue. The syllables, the harshness of the consonants, were somehow pleasing.

He reached out, and she drew her hand back.

"Your pardon, Kiriel. With your permission, I would like to examine the ring."

She laughed bitterly. "My permission does not seem to be the deciding factor. If you wish to examine it, you must examine it as it sits; it will not be removed."

He gazed at her, and she knew he was attempting to determine the truth behind the words she offered; the half-truth, the benefit she might gain by lying. It wearied her. It made her feel at home.

"I tried to remove the finger," she continued, dispassionately. "And the hand. I suspect that not even the removal of the arm would be possible, but I admit that I did not attempt that much injury."

"The loss of the hand would be danger enough."

She shrugged. "I would not attempt it now."

"You accept the ring?"

"I accept what cannot be changed."

His turn to offer a shrug. "Wise."

She held out her hand. He reached out to touch it, and the ring flared, brilliant in the shard-scattered clearing, a warning that seared the fingertips of the kinlord, driving him back.

He did not so much as grunt with the pain, and she knew that the pain was fierce. Knew also that it was beneath him; the whole of his attention was now absorbed by what could not be touched.

"Kiriel," he said quietly. "Do you know what it is that you bear?"

"A ring."

"Yes. One of five, if I am not mistaken. One of *the* five. I have . . . heard of them, of course. The Lord has heard. In the distance of the Northern Wastes, he has felt the echo of their brief awakening, but it is tentative; they slumber. If they had not, he would have found them years ago.

"All, I think, save this one."

"Indeed, you are correct in your surmise," a new voice said.

Kiriel turned. They all turned.

It was to Kiriel that Meralonne APhaniel offered a low bow. "Well met," he said softly. "Well met, Kiriel di'Ashaf." Rising, he added, "Well met, Lord Telakar."

Lord Telakar turned to the Member of the Order of Knowledge. "Illaraphaniel," he said softly, and his face was transformed.

"I wondered if you would be summoned," the magi said quietly. "And I wondered if I might encounter you in the heart of the South. I had not expected to find you here, so close to the Northern border." He paused. "Word has reached the Order of Knowledge. Word, and rumor, although I confess that rumor means little to most of my brethren."

"And what word?"

"The Cities of Man," Meralonne said quietly.

Telakar smiled.

"A young man of Arkosa resides within the High City; he does not speak Weston well, but it is our belief that he traveled with his Matriarch toward the Tor Arkosa."

"Our?"

"Mine, then. And I see that there must be some truth in that belief, for you are here."

"I am here," Telakar said smoothly, "in service to Lord Kiriel."

"Lord?"

"Kiriel di'Ashaf," Telakar replied, correcting himself.

Kiriel knew the slip had been no accident.

Meralonne turned to Kiriel once again. "I offer advice," he said wearily, "and only advice. Lord Telakar is not your enemy—but he is not, by the nature of his service to the Lord of Night, your friend. What you have done, what you have revealed, is a danger to you—a danger that you cannot understand.

"I would counsel you to destroy him."

"He serves me."

"Indeed. Let me accept, as truth, that premise. But in the presence of the Lord of Night, what does such an allegiance count for? If he is commanded, he will speak of all that he has learned from you, and what he has learned cannot be measured in simple words. If commanded, he will return to the North."

"Enough, Illaraphaniel," Telakar said, his voice thin and cool.

"And if he delivers word that you wear the fifth of Myrrdion's rings—the *only* ring forged in such a way that it might remain invisible forever to the Lord of Night and his endless gaze . . ."

"Yes?"

"It was said that not even a god could unmake what Myrddion forged," Meralonne said softly. "But I would not test it, if I had the choice. Because if the ring itself cannot be unmade, its bearer can."

"What is the role of the ring, Illaraphaniel?"

"In truth? I do not know. But did I, I would not share that information with one who could be so easily compelled to part with it. It is some part of Myrddion's vision, some part of his great plan. We were privy to the necessity of the creation, but not the insanity of the vision itself. We cannot say."

Telakar shook his head. The motion was strange enough that it drew the whole of Kiriel's attention. Her eyes widened; his expression made him look like a different

creature. "This . . . ah. I thought . . . this was an impoverished age," he said softly. "So empty of the grace and the
fire of man's magic, so gray and so lifeless. But now I see
that legends are waking. We may see a return to power of
the heroes of that era."

"Heroes," Meralonne said coldly, "are vastly overrated."

"Perhaps. But in the end, was it not a mortal hero who
rode into the heart of Vexusa? Was it not a mortal hand that
lifted sword, that dealt the crippling blow to the Lord of
Darkness?"

"So the bards sing, who sing of that time at all."

"And you?"

"I am no bard. I offer your lord my warning, that is all."
Telakar turned to Kiriel. "He is correct."

She frowned.

"He *is* correct, Lord."

"Do not—"

"Kiriel." He corrected himself with far too much ease; it
was as if he no longer had interest in the facade of power.
"He does not speak with enmity. He speaks pragmatically."

"Ah. And as the first of my lieges, what would you advise?"

"My destruction."

She was shocked into stillness. His expression *was* an expression, but she hadn't the tools to interpret it. Still, she
had no intention of destroying Lord Telakar. "I am not . . .
as my compatriots are. You have given me advice as I have
commanded; do not trouble me with it again."

He hesitated a moment, and again, his face wore an open
expression that made no sense to her. But he bowed.

"The ring binds me," she said quietly. "And if that was a
part of this Myrddion's plan, then he must have seen me at
the head of my—of the Lord's armies."

Meralonne said nothing.

"But of late, the ring is not as strong as it was; there are
times when I can almost hear the voice of the Lord in the
North; I can see the towers. I can feel the ice of Northern

wind. And when that happens, I can see as I once saw, feel as I once felt. Only then. It's how I saw you.

"Otherwise, I see as mortals see. If there are *Kialli* present, I do not hear their names."

"That," Meralonne said softly, "is why I chose to be sent to the South. And I will tell you now, Kiriel, that there is indeed such a presence, such a name, upon the plateau. But it is newly come."

"Whose?"

"I am not so familiar with the *Kialli* as it might appear," he said cautiously, "but I believe that we are visited, at some distance, by the Lord Ishavriel."

Shrouded in the darkness of city streets too poor to own any light but moon, Lord Ishavriel gazed toward the Callestan palace. Word had come to him; he had received it and departed the camp of the human Tyr in haste, and without *permission*. The word simmered uneasily in thoughts that already grew wild with leashed anger.

Silabras was gone. Lord Ishavriel had called him, in the softest of the voices he possessed, and his liege had failed to answer the summons. That failure was death; only death would prevent obedience.

And the death of Silabras was significant.

Isladar, he thought, and forced himself to be still, listening to the wind, to what the wind carried. But the wind carried no hint of Lord Isladar's presence.

He hesitated. Although he had been fully apprised of the intent of the Lord's Fist, he had not been present, and he knew—incompetence, utter failure—that Lord Isladar had escaped the trap set for him by Etridian, Assarak, and Nugratz. He had been injured in the battle; few indeed were the kinlords who might have escaped, once so engaged, uninjured.

But Lord Isladar was unique. Incomprehensible. The Shining City no longer contained him. And the plans he had made—in silence, in the millennia of existence in the

Hells—were not plans that Ishavriel was privy to. Did they include this treachery?

Silabras had not been blood-bound. His role in the heart of Callesta had been one that required subtlety and cooperation; it required initiative, the ability to wait. He had been given permission to feed only upon the grief that the mortals might offer their dead, and he was capable of gaining sustenance from that pain.

He was gone.

How? Ishavriel drifted toward the plateau. He took care to mask himself from the eyes of the strays that lingered in the streets of the city. The mortal, Alesso di'Marente, chosen as puppet and figurehead, claimed to have his spies among the Callestans—but it galled Ishavriel to rely upon them. Their words would be slow to travel, unadorned by magic; they would cross the valleys and rivers, the plains and forests, in days. And they might come to him if he waited like a patient beast of burden, a lowly soldier, at the whim of a man who defined himself on a mortal field of battle.

It was not to his liking.

He had failed in the desert, and that was costly; Etridian's servants had failed him again, on the desert's edge. This third failure was more than he could willingly bear. And had Silabras been given leave to operate without constraints, had he been *allowed* to walk, uncloaked, in Callesta, that third failure might never have accrued. The edges of shadow frayed about the *Kialli* lord. He gathered them carelessly.

Lord Telakar raised his head, listening. After a moment he met Meralonne APhaniel's gaze. Kiriel watched them both with ill-concealed hunger. What they had, she had once possessed. It had been months since she had missed it.

"I believe you are correct, although I would not have sensed it were I not alerted," he said at last.

Kiriel drew her blade.

And Meralonne raised a hand. It was a polite gesture, but it was an imperious one. "I do not understand your place within the Shining Court," he told her, his voice gentle, his eyes, steel. "But I believe that if you have not been revealed to Lord Ishavriel's sight, now is not the time." He threw back his mage's cloak. Beneath it, glittering with absorbed and hoarded light, he wore chain, a thin, thin mail that conformed to the lines of his body as if it were silk.

"But my place within the Court is quite clear," he continued.

Telakar's shadows grew deeper.

Again, Meralonne APhaniel raised a hand. Shook his head, the pale skein of his hair falling wild around his shoulders, an ivory mantle. No Osprey would have been allowed the vanity of hair as unfettered as his; no soldier, if Kiriel understood the dictates of the Kings' armies well enough.

"Not you," Meralonne said. "Do not draw attention that you will be unable to escape. Not yet."

"You intend to hunt him alone?"

"I intend to see the streets of Callesta by moonlight," the mage replied. "But the streets of the South are not as tame and tended as the streets of my Northern home, and I may require the weapons I have long carried."

He waited; Telakar's silence was grudging.

"Tyr'agar?" the mage said softly.

Kiriel started; she had forgotten, for a moment, that Valedan, his Ospreys, and his Commanders, now waited.

"Callesta is not my city, but inasmuch as it is within the boundaries of my country, you have my permission."

Meralonne bowed. "I will return," he said quietly.

"Hold."

They turned at once, the Tyr'agar, the Ospreys, the Commanders.

Ramiro di'Callesta stood in the moonlight beneath the

forked branches of perfect trees. His weapon was un-sheathed and unblooded in the pale light. He stood alone.

Ser Fillipo par di'Callesta and Ser Miko di'Callesta approached him; the Tyr'agnate sent them back with the simple gesture of a raised hand.

"Tyr'agnate," Meralonne APhaniel said, bowing with a perfect respect that he never offered Northern Commanders.

"I will travel with you."

"I would not advise it. If we find what we seek—"

"I do not require your advice. I certainly do not require your permission." Cold, that voice. "Ser Fillipo."

The Captain of the oathguards knelt at once, knees crushing grass, Serra Amara's grass.

"Remain. If I do not return, Alfredo is in your keeping. Serve him as you have served me."

Ser Fillipo said nothing; his head fell toward his knees, exposing the back of his neck.

What the Captain of the oathguards offered, the oathguards themselves need match. They gave the Tyr'agnate the gift of their silence. Obedience.

But more, Kiriel thought. More than that. She was diminished, yes, but she could sense the terrible anger that guided, that demanded, their silence. No Northern faces had contained anger so perfectly, hidden it so well; the Southerners understood weakness and strength, and they offered their lord only strength.

Meralonne APhaniel waited. If he was ill-pleased, he did not show it. "Tyr'agnate, our time is short."

Ramiro di'Callesta nodded curtly. "Lead."

"As you command."

Only when they had gone were words free to fly in the clearing. Duarte's magic could not contain them; Kiriel wondered that half the palace was not now alive with the movement of serafs, of cerdan, of the rest of the Ospreys who had not yet been called to active duty by the end of the quarter shift.

The Commanders spoke in Weston, and only Weston, and they spoke *quickly,* as if speed would rob their words of sense to the Tyran who slowly gained their feet.

"Primus, take the Sentrus. Take both of them." Commander Ellora AKalakar frowned. "Where's Sanderton?"

"Off duty."

"Get him."

Sanderton was the best of the Osprey bowmen. It was his single pride, and the Ospreys encouraged him in it, for he was one of the few who had been allowed entry into the Osprey ranks after the slaughter in the Averdan valleys. No one had been willing to tell Kiriel why, and after a few months with the Ospreys, she understood that she shouldn't have asked in the first place.

"Take bows. Take the weapons that were gifted us by the Churches. Follow them."

"Ellora—"

"Not now, Devran. We cannot afford to lose the Tyr'agnate."

"He travels with Member APhaniel," Commander Allen said sharply.

"One man. A mage, at that."

"Ellora. That is beneath you."

"You know how magi fight."

"I know how Member APhaniel fights," Commander Allen replied softly. "And I have had the advantage of traveling with one of his . . . students."

He paused. Ser Fillipo par di'Callesta had gained his feet, and gained his bearing; he shed silence now, and let hand fall to undrawn sword hilt. "You will wait," he said quietly.

Command, there. Kiriel found it amusing.

The Kalakar Commander found it less so. "We don't have the time to wait—"

"You *will* wait," Fillipo replied. As he spoke, the other

Tyran rose to join him, flanking him, the hands on sword hilts not a simple nicety of form.

"Are you so eager to lose your brother?" she snapped.

The faces of the Tyran were not so expressionless as they had been in the presence of their lord.

Kiriel smiled. The smile had edge.

Women did not give orders to men in the Dominion. Commander Allen stepped quietly between The Kalakar and the Captain of the oathguards. "Your pardon," he said, bowing deeply. "We mean no insult to your lord; we mean to offer no offense."

"None will be offered," Ser Fillipo replied smoothly, "if his request is honored."

"He made no request of us," the Commander replied. "And the will of the Tyr'agnate is subject to the will of the Tyr'agar; to this, I believe, Ser Ramiro kai di'Callesta would offer no argument."

Ser Fillipo was silent.

"Tyr'agar?" Commander Allen said quietly.

"No," Valedan replied.

The Kalakar rolled her eyes. The Berriliya was almost as still as the Callestan Tyran. But Commander Allen turned to Valedan.

"We are here at your behest," he said, with just the hint of anger in the words. "And we are here to *win* a war that the Dominion—and the Empire—cannot afford to lose. Do you understand what the possible loss of the kai Callesta entails?"

Valedan nodded. "He is irreplaceable. His son, the kai Callesta, is not yet the man his father is."

"Then you see a need for action."

"Yes, Commander."

But his tone called for the opposite.

Turning, he bowed to the Tyran; the bow was shallow, but it was not perfunctory. "These men are sworn to serve the kai Callesta with their lives. There are no others he can trust so completely; no others he would choose to have stand beside him.

"He ordered them to remain. We cannot, in deference to that order, choose to go where they have been forbidden to follow."

"They are *his* men. We are yours."

Valedan nodded.

"Are you aware of the risk you take?"

Again, Valedan met the eyes of the Callestans, and Kiriel saw that they were now with him, to a man, although the Commanders stood between them.

She had a glimpse, then, of understanding, some glimmer of a wisdom that was not—quite—her own. Valedan was not Callestan, but in refusing what was barely a request, he made himself less Northern in their eyes.

The Serra Alina di'Lamberto, dressed in the armor of the Northern soldiery, came to stand behind him. Although she wore no sari, no veil, bound her hair with no comb, she stood as a Serra might; at his back, to his right, witness to his whim, and servant to it. No armor she wore could rob her of the grace and the habit of a lifetime.

Still, she did not kneel as a Serra would be expected to kneel; she did not disgrace the Northern uniform that she had been commanded to wear. Did not forsake the role that she had been commanded, against her better judgment, to take.

Valedan was aware of her. Aware of the flaws in her Northern facade, and grateful for them. He found himself angered by the Commanders, by their Northern attitudes, by their inability to understand what was at stake.

She touched his shoulder gently, as if she were in truth his wife. Without thinking, he reached up and touched her fingers; she had removed her gloves. They chafed her skin, these things of chain and leather, and he had not the heart to order her to wear them.

To Ser Fillipo, he said, "Forgive us; you have spent time

in *Averalaan Aramarelas*. You know that the intent of the Commanders is honorable. But you know, also, that they come from a land where the bloodlines do not have the import and the significance they do in the South.

"They are not fools," he continued. "And they mean no insult to the Tyr'agnate. They honor his importance in this war; they believe that the winning of it will be much, much harder in his absence."

Ser Fillipo did not smile, but the line of his shoulders fell slightly. His hand did not leave his sword.

Valedan turned his attention to the Commanders who stood between them.

"His son," he said, sliding into Weston, "was not only killed by the kin—that much must now be clear—but defiled by them. Used by them. The Tyr'agnate has always understood that the Northern interest in the war is not an interest in land or Dominion, but rather, in the hand of the Lord of Night and all its manifestations."

Ser Fillipo nodded, although he did not choose to speak. His Weston, as his brother's, was flawless.

"It is now his cause, as well. Where he might have hesitated in the interests of the Terrean, he will hesitate no longer—and that serves you; it serves our cause."

"He has to survive in order for that to be true," Ellora snapped.

"No. The Tyran understand what they face now. They will carry word, *if* he perishes; those words will carry weight. Callesta will never stand with Marente, while any of the Tyran remain. If Ramiro falls, they have lost not only the kai Callesta, but their Tyr—the man they are sworn to serve with their deaths. They understand this. But it was his *son*, Kalakar. His heir. His kai.

"He has his duty to that son, and he has made this decision. This must be a private matter."

"But—"

"He has claimed that privacy. I will not sanction interference. He chose to accept Meralonne APhaniel's presence;

that is all he was willing to accept. These are *his* lands, and when I rule the Dominion, they will continue to be his lands. We are guests here, and witnesses; we are in the South. And in the South no one, no matter how close or how trusted an ally, may come between a man and his son."

He thought that Ellora might say, *His son is dead,* which would be unfortunate—but Commander Allen now raised a hand.

"We are here in your service, Tyr'agar," the Commander said gravely. "And we accept your orders. We will wait."

Ser Fillipo, the Captain of the Tyran, bowed to Valedan kai di'Leonne; he bowed low. "What you have learned in the North, I cannot judge," he said quietly—in Torra. "But the North has not displaced the South in your blood. Callesta is honored to stand beside you, Tyr'agar."

Hunter's Moon.

Northern phrase. Ramiro di'Callesta had heard it in passing, and although he understood the words, their conjugation was beyond him, a matter of culture, a different experience. But he walked beneath the moon's face now, and it was partially veiled, veiled as Amara had been.

Not since he had been a youth, unbridled, unmarried, and granted the sword of the younger kai, had he known such a dangerous anger; the Lord's fire burned him. Without care, it would consume him, and he was almost past caring.

It had been a long night, a night of revelation. And it had been the first night that his wife had come, unveiled, into his presence since his return to Callesta; had given him a glimpse of the heart that she had turned from him in grief and in, yes, anger. What she had—barely—forgiven was nothing compared to this, this defilement; what might it take to earn her forgiveness after she learned of the events of this night?

He knew her well. He could order the Tyran to silence, and they would comply; were silent now, in the wake of his absence. But she was the Serra Amara; nothing passed in the city of Callesta that she was not, in the end, aware of. He had the ability to be silent in her presence; he had the ability to counsel her to silence should he deem that silence wise. But the ability to lie had long since passed with the first blush of married passion, and with it, much illusion. She was his Serra. She was half of Callesta to the man who ruled its entirety.

Someone had once warned him of the folly of needing a woman. Any woman. He had seldom considered it folly, and even tonight, sword trembling in mailed hand, he could not consider it in that light. Moonlight.

Carelo. Amara.

He paused a moment.

The mage by his side paused as well, and turned a side glance upon him. The Northerners often spoke too much. This man offered nothing. Funny, that silence itself could seem so much like strength. He was silent; he had none. None but the rage that drove him.

Meralonne APhaniel lifted his head. Wind made his hair dance; strands of silver light, an answer, and a call, to the moon. Men fought; men were the Lord's. This stranger, this Northerner, was the Lady's.

But Ramiro felt no surprise at all when he lifted a hand and a sword came to it, shimmering, gathering moonlight until that light was sharp and blue, a glittering thing of Northern edges.

"I have announced myself," he said quietly. "Stand ready."

Ramiro nodded.

Lord Telakar raised his head in the silent clearing. "Lord," he said, invoking formality as he inclined chin.

Kiriel frowned.

"Meralonne APhaniel, as you call him, has just drawn sword in the streets of Callesta."

She nodded, as if she expected no less. Turned to Valedan, a question in her expression.

He shook his head.

Telakar watched this minimal exchange, fascinated by it. Fascinated by Kiriel, Kiriel di'Ashaf.

He had seen her when she dwelled within the twin towers of the Shining City; all of the kin had. The Lord had commanded their presence thrice, and three times they had gathered in the great basin at the foot of the ice and snow that formed the streets of that great edifice, the first of the Lord's works upon this plane. Her father beside her, she had been a thing of wonder, but dark, enrobed in the shadows that the Lord invoked by presence alone.

He had never once seen her like this: mortal. Human. The human Court denied her entry into their closed and feeble world. They did not fear her, perhaps because of her age, perhaps because she was surrounded, at all times, by the *Kialli*. As if the *Kialli* were the greater threat.

They were. They were, and yet, Telakar stood by her side, gazing upon the souls of the living as if they were gemstones, and he a jeweler who might make of them something memorable. Something truly beautiful.

He shook himself.

She understood the laws of the Hells, but she accepted the decision of the young man whose mortal title held all of his power.

Isladar, did you foresee this? And if so, why did you raise her, at such risk and at such cost?

He did not speak the name aloud.

Instead, he turned windward, toward the city that lay beneath them, contours of impoverished hovels shadowed by moonlight, even to his vision. And as he stared, as he listened, he felt it: another power, the hint, the whisper, of another name.

"Lord," he said softly, "there is another in the city streets."

Her frown deepened. "Who?"

"He is distant. Careful. I cannot say for certain."

"Kai Leonne?"

Valedan shook his head, with a grim look. "We have, I think, other work before us."

"What other work?"

"The bodies," he replied. "The bodies of the Lambertan assassins."

The man Kiriel called Auralis lifted his hand and smacked the center of his forehead with an open palm. The noise was soft, but it carried.

"Ser Fillipo," Valedan continued, "if you do not feel this compromises the orders of your Tyr, we will take the responsibility for exhuming their corpses."

The instant the sword was drawn, Ishavriel heard its voice. Cold voice, Winter voice, voice of ice and the Northern passages, it was unmistakable. It was both call and answer.

He cursed softly. Without hesitation, he lifted his hands; his sword came to the left, his shield to the right. They were of darker light, and the depth of their fires burned. Across edge and surface, if one knew how to read it, the name that did not compel him now shone beneath the veiled moon.

Illaraphaniel.

Illaraphaniel, in the South, and in the company of the mortals. He did not question his presence; it explained much. Too much.

"He is ready," Meralonne said.

"Moving?"

"Toward us. Tyr'agnate, if it will not demean you or unman you, I suggest that you seek cover."

"I did not come to cower," Ramiro replied, the bite in the words sharp as *Bloodhame*'s single edge.

"No. But you are Tyr'agnate, and you almost bested the Commanders in the South; you defeated the Ospreys."

"I was not the General upon that field."

Meralonne inclined his head, an unpleasant smile across his lips. "As you say; I will correct myself. The young Tyr upon the field," he continued, the irony heavy, "understood the value not of cowering, but of subterfuge. You are not a bowman. You wield the Lord's weapon, and with some ferocity. But this is the Lady's time. The Lady casts pale light and delivers you into shadow—into a shadow that does not devour you.

"You have learned the shadow dance. You know when to hide, and when to strike. Seek the vantage, and the advantage, of the terrain."

"While you stand thus?"

"I am beacon, " he said softly.

It was half the truth. Ramiro di'Callesta understood power, and he understood that the powerful offered, at best, half truths among equals.

He hesitated, warring with anger, with the visceral, terrible need to strike. To kill. The rage that rode him was almost his master.

Almost.

But had it been, he would never have survived his father, the former Tyr'agnate. And perhaps, just perhaps, that might have been a mercy.

The Lord knew no mercy. He judged his followers by two things: victory and survival.

"Move forward," Ramiro said, and his tone brooked no refusal. "Stand in the lee of that building. I will . . . be cautious."

"If an opportunity presents itself," Meralonne said, obeying the Tyr'agnate as if obedience itself had no cost and no value, "you will know when to strike."

Ramiro nodded.

He walked quietly; he had chosen the location because the building itself was unusual. It housed the Guild of the Callestan Cloth Merchants, and because of that, it was larger than most of the buildings in this quarter of town. Of more significance: it was three stories high, and both the second and third stories were girdled by large, open verandas over which the cloths of the various members were often hung in gaudy display.

But not at night; at night, the guild members most mindful of thieves caused those banners, those proud and prominent displays, to be carefully folded, and just as carefully concealed. He made his way up to the second veranda, and stopped there; crouched, knees bending, heels falling back into the flat slats of painted wood. Wood was seldom used in buildings such as these, but stone balconies of this size would have been costly; the merchants did not desire a finer dwelling than the Tyr'agnate's, and they made this clear by the choice of the materials with which they built.

Nor were they foolish or overcautious; such a slight, he could not afford to overlook.

Fire strode through the streets. What strays there were, on many legs or few, vanished before it, leaving silence in its wake. Callesta should have burned; it did not. The flame was focused, like the breath of ancient dragons; it skirted the ground, but did not char it, seeking instead other prey.

And fire answered. Blue fire, a single, slender line that was almost as fierce in its glare as the Lord's. Ramiro's breath was quiet, still; he watched, his shoulders hunching, free hand upon the rails. Through it, like a caged great cat, he watched, bore witness, bided time. But he did not pace; did not otherwise move.

Instead, as the red fire drew closer to the blue, he wondered. He had chosen, months ago, to break the peace of the swordhaven, to lift *Bloodhame,* to choose his war. Had *Bloodhame* lain, silent, enclosed in case and sheath, unexposed to the glare of the Lord, and the Lord's judgment, would his son now live? Would his kai now stand ready, at his father's side, on the eve of the first war he was old enough to be tested in?

Night thoughts, and pointless, but they came, and he allowed them entry. He had stood by his father's side in a very different war.

Ah. The fire stopped.

Clear as morning bell, dark as Lady's veiled Night, the creature spoke. "Illaraphaniel."

And the Northern mage bowed. "Ishavriel. It has been some time." The blue blade rose, not in threat, but in punctuation. "And do not, please, for the sake of my dignity, attempt to tell me that I meddle in things I do not understand."

"You meddle," the creature said softly.

"Indeed. A failing of mine. There is so little amusement left to me, I take what I can find."

"You think this a game?"

"A fine game," Meralonne APhaniel said.

Ramiro frowned. The words spoken, the language he heard, was Torra. And it wasn't. He could not repeat the sounds made by either man, although he could easily resolve them into meaning.

Mage, he thought, bowing his head at this unexpected gift.

"As always, you have chosen the wrong side."

"Ah. As always, *Lord* Ishavriel, the right side is defined by the survivors and the victors."

"If you wish to be among them—" He leaped. He leaped, and the air solidified beneath his feet, granting him an impossible purchase as he swung his blade in a wide, wide arc.

Meralonne APhaniel was not there to be bisected by it. He leaped clear, leaped up, his blade tracing a visible path in the night sky.

"You are without your shield," the creature said.

The Northern mage did not reply. Not with words, not with blade. But the winds came in at his call, at the slight tilt of his chin; the winds howled through his hair, lifting it wide as if it were the span of wings. Above him, moon, below him, the city.

His enemy flew back, striking a small building below; the stone cracked.

A man would be dead, Ramiro thought, had he struck the ground in such a fashion. But the creature snarled and rose.

Fire blazed from the tip of his sword, speeding like red lightning toward its target. The blue of blade split its foremost plume; flames lapped to either side of the Northern mage, flowing around him like a river.

But not without cost.

"I would offer you your life," the creature said.

"My life is not yours to barter with," the mage replied, laughing. "And I have heard far prettier offers, far more polished and courtly words. Did you not come here for battle, Ishavriel?"

He dove, then, ground rising to meet him.

Ishavriel stood his ground; the clash of swords was blinding. But the Callestan Tyr merely closed his eyes and waited until the light had passed him by.

Ser Fillipo par di'Callesta stood a moment as the color of the night sky changed. His hand ached; his arm shook. The Tyran gathered about him, silent as men, lost as children. He had but to give word, grant permission, and they would be gone.

Instead, he handed Ser Miko a shovel. "If this is not to take the whole of the evening, we will help the Northerners dig."

Ser Miko accepted the shovel far less willingly than the sword. Had there been no strangers present, he would have argued; they were half brothers, and not all of the words exchanged between kin were fair or pleasing. But he would not demean the rank that Fillipo held in the presence of Northerners. In the presence of the Tyr'agar.

Half of the Ospreys dug. Half waited, swords ready.

Kiriel di'Ashaf was among the watchers.

"Come, Miko," Fillipo said, speaking as quietly as he could and still be heard. "We must finish this before sun's rise. The Serra Amara has tended these grounds personally, and we would be well to be away when she discovers the damage done them."

Miko managed a feeble smile; it was better than nothing.

They fought; he waited, refusing to give in to the sting of bitter envy at the power they wielded so casually.

The ground broke at their feet, the air moved at their whim, fire gouted from between cracked stone, blackened earth. He could not survive this.

They were distant; too distant; the battle had moved, and moved again. No simple swordplay ranged this far; no simple battle for life or death traced such a large circle of destruction. He had thought to hide, to bide his time, to wait for an opening. The anger that had moved him this far was guttered; flames burned beneath his feet that were hotter, and colder, and brighter by far.

What place, he thought bitterly, had he in this war? What place had he, in the shadows cast by legends? What place, Callesta, or Lamberto, or even the kai Leonne? He closed his eyes, hands shaking now around the hilt of a blade that seemed dull, ordinary, a child's toy.

And then the wind changed; small stones and shards of glass flew past his upturned face, tracing thin lines of blood across his cheeks, nesting in his hair. He opened his eyes to the face of the moon, Lady's face, veiled but bright.

And he thought, as he met her distant gaze, that she waited in judgment; that she had seen things greater, and things far more insignificant than he; that all time had passed beneath her august gaze. And if, indeed, these were warriors of legend, if they were men—or worse—who could destroy whole cities when they came face-to-face— where were their kin now?

The whole of the Dominion, the whole of the Empire, was owned by the *insignificant*. Mortals ruled, mortals lived—and died—in places that would never know such glory as he was given to witness. And the lack of this knowledge did not impoverish them.

We rule here.

The moon's face. The sun's face. Between them, the hour of man, and it was coming; the sky was not so dark as it had been when he had ridden through the streets at the side of the kai Leonne; nor so dark as it was when he had seen the sacrilege done his son.

He rose, hand gripping rails; he watched. The winds had given him warning, and more, a reminder. He did not lose focus now, and the anger returned, primitive, a fire unlike the fire that ravaged the streets of his city. *His* city.

They passed beneath him, red and blue, dark and dark, and he tensed to leap, his sword before him, the curve of the crescent held up and toward his chest.

He would strike one blow, if that; he knew that he would be given no chance, no opportunity, for a second. He was not of the magi, not of the Sword, and for the first time in his life, he regretted it. But fleetingly.

He saw the creature draw back, saw his body shift, weight supported by his back leg, body lengthened to the side, shield out to absorb the blow offered him by Meralonne Aphaniel.

Before the twin blades met, Ramiro was in motion; gravity bore him down; no air sustained him, no wind broke his fall. One blow. One blow, for his son.

One.

What blue sword had failed to do, his sword did not; the creature, absorbed in the combat he had chosen, failed to notice something as insignificant as the Callestan kai. *Bloodhame* fell into the darkness behind the shield of the demon lord; it fell heavily, jerking with the force of a man's weight, a man's fall.

But the shield *fell*. The shield, and some part of the arm that had borne it.

The creature roared.

Had Ramiro voice for it, he might have joined its brief ululation, for the emotion it contained was kin to his own:

fury. Pain. Instead, he leaped to the side, rolling along the broken ground.

Meralonne APhaniel passed above him; he saw the sword of the demon and the sword of the mage meet for the last time.

Heard the mage curse, in a language that was utterly foreign, as the demon suddenly withdrew.

The moon paled in the night sky. The Lady began her passage into day. But the Lord had not yet come.

"Kai Callesta," the Northern mage said, his back toward the Tyr'agnate, his face toward the South.

Ramiro rose. Almost without thought, he removed his cloak; its edges now burned with the tongues of small flames, and he set it beneath the heels of his boots, grinding them, denying them further voice.

Then he rose.

"Meralonne APhaniel," he said, speaking in Weston, "I am in your debt."

The mage turned slowly. His sword was gone. The wind had left him; he seemed, for a moment, an old, an ancient, figure, weary with the burden of years.

"In my debt? I think not," he said quietly. "For Lord Ishavriel has lost his shield, and in the war to follow, that loss will count." He bowed.

He bowed, and Ramiro di'Callesta returned that bow, made of it an obeisance.

"You led him here," the Tyr'agnate said quietly.

"I?"

"I have . . . rarely . . . seen such a display. And I am grateful for the lack; I am not a young man, with a young man's dreams of glory. But I could not fail to notice that the battle was in no way contained; it had passed well beyond my reach."

Meralonne's gaze was cool. "It is said, among the Northern Commanders, that there are only two men to fear in the South. The Tyr'agnate of Callesta, and the man who now leads the armies of Annagar against us.

"You see too clearly, kai Callesta. I meant to burden you with no debt."

"Ah. That is very Northern of you, Member Aphaniel."

The mage smiled briefly. He bent his head a moment, and in the dawn light, untied the flap of his pouch. "I will smoke, I think, if it will not trouble you."

Ramiro nodded. "Forgive me if I do not join you."

"Indeed. It seems a habit that is out of favor in the South." He set dry leaf into the bowl of his pipe with meticulous care. Hard to see the warrior in the mage now; hard to believe that the hands that shook slightly as they conveyed pipe to mouth had wielded a sword of cold fire. "You see too clearly," the mage said again, "and you ask no questions."

"None," Ramiro replied gravely, gazing upon the broken ground, the guttering flames. "I have gathered wisdom over the years, and at some cost; I have learned that there are some answers that are better left unspoken." He smiled, and the smile was the sharpest of his smiles. "Was he important, mage?"

"The demon lord?"

Ramiro nodded.

"Oh, yes. You live up to your reputation."

"And that?"

Meralonne inhaled. "In the Averdan valleys, you chose to ambush the Black Ospreys. They were a small unit, and in the eyes of the North, one viewed with distaste; their loss could not dictate the course of the war.

"Why, then, did you choose to focus your efforts upon their banner?"

"In the South," Ramiro kai di'Callesta replied, "they were the only face of the Northern army that was clearly understood. I did not strike to damage the North, but to strengthen the South."

"They remember it."

"I remember it," Ramiro said, the smile gone from his face. He turned away. "Enough."

But the mage had not quite finished. "This kinlord was kin to the Ospreys. You have made a name for yourself among the enemies of the North, and it will not be forgotten; the *Kialli* forget little."

When they returned to the plateau, they found it little changed. The addition of the whole of the Tyran did not seem to crowd the damaged grounds; did not seem to crowd the broken frame of the temple door. The Ospreys were there in their full numbers as well, but they milled, like a small crowd.

This stopped when Commander Allen issued a soft command. All heads turned to Ramiro di'Callesta; in the soft glow of a carried lamp, he could see the momentary relief that changed the Commander's features. "Tyr'agnate," the Commander said, offering him a full Imperial bow.

Ramiro nodded. He was weary now. Whatever had driven him from balcony to ground had deserted him; the night was cold.

"Member APhaniel," the Commander added, turning to the mage.

Ramiro perceived that it was indeed the mage they waited upon. Why?

"Commander Allen." Meralonne was once again robed in the loose fitting garb of the Order; the sword was gone, and the mail of tiny chain links hidden. He bowed and reached for his pipe, the latter gesture robbing the former of due respect.

Not even Widan, Ramiro thought, with just a hint of humor, would dare as much. But the Commander, the Eagle, seemed familiar enough with this rough lack of respect; he paid it no heed. None at all.

"We have need of your services, APhaniel."

"The bodies?"

The Commander lifted a brow. Then he grimaced, and this, too, was completely unfettered. "The bodies," he said. "There were four. The days beneath the ground have been . . . unkind . . . to two of them. But the others seem whole."

Meralonne nodded.

"The Serra Alina di'Lamberto does not recognize the two."

"Then only two of the men served Lamberto."

"At best guess, none of them served Lamberto," the Commander replied, and this time, steel girded the words.

The mage shrugged. "This will not wait?"

Commander Allen's silence was answer enough. And it was the expected answer. It seemed that the Northerners had their own customs, their own dance of power. The manners that informed it were not Southern, but they were there, if one knew how to observe.

Meralonne lit the leaves in the basin of his pipe and then gestured; Commander Allen, himself, led. They walked between the ranks of the Tyran, smoke lingering in their wake like a pathway through air.

Ramiro met the gaze of his par. "Fillipo," he said.

"Was it done?"

Ramiro nodded.

"The bodies were disinterred. They have not been otherwise disturbed. If magic was used—by the Northerners—it was subtle enough to escape our detection."

He nodded again. He shed weariness, replacing it with a bitter curiosity.

Valedan kai di'Leonne waited beside Ser Andaro di'Corsarro, flanked by Ospreys, before the pallets upon the cleared ground. The open stone path that led to the temple served as bed; the Radann, some four men, Fiero among them, stood stiffly by his side, the rays of their office catching light as they moved. Dirt clung to the hems of their robes, dirt and grass; they carried their swords openly, forsaking shields for torchlight. But they bowed as the Tyr'agnate approached, and they retreated.

The kai Leonne did not.

Nor did Kiriel di'Ashaf or the Serra Alina di'Lamberto; nor did Alexis AKalakar or Fiara AKalakar. Commander Ellora AKalakar was likewise present; they formed the living antithesis to things graceful and feminine by their watchful, militant—and in two cases, sullen—presence.

But they ringed the kai Leonne, and for just a moment, Ramiro saw in them a ferocity, a fellowship, that reminded him in a way he could not explain, of his wives and their daughters.

There is very little, he thought dispassionately, *that these women would not do for your cause, or in it.* And then he smiled again, thinking that the same could be said of Serra Amara. He had—all of the South had—chosen the few weapons by which the Serras might fight, but having chosen to arm them so poorly, he still knew what they were capable of. He desired his wife now.

But he would not demean her by summoning her. There were other reasons why he did not wish to face her yet.

"Member APhaniel," Valedan said quietly.

The mage looked up. To Valedan kai di'Leonne, he offered a somber, perfect bow—a Southern bow, graceful to the last detail, and held for exactly the right length of breath, of heartbeat. *So,* Ramiro thought. But he said nothing.

"You are aware of what passed within the temple," the boy Tyr said quietly.

"Indeed."

"We wish to know how it was done."

"If I am not mistaken, Tyr'agar, you have seen it once before."

Ser Andaro di'Corsarro was pale. The light that shone orange upon the rest of the Ospreys seemed to discolor his face and his skin.

But the mage made his way to the side of the bodies, and he knelt there for some time, his expression shifting. He passed a hand over the sunken faces of the men that the Serra had called Lambertan. With a grunt, he rolled the first body over, dislodging it from the pallet. Armor had already been stripped from it. From the back, the black of a sword wound could be seen; the blood had long since dried.

"These?"

"Perhaps." He rolled the second corpse on its chest, and likewise examined back and spine, and then bid the Ospreys roll them back. He said quietly, "I will have to cut them open."

"Why those two, APhaniel?" Ramiro asked, choosing the Northern title.

"If, as you suspect but do not say, one of the four carried demons within them, evidence will almost certainly be found with these two."

"And not the others?"

"They are a different problem," the mage replied. "And they may offer different answers. But the Tyran and their presence would be significant here; were I to choose a method of conveyance, were I to desire their presence, I would control it personally." He glanced up at Kiriel di'Ashaf, and after a moment, she shook her head. "They are empty," she said quietly.

"Good."

Ser Andaro said, "When . . . my compatriot . . . was—"

Valedan lifted a hand, but Ser Andaro shook his head. "The body was his; the memories his. I would swear it. Cutting him open, wounding him, did not—"

Meralonne frowned. "You are correct, Ser Andaro. And perceptive. Our lore in these matters is poor; we are forbidden the study of ancient arts, and we gather information as we can. But you are correct. What . . . inhabited . . . the kai Callesta's body was not kin to what we witnessed upon the Kings' field. I am almost certain that the kai Callesta was dead before the demon moved.

"The kin do not easily inhabit living flesh, and not without a great deal of preparation; they can, however, *wear* it, for some time, and in a fashion. They can preserve it for their own use, if they have the self-control, but no more." He paused, and then drew his dagger.

Without another word, he cut across the center of the first man's chest; his blade was sharp, if short, and it passed with ease between ribs and sunken flesh. Too great an ease, the Callestan Tyr thought.

He peeled back the skin.

The chest cavity was hollow; the number of ribs too few. "Here," he said quietly.

"There is no heart," Valedan said.

"None, Tyr'agar." The mage rose, and bent beside the second corpse. This, too, was empty.

"We found only one demon." Valedan rose.

"If there was a second," Kiriel told him, "It is long gone. The plateau is free of the presence of the kin."

"So," Meralonne said, rising and stretching his shoulders, his long neck. His pipe flared again. "At least that much of a mystery is solved. It leaves another, of course. Tyr'agnate, is it possible for the oathguards to quit?"

Ramiro's scorn was only barely concealed. "They are not Northern guards," he said quietly.

"And is it possible to dismiss them?"

Ser Fillipo par di'Callesta, silent until that moment, said, "Yes. We call it execution."

"Ah. Then this must have been done in Lamberto."

"They planned well," Ramiro said quietly.

"Lack of organization has never been among their failings; they are not bound by mortal time; haste can be measured in decades, not hours. You are confident that the kai Lamberto is in no way allied with the kin?"

Ramiro kai di'Callesta said nothing. But he looked to the Serra Alina.

She, too, was silent.

"We are confident," Valedan said, speaking the words that they would not.

Meralonne rose. "They cannot do this easily," he said at last. "And not for long."

"Did they retain the memories of the men whose bodies they wore?" Ramiro asked.

Meralonne shrugged. "I cannot be certain. I would say no, but that would be conjecture, and we have no way of testing it."

"It would be best if this were not known."

"Indeed. It is the same situation in which the Kings found themselves: the cost of the fear and the panic would be too great."

"Can we protect our own against this?"

Meralonne shook his head. "As we protected the contestants? No. We offered them no protection in the end, kai Callesta; we offered ourselves early warning, that was all. But I will tell you again, this is rare, and it is costly."

"Not costly enough."

"Not yet."

"Kiriel di'Ashaf," Ramiro turned to the Osprey. "If these possessed my men, could you detect them?"

She hesitated. And then, as if ashamed, she lowered her head. "Not I," she said at last. "But—"

"Say no more. But I better understand your decision now, and if I do not rejoice in it, I accept it. Your creature—your servant—I wish use of him on the morrow."

She nodded grimly.

But the mage had not yet finished.

"These two," he said quietly, coming at last to the bodies that seemed freshly fallen. He paused before the first, looking up, not at Valedan, but at the Tyr'agnate. "Kai Callesta, with your permission?"

"You have it."

The mage looked down. And then he set his pipe aside upon the stone, and spread his hands flat against the chest of the nearest. He spoke words, and they were sharp and harsh to the ears of the Callestan Tyr; they were fully formed and yet completely unintelligible; they eluded the ear, and all memory. He could not hold them.

The chest of the man began to *unfold*. Skin rose, and rose

again, like tendrils of a plant, flesh-colored but thin and almost translucent beneath the lantern hearts, the billowing
smoke of torchlight.

Everywhere that skin had touched the mage's hands, it
sought to elude them, until beneath his hands, only one
thing remained, shining and wet in its exposure to the cool
of the night sky: a heart.

Not a living heart, but not—yet—dead.

Meralonne APhaniel cursed roundly in Weston. Reaching down, he caught the heart in his hands as the skin that
had risen now collapsed in a sudden effort to heal the
breach. It came too late; the heart was his.

And as he drew it from the chest, the body began to col-
lapse, taking the form now of dead leaves, long grass, bent
branches and twigs.

"It is *Allasakari* magic," he said quietly. "I begin to understand now."

No one spoke for a full minute.

"Two others must have traveled with the possessed
Tyran," he said quietly. "But they had no intention of dying
here. You will no doubt find—if you look—that two of your
own have gone missing, kai Callesta. They will never be
found; no more of them remains than this." And he lifted
the heart in the scant light. "It is a magic of seeming, only;
it has not the power to grant life, or even its semblance. But
it has served its purpose here.

"They may have served as witnesses to the assassination;
they could not afford to leave any real witnesses alive. Seek
them."

But his tone made clear that he thought nothing would be
found.

CHAPTER EIGHTEEN

THE Serra Donna en'Lamberto entered the courtyard with two of the Lambertan Tyran. Her husband's men, and trusted, they walked before her, swords sheathed; they were meant not as warning but as evidence of her significance.

She accepted them with an ease borne of familiarity, and in truth, she found them a comfort—but she would have to shed them before she spoke with the Voyani who waited. Her hands were steady; she drew strength from the formal posture, the rigidity of lifted chin, of elongated neck—forms that she adopted without thought, they were so necessary.

This was not her home; her home was the heart of the harem. Exposed, she retreated into the mannered dignity of a Serra.

And knew, as she reached the waiting women, that it was the wrong retreat.

The older of the two was no longer dark-haired; time had grayed the untidy spill of raven black, and lines had become engraved around mouth and lip. Whether these were due to frown or smile, she could not say; the woman herself betrayed no emotion, other than the mild look of irritation that seemed so common among the Voyani.

But when the Serra Donna left the Tyran and approached,

both women surprised her; they bowed. She did not kneel, although instinct bade her bend knee. Her husband was watching.

"Serra Donna en'Lamberto," the older woman said quietly, as she rose. "I am Nadia Yollanaan, Daughter of the Matriarch of Havalla. And this is Varya, my sister. We're honored that you could meet with us."

This last was said with a heavy irony, and the younger woman frowned openly. But she did not speak, and by her silence, Donna knew who was in command. Still, she gazed at the sister a moment; she, too, was darkened by sun, creased by wind—but the color had not yet been bleached from her hair, and the wildness was moored in her face, her dark eyes. In the full bloom of her youth, however brief, she must have been beautiful.

"Accept my apologies for my tardiness," she said quietly. "I received a message that could not wait."

"Was it welcome news?"

"No," she said quietly, discomfited by the boldness of the question. Squaring shoulders, she added, "It came from the Terrean of Averda."

Both women were instantly alert.

"And I will offer it to you, although it was private, in return for information."

The women relaxed. The Voyani were not true merchants; if they traded at all, it was in secrecy and herbs. But information was bartered often between the poorer clanswomen and the Voyani. "And that information, Serra?"

"I wish to know how something impossible might be achieved."

"If indeed it is impossible," Nadia replied cautiously, "it might never be achieved at all."

"Ah, you mistake me—I speak poorly. It has been a long day. I do not desire to achieve this thing; I desire to understand how it came to pass."

The sisters exchanged a look. Donna read much in what

passed between them, but it did not surprise her; the Voyani did not wear masks in the High Courts. Did not spend time in the High Courts, if it could be avoided.

"You will have to trust us," Nadia said at last. "For until you ask the question, we will not know whether or not we can answer it; you may be offering us information for free."

"I will take that risk," she replied quietly. "For it is said that the Voyani serve the Lady."

"It is not said beneath the Lord's gaze," Nadia replied quietly, lifting a hand.

That hand cast a shadow; the Lord was in the sky.

"If you will," Serra Donna replied, "I would offer you the meager hospitality of my quarters. I know that the Voyani are not accustomed to spending much time beneath roof or enclosing walls—but there is privacy in the harem that is not found elsewhere."

Nadia bowed again. "We have traveled in haste," she replied. "And although it is said that we neither bathe nor sleep, neither of these things are entirely true." Her smile was almost warm; it was certainly genuine.

Serra Donna returned a scant bow; it hid her relief. "Please," she said quietly, "follow me. The Tyran will not accompany us if you prefer their absence; you do not travel in the company of men."

"No," Nadia replied. "We do not. You are considerate, Serra Donna, but it is no surprise; you are Lambertan. If you are truly comfortable with their absence, we will gratefully do without; if there is difficulty in the domis, both Varya and myself are capable of dealing with it, and we will defend you as if you were Havallan." Her accent, indeed her choice of words, was awkward—but it was appropriate. To the domis, to the High Court, to the Serra.

She felt a prickle of unease take root at that.

Serra Donna bowed again, and turning, she offered the Tyran the agreed upon signal. They parted to allow her to pass, and they did not follow; they were perfect enough that they showed no concern, no interest all, as she left them behind. It did not surprise her, but it gratified her nonetheless, for she knew that Nadia of the Havalla Voyani was now slightly off her stride; she had expected neither offer, and had accepted both.

The Voyani women were offered access to the baths, and food was prepared in their absence; when they returned to the heart of the harem, Serra Donna en'Lamberto was alone—but her screens were not yet closed, and through them, the sounds of the children could easily be heard. She had arranged it, just so, but children were often unpredictable.

Nadia sank awkwardly to her knees, and Varya, even more so, but the cushions were soft and the food at a height that standing made awkward. Serra Donna herself poured both water and wine; she knew that the Voyani were not comfortable in the presence of serafs, and she therefore sent all of her serafs from the wing. The children, however, remained, a distant reminder of the things they had in common.

Only after the women had eaten did Donna rise and close the screens, sealing them with the silk flashing that requested—no, ordered—privacy.

"Nadia of Havalla," she said, as she resumed her seat, "we have had no word of the Matriarch. Have you?"

"Some," Nadia replied, with care. "But none of it from her directly."

More than that, Donna did not ask. Instead, she swallowed breath and shed dignity, in order to better accommodate her unusual guests. "I received a letter from the Serra Amara en'Callesta."

Nadia raised a weathered brow. It changed the landscape of her face. "How much does she say?" The tone was now completely neutral, if too blunt.

"Enough," the Serra Donna replied. "It is a Serra's letter . . . and it is not. She does not," she added, when Nadia opened her mouth again, "speak of the Northern armies, if that is what you mean to ask."

Nadia subsided, but her expression shifted again, and this time she offered the Serra the sharpest of her smiles. "So," she said quietly. "You know."

"My husband knows," Serra Donna said carefully, setting the water aside. "It is not given to the Serras to study the arts of war."

"Fair enough," Nadia said.

But Varya said bitterly, "No. Only to die by them."

The older sister turned a venomous gaze upon the younger; it was the first thing they had done that made them seem, in truth, kin. Serra Donna was careful not to smile.

"What, then, does the Serra Amara offer you?"

"She offers nothing," Serra Donna replied, with just a hint of reproval. "But she asks much."

"Be blunt, Serra."

Donna stiffened. "I was being blunt," she said coolly.

Varya snickered.

"But I will be more so, if it pleases you. Her son, Carelo kai di'Callesta, is dead."

The two woman stilled completely. That much information, it seemed, had not traveled between the two Terreans, at least not by the roads the Voyani walked. "How?" the older of the two asked sharply.

"Assassins," the Serra replied, serene now, the knowledge a sharp weapon. A weapon, she thought, with some regret, that could only be used once.

"What was the nature of the assassins? Is it known?"

It was not the question that Donna expected, if she had expected any at all, but it told her much. It changed the face of the conversation.

"To the Callestans," she said, with deliberate care, "it would seem that he was killed by Lambertan men. By," she added softly, "the Tyran that serve my husband."

"Impossible," Varya said, and from that moment on,

Donna felt that she must like this sharp-tongued, prickly woman.

Nadia, however, said nothing. She was not yet her mother's equal, but the potential now lay before the Serra, open to inspection. "Were there witnesses?"

"I think there must have been," the Serra replied quietly. "But although the bodies of the killers were identified by a source that both the Callestans *and* the Lambertans must consider above reproach," she continued with care, "the Serra Amara en'Callesta is cautious."

"How so?"

"She has asked me if my husband ordered this killing."

"And your answer?"

"Ah, forgive me, Nadia. I have not yet tendered a reply; I was late to meet with you because the information was of import enough to the Tyr that I attended him first."

Nadia frowned.

"My husband, of course, did not order the assassination."

Nadia nodded. If she doubted the words, the doubt was kept from her otherwise fluid expression.

"Yet the men who carried it out were, indeed, his men."

Impassive, the Voyani woman waited.

"We do not treat with Widan, except at need," the Serra continued, "and their arts are not our arts. But it is not my husband's belief that such . . . deception is within their capabilities."

"No," Nadia said quietly. "It is not."

"How, then, could this be achieved?"

Nadia looked toward the opaque screens. She bowed her head a moment. "There are two ways," she said quietly. "And I will offer you both, Serra Donna en'Lamberto, and more.

"If the killing itself was carried out by a third party, it would be a difficult—but not impossible—task to then leave the bodies of the supposed killers behind. The Voyani could do it, although it would carry some risk to us, and the witnesses could not be people with any sophistication."

Donna said nothing at all, but folded her hands in her lap as Nadia spoke.

"We did not, nor would we, assassinate the Callestan kai. Not now. Especially not now."

"And the other way?"

"The other way is not within our grasp," she replied. "But it is within the grasp of the servants of the Lord of Night."

The hands in her lap shook briefly; Serra Donna stilled the tremor.

"Even here?" she said at last, when it was clear that the Havallan would not continue.

"Even here." Nadia lifted wine, not water, to her cracked lips. "We did not come to barter with old wives or to offer fortunes and mystery, Serra. Were that our intent, we would never have approached the plateau." She drank; there was no grace in the bitter, deliberate gesture. "The wine is sweet."

"And the water."

"Nadia—"

"No, Varya." She raised her head and ran fingers through stiff hair. "We have come with word, and with an offer."

"What offer?"

"The Voyani have, among their number, people who can detect the servants of the Lord of Night. They are few," she added quietly, "and we do not expose them willingly."

"And word?"

But Nadia's face smoothed into lines of impassivity as she studied the Serra's face. A decision was being made; Donna knew better than to attempt to influence it.

"The Tor'agar of Marano," Nadia said at last, "arrived at your gates some days before we did."

Serra Donna en'Lamberto frowned. "Yes," she said quietly.

"He carried word, we believe, from the General Marente. No, Serra; if it places you in a difficult position, do not answer; it was not a question."

Serra Donna said nothing.

"The General Marente has made, in one action, enemies of the Voyani. We will not serve him; we will not treat with him."

Serra Donna nodded. She longed for the safety of her fan, but although it rested beside the cushions on which she knelt, she did not dare to draw attention by lifting it.

"I do not know what offer the letter contained; there was some discussion about whether or not it was wise to let the message pass." Another look passed between the sisters. "But in the end, we must have some faith in Lamberto; we did not intervene. And in the end, Serra Donna, we had pressing concerns; taking action against the Tor'agar would have hindered us in our other operations.

"Some small number of these servants of the Lord of Night have crossed the border of Mancorvo; they are some-place within the Terrean as we speak."

13th of Corvil, 427 AA
Dominion of Annagar, The Dark Deepings

Kallandras turned to Lord Celleriant when he stilled. Ahead, in the darkness, he could hear the clear sound of snapping twigs, dry branches that had fallen from the ancient trees that seem to gird the path chosen by the Havallan Matriarch.

"Celleriant."

The Arianni lord lifted his silver head. The night had waned; the moon had passed above them inches at a time; day weighted it as the horizon shifted toward light. "Now," Lord Celleriant said softly, "we had best be wary."

Kallandras nodded. He could not see what Lord Celleriant saw; that much was clear. But he knew how to listen; he could hear. The forest was devoid of the voices that would otherwise give it some semblance of life. Only dry branches spoke, at the behest of the weight of footsteps.

"Do you know this place?"

Celleriant offered the bard a rare smile. "I knew it in my youth, and it has . . . changed little. I am surprised."

"What dwells within this forest?"

"Now?" The smile dimmed. "The dead," he said softly. He spoke with regret; did not trouble himself to hide it in the folds of silken voice. "And the living—you, the others—had best be wary. But there is some benefit to this road. If we are followed here, it will go ill with the followers."

"Where will this path take us?"

"I do not know. It is not a path of *my* making." He lifted his head. Listened a moment. "Understand," he added, staring up at the bower of dark trees, "that in a place such as this—in any of the oldest places the world harbors—paths are made; they are not made, as they are elsewhere, by the simple expedient of walking them time and again. This forest lives, and the will to make an impression upon it—any impression—must be both strong and personal."

Kallandras heard nothing but the sound of Lord Celleriant's voice. It was almost enough. "We will fall behind," he said softly.

Celleriant nodded. Nodded, and drew sword. It came in the graying dark of early light, as bright as moon or stars in the clear, cool sky. Its edge traced a blue symbol in the air; one that hung there, like afterimage, burned into awareness and vision.

Kallandras lifted a pale brow.

"It is . . . my name," Celleriant said, answering the question that the bard had not—would not—ask.

"And you expect to meet someone who will know it?"

"This is an ancient place, a Deeping." Celleriant began to move, taking care to place his feet against the earth, grounding heel, bending toe. "The old woman has written her name, her blood's name, in the earth; she seeks to use what already exists."

"You see her name?"

"Yes. You don't?"

Kallandras shook his head. "I neither see it nor hear it, and perhaps that is best. I may cling to the delusion that mortals do not possess mystic names." But he, too, drew his weapon. As he lifted it, the ring that had come to him in the oldest of the mortal cities burned blue against his pale flesh.

"Be wary," Celleriant told him, eyeing the ring. "For the power that guides us is not a friend to the power of that ring."

The master bard of Senniel College bid the ring be silent, speaking softly and pleasantly; making a plea of the command. He cajoled, where another might have ordered, and in doing so, avoided an argument.

Celleriant watched him. "You are . . . unexpected," he said at last, when the ring was silent, its light momentarily stilled.

Kallandras looked up.

"It is the way of men of power, is it not, to rule?"

And shrugged.

"The wind is silent," the Arianni lord continued, "and if I judge its voice correctly, it will remain so."

"Be glad that it cannot so easily hear yours."

"Ah, but it can." He smiled. "It is not our way to speak softly to the wild ones, and we have ruled them for millennia."

"You are not mortal."

"No. But in my time, I have met many who are, and I have not noted that lack of pride comes with lack of longevity."

The bard shrugged. "Pride?"

"Where there are no witnesses, your words are your own. But where witnesses preside, your words are carried, and they are carried at the whim of the watchers. I would not speak so softly to the wild ones."

"Perhaps I trust the witness."

"Perhaps. Trust or no, it is not a gambit that I would chance. You are strange, Kallandras of Senniel."

"Perhaps. Perhaps it is something I learned in Senniel College."

"In Senniel? The college of bards?"

"Songs serve their purpose. Each is chosen to invoke either memory or emotion." He glanced up, along the hidden forest path. "I am not a man who is destined to rule. If I am seen as weak, it may even be truth."

"And this does not concern you."

"No. Should it?"

Celleriant's hair fell about his shoulders as he shook his head. "I have seen you fight," he said softly. "I have seen you kill. I would not have guessed that you could speak so quietly, that you could offer plea where command would also serve."

"Death is the Lady's," Kallandras whispered. "All else comes from me. Perhaps we have something to teach each other."

"I would have said no."

Kallandras smiled.

And then he froze, for he heard, in the road ahead, the sound of a short, terrible cry.

Yollana's voice.

The stag froze in mid-step.

Jewel had heard that phrase before, but she had never seen words given such visceral life; his foremost left hoof hovered above the ground between the impression of pale steps. The child dozed in her arms, legs to either side of the stag's great back, and Jewel tightened her grip just enough that the girl stirred.

She forced herself to relax, as much as she could, craning back, eyes squinting in the shade and shadow of forest at dawn. And what a forest: a ragged wall of trees that stretched from the earth to the heights so far above she could not see their tops without taking the risk of falling off the stag's back.

Jewel.

Stag's voice.

That was Yollana.

Yes. His voice was smooth and deep.

Should we ride back?

No.

But—

No. If she summons you, turn; if she does not, do her the grace of ignoring what should have remained unuttered.

But she—

No.

Her knees tightened, as if the stag were horse; his antlers rose, like cool tree branches, at the whim of his stiffening neck.

And then she, too, froze.

The stag was silent. Before them, in the winding curve of a path laid out by the feet of the dead, stood two men.

An old man, she thought, and a young one; their faces were obscured by morning shadow, although they were white as snow. Why was white the color of snow, anyway? Why was white the color of cold?

It is the color of mortal death, the stag replied softly. *When blood has ceased its flow beneath the shell of skin: when flesh has ceased all movement.*

That was rhetorical.

Ah.

You can see them?

I . . . can. But I do not think I see as you see, Jewel ATerafin.

I see an old man. And a boy.

I see merely the dead, and they are angry.

They're looking for something.

I doubt that. I doubt it much.

Why?

I think they know exactly where what they seek is to be found: they merely lie in wait. Do not, he added severely, as she shifted the burden of her weight, *attempt to interfere here.*

Interfere?

If you attempt to dismount. I will carry you as far from this place as I can before you touch ground.

She nodded; she had almost expected to hear those words.

For the first time that night, she thought of Avandar.

Viandaran is close by, the stag told her gently. *And if you manage to escape the safety of my back, he will be greatly annoyed.*

Well, at least that would be normal.

No, the stag said, the tone chiding. *He would be greatly annoyed at me.*

He's not in danger, is he?

He is Viandaran. By definition he is in no mortal danger. The stag paused; its breath came out in morning mist, sweet and damp. *But that is too simple an answer. Yes, Jewel ATerafin, he is in danger here. But it is not the danger you face.*

What do I face?

The old man stepped out, onto the path, and his eyes, his hollow, cavernous eyes, turned toward her.

Never mind.

Radann Marakas par el'Sol had heard screams before. He was not, had never become, inured to them; it was a sign of his weakness, a sign of the vulnerability that came with his gift. Or so he had often believed in his youth, when other men stood in the wake of such cries, unmoved.

But if he were honest, he might seem to be those men now, made of Lord's steel, affected by nothing but the corrosive quality of blood, the damaging rigidity of an enemy's armor.

He turned to the Serra Diora, and saw that she was as still as he; her face was smooth, her eyes no wider than they had been.

"Serra?"

She nodded, gracefully, delicately. At her back, looming like shadow, her seraf met the Radann's gaze. He held it only briefly; he was not a free man, to offer threat or warning in such an obvious fashion. Nor was he a poorly trained seraf, an embarrassment to a great clan; the glancing meeting of gazes was enough—just enough—to catch the Radann par el'Sol's attention.

"Are we truly upon the border of Mancorvo?" She asked the question quietly, but urgency marked the words; he wondered if it were his, placed there by the grim shade of early morn in a place that knew so little light.

Marakas gazed into the forest. He wondered if the Lord's light ever fell upon this ground; the bower of tree branches was high and terrible. But the trees had shed leaves—some passing reminder that all living things know season—and the light was therefore brighter than it might have been, the ground less barren, less devoid of color.

"If you had asked me at another time," he replied gravely, "I would have said it was impossible that these lands could border any Terrean of my acquaintance."

She did not smile; did not demur; he realized only after he had chosen to answer that she had not asked for permission to speak the words. They had come, unfettered, into the morning, and he had accepted them. As if they were equals, this Serra of the High Courts and he, a man second only to the Tyr'agar and the kai el'Sol.

No Lady's time, this; and no Lord's. She took advantage of laws older and more unforgiving than he.

She stiffened slightly.

"Serra?"

"I am well, Radann par el'Sol, and grateful for your concern."

He frowned. But he accepted the words as they were spoken; refused to seek the more obvious meaning behind their surface. Instead, he drew sword.

Light flared, and grew, in the clearing; cold light, white and blue. He had only once seen *Verragar* burn so brightly, and he knew—or thought he knew—what that fire presaged.

And yet . . . and yet he felt somehow that the kin were not present; that *Verragar*'s fire spoke of a different danger, a different enemy.

Skin white in the shed light of sword, the Serra Diora bowed her head. Lifting a graceful, delicate hand, she drew the mask of the desert traveler across her cheeks and lips, denying him the full breadth of her expression.

Kallandras.
Serra Diora. You are safe?
I am . . . safe. Are you distant?
I cannot see you, he replied, **but I can hear you clearly.**
The sword of the Radann par el'Sol is speaking, she told him, **and I think it best that you join Ona Teresa and the Havallan Matriarch.**
I think it unlikely that our presence would be appreciated.
It will not be. But that does not make it less necessary.

In the darkness, he smiled, and the smile lingered a moment.

"Kallandras?"

"The Serra," he said gravely, "has learned more than she knows in her journey alongside the Arkosa Voyani." He turned to his companion. "Lord Celleriant," he said gravely, "I think it time that we join the Matriarch."

"Past time," Celleriant replied.

The Serra Teresa di'Marano had learned the cadence of Yollana's injured step; had learned to shoulder the burden of this older, this powerful woman, as gracefully as she had shouldered any burden in the High Court.

But the familiar footfall had changed as the black of night gave way to gray and shadow, and twice now, she had had to exert some force—and a great lack of the grace for which she was known—to prevent Yollana's fall.

The third time, she failed in the duty that she had silently undertaken; the old woman's knees buckled quickly and suddenly, rounding toward the earth beyond the rise of knotted, ancient tree roots that time had exposed to air.

"Teresa," the Matriarch said, "leave me."

It was not a request. And the Serra Teresa was not Havallan, not a daughter who might be forgiven the crime of disobedience by the expedience of her necessity to the bloodline.

But she did not choose to hear the older woman's words. Instead, she shifted her arms—they ached now, with damp, with morning—around the old woman's waist, feeling the line of tobacco satchel, of hidden pack, of dagger hilt.

"Na'tere," the Matriarch said.

Her voice was devoid of querulous anger, of annoyance, of rage. It was devoid of almost all emotion; Yollana had closed the window that lay between them as firmly as she could.

Of all things that had happened this eve, this single act was the most disquieting.

"I have seen you through the Sea of Sorrows," the Serra of clan Marano said, bending to the older woman's ear. "I have stayed by your side while the Serpent of the ancient storm rode the winds above us; while the earth broke and bent beneath our feet. Will you send me away now?"

"Yes."

"Ah. Forgive me, Matriarch. I understand the cost associated with deliberate disobedience; I understand it better than you understand it yourself, for I have lived at its whim all my life. When I chose to travel with you, when I chose to step—for as long as our roads conjoin—upon the *Voyanne,* I made my vows."

"To whom?"

"Does it matter? If I say 'To the Lady' you will chide me; you will tell me that this is not the Lady's time. And you know that I make no vow to the Lord."

"You know me too well," the old woman replied, but again her voice was smooth as stone wall; no cracks or fissures there, nothing to read.

A reminder, if it were needed, that Serra Teresa di'-Marano relied upon what lay in the voice; that it had become a part of every conversation she had ever overheard or participated in. She felt the absence of Yollana in Yollana's words; she was alone with her own.

"I know you well enough," the Serra said quietly. "You fear to meet something on this road."

"I do not fear it," the old woman replied, snapping, coloring her words with annoyance. "I accept it as inevitable. I will meet what I meet, and if I am strong enough—" and she gazed at her broken legs, legs that could not support the whole of her weight without the humiliation of dependence, "—we will win through."

"And if you are not strong enough?"

Silence.

"Yollana, are we lost to this path if you cannot face what is here?"

"It is my . . . hope . . . that you will make your escape," the old woman replied, and the walls cracked suddenly as her eyes turned up, toward the Serra's face, "while they are otherwise occupied."

"Then you know me less well than I know you," the Serra said.

"You have your duty."

"I have done with duty. No, that is not true. I *have* my duty, and it is here, by the side of the Matriarch of Havalla."

"And your niece?"

"I have given her everything that I am capable of giving; she stands in the lee of Kallandras of Senniel College, a man who speaks with the very voice of the wind."

"He had best not speak with that voice here."

"If it is necessary," Teresa replied, "he will speak with all the voices he possesses."

"And?"

"And then we will see death, and know it."

Yollana shuddered. "I see death," she said, and her hand reached out, caught Teresa's, clamped tight. The gesture was involuntary, and Teresa did not deign to notice it, although she saw her fingers whiten at the strength of Yollana's grip.

"I tried," the old woman said weakly. "Bear witness, Na'tere, and remember: I tried."

"I understand. I hold you responsible in no wise for my action, for my decision." She bent, braced herself, and drew Yollana to her feet. And then, softly, she added, "That is not true. I hold you in esteem, and myself in your debt, for the road you offered me was the only road for which I am now fit, and you offered it without judgment or fear."

"Na' tere."

"Yollana?"

"Sing," the old woman said quietly. "Sing a song that is meant to soothe, to speak to, the loss of men."

She had no samisen, no Northern harp, no lute; she might find one at a word to Ramdan, a word to Na'dio, but in taking it, she would have to give over the burden that she bore.

She closed her eyes. The burden was, in some fashion, an instrument. "Yes, Yollana," she said quietly. And she lifted her face in the gray light, and she opened her dry lips, and she wrapped her words in their most naked form of expression: song.

They heard it.

Jewel ATerafin, the child in her arms, the stag upon whom she sat in relative safety; Avandar Gallais, in the shadows cast by old trees, older memories; Kallandras of Senniel College and the brother he had chosen in the fight of flight and blade; Stavos, Ramdan, the Radann Marakas par el'Sol, and the woman they chose to guard, hovering like common cerdan.

They lifted their heads in unison; her voice commanded the attention; drew it, coaxing and cajoling in turn.

The Serra Teresa di'Marano had been called upon to sing of loss, and she understood loss in some measure; she had forsaken her home, her family, the only life for which she was suited. The decades of perfect courtly grace honed the words she chose, coloring them, lending them a depth, a gravity, a majesty, that a child's voice could never contain.

They bowed head, these witnesses, and some felt tears sting their eyes and blur vision in the dusk of this new, this unknown world.

They were not the only listeners; not the only ones who were drawn to the song that she offered. They were, however, the only ones for whom trees, plants, the twisting roots of undergrowth, were an obstacle.

The dead came.

Teresa saw them first.

Had she been younger, had she been a different woman, she would have fallen silent, the strength of voice faltering in the wake of fear. She had seen death before; no one who made home of the High Courts could avoid it, no matter how careful their fathers or brothers chose to be. But that death was different: a thing of blood and flesh, a cessation of motion, something that could be touched, ascertained, made distant.

These dead, Yollana's dead, were hampered by no such forms. They were pale as morning mist, solid as vision; fear gave them their only solidity.

In her arms, Yollana of the Havallan Voyani stirred; in her arms, the old woman froze. The hand that Teresa held, the hand that held her, was tight now, so rigid it seemed that life had deserted it between the start—and the end—of the song.

But the song did not end.

Three ghosts. Three quiet ghosts, moved toward it.

A young man, one barely past childhood. A man in his prime. An old man, not yet bent by years, his face pale with beard's ghost. But all of their eyes were black and hollow, and their skin was the color of light on water, although no light pierced the trees.

They came, moving in time to the rhythm of her song, and she knew that she could not let that song falter. Not yet.

The man who wore the mockery of the prime of life raised an arm. Flesh hung from it loosely, as if it were poorly donned cloth. But it was not flesh that concerned her; his finger was part fist and part finger; he pointed at the heart of the Havallan Matriarch, and when he opened his mouth, he introduced the first discordant note into the Serra's perfect song.

She groped for harmony. Groped, phrasing the notes and the scales, as she tried to match, to gentle, his wordless keening.

He drew blade, and the blade was dark as his eyes. From it, dripping groundward, black blood. This, she thought, was memory; the memory of the dead. She knew how he had died.

He approached. Her song slowed him; she could see that he stepped in time with the notes that she sang. Seeing this, she modulated them, slowed her words, the power that they contained.

If he did not deign to notice her in any other way, he slowed.

The old man joined him, eyes as dark, hands darker. He, too, carried a dagger, night's dagger. It was not, she thought, the Lady's work.

Last came the boy. He was of an age with Adam, the Arkosan Matriarch's brother, but there was none of his inherent sweetness in this ghostly face; there was something akin to malice, something akin to rage, and the youngest face wore it most openly of the three.

Yollana, Teresa thought, very much afraid. *What did you do here?*

She did not ask. Could not afford to; the break in the words would give them room and time to maneuver. No knowledge of the dead was necessary; she knew what that would mean. Could see it clearly in eyes that were no longer—if they had ever been—mortal.

                    *   *   *

The Serra Diora di'Marano lifted her head. As she did, her shoulders dropped; her posture became the posture of the wife of Tyrs. She did not rise, for she had not taken shelter upon the ground, fearing the earth here, fearing the tangle of roots, the touch of these trees.

But she was not unarmed: She, too sang.

Who better than she to sing a song of loss?

Since her sojourn, her brief peace, in the towers of Arkosa, the dead had slept more quietly; her memories had stilled and gentled. She heard, in Margret's voice, the voice of the most beloved of her wives, and she was almost content. She had discovered, in the Sea of Sorrows, that the dead were not dead; that the wind did not contain them; that there existed, beyond the moment of a terrible, painful end, the possibility of another life.

That had brought her peace, in the only measure that she had known since the night of the slaughter.

Hard, to set that peace aside.

But she heard Ona Teresa's song, and she understood that the moment for peace had passed. She reached for memory, and memory came.

She sang of her own failure. She sang of her own betrayal. She sang of the terrible, terrible cost to her loved and her dead, and in that song, she made her first plea for their forgiveness since she had trod the desert sands at the side of the Matriarch.

They did not hear her, of course; they had never heard her.

But there were creatures upon the road who were more— or less—fortunate.

The Radann par el'Sol was speaking. She lifted a hand, an imperious hand, stemming the tide of his scant words. Although she knew grace—how could she not, who was the Flower of the Dominion—she knew also that it cost, would cost, time. And time was the thing she did not have.

They did not have.

She began to walk. At her back, to one side, followed

Ramdan; beside her, shoulder to shoulder, although his were broader and higher, the Radann par el'Sol. Stavos, blade drawn, walked before them, silent; he offered no interruption to the song she now sang.

They wound their way toward Serra Teresa.

Toward the dead.

Last, Kallandras of Senniel College lifted his head; pale curls, edges darkened by the dyes he had used to better disguise himself among the clans, shook a moment as he tested the wind.

Lord Celleriant, blade drawn, stood at his side. "Be wary," he said softly. "I have drawn blade, but it is not, I fear, a weapon against what we face here."

"What do we face?"

"Memory," the Arianni lord said quietly. "Mortal memory."

"If I recall my history correctly, mortal memory is a poor container for events; it lacks the steel of the Arianni, the fire of the *Kialli*."

"One day, I will ask you where you learned that history," Celleriant said quietly. "And as payment against that day, I will offer you my own experience. You are right: my memory is sharper and cleaner than yours—than any of yours—and it is far, far longer. But the passions of the Arianni, the passions of those who were once *Allasiani,* run to few things, and they are living passions. Few events in our lives have the significance of a simple birth or a simple death in yours; we are not moved by the mundane."

"This is hardly mundane."

"No? Three men died here, and those deaths define the path upon which we now stand."

"Memory of death—"

"Not their memory," Celleriant said softly, "but hers." He lifted his head. "The Cities of Man," he said quietly, "contained such ghosts as these. They were a punishment, and a monument, to the power of those to whom they had lost. In the cities of this diminished world, you build gargoyles and winged creatures, you decorate your buildings with the silence of stone.

"Such art, such work, was considered lesser by the Tors of the ancient Cities. What they built, what they contained, was meant to invoke no sense of grandeur; it was meant to invoke fear. It offered warning. And it offered death to the unwary, the unpowerful."

Kallandras nodded quietly. "I will sing," he said quietly.

Celleriant nodded, understanding the truth that had not yet been spoken: song was their best weapon.

And Kallandras of Senniel College was a bard without peer upon this poorly traveled road.

His voice joined theirs. Serra Teresa heard it instantly, and she gave over some part of her melody to its power, choosing harmonies that might better bring his voice to light. But she was shaken. She had heard him sing before; in the Court of the Tyr'agar Markaso kai di'Leonne, a man who had become a simple part of the complexity of Annagarian history, and in the Eastern Fount of contemplation. Then, he had chosen cradle song, overpowering her with her own desire for safety and simplicity.

Now, he chose to speak to the heart of loss, and his loss was the wind's sharpest voice.

Had she been better prepared, she might not have faltered. Indeed, she faltered only for a moment.

But were it not for her niece, that moment would have been her death. The dead moved in the gap between the fullness of her offered musical phrases, seeking an opening.

They were no longer a distant audience; they had found the strength to move, and move again, with each verse she offered. She laid her heart bare, and they slowed, but it was costly.

She sang of Alora, her brother's dead wife. She sang of the bitterness of their parting. She sang of her failure, her profound failure, and again, the men faltered. But they did not stop; they were close enough to Yollana of the Havalla Voyani now, and she drew them forward.

The strongest of the men reached them first, and stood at the feet of the Havallan Matriarch. Yollana, crouched to ground, lifted a face carved by wind and darkened by sun; her eyes met his, and she saw in those eyes something that Teresa herself could not see.

"The time has come, Andreas. The time has come at last." She made to rise, and Teresa rose with her, struggling with the weight of both song and Matriarch.

He nodded, grim, and the dagger he held shifted position in the palm of his hand.

Wordless, he came, and wordless, he remained. But the dagger itself moved; it struck Yollana full in the chest.

The Matriarch grunted, stumbling. Teresa almost lost song as she pulled Yollana to her feet, and held her swaying there. The hilt of the black knife protruded from her chest.

"You are free," Yollana whispered, choking on the words. On the words and more. Blood trailed from the corners of her mouth, darkening the wind's cracks, the sun's lines.

The man smiled.

The boy came next. Teresa could not look away; the whole of his face seemed absorbed by the shadow that had taken up residence in the hollow of his eyes.

"You betrayed us," he said, the sibilance of the last syllable louder than the Serra Teresa's voice. He lifted a slender dagger.

The Matriarch said nothing.

And the Serra Teresa's song faltered. If Yollana had chosen to armor herself against the gift—and the curse—that had forever defined the Serra's life, the boy felt no such compunction. She heard what lay beneath the surface of his words clearly, and she was stunned into silence by it: it was dark, terrible, a thing that might belong to the servants of the Lord of Night.

It was a costly mistake, that silence; the boy darted forward, the dagger swinging in a wide, a wild, arc.

But if she had lost song, she had not lost wit; her arm tightened around Yollana's midriff and she pulled the old woman back, unbalancing them both. A tree root caught the heel of her boot; she fell back and over it.

But the dagger had made its mark in the old woman's flesh; a dark, dark line appeared across the folds of her desert robes—robes that had been separated cleanly by the blade's edge.

Teresa looked up: the dagger was vanishing into the dusk, its shadow diminished by Yollana's blood. The boy looked at his hand, at the ghost of a blade that was already insubstantial. He howled in rage and fury.

All of the stories of the wolves that lived in the darkest and the deadliest of the Western forests came back to her then. She had come, in time, to understand that even the most simple of children's tales bore some element of older truth, and she wondered if the howling of those distant tales belonged, in the end, to men such as these.

But Yollana, wincing, pushed herself up from the dubious haven of the earth. Her hands were shaking, and her arms; her legs were buckled at an odd angle. She needed Teresa's help, and the Serra responded instantly, as if she were a puppet master in the silent plays of the High Court.

"Sergio, you . . . are . . . free," Yollana said.

He came at her then, at a run, his dark eyes growing until they consumed half his face. But his hands were ineffectual; they passed through her chest, her neck, her face. She flinched, though; the Serra Teresa felt the desert night in the passing arc of his arm.

The old man stood silent in the face of the boy's fury. He stared at the Matriarch. Of the blades she had faced, his was longest, darkest; it seemed to swallow all light until it re-

mained in his hands, the symbol of the absence of all things
that the Serra had ever valued.

She tried to find her song, and realized, belatedly, that although she had lost voice, lost strength, two others had not.

Kallandras of Senniel College came out of the tree's
shadows, and stood upon this slender, open road, his lips
moving in the fullness of his song.

And the Serra Diora di'Marano joined him, coming from
around the trunk of a different tree; she lifted her hands to
rough, linen hood, and drew it back from her delicate, white
face. Had she not had eyes that were perfect, lashes that, in
the dawn's gray, were full and thick, she might have been
one of the three, a ghost, an ethereal vengeance visited
upon the people who had dared to come to this place.

Yollana was bleeding. The blood was both dark and real;
it was warm to the touch, although it had dried to stickiness
where it nestled between the Serra's fingers. Had Yollana
been a young woman, the wounds would have been serious.
But the dagger that remained in her chest had missed its
mark; it did not reside in the heart's center. And the boy's
blow, a jagged cut, seemed clean.

If such a thing could deliver a clean blow.

The old man gazed at Yollana; he was far more restrained
than the boy had been, but more than that was hard to glean
from the emptiness of his eyes.

The Matriarch of Havalla looked up at him, met his gaze
as if it *were* a gaze. "Marius," she said, her voice as cold a
voice as Teresa had yet heard.

The old man nodded.

"Tell the bard to stop singing," Yollana whispered, a hint
of irritation breaking through the surface of her words.

"Is that wise?"

"No."

"I do not think you can survive another such blow,"
Teresa replied softly.

"If I'm lucky," Yollana replied, and again, some crack in

the facade of smooth voice let Teresa hear her terrible bitterness.

He moved forward; Yollana stood her ground, putting most of her weight against the Serra Teresa. "The road is closed," he said.

The Serra was surprised; the younger man had not spoken a word; the boy, few. But there was an intelligence in this last creature.

"The road," Yollana told him quietly, "is waiting. Step from it, Marius. Return to the winds, at last, if that is your desire."

"My desire," the old man replied coldly, "is simply this." He raised the blade.

And Kallandras of Senniel College stepped out into the road before him. He carried the Lady's weapons, one in either hand, and he crossed their blades before his chest, bowing briefly, offering this much respect.

"Have you not told them?" the dead man said.

"We do not speak of things Havallan to outsiders."

"Nor to insiders," was the cold reply.

She did not waver. "Not even to Havallans was it safe to speak of this."

"You trusted us so little?"

She was silent. The Serra Teresa arranged her weight with care, stepping to one side so that she might better judge her expression. To her surprise, she saw that the old woman's eyes were closed.

"I am . . . sorry . . . cousin. Believe that I have carried the weight of this. Believe that the stains have never left my hands." She lifted her head, opened her eyes, and met his again; his face was white. Dead.

Only the Serra Diora sang now, and her voice was soft. "Why?"

She flinched. "I had not thought . . . enough of you would remain . . . to ask that question."

"I am not Andreas. I am not Sergio."

"No. Of the three, you were—" She closed her eyes

again. "You were my cousin. The closest kin to the blood-line that could be spared."

"For this?"

"For just this." Her words were bitter. "Against this night, against this coming day."

"You saw it."

"Yes."

He drew closer. Kallandras let his arms fall to either side. "Tell him, Yollana."

"Bard," the Matriarch said, "stand aside. You cannot harm him, but if you do not step aside, he will harm you, and all of our losses will mean nothing."

"We cannot afford to lose you."

"You can," the old woman replied curtly. "There are other Havallans, and if I fall, my daughter will rise to take my place. We must reach Mancorvo, and we must reach Lamberto soon, or we will have lost the war."

Lord Celleriant stepped forward, and placed his hand upon the bard's shoulder, drawing him gently, and inexorably, to one side. "I understand now," he said softly. "She is right."

The Master Bard of Senniel College turned toward his companion.

"He can harm you. And although she does not understand it, you have the power to harm *him*. But that was not the price she chose. These three have hallowed the way; they have made it hers. But she must pay the price she bargained for, or we will be lost in the Deepings."

"The . . . Deepings?"

"The Dark Deepings," Celleriant replied. "The heart of the oldest forest in this world. I may find my way out, in time—but time is a luxury that you do not possess. Stay, and the forest will devour you." He turned to the Matriarch. Gazed at her, his brows furrowing slightly.

Kallandras bowed.

The old man drew closer to the Matriarch; the last obstacle had passed. "I could kill him," he told her coldly.

"Yes."

He lifted his dagger. "Havalla?"

"Tor Arkosa has risen," the Matriarch said simply. "And Tor Havalla must follow in the years to come. But there is no way home for you, Marius. You are doomed to the freedom of the dead. I had hoped—"

"That I would be Andreas, or Sergio, wild with anger and pain."

She was quiet.

"And I *am,* Matriarch."

He lifted the dagger and before she could speak another word, he plunged it, with care, into her left eye.

Teresa cried out in horror.

But the blade sank an inch, no more, into the curve of that eye.

Yollana did not grunt; did not cry out in pain. She stared at him now, from the eye that was left her, and in the growing light, Teresa saw the tears that trailed from it.

The dagger grew insubstantial as morning mist.

"You are free," Yollana whispered, choking on the words.

"And you," he said, with malice, "are not."

He stepped back, weaponless now; he had done his damage.

The boy was beside himself with rage. But the younger man watched in a cold silence, waiting until the oldest had joined their ranks.

As one, they lifted their arms, their fingers pointing toward her in accusation, and then the dawn came at last, and the rays of Lord's light that could penetrate the forest heights fell upon the ground, speckled and broken by branch and swaying leaf.

That light, scant and meager, took root. The footprints that had served as guide along this hidden path reached for it, broadening, lengthening, covered the surface of earth and the rounded curve of roots with a long, thin stream of light that stretched forward—and back—as far as the eye could see.

The Radann Marakas par el'Sol, absolutely silent until that moment, walked the path until it brought him to Yollana. He knelt before her, as supplicant, and offered her the open flat of two weaponless palms.

She understood what he offered, but lifted her left hand to her eye and turned away, forcing Teresa to turn as well if she wished to continue to bear the older woman's weight.

"I have healed the Arkosans in my time," he said softly, "and I have never spoken of what passed between us. There is a covenant between the healer and the healed that is not easily broken."

"Aye," she said, pressing palm into wound, accepting a blindness that would never pass. "But there are things that I would not burden anyone with, not even a man who has given his life in service to the Lord." She clutched her chest; blood trailed from her lips. "And there are things that cannot be healed," she continued quietly. "A price to be paid that cannot, in the end, be revoked.

"The road is open to us now. We must follow it while the light lasts; it will not last long, and if we are not quit of this forest before it fades, we will never leave it."

The Radann stood, brushing dirt from the front of his robe. He gazed at her a long time, and then said, "How did you quit it the last time? For you must have come here in order to . . . prepare the way."

"Do not ask," she said coldly. "Never ask. Never speak of what has happened this eve. Were it not for the war we have chosen—or the war that has chosen us—it would be my duty to close the way to you.

"Na'tere," she continued, her voice losing ice and strength.

"I am here, Yollana. We will walk this road together."

The Havallan Matriarch nodded, her good eye seeing the

road, and seeing it in a way that no one who had not made it could ever understand.

But she was tired, drained; she had no strength to spare Teresa the depths of her voice.

CHAPTER NINETEEN

MANY, many years had passed since Marakas par el'-Sol had made the journey through the Terrean of Mancorvo, and although it was held as truth that once a man entered the service of the Lord, he severed all family ties, Mancorvo was the Terrean through which he had journeyed most often at the side of Fredero kai el'Sol. It was in Mancorvo that he had been healed, had healed, had learned to see the Lord that Fredero saw.

He had thought to find it painful to return, for Fredero's ghost was strongest in the lands ruled by Lamberto. But the kai el'Sol had never made the passage through the forests that defined its Western border. No wise men did; no men of the Lord.

This was the accepted wisdom that governed Mancorvo, but Marakas par el'Sol had never understood the truth of that warning so clearly. He would not pass this way again, while he lived.

He saw dawn clearly when they reached the path's end, the unnatural light across the forest floor giving way, at last, to the shades and shadow of true day. Not since he had drawn *Verragar* for the first time had he felt the blessing of the Lord so keenly.

He bowed his head a moment; it was a gesture of respect,

as much of an obeisance as one could make to the Lord in the lands of the sun.

He was accompanied by the Serra Diora di'Marano and her seraf; Stavos had fallen behind, had taken up his quiet position beside the Matriarch of Havalla. He did not touch her—in Marakas' estimation, he did not dare—but hovered quietly by her side, as if he, younger in years, were father, uncle, or brother. The Arkosans and the Havallans were not friends. Although it was true that the Voyani claimed no home, they often chose to wander within the boundaries of a particular Terrean.

Arkosa had claimed Averda; Havalla had claimed Mancorvo. Although they traveled the merchant roads openly between these two places, they seldom met, and never as friends. But a bond had grown between the Arkosan and the Havallan Matriarch. A bond and a debt.

The Voyani were Southern in at least this: they accrued debt cautiously, and they repaid it—as they were able—in full. And so he labored, in silence, his presence almost ignored.

The Serra Teresa di'Marano was crutch and cane; she spoke often to the Matriarch, and the Matriarch responded. It was the Serra Teresa—if she could be called that, robed as Voyani, and darkened even now by exposure to sun and wind—who fashioned a patch for the old woman's lost eye; the Serra Teresa who placed it gently across her brow. The Matriarch allowed this.

And he, man of the Lord, noticed. He had the excuse of observing a person of power—for no one who holds power is beneath the attention of the Radann—but in truth, it was not power which drew him, not a desire to observe one who might be, might yet be, enemy. Instead, he felt pity, and the painful desire to aid.

His hands ached with it, as they had not done in years: healing denied.

The Serra Diora di'Marano glanced up at his face, and then reached out gently to touch his sleeve. Surprised, he

turned to face her, his chin lowering, his gaze falling. She
was delicate, diminutive; her height forced his gaze down.

"Serra Diora?"

"We are in Mancorvo."

Not a question. But he nodded quietly.

"Do you know where we are?"

"No."

"A pity. For I believe that we have been seen."

He lifted his head, turning toward the expanse of flat
land, green and broken by rows of trees that spoke not of
forest but of windbreaks. In the distance, he could make out
a stretch of flat dirt that must be road, and upon that road,
dust drifted up in a great cloud.

"We have been seen," Kallandras of Senniel agreed quietly. "Celleriant?"

"There are twenty riders," the Arianni lord replied softly.
He turned, then, and looked not toward the growing cloud
of dust, but rather, toward the only mounted rider in their
group: Jewel ATerafin and the child she held so carefully.

"ATerafin," Kallandras said quietly. "Perhaps it would be
wisest if you dismounted."

Avandar said nothing, but he came at once to her side and
offered her a hand. The gesture was, on the surface, the perfect example of the domicis art, but beneath the polish of
servitude lay the force of command. And there was only
one circumstance in which he offered—which he dared to
offer—command. She hesitated a moment, and he lifted a
brow.

"Ariel," she said quietly.

He nodded. The girl was awake, but barely, and she stiffened the moment Jewel handed her to Avandar. "It's all
right, Ariel," she whispered quietly. "He's a friend."

The girl's eyes were wide and dark.

"And he serves me. He is . . . like the stag. He will carry
you, and he will allow nothing to reach you if it means you

harm. Trust him," she added, without much hope. "Trust him as much as you trust me."

And then, before she could think, she added, "Not even Lord Isladar could defeat Avandar in battle."

The girl's eyes grew wide a moment, and then she nodded and turned away, burying her face against the domicis' chest.

He raised a brow above the tangle of her hair, but said nothing.

What would you have of me, Jewel? The stag's voice was regal. Calm.

Take Celleriant, she told him quietly. *Take him, and go.*

She thought he might refuse.

"I do not like this," Lord Celleriant said quietly, as he watched Jewel ATerafin dismount.

Kallandras smiled.

"The *Kialli* are abroad. Your human armies are scattered, and it is not easy to determine which is friend and which is foe."

Again, the bard smiled, but he offered no words.

"I do not like to leave you."

"Nor I, you. I think I will find no better comrade in arms in the breadth of the Dominion. But you—and the Winter King—are a part of a different world, and we are not yet ready to declare ourselves."

"I am capable of bearing a lesser glamour."

Kallandras raised a brow. "You are capable of donning the appearance of mortality, but when you move, when you speak, when you walk, you deny its truth. I have never seen you sleep. I have seldom seen you eat."

Lord Celleriant shrugged. "I require less of the earth than you and your kind."

"Indeed." He paused. Spoke again, privately.

Brother, when you are needed, I will call. You will know when to come.

It was not to Celleriant's liking.

"Remember," Kallandras said softly, "who you must serve. The ATerafin has made her decision, and it is not without merit."

"I have served the White Lady for all of my life," Lord Celleriant said quietly, "and she would never have divested herself of lords of power in enemy lands."

"She desires—is capable of—no subtlety. Jewel ATerafin has often been accused of the same, but she understands what is at risk in a way that you, my friend, cannot."

"I understand the *Kialli*. I understand the Lord they serve."

"And if our battle was in the Northern Wastes, you would be with us." Kallandras bowed then, with perfect, fluid grace, as the Winter King joined him.

"We will meet again," Kallandras said quietly. "The war has not yet begun in earnest."

"I have no desire to come late to that field," Celleriant said. He had sheathed his blade, and did not now condescend to draw it.

"And I," Kallandras replied, with more gravity, "have no desire to come to that field at all." He bowed.

Watched as the Arianni lord and the Winter King retreated into the outskirts of the forest.

The Serra Diora di'Marano had been raised in the High Courts. It had never been the intent of her father that she become bride to the kai Leonne, but he had had his pride; if she was never to be wife to a Tyr, she was to be—in all ways—the equal to the women who *would* occupy that position. She sang, of course, but she sang *well*; she read, and she could write in a hand as perfect and delicate as the Tyr'agar's Serra. She could serve sweet water and wine, could arrange flowers, hangings, the fall of chains of gold; she could make a room that was empty an elegant, even an opulent, place simply by becoming some part of its center.

And she could recognize, at a distance, the golden glint

of a half circle, six distinct rays rising above the sword that formed its horizon: the standard of a Tor'agar.

At her side, the Radann par el'Sol stiffened. His hand fell to his blade, but he was cautious enough not to draw it; twenty mounted men were not wisely antagonized before one knew their intent. Or perhaps even after.

As Serra, the option to draw such a weapon had never been granted her. She had a dagger, of course, but daggers in the hands of Serras were seldom considered weapons; they were defense of a last resort, and turned as easily inward as out.

She did not draw hers. Instead, she lifted hand, pulled hood from her face, touched the strands of hair that now hung there, untended by seraf, unadorned by jade or pearl, by flower or comb. Her clothing was almost inexcusable; she felt a pang as she looked at the heavy robes and saw them as they would be seen by the men who now approached on horseback: dusty, dark with the dirt of forest travel, of desert travel, of too little water.

She felt a moment's panic; her palm still bore a faint, red mark—a blemish made more obvious by the pale, perfect lines of a Serra's skin.

The fear—one she had not felt since she had stood at the heights of the Sen tower in the Tor Arkosa—told her that she had, at last, come home. It settled about her, familiar, unwanted.

It must have shown. It must have, because the Radann par el'Sol turned to her at that moment and lowered his head.

"I am sworn to defend you," he said quietly.

She nodded.

She nodded, and she felt grateful, for she had no other family here; she was a woman, without cerdan, without brother or father—and such women's honor lay at the mercy of the men they encountered.

Margret would have been angry.

She bowed her head, thinking it, knowing it for truth, and

finding in that truth the strangest of comforts. Margret *would* be angry, when she learned of it.

As the horses drew closer, the standard grew clearer. The six rays were unmistakable; the crescent sword the perfect horizon for the embroidered sun, and beneath it, in orange, red, and gold, a shield of fire.

The clan Clemente.

"The Tor'agar has taken to the road," the Radann par el'-Sol said softly.

She nodded. But she did not speak; she had passed the boundary of the darkest of forests, and that border, paid for by the blood of the Havallan Matriarch, had been closed against them. There was only one way, and that, forward.

She was once again a Serra of the clan Marano.

Garbed in desert robe or not, she knelt in the tall grass, and her seraf, her perfect seraf, came to stand by her side, choosing, carefully, where he might best plant his feet to protect her from the sun's glare.

No one joined her; Jewel ATerafin did not bow, and the Havallan Matriarch, supported by Ona Teresa, stayed her ground with a bitter twist of her lip. The child that had come to them, like ghost or doom, in the heart of desert night, was held fast in the arms of the domicis; Diora was alone upon the ground, knees bent in a familiar posture of obeisance.

But because she was gifted—and cursed—she heard the sharp intake of the Radann's breath. She did not glance up to see his hand tighten about his blade; it would not be seemly, and besides, she had a good view of the feet that trampled the slender stalks of dry grass, and saw that he had planted them firmly apart in a sword stance.

Such a stance would not be lost upon the Tor'agar.

The horses came to a halt; she heard their hooves slow and become silent. A moment passed; the sound of men's boots were less thunderous, and more dangerous, when they came. The Radann Marakas par el'Sol did not move; his shadow joined Ramdan's as the Tor'agar's men made

their way across the wilderness of land that had not yet
been cleared or tilled.

She had a wild, terrible urge to look up.

Could remember the time she had sat thus, in a dark, cold
desert night, when Adam of the Arkosa Voyani had come
bearing the instrument of Kallandras of Senniel College—
a gift, to her, that had almost cost him his life, and that had,
in the end, cost him the only family he had.

Could even she be changed in so short a time? Could she
be ruined, destroyed by the freedom and the conflict in the
desert's heart, her own laid bare?

No.

No. She was Serra Diora di'Marano. She understood
duty.

But it was hard, much harder than she had expected it
would be, to sit in silence, head bowed. To be *perfect*.

She did not pray to the Lady for strength or guidance; the
Lord reigned. Instead, she waited, her hands palm down in
the fold of her lap. Palm down, so that the imperfection
might be hidden, that it not trouble the sight of men.

Ramdan bent, still shielding her from sun's rays by the
breadth of his shoulders, his back. In his hands, pulled from
the robes of the Voyani desert, he held a simple fan. Painted
silk, spread by straight, slender jade spokes. She took it as
if it were an anchor; raised it in gratitude and hid her face.

"Strangers," a man said. She heard worry in his voice,
the vague edge of fear, the certainty of duty. "You have entered, without permission, the lands of the Tor'agar
Alessandro kai di'Clemente.

"Identify yourselves, and state your business clearly."

Swords were drawn. Clemente swords.

"I am the Radann Marakas par el'Sol, and these, my
companions, have come to your Tor's lands in haste. Accept
our apologies for the unsuitability of our dress and our
manner; we have been on the road these past weeks, and we
have seen little in the way of hospitality."

"You traveled the roads?" Disbelief in that voice. Suspicion.

"No," the Radann said quietly. "We traveled through the forests at the border's edge."

"The forest?"

"Indeed."

The Serra waited. Silence followed the single word; she wondered if the man would challenge the Radann's words. But the Radann par el'Sol was granted, by right, the symbol of the sun ascendant, and if it did not adorn his chest in the open light, his name carried its weight.

"Radann par el'Sol," the man said. His armor spoke as he bowed; she heard it clearly, the clink of metal against metal, the chaffing of surcoat. In the Southern Terreans, armor was rare. "We . . . did not expect . . . a man of your import. Your companions?"

"I will speak for them," he replied evenly.

"Then speak," a new voice said. A strong voice. Not, the Serra Diora thought, a friendly one. But this man spoke with the certainty of power: this man was the Tor'agar.

"Kai Clemente," the Radann said. "My companions are varied, but as you can clearly see, they are not a band of war."

"Give me their names, par el'Sol, and let me judge their worth for myself."

The silence was stiff. But the command in the words was almost laced with threat. Diora lifted her face, protected now by folds of translucent silk, her eyes seeing between the painted petals of lilies.

She saw, veiled in gauze, a man dressed in armor, his coat adorned with the full symbol of the rising sun, its six rays reaching to throat and shoulders as they caught light, glittering. His hair was dark; he wore a scant beard. His eyes, she thought, were dark as well, but the fan's folds hid their color, and she did not dare to lower it; he was not a man given to missing even the slightest of gestures.

"Very well, Tor'agar," the Radann replied. He turned and bowed to Yollana, the Matriarch of Havalla.

The old woman's nod was visible.

"May I present the Matriarch of the Havalla Voyani," Marakas said gravely, "and her cousin, Teresa."

The Tor'agar stiffened slightly. That he did this much showed the depth of his surprise; he was Court trained, after all. After a marked hesitation, he lowered his head. No other courtesy was demanded of a clansman of his rank; indeed, not even that much was necessary. But etiquette and prudence often diverged, and he had chosen prudence.

It spoke well of him, if nothing else did.

"The others?"

Again, the Radann par el'Sol turned, and again, he received a slight nod.

"Kallandras of Senniel College. He is . . . of the North."

"So it would seem."

"He travels with Jewel ATerafin."

"ATerafin? If I am not mistaken Terafin is one of The Ten Houses that have prominence in the Empire."

"Indeed, Tor'agar."

"The man?"

"Her domicis."

"I am not familiar with the term."

"There are no serafs in the North," the Radann replied evenly. "But there are those who choose—free of constraint—to serve. He is one."

"I doubt that, par el'Sol. I doubt that highly." The Tor'agar held the words for just a second longer than necessary, and then added, "Although it is clear that the claim is his, and not yours. And the other man is also Havallan?"

"He is Arkosan."

"Arkosan?"

"Even so."

The men who had ridden at the side of the Tor'agar were silent, but beyond them, their voices clear to Diora's strange gift, the others spoke. They gestured toward the forest, the forest heart, the forest height.

"It seems that old tales have some truth in them after all," the Tor'agar said. "But I notice that you have failed to introduce the last member of your party." And he stepped forward, into the shadows cast by the bower of ancient branches.

Marakas par el'Sol moved as well, interposing himself—with far less courtly grace—between the Tor'agar and the Serra Diora. His hand was on his sword, and Diora thought—for just a moment—that he might draw it. She held her breath; contained it in the same way she contained all motion. Remembering, now, how to wait.

Marakas par el'Sol glanced toward her; met the sheen of fan, the shadow of seraf. "Serra," he said quietly, "it would honor us both greatly if you chose to grace us with your presence."

As his words died into silence, the Serra bent slowly and delicately toward the earth, aware that there was no mat against which to place her forehead. Her hair brushed the undergrowth, revealing the curve of the back of her unadorned neck.

Ramdan was at her side in an instant, offering her a hand with which to steady herself. It was unnecessary; she had no need of his aid. But it was also necessary, for he showed himself to be a seraf of breeding and refinement, and by so doing, showed that the woman who owned his name was worthy of note.

The Serra Diora di'Marano rose quietly, unfolding as delicately as she had unfolded the fan, her movements both conscious and unconscious. The line of her shoulders both rose and fell, lengthening her neck, accentuating the perfect line of a back hidden by folds of stiff desert cloth.

Ser Alessandro kai di'Clemente met her gaze, his eyes widening as he recognized her exposed face. He gestured sharply, and his Toran fell back a step.

"I understand," he said softly, "why you chose to forgo the open road, par el'Sol."

"Will you allow us to pass, kai Clemente?"

"That is a complicated question," the Tor'agar replied, his gaze fixed upon the face of the Flower of the Dominion. "But you have been on a dark road, and you must be in need of rest and refreshment. Allow me to offer you the hospitality of my domis. It would be my honor to have such noteworthy guests."

She heard all the words that he did not choose to speak. None of them brooked refusal.

The Radann Marakas par el'Sol was no fool. "The honor," he said, bowing, "is ours."

The Tor'agar nodded. And then he bowed to the Serra Diora di'Marano, and gently offered her his hand.

If the cerdan were ill pleased at being unhorsed, they did not show it. Ser Alessandro offered horse to Yollana of Havalla and her companion; he offered horse to Jewel ATerafin; he offered horse to Kallandras of Senniel College, and to the Radann par el'Sol.

But he paused a moment, the line of his lips shifting as Avandar approached the horse upon which the Northern ATerafin woman sat so awkwardly. They spoke quietly, and he helped the child he bore into the saddle; the woman enfolded her in arms that were a shade too stiff. "You failed to introduce the child." He spoke quietly.

"We found her wandering the road in Raverra. Her parents are dead," the Radann replied. Again, his hand found the hilt of his sword.

"And you travel with her?" Ser Alessandro smiled; the smile was as sharp as sword's edge. "You have always been an unusual servant of the Lord, par el'Sol. It seems that the fate of the helpless and the barely free continue to be of concern to you. I am impressed. But the Lord's steel must hide beneath the gentleness of your demeanor. I would not have guessed, years ago, that you would have risen to the rank you now hold."

"The ATerafin has chosen to extend the protection of her House to the child; she eats little, and she interferes with nothing."

"I see. She is not a seraf?"

"She bears no brand."

"Good." He placed foot in the stirrup of one of Mancorvo's finest horses; a great, black beast with gold markings. "We must ride in haste," he said quietly. "Word will travel."

Marakas par el'Sol nodded. "You travel in numbers."

"Indeed. There are bandits upon the roads, and worse." His smile was grim. "Twenty mounted men might give pause to even the most foolhardy of outlaws."

The dwelling of the Tor'agar of Clemente was not so grand a dwelling as Marakas might have expected, for the lands in Mancorvo were rich. Yet if it was not grand, it was deceptive in its simplicity; it was built of stone, and the gates, great, rolling walls, were of steel and wood. Men stood upon the curtain walls that girded the city; men armed with spears and, to Marakas' great surprise, bows.

Ser Alessandro noted his surprise with an ironic smile. "We have learned that not everything that comes out of the North is evil."

"It is said that weapons of distance breed poor warriors."

"Indeed, I have heard it said," the kai Clemente replied. "If you are unfortunate, you will judge for yourself the truth of that adage."

Radann Marakas par el'Sol stilled a moment. "You are at war?"

"We are Mancorvan, but we do not border Averda. We are not yet at war, but we are not unprepared for it, as you have seen."

"The armies—"

"There are guests in great number along the Southern

border of the Terrean," the kai Clemente replied evenly. "The Southern border, and the Eastern one."

The lands claimed by the clan Clemente were neither.

"What word, Tor'agar, has come from the South?"

"Do you not know? For it is said that the Radann kai el'-Sol himself rides at the behest of the Tyr'agar."

Marakas par el'Sol stiffened slightly. But he did not deny the truth of those words. "The Radann are not Widan; what message travels, travels by roads that are easily seen by men."

"You were not sent."

It was not a question.

The Tor'agar turned a moment to gaze upon the Serra Diora di'Marano. "And you have come with a small party, indeed, to guard such a treasure. Come, par el'Sol. I was present at the Lake of the Tor Leonne at the culmination of the Festival of the Lord. I saw the hands of the Flower of the Dominion draw, from the waters of the Tor Leonne, the Sun Sword. I saw the ashes of the kai el'Sol scattered by the winds. I heard her plea, and I was not . . . unmoved . . . by its strength." His eyes narrowed. "But we had no word that she, jewel to crown, was no longer upon the plateau.

"Her presence here explains much."

Marakas par el'Sol offered no further words; none were wanting, and he was learned enough to keep his own counsel.

"My Toran will see to our horses," Ser Alessandro said, "and I myself will lead you to the rooms you will occupy for your visit."

He spoke to his men; the Toran came at once and took the bridles of the Mancorvan horses, and the horses, light-footed and ill-pleased to be so confined, went quietly at their command. He felt a twinge of envy; the horses of Mancorvo were indeed as fine as any in the Dominion, and although Marakas came from the Southern Terreans, he was the Lord's man: he understood their value.

But he did not understand their lord, and he was troubled.

Unbidden, memory returned.

The first time he had seen this man, and the last, Ser Alessandro had been the par, not the kai, and he had closed the eyes of a fallen friend in the aftermath of the kai el'Sol's bitter judgment. His *just* judgment.

He had also taken the unblooded blade of the son of the Tor'agnate of clan Manelo, and cut his own arm, so that the Tor'agnate might see his son's blade, and know that he had not died completely unmanned.

Ser Alessandro had offered no threat, no enmity, to Fredero kai el'Sol—but that was simple prudence, for Fredero was younger brother to Mareo kai di'Lamberto, the Tyr'agnate who claimed rulership of the Terrean of Mancorvo.

As if he were privy to that memory, Ser Alessandro turned. "Yes," he said softly, "I remember our first encounter. And I remember what occurred after the departure of the Radann kai el'Sol. The Tor'agnate, Ser Amando kai di'Manelo, was ill-pleased by the death of his son. Had the man who killed him not been Radann, there would be blood feud between their clans that might last generations."

"The Radann claim no kin-ties."

"Indeed. And it is folly to war against the Lord. Ser Franko chose his weapon and his course, and he suffered the Lord's judgment."

The words were smooth as stone; cool as stone, and just as hard.

"He was my cousin," Ser Alessandro added. "And almost brother to me."

Marakas par el'Sol closed his eyes as the gates of the city of Sarel rolled shut at their backs.

"I do not like it," Yollana said quietly, in the confines of a finely appointed room. There were no windows, although the edifice itself was of stone, and allowed them. The Havallan Matriarch, and her "kin" had been given quarters that suited the needs of Serras, and Yollana was no Serra, to be comforted by pretty, gleaming planks of wood, by jade-colored mats, by flat tables adorned with bowls and the pink blossoms of the trees of the Northern Terreans. Nor was she impressed by the painted fans that adorned the walls, by the translucent paper that, nestled in wooden lattice, was the only door to this half prison.

No open road here. No *Voyanne*.

But she was tired, and her injuries were grave; although she spoke her mind, as was her wont, her voice was weak. The Serra Teresa did not leave her side. Clothed as Voyani, darkened by more exposure to the Lord's gaze than she had had in the whole of her life at Court, she served as seraf, the grace of her movements uninhibited by the loss of the rank she had enjoyed as the unmarried sister of a man who served the Lambertan Tyr.

"What of the kai Clemente?" Yollana asked, waving away the slender bowl with its clear, sweet water. "Will he hinder us, Teresa? Does he mean us harm?"

Teresa was silent a moment; the water that would not be imbibed, she put to use cleansing the wounds that Yollana had taken at the hands of the dead. Those wounds were dark and ugly, but none so disturbing as the one that had robbed her of sight.

"He is not our friend," she said at last, when Yollana stilled enough to allow the Serra to remove the eye patch and treat what was left of the eye. "But I do not believe he knows, himself, what he intends for us."

Yollana closed her good eye. "And if he intends us ill?"

"There is little that we can do. But I think he will be cautious. He will not hold you, Yollana; he is prudent enough not to seek the enmity of the Havalla Voyani, not when he is so obviously prepared for war."

The old woman snorted. "Where is my pipe?"

"Here."

"Fill it, then," she said gruffly. "And get me some pillows. This place is too soft and too empty."

Teresa's smile was gentle. She was accustomed to com-

mand and dictate, and very few of those commands had
come so gracelessly into her presence. But she had obeyed
few as willingly as she obeyed this woman's. She filled the
bowl of Yollana's pipe. "There is no fire here," she said.

"I am capable of lighting a pipe," the old woman replied.
But her hands shook as she lifted it. "Na'tere, what will you
do?"

"What I have always done," was the serene reply.

"And that?"

"What is necessary, Matriarch. No less than that, and
possibly no more. If we must leave, we will leave; there is
not a force in this world that could contain Kallandras of
Senniel College if he chooses to speak, and if he bids the
gates open, they will open."

"Is he proof against arrows?"

"I do not know. But if any man is, I would say it is he.
He is blessed by the Lady."

"Aye, and cursed by her."

The Serra frowned.

But Yollana would say no more of the bard. Instead, she
said, "Where is your niece?"

To the Serra Diora di'Marano, grander rooms were offered. The light that had been denied the rest of her companions was offered to her; she was granted high windows,
and a seat of stone by their edge. But the seat itself was cool
in the open breeze, and the window looked down from a
height.

She had lived her life in Marano and in the Tor Leonne,
and had been surrounded, always, by things of beauty and
grace; in this room, with its vast ceilings, she found little
that was familiar. The floors gleamed, flat and new; the
walls were adorned with hangings, gold embroidered
everywhere above the standard of the clan Clemente.

But this was not the harem's heart; she was certain of it.
There was one door, and it, hinged and wooden; there were
no sliding screens, no slender halls, no passage to and from

the rooms of the Serra of the Tor'agar and her wives. No; these were men's rooms, and to her surprise, she found that she missed the orderly maze that lay at the heart of any harem in which she had dwelled, however briefly.

But few were the men who thought their wives in need of protection within their own strongholds; such doors as these were made for one purpose, and one alone: to keep intruders out.

Or to keep guests in.

Ramdan was by her side; the Tor'agar had, as was customary, failed to notice the seraf's perfect presence. But to Ramdan, silk saris had been offered, and fans that were larger and more valuable than the simple fan he had carried in the folds of his desert robes.

Those robes had also been replaced; he wore instead the loose, wide legs of seraf pants, the long, wide sleeves of silk that denoted his value. His hair had been cleaned and drawn back across the lines of his silent face; his hands had been washed. The dust of the road no longer troubled or disturbed him: he looked every inch the man that she had known for the whole of her life.

He had helped her dress; had taken from her the robes that had served her so well in the Sea of Sorrows. But he had not allowed those robes to be carried away; he had seen to their cleaning himself, and had seen to their care. She wondered if she would ever have cause to wear them again, and was not certain, now that she felt the softness of silk, saw the brilliance of blue and white, of silver and gold, that she desired to do so.

And yet there was a freedom in the anonymity and necessity of those robes that she had never otherwise known. She took the fan that Ramdan offered; she allowed him to brush out the strands of her gleaming hair. It had been a long, long time since she had had the luxury to see it thus tended.

When he was finished, he bound it carefully in combs of gold and jade; her combs. She had never asked him what he had chosen to take with him when he had decided to flee the Tor Leonne in the service of Ona Teresa. She never would; the bounty of the generosity of his choice was like a small miracle and she did not wish to shatter the delicacy of that illusion.

But she was fully clothed, fully prepared, when the knock at the door came. It was dull, that knock; heavy and thunderous, a plodding sound. Bells, gongs, things that were musical, had called her attention in the High Courts. Still, she straightened at the sound of the door, arranging herself with care upon the thick mats laid out before the room's single table.

The hinges creaked as the door swung wide. It was not a pleasant sound.

She bowed her head, listening; a single set of steps approached her, and it was mercifully free from the sound of metal.

"Serra, I would be honored by your company, if you would grant me that privilege."

She looked up then, lowering the fan to expose her eyes.

The Tor'agar stood just in front of the open door. He did not seek to close it, and beyond the thick frame, she could see the shadows of Toran reflected in the gleam of wooden floor.

She understood, then, that he granted her as much respect as he could, given that she had no cerdan, and no brother or father who might otherwise protect her. And she bowed her head, acknowledging both her helplessness and her debt.

"Accept my apologies for the roughness of your surroundings. I cannot offer you rooms in my harem; you travel without kin, and without cerdan of your own, and it would bring no honor upon you."

She said nothing.

"Speak," he said quietly, "if it pleases you. And speak freely; I will take no offense, and hope to offer none."

"Among my companions, the Radann Marakas par el'Sol

has offered his protection in the stead of my clan, and I have accepted it."

"The men of the Lord are not often given to the protection of Serras," he replied gravely. "Such matters, to men who have no wives, no mothers, no sisters, are often beneath notice."

"The oath of a Radann is never beneath notice, be that oath given to one as humble as I."

He raised a brow. "Perhaps."

He knelt on the opposite side of the table, and clapped his hands.

Serafs entered the room at once; they carried wine, water, and food. The food itself was spare; fruits from the trees of the North, soft bread.

"I must ask you, Serra Diora, how you came to travel to Mancorvo."

Very delicately, and with great care, she poured wine for the Tor'agar; when he lifted his goblet, she poured for herself, but she poured little and she drank less.

"I am not captive," she said softly. "I do not know how quickly word travels, but at the Festival of the Moon, the Tor Leonne was . . . besieged . . . by strangeness, and many, many people were ordered to flee."

"And you?"

"I was offered the safety of flight," she said, her voice gentle, musical, her words paced and imbued with a lightness and grace that had been absent from them for long enough they felt strange. "And I accepted what was offered; I did not know what would come of the night, and it seemed the Lady guided my steps."

"A prudent answer. I expect no less. But I am not unaware that it lacks . . . content."

She bowed her head at once, assuming the submissive posture. But she did not touch ground with her forehead.

"You travel with strange companions," he said, accepting the apology. "The Matriarch of Havalla. A Northern bard. A woman who is of import in the Empire. The Radann par el'Sol. Not even in stories and the idle whim of poor poets does such a fellowship often gather."

She was already weary of the interview, of the games inherent in the words. *Margret,* she thought, with a pang, *you have caused me some injury. It is not so easy to sing in a cage as it once was.*

But necessary. Very necessary.

"Where do you travel, Serra?"

"I think the Radann par el'Sol might better to be able to answer your question."

"He serves a kai whose loyalties seem well known," the Tor'agar replied. His voice had cooled, but he was not yet angered; she had said nothing that was improper. "Yet he is here, not at the side of Peder kai el'Sol, and more significantly, you are here." He lifted the goblet and drank slowly, his eyes never leaving her face. "And it is not my guess that the Tyr'agar would willingly surrender you to any other man. You are of import in this war, and he is no fool; he is well aware of it."

"I am not a warrior," she said quietly, as if it were not self-evident. "And of war, I cannot speak."

"Indeed, it is not of war that I have asked you to speak; I merely seek to better discern your intention."

"I would travel," she said quietly, "to my father's kai."

It was not the truth, but she lent it the force of her gift, honeying the stark words with the patina of honesty.

"Ser Sendari has sent you to Adano?"

"He is aware that I travel North," she replied.

"Is he not the closest and most trusted adviser to the Tyr'agar?"

She said, simply, "I do not know. I am not a part of the counsel the Tyr'agar chooses to keep."

"And yet it is said that Ser Sendari almost doomed his clan by refusing to grant your hand to the kai Leonne. It is just possible that he might see this as wise." He smiled.

The smile did not touch his eyes, and it did not enter his words.

"If," he continued, "Ser Sendari *di'Sendari* thought there was no danger of war in the Terrean. And I do not think that even he could be so . . . optimistic. Come, Serra. I was witness to your act after the death of the kai el'Sol, and I ask you again: What is your intention?"

"Let me first ask, if I may be so unforgivably bold, Tor'agar, the same question."

"You are indeed bold," he replied, but this time he did smile. A dangerous smile, but one that transformed his face, lending it a beauty that had been absent. "It amuses me. It is rare.

"I do not know what you have heard; given that you came to us from the shrouded hills of the dark forest, I cannot say for certain that you have heard much. The armies of the Tyr'agar have gathered. He has at his command the whole of the First and the Second army. The Third is scattered, and although some part of it has been gathered in his service, it has been left at the border. I do not believe he trusts the loyalty of those men; they served General Baredan di'Navarre, and rumor indicates that the General might still live.

"But it is clear that the Lambertan Tyr has no love of the Tyr'agar. Clear, as well, that he has less love of the Averdan Tyr. What is not clear—to many—is what will happen to Mancorvo. War is almost upon us, and many who now govern lands within Mancorvo believe that should a change of rulers be fated, they might preserve their clans—and their power—should they choose to ally themselves with the Tyr'agar."

And are you such a man? She did not ask.

"Word has reached Clemente that some measure of alliance was offered to Ser Mareo kai di'Lamberto. No word has reached Clemente of his response. But while many see the Lambertan Tyr as hopelessly honor bound, I have seen him in battle, and I have seen him in the political arena. If he is bound by honor, it does not make him helpless; he is canny."

"What would you have of me, Ser Alessandro?"

"The truth," he replied.

"I hold the Tyr'agnate of Mancorvo in the highest regard," she said softly, "and I owe a debt that no Serra could possibly hope to repay to the man who was once his brother."

He stiffened. "I owe that man a different debt," he said at last, coldly. Anger, there. A deep anger.

"The winds will make him pay it," she replied. "Or the Lady, if any hope of the Lady's mercy is true. He is beyond approach or reproach now."

"Indeed. But he dared much in this Terrean because he trusted the rulership of his brother."

"The Radann claim no family ties."

"Also true. And it was not family that he trusted; it was its sense of honor and justice. But such ties as exist among those born to Lamberto are at least as strong as blood; he disavowed the kinship that was obvious, but he could never disavow what he *was*."

"Would you see the Lambertans fail, then?"

"In truth, Serra Diora, it would not ill-please me."

She was silent.

"But I have always been pragmatic. Had the Tyr'agar intended to ally with Mancorvo, he would not now have his men stationed in the South and the East. If I were to guess, I would say that he originally offered some part of Mancorvo, and some part of Averda, to the Tyrs of Oerta and Sorgassa in return for their support. Any of the four Tyrs could choose to claim the Tor Leonne; it is clear that no one of them has, and it would take much support for the par of a lesser clan to do so. His offer to the Tyr'agnate of Mancorvo, while more recent, may change the balance of this alliance. But much depends on the reply that the Tyr will tender.

"Lorenza and Garrardi are therefore of import to the Tyr'agar, and against their support, a clan of Clemente's rank—and I labor under few illusions—is of little consequence. But not all that is of consequence is decided by either men, horses, or wealth. The more powerful of the clans will stand by Lamberto, for their own purpose. But a clan of little note? Such a clan might be left to rule as it has ruled for a century, if it offers its allegiance to another Tyr.

"You would be a gift," he added softly. "A gift and a sign of good faith, should I choose to return you to him."

CHAPTER TWENTY

SERRA Teresa.
  Kallandras.
  You are well?

We are both well. Yollana is . . . injured. Were it not for the cost to him, I would have her accept the offer of the Radann par el'Sol. The loss of her left eye . . . She turned to look at the older woman; sleep had come, and in its wake, the rigid lines of indifference had smoothed themselves into wrinkles and crevices. The weight of age descended with that sleep, and Teresa thought that waking would not lessen its burden.

But old, she was beautiful; she had done much in the name of duty, and would do much, much more if she survived. It was a harsh beauty, perhaps a Southern beauty, and there was no softness in it.

Where are you? she asked softly.

I have been given quarters adjacent to the Radann par el'Sol's. I believe we are in the Northern wing of the building; we have been given no windows, and cerdan patrol the halls with almost annoying frequency.

There are no cerdan here.

Ah. The Tor'agar does not wish to invoke the wrath of Havalla. He has some wisdom. Where is Diora?

I am not certain.

Kallandras' voice fell silent. She waited, but it did not return. Instead, she heard the sliding of screens, and saw that a young seraf—a girl barely of age—knelt beyond the grooved wood, her dark hair falling across bent shoulders.

She was not perfect; her posture was a shade too awkward, and her knees too thick to support it for long.

But she lifted her face, and the Serra saw it was a sweet face, a gentle one, rounded and curved with the chubbiness of indulged childhood. Whoever the Tor'agar's wife was, she was obviously not a harsh mistress.

The girl waited a moment in a growing, awkward silence, and Teresa realized that the seraf did not know how to address either of the guests. She could not use the honorific Serra, for it was known that the Voyani took ill to the titles of the clansmen, but robbed of that title, the child had no other to offer.

Poorly trained, indeed. And yet Teresa felt little contempt for the quality of her training; the hesitancy, marked and easily seen, was somehow endearing. *I have been on the road too long,* she thought critically.

"Child," she said. "Have you come with a message from the Tor'agar?"

"Oh, no," the girl responded quickly. "I have come from Serra Celina en'Clemente. She bids me offer you wine and fruit, if you will have it."

"We would be grateful for any such sustenance; we have come late from the road, and we are weary." It was entirely untrue; Yollana would be deeply annoyed to be indebted in even this small a fashion. But the Matriarch slept, and the Serra Teresa reigned for the moment.

"The Serra also wishes me to say that baths have been drawn, with hot water, if you desire it."

Teresa frowned. "My companion, as you see, is much exhausted from our travels."

The girl's eyes looked toward Yollana and froze there. The wounds had bled through their bindings.

"But tell your mistress that we are greatly honored by the offer of the bath, and if she would not feel insulted, I, at least would be grateful to accept the kindness of that offer."

The girl nodded at once, falling into the subservient posture. She could reach the floor with her head by rounding the curve of her spine, and only by so doing. Again, Teresa wondered at the Serra who had trained her, and her curiosity was intense. The Tor'agar did not seem a man prone to accept a lesser Serra as his wife.

The doors slid shut.

"I heard all of it," Yollana snapped, but only when the sound of footfalls had receded into silence.

"My apologies, Matriarch. But there is no way, with grace, to refuse the offer of the Serra Celina en'Clemente."

"And you don't want to, do you?"

Teresa said nothing.

"You want to go and bathe and sit in the heart of a harem. You want to feel at home."

"I will never be at home again in the heart of any harem," Teresa replied. She let the truth seep to the surface of her perfect words. "But I am curious. And it may be that we might gain information—and some small advantage—from such a meeting."

"Small advantage indeed. The women of the clans have no teeth and no claws; they exist at the whim of their husbands."

"That is the law," the Serra Teresa replied, and this time she offered the Havallan Matriarch the most perfect of her smiles. "But the Serra Diora di'Marano is such a woman. Tell me, Yollana, that she is without power; tell me that she is no more than pawn."

"Aye, aye, I understand your point. And I note the false humility you show when you fail to mention your own name. Learn to speak plainly, Na'tere. Learn to speak like a Voyani woman. You would find life among my kin much easier."

"Indeed. The Matriarch Maria of the Lyserra Voyani is treated with suspicion because of her inability to shed a lifetime of grace."

"A lifetime of subservience," Yollana snapped.

The Serra's smile grew more perfect, more graceful. It

was the only way she could clearly express her annoyance. "If you prefer it, I will rescind my acceptance."

Yollana snorted. "No. Go. But leave me here. I couldn't stand to listen to the endless, pretty words that Serras use. But I caution you, Serra, to remember what you are *supposed* to be while you are here: my kin. My cousin."

Teresa bowed. And her bow, unlike the seraf's, was perfect. Age had not lessened it. Nothing would.

The Serra Celina en'Clemente was waiting in the baths. The tubs, wide and deep, were filled with water; the room itself was covered in a fine, thick steam. Serafs waited with towels and the broken beads of fragrant oils; they were, like the girl who had come to Yollana's room, of less than perfect quality. They were not all young; one was older than Ramdan, and the damp in the room caused her movements to slow. All this, Teresa noted in a glance; she accepted the aid offered as she shed the robes of the Voyani, and sank into the blessed waters.

But she was ill-prepared for the Serra Celina's first words.

"Serra Teresa di'Marano, I am honored to have you as a guest in my harem."

She sank shoulder-deep into the waters; let them lap against the point of her chin as she lowered her head in a slight bow, an acknowledgment of the Serra's words.

"It has been a long time since I last saw you; no doubt you have little memory of that day."

"I confess that I have, indeed, little memory of it, and it is my profound hope that your memory of that meeting is kind."

"Could it be otherwise? You have defined courtly grace in the Terrean of Mancorvo for many years. Your serafs, those trained and chosen by you, have been in high demand, and held in high esteem, for those years. I was never so lucky as to own one, and I hope that you do not judge my own serafs by the standards you helped define."

She listened with care, accepting the oil that the oldest of the serafs offered. The skin that had not been exposed to the Lord's harsh glare was white, as white and perfect as it had always been; the contrast between her hands and her stomach was almost shocking.

"Did the Tor'agar recognize me?" Teresa asked quietly.

The Serra did not reply; reply enough. But the woman's voice held no malice; it held open curiosity and genuine respect.

"You come to us in a time of war, and I apologize for the conditions in which you find my domis; the grounds have been all but destroyed by the heavy feet of armed men; even the trees—the oldest of trees—were not spared."

She nodded.

"The woman you travel with—is she as she claims?"

"She is Yollana of the Havalla Voyani," the Serra Teresa replied with care.

"I saw her once. She was not so old then, but she was always terrifying. I was a foolish girl," the Serra Celina added, "and she had the Voyani Sight."

Something in her voice caught the Serra Teresa's attention; she turned to face the Serra Celina, and found green eyes intent upon her. "You are aware of the recent history of our clan?"

"I . . . have been much absent from Mancorvo of late," Teresa said, gentling her voice. "But I confess that I was surprised to see Ser Alessandro wearing the symbol of the Tor."

"He was not Tor when you last resided with your kai," the Serra Celina replied. "I take no offense, Serra Teresa. Although Clemente holds the rank of Tor'agar, my former husband, Ser Roberto kai di'Clemente, was not a man overly concerned with the grace and nuance of the High Court; he was seldom seen upon the plateau of the Tor Leonne, and seldom seen in the Court of Amar. He was like his father, Ser Rogos, in that. A practical man.

"A man," she added, speaking with both sorrow and obvious affection, "who was not embarrassed by the quality of my serafs."

"It is said," Teresa said quietly, "that the quality of the master—or the mistress—is best judged by the affection the seraf feels for him, or her, and I do not doubt that your serafs hold you in that particular warmth of esteem."

The woman blushed. She was, Teresa thought, a few years younger than Teresa herself, but vastly younger, and vastly more protected, than the Serra Teresa di'Marano had ever been allowed to be. Not a weapon, this woman, not a sword to be lifted at the behest of a clan.

"You are still Serra here? Ser Alessandro has taken no wife?"

"He has," Serra Celina replied quietly—too quietly. "After the death of my husband, I was uncertain of my fate. I bore my husband two sons, but only one survived; I gave him daughters," she added. "And he was perhaps foolish in his affection for them. Only one has married.

"Ser Alessandro is kai," she continued. "My second son was born to me late, by the Lady's grace, and . . . he was young . . . to be without regent. When Roberto died, Alessandro approached me, and he asked me to remain in the harem, with my son, and my wives, for he said Clemente had need of continuity, and a Serra who understood her people. I accepted his offer, as you can see. Ser Alessandro has confirmed my son as the clan's heir."

"You tell me much about your husband," Serra Teresa said. "There is much to respect in his action; there are few who would follow the old ways as closely as he has."

"Yes. And yet you saw the bowmen upon the curtain wall when you approached."

She nodded again. "The kai Lamberto would be ill-pleased by their presence, for he despises all things Northern."

She nodded again. "I have said as much, but my husband is a man who takes no counsel but his own."

The Serra was silent. "Serra Celina," she said at last, "what does your husband intend for us?"

"It is to speak of these things that I have asked you to join me," the Serra replied, "for there are things I feel you must know." She drew a deep breath, tilting her face up and into the comforting wreaths of steam.

"There have been rumors these past months; they have traveled across the Terrean, by merchant caravan and by Voyani caravan alike. I . . . am a simple woman. I have had some small business with the Voyani, Arkosan and Havallan, and although they are a rough people, they have been courteous and helpful when I have asked for aid."

And what aid, she thought, *would a Serra be unwise enough to ask of the Voyani? Or do you not understand the debt you incur when you accept their favor?*

"It is said," the Serra continued, lowering her voice, "that the Tyr'agar now deals with the servants of the Lord of Night; that he intended to honor the Lord at the height of the Lady's festival.

"Serra Teresa, you were within the Tor Leonne during the Festival season. Is there truth to these rumors?"

"There is . . . some truth to these rumors. Understand that it is unwise to speak of any rumors that involve men of power and the wars they play."

Serra Celina en'Clemente nodded earnestly, and Teresa knew, by the quality of that nod, that she in fact understood no such thing. She was not a girl, but Ser Roberto, and Ser Alessandro after him, had either been kind, or foolish, enough to allow her to retain the sweetness and the naïveté of youth.

"The kai Lamberto would never deal with the servants of the Lord of Night. Never."

That, indeed, was truth. "No," the Serra Teresa replied gravely. "Not while he drew breath. Not Mareo kai di'Lamberto, and not any of his children, nor his brothers."

"Aye," the Serra Celina said, rough word that showed her breeding. "And it is the brother that lies at the heart of the difficulty. My husband's cousin was killed by the kai el'Sol over the matter of a simple village seraf."

"The kai el'Sol was not a man to step outside of the

bounds of law," Serra Teresa said quietly. "And I find it
hard to believe that he would kill a man of rank over his
treatment of a simple seraf."

"She was not a seraf in name. But in all but name. She
came from the poorest of clans." Serra Celina frowned.
"My husband—my former husband—was a gentle man. He
sought wives among the villages within our domains,
but . . . he never sought to . . ." She bowed her head. Lifted
it. "Ser Alessandro has said very little, but word has come
to me from other sources."

The Voyani, Teresa thought. Perhaps the Serra Celina
was not so simple as she appeared.

"The kai Manelo had taken an interest in the girl, but the
girl was married."

"Ah."

"And her husband . . . was injured . . . by the kai di'-
Manelo. The kai el'Sol accused him of attempted murder,
and they fought."

That—that, Teresa thought, was more than believable.
"Ser Alessandro was fond of this cousin."

"They were kin."

"And he now seeks war with Lamberto over the death of
his cousin?"

"Not war," his wife said softly. "But his uncle, the kai
di'Manelo—"

"The Tor'agnate?"

"Yes. He was outraged by the death of his kai. He has
never recovered. He, as my husband did, ventured to the
Tor Leonne for the Festival of the Sun. It was not to the
Tyr'agnate's liking."

Adano, Teresa thought, had turned back.

"Understand, Serra Teresa, that I care for my husband.
He has been like a brother to me; he is a kind man. He has
made no demands of me, and he has been kind to my wives.
There is little that I would not do for him, if he but asked.
But I do not wish him to fall into the Lord of Night's
shadow, and I fear—" She dropped her head into her hands.

Lifted her face. "You travel with the Havallan Matriarch. She will not be detained, no matter what he might decide to do with the others. You must tell her—" She hesitated now, on the brink of treachery, her pain writ clearly upon the large, grand lines of her open expression.

Black hair clung to the sides of high cheekbones, and trailed the edge of her chin, the long line of her neck; she was lovely in a fashion, and Teresa thought she must have been more than lovely in the full bloom of a distant youth.

"You must tell her that the Tor'agnate Amando kai di'-Manelo has allowed the armies of the Tyr'agar free passage through his lands. They rest there now, waiting the orders of Alesso di'Marente."

Again, her eyes were wide, round. "I would not tell you this. I am aware of what it might cost. But it is said that, in the lands of Manelo, the cattle sicken and die. The horses will not remain upon the plains. And the serafs in the village have been plagued by unexplained diseases and injuries that swords alone cannot explain."

Teresa bowed her head. Lifted it. "You serve the Lady," she said softly. "We are, neither of us, warrior-born; the Lady requires no warriors. But she requires bold heart and dedication, and you have that in great measure.

"I thank you, Serra Celina, for your warning, and I thank you for the grace of your hospitality."

"My husband," Celina said, "has not yet allowed the armies of Marente passage into Clemente. He is Tor'agar; Amando is Tor'agnate, and he serves another. But . . . he is kin. And there is pressure upon Clemente. In rank, there is no question of superiority; Alessandro is Tor'agar, and in theory the more powerful of the two. But Amando has planned these many years for personal war, and he is well provisioned and well armed. If he threatens war . . ."

"Please, Serra Celina, say no more."

The past.
Amelia, his Serra, his only wife; their son, Jonas. Their

deaths, at a distance, while his hands waged war in the
name of a clansman of the High Court. Easy to remember
them here, in this spare, harsh room. Easy to remember all
of the dead.

Fredero.

The dead.

When the knock came, muffled by the thickness of wood,
Marakas looked up. Remembering the past, the gift of the
past, and the burden of the responsibility for it. The death
of a single man—a single unimportant man—had given
him back his life's gift and his purpose; he had not thought,
in truth, that he might be forced to pay for it. Or rather, had
thought the debt paid by the life of service that had followed, year after year.

But he did not flinch.

Instead, he drew back, away from the door. "Enter," he
said, pitching his voice so that it might carry.

The door opened, but only slightly; no one obeyed the
word that strayed the gray area between command and permission.

He moved toward the door, then, and saw that a seraf
knelt inches from its frame. A man, and not one comfortable with these heavy, graceless doors. He looked up as
Marakas approached, light in the halls gleaming along the
streaked black of his hair.

"The Tor'agar," he said quietly, "requests your company."

The halls of the *domis* were of stone and wood; Marakas
was aware that beyond them, in the heart of the complex, a
more graceful dwelling resided, for as he followed the
seraf, stone gave way to wood, and wood at last to the
screens and the sliding walls of a rich man's home. Flowers
adorned wooden tables, wooden pedestals; water lay in
gourds from which lily petals hung. And beyond these, in
the longest of halls, shields, adorned with the symbol of

rank and the colors of clan, rested above the last door. A shield. A shield of fire.

The seraf bowed at once to floor; Marakas glanced at his back, but did not choose to abase himself in a like fashion. He waited, his hands at his sides, his sword's curve part of the fall of his robes.

The door slid open; the seraf's hands moved it effortlessly in its recessed track.

Beyond it, seated upon a low dais, was the Tor'agar, Ser Alessandro kai di'Clemente. To either side, as much adornment as threat, stood men who wore the crest of his house: Toran. There were only two.

But there was no low table in this room; no hangings, none of the details which graced a hall that was intended for the hospitality of guests. There was a long, wide door upon the West wall, but it was closed; light came through the opaque cells of heavy paper.

"Radann par el'Sol," the Tor'agar said, voice smooth and cool. "I bid you welcome to the stronghold of the clan Clemente."

Marakas bowed, then. When he rose, he said, "Tor'agar, you honor me by your welcome."

The seraf did not rise. The Toran did not move.

Ser Alessandro's gaze was bright and dark in the silence.

"Enter," he said softly. "We have much to discuss."

There was no way to refuse the command. Nor was Marakas inclined to try. He stepped past the bent back of the unnamed seraf; the door slid shut behind him, punctuation to the decision and flow of movement. The room stretched out, from door to wall, as if it were a long and narrow passage between the heights of the mountain chain to the North of Mancorvo.

He approached the Tor'agar, not as supplicant, and not as ally, nor as penitent. But he was grateful for the absence of the rest of his companions. The Northerners might not understand the significance of this meeting, but the Southerners—the Serra Diora di'Marano—would. He wished to spare her the uncertainty, although he was not at all certain she was a woman who could be spared anything; had she not been among the Arkosans when the Tor Arkosa rose from the empty plains of desert death?

Had she not bent, hems drenched in the blessed waters of the Tor Leonne after the kai el'Sol's sacrifice, to retrieve the fallen Sun Sword, her arms strong in spite of the terrible weight of grief and loss?

He approached Ser Alessandro, and when he stood ten feet from the dais, he bowed stiffly and allowed himself to kneel. But his back was straight; he placed his hands upon his knees as he lifted his chin. Readiness, not supplication. "Tor'agar. You requested my presence."

"Indeed. We have matters to discuss; I am certain that you have questions you wish to ask, and I bid you speak freely here."

Marakas nodded. "We have been grateful for the hospitality offered by the clan Clemente," he said, neutral now. "The road traveled from Raverra was . . . a road that I would not willingly travel again, and my companions were much in need of rest."

"I would hear, one day, of that road—although I fear that such a tale would be costly." He frowned. "But the circumstances that drove you to take such a road are also of interest, for it is a road not suited to those in your care."

"You refer to the Serra," he said quietly.

"I do." He rose; the Toran did not move at all. Marakas marveled at their composure, for the serafs of Clemente did not possess it. "She is of value, par el'Sol."

He did not reach for *Verragar,* but he heard the sword's voice, the whisper of its keening edge.

"I have sworn oath, upon one of the five, to protect her," Marakas replied.

"From me?"

"From any man who would deter her from her final destination."

"Ah. And that? That is the question, is it not, Radann par

el'Sol? You have traveled the Terrean in the past," he added darkly, "on your errands of honor, at the side of Fredero kai el'Sol. Will you travel upon such a path again? You will find the going more difficult with the passing of the kai el'-Sol."

He shrugged. "A man is bound by his oaths," he said softly.

"Spoken as a clansman who has never seen the High Courts."

"Or a clansmen who has never valued them highly." Dangerous words; dangerous words to speak in the presence of a Tor.

But Alessandro smiled. Sharp smile, that, but it transformed his face. "Do you remember me, par el'Sol?"

"I remember you," Marakas replied softly. "I remember the honor you offered your dead."

"I bear the scar."

"And I; not all scars take root in flesh."

The Tor'agar lifted brow. "You have grown canny with words since last we met."

"A duty of my position."

"Indeed. I admit that I am surprised you retain that position; Peder kai el'Sol is not the man that Fredero kai el'Sol was. I would have said that he would have had you replaced with a more political man—a more ambitious one."

"I am not without ambition."

"You could not be, and still be par el'Sol. Men serve the Lord."

"Men," Marakas replied, taking the first of his great risks, "define the Lord."

Silence, then. One of the Toran turned to look at his lord, but Ser Alessandro's gaze was now fixed upon the Radann.

"The Lord," Alessandro replied, "values victory above all else."

"Does he? Were that true, the servants of the Lord of Night might have been given his blessing to march across the face of the Dominion."

"And you speak for the Lord, now?"

"I am Radann. I am par el'Sol. If not me, then who?" He touched the hilt of *Verragar.* "If victory were the only thing the Lord valued, he would not have intervened in the Leonne wars. He would not have chosen to bless the clan Leonne with the gift of the Sun Sword; he would not have granted, to the Radann who were not blinded by promises of power and Dominion, the use of the five."

"You make a persuasive argument, par el'Sol. But the clan Leonne is dead; the Sun Sword takes no other master."

"The clan Leonne," Marakas replied, "is not yet dead; the line has not yet perished."

Ser Alessandro's smile deepened, and Marakas was instantly on his guard.

"And so we come at last to the heart of the matter. The clan Leonne."

Marakas was silent.

"Where is this scion of Leonne to be found, par el'Sol?"

"I do not, in truth, have the answer to that question."

"And yet it must be the kai Leonne that you seek."

"And you, Tor'agar?"

"I seek what is best for the clan Clemente, of course."

"And the people who are beholden to Clemente?"

"What is best for the clan is best for the people."

Marakas said nothing, but memory intruded; memory was strong. He weighed his words carefully, understanding their weight and their cost. "When you traveled in the lands claimed by the clan Manelo, would you have made the same claim of the people there?"

Ser Alessandro's silence was sharp and cold. He walked the distance that divided them—the obvious distance, the one most easily crossed—and came to stand before the par el'Sol. "Clan Manelo," he said quietly, "was not my clan, and its people, not my people."

"And it is thus that you abjure responsibility for your actions there?"

"My actions there? Speak plainly, par el'Sol. Speak quickly."

"You would have seen a boy barely man murdered for a moment of self-indulgence."

"I saw just that," Ser Alessandro snapped, losing the perfect control that had defined his presence in this room.

"The kai di'Manelo was no boy," Marakas snapped back. "He was granted the gift of power by the expedience of birth, and his use of that power—"

Ser Alessandro slapped the Radann par el'Sol.

The blow rang out in the silence.

Marakas rose.

The Toran who stood upon the dais started forward; Ser Alessandro lifted a hand, the silence—and the fury—of the command inherent in the gesture unmistakable.

"I was not born to the High Clans," Marakas said, forcing a calm into the heat of his words. Fredero would have handled the discussion differently, but Fredero was gone, consumed by flame. "I was born to the low. I know what they suffer at the hands of men who claim power."

"And it is your duty to save them all?"

"It was my *duty* to stand by the side of the kai el'Sol. My duty," he said, "and my honor."

"Costly honor, that."

"It may well be. What do you intend, Tor'agar? We are within the bounds of Clemente. I have seen your Toran, and the cerdan that line the walls, and I have little illusion; the safety that we enjoy is entirely at your whim, and that whim has yet to make itself clear."

"Tell me of duty, par el'Sol. The kai el'Sol himself travels at the side of the Tyr'agar."

"He does."

"Surely, then, your duty is clear? Or do you serve the memory of a dead man?"

"It was never his memory that I served," Marakas replied, standing taller now, the weight that had bowed his shoulders falling away in a moment of clarity. "It was his vision. It was his goal."

"He would never have served at the side of the General."

"No. Never. He chose instead to draw the Sun Sword, in the Lake of the Tor Leonne; chose instead to offer proof of the General's illegitimacy."

"And now?"

"I am in Mancorvo."

"You have been in Mancorvo before."

"I will not leave it until I am called to war."

"You think that you have not been called to war?" Ser Alessandro laughed. And then, to Marakas' surprise, he drew his sword.

"Will you challenge me, Tor'agar? Will you ask the Lord to settle what has long lain in the past?"

"Perhaps." The sword did not glint in the sun's light; the sun had egress through the opacity of paper, that was all. The lamps were not bright enough to bring the edge of steel to light.

"Then let me draw *Verragar,* and I will accept the challenge you offer."

"Draw her, then," Ser Alessandro said softly. A challenge.

Without hesitation, the Radann par el'Sol complied. *Verragar* came from the sheath.

But the light that was denied the Tor'agar's sword shone bright and deep along the runnels and edges of the Radann's blade, and in the runes etched in steel, words now glowed, painful to look upon.

Marakas' eyes widened.

But the Tor'agar lowered his blade and lifted a hand to his brow, turning away, exposing his back.

"So," he said softly. Just that.

Marakas said nothing; he stared instead at what was written upon the blade, and felt its ancient fire with a hunger, and a clarity, that he had forgotten. Had had to forget; a man could not be scoured by such fires and retain their perfect memory, and live in the world.

"There are . . . envoys . . . within my domis," Ser Alessandro said. "They have come through Manelo from Alesso di'Marente."

Their eyes met.

"I would not have my people suffer as the people of Manelo have suffered," Ser Alessandro said. "Whatever else you choose to think of me, believe that." He paused, and then stared at the unsheathed blade. "And believe that the people of Manelo would not suffer as they do now were it not for the decision of the kai el'Sol a decade past. What he saved, in that village, he saved for death—for it is death that walks those lands."

"The kai el'Sol cannot be held responsible for the choices that other men make."

"But for his own? There were other ways to have resolved the difficulty. Any other man, save perhaps the kai Lamberto, would have in prudence chosen those instead. But the kai el'Sol sought to prove that justice prevails in these lands, and he has had his justice." The words were bitter, the accusation unadorned. "And what justice will you now offer, par el'Sol?"

"Tell me, Ser Alessandro, that the actions of the kai Manelo were just. Tell me that they were justified."

"I will not play those games with you."

"You play them now, and at some risk."

"Very well. The kai Manelo was young; he was unwise. He made poor choices—but not all of his choices were poor, and he was capable of largesse and compassion in his time. You judge him by the act of a single, ill-considered day."

"I do not judge him at all. Whatever else I may be, I do not claim to speak with the wind's voice; he is beyond my judgment. But I learned, that day, that rank alone is no protection against ill-considered action."

Ser Alessandro said nothing.

"There is no protection for Clemente under the rule of the Lord of Night."

"And under the rule of the Lord?" He laughed. "Where are your armies, par el'Sol? Where is the strength of the Lord now? In a handful of people who fled the dark forest?"

Marakas par el'Sol straightened. "Yes," he said softly. "In a handful of men—and women—who dared the forest to arrive in Mancorvo."

The Toran moved now, restive. Marakas spared them a glance because they had shown the strength of training, the strength of the kai's purpose. They stood, hands on swords, bereft of direction, waiting.

"The forests," Ser Alessandro said softly. "Do you know what they mean to Clemente?"

"No, Tor'agar."

"Do you know what they mean to those who live in the lands they border?"

"No."

Ser Alessandro's expression was knife's edge; sharp. Cold. But at last his shoulders shifted, his chin lowered. "The kai el'Sol would lend no credence to old stories, and older losses. He was the Lord's man, and such stories were perhaps—to a man raised in the heartland of the Terrean—children's stories. The tales of old women, the dark musings of Voyani seers.

"But they have significance to Clemente, story or no, and it seems that they have given you to us, when you were unexpected and unlooked for." He brought his blade up until it mirrored the straight line of his spine.

"Those stories?"

"Can a man who is a part of their nature appreciate them?" the Tor'agar asked softly. "It is not the Lady's time, but my thoughts are given to her now."

"And my companions?"

"They traveled the darkest road," the Tor'agar said. "They traveled it willingly, if I am any judge. Even the

Serra Diora. Perhaps especially that Serra. And they traveled that road to us, in the wake of the emissaries of the General Marente. The man who claims the Tor Leonne.

"Against his arrival, the bowmen upon the curtain wall wait. We have sought word," he added quietly. "And the simple people of the Clemente villages have sought more. They have looked to old stories for their wisdom and power, for they are bereft of any other. And it seems that some answer has been granted their prayers."

"What would you have of us?"

The Tor'agar stared at the unsheathed blade; *Verragar*'s edge seemed to converse in the silence between them. "You owe me a debt of blood. Pay it."

The sword whispered. The fire burned.

"And that payment?"

"Wield the sword."

"Gladly."

The Tor'agar turned to the two men who adorned the dais. "Adelos, Reymos," he said. "Open the war room."

They nodded in unison, and turned.

"Par el'Sol, forgive me my curtness; forgive the lack of hospitality you have been shown. What food we have, we have chosen to store in the granaries against the need and the movement of our forces."

"In time of war, much is forgiven," Marakas said quietly, his hand still tingling with the heat—and the ice—of blue fire. "But I must ask, Tor'agar, what you intend in the event—however small the chance—that we fail."

Ser Alessandro nodded grimly. "I will offer the Serra Diora di'Marano to the General," he replied. "And I will offer my formal allegiance to his armies."

"And if we succeed?"

"I will consider all debt between us repaid," was the even reply, "and I will put my forces in the hands of the Tyr'agnate of Mancorvo, against my blood-kin, the clan Manelo."

Again Marakas par el'Sol nodded. The Tor'agar turned,

but the Radann lifted a hand, calling him back with the force and the silence of that gesture.

"Par el'Sol?"

"Another question, a brief question," he said.

"That?"

"Which outcome is preferable, kai Clemente?"

The kai Clemente was still. "Is it not obvious?"

"If it were, I would not ask. Indulge me; I am not—as you have correctly guessed—a man of the High Courts, and the subtlety of the Courts often escapes me."

"I would not have brought you here, nor requested your aid, if I desired the allegiance . . . offered me . . . by my kin." His lips twisted in the curl of a man who has eaten something bitter and has not yet decided if the manners decreed by hospitality will be enough to force him to swallow. "I have been fond of my cousin," he said softly. "And I understand his pain. If the kai el'Sol were among the living, I would be . . . less certain of my answer."

Marakas nodded slowly. It was not the answer he would have chosen, had the choice been his, but it was shorn of prettiness.

"I will ask, in my turn, why the answer is of interest to you; it changes nothing."

"It changes much," Marakas replied. "The kai el'Sol went willingly to his death," he said softly. "On the eve of war, in the heart of his enemy's stronghold. You . . . resent him . . . for his part in the death of your cousin."

"Resent is a petty word."

"Perhaps. But were it not for that day, I would have followed a different course. I would not now wield one of the five; I would not now enter your war room with intent to wield it in your service."

"I have already said the necessity of such action would not exist were it not for the kai el'Sol's intemperate action."

"No. Nor would justice within the Dominion."

"You speak as a servant of the Lady," Ser Alessandro replied curtly. "The Lord's justice is delivered by sword."

"And it was, and it was not accepted as such by either Manelo or Clemente, although neither of you have stooped to accuse the kai el'Sol of dishonor in the fight."

"Justice is not static," Ser Alessandro said.

"No." Marakas bowed. "I will require the aid of my companions upon the road."

"Granted; you may take with you all but the Serra Diora; the Serra will remain within the safety of these walls."

A grim, grim smile touched the Radann's face. "There is no safety within these walls; *Verragar* does not speak so openly when the servants of the Lord of Night are not nearby."

Ser Alessandro's expression was soft as steel. "I would have this done with discretion," he replied. "For the clan Manelo is not, in its entirety, the man who now rules her."

"And his heir?"

"His heir," Alessandro said coolly, "is perhaps a man who might meet with your approval under different circumstances. He was not much loved by his brother, Ser Franko; nor was he much valued."

"And by his father?"

"His father understands the necessity of having an heir; the son understands the necessity of loyalty to his bloodline. Do not look for help from that quarter."

"Understood. I will leave you now, and I will return shortly. But Tor'agar?"

"What?"

The word was curt. Cold.

"I would hear, when we have time, of the stories of the dark wood."

To his surprise, Alessandro di'Clemente laughed.

Kallandras of Senniel College was waiting when the Radann par el'Sol knocked upon his door. The door opened silently; Kallandras met the gaze of the Radann par el'Sol and nodded.

He carried little, and of that, he left only his lute behind.

He did not ask questions, and it seemed odd to the Radann that a man known across both the Empire and the Dominion for the strength and the clarity of his voice should trade so little in words.

He came next to the room occupied by Jewel ATerafin, and hesitated a moment outside of its screen—for she had been given rooms better suited to the women of a clan than their men. But his shadow had drawn her attention, and she waited for no seraf; she shoved the screens to one side, rattling them in their groove. The child was huddled in the room's corner. Jewel ATerafin spoke briefly, and in Weston; the man who was her servant nodded. He lifted the girl in his arms.

"The Serra Diora?"

"She is to remain in the stronghold of Clemente, an honored guest."

The Northern woman almost spit, her expression was so clearly one of open contempt and hostility. But Marakas noted no surprise.

"We will take the child to the Serra Diora," the ATerafin woman said, in her rough and lowborn Torra. "If we can find her."

He nodded. He had not yet finished.

But he hesitated outside of the last door: the room in which Yollana of Havalla resided. He was no seraf, but he opened her door gently, and bowed at its outer edge.

She was awake; the wounds she had taken had not yet ceased to cause her pain, if they ever would. "Matriarch," he said quietly, "we have been summoned to a council of war. Will you join us?"

The old woman snorted. She was entirely graceless. "Na'tere."

The younger of the two women rose swiftly. "We would be honored to join you, Radann par el'Sol; give us but a moment." She knelt at the side of the Havallan Matriarch with the grace and form of a perfect seraf. But she lifted her head as she lifted the burden of the older woman. "The Serra Diora?"

"She is to be held in the safety of the domis," he replied.

The answer was not to her liking; it was not to his. But it was unwise to offer a lie to the Havallan Matriarch; she was canny, and she was easily angered.

"Stavos?"

"A seraf has been sent to fetch him; he is quartered in the outer domis."

She nodded. "Lead, then, and we will follow as we are able."

Brother.

The word traveled on the Lady's wind. Kallandras did not listen for an answer; none would be forthcoming.

It seems that we will fight; the ATerafin summons you, and the Winter King, should you care to join us. It would be best if you met us beyond the gates; the men here are easily . . . intimidated . . . by the unknown.

The words left a peculiar silence in their wake.

Ser Alessandro kai di'Clemente looked up from the table upon which the flats of his palms rested. The perfect line of bent back straightened as he rose.

"Par el'Sol," he said, nodding. "Matriarch. You honor us by your presence." He did not condescend to notice the wounds that darkened her clothing; if she chose to be present, she did not consider them worthy of note.

He gestured; command came easily to the rise and fall of hand. The hand then fell to the table; niceties were kept to a minimum.

"This," he said, "is the border of Clemente lands."

Marakas understood the invitation in the sparse words. He walked to the table and took his place at the side of the Tor'agar. Beneath his hands, a map lay, pinned gracefully across the tabletop. It was the only adornment a war room required.

"These are the forces of my cousin."

Marked in red, they were concentrated on the wavering line of the border closest to the city itself. "All of his men?"

"Not all. He has had the prudence to leave his city well defended against our enemies."

"And these?"

"Ah. The blue marks are an estimation, to the best of our ability, of the forces of the Tyr'agar within the lands Manelo holds."

"They are concentrated in three villages."

"Yes. They have built a rough stockade. The villages," he added quietly, "are those that have granaries. They supply themselves there, although we believe that they have some method of feeding themselves that does not rely upon the friendliness of the Mancorvan Tors."

"It is not a small number."

"No."

"And your own forces?"

"They are represented by the green. They are ready, upon my word, to close our borders."

"The red here?" Marakas placed finger lightly above the marks that existed within the Clemente border; they were not inconsiderable.

"My cousin," Ser Alessandro said quietly. "He has come with a small force to discuss our military plans. We have agreed to allow his troops to station themselves within the village of Damar." At the mention of the village, the Tor's expression darkened.

"And that village?"

"Ten miles to the south," he said quietly.

"How large is this small force?"

Ser Alessandro's smile was bitter. "To the best of our knowledge, three hundred armed and mounted men."

"A definition of small that only a Tor'agar would condescend to use."

Ser Alessandro's brow rose. "There were reasons he was

granted leave to remain within the fields and inns of Damar."

"There are blue marks within that village as well."

"Indeed, but those are of a less certain nature. We know that he travels with Marente advisors. We cannot be certain of their number; we cannot be certain of their strength. The men that my cousin claims as his own could be Marente's."

"The village of Damar is bounded by the Adane?"

"No; the river cuts through the village; the fields—and the buildings that house the officials the village boasts—reside on either side of the water." He reached out and lightly touched the ridges of dark terrain. "Damar is bounded by the dark forest on its Western edge."

"Can men be secreted within the forest?"

His smile was grim. "You have traveled it yourself; you are better judges than I."

Yollana grimaced.

Answer enough.

The men bent over the unfamiliar map; the Tor'agar allowed them their silent study, studying their faces in turn. Kallandras was still; Avandar was still; Marakas moved quietly from one side of the table to the other. The Havallan Matriarch did not seem to notice the map at all—but it was likely that she found it unnecessary. All of Mancorvo was, inasmuch as it could be, the wandering grounds of the Havalla Voyani.

"The road that we took from the forest?"

"The Western road. It is a smaller road, and it follows the West bank of the Adane. Here, and here, the Eastern road follows the East bank."

The Adane drifted toward the city of Seral. "This is where we crossed the river," the Tor'agar said.

"And if you travel to Damar?"

"We will take the Eastern road. Here," he added. "There is no river crossing until we are within Damar itself. My cousin is lodged, with the better part of his men, in the fields and houses of Damar; they are bound by the forest, here, and by the Western road and the Southern one, here."

"And the Eastern road?"

"If there is difficulty, the greater part of my forces will be stationed on the East bank. We can hold the bridges, should the unforeseen happen, and it becomes necessary."

"And if you want to drive them out of Damar?" Marakas asked quietly.

"That is our intent. But we do not know, for certain, where their forces are arrayed, and in what number. We will remain in the East until our meeting."

"Bridges?"

"Two bridges. One is wide enough to easily convey the whole of a merchant caravan; the other is a footbridge two men wide."

"Ferries?"

"Boatmen work the banks of the Adane, but not in great numbers; the bridges are considered safer. Only when the river swells in the rainy season do the boatmen show their true value, for the footbridge is considered unsafe at that time. The larger bridge is traversable."

"You are certain your cousin can be found within the Western half of Damar?"

"There is more room, and more to his liking, in the West; the Eastern half is poorer."

Kallandras of Senniel, reading the lines of the map as easily as he might have read music, now raised his head. "Do Widan travel with the Tor'agnate's party?"

"Openly?"

"Or not."

"One man wears the sword," the Tor'agar replied.

"And do the Tor'agnate's forces arm themselves, as your own appear to have done, with Northern bows?"

"To the best of my knowledge, no."

He nodded. "Is the Tor'agnate to be found in the village of Damar?"

"He resides there, yes. I offered him the hospitality of my city, but he chose to take the counsel of his advisor."

"The advisor?"

"A man who wears the colors of Marente," Ser Alessandro replied. No gift was required to hear the anger that lay beneath those words.

"And no messenger, no member of his entourage, is within your city?"

"That I know of? None."

Kallandras turned to the Radann par el'Sol. Marakas nodded grimly and spoke. "There is at least one."

"We cannot assume that he has no method of communication."

"No."

"If we remove him, you may be forced into a position of war," the Northerner said.

"And if you do not?"

"Then when we seek the village of Damar, he may be in a position to do great damage within your domis. The choice is yours. You may say that our intervention was entirely without your blessing or knowledge, but in order for such words to have effect—"

Ser Alessandro lifted a hand. "It is not to my liking, to be told how to wage war by a man who sings for a living." His voice was cool.

Kallandras, however, took no offense. Marakas wondered, briefly, if he was capable of taking offense; in their travels together, he had shown no sign of temper, no sign of anger, no sign of fear.

"I have received three messages from the Tor'agnate. I have returned two; he has been patient, but the tone of his third letter makes clear that his patience is almost at an end."

"What does he request?"

"My presence," Ser Alessandro replied coldly. "He wishes to meet in the village of Damar, to discuss the future of our place in the Terrean of Mancorvo. He has, at his

side, a man who is given leave to negotiate on behalf of the
Tyr'agar, and it is in Damar that my cousin feels such negotiations would best be served."

"Not a sign for lovers of peace," Kallandras said quietly.

"Indeed."

"And this meeting?"

"It is to take place on the morrow. Understand," he
added softly, "that there is a reason that you are viewed
with both suspicion and reverence among the more superstitious of my cerdan.

"They understand what is at risk; they understand that I
have no choice but to attend my cousin. But your presence
here—with the Matriarch of Havalla as traveling companion, and the bearer of one of the Five Swords of the
Radann at her side—has come upon a day of decision for
Clemente. You are seen as an omen."

"Omens are not guaranteed to be good."

"Indeed, as you say."

Kallandras of Senniel College inclined his oddly colored
head and fell silent. He was a strange man, even for a
Northerner.

"How many of your men will stand ready?"

Another voice. Another Northerner. Avandar Gallais had
quietly joined the table.

"Three hundred," Ser Alessandro replied, barely lifting
a brow at the interruption. "Here. And here."

"Six hundred men in total. Are they mounted?"

"They are all mounted."

"And the villagers?" Jewel ATerafin spoke for the first
time.

To Marakas' great surprise, the Tor'agar smiled. It was a
bitter smile, but not devoid of humor. "I should have
guessed," he said softly, "for they travel in your company.
It comes, always, to that, does it not? You will seek victims
no matter where you travel, and no matter who claims to
own them.

"Very well. The villagers are trapped within the bounds

of Damar. Some few have fled, where they are able; it is how we have the information we do have."

"And the others?"

"They may yet live. My cousin is not a fool, but he is not entirely capable of containing his cerdan."

"He expects you to say no, doesn't he?"

Ser Alessandro's brows rose. "In the North," he said at last, "are all women so blunt?"

"I don't know. I can only speak for me."

"No," Avandar Gallais replied. "Not all women are so blunt. But you will find that our men are often just as ill at ease with the social grace demanded by the Courts of the South. And Jewel ATerafin has asked the most obvious of the questions your answers offer; let me ask the second."

"And that?"

"The information the villagers brought you."

Ser Alessandro nodded again, his face growing grave. If he was ill-pleased by the broken currents of interrupted conversation, it did not show; Marakas suspected that he was in some ways relieved—for the questions showed an understanding of tactics that required no lengthy explanation. "Understand that the villagers are not serafs, but they are not of clans whose power might otherwise protect them. They are often superstitious, and in times of duress, will see what superstition suggests."

"Understood."

"It is said that in Damar, when the Lord has turned his face toward the night, fell creatures walk. There have been deaths and disappearances among the serafs, and among the poorest of clans, who are incapable of demanding restitution."

"Then let me speak bluntly, in the Northern style," Avandar Gallais said, although he did not veer from the use of Torra. "We are seven men—and women—and at least one of our number was greatly injured in the passage through the Deepings. You cannot intend us to destroy the whole of the forces arrayed within the village of Damar unless you intend the destruction and the loss of that village."

"And if I were willing to lose the village in its entirety?"

"No," Jewel ATerafin said sharply.

Avandar Gallais raised brows at what was obviously an expected interruption. "ATerafin."

She subsided. Hard, thought Marakas, to tell who was master, and who servant, here.

"I see," Ser Alessandro replied quietly, and it seemed to Marakas that he did. His gaze was now cutting where it rested upon Avandar's face, but it did not rest there long. "That was, indeed, not my intent."

"What would you have us do, Tor'agar? What would you have us achieve?"

The Tor'agar turned to Marakas, and only to Marakas. "Hunt what you must hunt, man of the Lord. Seek what only you can find. Destroy it, and you will have destroyed a greater part of the threat that is leveled—in silence— against us. We cannot fight what we do not understand."

"And the demon who walks within your own fair city?" It was the first time the threat had been given name.

"Destroy it," Ser Alessandro said, without pause. "If it can communicate with the forces the Tor'agnate has assembled, it will do so; I am willing to take that much risk with the fate of my village."

"Can I make a different suggestion?" Jewel now spoke through tight, thin lips.

"Please do," the Tor'agar replied, in a tone that should have conveyed warning and veiled threat.

"Why don't we time this so that we strike in tandem?"

"In tandem?"

"Let the Radann par el'Sol deal with the demon within the walls," she replied curtly. "But let him do so only when we're in position to attack the demons in the village."

"You have obviously never been on the battlefield, ATerafin."

She shrugged. "So?"

"Information of that nature is seldom easily conveyed; to attempt to time—"

"Kallandras is a master bard of Senniel College," she said coldly. "There is no better method of conveying information. No bird, no horsed rider, no cursed wind. *None.* I'm betting that the demon in the city will be easier to find than the demons in the village—if they've got half a brain, they'll be wearing human guise. When we know what we need to know, we'll let him know what he needs to know. He can strike at leisure; any warning the creature can send will be too little and too late."

The Tor'agar was silent a moment while he considered his options. His gaze shifted to the Radann par el'Sol. "Can this be done, as she claims?"

"I am not a Northern bard," the par el'Sol replied cautiously, "but in my limited experience with the Northerners, no claim they have made has yet been proved idle boast. If it were my city, and it were my choice, I would trust them."

Alessandro's gaze shifted. "Matriarch?"

"I have already placed myself in the debt of the bard and the Northern woman; if we are an omen here, she was a like omen to the gathering of Matriarchs. I, too, would place my faith in their claims, were I minded to incur a greater debt."

"It is said a wise man will accept the counsel of the wise. Very well."

"If you can spare them, Tor'agar," Kallandras said quietly, "I will take two bows."

"Two?"

The Northern bard smiled, but said nothing.

"I can spare a handful of bowmen."

"Will you risk them?"

"I am loath to send you on a mission within my domain with none of my own in attendance."

"We would, of course, be honored. But the line of command must be drawn before our departure."

"They serve me," the Tor'agar said quietly.

"Indeed. But you will not be present."

"Ah. I see that we have a misunderstanding, Kallandras of Senniel College. I will of course be present."

Silence, then.

CHAPTER TWENTY-ONE

SILENCE greeted the Tor'agar's words; silence punctuated by the grim edge of his smile.

"We have watched the Lady slowly raise her veil while we have debated the course of Clemente. There are those among my advisers who are not of the High Courts, and they have spent much time adorning the Lady's shrine with water, wine, and blood.

"It is said that the guidance of the Lady is a hazardous thing to the men of the Lord, and perhaps we shall see the truth of that in the evening to follow. But we will tender our answer to the Tor'agnate and his allies: the clan Clemente does not negotiate on its knees." His smile was slender. Cold.

"Can you give him that answer *after* we've started our own attack?" Jewel ATerafin asked.

"You will be in position," he said quietly, "for I will carry the answer myself.

"My men will travel with me, and in number; they have been prepared for this since we received information from the clansmen of the village of Damar. I should warn you that not a few of them were born to Damar. Their concern is no idle concern, and in the event of victory, they can be trusted.

"And you, gentlemen—and lady—will grace us with your presence." He stepped back from the map, surveying it with the intensity a circling bird of prey gives the low lands beneath its flat expanse of wings.

"Go now. Ready yourselves. Say what must be said to

your companions; if you require armor, it will be provided."
He hesitated a moment, and then turned to Jewel ATerafin.
"It is said that women serve in the armies of the North, and
if what I have seen here today is any indication of the
women of that strange Empire, I believe the words to be
true.

"But you are not of a size that would normally be considered acceptable for the ranks of the Clemente cerdan,
and if I bid all of my armorers to work in the scant time remaining us, they would not be able to produce anything that
would fit you."

"I'm not used to armor," she said; she was of the North
and did not notice his descent into bluntness. "But I don't
really need it. I have Avandar."

"Then let us hope that your Avandar is proof against steel
and spell, Lady."

She smiled. "Lady is a Northern title, but it's not one I
use. Call me Jewel, unless that causes some sort of political
difficulty."

He raised a brow.

"I'm called ATerafin when people feel the need for formality."

"ATerafin," he said, and he bowed. The bow was shallow, and it was short, but the fact that he offered it said
much. "We have weapons that might be of use to you. Long
daggers. Our swords, I fear, will be heavy for your hand."

"And all the wrong shape," she said quietly. "No, don't
worry about me."

"Will you go mounted?"

Her smile was peculiar. "Yes," she told him softly. "But
I'll spare you the horse." Just that.

"Then withdraw; we will meet again in the courtyard."

14th of Corvil, 427 AA
Terrean of Mancorvo

The Serra Teresa di'Marano sought the company of the Serra Celina en'Clemente one more time. She came without seraf, but she had long since learned to navigate the heart of harem mazes, with or without the benefit of a guide.

Her hand touched the screens beyond which the Serra Celina lay confined; her hands lifted the doors with deliberate care; her hands moved them, an inch apart, along their grooved tracks. She bowed there, in the small space made, and waited.

Nor did she wait long.

A seraf bid her enter at once, and the only awkward moment came when the seraf herself did not move quickly enough, and the Serra Teresa was forced to choose between stumbling or stepping upon the folds of her sari. She chose the former, but it pained her. Vanity.

The Serra Celina rose at once, and then made courtly obeisance to an honored guest, gesturing for privacy by the curt wave of fan. She received it instantly.

They stood, two women in an empty room.

"Forgive me for my interruption," the Serra Teresa said. "Forgive me my lack of grace; the circumstances are dire and permit little."

"You have spoken with my husband." It was not a question, and it was not a statement that the Serra Teresa had been prepared to hear. It seemed that the humble Serra Celina was yet a Serra capable of surprising.

"Say rather, that he has spoken with us," she replied softly. "And that the Radann par el'Sol, and the men who have traveled with us, are of a mind with his intent."

Celina's eyes closed heavily; she bowed her head a moment and strands of black hair curled round her cheeks with their full weight.

"Serra Celina, this night, no matter what we might otherwise wish, war will be joined. Battle fought. But although war is the affair of men, some wars are said to be more evil than others. I believe that the Tor'agar will grant the armies of the Tyr'agar no easy passage through his lands."

"I am glad," the Serra whispered, her voice shaking.

And Teresa heard the sorrow and fear in the words as clearly as if they had been spoken instead. "I ask a favor," she said quietly. "The Matriarch of Havalla is not well, and she is not fit to travel with the Tor'agar and the men he has assembled. Where she cannot travel, I do not seek to travel.

"But our rooms are no harem rooms; they are blessed with no windows, and no view of the Lady's face. By your grace—"

"Stay with me," the Serra said quietly. "I am not afraid to have the Matriarch within my harem, and I would—as any Serra would—be honored by your presence."

"I thank you, Serra Celina, for your kindness." She bowed again, her knees now touching floor, her shoulders flowing over them beyond the perfect line of her back.

Kallandras.

Serra Teresa.

It is done. I will remain in the domis, and if the situation here becomes dangerous, I will send word.

Word may well travel too late, Serra Teresa. Will you not reconsider? He did not say, but could have, that the power she had at her command was not the equal of his; that her voice might not travel the stretch to Damar, even to his ears.

She was grateful for this kindness.

You know the answer, but you are Southern enough to ask. No. I know how I may best serve, and I am no longer Serra, to be bound and hidden at the whim of my kai.

She did not mention the Serra Diora di'Marano; he did not ask.

But when she raised her face, she met the unblinking

gaze—the appraising gaze—of the Serra Celina en'-Clemente.

The Lady's time had not yet come; the light in the room was warm and gentle. But it was to the Lady that both women had claimed some small allegiance, and by the Lady that the Serra Teresa was now guided, in some fashion.

"Serra Celina," she said, "a question, if it is not too bold."

"I do not think you capable of too bold a question, Serra Teresa."

"You have not heard the question," the Serra replied, smiling.

"Then ask it without fear; I shall take no offense."

"The young man and the young woman over whom your husband's cousin perished—what became of them?"

"An interesting question, Serra. An unusual one. What do you think happened, given the outcome to the Manelo family?"

Teresa bowed her head. But she heard, in the words of the Serra Celina, some hesitancy, and something akin to both shame and pride; she did not press further.

Ser Alessandro kai di'Clemente came to her in the early morning, but this time he traveled by the side of the par el'-Sol. She heard their muffled steps only moments before the knock came at the door, and she had already made the obeisance his rank demanded when the door was opened from the outside.

"Serra Diora," the Tor'agar said, "after much discussion, and some misgivings, we feel it may be best to sequester you within the Clemente harem. But it has come to my attention that there are suitable companions for you among your own party, and in such a case, your name might not be damaged by placement among my own wives."

She bowed her head at once.

"If there is anything you desire, you may ask it of the

Serra Celina. She is aware of who you are, and she understands that you were once the wife to the man who ruled the Dominion. She is not . . . as you are; but she is kind and gentle, and she will do all within her power to see to your comfort while we are gone."

She looked up then, although he had given her no permission to rise, and met the watchful eyes of the Radann par el'Sol.

"Yes," he said quietly. "I will be occupied for a few days at the behest of the Tor'agar, and I may be unavailable for hours at a time. The Tor'agar is summoned to a meeting with the Tor'agnate Amando kai di'Manelo; the Northerners will travel with the Tor'agar, but the Matriarch and her companion are not deemed fit for travel upon the open road; they will be your companions in our absence."

"The Radann par el'Sol will remain within my domis. I do not believe he would be parted from you; he has given his oath, and I, of all men, am aware of what that oath entails. I have not asked."

"And the child?"

"She, too, will be taken into the harem." He glanced at the girl; she slept in a corner of the room, without benefit of blanket or pillow.

Serra Diora bowed again. Thinking, although she knew it was foolish and self-indulgent, that she would ask for the samisen when she was brought before the Serra Celina.

And that she would play it.

When Jewel, accompanied by Avandar and Kallandras, made her way to the open courtyard that stood in the lee of the great gates, the cerdan were talking among themselves in voices that were both heated and hushed. Silence descended upon them all when they caught sight of the Northern contingent.

Jewel wondered what the Tor'agar had told them, for she knew awe and fear when she saw it, even writ as it was upon foreign faces.

But when they turned their gazes toward the gates, she looked beyond their iron bars, and saw that it was no word from the Tor that had caused their muted conversation.

Lord Celleriant stood in the rounded glow of torchlight, and at his side, tines dark in the diminishing light of day, stood the Winter King. His eyes were round and dark as he turned toward her, and she felt some hint of his humor as their eyes met.

So much for subterfuge.

Celleriant stood just under seven feet in height, and every inch of it seemed a mockery of human frailty and the lack of beauty inherent in that condition; his hair fell to his shoulders, spill of silver, cloak of light; his face, unadorned by the leather and splint helms of the cerdan, was flawless, his eyes silver.

His lips turned up at the corners, and she lost breath for just an instant; hated herself for doing it. But traveling upon the open road at the side of the Arianni lord had done nothing to diminish the effect of his beauty—and only his absence, be it for a few short hours, had given her the illusion that she had developed some immunity.

He bowed to her, in full sight of the Clemente cerdan; he held that bow until she realized that he meant to hold it, awaiting her permission to rise. She gave it awkwardly, cursing in the silence.

The Winter King's laughter was rich and deep; a resonant, welcome sensation.

"Lady," one of the cerdan said, in awkward, broken Weston. "Open the gate?"

"Please," she replied, in the Torra that so ill-suited the High Court. "They are allies, not enemies."

The gates rolled open, creaking and straining; she waited in their center.

Lord Celleriant straightened, tossing his hair past his shoulder. "Lady," he said, in flawless Weston, his voice the perfect tenor. "You summoned me. How may I serve?"

Through gritted teeth, she said, "Cut it out." Her Weston

was clean, sharp, and very, very quick. She hoped that none of the cerdan could follow the words.

But he did not condescend to notice the ill-grace she offered his perfect bow.

"I mean it," she whispered, aware that no one else spoke. "Cut it out. Everyone is staring at me."

"They are perhaps aware that you wield a power that is seldom seen in these lands."

"Great. I want them to be *less* aware."

His smile was perfect. "I think it unwise," he said quietly. And then he frowned.

She turned; Kallandras had come to stand by her side, and his lips moved, briefly and silently, over words his gift protected from reaching her ears. He turned to her next. "ATerafin," he said quietly, "It is unlikely that you will be . . . unnoticed here."

"I don't—"

"You are a woman, and you will ride with the Tor'agar. The men are armed and armored as if for war, and they expect to see battle before dawn's light. If you did nothing but ride at the side of the Tor'agar, you would still be worthy of remark.

"But even without the Lord Celleriant, you would engender much comment, for if I'm not mistaken, you intend to ride the stag."

"I don't have much choice," she said grimly. "I'm not highborn. I never learned to ride horseback. Not well."

"Then accept the curiosity and the mute awe of strangers," he replied gravely. "Because accept it or no, you will receive it."

"Jewel ATerafin is not noted, among The Ten, for the grace with which she accepts the inevitable."

"Why, thank you, Avandar."

The domicis offered her a shadowed smile, and she realized that it was one of the few he had offered in a very long time. "Understand that the Tor'agar plays no game," he said quietly. "You've never been on the field in a battle."

"I've been in battles before."

"True enough. But you had the luxury of command in those situations; you have no such luxury here. While you can hear him, while he can speak to you, the course of the combat *is* his. Do not forget this."

She nodded stiffly.

The stag entered the courtyard and came to stand before her; she stood in the cage of his shadow, staring up, and up again, at the length of his neck, the length of his jaw, the proud lift of his head.

She could almost see the man in the creature, and as always, it disturbed her deeply.

Come, he said. *If I am to be servant, and I am not disturbed, you have no cause to trouble yourself.* He bent, his forelegs kneeling into the flagstone that seemed so out of place in the South.

She nodded and reached up, gripping his antlers in the palms of her hands. He rose as she slid over his neck and across his withers to the slight curve of his back. Then he turned to gaze upon the cerdan; Jewel turned as well, seeing them from the vantage of height and safety.

The Tor'agar had joined them in silence.

He met her hesitant gaze, his own unblinking. "So," he said softly, "it appears that we saw no mirage on the road."

"We thought it . . . best . . . to . . ." her voice trailed off.

"Had you arrived in the presence of any less a man of the Lord than the Radann Marakas par el'Sol, I think we would consider you as great a threat as the one we now face. But I am well aware of who his master was, and I know how far he will go in his odd pursuit of honor. You walk out of story, Lady, and the stories of the South are not kind."

"It seems very little about the South is."

Avandar's frown was a thing more felt than seen.

"Kindness is often ill-rewarded," Ser Alessandro replied gravely. "As you will no doubt see, should you remain in the Dominion. I have not asked you why you have jour-

neyed South, and perhaps it would be prudent to have such
an answer."

"It would take far, far longer than you have," Avandar
said, bowing.

"No doubt. But when we have the time, it is a story I
would like to hear." He turned to his cerdan. "Enough. The
gates are open, the stables are waiting. Bring me Quickheart, and ready yourselves; we ride to join the rest of
Clemente."

Moonlight crested the horizon before the sun's light had
faded; the dark of night had not yet banished crimson and
orange gold from view. Against this backdrop, the cerdan of
clan Clemente rode behind their leader and his Toran. They
were silent, although the hooves of shod horses spoke in a
clipped, steady thunder, the drumbeat of war.

Lord Celleriant went unmounted; Kallandras and Avandar accepted the offer of horses, and rode to one side of the
Tor'agar. But although the Arianni lord followed the paths
by foot, he did not fall behind; indeed he disappeared for
long stretches, following the road and the shadows trees
cast across it. Every time he disappeared, the cerdan spoke;
every time he returned, they spoke again. Only the Toran
and the Tor'agar seemed immune to his presence.

Jewel watched them all, nervous now.

She had told the Tor'agar she had seen battle, and she
had. But she had never seen it shorn of all her den. Never
seen it at the head of a small army. She might have said
something, but there was no one to say anything *to*.

There is me, the Winter King said quietly.

She had thought he would be amused.

Not this eve, he replied, his voice rich and somber. *Can
you not feel it, upon the wind?*

Feel what?

The servants, he replied, *of the Lord of Night.*

No. But as she spoke, she realized the words were a lie.

She could not see, could not hear, the enemy—but she was aware of them.

She wondered whether or not she should speak with the Tor'agar. In truth, she didn't much care for him. He was cold, and obviously fond of the rank he held.

Do not mistrust power so openly, the Winter King said.

Why not?

You will be one.

Great.

Power is the only way to ensure that your law and your justice prevails.

I thought you said I was weak.

You are. You have chosen weakness, he added quietly. *It is a choice that I could never have made.*

Would never have made, you mean?

They are the same, your statement and mine.

Understand, Jewel ATerafin, that the power you will wield will never be whole. It will be broken. It will be tested. It will never be a certain fortress.

You say this to me? When you look like—

I say it because I can.

I'm . . . sorry. That was unnecessary.

It is hard to choose the power you have chosen.

There is no other power, for me.

No. But . . . His voice, devoid of amusement, was stark and uncomfortable. *Great,* she thought, attempting to keep the words to herself. *I'm now only comfortable when I'm being mocked and condescended to.*

It will be hard not to be twisted and broken by the sacrifices you must make. It is easy—for you—to contemplate death. But only as long as it is your own. Learn to contemplate others. Learn, he said softly, *to be unbowed by them.*

I can't—

You can. The Terafin does.

You know nothing of The Terafin. You've never even met her!

I know, he said quietly, *what you know.*

Leave it alone, she told him. Just that. But she was uneasy again. How much of her life had she given him, in the silence of musing and thought? How much more of her past did he know?

She seldom gave him orders. And if she was honest, it was not what he knew that troubled her—it was what Avandar might also have gleaned.

If the Winter King heard her, he did not choose to acknowledge the thought. Instead, he turned his great, tined head toward the horse which bore the Tor'agar. Without order, he began to canter toward the stallion, Quickheart.

The stallion, unlike the men, did not view him with awe, although suspicion was there.

"ATerafin," the Tor'agar said. "Does something trouble you?"

She nodded.

His face, in the moonlight and lamplight, was dark. "Speak plainly, as is your custom. I will take no offense. In times of war, much is excusable, and much excused."

"The servants of the Lord of Night are ahead of us."

She spoke in Weston, out of habit.

After a moment, he replied, and his Weston, unlike her Torra, was strongly accented. "Do you know their numbers?"

She shook her head.

But he marked the hesitation in the gesture. "Speak," he said, the word inflected and brusque.

"More than one, I think," she said at last. "Or one very, very powerful one."

"Do you know much of these creatures?"

"More than I'd like," she said, without thinking. And then, when the Winter King's snort invaded the silence, she added, "I've seen them fight before."

"And one is a danger?"

"A big danger, no matter what its power."

He turned and lifted a hand, by gesture calling for a halt to the march.

She took advantage of it; she waved Kallandras forward. He came at once, in perfect silence. "ATerafin?"

"Has Lord Celleriant discovered anything?"

"Not to report, no. But he is . . . uneasy."

He looked anything but.

"Is this the same kind of uneasy he was in the desert?"

Kallandras stared at her for a moment, and then he smiled; it was a slight smile, but it seemed almost genuine. "Yes."

"And there were five. No, six."

He nodded.

The Tor'agar nodded as well. "Thank you, ATerafin." He turned to the Toran and spoke quickly and quietly; his words did not reach her ears.

But they didn't have to; their meaning was made plain when the Toran wheeled and rode back into the column. When they appeared again, they bore two bows.

They gave these to their Tor, and he in turn gave them into Kallandras' keeping.

"I need not tell you," he said, although plainly he did, "that these are of value to me; we have few fletchers in the South, and they are not of note."

"The bows are of Imperial manufacture?"

"Indeed."

"We will return them to you before we depart these lands," Kallandras said. He bowed. Something about the bow was subtly wrong, but it wasn't until he rose that Jewel realized what it was: It was entirely Southern. It suited him.

The Tor'agar was silent. At length, he said, "I do not like this. I had hoped that you might strengthen my men by presence alone.

"I release you," he said coldly. "From my command and my service. Go as you will; do what you must."

Kallandras nodded. "The ATerafin?"

"She, too, must follow her own course." He was silent a moment, weighing words. At length, he shifted into Torra. "We will buy time, if that is possible. My cousin will not . . . attack . . . before we have finished negotiations in Damar. But I do not know the servants of the Lord of Night; I do not know the intent of Marente. I cannot say what they will do.

"I am the Lord's man; I can guess. Whether they stay their hand or not will depend in large part upon what we are seen to do—and if we are seen in the company of . . . the ATerafin's mount, and her liege—"

"Understood," Kallandras said. "Avandar?"

Jewel turned to look at her domicis. It was funny; he had shed the menace and strangeness of the desert and the mountain, and she had chosen to allow it; she accepted his presence as if he was still a complicated, condescending domicis.

The stag moved beneath her stiff legs; the night was cool.

Avandar's profile faced her; no more. But his expression was distant, his eyes dark; he seemed taller in the shadows of night.

He swiveled his gaze; caught hers and held it. "What would you have of me, ATerafin?"

A hundred answers came to her lips, and a hundred answers died before leaving them. She could not see the whites of his eyes. She could see something akin to gold instead, and it burned. Her hands gripped folds of skin and fur as she met those eyes and held them.

"Avandar Gallais," she said.

"Yes?"

Not enough, Jewel, the Winter King said, and his voice was the soul of ice.

"I want you to be Avandar Gallais."

"Is that not what I am?"

She lifted a hand then. Lifted an arm. It burned in the cold of night, and she knew which arm she had lifted; what lay upon the surface of skin, beneath the folds of rough cloth.

"It's not all that you are," she replied. "I—I know this."

She bit her lip and let go of fur for long enough to shove the hair out of her eyes. "But this is all that *I* am, and I . . ."

He waited. In silence, the time passed, and it was time they did not have. She knew it.

But she was afraid. It was night. Night now. Maybe in the day—

Pretend, she thought. *Pretend, for just a little while longer, that that* is *all you are.*

But she couldn't bring herself to say the words, because even thinking them, she despised them.

"How many people are in the village?" she asked instead, and felt the Winter King's bitter disappointment. Surprising, how much it could sting.

Avandar seemed to grow taller. The arm he had lifted—and he had lifted his arm, although when, she couldn't remember, fell back to his side. He offered his profile for her inspection, but it might as well have been a wall.

The Tor'agar frowned. He was not a stupid man; he was aware that something had passed between these Northerners and the stag that was both significant and beyond his grasp. It did nothing to improve his temper.

"Ten thousand," he said curtly.

Ten thousand. She thought of telling him that "village" was not the word she thought it was, at least not in the North. "How many—" she lifted her hand. "No, forget it. I'm sorry." She ran the back of her hand across her eyes. "Tor'agar."

"ATerafin."

"We'll find the kin."

"Kin?"

"The—the Servants of the Lord of Night. We'll find them. We'll kill them. Or send them back to the Hells."

He waited, sensing that she had not yet finished. He was right.

"But we don't do this for free."

The stillness that enveloped his face robbed the clearing

of the last of its warmth. "What would you have of me, stranger?"

His Toran urged their horses forward; their Tor sent them back with a gesture, his hand a mailed fist.

"I . . . I don't know," she answered.

"We do not have the time for games, ATerafin."

"I know."

What do you want, idiot? She cursed herself in the silence. *Tell him to free all the serafs in his precious village if we manage to save it?*

He'd never agree. She *knew* it.

But she found words, ashamed that she could. "The Serra," she said. Her voice was remarkably calm.

"What of the Serra?"

"The Serra Diora."

"What of her?"

"She has to go North. North and East."

Silence, then.

"And I want your word that you will do everything in your power to see that she gets there. Everything."

"I will offer you my word; the word of Clemente. But in return for your service this eve, I will also place one condition upon this oath."

"And that?"

"I want to know why."

"Why?" It seemed obvious to her. "Because if she doesn't, we'll lose this war. And I think you're beginning to understand why we can't afford to."

Too late, she realized that she should have had anyone else offer these words, this warning; she was, after all, a woman, and these lands were within a Dominion that granted women little.

"ATerafin," Avandar said. It was almost a blessing. She turned to meet his gaze, wary now. "In the South, men do not swear binding oaths to women."

His expression was familiar; he was annoyed. Damn him anyway. He was right.

But the Tor'agar raised his hand again. "I swear an oath not to you," he said quietly, "but to the Lord, the Lady, and the forest which borders these lands. I will not surrender my dominion to the Lord of Night; I will not allow any battle against him to falter. I confess that I would not normally accept the word of a Northerner in these matters. Or perhaps in any other. But you ride a great stag, and you command a servant of the Lady.

"Among the common cerdan, you are her signal, and her blessing."

"You are not—"

"No. I am not. But I am one sword. The swords that will be lifted this eve will be lifted by men who are not so cautious."

"Have you horn?" she asked him quietly.

"I have."

"Wind it," she said, "if we are needed."

"I think," he said, "If it is winded, you will not have the opportunity to reach us."

"We will."

He bowed. "We understand the war we have prepared to fight. I pray you understand as well that war that you have undertaken."

She closed her eyes. "Kallandras," she said.

"ATerafin."

"We enter the forest."

Only when they were well away from the body of the Tor'agar's army did someone speak.

To Jewel's surprise, it was Lord Celleriant. "Lady," he said, bowing, "this is not the safest path."

"It's the only path," she said quietly.

"There are others. The village—and it is poorly named, if my understanding of the human word 'village' has any meaning—is large; there are many ways to reach it, and none of them are as dangerous—"

"They are *all* dangerous," she snapped back. "And they're all guarded."

Arianni gray met common brown. Gray fell first.

She had been taken by the words; they had left her lips without any conscious thought on her part. But once they had, she *knew* them for truth.

"Very few are the guards that could deny us passage," Celleriant said softly.

"We want to choose the fight," she snapped back. "On our own terms. We don't know who—" She held up a hand, demanding silence.

Since none of the men who regarded her now were *ever* talkative, it wasn't that hard to get it. *Think, damn it, think fast.*

Avandar stepped into her path. "Who guards the paths, Jewel?"

"Ahead of you," she whispered. Aie, she hated her gift. *Hated* it. "How many roads, Celleriant?"

"Seven," he said quietly.

"You haven't missed any?"

He shook his head. "They're cut through the fields and the edge of the Deepings, and this close to the dark forest, life has its own voice. It is not," he added, "a gentle one; but it is not . . . yet . . . awake. I hear the silence where life has been cleared as if it were a scar; the paths are seven."

"Does that include the bridges?"

"No, Lady. The bridges are within Damar."

"And this road?"

"It leads to the East. The only way to reach the West is through the forest, or across the river itself, within Damar."

"There's a bridge in the forest?"

His smile was cold. Far too cold.

"There is a passage," he said quietly. "I would advise against it, were you any other mortal."

"What the Hells does that mean?"

"It means," he replied, drawing his sword from the air in

front of his slender breast, "that you should not dismount until we are clear of the trees."

"And Kallandras?"

"Kallandras, as you call him, has walked a darker road than this in his time, if I am not mistaken."

She didn't like the way he said the bard's name. It was almost possessive.

Seven paths. "The forest—that's not a path?"

He laughed. The sound was beautiful. Funny, that beauty had come to be synonymous with things that were distant and cold. "It is not one of the seven," he replied. "I ask again, Lady, that you choose a mortal road."

"Seven paths," she said, lost in the number, the two words. "No"

"No?"

"They're guarded. There are at least seven of the kin on the edge of town." She said the words as if she were groping her way toward truth. She was. "They're probably there to make sure that no one else escapes."

He nodded. "We can—"

"Yes. We can. But not without announcing our presence."

"It is not our way to skulk."

"It *is* our way to skulk," she snapped back. "Are there so many of the kin?"

"They are many, in the Hells."

"Here, damnit. Here. Are there so many that they can just be sent out in numbers to capture one lousy village?"

"That is the first intelligent question you've asked this eve."

"Thank you, Avandar."

Kallandras raised his head; until he did, she had not noticed that he had bowed it. "No," he said. "I think that this village is of import."

"Or something in it?"

"Or something within the Torrean."

She was silent as she absorbed the words. "They can't . . . know . . . that we're here."

"Not us, no."

"Then what?"

"It is said—in the South—that the Sun Sword was crafted to be demon-bane."

"You think they—"

He shrugged. "Understand, ATerafin, that although they were rare, the immortal races were not without their seers."

"But—"

"I have had some experience," he said, and the complete neutrality of his tone was chilling.

"Lord Celleriant?"

The Arianni lord was gazing at Kallandras. After a moment, he bowed; his hair draped across his left shoulder. Across his right, he now carried a Northern bow. "I will lead," he said gravely.

She nodded. But she looked to Avandar.

He said nothing. His eyes still glittered with golden fire. A little, she thought, like the sun—the afterimage of the flames was burned into her vision for minutes, obscuring all else.

"Well, Adelos?" Alessandro kai di'Clemente said, when the strangers had disappeared into the forest's depths.

"Tor'agar," Ser Adelos said, inclining his head. He could not bow without dismounting.

"Reymos?"

"Tor'agar."

"Come. Your silence is unpleasant. We are not among outsiders now. Tell me."

The two men shared an uneasy glance. Alessandro waited for Reymos to speak. He assumed it would be Reymos, for Adelos often left the difficult words to the more quiet Toran.

Reymos ran a hand through his beard and cleared his throat. "I trust them."

"Good. Adelos?"

"I concur."

"But?"

"The man—the seraf—that serves the Northern woman."

"Yes?"

He shook his head. "I would not anger him. Not if you offered me the whole of the Terrean as reward."

Alessandro nodded again. "Come. We have two hours to travel before we arrive in Damar, and Ser Amando is not known for his patience."

Adelos spit to one side.

The Tor'agar smiled bitterly, but said nothing; although his Toran were, measure for measure, men of the Court, they had not been born to the Court, and some of the habits of old returned to them in times of duress. Fear, they had mastered. Distaste. Exhaustion. But anger?

Perhaps, in the end, he was his father's son. The time spent in Manelo, the time spent in the Lambertan stronghold, had given him the appearance, the carriage, of high nobility. Certainly his title and his birth spoke of both. But he found no disdain for the men upon whom his life depended.

"Adelos, tell Carvan that he is to keep all but a handful of his men sequestered in the Eastern half of Damar. Have fifty men prepare to secure the bridges when we arrive."

Adelos nodded.

But Alessandro noticed that the Captain of his Toran had let one hand drop to the sash at his waist; it hovered, in darkness, around the slender curve of silver horn.

In the night, the woods seemed dark and devoid of life. Although no snow was upon the undergrowth, no ice upon the branches, Jewel felt Winter in the air; she shivered upon the back of the Winter King.

Lord Celleriant knew no such cold. Although he stopped frequently as he traversed the thick of trees grown tall and majestic in the fringes of the forest, he did not notice the weight of their impenetrable shadows; he was at home in this place. Still, he did not lead them into the forest's heart; where he strayed, he kept the flats and the plains of Mancorvo to one side or the other, as if they were anchor.

She could not have done as much; the trees seemed to absorb the whole of her attention, and any glimpse she had of the cleared lands began to seem strange, drab, almost repulsive. She could not have walked in safety here.

The Green Deepings were his home, the Winter King offered, in silence. Warmth nestled in the words. *And in some fashion, this forest remembers them. He need know no fear here.*

No fear that is not for you, Lady.

Don't call me that, she said, but her heart wasn't in it.

Celleriant raised a hand. The Winter King came to a stop. Jewel noticed that the stag's hooves were placed, with care, upon the ground; that although he moved quickly, he moved with a precision that spoke of dance. Dangerous dance.

She heard voices in the fringes of this forest.

Whispers, things that carried words just beyond the edge of her hearing.

Do not listen, the Winter King said sharply.

I'm not an idiot, she said, as sharply, although her hands gripped his fur. *And anyway, I can't hear a damn word they're saying.*

No; that wasn't true. She could hear a voice. One voice, resolving itself now into something that tugged at memory.

The darkest of memories. Her rage.

She couldn't help herself; she turned back.

Saw the dark trunks of trees, like an iron wall, extending into the distance for as far as the eye could see. Which was, all things considered, far indeed.

Jewel, the Winter King said quietly.

Carmenta.

She heard the Winter King's voice. Was grateful, for the first time, for the *way* she heard it. Because sound was lost

to the snarling, agonized accusation in a voice she hadn't
heard for half a lifetime: Carmenta's voice. Carmenta,
whose gang had once controlled the streets of the twenty-
sixth holding.

You killed me, he said. She searched the darkness for
him; the darkness was—for the moment—merciful.

"Yes," she said out loud, her voice much thinner than
she'd've liked. "I did."

The voice was silent a moment. She had no illusions; it
would start up again, and soon.

Jewel ATerafin, Jewel Markess, Jay.

Three women, one woman. She had never lifted dagger
in anger, although she'd certainly lifted hand—or pot, or
whatever else happened to be in easy range. She had never
played the games that the House Council immersed themselves in. Prided herself on that, but in silence, especially
when Avandar was around.

But she *had,* just once, killed. She had given a demon the
location of Carmenta's den. And she had *known,* when the
words left her lips, what that would mean.

No, she had known before they left. She had taken their
lives in payment for Lander's. Her den-kin. Carmenta's
gang had chased him into the labyrinth that lay beneath the
sprawl of the hundred holdings in Averalaan. The maze had
swallowed him whole, and she knew now that the death he
suffered had been slow and terrible. They had never found
his body.

"Yes," she said again, but quietly. "I killed you."

There was no triumph in the words.

She felt the Winter King beneath her stiff legs; he had
stilled.

Not in self-defense.

No, she told him flatly. *Revenge.*

Ah. He was surprised. She took no pleasure from it. It
had been many, many years since she had taken pleasure
from the death.

But not none. Not none. She closed her eyes; the voice grew sharper.

I didn't kill your den-kin, it said. And it spoke inside her, the words contained, as the Winter King's words were, but made of ice.

She could have argued. Even wanted to. When she had been sixteen, she would have. And what would she have said? *Yes. Yes, you did. You killed him. You forced him into the maze. You sent him straight to the kin.*

It was true.

You wouldn't shed any tears if you'd killed me, you bastard.

That was true, too.

But sometime between the then of lean streets, terrible cold, and fear of starvation, and now—even the ridiculous now of being seated upon the back of a creature that hadn't even been one of *her* childhood stories—she had lost the ability to make that argument stick.

Because it made her Carmenta.

It was the only thing that she had ever done that made of her life something akin to his.

"Yes," she said again, into the dark that was suddenly too familiar. "I killed you."

He came out of the shadows then, her acknowledgment giving him form and shape. His face—aiee, what was left of his face—was twisted and broken.

Rage she could have accepted; it would have given her something to fight against. But all she saw was his fear and his torment. She had killed him. She had brought him to this.

"They killed us all," he said, the words coming from broken lips. "Do you know how?"

"No."

But it was a lie. She *did* know. She had, through the auspices of House Terafin, requested the reports of the magisterial guards. She had read them, their cold, precise language understating the horror of those deaths. Two bodies were beyond identification. None of the bodies were in one piece.

"We never hurt you," he said.

"You did," she snapped back. But it was hard. Her memories of Carmenta had been of a large, brutish giant with an ugly face, an ugly laugh, the scars of old fights adorning his jaw.

This—this Carmenta—was a child. Not a small child, never that, but a boy.

Jewel. The Winter King's voice was deep and deceptively gentle.

What?

Do not do this.

Can you see him?

No.

Can you see anything?

The Winter King was silent. She thought he would remain silent. Didn't want him to.

And he heard that desire. *I was the mount of the Winter Queen,* he said softly. *And I have seen much, much worse in the Deepings. But I am some part of them now. They do not speak to me with human voices.*

She turned then, stiffly, and looked ahead. Celleriant's hair was like a sheen of winter snow. By his side, Kallandras of Senniel College walked. His steps were light, quick, elegant; his legs did not shake and his feet did not hesitate.

"Kallandras," she whispered.

He turned. His eyes were wide, unblinking in the mask of his face. "ATerafin?"

She wanted to ask him. If he could see anything. Hear anything. But what could he hear? What did a master bard know of death?

Unbidden, another memory returned. Henden.

The song of the bards of Senniel College.

What had Kallandras of Senniel offered to the dying? What had he offered to the victims whose tortured cries were slowly destroying the morale and the spirit of *Averalaan?*

Death.

Simple. Merciful. Quick. But death, nonetheless.

Had she forgotten that? How?

Yet he did not seem tormented. He did not seem to be caught in conversation, to be speaking to ghosts. No; maybe they were hers. Maybe that was how the forest spoke to her.

The Winter King said nothing.

"It's . . . nothing," she said lamely. But before her attention left him, she saw that Lord Celleriant had reached out to catch the bard by the arm; that a slender, perfect hand, a long arm, had wrapped itself around the bard's shoulders.

The boy had come to her side, and although his feet left no mark upon the ground, neither did hers; he kept pace with the stag. He spoke.

She wanted to lift her hands to her ears; to stop the words from reaching them. Wanted to cry out or snarl in fury because fury was easier than anything else.

But she didn't.

"Yes," she heard herself saying. "Yes. Tell me how you died."

Hating him. Hating him, but not as much as she hated herself. This had been her only act of willful murder. This was the death that she could have prevented by the simple expediency of silence. But she had been so angry that she had wanted the justice of his death. An eye for an eye. Lander had been worth a hundred Carmentas, and she had never been able to face the fact that she could not protect her own. Not then.

Not now.

A hundred things came between her and this ghost.

I only did it once.

We were already at war.

I thought it was necessary. I thought we would be going back. I was protecting my own.

I'm not as bad as Haerrad—

Or less. She understood the danger here.

Yes, she said flatly. *I killed you. I enjoyed it, for a while.*

She curled up on the back of the Winter King, the night so cold she might as well have been in the desert.

The ghost stopped speaking. And smiled.

She wondered if the others might come back to haunt her; none did. No Duster. No Lefty, no Fisher, no Lander. Just Carmenta.

She swallowed, and said out loud, "It's part of what I am. But I swear that it's not all that I am. And it will *never* be all that I am. If you came to remind me," she added softly, staring at the mutilated, oddly peaceful face, "I've been reminded. If you came to torment me, you can stand in line."

"Lady." Celleriant's voice, clear as a bell.

She looked across a slender clearing and met the startling clarity of eyes that the darkness should have concealed. He bowed.

"You are . . . more, indeed, than you seem."

"And less," she said sadly.

She wondered what Haerrad would see, if he walked these roads.

And wondering, turned.

Avandar.

She forgot to breathe then.

Avandar Gallais stood at the very edge of her vision. He looked up, as Celleriant had done, but the fire in his eyes was guttered.

"Viandaran has walked roads darker than this," Celleriant said quietly. But he, too, turned.

"Avandar?"

Silence.

What's wrong with him?

The Winter King didn't answer.

What's wrong?

The absence of his voice was frightening.

"Is every single road going to be like this one?" she

snarled, to no one in particular. She wrapped her hands
around folds of warm fur and then tensed; her legs tightened and she braced herself for a fall.

The ground beneath her feet was harder than it looked
from a distance.

The shadow of the Winter King's great tines fell like a
net at her feet; he had turned; she could feel his gaze upon
her back. She expected him to try to stop her. Expected
some warning, some grave discussion of the danger she
faced just standing on the ground.

Nothing.

Squaring her shoulders, she began to walk toward Avandar Gallais. The distance was not great, but she was aware
of it because in times of danger, he never stood more than
ten feet from her back.

Fair enough; the danger wasn't hers.

He can't die, she thought, knowing that what she was
doing was absurd. *He can't be killed.*

True. All true.

There were other truths, glimpsed in dream and vision,
that she didn't want to approach. But they led to the one
question that occupied her as she walked.

What could make a man want to die so badly he was willing to destroy an entire city on the off chance he'd be
killed?

Ask him. The ground beneath her feet was uneven; the
night was unkind. She stumbled twice, but righted herself
before her hands hit the ground.

"ATerafin," Avandar said. "Go back."

She nodded politely; it was a habit she had struggled to
form over the last few years, and although it was best suited
to the Terafin Council Hall, she wasn't above using it here.

The Winter King still said nothing, and she took that as a
good sign. Or as a sign, at any rate.

She walked until she stood two feet away from Avandar,
and then she stopped.

His face was about as warm as steel. Luckily, she was

used to that. "Avandar," she said quietly. "Come on." She
held out a hand, palm up.

He stared at it.

Okay; he wasn't going to make this easy. He almost
never made anything easy, though, so it didn't come as
much of a surprise. She reached out and caught his hand—

And cried out, falling back as fire lanced up her arm,
consuming the length of her sleeve. Shock held her still for
a moment; it was followed by anger.

Bright anger, clear as the night.

She looked up at his face, and the anger died as suddenly
as the fire had; his eyes had not changed; the line of his jaw
hadn't shifted. She saw almost nothing there that she recognized.

Just don't start speaking in tongues, she thought sharply,
not much caring if he could hear her.

She reached out, slow now, and cautious.

Felt something as she once again reached out for his
hand. This time, she saw a tremor about his lips as he set
them in a narrow line. And this time, there was no fire.

Not that it did much for what was left of her sleeve. She
looked down at her arm; that was a mistake. The brand, the
hated and unmistakable mark upon her inner wrist, was
glowing brightly. Red, red, gold, and silver.

This time it was Avandar's sleeve that caught fire; Avandar's sleeve that was consumed by flame.

In the dark of Southern night, she saw for the first time
the brand that he, too bore: red, red, gold, and silver. Twin
to hers, it seemed smaller as it rested against his skin—but
it was the same size, the same shape; it was their arms that
were different.

She reached out to touch it, drawn to its strange familiarity. But it was *hot,* and she withdrew her fingers before they
suffered what cloth had suffered.

Celleriant's voice formed no words, but it carried in the
stillness, intake of breath that was more than simple breath-
ing.

And she knew that something was wrong.

She touched his hand carefully; it was warm in hers, and she knew that meant hers were cold. "Avandar," she said, speaking as gently as she knew how to speak.

His eyes flickered. A hint of gold, like dying embers, caught and held her attention. "Jewel."

Not ATerafin. Not the comfortable formality of the distant House. "What . . . is . . . this mark?"

"It is mine," he replied.

"It's the same."

"Yes."

"But—"

Silence. He had no intention of helping her.

No; be fair. His gaze was caught by something beyond her. She wondered if he heard his dead. Had no doubt at all they existed.

"Have you ever . . ." She hesitated. Decided that she really didn't want to know. She lifted a hand—her left hand— and the Winter King walked forward.

I really hate to do this, she began.

Then don't.

But you're going to carry him.

She could feel the Winter King at her back. "That isn't a request," she added.

He will not ride.

He damn well will.

If he accedes to your . . . command . . . I will bear him, Lady.

Don't. Call. Me. That.

Grinding her teeth, she turned back to the man who was her domicis. "Avandar."

No answer.

Avandar.

No answer.

She started to worry.

CHAPTER TWENTY-TWO

THE Radann par el'Sol was granted the freedom of the domis. More significant, he was given the freedom of the city. While in theory it could not be denied him, in practice there was much a Tyr or Tor could do to impede his progress. The Tor'agar had chosen no such restraint, and Marakas was glad of it.

Before he began his hunt, he sent word to the Serra Celina en'Clemente, and she in turn carried that message to the Havallan Matriarch. It was brief; he could not afford the length that pretty words required, and for once—perhaps for the only time—was grateful that the Voyani Matriarch in fact required none.

Prepare.

If there was safety—if indeed, injured as she was, she could provide some scant protection for the women and children of the harem—it would be in her hands.

His own were heavy with *Verragar*. His ears were absorbed with her whisper, her quiet, ceaseless determination. He had been left with a map of the city, one used by the tax collectors a Tor'agar often employed; he knew where the small temple of the Radann was situated. It was to that temple he now repaired.

The day was gone; the moon, bright as she crested the sky, declared the Lady's Dominion. Not the time to seek the Radann, and in truth, if the temple were under suspicion from spies of a foreign Lord, it would be now, in the darkness. The servants of the Lord did not—as legend said—

shrivel at the touch of the Sun, but they worked best in the shadows that hid their true nature.

The kin were abroad in the city. The light of the sword attested to this fact, and the Radann par el'Sol walked the city's streets, measuring her brightness, the strength of her voice. Listening, now with instinct, now with deliberation. In the Tor Leonne, such a hunt had been easier; the Tor Leonne was his city, and he had, at his side, men of like mind, swords of like voice. This place, with its flat plain, its negligible plateau, was a place of unknowns.

But unknown or not, it was where his duty lay, and of all the duties he had undertaken, it was the cleanest and the clearest; he approached it with a strange, a complete, joy.

Only as a child had he been absorbed with questions of Good and Evil, of Right and Wrong; as an adult, his quest for Justice had shown him, time and again, that judgment was faulty, that men were complex. There was comfort in this return to those early beliefs; comfort and a purity that he found he still desired, decades and so many deaths and bitter truths later.

He went to the temple of the Radann.

It was not so large a complex as that which housed the Radann kai and par el'Sol upon the plateau of the Tor Leonne; it boasted no rights to the waters of the Lady. It had—from the appearance of both city map and outer dwelling, no vast, stone garden, no small fountains, no areas in which the illusion of complete privacy—and it was an illusion—could be fostered.

But he was familiar with temples such as these, for it was to such a place that he had first come, bereft of all but the poorest of swords and the clothing upon his back, to make his offerings and his oaths, forsaking the family of his birth.

But he had not come at night.

Had not come bearing the sun ascendant, with its eight full rays.

The outer gate was closed, but it was manned; he sheathed *Verragar,* and approached the servitor at the gate.

The man was old; his hair was dusted with Northern frost, and his skin lined by days beneath the ferocity of the Lord's glare. But age had not bowed him; did not bend him now; he turned his attention upon the Radann par el'Sol, lifting a lamp as Marakas approached.

When he saw who stood in the light's glow, he lowered the lamp, or rather, he bowed and the light went with him.

Marakas did not bid him rise; he waited, and the man rose on his own. "Radann par el'Sol," he said, recognizing the insignia, and not the man who wore it.

"Radann el'Sol," Marakas replied. "It is late, but I must speak with the Radann in charge of the temple. It is Santos el'Sol, if I am not mistaken?"

"He still presides over the Radann in Seral," the servitor replied grimly. "And he had some warning of your presence here. He expected you earlier," he added, opening the gate. "But day or night, he waits upon your command. Follow me."

Marakas bowed and entered.

The Radann Santos el'Sol was much like the servitor at the gate; weathered, aged by sun and wind, but unbowed. He was not perhaps as perfect as the High Courts would expect; his robes were rumpled, and his hair flyaway with sleep. But his eyes were both dark and sharp when Marakas entered his presence.

"Radann par el'Sol," he said, bowing.

"Radann Santos el'Sol," Marakas replied.

"We had word of your arrival."

"The Tor'agar?"

"Ah. No, not through the Tor," Santos replied. "He has been occupied of late with preparation for war, and it is not his way to ask for counsel. Or offer it."

Marakas nodded. He did not ask how word had traveled; it was not his business.

"We have had little word in the Torrean," Santos continued, "But of the words that have reached us, none have been more troubling than the news of the kai el'Sol."

"Peder kai el'Sol travels with the armies of the—of Alesso di'Marente."

Silence, then. With caution, the Radann Santos said, "It was not of Peder kai el'Sol that I spoke. Forgive me."

Marakas lifted a hand. "There is nothing to forgive," he said softly. "My own allegiances are—in the Terrean of Mancorvo—well known, in life and death, and I stand by them."

Santos' eyes widened slightly; his boldness had been far surpassed by the Radann par el'Sol's. But after a moment, the older man smiled, and his shoulders seemed to slump slightly, as if he carried a great burden and was at last allowed to acknowledged the fullness of its weight.

"I told them," he said softly, "that you were Fredero's man."

"But you were surprised to find me in Seral?"

"Yes," Santos replied gravely. "But not because you do not travel with the Radann kai el'Sol; rather because you arrived at the side of the Havallan Matriarch. She is known in this Terrean. Even to me, she is known." He seemed about to add more, but hesitated.

"Speak freely," Marakas said. "I am no more a man of the High Court than you, and wherever possible, I shed its burden."

"You came from the Lady's forest," Santos said. "I am . . . a man of the Lord . . . but I was raised in the Torrean. Very, very few are the men who enter that forest and leave it again. But if there were one such among the living, I would guess it would be you."

Marakas was uncomfortable with the awe the words contained, but he held his peace. He had grown to understand that such awe was a gift, and no gift of its kind could, with grace, be refused.

"It is not of the forest that I would speak," he said softly, and with the force of truth. "I am not permitted to speak of it openly, and if I had the choice, it is not a road I would take again."

"Of course. Of course, par el'Sol."

"The Tor'agar has ridden to Damar."

Santos el'Sol closed his eyes. The lids were thin, veined in rich blue, a rich purple. But they were steady. "We expected as much," he said quietly, and opened them. "Among his cerdan travel some ten of our number. They go to war."

"Aye, war. But it is of the nature of that war that I have come to speak." He rose to his full height, placed his hand upon the hilt of *Verragar,* and drew the sword.

Its light was much diminished in this hall, but it was unmistakable. The Radann Santos el'Sol stared at the length of the blade for some time.

"So," he said at last, the word an echo of the Tor'agar's word. "So." He bowed. "I will don my armor," he said quietly, "and summon the Radann left at my disposal."

"The crest must be seen," Marakas said quietly.

"It will."

He could have refused the Radann's offer; he had fought with the demons of the Lord of Night, and he knew that normal swords counted for little against them.

But not for nothing. And Santos par el'Sol was the Lord's voice in this Torrean. The weight of his presence could not be underestimated.

"We hunt," Marakas said, as the older man reached the door. "And what we hunt, we *must* find before dawn."

"Understood, par el'Sol. While you wield one of the five—"

"*Verragar.*"

"You will be noted; if your face and your name are not known, the importance of what you wield will be."

Avandar.

Jewel Markess ATerafin, comfortable now in all three names, stared at her domicis. She must have called the Arianni lord, for he traveled down the unseen path, careful to drag Kallandras with him, until he stood by her side.

"What does he see?" she asked him softly.

"What did you see, Lady?"

She hesitated for just a moment; she did not trust Celleriant. Could not. She had seen him on the Winter Road, and although she had seen him countless times since then, the road was strong this eve. She *knew* what he was capable of.

But trusting him was not an issue, here.

She had learned that secrets weighed her down in ways that she could not afford to be weighed down. Had the den appreciated her honesty? Yes. But in truth, she was honest because it best suited her. If she spoke openly, nothing that lay in her past could be wielded, without her consent, as a weapon against her.

"I saw a boy I had killed."

He nodded.

"Is that what he sees?"

"I would say that he sees far more than one," Celleriant replied.

She glanced at his face; his expression was neutral. He took no joy and found no horror in his statement; it was bald fact, unadorned by malice or concern.

"But he's seen them before," she said faintly. "And I've never seen regret in him."

"Mortals are strange, even those that cannot die," Celleriant replied. "They take comfort from their strength, and they resent it, in turns. Both emotions are true."

"Can we define strength as something other than killing?"

"We can define strength in a myriad of ways," he replied, bowing slightly. "But I ask your pardon; I attempt to define strength in the way that the Warlord has defined it for millennia. It is by the fear of death that he wielded the greatest power."

"Can he hear me?"

"I do not know."

"Can we move him?"

Celleriant was silent. After a moment, he said, "Perhaps you can. I think it would be unwise for anyone else to try."

And unwise for me to. But she didn't say it aloud; there was no need.

The Winter King waited.

"Kallandras?"

"ATerafin."

"Can you speak to him?"

"What would you have me say?"

"That we are on this road, and we need to move."

She felt what she seldom felt when Kallandras chose to speak in the tongue of bards: the tingle at the base of neck and spine that spoke of power being shed. But a glance at his face revealed as much as a glance at Celleriant's: Nothing.

The Arianni lord was not human; he did not say *I told you so.* She wasn't sure what she would have done if he had. Couldn't imagine his cruelty descending to that level of pettiness.

Avandar did not move.

"ATerafin," the master bard said quietly, "if he hears me, he either chooses not to answer."

"Or he can't?"

"Or he cannot."

This is my fault, she thought. It was true.

But it had happened before. It would probably happen again. What could she say? It had seemed like a good idea at the time? It had.

She took a deep breath. He wasn't dead; wasn't dying. Short of that, there was no point descending into guilt. It wouldn't do either of them any good. Later, maybe. When she had time. But it was tempting, that paralysis, that internal conflict. Tempting, because she had the choice of that and fear.

You're afraid of Avandar.

Big surprise. *I've seen what he did. I know what he can do. How could I not be afraid of him? He was a monster.*

Is he a monster now?

Yes. Yes. Maybe.

She wasn't the type of person who said "I can't judge." Judgment—her own—had saved not only her life but the lives of her den more times than she could count. She lived by that judgment, by that ability, and to set it aside was something she wasn't capable of.

What are you afraid of right now, damnit?

Harder question. Because the fear wasn't a clean one; it was muddled. Muddy.

There was only one way to get clarity here.

Steeling herself, she reached out and touched him. Her right hand. To his right.

The trees vanished.

Pain did that.

She stood by the seawall, Avandar at her side; the night was moonless and dark.

At least, she thought it was the seawall; the ocean's voice was a crashing thunder, a horrible rumble of wave. No one with half a brain stood here in a storm; the water could easily crest the walls.

No. No, that was a comfortable thought. The truth followed quickly on its heels. That wasn't the ocean's voice. It was the thunder of a crowd. A mob, each voice subsumed by the whole, individual words lost to its shouting, its terrible anger.

She turned, clenching her hands into fists. One hand. The other couldn't quite close.

Of course it can't, idiot. It's holding Avandar.

She could see him clearly.

And after a moment, she could see some part of what he saw. Steel yourself was such a useless expression; all the steel in the world couldn't prevent her from blanching.

He gazed at her, almost unaware of her grip on his hand.

But his frown, while not the familiar one, was the first expression he offered her. There was something else in it, but it took her a moment to recognize it for what it was because she couldn't remember ever seeing it on his face before. Fear.

She even understood it.

"No," she said quickly, before he could speak. "No, I'm not dead. I'm not one of your dead."

She thought he would turn from her then. But his eyes remained fixed on her face.

"Avandar?"

He lifted his free hand and cupped her chin in it. She would have drawn away had they been in any other place. Had he looked at her in any other way.

But his face was rigid, and the hand beneath her chin was shaking. Not a lot, give him that, but it was the first time—

The first time that she thought he *needed* her.

She stayed her ground.

"Avandar," she said. And then, after a long pause, "Viandaran."

"Lady."

Not the word she wanted, but it would do. She was surprised she could even hear it; the voices of the dead were *so* damn loud.

"We can't stay here," she told him.

His eyes narrowed. She didn't much like the look.

"Viandaran," she said again. "They're already dead. The dead can't hurt you."

He laughed. "The dead," he said, the words soft, "are the only things that *can* hurt me. Have you forgotten, Lady? I cannot die. I will *never* die."

So much truth.

"Do you want to?"

"Can it be you do not know?" He turned from her then, releasing her chin, and his hand swept out in a grand gesture, encompassing the ghosts that she could hear, but could not see. "How else am I to escape the past, Lady? How else am I to know peace? Or can you grant me absolution from my sins?"

"Are they?" she shouted back; the voices, as if sensing the weakness in the Warlord, grew louder, grew frenzied. Or maybe it was her; maybe the frenzy was entirely contained.

"Are they?"

"Sins!"

He stopped then. His eyes were dark and clear.

Afraid to lose him, she continued. "You've walked darker roads than this. You've seen the dead before. Why are they stopping you *now?*"

"Should they not?" His voice was soft; deceptive. "If I am not mistaken, Lady, you met only one upon your road, and you could not continue. What might you do if faced with *them?*"

The curtain fell away. The darkness parted.

There was almost no distance between Jewel Markess ATerafin and the mob.

Her heart stopped. For just a moment, it stopped; her mouth was frozen, and her eyelids refused to budge.

What was the first comfort she offered her den? *The past doesn't matter.* But against such a past as this the words were a thin, fragile shield. She couldn't even lift it; couldn't offer it to him.

Even Haerrad, she thought, if he were forced to walk this road, wouldn't face what Avandar now faced. And Haerrad, she would leave to the wolves with a fierce joy. Could she do any less here? Could she?

No.

But she could not let go of his hand.

Was bitterly aware that had he injured any of *hers,* she wouldn't have come here; wouldn't have touched him; wouldn't have taken the risk.

And yet there were men, and women, and children, that he had hurt just as much; was she to forgive—and forget—

those deaths, that pain, because he had never done anything to *her?*

"You understand," he said quietly. He started to pull his hand back, and she almost let him go.

"Yes," she told him. Because he had seen the truth and she didn't much feel like lying. "I do. But what you do *here* won't bring them back. And it won't give them peace."

"And your own dead?"

She shook her head. "He only . . . needed me . . . to acknowledge what I'd done. To understand it."

"You understood it already."

"Yes. And no. I . . . can ignore it. I have, for years. I've taken it out once or twice. I've used it against The Terafin, the only woman I've ever served, and ever want to. But I'm not ruled by it."

"But you are, Jewel."

Her name. She started to pull him away from the crowd, and he took a step as she pulled.

"Am I?"

"Yes."

"Tell me how." *Tell me how,* she thought, *as we get the hell out of here.*

She thought to make a pretense of listening, but she found the words compelling. Almost as if she actually cared what he thought, which was strange, given how much of her adult life had been spent convincing him that she didn't give a damn.

"You let his death define you."

"Gods, I hope not."

The corner of his lip turned up. It wasn't quite a smile.

"You let it rule what you will—and will not—do. Haerrad is a danger. Rymark is a danger. At the very least, those two would always be a threat. But while the others play their games of power, familiarize themselves with the assassins and the poisons that they *will* use in the war for the House, you hide. You caused the one death—and a death, in the end, that no one but you regrets—and having faced it, having paid no other price—"

"I paid a price," she said coldly. "And it's as much of a price as I'm willing—ever—to pay."

"And was it not a just death?"

"No."

"Did he not cost you at least one of the family that you so value?"

"Enough, Avandar."

"No. Not enough."

"If he had lived, he would have made no difference."

"Not to you. But to those who took your place in the twenty-fifth holding? Did you not, by his death, ease their future suffering?"

She was white now. "It wasn't a clean death."

"No. But in the end, clean or no, death is death." He turned away again.

She hadn't finished. "It makes a difference *to me*."

"Justice, in its rudimentary form, is a wergild. Justice, in the absence of a wergild, is an eye for an eye."

"Great. So we all walk around blind."

His brow rose as she spit.

"An eye for an eye," she continued, "makes me no better than Haerrad."

"Ah, but it does. You did not *start* the hostilities. It can be argued that you finished them."

"It's too easy to argue that," she snapped back. "It's just too damn convenient."

"You don't trust yourself."

Not a question. She shrugged. Shoved hair out of her eyes. "Yes. Yes I do. And I want to *continue* to be able to trust myself. I want to know who I am. I want limits. I want rules."

"Why?"

"Because without them, I'm no better than—"

"Me?"

"Yes," she said, softly now. "Yes." She tugged at his hand.

"Is superiority so important?"

"Yes," she said again. A third time. "Because without try-ing to achieve it, what's the point? I know I'm not perfect. I'll *never* be perfect. But if I don't try to be as perfect as *I* can be, I might as well just *be* Haerrad.

"I met Carmenta tonight. But really, he was just *me*. Some part of me. I don't want to add to him. Not even for the House. I want . . ."

"You want what a child wants."

"Maybe. But it's *my* goal."

"And of me?"

"What?"

"What do you want of me? If Carmenta was simply some part of you, what of my dead?"

She shook her head. "I don't want them."

"They come with me," he said quietly.

Her arm ached. Her hand had gone from warm to some-thing just shy of burning.

Could she accept it? She closed her eyes.

"Let's just start with this," she said, almost to herself.

"With what?"

"I don't want you to add to them. Can you understand that?"

"What difference will one or two make?"

"I don't know. Maybe none." She shook her head. "No, that's not true. It will make a difference *to me*. No. Don't say it. You can say it when the village is safe. Just don't add to them. Don't—"

His eyes widened slightly. His hand tightened around hers, and this was a shock: it was the first time he'd re-sponded to her grip. He turned to look back at the dead. "If every single one of them were given permission to unbur-den themselves," he said softly, "you would be dead before they finished." And then he smiled; the smile was bitter. "I . . . begin to understand."

"Good. Tell me, because I don't."

But he shook his head, reasserting himself; becoming, again, the man that she had known for a decade. "My apologies, ATerafin."

Celleriant was waiting when Jewel turned around. The look on his face was an odd one. "What?" she said, more sharply than she'd intended.

He rewarded her with the lift of a brow and the faintest of smiles. "I will say no more than this, Lady. But I will say it. Were you to stand against my—against the Winter Queen upon the Winter Road, she would sweep you away without notice. But you forced her to stand a moment, and what she saw when she did, I only begin to see now." He bowed.

In the cold of night, she felt a sudden warmth in her cheeks. From just a smile and a few soft words. She was *never* going to take him to Court.

"Was I gone long?"

"No. Do not fear; the village—and the rendezvous—are well within our means now."

"Good. Avandar, you ride."

His brow rose.

"That wasn't a request."

"The road will not hold me captive again; not this eve."

"No. It won't. Because you'll be on his back." When he made no move, she snarled. "I already asked him, and he said it was all right. *Get on.*"

The second brow rose to join the first.

Lord Celleriant's hand tightened slightly, but he made no other move.

"ATerafin," Avandar said at last, the word heavy with multiple meanings, "at your command."

To her surprise, he climbed upon the back of the Winter King, and the great stag rose. Funny, how tall he seemed when viewed from the perspective of the ground.

"Okay," she told them all. "Let's move."

*   *   *

Ser Alessandro saw the lights of Damar before his men
left the road. They were many, and he found their presence
disturbing; the eastern half of Damar was seldom so well
lit. Oil was expensive; tallow expensive; the gathering of
wood a distant second to the tilling of fields, the gathering
of food.

Proof that the villagers did, indeed, fear the night, this
new darkness. The villagers of Damar were not given to
such overt displays of fear—for they lived in the lee of the
forest.

Had lived in it, for all of his life. In Damar, there were
stories and legends that predated the Dominion. He had
heard some of them, in his time—but not all; they were
common stories, and he was not a common man.

Still, he had stayed for some time in the village, hoping—in his youth—to glean some knowledge of the mys-
teries that lay beyond the Western bounds of Damar, the
borders defined by forest.

He looked upon it now, and as it approached, as he did,
he felt the strength of shadow, the cold of night. In the Eastern half of the village, with its low huts, its wooden homes
supported by hidden stone, its flat roofs, he saw only what
he chose to see: light, evening light. The fields that lay
across the bounds of Damar spilled past them into the
plains; the village had no walls. But where the scarecrows
stood, the lanterns were also burning; in the drier seasons,
this presented risk.

It was not dry yet.

No movement in the rough streets of the town distracted
him, and his eyes, accustomed to silver moonlight, passed
beyond them, tracing their egress. There were stone-bol-
stered causeways—those that led to the wide bridge, and
those that led from the main road; the roads to the West
were of necessity small; they were almost never taken.
They were certainly not maintained.

The divide between the East and the West became
clearer; the river seemed almost still in the flat of its bed,

glittering like twisted blade. The roads, two, seemed all that Damar had in common.

But they had not been built by the Easterners; they had been built for the use of the West, where the merchants, the craftsmen, and the elders lived.

As if in defiance of the old forest, Damar's heart lay upon the Western bank, in the form of a market. It was situated farthest from the shadows and bowers of ancient trees, hugging the banks of the Adane. But as the village had grown, the market had grown, its messy half circle widening in time. Old buildings still rose along the streets of the market center, and the tallest of these were reserved for those who had power or money—as such things were defined by a village. In the foreground of those buildings newer structures lay: stalls, small shops, the fount of contemplation in their center, its carvings almost too ornate for the village itself. He often wondered who had commissioned it, for along its surfaces, forest creatures ran, caught in the act of flight, and in its center, a woman stood, a bow in her pale hands. They called her the Lady.

But they did not speak of her often, and never to outsiders. He wondered what the Northerners would make of her, should they notice her at all. They might not; it was true that the statue was unusual, but true also that familiarity robbed it of its grace and its unique power. The villagers went about their business in the hours of dawn, and all of the hours that led to dusk, passing before her arrow without noticing that it was near to flight. The merchants were not troubled by her shadow; the farmers cursed and shouted openly before her chiseled gaze as they battled their way to their stalls, their carts and wagons moving poorly in the clogged streets.

No need for wells, either to the West or the East; the Adane provided all of the water Damar needed.

And when the banks were swollen in spring, the market stood yards away from its currents. Once, perhaps twice, those stalls had been flooded—but they had never been swept away; they endured much.

It was in the market that he would find his cousin; he felt certain of it. It was the only place in Damar in which people habitually gathered in great numbers; the only place in which the whole of the village lay visible. Even at night. Perhaps especially at night.

And on this one? Lights glimmering everywhere? Yes, he thought. There.

Ser Adelos frowned.

"Too much light," Ser Reymos said. Alessandro nodded. "The column?"

"They'll clear the forest in ten minutes, Tor'agar."

"The archers?"

"They'll like the light."

"Good. When we arrive at the bridge, call a halt. If there are men in the streets, clear them; make sure they return to the shelter of their homes."

And let those homes, he added silently, *be* shelter, for the eve.

Quickheart nickered; his forehooves skittered against the ground in a nervous dance. Alessandro leaned over and thumped the horse soundly, hands wide against the curve of dark neck. The words he spoke reached the horse's ears; they were gentle, even, simple.

Quickheart was slow to take comfort; a bad sign. Ser Alessandro wondered how the others would fare; few were the horses that were so steady in time of crisis, so inured to the sound and the dangers of battle, as Quickheart.

"You sense them," he said quietly. "You sense them, don't you? Well and good. Be alert, Quickheart. Be alert, and if necessary, be fleet of foot."

The village lay before him.

He followed the road, watching the lights. Something was wrong, but it took him a moment to realize what it was. All of the noise that slowly filled the village came from his men; there were no insect sounds, no night birds. Even the river seemed sluggish and meek as it traveled the course of its bed.

He saw a lone dog at the village edge.

Quickheart was so skittish that he reared at the sight of the animal. Alessandro rode the movement, tightening his knees. The dog retreated. Wise, that.

"Reymos," Alessandro said, when all four of Quickheart's hooves were again upon the ground, "I will travel to the Lady's shrine."

Reymos nodded.

The Lady's shrine was in the Eastern half of Damar. It was a small shrine, but even in the glow of moonlight, it looked well-tended. The stones that circled ground hallowed by moonlight were swept and cleaned; the plants that adorned the base of those stones, weeded and arranged with care. He wondered what their colors were; the night made them midnight blue, white, and dark shades of gray. Against the backdrop of night, they formed the perfect colors of mourning.

They would have need of them, before dawn. Ah.

He shook his head; raised his hand and swept his eyes clear of the road's dust. With it went resignation.

He would not easily surrender to death the men in his care.

Radann par el'Sol, he thought, with a trace of bitterness, *we are all infected by the blood of Lamberto.* It might have eased the Radann's mind, had he spoken so openly—but he had no desire to offer that man any peace.

The stone bowls were not empty; in fact were so full, Ser Alessandro was reduced to making the offerings in the ground beyond them. He took water and wine from the flasks tied to Quickheart's saddle. Unstoppering the skins, he offered the whole of their contents to the Lady, pausing only a moment to taste what lay within. The water must be sweet, and the wine unsoured; the Lady's favor, this eve, was important. As he did before no other woman, be she

fair and terrible, be she wise and powerful, he now offered
his full obeisance to the moon's bright face. Then, kneeling,
he drew dagger and offered the last of the supplications,
and the most powerful: his blood. The blood of Tors.

*I am the Lord's man, Lady, but even the men of the Lord
surrender to you the things that are yours. I have followed
the old ways. I have honored my mother and your daughter,
my kai's wife: I have offered shelter to the Matriarch of
Havalla. I have shed no blood of yours within Sarel: I have
caused no blood to be shed that would dishonor your name.*

*Guard your people. If you desire blood, accept the offer
of my blood in their stead.*

He raised hand to forehead, bent low; his hair grazed
ground before his skin touched it. The earth was cold.

He stayed there for three full breaths, and then he rose.
He spoke her name once, aloud. Brought his right arm to
his chest in salute before gaining his feet.

Then he turned and made his way back to Quickheart.
Reymos stood to one side of the horse, his face turned toward the village's many homes.

He looked back only when Ser Alessandro was almost
beside him.

"I have made the offerings," Alessandro said quietly.
"Gather the Toran; we will ride across the bridge when the
men are assembled."

"Tor'agar." Reymos bowed.

The leaves were thick and the branches, low-lying,
seemed to reflect not moonlight, but night; they were dark
and cool as they brushed Jewel's face. She took care not to
break or damage them as she pushed them aside. They
seemed, to her, living things in a way that not even the great
trees in the Common were: rooted in place, they seemed a
cold audience, a severe crowd.

She hated crowds, but she did what she could not to invoke their anger, for the mob lay at the heart of every gathered crowd she'd witnessed.

As a child—and she would have hated to be so described—she had learned to skirt the edges of such gatherings, slipping hands into pockets, sliding dagger's edge along leather thongs in order to retrieve the purses that held silver and copper crowns. But she had taken only what the den needed, no more; she had learned to cause no other harm.

Funny, that such a furtive, desperate life could feel so much like the right one in this place.

She was aware of Lord Celleriant's regard, for he paused often—to wait for her to catch up—and watched her progress through the thin woods.

"Have you walked the Green Deepings before?" he asked her.

She jumped at the sound of his voice, for he had come upon her where the trees were thickest. "Yes."

"When?"

"You were there. Yollana led us."

"Ah. My apologies. I meant, perhaps, at some earlier time."

"Oh. No."

"Yet you walk with such care." He reached out; his hands touched leaf and branch as if caressing them. They seemed to bow and shiver with unseen, unfelt wind; they rose above the line of her brow, the unruly strands of her tangled hair. "Why?"

"I don't think the trees here would take kindly to anything else."

He lifted his face and spoke; the words were complete gibberish to her—but they were musical gibberish, beautiful and complex in the rise and fall of fleeting syllables.

"What did you say?"

He offered no answer, pretending not to hear the question.

But after silence once again descended, the branches seemed to rise, and although leaves brushed the skin of her face, the rise of her cheeks, the exposed back of her neck, they did not cling or tangle.

"Remember this," he said quietly. "If you ever have cause to walk the Deepings again."

"Remember what?"

"Your caution. The trees have little love of men."

She nodded. She wanted to be flippant, but she knew that anything she said would come out in a thin and shaky voice.

"Could you make it safe?"

"Make what safe, Lady?"

"The forest."

"I am safe within the forest."

"For others. For the villagers. Could you do for them what you just did for me?"

"You misunderstand me," he said quietly. "What I said was not said for your benefit, but theirs." His gaze lingered a moment upon the great, standing trees. "I am not their master. Not even the Winter Queen would make such a claim."

"But you—"

"I merely drew their attention to your passage; what they gleaned from their attempt to observe you is entirely their own."

She stared at him, and he turned. The smile he offered her was a dark one. "Do not think of me as a gardener, as the keeper of tame trees and tame, silent plants. If the *Kialli* make their home in the Northern Wastes, we make our home in the wild places, and in the wild places, you have no friends. Not even these," he added, his gesture taking in the forest's many trees. "Perhaps especially not these."

She wondered, then, if she would ever understand him.

The forest was still dark, but it was silent now. No ghosts intruded upon her passage through the Deepings. She wondered if they had been laid to rest. Or if, like any other living presence, they required sleep and shelter before they gathered the strength to return.

Here and there, the trees broke, opening a window into the plains beneath moonlight. She saw no village, although a lone building sometimes suggested itself in the pale gray of landscape. No lights, though; no sign of movement. Funny that she found the lack disturbing. In the desert, the endless heat and cold had demanded her full attention. But here, in the Torrean of Clemente, the weather itself was not a threat, and she felt the absence of Averalaan keenly. City girl.

Or perhaps she missed the simplicity of her old life, even its darkness and its violence, for it was not the Terafin Manse that she longed for; not the Terafin manse that she missed. It was the streets of the twenty-fifth holding.

Memory, she thought. We choose it. We let go of the things that don't suit us.

She had never imagined, in the spare, terrible struggle of life with her den, that there would come a time when she yearned for its stark simplicity.

What I would tell that girl now, she thought, as she continued to tread her careful path. If I were Evayne. If I could walk between then and now.

"ATerafin."

She looked up. Met Avandar's shuttered gaze. "What?"

"Damar."

Verragar's voice was strongest in the citadel of the Tor. Marakas had feared to find as much. He and the Radann who had chosen to accompany him walked with quiet deliberation through the streets of Sarel, their steps lighter and more certain than the heavy fall of cerdan boots across a curve broken by wall and fount, by gate and building. But after some distance, broken and awkward as it was, their steps traced a circle whose periphery enclosed the heart of Clemente's power.

The Radann felt no love of, and no responsibility for, the Tor'agar. He had made his interests clear, and the past that existed as wall or gap between them would not, by the ac-

tion of an evening, be bridged, although it might be forgiven.

But he had left his domis in the care of the Radann par
el'Sol and had led his men to night's war, when the only
Lord that lay in watch was the one they both hated and—in
the privacy of moonlight—feared.

"Santos," he said, his grip upon *Verragar* too tight.

The Radann bowed head once.

"We can afford to offer no warning."

"You think the servant of the Lord of Night is within the
Tor'agar's domis."

"I think he must be. But we have heard no sounds of battle; no sounds of slaughter. None of the serafs have fled."

"Perhaps they were given no chance."

"Perhaps. But . . . I believe that the servant of the Lord of
Night seeks to pass as human; there are few who could un-
veil him if such is the case."

"But why would he—"

Marakas waited. After a moment, Santos el'Sol nodded.
"Of course. Not even the General Marente would willingly
be seen to associate with the envoys of the Lord of Night."

"Indeed. He will guard his actions with care, unless he
knows he is discovered.

"It is therefore imperative that when we find him, we
guard our knowledge with equal care until the location is
empty of all but the warriors of *our* Lord."

Santos bowed. But his smile, as he rose, was grim. "It is
seldom," he told the Radann par el'Sol, "that the Serras invite the Radann to inspect their territory."

"Indeed. But I do not believe that we will find our enemy
in the midst of the women. The Tor'agar spoke—briefly—
of an envoy within Sarel. It is there that we will find what
we seek."

"And when we find what we seek, par el'Sol?"

"Then," Marakas said grimly, as a man does when he
speaks truths that are unpleasant, "we wait."

*   *   *

Ser Alessandro kai di'Clemente surveyed the men he could see in a grim silence. They stayed to one side of the bridge, by his command, positioning themselves along the East bank. The buildings in the East provided some cover, but it was scant; cover in the West was better, but it was denied them.

Orange light, surrendered by oiled wood and swinging lamp, lent glint to helm and revealed in chain a warmth of color that was in no way warm; it drew the eye. War colors, in the night. No camp had been made, although some precautions had been taken upon the Eastern road. If the Tor'agnate was canny enough to split his forces, it would not be by the Eastern road, or the thin windbreak provided by its scant trees, that they would catch Clemente unawares.

But across the river, the slender ribbon of Western road stretched into moonlight and darkness to either side of Damar. The shadows in the lee of the old forest lay across it like a shroud; even the waters seemed to shun its banks.

It was not always so, and it seemed an omen.

But of what? He was not a woman; not of the Lady. He could not say. Yet it seemed that something lay poised within the Deepings, and he felt the certainty of its presence like the cold, sharp cut of a perfect blade.

Let it, he thought, be our allies. Let it be only our allies.

The stag. The forest lord. The Northern strangers.

Wind replied. Wind caught his hair, the edges of his surcoat, the strands of Quickheart's mane. Even when the sun was absent, the wind's curtain fell; neither light nor darkness were proof against its voice.

Reymos and Adelos brought their horses to either side of Quickheart.

Above the sound of hooves, the nickering of nervous horses, the muted speech of men, above the quiet flow of water through the riverbed, came the voice of rolling thunder.

Ancient thunder; the greetings of the Tors of the plains.

"Tor'agar," Reymos said. "He has brought the drums of war."

"His drummers do not speak of war yet," Alessandro replied, his words riding the crest of the steady rhythm.

"But they speak."

"They introduce our presence."

"Should we choose, we might introduce ourselves in a fashion of our own devising," Adelos added. "Such drums have not been sounded in Damar since—"

"Enough." The Tor raised fist; the words ebbed into silence. But the drums demanded response. By gesture alone, Alessandro called six more of the Toran forward. He had intended to travel with two; he now chose a complement of eight. More would be insult.

Less would be unwise.

Celleriant raised his head. "ATerafin."

She frowned. "Thunder?"

"Drums," he replied. "Kallandras?"

"Drums." The bard frowned. "Among the plainsmen, drums were once a form of warning. Over time, they became a form of . . . greeting. But only between the tribal lords. The ruled did not choose to dare the drum's voice."

"Kallandras, is there *anything* you don't study?"

"Senniel encourages diversity." He offered her the briefest of smiles.

"So . . . what we're hearing here is?"

"Is not a tribal greeting," Celleriant replied, although she had offered the question to the bard.

"No," Kallandras said, nodding. "Invocation?"

Celleriant's gaze was fixed upon the distant source of the drumming.

"Invocation," Avandar replied. "Be wary, master bard. Be wary, lord of the Green Deepings."

Celleriant nodded.

I hate being ignorant, Jewel thought.

They are claimed by their element, the Winter King

replied. *They hear what the element hears. Although I do not understand how the mortal survives it, it is clear that he holds sway over air.*

And the other?

Lord Celleriant is of the Arianni. Air, the Winter King said, but he spoke the word with less certainty, as if testing it. *And earth, almost of a certainty.*

You think they'll summon fire? She spoke of the enemy, unseen and unknown.

Fire? No, ATerafin. Unless it suits their purpose, it is not the fire that they will invoke.

She turned, then. Beyond the trees at the edge of the Deeping she gazed at the riverbank.

She lived by the ocean. She understood the power—and the fury—of water.

CHAPTER TWENTY-THREE

SER Alessandro kai di'Clemente crossed the bridge at the head of the tight formation of his Toran. It was more difficult than he had imagined, for Quickheart attempted to stay his ground and brought his hooves up short at the edge of the bridge's gentle slope. Reymos and Adelos had as much luck with their horses, but they were men of Mancorvo. The horses stilled beneath their knees and obeyed their silent command to walk forward.

But their nervousness was lost to the determination of their riders, and when the river was behind them, Alessandro squared shoulders, hand falling to the hilt of his father's sword. Damar was home to much history, much loss.

But it was his. He did not therefore choose to approach his cousin as supplicant. But he did not choose to approach in obvious anger; the greater part of the kai Manelo's force lay within the West of Damar, and that force did not serve Clemente. Prudence did, and prudence had served him well in the past.

Even if he had cause to regret it.

Lady.

Could he have stopped his cousin's obsessive whim on that single day of folly in the Torrean of Manelo? Could he have done more to deter him? Could he have seen the value that a simple half free clanswoman might have had to the kai el'Sol on that one day?

And if not—and he had not—could he not have lifted sword in his cousin's defense?

As he cleared the bridge, the Western half of Damar

stood revealed, and it was a much changed place. Some fires had burned too near the walls of buildings, blackening their surface, and the center of the village, reserved for the wagons and stalls that farmers built, had been cleared for Manelan use. At the heart of the market, built up from new wood, a platform rose; it was surrounded by the shoulders of cerdan.

Of the fount of contemplation, there was no sign.

He almost stopped, then, and his hands became fists. *They would not dare.* But they might; the fount itself was of little value; its history of less.

The Tor'agnate, Ser Amando kai di'Manelo, stood on the platform's height, arms by his sides, helm raised. He wore sword, surcoat, a shield upon his back; he stood beneath the lee of a banner that the wind barely moved. In and of himself, he was remarkable—but he was not alone: to his left and right, the drums stood, and behind them, men with flattened hands, beating asynchronous rhythm. The men were not armored and armed; they wore robes.

The first sign.

The pulse of the drums was loud and insistent, like a heartbeat that was somehow devoid of life, but not of blood.

They made their demand, as he approached them.

He bowed to their pressure in silence as Reymos allowed the weight of the Clemente banner to fall, at last, in the silver and gray of moon's light: the colors of Clemente. They were dark, here; they existed in spirit and memory, but the lamps did not give them the voice of hue; only the gold embroidery of the rising sun caught light, but the light was that of fire, not of day.

Ser Franko kai di'Manelo's father awaited him, like a final judgment.

Yes, he thought, bitter now. He could have attempted to deter his cousin; to distract him. And failing that, he could have raised sword against the kai el'Sol. Of the two

cousins, Ser Alessandro had always been the better swordsman.

But he had done neither. Had chosen to do neither. He
had offered his cousin his blood after the fact of an ignoble
death, but that was all. Not even the vengeance laid upon
kin was within his meager ability.

He had hated the kai el'Sol. He had raged against him in
the bitter heat of silence. He had all but vowed his revenge.

But he had taken the girl and her husband from the Torrean of Manelo, and he had brought them here. He no
longer remembered their names; they no longer used them.
That had been wisest. He wondered where they were, this
eve; if they hid in hovel or hut, if they slept in a simple bed
beneath a flat roof, surrounded by growing fields, sleeping
fields.

Or if they had already perished; if Ser Amando had managed by some trickery or torture to find them here.

For Alessandro had chosen to bring them to Damar.

To leave them in Manelo was to guarantee their deaths,
and in the end . . . in the end, although he hated the price
that his cousin had paid for his crime, he accepted the judgment of the kai el'Sol. He could not speak to them; not to
the girl, and not to the boy who had tried to protect her and
had almost died a failure. But he could not leave them to
die.

Sin against honor.

Sin against kin.

What would he pay, in the end, for the folly of that
choice?

"Ser Alessandro kai di'Clemente seeks words with Ser
Amando kai di'Manelan," Ser Reymos intoned, over the
beat of drums.

The line of Manelan Toran stood unbroken before the
dais; the drums answered, louder now, a threat and not a
greeting.

Alessandro waited with a patience he did not feel. Such

was the way of the High Clans: to wait; to hide behind the
perfect composure of waiting all anger and all fear.

"Ser Amando kai di'Manelo," one of the Toran said,
"will speak with you now."

The drums roared; their beat grew loud now, wild. The
horses reared in terror.

Beyond his back, Alessandro heard something like the
rumbling movement of earth; heard above it the cries and
shouts of voices made unfamiliar by fear. He could not
turn—not easily—until he had mastered Quickheart. But he
did not need to turn in the saddle, for Quickheart's leap was
a dance, a circular movement that almost unseated him.

Part of that dance brought him to the East, where
Alessandro could see what he had heard, although in that
instant neither made immediate sense to him.

The water in the river had risen from its bed like a wall,
sundering bridge from either side of the village as if the
wood and stone that anchored it were kindling and pebbles,
children's toys.

They crested the edge of the forest as if the forest itself
had finally chosen to draw curtains and reveal the outer
world. Jewel stumbled over a root and bit her lip; she
righted herself, palm planted in damp earth. But she did not
curse; did not cry out. There was a watchful silence in the
village of Damar that reminded her of storm laden sky before the beginning of a torrent.

Avandar offered her a hand, and she accepted his aid before she realized what it meant: he had dismounted. Her
eyes narrowed, but he shook his head in warning, and she
subsided. Time, later, for argument.

Celleriant lifted a slender arm. In the distance, she could
see the village wall rising into the dark of horizon.

And she remembered, as she looked at its odd shape, that
Damar *had* no walls.

"Yes," Celleriant said quietly, seeing the shift in her expression. "The river has risen."

"Where is the Tor'agar?"

"I cannot see him," the Arianni lord replied, after a pause. "The dwellings are in my way."

Hers too. *Now what?* she thought, watching the moon's light against the surface of moving water.

"Now, ATerafin, we play a dangerous game." Avandar's voice was soft.

So what else is new? Her legs ached. She wasn't sure why. "If they see us—"

"I believe we will know if we are spotted. But we have the advantage of numbers here," he replied. Distant.

"Advantage?"

"We ride no horses, we wear no armor, we carry no banner. We are five, but the men who are stationed here will count us three; they will see threat in neither you nor . . . the Winter King. Unless," he added softly, "you choose to ride him, in which case, they will see a threat in the two of you that will diminish ours."

It occurred to her, as he spoke, that he knew the name of the stag. The name he had been known by before he had chosen to accept the offer of the Winter Queen, before he had lost her dangerous game.

Yes, he said quietly. *I believe I do know it.*

Tell me? she asked him, without much hope. It evoked a grim smile.

If you wish to know, do not ask him. Command him. He is yours, Jewel. Arianne did not release him—she gave him to you.

But he knew she wouldn't.

She knew that he knew.

I'm that predictable.

Yes. But predictability is not always a sin, ATerafin. When you choose to trust a man's word, why do you trust?

Which man?

He smiled. *Why does it matter?*

She hesitated and then snorted. "All right. All right, I get it. You can stop the lesson now."

He bowed, expression grave. "Not all lessons are so easily halted, but I, too, am in your service." And rose. "And as we are all in service to you—all of us save the master bard—we now await your decision. Which way, ATerafin?"

Bastard.

Warm air blew across the back of her neck. She turned to meet the luminous eyes of the Winter King. They were striking, the silvers and grays of night. More so, she thought, than they ever were when the sun rode the sky. She heard the question he didn't ask, and she nodded; he knelt.

She lifted herself across his back and held tight to his antlers as he rose.

"All right," she said curtly. "Kallandras?"

"ATerafin."

"Do you want to split off with Celleriant, or will you follow my lead?"

"I think it wisest that we remain together."

She nodded. "All right," she said again. "That way." It was time to play the game by instinct.

Instinct. She smiled a moment and turned to catch the frown forming on Avandar's lips.

"Remember, ATerafin, that it is always wise to have a goal before one sets out."

"Wisdom and being here have almost nothing in common," she replied.

The Winter King's laughter was silent, but she felt it and took comfort from it.

Ser Amando kai di'Manelo stepped out from behind the ranks of his Toran; he crossed the height of the dais slowly, and with perfect grace. He removed his helm, and his hair, even by moonlight, was silvered; age was his mantle. He wore a beard, long and thin; like to a Widan's beard, and not a Tor's. His ears were pierced with rings.

Only in the plains of Mancorvo could a man be so adorned without risk of scorn or derision. They were war rings, as much a part of the ferocity of his face as the scars he bore.

At his side, tucked into the dark silk of broad sash, Ser Amando kai di'Manelo wore two swords. They were his finest adornments; their sheaths glittered brightly, even in the half-light. The Clemente war sheath was more practical. Alessandro had chosen to wear it for expediency, but he regretted the lack of formality now.

He was aware, however, that formality was far more than simple dress. Quickheart had stilled, but it had taken effort; the Manelo Toran were witness to that effort, and it was a costly humiliation.

Or perhaps not; he noted as he dismounted that there were no horses present. The Tors of Mancorvo did not divest themselves easily of their mounts.

Nor did they divest themselves of their men in time of war. Alessandro did not spare a glance to the obscenity of the river, although it cast an odd shadow at his feet; the shadow spoke of its height. What was done was done; he railed against it at his peril.

Reymos and Adelos were likewise silent. They would fall here, if he chose a poor word, offered a poor gesture, but they would die like men; their hands were upon the hilts of their swords, and although the blades had not yet been drawn, such a gesture did not proffer disrespect.

"Ser Amando," Ser Alessandro said. His chin dipped; he did not offer a formal bow.

Reminder of the difference in rank between the two clans. More of a reminder could not, in wisdom, be offered.

"Ser Alessandro," Ser Amando replied. He, too, forbore a bow. "I had almost despaired of your presence within Damar. The speed of your response to my requests was . . . uncharacteristic, cousin."

"Indeed. I was detained in Seral. Preparations for war are time-consuming, but you must be better aware of this fact than I."

Ser Amando revealed the grimmest of his smiles. "Must I? We are both the Lord's men."

"Ah," Alessandro said quietly, seeing the opening. "But which Lord, Ser Amando?"

Jewel's head snapped up.

"ATerafin?" Avandar and Kallandras spoke as a single person.

"Something bad just happened," she told them. "And no, don't ask me what." She edged the stag forward. "But we've just lost a lot of time."

The smile ended abruptly. Alessandro was not grieved to see it pass. He stood at his full height; Amando had the advantage given him by the dais, no more.

"Surely," another voice said, "*the* Lord."

A man joined the Manelan Tor upon the wooden platform. That Alessandro's hand did not fall to blade spoke well of his self-control; everything about this stranger spoke of power. "Ah. Forgive me, cousin," he said, emphasizing the kinship, "but I do not recognize your adviser."

"Enough."

The burden of silence was not difficult to shoulder.

"The man is Widan," Amando said coldly. "An ally of the Tyr'agar."

Alessandro studied the Widan, his eyes narrowing. The man was tall; taller than the Tor'agnate of Manelo. His build was slender, but not slight; indeed, nothing about him gave the impression of a small man. His hair was night dark, and it fell about his shoulders, unfettered by braid.

But his chin was smooth; no beard descended from its sharp line. Widan?

No.

"He does not choose to wear the Sword of Knowledge."

Ser Amando frowned. "Will you play at games, Alessandro? I am disappointed. Of my son's kin, he counted you closer than brother.

"He does not wear the Sword, but the river is his work; what other proof of his claim is required?"

Here and there, dirt track had been worn through grass; it was covered in layers of straw and mud, like a dense imitation of stone. The tracks that were little worn were not wide; Kallandras found them, and Kallandras led the way, walking a few paces ahead of Jewel, no more.

Buildings now added a texture to the scant light; lamps were lit, and Jewel doubted that they always burned this late. Shadows stirred to one side of the track.

They were familiar to Jewel because, in her youth, she had been such a shadow. She lifted a hand; the stag was already still beneath her.

"We mean no harm," she said, speaking quietly but clearly into the empty night. "We travel at the behest of Clemente."

"Clemente?" A voice. A woman's voice.

"Clemente," Jewel said more firmly.

"The Tor does not travel through the forest," the woman said, and the shadows resolved themselves into a single form.

"No. We do not travel by his side."

The woman nodded. "We know."

The villager approached now, lit by moon; she carried neither torch nor lamp. Nothing, Jewel thought, that might give her away to the casual observer.

Jewel had walked as carefully through the streets of the twenty-fifth holding. But they had never been so quiet, those streets; even at night, the taverns' noise spilled into the cobbled stone, and the loud, varied voices of men who indulged in smoke and alcohol provided some cover for the sound of moving feet.

"We?"

"Not all of the people of Damar are in hiding," the woman answered.

"No," another voice said, older but definitely feminine. "Only the smart ones."

The woman in the road froze, but not with fear; although Jewel could not yet see her face—might never see it clearly—she thought she sensed irritation in the stiffening of posture.

"There is no good place to hide," the younger woman said, and her tone conveyed clearly what her posture had hinted at. "Surely Maria's and Serge's deaths made that plain."

Silence.

"The Tor'agnate is here," the figure said. "But he is . . . alone."

"Alone?"

"He has seven men by his side."

"Impossible," Jewel said flatly. But it wasn't—and she *knew* it.

"As impossible," the woman replied, "as a woman riding a creature of the Old Forest. As impossible," she continued, "as a woman who is clearly served by one of its lords."

Almost against her will, Jewel smiled. "How? How was he isolated?"

"He crossed the Adane," the woman replied. "And the river itself was raised from its bed as the Tor'agar and his escort stepped off the bridge."

"But—"

"The river destroyed the bridge; it destroyed the narrow foot passage as well. The rest of his men will not be able to cross the river unless they turn East and make for the bridge near Sarel."

Which would mean they'd have to leave Damar. Jewel knew just how likely that was.

The woman lowered her head. "By then, it will be too late."

"Too late for what?"

But the stranger fell silent. Words had power. She had said enough.

"You are not a war host," the older voice said. Another form separated itself from the shadows by the simple expedient of motion. She wore a heavy robe, and a veil covered her face.

"No," Jewel replied, cautious now.

"Then if you cannot summon an army from the shadows of the Old Forest," the woman said, "leave Damar."

"Why?"

"Because an army *is* gathered here." The younger woman tried to regain control of the conversation. Jewel wondered idly if they were related. "And without an army, you cannot stand against it."

"We'll take our chances." She turned to look at Avandar.

He met her gaze, and his frown reminded her of the desert. But he turned to the women. "How many?"

"We don't know," the woman replied. "We don't . . . count . . . that number of men."

The frown tightened.

"ATerafin," Kallandras said quietly. "With your permission?"

She nodded.

He approached the younger woman. Something about his silent, graceful movement was almost timid; his approach provoked no fear, caused no retreat. "I will not ask you to lead me, but tell me where these men can be found. Are they within Damar?"

She nodded. "Some hundred men came to this village four days past; they occupy the Western half of the village, but they do not stray to its borders, or we would not be here. The others came to the village this morning, in numbers; we believe they encamped a few miles outside of Damar until now."

"Where are they?"

"They are not hard to find: they line the banks of the Adane, and they cleave to their Tor. We can lead you some part of the way."

"Let us go," he said quietly, his voice carrying first to Lord Celleriant.

"Kallandras." Avandar lifted a hand.

The master bard turned.

"Remember: do not seek to speak with the wind's voice."

He nodded.

"We desire your presence upon the field," Ser Amando said. He did not move from the vantage of height. "I, of course, have no doubt of your loyalty, but my allies are less trusting."

Alessandro said nothing. His hand did not stray from the hilt of his sword. He weighed the past against the future, aware of the edges of either. The Northern sword might not be a man's weapon, but it was a weapon that served metaphor: it had no safe edge.

If he died here, he died. His heir was safe within Sarel.

"I have long valued the trust you have placed in me," he said, tone neutral. But he raised his head to meet the eyes of his kinsman. "I am a simple man," he continued, when Ser Amando nodded. "But the presence of the . . . river . . . does not seem to me a great indication of faith."

"But it is, Ser Alessandro. Were the bridges to remain standing, your men might be tempted to cross." He lifted a hand then, and held it aloft.

Lanterns began to converge upon the dais, revealing, as they burned, the metallic sheen of the men who carried them.

"You took the time to gather your forces," he continued. "You have always been a prudent man. But I, too, understand the value of preparation."

Alessandro gazed upon the forces of Manelo. They were greater in number than even his spies had indicated; he wondered—for he could not see beyond the press of men who now lined this open causeway—how many of these men served a different Tyr.

"I will not see your forces squandered needlessly," the

Manelan Tor continued. "And I thought it best that they remain where they stand."

"I . . . see."

"They serve you," he continued. "They are not serafs. They are among the finest of the plainsmen. Lead them. Lead them to war against the enemy of the Tyr'agar, and the river will fall. You may rejoin your men when we have completed our negotiations here."

The double edge of the Northern blade was a metaphor, but so, too, the single edge of the South: Alessandro came to his grim decision.

He smiled. "Then, cousin, there is much to discuss. I have a visitor in Sarel who may be of interest to the Tyr'agar."

Kallandras chose his position with care. The packed straw and mud of road gave way to wider venues; he avoided these. The woman who traveled by his side had once again rejoined the shadows that kept her hidden; she had led him only as far as the light permitted.

But the light in the distance had suddenly grown bright; he could make out the individual flickers of lamp flame, and these were too numerous to count.

He whispered his thanks to the nameless stranger, but he did not wait for a response that he knew wouldn't come; instead, he began to climb. The roofs of the houses were peaked, and sometimes the slope from the peak was a sharp decline of wood; they offered him little trouble.

In Averalaan, or in the streets of the Tor Leonne, he might make his way from roof to roof in silence, unobserved by the men who stood sentry. Here, the gaps between buildings was large, and the finer homes were fenced in.

The fences were meant as decoration, he thought; as a way of demarking the subtle rank of lower clansmen. They were easily traversed; the Southerners valued privacy, and often built hedges against the fence wall to facilitate a sense of isolation.

He used both without pause, seeking safety and height.

The bard-born were gifted with voice, and with *the* voice. In the South, shorn of the title of Northern diplomat, such a gift often meant death.

But in the South, so much did. What he had made of his gift would be at home, here.

He slipped over a balcony rail.

The distance was great, but the press of men who now spilled into the city streets leading toward the Adane were mercifully silent.

He waited a moment, crouching against the wooden rails, the smooth slats beneath his feet dry and cool. Then he rose again, ascending to roof; there were only three buildings in the town that were tall, and he had chosen the one closest to the water.

There was some risk in the choice, but there was always risk; he felt the passing feet of men as clearly as he heard them. They patrolled, he thought, and this surprised him. He listened.

The wind's voice was silent, but the voice of the water was the storm's voice, chained to ground and unhappy in its captivity. The wall that rose from the riverbed towered above the tallest of the buildings, shimmering in moonlight. He could see the banks and the bed itself, shorn of the water's movement: the river had gathered itself, condensing its strength and power in a stretch of wall that traveled a few miles, no more.

He felt its presence.

The ring on his hand glowed a pale white against the darker shade of night skin. He did not respond to the heat. Instead, he responded to the warning offered him by Avandar Gallais.

But not for the first time, he wondered what the cost of bearing this ring would ultimately be: for he disliked the

water, with its blind, groping presence, its contained rage,
its threat.

No; dislike was a petty word for something so visceral,
and if the bards of Senniel were trained to song, they were
trained to words as well. He did not name what he felt because it was so incongruous. He had been raised to think
carefully, to deliberate quietly, even to kill dispassionately.

To kill in any other way was simply self-indulgent—a
service performed for self and not for the Lady.

He shook his head, clearing it. He did not listen to the
voices of the brothers he had lost, although they were there,
as they had always been.

Instead, he looked. The army that stood at attention along
the Adane broke in one place: its center. The streets of
Damar led there, ending in a wide, semicircle which he
knew must contain a fountain of contemplation. It was lost
to the bodies of men, the gleam f armor. What now
claimed the half circle's heart, raised against the stones of
this thoroughfare, was a long platform, and upon it, four
men.

Ah, no, five.

The fifth, he recognized.

"This is true?" the strange Widan said sharply to the
Tor'agnate of Manelo.

Alessandro did not dignify the question with a reply; the
Tor'agnate dignified it with the simple narrowing of eyes.

The man in Widan's robes noticed neither.

As if, Alessandro thought, he was ill-versed with the customs of the Court.

"Tor'agar," the man said, into a silence that grew in
weight and meaning, "is it true that you have the girl in
your domis?"

"If," Ser Alessandro said quietly, "the Widan accuses me
of lying, perhaps there is no point to these negotiations."

They were not words that should have had to be spoken,
but their truth was immutable. Not even Ser Amando,

clearly annoyed by Ser Alessandro's hesitance, could have been so careless with his words.

And still, it was the Widan whose thin composure gave way to anger, and there was no subtlety of expression, no stillness of gesture, no cutting silence in his display; his brows rose in obvious, and ugly, displeasure.

"You are in no position—"

"Widan," Ser Amando said, lifting a hand.

It would have silenced men of greater power. Indeed, it would have silenced the Tor'agar, had he been fool enough to require such reminder.

But the Widan's mood was impenetrable. "Ser Amando," he said, his tone kin to growl, "we have no time for games or wordplay this eve. The Tyr'agar is already on the move, and he requires—"

"Yes?" Single word. The sharpest yet spoken.

No, thought Alessandro, as the Widan's brows drew in, and the line of his beardless jaw tensed, this man was not of the South.

"He requires proof of the loyalty of his servants. The girl is of import to the Tyr's war, as you well know. If she is, indeed, within Sarel, we must go to Sarel in force, *now.*"

"She is one *Serra,*" the Tor'agnate replied, his voice as cold as the sheathed blade by his side. "And we speak of things that matter to *men.*"

"What she bears—what she is rumored to bear—matters greatly to *men,*" the Widan snapped.

Had Ser Alessandro not felt silence prudent, he would have been enveloped by it regardless; he was—as much as any man of the Court could be—shocked.

But the measure of this Widan's influence was made clear by the Tor'agnate's next words.

"Do you think that the men of the South are not capable of confining a simple Serra?"

"They have *failed* in every attempt to confine her. They have *failed* in every attempt to find her on the road. She must have passed through your Torrean, Ser Amando, but

she passed without note although your men were warned to
watch the road against her coming."

Not even Ser Amando could ignore what had just been
said, but again, to Ser Alessandro's surprise, he made the
attempt. "As the circumstance of her arrival has not—yet—
been discussed, it cannot be said for certain that she passed
through the Torrean of Manelo. Widan." He gestured; one
of his Toran stepped forward, passing the Widan without so
much as a glance of acknowledgment. His bearing was
rigid with the anger that Ser Amando himself did not deign
to express; his hand was upon the hilt of his sword.

But he was Toran, and if his lord chose to take—to acknowledge—no insult in what was obviously insulting, he
could not publicly attack the Widan.

Instead, he knelt stiffly—and utterly formally—at the
feet of Ser Amando. A man, Alessandro thought, of worth.

In his hands, he held a round, unmarked medallion.
Wood, pale, unadorned, it waited the cut of two swords.

And those cuts, either of them, would never be made if
the Widan continued his prattle.

The Lady, thought Alessandro, knew mercy in her fashion. Time was indeed of the essence. He lifted his gaze to
the West.

The Torrean of Manelo was not bounded by the Deepings, the ancient name for the Old Forest. Its superstitions,
its stories, were therefore no part of Manelan culture,
Manelan knowledge. It was a forest; and like other forests,
a matter of fact, of nature.

I am committed, he thought.

"How simple could this *Serra* be, to escape the Tor
Leonne itself? I tell you, she is a threat."

"And I," Ser Amando said, gaining inches as he at last
unveiled the anger that any Tor would feel under such circumstances, "tell *you,* Widan, that there are matters that
must be decided before we leave Damar. If you cannot offer
advice that does not conform to the negotiations *I* have chosen, leave the dais."

For just a moment, the Widan grew in height, and the height he gained by the simple expedience of shifting posture was both remarkable and unsettling. His shoulders were broad, if slender, his arms long. He wore no sword, which was unusual, and no armor save for his robes and the distant rise of water in the hollowed bed of the Adane.

And then he smiled.

"As you wish, Tor'agnate. But time *is* of the essence." He turned to face Alessandro. "Strange things live in the edges of the Deepings," he said, voice cool. "And on a night such as this, the forest cannot contain them all. Speak quickly, Tor'agar."

"Widan."

He turned, bowed stiffly, and left the dais.

But as he did, the waters stilled. They stood now, clear as poor glass, the thunder in their movement silenced.

Beyond them, Alessandro could suddenly see the distorted figures the men of Clemente made, viewed through water defiled by strange magic.

Worse, he could hear their sudden shouts. They had turned their attention—and their formation—from the West of Damar; they were running now, some horsed and some on foot, as if they prepared for battle.

As if it were already upon them.

Ser Alessandro stiffened. The bridges were gone, and even had they not been, the men of Manelo now stood between himself and the men who followed his command, even to their own deaths.

He turned his gaze upon Ser Amando. The Tor'agnate was not as impassive as he should have been; his brows rose faintly in surprise, and his lips curved in frown.

"Widan!"

But the Widan's smile deepened, revealing at last its full edge. "If the negotiations are swift, Tor'agar, Tor'agnate, you will be in time to lend aid to the men across the Adane. If they are not, there are no guarantees."

"We need those men!" Ser Amando's voice was too high, his words too quick.

"We need the girl," the creature said, eyes glittering strangely. "We need the girl and the sword she bears."

Jewel knew Kallandras approached long before the night revealed sight of him. She stiffened upon the back of the Winter King, but he, too, was already still with the peculiar tension that spoke of coming battle. He did not speak to her. He did not look away.

The bard appeared from the shadows, but he moved so swiftly from wall to wall that the glimpses caught might have been the product of fancy, of desire.

"**ATerafin,**" he said, his voice carrying the distance that power granted him. "**The *Kialli* are at the Adane. And they are, I fear, beyond it—beyond our easy reach. The men of Clemente are now engaged in battle upon the Eastern bank. I do not think . . . it will go well with them.**"

She turned to Lord Celleriant.

The Arianni lord met her gaze briefly, but his eyes sought the shadow for some sight of Kallandras. She didn't understand what now existed between these two, but she knew better than to question it. "Celleriant."

He bowed.

"Kallandras is coming."

Bowed again.

"Arm yourself," she said quietly. "But be careful. I think . . ."

A silver brow rose.

"I think that the two of you are meant to cross the Adane. I think you're needed on the far bank of the river."

"It is not so easily crossed," he told her quietly. "Neither for Kallandras nor I."

"I didn't say it had to be easy. Is it possible?"

His answer was a slender smile. He lifted a hand, and his blade came to it, denying the night and the darkness while retaining some part of its secrecy. Blue light lined the contours of his face, the point of his chin; blue light glinted off the strange coat of mail he wore.

"Yes," he said, as he lowered the blade.

"And what of us, ATerafin?" Avandar's question was reasonable and quiet; he spoke in the same tone of voice he might have used when the walls of Terafin had enclosed them.

"We're here," she said, voice too quiet. "*This* is where we have to be."

He bowed.

Kallandras came, at last, to join them. He glanced first at Jewel, and then at Celleriant, and when he saw what Celleriant wielded, he closed his eyes.

"What did you hear?" the Arianni lord asked. Not what did you see.

"Baying," the bard replied, shorn of the length and prettiness of words, the power of voice. "Above the cries of the Clemente men."

"How many?"

"Four at least."

"And all upon the other side of the river?"

"There may be . . . enemies . . . upon the Western bank; they are not yet set in motion. But upon the East, they have been unleashed."

"Will the Clemente men stand?"

"They stand now," Kallandras replied. He, too, drew weapons, but he drew them from the slender sheaths that adorned his thighs.

"They do not know what they face."

"They do not know. But they are superstitious. They have lived in the lee of the Deepings for the whole of their lives."

"My lady feels that our role in this battle is upon the Eastern shore."

Kallandras paused a moment, and then he nodded.

"How far does the river's wall extend?"

"The length and breadth of Damar. If we are to cross the river at a point where the element is not yet wakened, we will lose much time."

He did not say—because he did not need to—that it was time they didn't have.

"Avandar," Jewel said quietly. "How much of a risk is the use of—of the other magic?"

"Ask Lord Celleriant," the domicis replied. "He is versed in the art; I have merely had the experience of long observation."

But Lord Celleriant simply glanced at Jewel.

After a moment, she said, "You two don't use drums." Just that.

But it evoked a rare smile. "Very good," he said softly, the words strangely intimate.

"Is water more difficult than air?"

"Not to an adept," he replied, gazing toward the river. "Within the Deepings, there have only been three who were born to the caul."

She did not ask their names; short of a command, she was sure he wouldn't give them, and she found herself reluctant to break the strange warmth of his mood.

"The *Kialli*?"

"Understand that they once walked this world. They claimed it and they destroyed it, as we did." He turned away from the river, the light of the water captured in his eyes. "But they have returned as strangers to these lands; they have memory and they have power, but they surrendered kinship when they made their ancient choice."

"You're saying you have an advantage."

"Indeed." He turned to leave. Kallandras joined him.

They walked ten feet, twenty feet, leaving no mark against ground, and then the lord of the Green Deepings halted in mid-step, as if compelled. He turned slowly again, toward her, and he bowed. Something about his face was different, something was now familiar to her.

She was afraid, not for the first time, of beauty.

"The advantage," he said softly, "may be measured in lives." His words, soft as velvet, carried the distance between them.

She understood.

"How many?"

"I do not know. It has not been my concern, Lady."

"Until now."

He hesitated, and the hesitation was like a scar across his brow, the tale of some previous battle. But after that brief pause, he bowed, and his glance grazed the profile of the bard's face before he looked at her again. "We are . . . to cross the river . . . to intercede on behalf of those who cannot speak with the voice of the elements; who cannot stand against the power of the *Kialli*. It is to save the lives, and not the territory, that you wish to send us to battle."

She nodded.

"It is not . . . a command . . . that has ever been given in the Winter," he told her quietly, eyes clear, their silver lost now to distance. "Not for the sake of mortals. It would be like risking all to save cattle."

The words themselves called for a rough reply; the tone, the simplicity and the honesty of it, called for silence. She struggled between them, and let silence win, although it was a near thing. "I wish I could have seen the Court in Summer," she said quietly.

He closed his eyes.

When he opened them again, he was Lord Celleriant; his eyes were steel.

"If the men cannot be moved from the riverside," he said, his voice cool, "we will save more than we doom—but while the *Kialli* grip upon the water is poor, I do not think that they suffer under the constraints you place upon us."

"Kallandras?"

He nodded.

When they left, she looked to Avandar.

He waited; she felt the ache of the sigil against her right

arm. That, and the weight of memory, of dream, of the sight
of the Warlord.

She hated that man.

But it was that man she needed. He was not kind. "What
orders would you give me, ATerafin?"

"I don't know," she said, rougher in tone than she had intended. "You can't stand against the whole of their army."

He laughed. It was not a pleasant sound.

"Do you understand, ATerafin, why I chose the life of a
domicis?"

"No."

"No? It was to avoid such a conflict. Power is not easily
put aside, and when it has been—with difficulty—there is
danger in reclaiming it." His dark eyes were open; they
were night, and the night seemed endless.

"I want you to protect this town," she told him quietly.
"The same way you protected the Voyani in the desert."

"The desert," he told her, "is gone. What remains is more
complicated. There, there were no buildings, no hovels, no
farms; there, the people you wished to protect were gathered in the open. We faced the storm, and the creature that
rode it. Here, ATerafin, the living hide, and they number not
in the tens, but in the thousands."

She nodded.

"You will lose some of them," he said evenly. His gaze
was cold.

She swallowed and nodded again. "Better some than all."

He bowed. When he rose, he held a golden sword, light
pouring and swelling through the red glow of flesh.

"They're counting on us," she whispered. But she was
afraid. Her hands shook as they clung to the tines of the
Winter King's crown.

Jewel, the stag said. *Think carefully. Think long. There
are many ways to lose a battle, and the worst of them do not
end in death.*

"Let's go," she told Avandar. "Hide us, for now."

Avandar gestured. She saw light; orange and blue cascaded down the length of his arms, billowing like cloud, like hidden fire. She stiffened as it touched her, but she held tight.

"This will protect us against the vision of men," Avandar said. "But against the *Kialli*, no power of significance remains hidden."

"It'll do."

The Tor'agnate of Manelo was silent.

So, too, the Tor'agar of Clemente.

Against the screams and shouted orders of the Clemente cerdan, words were too much of a shroud. They contained an anger that would add fire, and death, to the battle that now raged, distorted by water.

But silence offered no answer; silence was not a weapon. Ser Alessandro kai di'Clemente raised his head. "Will you kill me, *cousin?*" he said softly.

Ser Amando returned his cool gaze. "It was not my intent."

Alessandro weighed the tone behind the scant words. Anger, there. Anger and not a little fear. The Widan—if he was Widan—ruled here; it was clear to Alessandro. But it was also clear to Ser Amando, and the illusion of command—necessary illusion, like all titles, all power, in the Dominion—had been stripped away with a brutal disregard for the consequences of the loss.

It was night, the Lady's time.

But even at night, no Tor could afford to be unmanned in the view of those whose loyalty strength alone ensured. By such a crisis, men were judged.

Ser Alessandro could not even guess at the magicks that imperiled his cerdan, for the water was not like a Northern window; it moved constantly.

He waited with a patience that was entirely facade.

"The medallion," Ser Amando said at last. Just that. His Toran hastened to obey him, but they, too, were shaken by what had transpired. Robbed of grace, they fumbled, and speed robbed them of even the dignity their rank demanded.

"So," Alessandro said quietly.

Ser Amando bowed head. Acknowledgment.

It was a bitter gesture; among men who are no longer allies, truth is an expensive luxury.

With the medallion came the rest of the Widan. There were, in total, five, but only two wore the proud Sword, edge glittering with rubies arranged as if in fall. He met their eyes, but he could not hold them; they skittered away from his face as if in shame. Or fear.

And what, he thought, engendered fear in Widan?

The other three.

Ser Alessandro drew his sword. By his side, standing with the grace of purpose that now eluded the Manelan Toran, were the two men he trusted with not only his life, but his death. It would not be the first time; it would not, even if they had victory here, be the last. He had never placed faith in soldiers who had not taken to the field.

The medallion lay before him.

"What oath, cousin, would you swear?" he asked softly.

"That if you offer your allegiance to the Tyr'agar, your men will be spared, your lands will be yours to govern, your people and their supplies will be bartered for instead of taken."

"And can you offer this?"

He said nothing. Instead, Ser Amando kai di'Manelo unsheathed his blade. He lifted it, its crescent flashing orange in the night light, the artificially contained fire.

It fell in a single stroke.

And it missed.

The Manelan Toran drew a single shared breath, ragged around the edges. The silence stretched out in a circle as men turned inward to stare at what they could not clearly see.

Ser Amando grimaced. When he lifted his sword again, the blade shook.

The shouts of Clemente cerdan mingled now with screams: Alessandro knew death when he heard it.

Still, he waited, watching the man he would never again claim as kin.

The blade fell, and this time, shaking, it made its mark. The mark was not clean; the wooden circle clung to the blade's edge as he attempted to raise it.

Toran interceded; their hands touched the medallion that was meant to be cut by blade alone. They pulled it free; set it upon the stone pedestal that was meant to contain the oath wood.

Ser Alessandro kai di'Clemente raised his sword.

He drew breath; his gaze slanted toward the West, and the North, toward the forests that had bounded his clan's lands for centuries. Out of that forest had come the people who might one day be legend; out of that forest, the first hope and the first fear.

But he had met them, these visiting strangers; he had taken their measure.

Against what now stood at his back—river water, raised as wall—their fleeting promise withered like false spring.

"I have hated the kai el'Sol in my time," he said quietly. "For the death of my cousin. For the loss of his life." Truth. To be used now, like any other weapon.

He met Ser Amando's eyes; was surprised at how they flickered.

But I better understand him, cousin. I better understand what I refused to understand that day, that year, the years that followed.

He lifted his sword. Met the eyes of the Tor'agnate without flinching or wavering.

His blade fell. Splinters of wood flew across the dais.

A sign.

Not even the Toran moved. Alessandro's sword rested a hair's breadth above the grinding surface of stone.

The Widan who was not Widan spoke.

"Another medallion, Tor'agnate?"

But Ser Amando stared at the wreckage and understood. His eyes narrowed. "Kill him," he said softly.

His last words. A fitting epitaph for a man who would serve the Lord of Night.

Alessandro struck as the swords of Manelan Toran crested scabbards, filling the silence left in the wake of shattered wood with the song of steel. Amando began to bring his sword to bear, but the movement was slowed; clumsy.

The Lord's men could not afford hesitation.

And Alessandro kai di'Clemente was the Lord's man. The Lord of Day. His sword's edge bit metal and flesh, seeking the short length of exposed neck. Finding it.

Adelos and Reymos were a step behind him; they were three, and they fought without expectation of mercy. Not for death had he come, but he accepted it: it was the sword's only law.

They did not discuss tactics. They did not discuss strategy.

As they approached the river, the master bard of Senniel College and the lord of the Court of the Green Deepings spoke with the nuance of motion and gesture. They did not pause; they did not spare more than a glance at the wall of water that waited them, cleaving the town in two.

Celleriant moved toward the water, tensing for a leap. The breeze began to gather beneath the strands of his hair, pulling at his tunic.

Kallandras caught his shoulder, and Celleriant's legs lengthened, losing tension and the strength of motion's beginning; a brow rose in question, wind dying as water began to rumble in response.

Brother, the bard said softly, **a change of plans.**

"The mortals oft had a saying about battle plans and the length of their survival."

The bard smiled. Lifting a hand, he pointed into the thicket of men that surrounded the dais and the Tors.

And the drums.

But death has many guises.

And into the Widan, it came, fair-haired and white, swift as wind, unlooked for.

The two who wore the Sword jumped back, unarmed, their hands raised in the complicated weave of dancing fingers and harsh words. They peeled away from the three who stood, beardless and tall, the robes of men of knowledge a poor fit for the length of their bodies, the growing width of their shoulders.

The Manelan cerdan gave way before the two Widan who had chosen flight, absorbing them whole into their ranks; they drew swords, but they did not know which way to turn: toward the man who had killed the Lord to whom they owed their allegiance, or toward their backs, where swords now spoke with voices that could not be denied.

The Clemente Toran were already at work; if they were few, they took advantage of chaos and uncertainty. It was the very essence of battle.

Ser Alessandro, given the vantage of height, drew his bloodied sword from his dying kin. He did not clean the blade; did not sheathe it; instead he took a moment to clearly see what the cerdan could not: Two men.

Ah, Lady, two Northern men.

One bore blue sword, blue shield; he walked—or so it seemed—in the air above the shoulders of the armed Manelan guards. Where his blade fell, it fell in silence, and when sword was raised to parry, metal shattered.

He was not mortal; did not look mortal; his hair was a thing of wind, a cloud and a storm. No man could fight thus encumbered. No man.

By his side, hair drawn back, was the Northern bard. In his hands he carried the weapons of the Dark Lady; they moved as if they were an extension of his body. Alessandro was frozen for a moment in recognition. The Dark Lady. *Kovaschaii.* He had never found a circumstance so dire that he had been willing to call upon the brotherhood; did not, in truth, know how to begin.

Bard, he thought. Northern bard. The words made no sense; they were foreign words, Northern words, nonsensical syllables.

And this bard offered no song; his lips were set in a slender line, and his expression was so still it seemed a mask had been set about his face—a mask of flesh, pale and reposed.

Two men. Against such two, the cerdan of Manelo retreated, shouting orders, raising a cry kin to the cries across the shattered bridge.

The bard brought his weapons down, seeking neither flesh nor armor.

In the night, the stretched skins of the drums that had beat greeting and warning *screamed*.

CHAPTER TWENTY-FOUR

HAD Kallandras been another man, had he in truth been born to the North and the halls of Senniel, or had he been entirely Southern, had he been raised in the domis of his father's clan, the screams would have stilled all movement, all breath.

Although both of these men were some part of the man he had become, he had given his youth to death, and the passage of years, the songs of the bardic masters, had not deprived those lessons of strength: he leaped clear of the drums. But the gift of the magi, the weapons he bore, gained a sudden weight, drawn to the sounds of pain and death. They struggled against his tightening grip.

They were not his only weapons; had they been, he would have fallen; they rose too slowly to parry; the skins of the drums had closed around their edges, and whether it was the blades that clung or the instruments, the result was the same.

He struck out with his foot; caught an arm wielding blade just above the bend of elbow. A new cry joined the fading screams of drum, but it was brief.

He leaped up, into air, and his blades at last came free, but they were heavy in his hands, and their shape seemed to shift and change as he moved. He vaulted, shifting his weight to land, tensing his knees to leap again before his body acknowledged the full weight of gravity. Around these movements, steel, the dance of the blade, the promise of death.

The drums were beyond repair.

The makers of those instruments, however, came quick to the fray.

They shunted aside the unwieldy robes of the Widan; they dispensed with the pretense of diminished height. They were three, and they drew swords with the same perfect grace that Celleriant had: red fire to blue.

The Manelan Toran raised cry; their swords lost unison, and for a moment, purpose. Those that crowded the Widan at the dais' edge paid for their duty with their lives; the red swords took them all.

They should have had quick deaths.

Kallandras did not pause to bear witness; he had seen death before, and he understood what he did not see. Instead, he took care not to join them.

But he was grateful for these kinlords and their red, red blades; his own sprang free of their unnatural weight as if called to battle. In the darkness, he could see the faintest trace of light across their edge—and it, too, was red.

Not even in the desert had the blades come to life.

They roared, or seemed to roar, as he raised them; they parried the sweeping arc of two swords. The third did not fall.

Instead, the water did.

From the back of the Winter King, she saw the river.

"Avandar!"

He acknowledged her without a word or a backward glance, for he saw what she saw; the river water gathered, losing the shape and form of wall. It rose, in coiling arms, limbs clear and undulating in the moonlight. Too many.

Too late. She could not tell who spoke.

"Too late? Why?" Her knees bit into the flanks of the King. But he would not go forward.

The water is a difficult element, the King said. *The most difficult to contain.*

"I thought the earth—"

Earth is the most difficult to call, the most difficult to wield; it sheds its form slowly. No one in need of haste will depend on it. Air and Fire come quickly, he added, *but they are almost formless; Water is heavy, and if it can be held to form, the destruction it brings is vast. Be grateful that we are by a river and not an ocean; be grateful that the river is long and thin.*

Gratitude was beyond her. Fear was not.

The watery limbs became tentacles.

"I don't understand!"

Did you not hear it, Jewel? The drums that were used in invocation were . . . wounded. The power that they exerted over the water's form was greatly weakened, but it was not broken; what they summoned remains. You see the water now as the water itself desires to be seen.

"Kallandras," Avandar said quietly, "Or Celleriant. They must have chosen to break the hold the *Kialli* have over the river. They failed," he added, as if he spoke of the downturn in market prices. "One, at least one, of the *Kialli* must have been an adept. If he does not release the water, it will not subside—but he has imperfect control."

She could see, for the moonlight was merciless, the sudden fall of liquid; could hear the crash of sundered timber in its wake. Water rose again, thin and graceful; in its center, she saw the flailing limbs of an armored man and cried out.

He is your enemy, the Winter King said coldly. *He is not of Clemente.*

She didn't tell him that she didn't care; he knew it, and it angered him.

Instead, Jewel caught tines. Pressed her thumbs into the sharpest of their points. Blood ran down her palms.

Go, she said.

There was no pretense of request. The Winter King leaped forward.

Kallandras was aware of the water.

It had a voice, and although he had never heard its waking strength, he had weathered storms in the lee of the sea-wall beyond which Senniel rose like a maker-made cliff. He had watched boats in harbor tossed against the rocks and the timber docks; had seen sails ripped from their moorings go to their resting place in the crook of waves made wild by storm.

Such storms had almost prepared him for this one.

Almost.

But bard-born, he was caught by the water's voice: by its rage, its fury, its sense of betrayal.

In the desert, water had been the source of life, its absence the source of death.

What life this water offered had been scoured clean. It spoke with death's voice.

Upon his finger, Myrddion's ring began to burn.

He could not heed that burning; the two kinlords did not; they drove themselves against the blades, and he was forced to meet their attack.

They were angry; they did not trouble themselves to hide it.

He had been taught, time and again, that anger was a fool's preserve; that in combat, there was only the blade dance and the blade's song; the tracing of the stars, the points of the Lady's circles.

His masters, he thought, had never faced *Kialli* lords.

They drew blood.

Lord Celleriant stood a moment between the scant safety of two mortal dwellings—the tallest that stood upon the edge of the river's banks. They would not last, and indeed, in this mortal geography, they were a poor choice of hiding place.

If, that is, one thought to hide from the elemental water.

Only the Winter Queen could now speak clearly to the rivers; only the Winter Queen could control, with contempt and ease, the water's anger, the water's fall.

In his youth—and that youth so far beyond him it returned at unexpected times—he had seen Arianne lift white, white arms in the splendor of Summer sky; had seen her walk into the stream of rushing foam and roaring water made by the falls of Lamentine. Hair streaming down her shoulders as if it, too, were liquid, she had laughed, raising hands as if to catch the bounty of the falls.

And the falls had . . . stopped.

The water ceased its roar, pausing, trapped in place against the sharp edges of broken rocks, and the smooth contours of worn ones.

Others, greater lords than he, had taken the Queen's challenge, but where she stood triumphant and at ease, they labored, the gray of their eyes turning now to silver, and now to gold.

Aie, she was gone.

Beyond him, for his failure in the cold of Winter.

But she could not command memory; he took what he could, as if he were mortal beggar in need of crumbs.

His blade he now lowered. His heart was its sheath; blue flame flickered and died, as if guttered by water.

He watched Kallandras as he danced between the kin-lords, and it brought a smile to his lips; a thin smile, but a genuine one.

The water struck the roof of the building on his right; he sprang clear of the falling debris, waving a hand to flick the timbers and shingles to one side.

It was not a casual gesture.

If he had any hope of returning to the Summer Court—or the Winter one—it lay with the mortal woman, Jewel ATerafin.

And she had commanded him, clumsily and without an understanding of the binding force of words, to use his power to *preserve*.

Brother, he thought, lifting a hand as if to touch the mortal bard, *your guess was wise; the drums were the source of their containment.*

But they were not the source of their power. It is true: the

*world does not lie easy beneath the hands of those who
chose to forsake it.*

Ser Alessandro kai di'Clemente had cause to be grateful
for his Toran. Adelos threw himself bodily across the man
he had offered his life to as the water passed above them,
flattening the dais that now seemed such a paltry, flimsy
conceit. The body of the Tor'agnate was crushed in that instant, and only by Adelos' reflexes did Alessandro fail to
join him.

But he could not hold Adelos; could not prevent the
water from taking him. He watched in a grim silence as one
of the two men he *trusted* drowned in the moving column.

And then he picked up fallen blade, caught Reymos by
the wrist, and began his retreat. Few were organized
enough to stop it.

One man stood against the river, hands raised in fists.
The cloak that had hidden him—the cloak that had *disgraced* him—he cast aside; the water reared the greatest of
its many tentacles above his head, seeking him blindly. He
did not duck, bow, hide; he did not seek to evade; he stood,
a challenge to the majesty of the wild element. Debris gathered at his feet, sloughing off his back and his raised fists.

He spoke to the river water in a voice both ancient and
broken with disuse. But the water's response was simple
rage; without the binding of drums and blood magic, he had
no hold upon its depths.

Once, once he had.

He was bitterly aware that among the *Kialli* there existed
lords of power whose will, and whose memory, held the
skills of their shattered past—bitterly, because he was not
among that number. Oh, his memory was intact, but everything else about his past had been burned away in the Hells.
This mockery of magic, this bastard summoning, was all
that was left.

That, and his sword. The shield, too, failed to come at his call.

Water took the mortals in number; what had been an army was broken by the sluggish whim of the living river.

He despised them, these broken, terrified *men*. Death took them all, soon or late; he could not understand their significance in the plans of the Lord. Could not understand the need for secrecy; the need to hide.

The water struck him.

He rose in its fist; felt it wash across his face; felt it exert the sudden pressure of an almost unimaginable weight. And he smiled.

What need had he of air? Only the living need draw breath.

He rose, encased in water; fell, encased in water. The ground at the river's bed grew dry and cracked as the element summoned what it needed, and he exulted a moment in its raw fury; it was kin to his own.

The Tor'agnate was dead. Dead by the hands of mortals, by the hands of the clansmen. The Lord would be ill-pleased—but if the other Tor had offered truth, if the Sun Sword could be found, such a loss might be forgiven.

He let the water play. There were deaths on both sides of the river that could no longer be avoided.

Against the water's rage, Lord Celleriant had several weapons. But only one might accomplish the task set him by the mortal he had been commanded to serve.

Viandaran's warning was just, and justified; the elements hated each other with a strength that rivaled the enmity between the *Kialli* and the Arianni. But the Arianni had one advantage: they were of the world. Even hidden, even imprisoned upon the old ways, the wild roads, they were *of* it.

He called air, and it came, its voice a roar.

The drums had been a gamble.

An expensive one.

Kallandras had failed before. In his youth, in the
labyrinths of Melesnea, and beyond it, in the streets of the
Tor Leonne. But each failure had failed to buy his death; instead, it had brought his brothers, their varied voices and
experience the steadying influence, the salvation, he required.

The voice that came to him now was none of these.

But he recognized it: the voice of the elemental air. His
hand burned; the ring grew bright enough to blind. To a
man who relied upon vision it might have been fatal, but
Kallandras had been trained to darkness. He leaped clear of
death, and the eddying currents of the air carried him above
the shoulders of the kin.

Their voices joined air, a howl of anger, a hint of fear,
blended into the harshness of a language he barely knew.
And harmony to it, harsh and beautiful, wild with the promise of death, a brother's voice.

Allele.

Across the wilds of storm made now of wind and now of
water in a mockery of nature, he met the eyes of an Arianni
lord of the Green Deepings.

He could not bow; the fleeting gaze was salute enough.
The kin rose to join him, finding easier purchase in the shelf
of wind than they had upon the ground.

Kallandras frowned. The wind drove them back, toward
ground. Into it.

The water rose as well.

Avandar Gallais struggled to sheathe his sword.

Jewel was aware of the motion although she couldn't see
it; he was behind her. The Winter King's stride had carried
them to the edge of the water's range—and it was wide.

But she could almost hear the voice of the blade; could
feel its weight, and its warmth, in her right palm; could feel
the pain of its denial against the scarred flesh of her fore-
arm.

You play a game you do not understand, ATerafn, the

stag said. He had never called her by title before; the rebuke
stung.

Avandar, she said, calling him in a way that diminished
distance.

He did not reply.

She looked back. Gray mist radiated outward in a nimbus
of light, and at its center, nothing. Avandar was gone.

There was no way to ford the stream. Although the
riverbed was dry and cracked—a hint of the desert and its
multiple deaths—the water roved freely.

Alessandro kai di'Clemente would never see water again
without remembering the destruction of Damar.

But he would see it without fear. He would see it as the
Lord's man. He paused on the periphery of flight's edge,
drew breath, turned back.

There, in moonlight—the lamps had fallen, and lay
crushed upon the cobbled stone and broken earth—he saw
the Northern bard. Saw what the bard faced: red swords,
red fire. Nothing natural. Nothing that the forest birthed.

He had offered the Lady his prayers, but he was of the
South; he accepted her answer with a grimace. His men,
upon the far bank, were scattered, but he heard the orders
and the sounds of steel that spoke of retreat, not rout. Pride,
there; pride for just a moment. Clemente produced *men.*
The Manelan Toran were either dead or dispersed; they had
failed in their sworn charge, but they had not chosen to seek
the death that awaited the failure of such profound oath.

He met Reymos' eyes in the darkness.

Ignored what he saw in them; he could offer his man that
much dignity.

But he could not make noble what was ignoble. He steadied himself, found strength remaining in the bend of tensed
knees, and ran.

The water struck the ground ten feet before him; he froze
and before he could run again, he was caught.

But not by water: the air held him.

"Tor'agnate," a foreign voice said, the syllables cold and too clear, "not on the West does your battle lie."

He flailed for just a moment, and then stilled as he rose. The water roared and rumbled as it passed beneath him; tendrils slammed into his legs with enough force to bruise.

And then he was clear of the banks; clear—for a moment—of the water. He heard a grunt at his side, and saw that Reymos had likewise been carried above the din of battle.

Quickheart was lost. He could not hear the horse; could not see him in the darkling night. *Home,* he thought, and it was a prayer. But it was all the prayer he spared.

For he could see, thirty yards away, what his men fought.

Celleriant fought the water. To force the air to accomplish the simple task of setting a commander among his forces had been costly, for the water was its enemy, and it sought nothing but battle. Sought to destroy anything that came between it and its rightful prey.

He was no youth, no stripling; the dawn of the world was beyond him. He could not be shaken by the simple anger, the visceral desire, of elemental air. He understood its heart; it was his own. For he had, by command, no choice but to turn his back upon the red blades of the kin, and they called him, a challenge and an insult that none—not even the Northern bard—could comprehend.

Winter was his heart. Ice. Cold.

In the Winter, the wind was death.

But his lady had commanded him to preserve life; he struggled to forgo the wilderness of the road that had defined him for millennia.

They will die anyway, he told her, silent, aware that his words would not carry the distance—the many distances—that separated them.

Aware, as his gaze turned to follow Kallandras a moment, that although the words were true, they contained the beginning of a falsehood. Lies were weapons; subterfuge a game. But what grew now was something foreign, something that defied his nature, his birth.

He lost the air a moment.

He paid.

They were like dogs.

Dogs grown in size, dogs whose eyes held the patina of fire's heart. They had jaws the size of a horse's head, teeth the length of daggers; they spoke with voices that might—once—have been human.

It was their speech that was, of all things, most disturbing. Ser Alessandro understood it. Felt the exultation that tainted the words and the challenge, the triumph, of the short bursts they made of words. Crossbow bolts were less effective.

They broke ground with their forepaws; severed limbs with their hind legs; they paused only to savor death, and the pause was brief.

He counted seven.

Against one, two, his men might stand, but against seven? He knew. Before he drew horn from sash, before he drew breath to wind it, he knew.

Not for Alessandro kai di'Clemente the madness of battle; not for Alessandro, the Tor'agar of Clemente, the wild exuberance of struggle and death. He stood, unchanged and unchangeable, as his men fought, and when he finally winded horn, they understood two things.

That their Tor was alive.

And that he was at their side.

Ser Amando had been correct in one way: These were men of the plains, and they served their Tor. They drew strength from his presence. They fought.

Where is he? she asked wildly.

The Winter King was silent. Above them both, the water trembled like a tower made of liquid crystal. She heard its voice; knew where it would fall. Knew who it would kill, although when she spoke the name, it had no meaning to her. A man's name. A clansman.

But she also knew that it would fall slowly. That it would fall blindly. What it sought, now, was above it, and around it.

Avandar warned us, she thought.

Yes. But in this at least he was mistaken.

Where is Celleriant? she asked again.

Where you sent him. ATerafin.

Take me.

You are my care, he replied.

Take me, damn you.

She had ridden him across the heart of the desert. Had ridden him through the heart of the Serpent's storm. She had ridden him through the Old Deepings, past the death that awaited Yollana of Havalla should she hesitate. But not until this evening, in the village of Damar, did she understand the force of the Wild Hunt.

Because he leaped up, above the reach of ground, as if gravity and weight were beneath his dignity. His hooves struck nothing; they fell in a silence that spoke of the death that at last ends pursuit.

Nothing escaped the Hunt, she thought, and the ghost of her Oma's voice remade old legends that memory and peace had fragmented. Nothing escaped, not even the King.

She clutched tines; her throat allowed the passage of air only when she gasped.

The Winter King, silent with the weight of command, took her beyond the reach of water, through the wail of air, and out the other side.

He offered no warning; her knees shook with the force of her grip, although she *knew* that he would not let her fall. Could not. It was some part of his transformation.

But he landed *in* the midst of battle, and she had just enough foresight—and she, gifted, born and cursed with knowledge—to unclench fists from antlers, one did not grab blade's edge for safety when the blade was being wielded.

What the blades of the Clemente cerdan were too slow, or too dull, to pierce, the Winter King did.

The voices of the kin—for these creatures could be nothing else—were raised now in anger and pain. But beneath it, a testament to the perception of her gift, she heard exultation.

They turned to face the stag.

The *Kialli* lord saw. The water that had taken him spit him out like refuse, a thing beneath its power and its concern. For a moment, anger governed him; anger lasted long enough to be transformed.

He recognized Lord Celleriant, blue fire burning along the fine trail of winter hair. The kinlord summoned blade, and it came, but he did not take to air; flight—even such flight as he had attained when he first woke upon the plain—was denied him.

Envy was a bitter blow; it struck him in a way that the elemental water could not.

His sight was not obscured by liquid, not riven by the debris the gale lifted. The hounds were at play; they would not now be called from battle by any lesser voice, and the Lord was in the Northern Wastes, upon the throne.

He had come to mortal lands with contempt; had worn it like vestment. It left him now. What remained was war, and the command that had been given him by the Lord's Fist.

The Manelan men were lost, but they were the least significant part of the forces that had assembled.

Shaking, fighting desire and the call to combat, he gathered the seeming that had protected the mortals from knowledge of who—of what—he was; he donned it clumsily, but he *did* don it.

He had expended power; but the power was not yet exhausted. With a snarl, Landaran of the *Kialli* left to gather

the army of the man who claimed dominion over all these
lands.

She felt the edge of nightmare tug at consciousness.

It wasn't unexpected. Demons, in all their dark glory,
were never a sight that she could be prepared for; not even
the worst of her memories—and she bore them all, like
scars—could contain the reality of their presence, the darkness of their shadows, the red, red light of their weapons, be
those weapons fangs and breath or bright, bloody blade.

The Winter King did not let her fall. Although he leaped,
lunged, danced across ground inexplicably cracked and dry,
she remained upon the safety of his back.

Discovered that safety, upon his back, was not guaranteed when the claws of one of these creatures slid through
the stiff leather of boots, the pale skin of calf, the flesh beneath it.

She accepted the pain. Clung to it.

But the nightmare descended anyway.

The Warlord was upon the field.

And a small field, a pathetic field, such as he had rarely
condescended to take. The blade that he had not drawn in
centuries now welded itself to hand; it moved as if it were
finger, knuckle, flesh. He did not struggle with it; did not
reach for skills that in another man might have become
slow and painful with disuse.

This was what he was.

This was what he had not died for, over and over again;
what he had given up the gift of the gods to obtain. He drew
himself up to a height that he had not felt for so long it
seemed an act of transformational magic. And then, with a
smile, he turned toward the kin, the mangy dogs that now
ran free across the terrain, scattering and killing as they
chose.

He saw the stag, and for just a moment, looked for Arianne upon the field. Saw, instead, Jewel ATerafin, dark

curls obscuring brown eyes, head bowed with the effort to control her fear. The blade fell a moment as he studied her face.

He had agreed to serve her.

He could not remember why.

But she could.

She did. What she had not said, time and again, she said now. *Viandaran.*

His name.

She had seen a god before, in the ruins of the foyer of the Terafin Manse. She had seen the children of gods in the Stone Deepings.

But what she saw in Avandar moved her in a way that those born to immortality had not moved her. Memory was a poor container. Reality was stronger.

She had seen this man in nightmare. She had seen him kill to exert authority over a wayward son. She had seen him—ah, this, too, in the present, relieved of the haze of memory—stand down to let their greatest enemy destroy one of the Cities of Men.

But she had never *seen* him. She knew it because she saw him now.

He was not Arianne; he was not Bredan; he was not Allasakar. But he was beautiful in a way they were not, for he was broken.

Time, now, to face truth and have done: She had gathered the broken to her, time and again. But she had refused to acknowledge that Avandar Gallais—that Viandaran—was one of them.

Why?

The Winter King spun, lifting hooves from all contact with earth. He was warm beneath her thighs, and his voice was silent. She wanted him to turn around, to turn again, to give her sight of Avandar.

But she wanted to live, and she knew that the blood that

fell, absorbed instantly by parched ground, drew the kin.
That and the pain.

The fear that she felt was a fear that the kin could not use;
she had learned that much of their nature.

Twisting, holding, she tried to see through the wild
strands of unkempt curls.

But Avandar was gone.

Alessandro kai di'Clemente drew his men back. He had
lost some quarter of their number; would lose more before
the battle's end. But it *was* a battle now. The stag that had
leaped into the midst of the creatures had killed one, and injured another. Hard to say if the injury was mortal; there
was blood, but it was dark beneath the night sky; he could
not say with certainty what its color was.

He raised a hand, bringing horn to lip. He knew that over
the din of arms his voice would not carry, but the horn song
would.

Archers came at his call, their ragged line forming up
into something more graceful. Their bows were strung; they
had arrows ready. He raised a hand and let it fall.

The strings quivered.

The creatures snarled, as if pricked by insects. Two
turned to leap into the line of men.

Alessandro joined those men, pushing through the ranks
to stand at their head; the line wavered a moment.

Reymos came, sword given over for the greater burden
of the banner he now carried. Unfurled, silver and gold
caught moonlight, marking the presence of the Tor.

The men held their ground. The moon looked on.

The foremost of the beasts drove into the line, and it
broke, not by flight, but by impact.

Run, the creature roared.

Stand, the horn replied.

Of such a conversation are stories born.

But legend is born from something else entirely.

As the creature tensed, as its jaws snapped around the

metal gorge of an armed cerdan, a strange silence fell, and into it walked a man wielding a sword the color of the sun.

For a moment, it seemed that Leonne had returned from the grasp of the winds to offer support and succor.

But the man's eyes were dark, and they passed above Clemente as if it were beneath his notice.

He spoke in a language that Alessandro had never heard, and had no desire to hear again, and the beast swiveled, turning to face his death.

And the man said, "The Warlord has taken the field." For the benefit of Clemente.

The Warlord.

Lord Celleriant held the water. He did not argue with the elemental air, but instead gave it the play it desired. Only when it swept across the paths of men did he nudge it back toward the oldest of its three enemies, and although it grudged him even this interference, it heeded the warning.

He did not attempt to protect the dwellings along the river's edge. If men were foolish enough to hide in them, they earned their grave. But he contained the combat, forcing the water's reach to the heights; what had been a several-tendriled foe was now a pillar.

It struck at him, and the air was only barely quick enough to respond. He was not grateful; he was not afraid. Instead, he felt something that he had never felt when he had chosen to enter combat: uncertainty. The rules of this battle were not the rules that had governed the whole of his existence, and he discovered that the Arianni were not as . . . flexible . . . as mortals.

Although he took no joy in death, the wild exultance of the Hunt had been solace and pleasure; these were gone. Gone, too, the worthy foe: the battle was beyond him; he held its fraying edges, no more. He bore witness, he made boundaries; his hidden sword was a weight and a decoration, like unto the banner now held, at such personal risk, by the Clemente Toran.

But he understood the importance of such a conceit, and at some cost to himself, forbid the wind to carry it out of their grasp.

Avandar was gone.

What remained had little in common with the man she had known; little in common with the man he had slowly become over the passage through the Stone Deepings and beyond. His hair was dark, his skin pale, but even these were of a hue that defied recognition.

He walked into the kin and they parted, jaws snapping, voices raised in something she had never really expected from them: fear.

Two fled.

Or tried to flee; light blazed from the sword as he swung it. He swung it yards from where they leaped; yards from where they fell. But the arc of the sword was larger than the sword itself, and the light, golden, was a corruption of every summer that Jewel had been graced—she knew it as grace now—to see. The kin were cut in two, and lay twitching and crawling upon the open ground.

The Winter King had gored a third, crippling its hind legs; its jaws were danger enough, for its neck was prehensile. It snapped at its foe, but the King, unwounded, was faster, leaping lightly into the air and touching ground only long enough to strike.

She wondered if he had ever held a sword like the War-lord's.

Yes.

She could see its ghost in the play of his limbs, the supple bend of his neck; his fur was warm armor beneath her hands.

She heard the fourth cry, the fourth mewling sound of a creature being consumed—and slowly—by flame, and although she had seen what the kin had done here, she flinched. It seemed to go on forever, blending with the howl of wind until at last she could no longer separate the two.

The Winter King stopped. He took to ground and stayed there, and Jewel was free to turn, free to look at the east bank of the Adane.

She was grateful for the moon's light; it was pale and silver and it hid the color of blood. Of all blood save that which now graced the Warlord.

The Clemente cerdan stood as the Winter King did; they bore witness, as if afraid to attract the attention of the man with the golden sword. Some fell to ground, but whether this was out of respect or due to lack of blood, she could not say; she hoped it was the latter.

Jewel, the Winter King said, his voice a thing of ice.

She shook her head, understanding what he asked.

The Warlord turned his gaze toward the West bank. He lifted his sword; buried it in the dry ground with enough force that the Winter King stumbled a moment.

Out of the earth came a bridge. It was wide, flat, a thing of rock.

Mortals can't contain the elemental forces. She had heard this somewhere. She had known it for truth.

His curse, the Winter King whispered.

In awe, she watched. What the water had sundered, he made whole, and she was not surprised to see that the rock's curve and width began to smooth and lengthen; that it grew rails, things that stonesmiths might once have made in the glory of the haunting and terrible cities that had defined power, for men, when the gods had walked the earth.

He took to the bridge, but she saw as he did that he turned toward the men of Clemente.

She *knew* he would command them.

She knew they would obey; what else was left them in the face of the power he now displayed? Power defined men in the South. Power elevated them; lack of power destroyed them.

Without thought, she leaped from the back of the stag.

Heard his voice, a clear warning that reverberated

through her limbs as if she were struck bell. Music there, and worse. She knew what bells tolled.

"Avandar!" She shouted the word; it was almost lost to the gale, for the air's voice had not stilled, and the water's had grown loud indeed. Neither air nor water troubled him, and if the earth did, it did not show in the cold, smooth lines of his face.

He did not turn; did not give any hint that he had even heard her.

And her instinct failed her—as it sometimes did—because the fear that she felt was suddenly too loud. He turned from her toward the bridge, and beyond his shoulder, she saw that Kallandras fought a single kinlord. The kinlord had the advantage of height, of reach, but Kallandras had something else—something that she was certain had not been defined or refined in Senniel.

His fight was a dance; not even the storm could deprive it of grace.

But she could not watch; her eyes turned to Avandar's back. He had not yet summoned the Clemente cerdan.

She could not afford to let him do that.

Yet when he turned, at the height of the bridge's curve, she froze again; she did not know how she—how anyone—could stop him.

For just a minute, wasn't sure that she wanted to.

Truth, too much truth this eve. *"Avandar!"*

Was not sure that she wanted to because he seemed unstoppable. Remote, broken, a killer. Maybe even her killer, if she could reach him. She wore his mark. He—wore it, twin to hers.

And he would be a killer that she never need fear—not the way she had feared Duster, in the end. Because in the end, Duster had died.

Yes, the Winter King said. Unfair, that a single word could say so much.

Lefty had died. Fisher had died. They had all left her.

Nothing she had done, nothing she *could* do, could prevent their desertion.

Teller could easily have been killed had Haerrad not chosen to offer warning in a way that would clearly show the cost of open warfare. The fear of that had almost destroyed her. And it would, she thought, bitter now.

She shook her head; hair was already arrayed against vision, and she did nothing to push it out of the way.

Avandar lifted his arm, his sword arm.

And she lifted hers, struggling a moment with the button that held shirt to wrist.

"Viandaran!"

The words that he might have said did not come. Instead, he looked at her for the first time since he had drawn sword and taken up the mantle of the Warlord.

Enough, she said softly, as if speaking to a wild creature. *Enough, Viandaran. You have done enough here.*

He lifted his arm; she could not see it clearly, but she felt hers respond. Warmth. Heat.

Everything would change. She knew it.

But everything did, anyway.

You swore yourself to my service, she told him, arm burning as if the brand itself were being applied for the first time, or as if the pain of it had been delayed until she had at last accepted its presence.

I . . . serve . . . you?

We serve each other, she replied. Raw now. Words she hadn't spoken for so many years they made her feel young and vulnerable.

He stood. It was not an act of hesitation.

The Clemente cerdan began to gain their feet, to find their weapons, to find their ranks. She heard, above the din of so many different storms, the call of horn; heard it answered.

Harmony, she thought.

I've seen your dead, she told him.

Lady, he said, although the word itself was composed of

syllables that she had never heard. *The servants of the shadow god leave no ghosts.*

No, she said, because it was truth. *They leave scars. You've done enough. I—I asked for too much.*

How much was too much? The words seemed small, irresolute, the whimpering denial of a child.

But because they were true, she stood behind them.

Golden light shrouded his face, his features; made him hard to look upon.

I am not Avandar Gallais, he told her.

I know. She took a step forward; bent her head into the driving wind. Something struck her in the shoulder, but not hard enough to knock her off her feet; she glanced back to see the flat of a board. Some part of a building that had not survived the night's work.

But you're not the Warlord either.

Am I not? Sword, now. Eyes too bright to be dark, although they looked all of black.

No. Because if you were, you would never have taken the name Avandar Gallais. You would never have come to Terafin. You would never have been—

The blade lowered a fraction. She had all of his attention now, and she found that she didn't *want* it.

Mine.

Everything, everything, would change.

She made her way to the bridge. The debris that swirled lazily in the air no longer touched her; it swooped past her face, shadowed her steps, ruffled her hair—but it caused her no harm.

His work, she knew.

Do you understand what you are saying?

As much as I ever do.

His brow rose a fraction. It was almost familiar.

This is a war that you cannot fight, ATerafin. This, these—they are not enemies against which you or your den can stand. Will you take that risk? Will you disarm yourself?

Could you protect them? she asked. *Could you, when you
couldn't even protect—*

Silence.

Funny, how much she wanted the answer to the question
she suddenly didn't have the courage to ask.

*Put up the sword, Avandar. Viandaran. Whatever you
want to call yourself. Put it up. You should never have
drawn it.*

Oh?

Because now, she continued, the words carrying themselves beyond volition and intention, *now they'll know.
Where you are. What you've done.*

Ah. Yes, he said. He *will know.* And he looked to the
North.

No, she thought, the City coming unbidden to mind. No.
But she *knew* that the god in the North could grant him
what he desired, what she had *never* desired for her den.
Death.

"Avandar." Close enough. Close enough to touch him.
The blade was between them, its edge a thing of light.

He looked down at her.

She reached out, arm shaking, and touched his chest.
With the flat of her hand. She stopped there, staring up at
his eyes, her hand illuminated now by the red, red light of
a brand that was glowing in the recess of night, in the light
of sword.

His hand touched the back of hers.

His fingers lifted her chin, forcing her eyes up.

"Are you afraid, ATerafin?"

"Yes."

"Good." His smile was cool. Foreign.

And she realized, as he offered it, that the hand that
touched her chin was the hand that had borne the sword.

Ser Alessandro kai di'Clemente waited out the storm. Although the plains seldom saw a storm such as this, he felt
the danger of it at great remove; the beasts that had harried

and killed his men were dead; the Widan—or whatever it
was they styled themselves—gone. If victory was counted
in a hundred dead, he had victory. The Adane had exacted
its price along the riverbanks. His boot hit hard ground,
kicked up rocks that had struggled to broken surface. He
wondered what would grow here, in the months that followed, if anything did.

Reymos was by his side. His forehead was covered in a
sheen of red; slick and shiny, it stopped at his lids. The banner of Clemente he bore with a quiet determination, but his
hands shook with fatigue.

"He will pay," Alessandro said quietly. "For Adelos. For
my men."

Reymos nodded. No other words need be said.

But other words came. Practical words. "The Tyr'agnate," Reymos said quietly.

Alessandro nodded. Not even a Tor'agar could kill the
head of a ruling clan with impunity. "We will inform him of
the night's events. Look," he added.

The river was subsiding.

If, by subsiding, one meant shrinking back into the containment of its bed. It was slow to yield; it reached out to
destroy what was within its reach—but almost nothing was.
Wooden planks, men's swords and shields, the detritus of
old buildings—these were pulled in by the force of the
water, to be carried or hoarded in the movement of its
stream.

But the bridge made by the Warlord remained unmoved
and untroubled by the water that lapped at its curve.

Upon the bridge, sword sheathed, the man stood, the
Northern girl in his arms.

Calm came slowly to the Lady's Night. Silence descended.

Across the width of new bridge came the Northern bard;
his chest was red with blood, his arm wounded, but his expression denied the existence of injury. He paused at the
back of the Warlord, and the Warlord turned.

What he said, no one could hear, and Alessandro bitterly regretted it. The bard's speech was short; the Northern woman nodded and he stepped around them, tracing a clear path toward the ruling kai of Clemente.

He bowed before him, feet steady above the wreckage of buildings. The bow itself was perfect; it accorded Alessandro the full measure of respect due his rank. In spite of himself, Alessandro felt the debt he bore grow subtly.

"Kai Clemente," the bard said, choosing the less formal title, as if to alleviate some of that burden.

"Kallandras of Senniel," the Tor'agar replied.

"If your negotiations within Damar have been completed, I would respectfully suggest you withdraw your forces."

Alessandro raised brow; a question.

"Not all of the men sent to Damar were stationed within it; not all of them were gathered by the Adane. Sarel offers some safety against their numbers—but that safety diminishes with time." He paused. "With your leave, kai Clemente, I will bespeak the Radann par el'Sol; I believe he has duties to which he *must* attend."

Alessandro nodded at once.

But the horses were scattered, and he had no idea of how many had survived the onslaught; the return to Sarel would be slower and more cumbersome than the arrival in Damar had been.

He lifted horn to lip, drew breath.

But before he could wind it he heard the voice of another horn, its song raised in cry of war.

He closed his eyes. "How many?" he said softly.

Kallandras of Senniel turned to the South and listened a moment.

"Many," he said softly. "And they are close now."

Weary, Alessandro blew horn. But it was not the note he had hoped to sound.

The forces of the Tyr'agar had begun their march into the town of Damar.

CHAPTER TWENTY-FIVE

LORD Celleriant descended slowly. He had turned to face the South, and he observed the march of lights from the distance of height; his sight was keen, and his instinct gave him numbers.

He did not fear mortal armies, but he knew that he had spent the better part of his power in an act of preservation that now seemed futile. For Viandaran had sheathed his blade—against all tale, all legend, of his time before the fall of man—and stood, cloaked again, his power shuttered, his head bowed over the head of the ATerafin woman, his arms, incongruously, around her.

His was not the only blade of power upon the field; Lord Celleriant's was a bright slash of blue against the vision as he touched ground.

Kallandras of Senniel College stood five yards to the west; their eyes met. The blood that adorned the bard was like a poem, and Celleriant desired the privacy—and the leisure—in which to appreciate it; he had neither. Not for the first time would he curse the hurried pace of mortal life.

And death.

He stepped lightly above the fallen, and knelt a moment to close the eyes of a dead man.

When he rose, Kallandras was at his side, his brows lifted slightly in curiosity.

"It is a mortal custom," Celleriant said.

"Yes," Kallandras replied, no more.

But they were watched; Lord Celleriant was aware of the observers. He did not intend to answer the question Kallan-

dras had not asked, although he was as aware of it as he was
of the regard of the Clemente men.

But he said, "It is reparation for failure. He died by the
water's hand."

Kallandras said, "The dead are dead; their eyes see nothing."

"That is not what the mortals of old believed."

"It is the truth."

He shrugged. "It is reality. But . . . all custom, all
pageantry, all ritual, are based in things that hold deeper
truths at their heart. Come. They gather."

He walked toward the lady he had been given to serve.
Bowed, although the bow was a war bow, and not the ritual,
perfect abasement of a distant Court.

She was slow to detach from the Warlord, or perhaps he
was slow to release her, but she did turn. Her eyes, living
eyes, were round and wide.

"There are a thousand men," he said quietly, "who march
even now through the streets of Damar."

"The villagers?"

She could surprise him by the simplest of questions.

"I did not think to look."

It was true; armor's glint, and sword's, had captured his
attention, as if he were magpie, and they, treasures to be
gathered when the night's work was done and the story at
last told.

"ATerafin," Viandaran said quietly. "The villagers present no threat to Clemente; let them fend for themselves a
while longer."

She stiffened; her lips opened, presaging argument.

But they closed again as she nodded. She let go of Viandaran completely, and gained two inches in height as she
squared slender shoulders.

As if she were of the North, as if the South had no part
of her blood or her heritage—and it was there, to Celleriant's admittedly untutored eye—she marched toward the
Clemente Tor who had just lowered horn.

                              *   *   *

"You have my gratitude, Lady," he said, offering her a bow that was in essence foreign.

As was she; she did not seem to note the significance of the gesture. And perhaps it had no significance to one who could command such . . . men . . . as hers. "Maybe," she said quietly. "But there are a thousand men marching through the streets of Damar. They'll be here soon."

"They come from the South?"

She nodded.

"Then they will be forced to the Eastern half of Damar."

"Why?" Her eyes were too wide. He looked at her, and he saw a woman, a tired, frightened woman. But beyond her, he saw . . . the Warlord. He did not pity her, and he did not despise her; that he did not understand her was a mercy.

Almost gently, he said, "there are no roads upon the Western bank; they will not chance the forests at night, even if they do not understand our customs. They will arrive by the Eastern road.

"We gather beyond the bridge," he said, looking at the edifice of perfect stone with something akin to wonder. And weariness. "If we can hold the bridge for some time, we may give them cause to regret their presence in Mancorvo."

"You assume," the Northern bard said quietly, "that they will content themselves with your destruction. If they choose to ignore the bridge, they can march upon Sarel."

"They will not leave us at their backs," Ser Alessandro said evenly. "They will seek the advantage of numbers to destroy our forces here before they proceed."

Jewel ATerafin frowned openly, but the battleground was already such a strange, destroyed place that it mattered little. "That makes no sense," she said.

Reymos, bleeding, bridled. But Ser Alessandro nodded, bidding her continue.

"If I were them, I'd leave some small number to contain *us*, and I'd ride to Sarel. If they take Sarel, you cannot win, even if you survive."

"ATerafin," Kallandras said quietly, "they are led by *Kialli*, whether they know it or not. We *are* too great a threat."

"Can we win?"

"I cannot say." Ser Alessandro gazed at the silent sky, and then at the stag, at Lord Celleriant, at Kallandras of Senniel. "But . . . against their numbers, without some greater intervention, I would say that the possibility is slim. We can retreat, but the retreat would be costly, and there is no guarantee that it would not become a rout; once they cross the bridge, once they enter the Western half of Damar, we are outnumbered."

"What if they try to cross the river to the West?"

"If they choose to cross the road beyond Damar, we have no way of defending it; they will come late, but they will come at our backs; we cannot hold bridge and land, both.

"And they have seen no battle, if I am not mistaken; they come fresh to the fight."

"You are not mistaken," the Old Forest lord said. "And . . ." he gazed a moment at the man upon the bridge, and then turned back. "I am spent; you will have my sword, and it will count for tens of men—but more than that, I cannot in safety offer; were I to unleash the wind, it would take more from you than it would preserve."

Alessandro bowed head, accepting the inevitable.

"Then we will hold the bridge," the Tor'agar replied. "Until we have, ourselves, none who are up to the task."

The Serra Teresa di'Marano looked up, neck snapping in a parody of grace. Her eyes were wide and dark; they gazed into the center of the perfect, spare room as if she could see a ghost that did not choose to haunt the room's other occupants.

But the Serra Celina en'Clemente, lamb or no, was not unwatchful. Her eyes rose as the Serra did.

"Serra Teresa?"

The Serra's grace returned, but she did not sink back into

the fold of lap and rough Voyani cloth. Instead, she turned
to the Matriarch of Havalla, her gaze skirting the upturned
face of the Serra Diora di'Marano.

The Serra's fingers lay still against samisen strings,
where a moment ago, they had moved; she did not otherwise acknowledge the change in the Serra Teresa's demeanor. Was not otherwise acknowledged.

"We must speak," Serra Teresa said quietly to the Havallan Matriarch.

Serra Celina rose at once; after a heart's beat, the Serra
Diora did likewise. Grace, Celina thought; exquisite grace.
For she knew the Serra Diora had traveled through the
Deepings at the side of both of these women. Celina
reached the sliding screens of the interior room, and paused
as she waited for the seraf without to slide them across their
recessed rails.

The seraf did not respond.

First fear. The night had fallen, and its hold was strange;
she could taste a wildness in the wind that wound its way
through open screens and veils of incense until, in subtlety,
it reached the harem's inner heart.

Best not to hear the words of the Voyani; best not to notice the words of their Matriarch. She pressed her hands
against the screens, determined now to perform the menial
task left her by the absent seraf.

But before she could open the doors, the Serra Teresa
spoke a single word. "No."

The Havallan Matriarch, crippled, rose by the grace of
the Serra Teresa di'Marano and made her way to the single
lamp that burned upon the low table, its shadows long and
wavering.

Celina was quiet; it was in silence that the most oft used
refuge of women lay. But the Serra Diora glanced once at
the swirling fiber contained in the opacity of screen paper,
and then she bowed and returned to her place against the
wall.

Without asking leave or permission—and in the end, what Voyani woman knew such grace—the Havallan Matriarch took a slender stick of wood from the dirty folds of clothing she had been unwilling to surrender to the ministrations of the serafs.

The scent of sweat, of blood, of road, lingered in the room in spite of the costly oils and incense that Celina had chosen to burn; her husband would be ill-pleased at the expense, she thought.

And knew herself a foolish woman to think so.

The wood was a sweet wood, but it was not a soft one; it was slow to take fire from the lamp, and Celina thought the lamp itself might gutter before surrendering any share of its flame.

But the stick took fire and began a hesitant crackle, and only when it spoke thus did they speak.

"Serra Celina," the Serra Teresa di'Marano said quietly, "I have traveled long upon the *Voyanne* at the side of the Matriarch, and in return for my aid, she has gifted me with some measure of the Voyani lore.

"What I say, therefore, is of the Voyani, and if you will have peace between her people and yours, you will hide the source of the words while you live."

Celina nodded.

But she sat, knees shaking into the soft mat that held them, hands now bunching in graceless fists around folds of pale silk. Orange, it looked, in the fire's dim light. Orange and shadow.

"Send for your son," the Serra said. "Tell him to man the curtain wall with the archers the Tor'agar left behind."

The Serra Celina gazed into the fire, into the dwindling length of stick. "I am not a man," she said at last, and softly. "It is not from me that he will take his command."

"Tell him," the Serra Teresa continued, as if the necessary and formulaic words had not been spoken, "that the forces of Alesso di'Marente have gathered a thousand strong in Damar, and that they will march—if unhindered—to the very gates of Sarel."

She closed her eyes. Thought of her son.

"Not all of the Clemente men were seconded; those that can fight must be ready to fight. Summon the Radann," she added, "for their foes are on the field."

Bright Lady, Dark Lady. She bowed her head.

"And Serra Celina, I bid you be deaf to the sounds of battle that you hear within your domis; seek only your son; deliver only this message. Return," she added quietly. "We will be waiting, with the child."

The child. For a moment, Celina's expression softened into lines of gentle worry. But the child had not heard; her breath remained steady, an even, gentle sound.

The Radann par el'Sol heard the words as if they were the voice of god. Clear, clearer than the roar of winds in open desert, they came to him as he stood in watchful silence with his gathered Radann, his men of the Lord.

It is time, Radann par el'Sol. Draw your blade. Do what must be done.

And what of you? he whispered, his lips barely moving. What of the kai Clemente?

But there was no answer; his voice was not like unto the Lord's; it traveled the brief span of air allowed men who must breathe to exist.

Turning to the Radann he lifted finger to lip; they nodded in the dim light. Around them, the domis of the clan Clemente slept; cerdan manned the gates, but they gazed out, toward the sleeping road, and the shadows of the Old Forest.

He placed his hand around the hilt of *Verragar*, and after a brief pause, he drew the sword. It shamed moonlight; it shone blue.

Radann eyes widened; heads bowed in respect. The swords that left sheath in reply to his own were dull glints of moon-touched sharpness. But they were men's weapons, all; Marakas par el'Sol felt not empowered, but humbled, for they drew their weapons as purposefully as he, and theirs was the greater risk.

"Not so," the eldest of the Radann said, divining the thought that Marakas did not hide behind courtly expression. "The only risk that matters is failure."

Marakas bowed to these men, rank forgotten a moment as the voice of the Sword became his own.

He began to move, and they followed in silence.

The Serra Celina returned to the heart of the harem, her face as pale as the powdered Serras of the Highest Court in the land. No artifice gave her color, and she paused a moment to gather breath, strands of her hair falling across her face like shadowed web.

"My son—" She was not used to running.

Which of them were, who lived in the harem?

The Serra Teresa di'Marano waited.

"My son bids me ask, what of my husband?"

The Serra Teresa shook her head. Had it been in her power, she would have lied. But the war had not yet come to the harem's heart, and only when all hope was gone would she use her gift in that way.

Instead, she said softly, "Serra Celina?"

The Serra nodded.

"If it is not too bold a request, and not too difficult a burden, I ask that you take the child. I must tend to the Havallan Matriarch."

The Serra's brows rose, and then she nodded. Was she grateful? Perhaps. Or perhaps she simply accepted the Serra Teresa's words.

She lifted the sleeping girl, settled her in her lap, and bowed her shaking head.

Verragar spoke in a voice that grew louder and louder; Marakas wondered—briefly—why the light of the blade did not blind, as the sun's light did. But gazing at the blade did not make the shadows darker; when his eyes returned to the halls, they seemed clearer. Harsh, bereft of all softness.

He had expected to find Clemente cerdan throughout the domis, and he did—but their numbers had been winnowed greatly. Here and there, a single man stood sentry, blade drawn.

None hindered his passage, or questioned it; in the light of the moon, even the serafs were absent; the domis seemed hollow. Sleeping.

One could be lulled by the silence.

Cozened by the stillness.

Even one as watchful as Marakas par el'Sol.

He heard *Verragar*'s voice; saw her light flare, bright now as sun, the most urgent of her warnings, and glanced ahead at the closed doors—Northern doors—that separated the dignitaries from the rest of the domis. He nodded, moving forward.

And almost died when the wall exploded outward at his back.

They felt it, in the harem's heart.

They *saw* it, in the flicker of lamplight, for the color and the dancing tongues of the flame seemed to lap a moment into a solid shape.

Yollana cursed; lifted her hand to the dark patch across what had once been eye. "Na'tere!"

Serra Teresa stood at once, lithe as a young girl in the first blush of harem's youth. Her hand was upon the hilt of a dagger, concealed until this moment against need. "Serra Celina," she said, "I charge you with the safety of the child. And with the mercy of her death, if it comes to that." She turned to her niece. "Na'dio," she said softly. "You have the sword?"

The Serra Diora di'Marano nodded, eyes watchful, hands still.

"Watch, then," the Serra Teresa said tersely. "Wait."

Ah, waiting. A woman's game. The Flower of the Dominion nodded again.

Celina's eyes were wide, and her skin as pale as moon. Her son was no boy; he manned the walls; her daughter ruled a harem of her own in a distant city. She thanked the Lady for this small mercy: none of her own faced the threat this child now faced.

None of her own.

The child stirred, and Celina reached out gently, stroking hair and brow. But brown eyes opened; lids grew light as flickering lamp. She sat. The Serra's arms tightened, preventing retreat.

The Havallan Matriarch now rose to her feet; her stance was shaky, and the Serra Teresa did not come to lend her strength. "Na'tere," she said again. "Take the satchel. Inscribe the smallest circle you can that will contain us all." She pulled the leather pouch from her belt and tossed it.

The Serra Teresa di'Marano fumbled with the leather knots that held the satchel closed. She opened her hands to ash, gray and fine. For just a moment, her brows rose; she met the eyes of the Havallan Matriarch.

But the Matriarch did not confirm the question the Serra would not ask.

Instead, she said, "All magic is a matter of life and death, and it exacts its price."

Two men did die. The creature—for if it had ever been graced by the shape of man, all grace was past—drove long hands *through* the length of the Radanns' blades, shattering steel as easily as he had splintered broad wood beam.

Marakas could not turn in time; could not and *did*. *Verragar* moved his hand, became the force by which he might steady himself to meet the creature's charge.

He discarded the dead like gloves, throwing them with ease into the men at whose side they had labored in the halls of the Radann. And then he turned to face Marakas, his jaws stretching into something akin to smile.

"You are too late," he said, tongue flickering pass the ragged edge of exposed teeth. "If the Tor'agnate returns, he will return to a mausoleum."

"I am not the Tor's man," Marakas replied, raising blade and bending into his knees. "But the Lord's."

"There is only one Lord in the Dominion."

The Radann par el'Sol offered the grimmest of smiles. "Indeed," he said softly. And struck.

The doors did not shatter; they slid. They slid as if at the hands of seraf, and indeed, a lone seraf now knelt in the hall without, head to floor, dark hair braided down the length of his spine.

The women stood in the center of a circle of ash, pale and light. A strong wind might sweep it away, exposing mats.

"Serra," the seraf said quietly. "The kai Clemente bids you follow."

But Yollana of the Havalla Voyani smiled grimly and lifted her pipe. "She will not follow where you lead," she told him, voice cracked with smoke and age, a texture that invoked a rough sense of beauty. "Leave."

The seraf rose, lifting youthful, even beautiful, face.

His eyes were hard and dark as ebony.

Yollana spoke a word and threw the pipe to the mats. They were soft enough to yield, but the pipe shattered on contact, and embers of what it contained now flared, bright and gold, in the circle.

Through the haze of summer light, the seraf's features changed; the bones of his face grew long and fine, the hair at his back dark, wild, a moving cloak. The winds, cursed in the South, buoyed him; he moved, and they whispered at his whim.

But although they felt it, heard it, although the room lost all warmth as he drew breath, the ash that lay upon the mats did not so much as quiver.

"Yes," Yollana said. "There still exists in this world the power to defy you."

The seraf—not seraf, not human, but not quite monster—
laughed softly. "Clever children," he said, and reaching out
casually, he brought the door's frame down.

The creature seemed surprised that the sword struck the
hard shell of demon flesh; that it pierced it, fraying the
edges of what looked like flexible chitin with a burning
blue light. But although the sword took him in the heart, it
was said that demons had none.

Marakas had just enough time to pull the blade free before the creature struck. Long claws raked armor, shredding
it as if it were gauze. No blood was drawn.

Not by *Verragar.* Not by demon.

"You have one of the lesser swords," the creature hissed,
"given to men too weak to survive the making of their own.
Do you think to stand against us?" He drew arms back, and
when he lifted hand—and claw—again, he carried a mas-
sive, red blade.

"Be honored," he said. "I have killed many, many mortals since my return, and I have raised sword against only
one."

His expression was not mortal; was not human. But the
arrogance in his voice made the contorted lines of his face
clear.

He struck; there was no grace, no dance, in the motion.

No grace or dance in the parry.

But where the blades met, fire burned, and the fire was
real.

The roof buckled with the loss of door and frame, teetering and creaking like an ancient, living thing. Beneath its
sudden curves, the golden fire grew brighter.

"You cannot enter the circle," Yollana said.

The man—the demon—laughed. "No, little mortal," he
replied, "*you* cannot leave it. The whole of your lives are
enscribed in your circle; to leave it is death. And I need not
touch you—any of you—to kill you. You are the definition

of fragility; there is none of the greatness of the old world
in you."

The Havallan Matriarch nodded. "And none of the taint,"
she whispered. "Be careful when you seek the weak, creature of the Lord of Night."

"You are *all* weak," he replied. He reached out again, and
the wall folded.

Fire. In the domis.

It lapped at floor and wall, at screen and the lattice that
held opaque paper in place. The flowers in the vases that
lined the hall in sparse and elegant display withered in the
heat of the flames.

The Radann cried out; warning blended with fear.

But Marakas par el'Sol was beyond them. The flames
touched him, lapping at robe, blackening chain; they took,
once again, hair and the sparse beard that had struggled its
way back from the cleansing in the Tor Leonne.

But they did not touch his face; did not obscure his vision. Instead, they *honed* it. He stood, as the demon did, his
hands upon an ancient blade: he saw, as the demon did, the
only enemy worth facing.

He swung, and the demon parried; he parried as the
demon swung. His blade sliced clean through extended
claws, for the creature had chosen to fight with both hands,
much like a man who chooses dagger over shield.

The Serra Teresa di'Marano rose. She spoke a few
words, but although her lips moved, they offered no sound.

"Ona Teresa—"

The child in the lap of the Serra Celina rose suddenly, as
if startled from harbor; her face was pale, and her hands
stiff. But her knees were bent; she crouched on the ground,
looked up, and met the eyes of the creature.

His smile was soft; an invitation. The whole of his threat
was hidden a moment beneath the curves of that sweet ex-

pression. He offered the child a hand, and Celina reached
for her.

But she was swift, this unnamed orphan; she dodged past
the Serra's shaking, fearful grip.

For just a moment, mouth dry, Celina thought that she
would accept what the stranger offered. But the moment
passed; the child turned suddenly, swiftly, on heel and
leaped toward the back of the circle that had been traced
with such care across the perfect floor of the harem's heart.

And the Serra Diora rose swiftly, as swiftly as the child
had, and as unexpectedly. She could not—quite—reach the
child, but her words could. And did.

"Ariel, stop."

The child froze in mid-motion, and the Serra, graceful
for someone who moved so quickly, caught her shoulders.
Her hands were smooth and steady, and her voice dropped,
as her head did; her lips were by the child's ear.

"He'll kill us," the girl said, her voice high and terrified.
"He'll kill us all—and Isladar's not here. There's *no one to
stop him.*"

"Hush, hush, Ariel," the Serra Diora said softly. She
drew the child into her arms. **"He will not kill us. I give
you my word. I will protect you."**

The Serra Teresa lowered her head a moment, and when
she raised it, she smiled. It was a Court smile, shorn of the
honesty, the vulnerability, that Celina's smiles oft exposed.

The Serra Diora stiffened. What she saw in her Ona,
Celina could not say. "Ona Teresa, don't—"

The Serra lifted a hand; the niece fell silent.

"The samisen," the older Serra said softly. "Na'dio.
Play."

"I—"

"Ariel will sit with you, if you play. She always has."

The Serra Diora shook her head again. "Ona Teresa."

In all of this, the stranger stared, his slate gaze moving
first from the child and then to the women, as if he were
tracing the lines of a triangle that contained them all.

"Ariel," the Serra Diora said quietly. "You must help me, now. Sit in my lap, and I will place the samisen in yours. We will play it . . . together. Will you do this? The circle cannot be crossed in safety. If you but break it, he can walk in."

"He doesn't *need* to walk in—I've seen them—I want my—"

"He will walk in if he can. Do not open the door for him. Do not fear him. It is fear that he needs."

The child crumpled, and the Serra drew a deep breath; she pulled flat, dark hair from the child's forehead, and kissed her gently. Her eyes were wide and red, her face wet and slick in the summer light.

It was almost too much for the Serra Celina, whose wives were somewhere in the domis. Somewhere where there was no circle, no ash, no Matriarch.

After a moment, silence gave way to sound: the strings moved. Celina watched, fascinated, as the young Serra began to play. She did not sing, and because she did not, it was a moment before the Serra Celina recognized the lay of the Sun Sword.

If the creature understood the challenge she played with such perfect, cool grace, he did not acknowledge it—and he was, Celina thought, a man; he did not ignore the overture of battle where knowledge was within his grasp.

His ignorance calmed her.

The circle was a boundary. But it was the least of the boundaries that had defined her life—and her survival—in the Dominion of Annagar. Teresa had no sword; indeed, no woman of worth in the Dominion ever held one, unless it was sheathed, and intended for use by a son. A husband did not leave his blade to the hands of women, not even his wives.

Aie, she had learned those lessons well. Not even en-wrapped by Voyani robes, shrouded by dust and the multi-ple scents of travel upon the open road, had she been able to shed the lessons that had guided the whole of her life, from cradle to this moment.

She thought of those lessons now, of their import; she moved with the delicate grace of a Serra as she raised dagger in the moving air. Flecks of ash rose to greet its silvery flat.

The dagger was a woman's weapon. Poison was a woman's weapon. Silence. The ability to wait, to endure. Words were a woman's weapon, if they were placed with care and humility into conversations whose power might otherwise be above them.

All of this, all of it, was her truth.

But she had others.

She bent to the fire that had bloomed from the shards of Yollana's pipe; bent there, as if the golden light were of the Lady and not the Lord. But she offered no prayer, no song, no supplication; she acted as a man acted, and took what she needed.

The blade passed through the fire.

The fire clung.

"Na'tere—" Yollana began.

But the Serra met the Matriarch's eyes, and it was the Matriarch who retreated into silence.

"Ona Teresa."

She did not look at her almost-daughter. But she spoke a single, private word. **"No."** She paused a moment, almost weary.

"Let me help."

"You have, Na'dio. Your song and the child in your arms strengthen me. I know what you are feeling, and it is a gift; protect *this* child. Protect this harem. You have your duty. And I . . . have long been absent from mine. Stay. Wait. If I fail, you are their last defense."

She, who had claimed no obvious power, gathered power now.

She had thought, when she had taken the robes of a man

and had walked away from the Tor Leonne, that she had left the old life behind. It had been truth.

But truth was subjective; the moment, the demon, the heart of the Clemente harem—her own forever denied her by her father and her brothers—now gave lie to what had been so bitter, so difficult a sacrifice.

Because she was silent, graceful, dutiful; she was Serra Teresa di'Marano.

"Demon," she said, as she rose, the fire lingering upon the sheen of blade's length. "It is said there is power in names, and in naming."

He laughed. The sound, to her ears, was exquisite—a thing of such texture and such beauty she might have listened to it until he chose to end the symphony by the simple expedient of death. She almost did.

She might never hear beauty of its kind again.

"You have not the skill or the sight to name *me*," he said, "and therefore, to you, little one, names have *no* power."

"Ah," she said quietly, her voice the voice of the High Courts, modulated and apologetic. She held the dagger almost carelessly, as if aware that it was no weapon against a man who could, without effort, bring down walls and ceiling on a whim.

She skirted the edge of the circle she had inscribed upon the mats; saw its edge, in a trail of diffuse dust, an inch away from the toe of her boot. "It was not your name of which I spoke."

Before she could retreat into hesitation, before the earlier lessons of her life—before *her life*—could reassert itself, she lifted foot and crossed that line, exposing herself.

The man smiled; his smile was breathtaking, and deadly in the way that the smiles of powerful men had always been.

"Come here," he told her, lifting a hand, curving a finger.

She obeyed; obedience was natural.

But what lay behind it, what had always lain behind it, was natural as well. Robart, bard-born and foolishly naïve, had taught her the use of her curse; had named it gift, a blessing. He had counseled her long in the gathering of its power, and she had learned.

Be wary, child, he said, from the distance of years, his words blurred by the fickleness of memory. *Power such as you wield must be gathered gently, and used gently. There is a risk, with power, of using too much.*

Risk. And what risk was greater than this? Dark eyes, fire, shadow. Death.

She walked. She appeared to struggle with each step, and in truth, it was more than simple appearance; she needed time, and she knew—for she could hear it in his voice—that the struggle, helpless and futile, would please the creature. Would feed him.

She offered him that much.

And while she walked, she heard Robart's voice. His old stories. His cautionary tales about the danger of reckless use of the voice.

Your gift is strong, he had said, *but think of it as a vessel; think of it as Northern crystal. Northern glass. It will hold even the most corrosive of elements, will gather and contain the most deadly of poisons—but once cracked, it will hold nothing.*

She gathered the power, thinking of herself as that crystal, as that clarity through which light shone, and in which the most dangerous of elemental liquid might, for moments, be contained.

"Come, mortal."

And she thought of shattered glass; of its new shards, edges sharp enough to catch the unwary, seeking blood.

She reached him, and as he reached for her, she let loose the force of the power that had destroyed the life she had been born to, day by day and year by year, until only this moment remained: outcast by choice, at the side of the Voyani, victim to sun and wind.

To sun and wind.

But not to man.

"HOLD."

Not even his brows rose; she felt the word leave her
throat, and she knew that she would not speak another word
this eve, if she could speak again at all, without a voice as
broken and cracked as Yollana's had become with time.

Her hands shook.

Old memory.

She ignored the warning that all memory contained,
hoarded as it was, examined and sorted in the recesses of
dream, of nightmare, of history.

As she had done once before, she raised dagger against a
servant of the Lord of Night.

This one burned.

The Radann had retreated. He was no longer aware of
their presence. The duty of battle had passed beyond them,
but other duties remained: the domis burned. And in it, unaware of the death that followed flame, cerdan, seraf, Serra;
the wives of Clemente.

He saw the battle not as swordplay; it was too raw and
too wild for that. It was a thing of fire, and in its heat, all
vision was reduced to the bare essentials. Not even the wavering of desert mirage had prepared him for this.

He did not face a minor demon. He did not face the creatures that had troubled the Tor Leonne.

He faced a lord, and knew it.

He had turned away from the path of the healer to enter
the service of the Lord; he had turned back to it, to better
serve the one man who defined the Lord in his eyes. That
man had also faced the fires, willing to be consumed by
them: could Marakas do less?

Yet he felt no pain, in the heat of these flames; he chose
his footing with instinctive care as floorboards parted and
blackened beneath him.

He took wounds, he offered them; he became aware that
this was the whole of the only conversation allowed be-

tween what he had become and what the creature had always been.

And if this was to be his last discussion, he entered into it freely and with a ferocity that the High Courts could never, ever, understand.

As the ceiling above gave way to fire, as the walls dissolved, flames opening windows into the rooms beyond, he cried out a single name.

Would have been surprised to know that it was not *Verragar*'s.

Serra Celina en'Clemente stared; her gaze hovered over the lids of a child's closed eyes. Smart child, she thought, with a trace of chill; wise child. Her own, she knew, were round; she could not contain her expression in the rigidity of the court—any court, even one as lax as Sarel's.

The creature screamed; his voice was the wind's voice, but worse—much worse—was the Serra Teresa's face, for the rigidity denied Celina was there in every line; her cheekbones and her chin formed a steel cage for everything else.

The fire consumed the demon, the gentle glow of Summer devouring red and black; making ash of flesh in an instant that seemed to go on and on in a scream of pain and denial. It should have been a comfort, that cry, for it was death's cry. But the Serra Celina was—had always been—a weak woman; if she understood the need for death—and she did, how could she not?—she had never understood the need for *pain*.

The Serra Teresa seemed unaware of the damage she had caused. She lowered shaking hand; the dagger's blade was gone.

"Na'tere," the old woman said, her voice almost gentle.

The Serra shook her head. She did not try to speak. Instead, she sank to her knees, outside of the circle, apart from them in ways that the circle itself could not account for.

"Na'tere," Yollana said, voice stronger. Angrier, or so it seemed to Celina.

But the Serra Teresa did not, could not, hear; she sank further, folding perfectly straight back over the bend of flawless lap. Her hair was a dark spill that caught lamplight and the remains of fire; dusted by ash, it cloaked her.

She gathered her arms around her shoulders, and beneath the curtain of hair, she began to tremble.

What woman would not, having faced what she faced? What woman would not, having exposed what she exposed? Celina felt the room waver, but it was the artifact of water, the quick pain of tears. These, she was strong enough to hold.

"Serra," the Voyani Matriarch said.

It came to Celina that the Matriarch spoke not to the Serra Teresa, but to her. She nodded.

"Take the child from the Serra Diora," Yollana said. "Take her, and let us see to the—see to Na'tere."

It was not a request.

What will you do to me, old woman? Celina thought, as she rose.

But before she could take the child, the Serra Diora rose. She set samisen aside, and with it, some of the poise of her former station. Her eyes were perfect; round and dark; her lips were pale in the darkening light.

"Serra Celina," she said quietly. "Ariel."

The child's eyes flickered open.

"The demon is gone," she told the girl.

The child nodded. She was stiff now, and words had once again deserted her; a mercy.

"Stay with the Serra Celina. Stay in the circle. The Serra Teresa needs me now. I will not be far away."

The child nodded again; she allowed herself to be lifted, allowed herself to be given to the Serra Celina. Celina was almost shocked at the weight of the child; it had become nonexistent. She caught the girl's hands in hers, noticing for the first time the loss of fingers. It made the burden seem more precious somehow.

The Serra Diora walked with care, lifting the silk of sari until she reached the circle. Listening a moment, she said, "Do not leave this haven." But she spoke without looking back. As her aunt had done before her, she now stepped across the barrier that had kept the creature out; she left no evidence of her passing in the fine, fine ash.

She reached the Serra Teresa and knelt by her side, the flat of her flawless hands touching the flat of the older woman's exposed back.

Then she rose. "Matriarch," she said quietly.

Yollana grunted.

"Give me the waters of the Tor."

Yollana reached into the folds of that same robe—as if it were haven to treasures, time, legend—and withdrew a waterskin. She hefted it with as much care as she could, and then, shifting bent shoulders, threw it.

One eye did not see as clearly as two; the skin flew wide, across the back of the Serra Teresa, and beyond the easy grasp of the Serra Diora.

But the Serra said nothing; she rose quickly, retrieving what she needed.

"How is she?" the Havallan Matriarch said. All defiance, all certainty, all sense of the mystic, had fled her, as if it were invoked by the presence of the Servant of the Lord, and bound to him. She remained an old woman, half-blind, crippled and far from kin.

Serra Diora di'Marano shook her head.

Answer, Celina thought, enough.

Healing was not a man's gift. Not the Lord's gift. It was too valuable to be stigma, but too suspect to be revered; it was used by the powerful, when they had access to it, that was all.

But were it not for the Lady's gift, Marakas would have been consumed in the fire, for the fire that took hold of the domis was natural. He felt the smoke twist his lungs, depriving him of breath; felt the skin on the backs of his hands go the way of his hair and his robe; felt the chain shirt take heat and hold it until it threatened to blister the flesh it protected.

But he felt, as well, the resistance of his body, the instinct of its defense. The creature was beyond the touch of fire; he inflicted it, but he did not suffer its grace.

Nothing was burned clean; there was nothing to be cleansed. Of all fights he had yet undertaken, this was the clearest, and he valued the clarity while it remained. He struck; he struck; he struck. *Verragar*'s voice was a roar that the creature responded to; *Verragar*'s speed was such that the Radann el'Sol tracked its movement by the sudden jerk of shoulder, the sudden lengthening of arm.

But when *Verragar* severed the arm that held the sword, the fight was over; flight remained.

He pursued as he could, but he was tainted by mortality, by something his sword both understood and decried. The creature retreated into the heart of the fires it had summoned, and the blood that fell caused the flames to billow, like cloud or curtain.

It was gone.

The Radann were scattered or dead; in the distance, above crackling wood, sundered timber, bodies spoke with fire's voice.

They were beyond him, now. Fire's death, the worst of deaths, he could not heal without cost—and in battle, he had only one choice.

Walls rose around him, moving back and forth as if at the dance of wind. He raised *Verragar*.

The sword sang.

His sword, he had thought it; and it was. But it was more. What the demon had summoned, the blade now summoned as well, but where the fire had scattered at demon whim, it coalesced at blade's, becoming a concentrated thing, something that went from orange to white, from white to blue:

blade's edge. And blade's edge shone, hot, as the fire flew
to it; his palms blistered with heat.

But he held the sword, for he knew that it had no voice
and no power without a wielder. One by one, the red-and-
orange lights that demarked the boundaries of the creature's
reach guttered; all flame came to *Verragar,* and Marakas
was content to hold it.

It was over.

He could see the moon's full face above the broken
columns that had once supported roof. But he could see, as
well, as if it were a small doll's house lacking the final wall
to seal it from prying eyes, the remainder of the domis; the
edge of fire had blackened wood, and the smoke had grayed
walls in a wash of shadow and soot, but it stood.

As he did; they would both need repair.

The Serra Diora di'Marano spoke to her aunt. She spoke
in a voice that she had used since childhood, but strengthened it with experience, much of it bitter. No one else could
hear her; and as she bent over her Ona's back, no one could
see her lips move over the ceaseless flow of words.

Ona Teresa.

She was no healer. Had never been one. She had gift, yes;
she had even used it. Only once had she used enough of it
to lie as the Serra Teresa did, shaking with fever. But it had
been the work of hours, of the hours of a first, a terrible
labor, her voice extending from start to finish by the dint of
will and the terrible fear of what would happen if she
stopped singing.

Ona Teresa had uttered a single word. Just one.

Could one word do such damage?

She closed her eyes, hating the lie that she told herself by
the simple expedient of asking the question. She was born
to the gift; she had *heard* her Ona's word, and she had
known, then, what the cost would be.

Had refused to know it.

The cool night breeze that swirled through the cracked

and broken roof didn't touch the heat; it was shunted to either side by the strength of fever's grip.

Ona Teresa, Ona Teresa, I'm here. Speak to me.

Truth, she had learned at the side of Margret of the Arkosa Voyani, need not be bitter.

But it was, this truth.

She could have left the child with Ona Teresa; she could have attempted to fight the demon. And why had she not? Because Ona Teresa had commanded her?

No. No. She turned a moment to look at Ariel, and she saw the whole of the girl's pale, peaceful face. She had stayed in the circle because—for just a moment—she *wanted* to protect that child. Those wives. Because it was an answer to the past that had defined her, had destroyed her, had birthed her. She wanted to hold that girl.

Because she could now do little else or the Serra Teresa di'Marano, she mourned.

You never had wives.

I did. If even only for a brief time, I did.

You gave me what your gift denied you. You protected me from the weight of its curse, as you could. You lived by, and with your curse, and in the end, it was your only power; your only company. What have you done? What have you done to yourself?

Her eyes were wide; she dared not blink. Blinking would cause the tears to fall, and Ona Teresa would not appreciate them.

Her hands unstoppered the waterskin; she struggled a moment with her aunt's shoulders; tried to turn her over, to unfold her. The tremble had grown, and grown quickly. She felt the Serra Teresa's resistance, although another might not have been able to discern what was will and what, reflex.

These were the fevers the talent-born faced. Kallandras of Senniel College had told her that once. He had told her more, but the rest eluded her now.

Kallandras!

Nothing answered; even the wind was silent.

In the Dominion, no Serra feared silence. Silence was a retreat; silence was a platform; silence was a gilded cage. All waiting was done in silence, and only with permission or invitation did the confines of that waiting allow for the things that she had loved best: song, the sound of samisen strings; the fuller, wilder notes of Northern lute.

The talent that had been curse had informed the whole of her life.

Ona Teresa, you must drink. You must take the waters of the Tor. Ona Teresa, please.

She had learned to hide the gift. It had come easily, with time; hiding was something that any Serra of the Courts must learn, and the secret itself was secondary to the need to keep it from the eyes or ears of the powerful. *What man would accept you, if he knew that he might, by a single spoken word, be unmanned? What man would allow you to live?*

The woman who shivered, head now bumping against the fold of her lap, had been the one who had made clear what the cost of discovery might be. As a girl, the cost seemed transparent; as a woman, for the single year she had had a harem of her own, a harem's heart, it had been a tragedy beyond compare.

Ona Teresa, drink. Command, in the single word. She hated to use it.

Hated to see it fail. The Serra Teresa, so graceful in life, now gasped at air and liquid like a dying fish.

Angry, suddenly angry, Diora looked up. "Serra," she said coldly. "Matriarch. Leave us. Now."

But they couldn't; she realized it after the words had left her. The circle had not been breached; the battle—if there was one—might still require a wall behind which to stand.

And the Serra Teresa's grace, her elegance, her absolute control, was a simple casualty of war. Not even death would have taken that from her.

But that casualty was not the worst.

Diora had learned to hide gift; had learned to hide heart. As she trickled water into the mouth of her aunt, as she struggled to hold snapping neck up, so that water might travel to throat, she realized that these two—gift and heart—were not separate.

Had she been forced to hide her particular song from her wives, she would never have loved them; they would never have loved her. They would never have known what she was, and the unknown could—at best—be worshiped, at worst, feared.

They—Serra Teresa di'Marano and Serra Diora di'-Marano—had called the voice a curse. For all of their lives together, the one exposed and the other hidden, they had commiserated in a fashion acceptable to the Courts; they had enfolded their words in silence.

Had spoken, she realized, not to ear, but to heart.

She would lose that.

Had lost it.

Realized it now, for truth. Ona Teresa had gathered all of the power she possessed and thrown it into the single word; had gathered *more,* and used that as well.

For a moment, the Serra Diora's perfect hands shook; the liquid failed in its slow trickle.

She would be able to speak to the heart of a woman who had been almost a mother to her, but that woman, this woman, would never tender reply.

A thousand men did not come to the bridge. Hundreds did; but Jewel ATerafin knew, by the frown across Avandar's still, observant features, that the Marente forces had, as Ser Alessandro feared, been split.

"How long," she said softly, "will it take the rest to ford the Adane?"

He frowned. She saw the lecture come to his lips and leave; he offered her position—tenuous and strange as it was—no insult in front of the Clemente forces. Whether that was for her sake or theirs, she couldn't say. Didn't much care, as long as he answered the question.

"Hours," he said, "if they are horsed; the bridges are meant for wagon traffic, but they are not meant for the hooves of warhorses moving at speed. They travel at night," he added, "and they will use some caution; if a horse slips on the bridges, it will be costly."

But she shook her head. "The Widan," she said quietly. "And the kin."

Quietly, though. The words didn't carry.

CHAPTER TWENTY-SIX

MARAKAS par el'Sol made his way to the courtyard.
The battle was over, and as he took each step, as he
walked away from the physical location of the creature's
ambush, he felt that he was walking out of the heart of legend; his memory could not contain more than the shards of
what had occurred, and how.

It was not a land he desired to leave, and yet, once he had
gone beyond it, not one he desired any return to. Such par-
adox would haunt him, time and again, in the course of the
war. He was uncertain of the fate that had befallen the
Radann he had led here. But he could count the bodies—or
the remains—that he could see, and he knew that not all of
his companions had fallen. Sometimes retreat was wise.
Sometimes it served some other purpose.

The halls were silent, but as he traveled them, the evidence of fire vanished; the flowers rested in their containers within the long dishes, the tall vases, that punctuated
evenly spaced trestles.

Verragar had fallen silent; he held her with care. The
skin that fire had blistered had fallen away; blood adorned
her hilt, seeping its way into the winding bands that composed it. His body would soon halt the flow of that liquid;
it had already dimmed the pain to a bearable level.

And the battle was not yet done.

Although *Verragar* was simple sword now, dim and un-
stained by anything but the black of soot, he held her knowing the sheath was not yet her home.

Life seeped into the halls as he ventured farther and far-

ther from the radius of the fire's destruction; he saw dim
lights beyond the opacity of screens; heard the huddled
hush of muted seraf voices; heard the cries of their children,
gathered in arm and lap, and muffled, but not extinguished,
by the guardians who had swept them into their refuge.

Beyond these rooms, he heard the voices of Clemente
cerdan. They did not seek the safety of silence; their voices
punctuated and destroyed stillness, giving command and
order to chaos.

It was these voices he sought; these and the men who
used them.

They were not few in number, but they were not more
than twenty; he met them just within the doors of the great
hall. They paused when he emerged, and stared, and he realized that he no longer bore the insignia of the Radann par
el'Sol; the sun emblazoned in gold upon dark fabric had
been burned clean by fire, and little of it remained.

What did, rags and strips of fire-edged cloth, told a different story.

He held his sword up as they approached, and they halted
some five yards away.

The foremost of their number executed a perfect, military
bow. "We were sent to your aid by the Radann," the man
said, his helm gleaming in the torchlight.

"Your aid is required upon the walls," he replied, his
voice parched and dried by fire and smoke. He forced clarity into it with will. "The domis has been damaged, but only
the Lady's face now disturbs its halls."

A few men spoke in the last rank; the men closest him,
those who could see what fire had wrought, offered him the
silence of awe.

"We were well served by the Lady," their leader said, rising, "when she sent you to us from the lee of her forest."

"Let me join you," he replied, "upon the walls. It is there
that the battle—if battle comes—will be decided."

"You killed the creature."

"There were two," he said quietly, for he was a modest

man. "And *Verragar* does not sense another presence; if the
second is gone, it is likely that you now owe a debt to the
Havalla Voyani."

The circumstances were dire enough that these words
evoked no unease.

The cerdan bowed again. "We would be honored by your
presence, par el'Sol."

"And I," he said, courteous, although the words still troubled his throat, "honored by yours. Come."

The torches were not so bright as the moon.

The Radann par el'Sol bowed his head a moment at the
Lady's bounty; even the wind's voice was still. As he left
the domis, he found the Radann who had retreated into the
halls not yet destroyed by demon fire, and he lifted a hand
in subtle command, forestalling their bows. It was not what
etiquette demanded, and even upon the battlefield, perhaps
especially upon that field, etiquette was a thing of import.

Yet he had no desire for it; it separated him from those
who offered obeisance, creating a distance that seemed un-
earned in the lull.

Storm's eye, he thought.

Voices replied, carrying with it the end of peace: the men
upon the walls raised horn. He was not familiar with all of
the Clemente calls—indeed, each Tor, and each Tyr, used
the horn's voice as if it were a private language.

But this once he had no need; what he did not know by
rote, he understood by instinct.

The Clemente cerdan tensed. Upon the walls, the archers
lowered bows, pulled strings, bent straight shafts of tapered
wood until they resembled a single-stringed harp; war's instrument.

They drew fletched arrows, the weapons—the cursed and
hated weapons—of the North. But they did not send shaft
into darkness; they waited.

He mounted the slender stairs that led to the curtain wall;
they were narrow but solid, and they did not creak or

protest his weight. As he drew even with the archers; the bowmen glanced at him—at the naked chain shirt, the fire-shaved face, at *Verragar*—and made room among their ranks.

From the highest point in Sarel, Marakas par el'Sol looked into darkness, and the darkness answered him in a fashion, birthing orange glow: lamps and torches, flickering as they moved. He could not count them all, but he could see, by their spacing, that they went on into a distance that his eyes could not yet penetrate.

But he frowned as he watched, and after a moment, he said, "Damar is to the South?"

One of the bowmen nodded grimly.

The frown grew.

"But these men—"

"Yes. From the North."

"And in number," he said softly.

"If they mean to take Sarel," the bowman replied, "we will make it costly."

Marakas nodded. "The kai Clemente?"

"Across the gate," the man replied. He did not speak again; the moving army—and it was an army—absorbed the whole of his attention. Well before they reached the gate, they would be in range of the arrows that had been drawn in Northern fashion, against such an attack.

In the dark of a night such as this, mistakes could be made. But the men of Clemente showed no outward signs of the nervousness that could lead to disaster; they waited, bows not yet drawn, watching for some sign of banner, some hint of the identity of the foe they would face.

The army approached, and it gathered speed—or so it seemed to Marakas, suspended between battles, between the imperative of two different types of survival.

But although the men drew close, they unfurled no banner, made of themselves no certain target. Marakas looked across the gap the gate occupied; he could see that the kai

Clemente stood, hands upon the crenelated stone, back bent, head forward, as if those extra inches could bridge the gap between anonymity and identity.

Now, the bowmen drew arrows, lifted bows, pulled strings; they prepared, aiming as they could between the bowers of the trees that lined the road. But they did not fire.

Nor did the kai Clemente give the order that might have released arrows' flight; he bent farther forward, craning neck. Not, Marakas thought, a risk that the Tor'agar would have taken had he been present.

The army did not halt, and every foot covered diminished the usefulness of the archers present. If they were a weapon, they were sheathed. Although the kai Clemente lifted hand, and with it silver horn, he did not play it, did not bring it to his lips.

A breeze blew, strong enough to slant the torch flames.

The kai Clemente shouted for light, and more torches were lit across the length of the wall upon which he stood. The archers themselves brought no lamps and no lights that would obscure their vision.

But the fire exposed their presence to those who now approached.

The unidentified army spoke with the voice of horns.

Marakas watched as the flames that moved above the helms of armed and mounted men now shuddered to a stop; like a wave, he thought them, against rock.

Some three of these lights gathered; men detached themselves from the body of the army and began to move—slowly—toward a gate locked and barred against their passage.

As they approached, Marakas felt an odd twinge; his fingers spasmed awkwardly around the hilt of a blade that—at this height—would be useless for some time.

He gazed at the flat of *Verragar,* the blade was nascent now; simple steel, with a glimmering of light that spoke of edge. The light was odd. Not blue, but gold, and at that, faint, as if it were a thing at once liquid and fire.

He frowned.

The kai Clemente brought horn to lip, and in that moment, the Radann par el'Sol understood what the blade knew, and he lifted his voice instead.

"Kai Clemente!" he cried, all formality forgotten.

The younger man turned at the sound of his name, at the use of a familiar title carried by a stranger's voice. But the horn did not follow.

Marakas made his way to the stairs and almost flew down them, his left hand anchoring itself to the rough surface of wall, his right hefting blade.

A moment, no more, and then the kai Clemente made his way from the heights as well, surrendering view to the urgency of the Radann's unspoken request.

They met upon the stones carved in the colorless crest of Clemente, boots skirting the edge of the rising sun and the grooved representations of its six rays.

"My pardon," Marakas said, bowing as formally as a man thus accoutred could bow. "Ser Janos kai di'-Clemente."

But it was not for nicety of perfect title that the young man had descended; Ser Janos waited until Marakas rose, his lips pressed into a thin line within the folds of his slight beard.

"The gate," Marakas said. "The gates must be opened."

The boy was not son to Ser Alessandro; he had none of the older man's fire, and none of his history. He hesitated only a moment, and then he bowed. "As you request, par el'Sol; the clan Clemente is in your debt this eve, and our trust has not yet been misplaced." He turned to the men who manned the gate, and he barked a sharp order. They were better trained than he; they obeyed without hesitation.

"Who are they?" Ser Janos said, offering the bare hint of doubt as the grind and creak of the great gates muted the words.

"I do not know," the Radann par el'Sol replied. "But one among them carries *Balagar.*"

"The kai el'Sol is there?"

Marakas shook his head softly. "No. And if he were, I would not now counsel you to take this action."

"But *Balagar* is—"

"Yes."

"I don't understand."

"No more do I. But there is a reason, Ser Janos, that the Hand of God now numbers four; *Balagar* has not been wielded since the death of Fredero kai el'Sol."

He waited, blade drawn; the kai Clemente dropped hand to sword hilt, but did not likewise arm himself. He drew breath, straightened the line of shoulders that had rested too long in an awkward position, and drew himself to full height.

He was not a short man, although he was not a large one; his face was pale in moonlight, as if he had spent too much time in the Lady's Dominion, and not the Lord's.

But for all that, when the great gates were at last silent, he retreated into silence as well, taking the mantle of the Tor'agar upon slender shoulders.

Wondering—and Marakas could read this clearly as he reached out to touch the kai Clemente's weaponless hand—if that mantle were now his in fact, and not in waiting. The grief and fear in that fleeting glimpse surprised Marakas, altering his opinion not of heir, but of the man who ruled Clemente.

The old ways, Marakas thought: Ser Alessandro had accepted the family his brother had left behind with grace and the strength of a man's affection, and Ser Janos feared to be diminished by his loss.

The Toran who had not been ordered to the side of their Tor—and they numbered a scant four—now hastened down the steps; they formed a small square, two men deep and two wide, on either side of the kai Clemente.

In the moonlight, the riders approached the gates, and as the gates opened, as the archers failed in their fire, one man at last lifted pole and wound banner, and the banner fell like judgment in the blaze of torchlight.

Horse rode across a green field, mane flying, hooves unfettered; upon his back, no man, but rather sword and shield. Beneath his feet, the crescent hill of Southern blade, and above him, rising over the crest of distant hill, the sun with eight rays.

Marakas bowed at once; Ser Janos was a breath behind, but his knee touched ground and his head fell as if the weight of the evening's work could finally be laid to rest.

The Toran did not bow in kind; they offered the obeisance armed men could who did not wish to forsake their chosen duty.

But they offered no insult as the banner flapped in a passing breeze; they held their ground as the foremost rider dismounted, aided by a man who wore the robes of the Radann.

Ser Mareo kai di'Lamberto adjusted the fall of his sheathed sword and executed a brief, but perfect, bow. "Well met," he said quietly, as the heir to the Clemente Torrean raised his head to meet the eyes of the man to whom they all owed their allegiance.

"Tyr'agnate," Ser Janos replied, in carefully modulated tones. He did not rise until the Lambertan Tyr strode into the courtyard, beneath the watching eyes of the archers of Clemente.

Tyran joined their lord; they numbered four. The smaller number of chosen men was a gesture of faith, a gesture of trust in a liege.

But the gaze of the Tyran lingered upon the walls above, and their expressions were cool.

"You are prepared for war," the Tyr'agnate said quietly.

"As you see," Ser Janos replied, showing the first sign of hesitation, as if only now remembering his Tyr's great disdain for *all* things Northern.

"And that war?"

"It is not with you," the younger man replied, discomfort

choosing the words. Ser Alessandro would not have been so
easily moved to nervousness. "Clemente honors its oath
and its pledge."

"And Mancorvo," the Tyr'agnate replied, from a distance
that the scant yards could not quite encompass, "will do no
less."

There fell an awkward silence, and such silence, allevi-
ated often by the presence of women, might have been left
to linger.

But Marakas par el'Sol chose that moment to break it. He
rose from his bow, revealing the smooth skin of his face, his
head, the lack of Radann robes and the adornment of the office he held.

But he raised sword, and as he did, the man who had
aided the Tyr'agnate now lifted head.

"Jevri," Marakas said softly.

"Radann par el'Sol," the servitor replied, tendering a
bow of genuine respect.

Marakas knew, then, who wielded *Balagar.* Wondered
that he had not known sooner.

"We have met the Servants of the Lord of Night,"
Marakas told the Tyr'agnate, "And we have triumphed, but
at some cost. It was against further attacks of this nature
that the walls were manned."

"Further attacks?"

"The Tor'agar is not resident within the city of Sarel."

Mareo kai di'Lamberto nodded.

"He took the better part of his forces, and traveled North
toward the village of Damar."

"And there?"

"The Tor'agnate, Ser Amando kai di'Manelo, requested
the presence of the Tor'agar; he had issues that he wished
resolved through negotiation."

"The nature of the negotiation?"

Marakas' eyes went to the road beyond the Tyr's back;
the words were rendered meaningless by the glance.

"Within the Clemente domis, two Marente envoys were housed."

"Would I be in error if I assumed that they are no longer present to be called upon?"

"No, Tyr'agar."

"Good. But Ser Alessandro has not returned."

"No. The better part of the Manelan forces gathered within the West of Damar, and the Tor'agar believed that some unknown number of Marente soldiery also camped within easy reach of the village."

"Then perhaps we will join him there." He asked no permission; none was needed. "Do you fear another attack, par el'Sol?"

Marakas considered the question carefully, and then he shook his head.

"Then if you will join us, join us; we travel in haste."

Verragar was keening as it trembled in his hand.

Avandar had constructed a wall of sorts. Before he began, he caught Jewel by the arms and lifted her almost gently, placing her upon the back of the Winter King. She held her hands in her lap; the stag's horns were stained by something she had seen at a remove: demon blood. It looked black, in the moonlight; she did not want it on her hands.

If you give the Warlord leave, the Winter King said quietly, *he will stand against your enemies. Lord Celleriant expended much in his battle to contain the water, and the Northern bard is human.*

She shook her head.

I almost lost him, she said softly. *And I don't have the strength to call him back again. Not tonight.*

Maybe, she thought, not ever.

To her surprise, she felt the stag's approbation. Together, they watched in silence as Avandar worked, lifting dirt and the stones that lay beneath it as if it were whole cloth. He placed these in the streets between the buildings of Damar;

drew them from the sloping bank of the now quiet river, and stretched them wide along what was only barely road.

Dust billowed out in clouds; the riverbank was parched as baked clay.

"It will not hold them long," he told her quietly, raising a brow. Asking the question the stag had asked, but without the attendant words.

Her tired smile was all her answer. *I don't want to lose you. I don't want to lose you again.*

You may die, here, he replied, his hands momentarily still. *And, ATerafin, the chance that I lose you is greater.*

What you do when I die is up to you. Everything changed. "But not before?"

She shook her head. "Not for me. We'll find another way."

The last half of her words were lost to a shout of dismay; the Clemente archers discovered—as did the men who now fell to knees, hands upon the exposed length of slender shafts, that the General di'Marente had learned from the armies of the North as well.

The first volley was deadly; the second far less so. The wind caught arrows in flight, changing their trajectory; it could not send reply in like fashion, but it spared the Clemente cerdan who fought across the bridge. Kallandras of Senniel, bandaged now, had lifted arms as if in greeting. His smile was slender, deadly.

She didn't care; she wanted to watch it forever.

It was so much better than everything else that demanded her attention.

Jewel had never seen carnage like this. The bodies upon the bridge had made stone slick with blood, and where there was no room to fight, men—on either side—slid and fell, to be speared or cut down as they struggled for footing. Bodies were thrown into the Adane, and some struggled a moment with the water and the weight of armor before at last sinking beneath its moving surface.

Avandar, can you bring the bridge down?

He was silent a moment. *Yes,* he said at last, *but it would not be wise.*

Why?

If there is no bridge, the forces of our enemy will not be split; they will withdraw, and join the moving force.

But then we can retreat.

Yes, he said quietly.

She didn't like the tone of the yes. *But?*

It was a . . . gift . . . from the older magics, he said at last.

From the elemental—but—

Eyes that were not quite brown met hers. *A gift,* he said again, quietly. *And such gifts, once bestowed, are best appreciated. What you ask can be done, but not without cost. If the water is the most difficult of elements to contain, it is not the most difficult to command.*

Jewel, the Winter King moved restively, *look at the bridge. And look at the walls.*

She did. And she knew he was right. The bridge was whole, a single piece of work. But it was not rough, not elemental; it was crafted, its stone lattice, the exposed sides of its rounded curve worked, as if with chisel and time, into a thing of beauty.

And the wall? Dirt, rock, something thrown up, like tarpaulin, against sandstorm or the careless fall of water. Not, she realized, a gifting—simply a faster, more efficient form of digging and building.

Very few of the Arianni, and very few of the Kialli were so adept at making requests of the wilder forces.

But he's human, she said, defiant. Stupid.

He will never be without power, the Winter King continued. *But the depth of his power, the height, must be denied if you wish to keep him.*

She was silent for a moment, and then she said, quietly, *You were human once.*

Yes. And perhaps that is why, little Jewel, I take some interest in the fate of Viandaran. Although he was never ruled, never owned, he has been trapped for far longer than I.

*   *   *

The walls were not of a single piece of stone; the dirt, pulled up, was mired in roots and branches, stronger for it, but less malleable.

Jewel watched Avandar's work in silence, and when it was finished, she exhaled heavily, as if she could claim some part of the exhaustion of his labor. He did not return to her side; instead, he waited while Clemente cerdan came to stand behind the walls. They had no windows, and were offered no easy view of the roads they had now sealed, and the buildings upon the Eastern bank—those that remained standing—were not as fine, or, more significant, as tall as those upon the West. But the roofs were tall enough, and firm enough, to support the weight of men, and men were lifted by foot to shoulder, and from there to building's flat, to watch. They disappeared from view as they gained the height.

Jewel understood why; the arrows that the wind did not dislodge flew above them.

Words traveled from height to ground; words were carried from building to Tor'agar. He listened, grim, and offered words of his own in response; like arrows, they were often taken by the breeze; they did not reach Jewel's ears.

Her hand played with the haft of dagger hilt as she watched; she did not draw her weapon. All of her skill with a blade—and it was meager—was not meant for fights of this nature; gone were the narrow alleys of the twenty-fifth holding, the walls of buildings looming to either side. The shadows in Damar were broken by moon and light, and the silent memory of the alley, by the hoarse shouts and cries of men.

And the screams.

Not all of the dying screamed. Some had no throat for it, and the gurgle of their final words were lost with their lives. Nor did all of the living choose to cloak their combat in sound.

Kallandras of Senniel College was utterly, profoundly

silent. Celleriant of the Green Deepings was silent as well, although his blade drew the eye, time and again, as it rose and fell.

He did not stand upon the bridge, but instead, upon the rail, and several times in the fight, he was forced to leap up, and into the Adane to avoid the play of spears, the swing of crescent blade. He seemed heavier, to her, than he had been—as if some essential joy was absent from the battle.

But joyless or no, he fought, and Kallandras shadowed his movements, touching water as well, but failing to sink beneath the rush of its current. The wounds he had taken at the hands of the kin were joined by others; he retreated and returned, as if such actions were part of a graceful dance.

Two such men as these could hold the bridge, she thought, for a long time.

But they wouldn't. She *knew* it, and spun, knees digging into the haunches of the Winter King.

Fire limned the edge of the Southernmost wall; dirt and stone flew up, as if they were, by fire, made liquid for a moment.

The cerdan retreated, but Avandar Gallais stood in the rain of earth, his hands spread wide, orange light seeping from his fingertips.

Kallandras leaped clear of the bridge; the soles of his boots skimmed the surface of a water now deprived of voice, of anger. He called for the wind and it took him above the din of battle, above the flat roofs of Southern dwellings; above the archers whose bows must be spent— they were silent.

He could see the Marente forces; they had gathered behind three sections of the wall that Avandar had pulled from the flattened mud and stonework of Damar's streets. They were led by men on horseback, but they hung back; they waited upon the work of Widan, of magecraft, the Sword's Edge.

He could hear the words they spoke—when they spoke at

all; they hoarded night words and night thoughts beneath
the grim press of lips. Lady's time.

Turn back, he told them, using the fine edge of his
power. **Turn back or the Lord will devour you; there will
not be enough left of you for the winds to claim.**

The words came from no discernible direction, or from
all; the three mounted men froze a moment, gathering the
reins of their horses in mailed fists.

He sent his words out again, choosing as targets the
Widan who worked against the walls.

Two froze a moment, but the third—ah, the third—
looked up. An umbrella of flame lit the sky, the point of its
center the spot where Kallandras had chosen to hover. He
dropped, folding his shoulders, his neck, curling his head
into the shield of bent arms. The air caught him before he
struck ground, and a trail of fire clung, like burrs, to the
longest strands of his hair.

Lord Celleriant, he said, shifting weapon's weight, **I
have found the last of the** *Kialli.*

Ser Alessandro kai di'Clemente counted the fall of his
men. Spoke their names, one after the other, as if naming
were a thing of legend, and had power. It was the Lady's
time, and if there was a time for such a power, it was now:
he surrendered to her the things that he valued: his men. His
horse. His sword.

He sat astride a horse not his own, and honored his rider
in so doing, although the rider had not lived to see or acknowledge the honor; he lay beneath the moving water.

A calm was upon the Tor'agar; a calm made of names, of
inevitability. A spray of pebbles, dusted with dry earth, clattered against the shoulders of turned armor. The Marente
forces still had their Widan, but although Clemente forces
had never dallied long with the Sword of Knowledge, they
were not helpless.

Not yet, and not while they stood.

He spoke another name, the fingers around the hilt of his

sword growing numb with the ferocity of what seemed idle grip. Soon, he thought, he would join them. But not soon enough; there was no room upon the bridge, no worthy death there. Still, death, he thought, would come, did come.

He heard the shortened cry of the only woman upon the field, and he did not even turn to acknowledge what it presaged; he knew. One wall, one at least, had fallen.

And a miracle, he thought, raising sword to the light of the falling moon, the grace of the Lady's brightest face, that it had not fallen sooner; that it had, in fact, stood at all.

He lifted his horn in his left hand, brought it full to lips; tasted cold silver, as if it were the very Lady's kiss. He called his men to him, those who remained, and they came, injured or whole, the clank of metal against metal, the labor of breath, the only honor offered him.

More than enough.

He spun horse around on short rein; saw that one wall had, indeed, been breached. But the breach was narrow, and in the gap stood the two Northern men, both fair of face, both dancers whose weapons seemed to add to their grace, their deadly steps. He could not recall the exact moment they had deserted the bridge.

He sounded horn again and urged his horse forward.

Horn answered him. A single long note.

And following it, others, lesser, shorter, but distinct: a song, a war song unlike the clamor of drums.

His gaze grazed moon, his horn fell slowly from his lips; just as slowly did his men look up to see his face, to see that the horn was now, once again, in his lap.

Reymos hesitated for a moment, but only a moment; he raised horn now, and in reply the Clemente call sounded across the rise and fall of the gathered huts and dwellings. Alessandro was surprised that Ser Reymos had breath left with which to make the urgent call of horn so loud.

The Clemente cerdan turned to him, turned away, listening for the play of distant horn, the sound of distant hooves.

As if, Alessandro thought, they did not walk in a dream

of the Lady. As if they were upon a clear field, upon the open plains in the heart of Mancorvo. As if the notes they had heard had been, could be, real.

But when they sounded a second time, he, too, turned, reins in hand, sword in hand, horn once again idle at his belt. Not for the Tors or the Tyrs the song of that call; no man of worth sounded his own praise.

From the North, where no wall had been erected, the first of the horsemen appeared, their gait slowed by the fall of buildings and the bodies that adorned the slender road. And the foremost of the men carried, with pride, a banner that even in moonlight no clansman could fail to recognize.

He bowed his head.

The Tyr'agnate, Mareo kai di'Lamberto, had come.

Steel is a miracle.

Fire is a miracle.

Horses are a miracle.

Cloth, the weave of something grown from plant or worm; gold, from stream or Northern mine; silver, border of chained links that stop wind from furling the banners away from mortal sight.

The sunlight seen through moon is a miracle. Blood, when it flows, and when it stills; breath, when drawn, and when it ceases to be drawn.

Miracles. Offerings.

Who can say that in the Dominion there are no prayers, and no answers, that power alone decides who is fit and who will fail?

Men. And men say much.

Even in silence, wielding blade, they speak.

The walls fell in concert as the forces of the Tyr'agnate streamed past the wounded and the dying. Silence—if silence could be the thundering of hooves, the sound of drawn blades—reigned, and ruled; no words were spoken, no threats exchanged. Threats were idle pleasantries in the

South, and the time for pleasantry—if it existed at all—had vanished.

They brought the sun with them. One man wore it openly; orange flame fanned the sheen of golden surcoat above his breastplate, and his sword spoke the language of Day.

Honor bound, he was called, this lord of Lamberto. Honor bound, and as one bound, lessened by stricture, weakened by it.

But strengthened by it as well.

He moved through the ranks of Marente cerdan as if they were already dead. His blade shattered blades; nothing stood in his way. He was not a young man, but the age that rested upon his face had hardened it, granting it the lines and fullness that no youth could own.

Ser Alessandro kai di'Clemente watched a moment, hand numb, the names of the dead lost to the rush of the living, and he realized that he had seen this man before.

Not in the Court of Amar, not within the vast expanse of the circle, the domis within which resided the most powerful clan in Mancorvo. Not in the Tor Leonne. Not in any of the dwellings within which the rich and the powerful resided.

But in a village in the Torrean of Manelo, wielding the *same* blade, and in the same cause: Justice. Honor.

He bowed his head a moment.

Kai el'Sol, he thought. *Fredero kai el'Sol*.

Alessandro had loved his cousin, Ser Franko kai di'Manelo.

He bowed his head, leaning into the wind, into the roar of a battle he had not yet joined. Yes, he had loved his cousin. He had hated the man who had killed him over a single, willful *mistake*.

But men make mistakes. And some mistakes end them; the truth of the Dominion. Costly. Clear.

The night air was cool and clean; he drew it into his

lungs, held it a moment, and expelled, straightening the line
of his shoulder, guiding the horse beneath his knees.

"Come!" he called, lifting sword, rallying the cerdan
who remained. "Let us not leave *all* of the Lord's glory to
Lamberto!"

CHAPTER TWENTY-SEVEN

NOT for the first time, she was trapped within the confines of a harem, waiting for armed men to finish their night's work.

The circumstances were different.

No one turned their last spoken words into the deadliest of all the weapons ever to be wielded against her.

Her wives were dead; her son dead; her father, alive, but taken by wind. She had thought she had nothing left to lose; had fashioned the whole of her life into a weapon on that premise.

But her hands lay against the damp skin of the Dominion's foremost Serra, giving lie to that: she learned, this eve, and bitterly, that there was *always* something to lose.

She did not cry; she did not struggle; she did not unfold the delicate bend of her knees. But she spoke three soft words to the woman she did not look to.

"Where is Ramdan?"

Remembering, as she said it, that not all losses were hers.

The outer rooms of the harem—three—were open to sky, and although the wives of the Serra Celina did not fear the Lady's gaze, they knew the cost of exposure to the Lord's; they retreated into the harem's heart as the pale pink and blue of dawn added color to the sky, changing the pallor of wood, the pale, jagged edge of column's broken heart.

But here, too, they found destruction, and at last, they gathered in the gardens that were, in theory, surrounded by rooms occupied by the wives of the harem. They were a pretty whirl of chittering noise and plain silks, and they shivered and clung to one another in either youth or fear.

Serra Diora di'Marano watched them ambivalently.

They were not her father's wives; not hers. They could not see when death had passed them by; they were caught by the fascination and fear of its shadow in the failing moonlight, and they asked the Serra Celina for words of wisdom.

But the Serra Celina held fast to her charge, and although she clearly held her wives in regard, the force of her affection was blunted—as it should be—by the presence of strangers; by the Havallan Matriarch, by the Serra Diora, and by the woman who huddled in the throes of seizure upon the damp ground.

Teresa lay like shadow between two standing stones in the garden; they provided no shelter, and no shade, for they were set in the garden's center, like tall, stone sentries; the carved faces turned outward on either side bore no witness, made no judgment.

Serra Diora would not leave her aunt's side. She labored, the waterskin slowly emptying, the power in her own voice becoming thin, as she bespoke the Serra Teresa. As companion, she had Yollana, and Yollana offered no words, no interference, no misplaced kindness. Instead, the wreath of slowly moving pipe smoke gathered in the air like cloud, dense and familiar; she watched, and she stood guard in her fashion.

There was some comfort in that; there was comfort in nothing else.

The sun could not be seen; the horizon was denied the harem garden. But its effects lightened the sky by slow degree, presaging the passage of the Lady, the advent of the Lord. What was hidden by night and silver light was now to be exposed; the damage done the domis was not light.

But it was nothing; it could be rebuilt.

She brushed matted strands of hair from her Ona's face; felt the heat beneath the clammy surface of skin, the terri-

ble asymmetrical shaking, like heartbeat gone askew and
traveling to the outer reaches of the body in its wild flight.

She heard the wives raise voice; heard the sudden absence of their muted whispers. Fear came and went; she
was sensitive because she listened for any sound—any
sign—that the Serra Teresa might somehow wake whole
into the world. Only then, she thought, would she know that
the night had truly passed.

And then she heard the sound of armor, and interposing
herself gracefully in the gap between the standing stones,
she rose, lifting chin and dropping hands in a semblance of
courtly grace. Yollana did not trouble herself; she lit her
pipe and inhaled, watchful now, her one eye more menac-
ing than both would have been.

Men entered the garden, but they were few.

Three, four, five. She counted them by the sound of their
boots, for she could not look up to meet their gaze; she
wore no veil, and she had no desire to see what she feared
in their faces.

Two men approached, the length of their stride broken by
grace and silence. She knew them for serafs by the fall of
their step, and waited. Ramdan bowed to ground before her,
and he did not rise. She closed her eyes.

"Serra Diora," he said. Just that. What she heard in his
voice was night. She had never thought to wonder just how
much he understood, how much he knew; she did not wonder now. Instead, she accepted the smooth surface of his
impenetrable voice as the answer to that unasked question.
He knew.

He held out his hands, palms up, as if in plea. Her answer: she passed the waterskin that held the waters of the
Tor Leonne into his keeping. There were no other hands
that she trusted with the task; no other eyes that she would
willingly expose the Serra Teresa to. She did not speak; she
did not step aside.

It was awkward.

But the man by his side was not known to her; not known

to the Serra Teresa; she offered her aunt what meager protection she could.

Discovered that she was wrong when the second seraf also fell to his knees; fell low enough that she could see the stylized—and indistinct—halo of sun's ray upon his right breast. No seraf, this. Radann.

Servitor.

As he knelt, his head bowed, she waited; absence of breath informed her posture, made of her a living stone, a living monument.

His hair was a pale sheen of white over something that had once been black; she could see the sun-darkened skin of exposed neck as it fell to either side. She knew him, then. Although he had never bowed this way to her before, although he had never offered obeisance in such a way to any woman in her memory, she knew him.

"Jevri," she whispered.

He lifted his face.

Jevri el'Sol. Jevri kep'Lamberto.

It was the latter name that owned him, although he wore Radann's robes. No slave could serve the Radann. No slave could serve the Lord.

And no man, she thought, could be free of a lifetime of service to the kai el'Sol that Jevri had served.

"Serra Diora di'Marano," he said, bowing his head again.

Gently, she said, "Radann do not bow to a simple Serra." It was not her place to speak so, but although he wore the robes, they did not, at the moment, fit.

He rose in silence, and offered her not a smile, but something akin to it. Some quiet crinkling of skin around eye, some lessening of the grim silence that held his face so smoothly in its grip. "It is not the Lord's time," he said softly. "Nor, by the light, the Lady's. And in man's time, Serra Diora, men must do what they must."

She was not careful, this eve. Or rather, she was, but all of her care was turned toward the Serra Teresa; she had little left for herself.

"Do you travel with the kai Lamberto?"

A gray brow rose; he bowed head again, a quick and graceful dip of chin, so unlike the movements of the lesser Radann, the men culled from poor clans.

"Is he here?"

"He is in the garden," Jevri said quietly. He turned a moment, but she could not see where he looked; the breadth of his shoulder was wall, not window. "The Serra Celina speaks with him now."

"The Tor'agar?"

"Has returned. He is injured, but the injury is minor; he fails to acknowledge it, even now, to the rue of his young kai." His smile was brief. "The physicians will suffer greatly if they fail in their charge; I have never seen a boy take such desperate command in an infirmary."

"And Marakas par el'Sol?"

"He, too, has returned."

She hesitated. He marked it. They were still a moment, resting in the safety of the web of deceit the powerless often spun. But she was not without power; nor was he. And she knew, as perhaps few others did, just how much knowledge a seraf could have, and hold in silence. "Send him to me," she said at last.

Jevri bowed head to ground and rose. And he was perfect, she thought, as she watched him walk away; the perfect seraf; the Lady's man.

When she saw the Radann Marakas par el'Sol, she recognized him.

She had seen him thus once before, at the side of the Radann Peder par el'Sol, come new from battle, and reborn in flame. The Lord's man.

It was not the Lord's man she wanted now.

She bowed to him, shedding the unnatural stiffness that she had donned for the Serra Teresa's sake. He knelt before her, skin smooth and glossy with sweat, with lack of hair, new and pale like the face of the moon. She said nothing,

and after a moment, he rose, aware of other eyes in the
courtyard, be they at his back and distant.

She listened for words, and heard none.

"Serra Diora," he said. He did not rise, but the position
lost the mien of subservience.

She had played many games in her scant years at court.
So, too, had he. But the time for such games had passed.
She allowed him to observe the Serra; it was Ramdan who
at last chose to curtain Teresa by interposing his back between them.

"What happened?" Marakas par el'Sol asked quietly.

So many years of caution. So many years of silence. She
had commanded his presence, and he had come, abasing
himself before her, all nicety of form and title set aside. But
she could not bring herself to speak the truth. Her own secret, she might choose to offer, but this was not—quite—
hers.

Yet an answer was expected. Words slid past; she
grasped at them, but coherence fled with them. This was to
be an evening of awkward silences, awkward pauses; she
had no strength to fill them.

Failing in the one duty, she waited.

And then, after the pause had grown almost exquisitely
painful, she reached out and caught his ungloved hands in
her own. His eyes widened; she thought he would pull back
as she felt the muscles of those hands tense in hers.

But they tensed to hold, and she remembered the only
other time he had touched her. He had healed wounded
palms; wounds made by the sharp edges of the Heart of
Arkosa. And he had tried, in that brief contact, to better
glean an understanding of her thoughts, her intentions. He
had angered her then; she had retrieved her hands, and she
had never raised them where he might touch them.

As if he remembered that single contact, and the reasons
for it—all of them—he waited until she met his eyes. She
was mute, still mute; all that she offered him was the contact of two palms. But in hands, much could be read: hers

were pale and soft; uncallused, unmarked in any obvious way, although the scar that she'd taken in the desert was there if one stood close enough to look.

His hands were rough; darkened by sun, cracked by wind; they were older than his face. Laborer's hands. They surprised her.

"A demon," she said quietly, surprising herself. "She faced a demon."

"It injured her?"

She shook her head. Lifted the hands she held with care, turning at last toward Ramdan's unbowed back.

Perfect seraf, he stepped aside. The Radann par el'Sol shifted his weight, easing his scabbard to one side. It lay against the flat earth, the smooth stone, becoming darker as the sun rose. There was so little time.

She surrendered his touch to the Serra Teresa, placing his palms against the older woman's face. "Help her."

"If it is within my power, Serra Diora."

And if it was not, then whose? She placed shaking hands in the fold of her lap, and waited, her knees catching sun and light.

He touched the Serra's face.

He was gentle; could afford to be gentle; her eyes were closed, and her body shuddered at fever's whim. What she saw, what she noted, he could not say, but he knew that the fever itself was strange: her skin should have been dry and hot to the touch. It was not.

She had taken no wound.

None. But she had defeated the creature of the Lord of Night; that much was evident by the Serra Diora's closed, cautious expression.

How?

Ah, he thought, as his own hands took some of the warmth from her face. So much was hidden in silence. So much, hidden beneath the perfect seeming of a Serra of the High Court. She was not, could not be, Widan.

Was not healer, for if she were, she would not lie here.

What power might see the death of a Servant of the Lord of Night? She carried no obvious weapon; no great sword, no blessing of the Lord of Day. She was small and delicate, even clothed as she was in the rough wear of the Voyani.

Serra Teresa.

She moved, as if to avoid the touch of his hands. He hesitated.

And then the Serra Diora joined him, her hands touching his, pressing against joints, knuckles, the rounded veins of dark skin. She did not speak. And he, now caught in the healing trance, could not.

She watched his face.

His lashes were gone; his eyelids, white, blue, and green, flickered as if at the behest of dream. The line of his jaw, shorn of beard, grew pronounced, although his face was long of line, and not given to width.

The hands beneath hers were warm, the dawn, cool. Ramdan cast a shadow above their bent backs, and when she dared look away from his face, she watched that shadow lengthen. While she watched, she spoke.

Silent, lips moving, power leaving her in a trickle. **Ona Teresa. Ona Teresa. Ona Teresa.**

The Radann's hands moved, and she moved with them, shield and guardian. But he did not speak, and the Serra Teresa did not answer.

Silence swallowed time; the colors of the rock grew grayer and brighter around the edges of the shadow Ramdan cast.

And then she felt Marakas par el'Sol's hands clench, his fingers curling protectively up into his palms. His lids opened slowly, as if they were blossoming—a black flower, a dark one.

Color returned to them slowly, the band of iris growing around the shrinking pupil. But he shook his head, retrieving his hands.

She swallowed. "You can't—"

"No."

"But—"

"The injury she has . . . done herself . . . I cannot heal."

"Will she recover?"

Silence. Not the answer she desired, nor the one she hoped for. And, of course, she had had hope; had she none, she would never have called him.

"No, Serra," he said softly.

"And you can do nothing."

"No."

Diora heard what the Serra Teresa would never hear again. Truth. She bowed her head.

Lifted it as he spoke again. "It is beyond me," he told her quietly. "I . . . have been gifted . . . by the Lady. I have labored under the burden of this gift for the whole of my adult life. I have called the dead back." He looked away from her, turning clenched fists around as if inspecting them. As if, she thought, he might better understand the failure if he could attach it to something physical.

"Understand, Serra, that we live in the Lord's Dominion. What we know—what I know—is not what the Lord knows. Had the Serra broken arm, or leg had she suffered injury in defense of the domis, I could be of aid. Had she," he added softly, "you would never have called me. You know much. Of me. Of my gift. But the injury she has taken is not one that I can touch. I do not understand it, but . . ."

He shook his head. "The Widan do not suffer themselves to be healed often."

"She is not Widan."

His brows, absent from his face, would have added much to his brief expression. "No more am I," he said quietly. "But I understand this much: she suffers from Widan fever. If she survives it—and I am not certain that she will—the injuries and scars it leaves will be upon those things that cannot be touched." He bowed. Rose.

"I should not say more," he continued, and she knew

from his tone, from the texture of his voice, that he would, "but I think you might have a different answer if you spoke with the Northerners."

"They are not healers."

"No. But in the North, it is said that all arts, no matter how vile, are understood. Tell them that I do not have the power to touch what must be touched. But tell them also, that I believe that if I were more blessed, I would."

She shook her head. "Radann par el'Sol," she whispered.

"Serra?"

"How long will this fever continue?"

"Three days," he replied. "Perhaps four. If the fever breaks, it will break by then; if it does not, it will consume her."

She bowed; she bowed as low as she could, listening for the sound of his retreating steps. Only when they had passed, in safety, beyond her did she rise again.

Ramdan stood by her side. She felt the fall of pale silk before she saw it touch her shoulders; he had brought her veil. Of course.

She lifted hands, exposing the pale scar left there by storm and ship.

As a young woman, as the wife of the kai Leonne, she could never demean herself as she did now; she took the veil from him and began to wind it about her head and shoulders. Labor of her own hands.

She had learned this, in the Tor Leonne, in the months of her isolation. Had learned it, in a different way, upon the road that led to the Tor Arkosa. This, this third time, was a blessing, for it was a choice. Her own.

"Ramdan," she said quietly. "Tend the Serra Teresa."

He bowed.

"I will have the services of the Clemente serafs. Your services will not be required until we leave Clemente."

She did not look at him. Could not. And perhaps he understood why; he was silent in his acquiescence. He had al-

ways been silent; she had assumed this to be some part of
the natural grace the best of serafs showed.

But she wondered. She listened to the rustle of fabric as
he bent; watched the play of shadow across stone and earth.
How much did he know? How much had he always known,
that he could offer the exquisite mercy of silence to one
who could hear beneath the facade of perfect words?

Kallandras.

The master bard of Senniel College looked up. The
physicians retained by Clemente were a sedate and quiet
group compared to those retained by either Senniel or the
Kings of Essalieyan; they chose words with care, and used
them with a caution lost upon Northerners used to the
caprice—some would say the idiocy—of Northern patients.

Of all the things that reminded him of the home that Senniel had become, none were as strong as this. He smiled a
moment, and lifted a hand as the physician peeled away
strips of bloodied fabric. The wound beneath them was
ugly, but it was not deep, and it had not yet become infected.

"I am capable of cleaning and dressing simple wounds,"
he said quietly, desiring privacy, "and the same cannot be
said for the Clemente cerdan."

"The Tor'agar gave his orders, Ser Kallandras."

Kallandras nodded, smoothing all evidence of amusement from his face. "I heard them," he said softly, weight-
ing his words with a hint of compulsion. "But I, too, have
my duties. Will you not tend to your fallen?"

The man hesitated, running fingers just washed through
the length of his beard. He desired it; that much was clear.
The Clemente forces were not so large that the physicians
could be assured of finding no friends among the fallen—
and some of those might yet be saved.

"I will speak with the Tor'agar," he continued, admiring
the man's tenacity. Few fought such an unrecognized compulsion for as long as he had. "And in truth, I, too, have or-

ders. When you have finished, I ask that you inspect my work." He lifted the wet cloth in his hands.

The doctor hesitated again, and then he made his decision. He offered a grim bow, shaded it with just a hint of gratitude and impatience, and was gone.

Serra Diora. Forgive me my silence; I heard you upon the field, but I was occupied in a dance that could not be interrupted. What has happened?

Ona Teresa. Two words. But he heard what lay beneath them. He rose as the doctor grew distant.

A moment, Serra Diora. Where are you?

I am in the harem.

And will I be granted access to the wives of the Tor?

She did not reply. By her silence, he knew she meant him to grant himself that access, were it to be denied him. Frowning, he began to walk.

Celleriant stood in his way. "Kallandras," he said quietly.

"Lord Celleriant."

"Ah. Formality, then."

"The battle is over," he replied gravely. "And we are in the South. Here, formality rules all."

"Here," Lord Celleriant replied, not moving, "the word of the Tor—or the Tyr—rules all."

"We acknowledge our rulers," Kallandras said quietly. "But we find elasticity in the rules themselves. I am called," he added, grave now.

"I know. I would accompany you."

He hesitated.

The Arianni lord marked that hesitation. But he did not turn; did not leave.

Kallandras smiled; Lord Celleriant returned the brief play of lips. Neither expression was genuine, and both knew it.

"This is not a battlefield," the Arianni lord said quietly.

"No. And away from the field, I have old ties, and old responsibilities." He could have pushed his way past Celleriant, and knew it.

"So, too, do I. But were I in the Summer Court—and perhaps even the Winter, I do not know—I would be honored by your presence."

"Until the Queen spoke."

"If she were present. I have been among your kind for a short time, but I have begun to learn that this elasticity of which you speak has its . . . charm."

"Yes," he said quietly. And then again, "Yes."

Lord Celleriant stepped aside, and when Kallandras began to walk, he fell in beside him; their strides were of a length, and the fall of their steps, to an untrained ear, might have been that of a single man.

The Tyr'agnate and the Tor'agar stood to one side of the screen that led to the garden; the early gray of dawn had given way to the muted colors—the green and the gray—of the stones; the pale clarity of water, its surface glimmering faintly; the black of hair not yet caught in combs; the pale white of harem faces.

Kallandras bowed, first to the Tyr, and then to the Tor.

Ser Alessandro kai di'Clemente shook his head. "Not here, Kallandras of Senniel."

Kallandras rose.

But the kai Clemente felt the need to add words to what was obvious. "Were it not for the aid of the Old Forest, were it not for the presence of Jewel ATerafin and those that serve her, Clemente would now be ruled by an untested Tor in a time of war. You owe me no loyalty," he continued, his voice perfect, his posture at odds with the dressing his wounds had been given, "and owing nothing, you have risked all.

"This is the heart of Clemente," he continued, raising an arm. "And I give you leave to traverse it. Walk with care, but walk freely."

Ah. Kallandras glanced at Ser Mareo kai di'Lamberto; his face was cast in stone, gray and cold as the edges of the rocks half hidden by tree and flower.

In the South, no man hated the North so openly.

"Were it not for the arrival of the Tyr'agnate, all that you feared might still have come to pass."

The Tyr'agnate did not condescend to speak. His hand rested upon the hilt of his sword, and his lips were set in a narrow line. But he did not gainsay what the kai Clemente openly offered.

"The Matriarch?" Kallandras said quietly.

"She is well, I believe. She speaks to no one."

The Tyr'agnate was silent.

Would be, Kallandras thought, for some time. He bowed again, the North giving way to the South in the grace of the gesture.

"My companion?" he asked.

"He is welcome," Ser Alessandro replied. But Kallandras heard the doubt the surface of words did not offer. He wondered what truths the legends of Clemente contained. He stepped away from the man who ruled and the man he served, and passed through the garden, following one of the narrow paths hidden among the fronds of plants not native to the Mancorvan plains.

The women fell silent in ones and twos.

He did not meet their eyes; did not look at their faces; did not otherwise acknowledge their presence—he understood what freedom within the harem entailed, and he took care, in the sight of the Tor, not to abuse the privilege.

But he had other reasons.

And one of them waited, knees pressed into unrolled mat, head bowed against the growing light of sun, the press of day. He approached her with care, and when he stood some ten feet from her, he spoke her name.

She looked up.

"Kallandras," she whispered.

He could clearly see the exhaustion that lay against the fine features of her face; could see the circles beneath eyes that were almost always perfect. Her hair was bound, and her posture flawless, but those were the only things she maintained.

"Serra Diora. I came in haste."

Her smile was perfect. Vacant.

"Ona Teresa is . . . indisposed."

He drew closer, his steps light and deliberate. By his side, white shadow, came Lord Celleriant.

Her expression shifted as she saw him; it was a subtle shift. Nothing as unpleasant as surprise marred her manner.

"I trust him," he told her quietly, exposing much of himself in the act. He did not hide what his voice contained, although he was not certain what she would hear of himself in the words.

She exposed nothing of herself in reply; she nodded, the nod itself so regal it placed a distance between them.

He accepted it.

Because beyond her, he could see Ramdan, and beside Ramdan, he could at last see the Serra Teresa. It surprised him, and it should not have; for no other reason would the Serra Diora have summoned him.

The desert had scoured her clean, he thought, as he surveyed the contours of her expressionless face. She had emerged from the Tor Arkosa a different woman; wiser in some ways. But much more vulnerable. He did not know if she was aware of the change; the young often saw clearly only when their vision was turned outward.

But if she was aware of it, he wondered if she thought it worth the cost; with life came pain, and she had chosen to live.

He stepped past her; came face-to-face with Ramdan.

The seraf was not cerdan. Not Toran, not Tyran. He bore no sword, for serafs were granted no weapons in the Lord's Dominion. Still, as he could, he stood watch.

Kallandras offered him a shallow bow. More than this, and he would pass from genuine respect to hollow mockery. Ramdan seemed impervious to all compliment. As the Serra

Diora before him, his gaze passed to, and lingered upon, Lord Celleriant.

And as she had done, he said nothing. Old habits were his by nature, and not by the dint of effort. He stepped aside, and the bard knelt.

And closed his eyes.

A healer was summoned, Diora said. Her voice was flat, uninflected in even this intimate a form of communication. It surprised him, and little did. Her power, he thought, was greater than even he had guessed, so many years ago.

The past held him. If he did not look upon her, he could see the child that she had been when he had first heard the clarity, the purity, of her singing.

A healer? Here?

Here.

He did not ask who; he knew she would offer him nothing. Needed to offer him nothing.

And the healer said?

That he cannot help her, Kallandras. Ah, a crack in the armor.

He nodded.

Is it true?

You must judge, Serra Diora. You heard the words he spoke.

Silence. Then, **Years ago, you made a man heal a woman against his will. She was dying. Could you not now call the winds? Could you not grant to Teresa what you granted Lissa en'Marano?**

All distance burned away in the heat of her words, as if it were the paper in the screens of the harem's doors. He bent, and touched Serra Teresa's forehead; it was slick with sweat. Her eyes were closed; he opened them with care, and saw that they were wide, unseeing. He knew, then, what she had done.

The demon, he said quietly.

The Serra Diora nodded.

This is beyond the ability of a healer, he told her quietly.

But *why?* **She is not dead. She is not—yet—dying—**

It is not the body that is injured, Serra Diora. It is the gift. And the gift itself cannot be made whole.

You know this.

It is a truth often held by healers. If the fevers had destroyed her body, the healer might tend the injuries; it is done in *Averalaan Aramarelas.* But . . .

It would not heal the other damage done.

No, Na'dio. He paused, and then offered her the only kindness he could. **She knew what she did; not by accident did she arrive at this pass. She chose, Serra Diora.**

Celleriant came to kneel beside him; their knees were an inch apart. The Arianni lord touched the Serra Teresa's face.

"She is important to you?" he asked quietly.

He needn't have asked; he knew the answer.

But if they were brothers, they still answered the dictates of their nature. Kallandras nodded, exposing weakness with the grace of a man for whom weakness meant little.

"I do not have your gift, Kallandras," Celleriant said. "I cannot cloak my words in silence; I cannot make the silence mine. Would you have me speak?"

He weighed his answer with care.

But before he could offer it, the Serra Diora did.

"I would have you speak," she told him gravely. "And I will bear the responsibility for the words offered, if they return upon the wind."

"Among my kin, there is only one who might be of aid, and . . . her aid is costly. Always."

Diora's gaze lingered upon his face, the lines of his cheekbones, the fine, slender point of his jaw; she glanced at the Northern white of his hair, at the silver-gray of his foreign eyes. She knew of whom he spoke. "No. She would accept no such aid, be burdened by no such debt."

"She is wise."

The Serra turned, but Kallandras reached out; fully ex-

tended, his arm brushed the rounded curve of her shoulders.
She had drawn them in, as if to ward off a blow.

"He would not have spoken," Kallandras told her, "if that
was all he had to offer. Be patient, Serra Diora. Understand
that he speaks as he can, and as he must; his language and
ours are not, and will never be, the same, no matter how
similar the words first appear to be."

The Arianni lord raised a silver brow. But he nodded
gravely. "In all things," he said, "even this, there is a price.
Be it small, be it paid in momentary pain, it must be asked."

She did not understand this; he saw it, although her expression did not shift. Perhaps because it did not.

"Among my kin," he continued, as if there had been no
interruption, and no graceless explanation offered, "there is
only one. But we are not healers. That was never our gift.
And many are our gifts, Serra. We speak with the wind. We
speak with the water. We move—when we can be heard—
the very earth. Even fire will dance when those who have
the power summon it.

"But the lesser arts, the mortal arts, are *not* ours."

"And you know of them?"

"What is left us, in eternity, but study? Yes. Yes, we
know of them."

She did not ask him how. Nor did Kallandras. They
waited, audience, and captive.

"Why?" she asked at last, daring much.

"It is part of our oldest histories," he replied. "You are
aware—perhaps?—that mortals have souls. You are not
aware of what those souls are. They are some part of the di-
vinity of the gods, captured fragments made flesh. In some
mortals, those fragments have power. In the North, they
know the names of these powers: bard-born," he said first,
gazing at the Serra and then to Kallandras. "Healer-born.
Mage-born. Seer-born. Maker-born." He paused, and then
said quietly, "There were others. Perhaps there still are; the
powers granted mortals were often subtle, and they eluded

the naming. At the height of the Cities of Man, such power existed in mortals that might challenge the mastery of gods.

"And among the mortals, in the time of the Cities of Man, there were those who might heal the injury she has sustained."

"A healer has come—"

"A human healer?"

She nodded.

"And he could not aid you."

Nodded again.

"Understand that, as with all gifts, some are greater and some lesser. I did not say that all healers were capable of this task; only that some existed—in a world that the ghosts of the Cities remember—who might." He brought his hands back to his sides. "But the fevers burn," he said softly.

"She will survive the fevers."

He raised a delicate brow. "You are not a seer," he told her gravely.

"No. But I will not let her go; not that way."

His smile was slender. Cold. Nothing about his face suggested kindness. "You are without mercy," he said softly. "There are those who, blinded, lose all desire for life—and in her fashion, she has become one such. But . . . If you can carry her, and if the fever does not devour her, there may be one who can answer her need. He is not here," he added softly, "but you have seen him; when you see him again—if ever—you will know."

"Who?"

But the Arianni lord fell silent, and as the silence lengthened, it became clear that he would not speak again.

Kallandras wondered if she would attempt to force an answer from him; she was weak, spent—and desperate.

The bard lifted hand and voice both. **You carried the Sun Sword, Serra Diora. You carried the Heart of Arkosa. Believe you will carry the Serra Teresa for as long as she must be carried.**

He bowed.

It was easier, to carry the Sword.

Yes. This is the price you pay, when you walk among the living and think of things other than death.

She waited while Kallandras gained his feet; the Arianni lord joined him, moving with so little effort he might have been a seraf. In another world, another Court. She heard the ice in his voice; he did not trouble himself to hide it. He was cruel; there was nothing about his presence that suggested kindness.

But there was little about Kallandras that did either. She bowed to them both as Ramdan once again knelt by the Serra Teresa's side.

"The kai Lamberto is waiting," Kallandras said softly.

"I know." She rose, taking the hand he offered. "Has he spoken with you?"

"Not a word."

"Ah. You are . . . from the North."

"Yes. And I see the truth of his disposition without the need of words; he will not be a willing ally, Serra Diora."

"No. Nor will he ally himself with the Servants of the Lord of Night."

Kallandras' smile was slender. "Nor that."

"Has he come for the Sword?"

"I do not know if he knows that you have it in your keeping."

Her eyes skirted the distant figure of Jevri. "I think," she said softly, "that he will know. He was never a fool."

"He could not be, and rule in the South."

She nodded. Gathered her silks about her slender shoulders, arranged the fall of her veil, hands calm and still with familiar motion.

The harem fell away; for a moment she saw walls, stone walls, smooth and bare of window or door. In such a room, she had bided her time, reinforcing the oldest and most important of learned skills: the gift of waiting.

But the time for waiting was done.

Mareo kai di'Lamberto was not a young man. Nor was he a man who sheltered beneath fan or bough; his face was lined and creased by exposure to sun, to wind; the plains boasted no desert, but she saw sand in his eyes as he turned toward her, his arms across the breadth of his chest.

She stopped ten feet from his shadow and knelt before him. Her knees were already dark with earth and dew; she would not trouble Ramdan to bring her those things that Serras of import were accustomed to.

His brow, streaked with the silver of age, rose slightly.

"Serra Diora."

She nodded. Her hands held no fan; she offered no resistance to the appraisal of his gaze. He did not bid her rise; did not offer her the freedom of speech. He was the Lord's man.

"Serra Diora . . . di'Marano?"

She let the silence serve as emphasis before she broke it with her delicate voice. "Serra Diora en'Leonne," she replied. A challenge, a soft one.

"The kai Leonne—both of them—lie dead and buried upon the plateau. Will you lay claim to a marriage of the dead?"

"Not of the dead, Tor'agnate."

"And does your father's clan have no claim upon your name, no claim upon your person?"

"As is our custom, my father's clan," she replied, even now, dagger steel dancing between the delicate syllables, "ceded me in marriage to Ser Illara kai di'Leonne."

"And your father had some hand in his destruction."

She said nothing. He expected no reply.

Or perhaps he did; something about his expression was wrong, some thinning of lip, some narrowing of eye. She straightened her back, lowered her chin, placed her hands, palms down, upon the fold of lap. She was a Serra of the High Courts; he was a Tyr. She had been raised to sit in the presence of men such as he. Raised to understand their moods, to read them as clearly as if words were painted in ink across the lines and hollows of their faces.

She would anger him, she thought, but that anger must be one of her choosing, and the timing of its invocation, under her control.

But she did not know him now. It had been many years since she had been a child in the lee of Amar.

"You have nothing to say of his treachery?"

"I am a Serra, Tyr'agnate. You ask me to speak of the games of men, and I have little experience from which to speak wisely."

"Indeed." But he was not moved; not cajoled. "Jevri."

Jevri el'Sol came to stand by his side. By it, and not within his shadow.

"Tell me what you know of the Serra Diora."

The old man hesitated, although the hesitation was marked only by the Serra. She was practiced in the same art; could gather strength and thought in the same subtle way.

She listened now. Wondering as she did what Ona Teresa would hear, if she could sit thus.

"I made her two dresses," Jevri el'Sol said quietly.

It was not what she expected to hear; it was not, she saw, from the lift of thick brow, what Mareo kai di'Lamberto expected either. But he did not turn to glance at Jevri, and because he did not, she could not.

"A dress," the Tyr'agnate said, meeting her eyes, his own a brown so dark they might have been all of black, "is something that any woman might wear. It tells me little."

"A dress, yes," Jevri replied, and his words carried stung but measured pride. "But upon any other woman, such a dress would fit poorly."

"They made poor use of a Radann."

"They made the use that I desired, Tyr'agnate." Mild rebuke. It surprised her. "She wore the first dress upon the day of her wedding to the kai Leonne. You saw it; all of the clansmen of the High Court, and many of the lower, saw it.

They did not see her face; they did not see her eyes, could not hear her voice. But they marked her by what she wore."

"They marked her by the husband."

"Indeed."

"And the other dress?"

Ah. She understood now.

"The Lord's Consort," Jevri replied.

"And when did she wear it?"

"At the Festival of the Sun."

"And was it noted?"

"It was noted. It was a finer dress than her wedding dress; it was a significant dress."

"A risk, Jevri."

"There was no longer a Leonne to offend," the servitor replied mildly. "And it can be argued that the Lord's Consort serves *the* Lord, and not *a* Lord, be he the Lord of the Dominion."

"It can. What occurred there?"

"She sang the lay of the Sun Sword, Tyr'agnate."

"Bold girl. It is said that the man who claims the Tor Leonne cannot draw the Sun Sword. It lies in its haven, sheathed and waiting."

"It is said that not all rumor is as capricious as wind. In this case, it is true: the General Marente could not pull the sword from its sheath."

"And as proof of this?"

"The kai el'Sol drew the blade in front of the assembly of the clansmen; he stood in the waters of the Tor Leonne, and he made his challenge for all to see."

"And then?"

"It consumed him utterly."

Dry, dry words. His eyes would be dry, she thought, if she could see them. But beneath the thin flutter of those empty words she heard what he did not say.

"And then?" The anger in the two words.

"The Serra Diora entered the waters. The Serra Diora retrieved the fallen blade."

"And?"

"And she asked that the clansmen hear the plea of a weak, of a foolish woman; that they choose for her no course that would dishonor the memory of her much loved dead."

"Surely no woman is allowed such a demand."

"Kai Lamberto."

"And yet . . . the clansmen acceded."

"Kai Lamberto."

Now his gaze was upon her face with all the ferocity his words could not be allowed to contain. "You are, as you have said, a Serra, and ill-trained in the arts of war. Let me tell you then, Serra Diora, what you will not hear as *Serra*."

She nodded quietly, attentively. Every gesture that she offered this man was perfect, for in perfection lay her only protection.

"The servants of the Lord of Night lay in wait within the village of Damar. They numbered ten. *Ten*. And within Sarel, it is said that two fell."

She nodded again. Her throat was dry, and her eyes, dry as well; she could not blink. But she had suffered far, far worse in time of peace.

"Twelve, Serra Diora. Twelve of the Enemy's servants. Not even in the oldest of our histories did nine walk abroad so openly. Nor do they walk openly now; it is not to serve the Lord of Night that the Terreans will take up sword and drum, banner and horn.

"I am curious. My wife, Serra Donna en'Lamberto, is a woman of some instinct and intuition, and over the years, I have learned to value that gift."

Perfection was her only protection. But it was not enough.

"Tell me why you think the Lord of Night would send twelve of his servants into *my* Terrean. Tell me why they chose to hide within Clemente at the exact moment of your arrival."

Jevri cleared his throat. It was graceless; it was beneath him.

She almost loved him for it.

"Jevri?"

"It is clear to me, from my brief conversations in the infirmary, that the Manelan forces could not have been aware of the Serra's presence before they marched."

"Ah. I see." He smiled. It was a dangerous smile. "So they were not aware of her presence, and yet they were here, as is she. Serra Diora?"

"Tyr'agnate."

"Why are you here?"

"This is where the Havallan Matriarch chose to lead us," she replied. Careful now, embroidering her words with the patina of felt truth.

Ah, but he was a canny man. A powerful man. Such a difficult combination.

"And if you were free to travel, Serra Diora, where would you now go?" She took a breath, squaring shoulders, bracing herself, as she could, against the garden floor.

"To the North," she said softly. "And the East."

"To Averda."

She nodded, regal now, the compliance of her earlier posturing discarded.

"And what waits you, in Averda?"

"Duty," she said softly.

"Duty. Surely, your duty is to Marano?"

"I am en'Leonne," she replied evenly.

"So."

He did not speak again.

Nor did she.

But another man did.

"Serra Diora," Ser Alessandro kai di'Clemente said softly. He bowed.

She looked up at him; saw the shadow of beard across his jaw, the shadow of night beneath his eyes. He bled through the bandages that physicians had laid across his sword arm, but the wound served to strengthen his presence.

"I am in your debt." He spoke as if he had heard none of the conversation that preceded his words.

"A man is not in a Serra's debt," Ser Mareo kai di'Lamberto said, neutral now, his face hooded.

"But even a man can stand in the Lady's. I am beholden to the Lady for her intervention." He paused and then turned to the kai Lamberto, the man who owned his oath. "And I swore to the Lady that if we had victory upon the field, I would see the Serra to her destination."

CHAPTER TWENTY-EIGHT

SERRA Teresa slept, surrounded by the quiet elegance of a room that the Northerners would call empty.

Ramdan rearranged her sleeping silks with care. He patted her forehead dry, and when she stirred, he raised her head to his lap and dripped water between the cracked surface of her lips. All this he did in silence; the silence was oppressive.

But to break it required strength.

Serra Diora sat with a samisen in her lap. It wobbled when she moved; her hands stilled the strings. She had no heart, no voice, for song, and were it not for the presence of Yollana, she might have slept.

But Yollana did not sleep. She sat upon jade mats, her expression composed of the intricate lines of age and injury. She watched Ramdan.

Diora watched her.

The domis was not silent; beyond the screens that paid lip service to privacy, serafs toiled with lumber beams, with toothed saw, with oils and perfumes. She could see their shadows against the lattice of paper and wood that formed the interior face of a sliding screen. A roof had already been erected above the harem; it was the first roof to be so raised.

Thus did Ser Alessandro honor his wives.

"Well, Diora."

She set aside the samisen and rose, clutching the Matriarch's pouch in her slender hands. As Serra Teresa had done, Diora now did: she tended the Matriarch. Yollana might have demurred; she was not a woman who willingly exposed weakness, even when weakness defined her. But she understood why Diora saw to her needs, and she accepted the gesture.

"Will you tell them?"

Diora pulled the pipe from the cracked folds of worn leather. The bowl was dull with sweat and dust, but Yollana would take no other.

"Diora?"

A Serra would have understood the answer. Yollana was Matriarch; bold and blunt as a lowborn clansman.

"I will tell them nothing," she said softly, "that they do not already know."

"But the appearance of ignorance is a matter of life and death among the clans. You are no Celina; had you been raised Voyani, you would almost be my equal. What do you intend?"

"What I have always intended, Matriarch. I will go to the North, and the East. I will carry the Sun Sword to the only man who can wield it."

Shaking hands cupped pipe; dried leaves caught flame that existed only in the pause between unintelligible words. "He is not happy."

She did not pretend to misunderstand. "No."

"Will he aid you?"

"I . . . do not know."

Rings of smoke rose above them, gray halos.

Ser Mareo kai di'Lamberto was given rooms in the domis that were—slightly—beneath his status as the reigning Tyr. The need for this was plain, and he was generous enough to offer an acceptance of the circumstances that was deeper than the scant words he spoke.

His Tyran were given rooms that bordered his; his men were encamped on the eastern side of Sarel. Both awaited his word in silence, for they had seen the archers upon the walls of Sarel, and they understood what the presence of Northerners within the surviving Clemente forces meant.

He gave them nothing.

Instead, he retired to his quarters. He took food and drink from the serafs who had been handpicked to attend him, and he paid no heed to the subtle inferiority of their service; it was beneath a man of his rank.

But he did notice.

He noticed much.

They were off-balance, Ser Alessandro, Marakas par el'-Sol. They were grateful for his intervention, and concerned enough with staunching their own losses that neither had come forth to ask him the only question he himself would have considered of relevance in their position.

Why did you travel to Sarel with an army?

Ah, but the old woman knew. He allowed himself a smile in the privacy of his chambers, protected from the gaze of the Lord. One eye covered in a dark patch, legs useless, hand cupped around an obscenely masculine pipe, she had met his gaze, held it, demanding the answers that men had not yet demanded.

She was the heart of his problem; of all the people he expected to see within the confines of the Clemente harem—and he was canny—Yollana of the Havalla Voyani was not among them. He would have been only marginally more surprised to find Alesso di'Marente there, although his welcome in that case would have been less measured.

That would have been too simple. Marente, by the nature of his occupation of Damar, he could afford to offend; it would cost him nothing. But Yollana of the Havalla Voyani?

No.

He was almost certain that this was why the Voyani had always chosen women as leaders—they knew how badly it discomfited the more powerful clansmen.

He reached into the folds of his robe and touched the crushed and folded scroll that he had carried this distance with him. It was a letter given him by his wife.

His wife was a Serra of the High Court, but she was also

a woman; she was not so canny or harsh as the Serra Amara
di'Callesta, nor was she as shrewd as the Serra Teresa di'-
Marano, the woman who—rank or no—ruled the Serras of
Amar. Even in her absence.

Perhaps especially in her absence.

*Where is the Serra Teresa di'Marano, Mareo? Surely
they would not keep her from her kai.*

It was not that his wife was a lamb. It was not that she
was, as the Serra Celina, given to the foolishly feminine.
But when she joined him in his war room, she felt no need
to deny the grace and the softness that defined her sex. She
did not trouble herself to hide her horror or her anger; did
not consider it demeaning to plead or beg for compassion or
pity if she deemed it just.

He had said as much, before he had left her to travel to
the South.

And she? She had offered him a momentary frown, a
longer silence. *Mareo,* she said at last, *surely you must understand the reason for this?*

With Donna, there was always reason. Before there was
anything, there was reason, and it was sweetly and gently
offered.

"No," he told her, taking her hands in his and kissing her
palms. There were no serafs present, no other wives, none
of his sons or daughters. He often found that the example
she must set before the people she loved and fretted over introduced a distance between them, and he desired no distance.

She smiled, but the smile was tinged with sadness. It
moved him; it always had.

And he had no doubt that she knew it; had no doubt that
she hoarded some of that sadness against future need, afraid
in the hidden part of her heart that to use it freely would be
to destroy its power.

He had never asked.

"I trust you," she replied, freeing one hand and running
it along the side of his face.

"And the others?"

"The Serra Teresa has no husband."

"She has father and brothers."

"A father—or a brother—must in the end choose one of two courses: to keep his daughter or sister, or to offer her in marriage to another clansman. But a husband? If he is not a man to kill wives, never." She retreated a moment into silence, and then said, "She would have been different, had she been allowed to marry."

"Ah." He shrugged. It had long been a source of discontent for his wife, but she was wise enough to hold her peace in the presence of the kai Marano, past and present. None of the jealousies that plagued lesser Serras had ever troubled his Donna.

"The Serra Alina likewise had no husband."

That chilled him; annoyed him enough that he withdrew. Mention of his sister was guaranteed to have this effect, and he knew that she was aware of it. But she spoke; he listened.

"So this harshness is something that men are wise enough to avoid." He shrugged.

"The Serra Amara has a husband," she continued quietly. "And perhaps, in the privacy of their harem, she offers him what I offer you."

"You don't believe that, Na'donna."

"She and I are not the same. Had I the choice, I would never have married Ser Ramiro kai di'Callesta—and what choice, in the end, are we offered? Our fathers decide. Our brothers. And they decide for reasons that a Serra's heart and sensibility count little against."

"She would never have refused him."

Serra Donna smiled. "No. I believe you correct in this. And she is proud of her husband. I am proud of mine. But Callesta and Lamberto are not the same."

"Serra Amara and Serra Donna are not the same."

"No." She knelt then.

He frowned.

"Na'donna, it may be months until I next see you. Will you spend the scant hours left us speaking of things unpleasant?"

"Out of the most unpleasant things, gardens may grow, and peace and repose may be found there."

She so seldom showed signs of steel. But it was there, if one knew her well enough to see it. "What is of such import, Na'donna?"

She rose. "I have a letter," she said at last. Hesitance marred the pretty words.

"And is what you have to say so unpleasant that you trust it only to ink and paper?"

She met his gaze, her lashes lowering like half-veil. "It was not," she said at last, "written by me."

He was on his guard then. "Who sent you this letter?"

"The Serra Amara en'Callesta."

He relaxed, but only marginally. "So," he said quietly. "You wrote her."

She nodded. He did not ask her what she had said. "And what does the Serra Amara say?"

"You might read it, Mareo." She drew the letter from the folds of her sari and held it out to him; he could see the fine grain of the paper that the Serra Amara had no doubt made with her own hands.

His hands remained folded in his lap.

She waited; in that, she was as all Serras but the very youngest. After a moment, the words in the air between them lessened in force and impact by the quality of the silence, he looked away from the brush-stroked lines.

"Tell me about this letter," he said at last, wanting very much to speak about almost anything else. They had so little time.

"It is political," she said quietly. "And it was done by her hand. No other hand, save one, is both so bold and so elegant."

Because he did not wish to hear his sister's name spoken again, he did not ask her who the second person was.

"Were it informal, Mareo, she would have written it in ink, with feather or quill; she meant to make a statement."

"A long statement."

She said nothing.

"Humor me, Mareo." She added delicate plea to the smoothness of voice; no whine here, no grating, annoying snivel.

"I have always humored you, Na'donna," he said, relenting.

She knew that there was often a price to be paid for such surrender, and she was cautious now. Her eyes hid nothing.

"But humor me, Serra Donna. Translate for me."

"She speaks of the Serra Alina di'Lamberto."

"And the Northerners?" he said, hearing the name. Hating it. Always, *always,* she returned to haunt him.

"Yes," she said, speaking starkly. Aware that her response was not the response he expected.

"So," he said softly. "She admits their treachery openly. I am not a Serra, Na'donna. I am not given to delicacy and introversion. Tell me."

"The Serra Alina was given leave, by the Northern Kings, to travel," his wife said quietly. "And she chose to travel. The Serra Amara does not say why."

"And she traveled alone?"

"No."

"Does the Serra Amara choose to divulge the names of her traveling companions?"

Silence again; heavier now. "You might read what is written, Mareo."

Yes. Yes, he might. But his hands closed the more tightly over the rolled parchment, changing the curve of its shape. It was so unlike Na'donna, to force him to admit that he could read what was written within.

"It is *not* in the Serra's language," she said quietly, as if divining the momentary pettiness of his dissatisfaction. Still, she spoke gently, almost apologetically.

"I do not think that the Serra Amara en'Callesta would

have chosen to write *this* letter to the wife of the man who killed her son. She is . . . careful . . . Mareo. But she offers no accusation."

"No. Of course not. Women have no place upon the field of battle." The words were heavy with irony.

His wife rose. The incense in the brazier had burned to ash, but the sweet ghost of its scent lingered. She turned her back upon him, tending it with care. Showing him that grace had not left her hands, her arms, the gentle tilt of her neck.

"Na'donna, speak plainly."

Back turned to him, face hidden by work that would have been better left to seraf hands, she obeyed.

"I think that it is no coincidence that you have gathered a third of your men. I think that it is no coincidence that you travel with Jevri el'Sol, and those men you could gather in haste. I think that the presence of the Havalla Voyani, here, in Amar, is proof enough that what we face—what *you* face—is not the battle that we had intended."

He hid nothing from her.

But she saw without seeing; her hands cupped the brass base of the small, lightless urn.

"And I think that your greatest challenge is in none of these things. No, the Serra Amara did not choose to openly speak of all that she knows; no more would I, in such a time."

"If ever, to that—"

"If ever, to the Serra Amara, who sees much and forgets nothing."

He accepted the gentle correction.

"The last of the Leonne clan has taken the field."

Silence was a gift. A cold gift, like the edge of a sword that has not yet been drawn in battle.

She hesitated, and then she withdrew the hands that steadied her. But he gazed now upon the pale blue of her sari. It was a meager gift of color, but she would not face him; he was denied the warmth of her eyes. "The Serra

Amara thinks highly of him. Highly enough that she was willing to mention the name of the sword he now bears."

"The sword?"

"It was . . . it is . . . the kai Callesta's sword."

Ah. "And the boy is already so much of a Callestan pawn that he was willing to take the sword?"

"It was not offered him," she replied. "He asked for it, Mareo. When he paid his respects to the first of the fallen, he asked it, as a boon."

"He asked it?"

"So she says. And I believe her. Not to sing his praise did she write this letter, but his praise is there, if one reads what is written; she took no pains to hide it."

"He did not travel from the North alone."

"No. He travels in the company of Ser Anton di'Guivera." She paused while the name played itself out in the cadence of her voice, in its soft echo. "She says that Ser Anton di'Guivera speaks highly of the kai Leonne; that he serves him completely, and with regard. He also travels in the company of Ser Baredan di'Navarre."

"Both good men," Mareo said softly. Stiffly.

His wife nodded quietly. His words did not catch her; did not disturb the graceful flow of her words. "He has taken the pledge of allegiance offered him by Ser Ramiro kai di'-Callesta—and his par, Ser Fillipo par di'Callesta."

"Ser Fillipo?"

She nodded.

"Continue."

"He is waited upon by the Serra Alina di'Lamberto."

He knew what she would say next. Almost raised hand to stem the flow of her pretty words.

But he was not a coward; he bore the weight that settled around him, and within him, as if it were inconsequential.

"He has come with the Northerners. He has chosen, as his cerdan, a Northern unit."

"You do not speak with anger, wife," he said, cold now.

Angry himself. "You do not speak with the quiet outrage that . . . I might otherwise expect. Why?"

"Because . . ." She turned away again, withdrawing her hands, almost withdrawing the pleasant cadence of her voice. "She speaks, last, of Northern ignorance, of Northern folly. The words are her words," she added quietly, "but I see Na'ali in them."

He almost rose, then. He almost said, *Do not use that name in my hearing*. But she sat, so pale, so stiff, her hands in shaking fists; stricken, as he was. Just as he was. "Yes," she said without preamble. "She speaks of the death of our son."

The sound of clenched fist made no noise in the harem.

It made no noise in the chambers given him for his use by the Tor'agar of Clemente. But the paper did, bending and folding at his whim, as much like a Serra in seeming as it was in substance.

Pretty strokes, but bold, as Donna had said. He read the letter by lamplight, unwilling to expose its contents to sun. He had not yet reached a decision.

But Serra Donna had.

It caused him pain, as all old wounds did in their time. *Am I now to surrender the life of my son to . . . these? Am I now to be unmanned, to be weakened in blood and oath?*

They thought him a child. My son. My oldest son. They thought to spare *him.* Lady, it was almost beyond belief. Would have been. But his wife believed it, and his faith in his wife was one of the few unshakable tenets upon which he had built his life. *They killed him, Na'donna.*

She could not answer. She was ensconced within the safety of Amar, in the heart of the harem that was hers to rule, the Havalla Voyani by her side as protection against the servants of the Lord of Night. And he had not chosen to ask the question that troubled him now, for he knew what her answer would be; she had given it, when she had given him the letter.

* * *

"Was that wise?"

Ser Alessandro kai di'Clemente looked up; met the unadorned lids of his guest. Although he understood that some magic had transpired that could burn away all trace of hair and yet leave no mark upon skin, he found the sight of a hairless man disturbing.

But it was not for this reason that he chose to look away.

Wise? No, he thought. How could it be? His statement was almost a challenge to the authority of the Tyr who had, with his army, saved Sarel from the forces of the distant General Marente.

But he had chosen to take the risk; had taken it. Did not—yet—regret it.

"Ser Alessandro?"

"For a man who speaks little, you have a love of words," he replied, shading his own with something akin to smile. "And like many men with such a love, you ask a question to which you already know the answer."

He was rewarded by the Radann's smile, and surprised by how it robbed his face of years. Seldom was joy considered a thief, although in the Dominion it carried with it the weight of hidden debt.

"It was not wise." He shifted in place, and regretted the motion almost before it was complete. The wound he had taken was not yet finished bleeding. Perhaps, exposed to sun, it might. But he exposed little to sunlight, this day. Although the flowers of the garden were pink and white, and the leaves themselves beryl, emerald, jade, he walked a while yet in the lee of the Lady's shadow; the colors that spoke of the Lord failed to move him.

Thus did he acknowledge the greatest of his debts.

"But I have often been accused of lack of wisdom. In youth," he added, the momentary sting of his cousin's death swift and unlooked for, "and even as an adult." No, he thought again, testing his past, finding in it much pain but—at last—little anger. *We are done with the past, par el'Sol.*

"And as the kai Clemente?"

"I am little interested in the ways of power; the cost is high."

Marakas fell silent.

It was the hand of the par el'Sol that had raised the Tor'agar, fallen, from the field of wreckage and cracked, broken ground, and the Radann was almost shamed to admit that he had become political enough to use his gift. The healing was brief; he could not do more without the Tor'agar's consent—or knowledge. But he had, now, a sense of the man that Ser Alessandro kai di'Clemente had become.

He therefore did not speak with the Tyr'agnate; he knew that Alessandro, injured or no, would say all that need be said. Thus was the past laid, at last, to rest.

"What will the Serra Celina say?"

Alessandro's smile was a small revelation. A window had been opened briefly; a gesture of truce, or perhaps even peace.

"She has spent the evening in the company of the Serra Diora; she approves of my decision." He shook his head, turning. "She has spoken little of what occurred in the harem," he added. "But she has spoken enough. No wise man hoards debt, and I have incurred a great debt in the passage of a single evening." He closed his eyes; for a moment, the battlefield of Damar encompassed the whole of his vision. Moonlight was kinder than sun; it veiled the sight, muting the harsh colors of the dead. But veiled or no, he knew their names. All of their names. He shook himself. "I count my debt thus: to the Havallans, to Marano, and to the Lambertans; to the Northerners, who owe no allegiance to the South; to the Radann." He inclined his head.

"I count you in no debt, Tor'agar."

"No. You wouldn't. But a man measures the worth of the gifts offered and the sacrifices made; he does not let the whole of the tale reside in the hands of others. It is *my* debt, Radann par el'Sol." Again, he offered a weary smile.

Marakas found it moving.

"Perhaps I speak to alleviate some little debt. You asked of the Serra Celina, my wife. Let me speak of her, briefly. The Tyr'agnate waits, and if I am not mistaken, he has not yet made his decision.

"After the death of my kai, my cousin, the Tor'agnate Ser Amando kai di'Manelo, wished me to dispense with Serra Celina; he did not feel her a suitable Serra for a man of my capabilities, for he desired to see me take my place at Court, which my father and my brother had chosen to forsake. We discussed this for some time before I returned to my domis, and the winds that night were almost silent.

"She was waiting for me. Had she been canny, she might have had her son by her side, but she wished to cause him no pain. She was pale, par el'Sol." His face rose a moment in the slowly moving shadow, the contours of nose, of cheek and chin, catching some hint of the light. "Delicate, not in seeming, but in truth. All of her ferocity—and there is little of it—is bent toward the protection of those she has chosen to care for: her serafs, her wives, her children.

"My cousin's words were much with me, that eve. He spoke to me not as distant kin, but as father to son, and in truth, we had more in common than my father and I. He was not overly fond of my father, and he likewise held my brother in lesser regard.

"I saw the wisdom in what he said. She is not a wise woman; she is no longer counted beautiful among the men of this land. She was oft indulged by my brother, and clearly indulged by her father before him.

"I saw the opportunity to remake Clemente in *my* image, and not in the image of my father or my kai. They were not men comfortable with the High Courts; they were seldom seen in Amar, and seldom upon the plateau of the Leonne Court. But should I choose to take my rightful place in the Courts, I might better be served by a woman of cunning and grace.

"I intended to tell her as much, and she saw that in my

posture and my expression. But she did not plead or argue. She bowed her head a moment; her hair was unbound and it formed a curtain, a veil, between us.

"I thought she might speak. I knew if she did, it would be difficult. But she had often spoken on my behalf when my *kai* was annoyed with my pretension and the company I chose to keep. I could not bid her be silent.

"And she asked me only one question."

Marakas nodded, unwilling to break the flow of the Tor's words with his own. Words in the Dominion were rare, especially given during the Lord's time. His silence acknowledged their gift.

"She said, 'Will you grant us the use of your mother's *domis*?' Her hands were in her lap, and they were not still; they were not perfect. She could not school her expression, and I knew it cost her much to say the words. She looked lovely to me then.

"I did not answer the question she asked. My mother had been dead five years, and the *domis* that she occupied had seen no use. It was not small, but it was not the harem in which she had presided during my brother's reign. I asked her, 'What of your son?'

"And she said, 'He knows what waits.' Just that. But it was enough. There was death and mourning in her voice, and a dignity that I had not thought she would possess."

Marakas did not speak. But he, too, bowed his head a moment. The son was not yet of age, but heir to the father, and if Ser Alessandro was to rule without question, he could not then leave that boy alive.

Yet he had. Clearly, he had.

"I do not love her as my brother loved her. But I do not love her less; she was as sister to me while he lived. I bid her rise, I bid her summon her son. I drew the sword of Clemente and spoke its secret name in the harem's heart. It was . . . a test. But she rose, and she left the room while I waited, and when she returned, her son came with her.

"And he seemed to me to be my brother in his youth;

dour and determined to go to his fate shorn of dishonesty. He was then twelve years of age. Not yet a man, but by his quiet action, no longer a boy."

His hand fell to his sword as he spoke.

"Ser Janos kai di'Clemente knelt before me, exposing the back of his neck. 'Do you offer me your life, Ser Janos?' He looked up at me, his eyes Roberto's eyes, his expression . . . mine. But he said, 'For the good of the clan, I offer it willingly.'

" 'Then offer it upon your feet, boy. Offer it with sword in hand.' He had no sword of his own; no named blade. I . . . gave him mine."

Marakas closed his eyes. This was, he thought, a song. Not the song of the Serra Diora, nor a song that might play well in the Courts in which the Lord ruled at his harshest. But there was a beauty in the simple meter of a man's voice, a man's memory, that hallowed the words. That made them. All of his judgment was undone; he repented of it, of his anger in the past, of his accusations. All. He took the gift of beauty offered him, and he treasured it; he would always treasure it.

"He was no fool; he rose at once, clumsy now, the grace of acceptance forgotten. He looked younger than his years, where a moment before he had looked beyond them.

" 'I will have no wife, but the Serra Celina,' I told him. 'And, Na'jano, I will have no kai but you.' "

"He was young, but he was cautious. He was afraid of hope, afraid to return from the state of death that he had managed to achieve, afraid to lose the peace and the determination of that acceptance. Twelve years," he added, shaking his head. "I would not have been such a boy, at twelve. But . . . I would have had Roberto as my guide, and he would not have laid down his life if it meant the loss of mine.

"His mother said nothing. Instead, she watched as her son accepted my sword. His eyes didn't leave mine; I thought he might drop the sword, or at least cut his foot with its edge, for he lowered it too quickly. But he lowered it point first, and the heft of the blade drove it a half inch into the mats. He knelt, knees to either side of it, and he raised his face, and he lost years as the minutes went by.

"'Na'jano.'

"Ser Alessandro.

"'I am not the man your father was. What I make of Clemente will not be what he made of it. You must be certain that you understand what this means, for when I die, the responsibilities of the Torrean will devolve to you. Will you serve me? Will you be the kai Clemente to a kai such as I have become?'"

"He is your kai," Marakas said quietly.

"Yes. No fool, he; he agreed to all that I asked. And his mother agreed to all that I offered."

"If I am not a poor judge of character," Marakas said, after a moment, "what you granted when he was twelve has marked him. You are his kin, certainly, but you are more than that: you have become his . . . hero."

Ser Alessandro laughed. "Such a quaint word, that."

"Yet it was not to the Tyr that he went when we returned from Damar; not by the Tyr's side that he stood; not for the Tyr that he demanded much of his physicians."

"Aye, perhaps. And perhaps I value his foolishness. But I have wandered, par el'Sol. What I offered the Serra Celina, she understood, and she likewise understands that, risk displeasure of my Tyr or no, I will do what I must, will see the Serra Diora—and the sword she bears—to the last of the Leonnes."

Silence, then. Measured. Profound.

"You did not speak of this—burden—to the kai Lamberto."

"No. It is not my burden to speak of." He rose. "My men are severely depleted; I can take but a handful if I do not wish to strip my city of defenses it may need in future. Will you travel with us?"

"Of course. I, too, have a debt to pay."

                    *   *   *

The heart of the harem had been moved to less elegant quarters, the privacy of the wives now enforced not by the presence of opaque walls and sliding doors, but by men, armed and armored, who bore the Tor's crest.

When the seraf came, she was ready.

She had accepted the aid of Serra Celina's wives, and they had bound her hair in gold and jade; they had offered her saris and silks, and had retrieved from her meager belongings the golden bracelets and chains that spoke of her former wealth. These, Ramdan and Ona Teresa had offered her when the Tor Leonne was miles at their back, and the road before them broken by the thousands of men and women who had chosen the prudence of flight beneath the moon's fullest, brightest face.

She wore them, missing the rings that had once adorned her hands. Missing, more, the woman upon whom she had impulsively bestowed them. *Margret,* she thought. *What would you say? What would you do were you now within this harem, this domis?*

Thinking about it brought the first smile of the long day to her face. Margret was a Matriarch, and if Arkosa chose to spend its peaceful months wandering the length and breadth of Averda, a clansman of note dared to offer her no threat when war had already begun its slow march across his Torrean. Would she sit? No. Would she allow the serafs to demean themselves by tending her? Would she accept the touch of their hands, the bowls of water, the application of powders, kohls, perfume?

Each question anchored the smile, made of it a rueful map by which the canny might find their way to her hidden heart.

No, and no and no.

Margret had most reminded her of Ruatha, of the dead and the lost, but in the end, Margret was none of these things: she lived, breathed Voyani fire, spoke like the most impatient and graceless of men.

But she no longer dismissed all clansmen, all clanswomen, as people beneath note or desire.

The Serra Celina herself gave Diora her fans, as fine as any that she had possessed as the Serra Diora en'Leonne; she brought sweet water and the fruit of the trees that lay hidden behind the cultivated wilderness of Sarel, as if she were seraf. Or as if Diora were a visiting clansman of great power and significance.

All this was offered in silence, but the gift that she most prized was the samisen that was placed in her lap.

For when she played, Ona Teresa's shuddering convulsions seemed to abate for a time, and Ramdan, never less watchful, could withdraw into the perfection of a seraf's subservience.

She therefore followed her own inclination, her own desire; she played.

The music brought her many things.

It enforced all silence save her own; it created a distance between her and the rest of the women who gathered here, drifting in ones and twos beyond the periphery of her awareness; it gave her an audience, even if that audience wisely sought shadow, abjuring the harsh sunlight that filtered through the exposed gap of broken screen.

The audience grounded her; she accepted its presence with perfect grace, drawing strength from the fact of it. Hours, days, even months, had been spent in such repose, and when she retreated into music, all war was held in abeyance.

But the harbingers of war did come, finally.

She stood in their shadow, and lifted her head when the notes of the mournful song at last ceased its plaintive echo.

Kallandras of Senniel College bowed. "Serra Diora," he said gravely, kneeling before her as if he did not understand how this gesture unmanned him in the presence of the Clemente wives, "I have brought what you commanded."

He laid the awkward runed box at her feet.

She would have thanked him, but the momentary anxiety

of its presence robbed her of some little grace; she set the samisen to one side, to better carry the Sun Sword, hidden in the last of its havens. A man's sword.

The strange, tall lord stood like white shadow at Kallandras' side, but he did not demean himself by kneeling.

"I . . . thank you, Kallandras," she said quietly, speaking not in the private voice, but in her own, shorn of power.

"Thank Yollana," he replied, with the hint of a smile. "If you dare. She is . . . in a poor mood."

"She is the Matriarch of Havalla," Diora replied, smile bleeding into the edges of her face as she thought of the other Matriarch she now loved. "And she has had some word from her daughters, if I am not mistaken."

"I believe," he replied, equally grave, "that if you *are* mistaken, so too are any of those who serve Clemente who still know how to listen."

"And a lot of those who don't serve Clemente," another voice said. Her Torra was rough, accented by the fields, by labor, by the spurious freedom that was Voyani wandering.

Diora looked past the kneeling form of the Northern bard and met the open gaze of Jewel ATerafin, woman of the North.

By her side, Ariel stood. Her smile was shy, and it was hesitant, but it transformed her waif's face.

"Ariel," Jewel said quietly, and the girl slid to ground, her legs forming lap before the Serra Diora, her posture exposing the sharp lines of shoulder blades, the slender nub of uncounted ribs.

"She thinks you have a beautiful voice," the Northerner continued, blithely unaware of the embarrassment her words caused the child.

Serra Diora smiled gracefully, although she lifted her fan and let it hover just beneath the curve of her lips. "She is gracious," she said.

Jewel ATerafin turned a look upon the child's back, an I Told You So that the child herself failed to witness. She was no court seraf, this child; all of her grace lay in her youth, and the obeisance that came so naturally to her was tinged by the simplicity of awe.

"Please accept our apologies," Jewel continued quietly. "But Yollana thought it best that we avoid all presence of the Tyr'agnate. He is rumored to . . . hate . . . things Northern."

"It is no mere rumor," Diora said softly. "But perhaps the legend of his hatred is much exaggerated."

Jewel raised a dark brow, and then shunted unruly curls from the sides of her face. Hair such as that, Diora thought, would never be given free reign within any domis of note; it would be attacked with irons and heat, brought into a semblance of straightness; no Serra allowed herself to be so publicly unkempt.

But it suited the woman. She wore vest, shirt, pants; she dressed as if she were already claimed by the *Voyanne* that her ancestors must have deserted.

"There is no wiser woman than Yollana of the Havalla Voyani," Diora said gravely, "and her advice—when offered—is to be treasured."

"Or feared," Jewel ATerafin said, the gravity of her words displacing the oddity of her appearance. "And heeded."

Diora smiled again, this time bringing the fan up to the periphery of vision. "And heeded," she said, agreeable as only a Serra might be.

"But we're here."

Again she smiled. Jewel ATerafin was not like Margret of the Arkosa Voyani; not for her the barely hidden depth of anger, the sudden well of fear. The shadow she cast in the harsh light was not one thing, but three: It spoke of herself, the beast she could command in silence, and the man who served her.

Only the man was present, and he had been attired in the finery of Court serafs.

"We're here," Jewel said again. "The kai Lamberto will

come, soon, and when he does, we will either fight or depart."

No question, now, of which was preferable. The Northern hand, lined and darkened by too much exposure to sunlight, rested lightly against the pommel of an obvious dagger.

"Are you ready?" Jewel said, surprising in her frankness.

Diora nodded. With care, she lifted the only burden of import. "I am ready."

"Good. Because he has just entered the room."

The warning was unnecessary; the women of Clemente chose to abase themselves as he passed, and she could see the fact of that passage in the supine bend of exposed back, exposed neck, the fall of black hair.

He came with Tyran; two men that Diora had not yet seen. They strode an arm's length from his back, their step in time with his, their hands by their sides.

Kallandras did not rise; Celleriant did not kneel.

And Jewel ATerafin hesitated a moment before she chose to join the bard, and not the lord who served her.

"Serra Diora," he said, his eyes passing above the Northerners as if they were beneath notice—or contempt.

"Tyr'agnate." Her own bow served to protect what she now carried.

"If you can be ready, we leave upon the morrow."

She was to be accorded the trappings of the rank assassination had taken from her: a palanquin was brought, and it was carried by Lambertan Tyran. She saw it clearly, and with surprise; it seemed a foreign thing, an enclosure, much like a gilded cage.

If Ser Mareo kai di'Lamberto noticed her hesitation, he did not show it; he waited, his hand the hand that drew beaded curtain to one side. An honor.

He waited thus, and she kept him waiting for as long as it took to offer her thanks to the Serra Celina. But the Serra Celina was unnerved by the presence of the Tyr, aware of the shortcomings of her court and her serafs. She bowed to the Serra Diora, as she had not done in the harem, and then, rising slowly, retrieved something from the serafs who waited in her shadow.

This she pressed into Diora's open hands.

A samisen.

A good one, wood well oiled, top covered in fine wooden inlay and a hint of gold. Diora was seldom speechless, but words deserted her as her fingers clutched the underside of the instrument. She lifted her face, exposing it to the Serra Celina.

The Serra blushed. "It isn't much," she said softly, so softly her words might not carry to the men who waited. "But it—"

"It is a very fine instrument," Diora said, willing herself to return it. But her will was weak; her hands tight. "Too fine an instrument for traveling. I am honored, Serra Celina, but I—"

"You play it far better than I," the clanswoman said, with warmth. "And having heard it in your hands, I don't think I could bear to listen to myself—or my wives—coax awkward tunes from its strings again."

Diara opened her lips to speak, attempting to choose the right words.

But the Serra shook her head. "I want you to have it," she said, firmly now. "It is my gift. To you. To the Serra—to the woman who walks at the side of the Matriarch of Havalla. We are in your debt, Serra Diora, even if it is a debt that we cannot acknowledge and can never repay. This is a token, and only that. But if—" She shook her head.

"If?" Although she had been impatient, at times, with the volume of the words Celina chose to speak, she surprised herself; she desired to hear what the Serra had not yet said.

"If the Lady blesses you, if the war you *must* fight is won, it would honor us all to hear you play it upon the plateau."

"I am not a warrior, Serra Celina, to be called upon to fight."

"No more was the Serra—was your aunt." She caught the strands of hair wind had pulled from combs, her fingers shaking as the words left her in a rush. "I have taken the liberty of sending my own palanquin with my husband's men. It will carry two, for I travel at times with a seraf for company."

"Then that is all the payment any debt requires. I cannot take this."

"She listens for your voice, Serra Diora."

Diora frowned, but the expression was lost to the pleated fold of fan.

"If you will not take it for your own sake, take it for hers, and if you will not incur debt on her behalf, please, take it for mine. I ask it, who have no right to ask anything further of you. I know what you bear."

She had no strength left to argue, and no desire at all. But the bow she offered the Serra Celina was far too deep, and far too obeisant, and when she rose, she clutched the samisen to her in a way that she had never once held the Sun Sword.

"Please, keep him safe," the Serra Celina whispered.

Diora nodded. She did not offer politeness; she did not deny the ability to do what men could not do. And the Serra Celina understood that the silence was her vow.

"The Serra Teresa is already within my palanquin," the Serra Celina said quietly. "She cannot walk; nor can she be called upon to ride. If you accept what Lamberto offers," and she nodded to the palanquin, her eyes shunning the sight of the man who still waited, beaded curtains in his mailed fist, "I would be honored if you would allow the Matriarch passage at the side of the Serra."

"It is my honor," the Serra Diora replied, thinking that Ramdan would have been the kinder companion. "And my debt."

Diora rose, and turned toward the Lambertan palanquin.

But as she made her way toward it, someone brushed past her in haste, his feet heavy against stone.

Ser Janos kai di'Clemente.

He came to stand before the Tyr'agnate, and he bowed, his hand upon the hilt of his sword. "Tyr'agnate," he said, youth in the earnest folds of his expression, "I beg leave to travel with your men."

"It is not of me that you must ask permission," Ser Mareo kai di'Lamberto replied, but not unkindly.

The boy who was not yet man, but no longer child, frowned. Serra Diora could see his expression clearly as she approached it, and she smiled in spite of herself. Ah, she had lost caution in the desert, and perhaps it had died there; things moved her now in a way that they had not done since the night of fires and the death of her wives.

"I have asked my uncle," he said quietly.

"He is your lord," the Tyr'agnate replied gravely. "Are you so eager to see battle?"

"My Tor is injured." Ser Janos straightened the line of his shoulders; they were gaunt, but time would fill them. If he survived.

"He is not unmanned; he is capable of riding, and of wielding sword."

"And most of his Toran perished in Damar."

The Tyr's expression became grave, but his words held the faintest hint of amusement if one knew how to listen. The boy did not; the Serra did.

"You are not, and will never be, Toran, Ser Janos."

"But I am kai Clemente."

"You are."

"And he will not give me permission to join you."

"Ser Janos, have you noticed my kai among the cerdan?"

The boy's frown was swift, and it lingered. "No, Tyr'agnate."

"Good. He is not present because I refused his request." Shoulders fell.

"I need him in Amar."

"But there is no war in Amar."

"There is no war *yet,*" the Tyr'agnate replied gravely, and the Serra Diora heard what the young kai could not: the edge of untruth. It was not, quite, lie. But close enough to surprise her; he was Lambertan.

But even so, unexpectedly gentle. "But in time, it may be that all of our cities will be besieged and embattled. I will not leave my wives and my daughters at the mercy of our enemies; my kai has the force of my law behind his words.

"There is no man that Ser Alessandro trusts with such a responsibility," he continued, "save you, yourself. We are warriors, yes, but we are something else: leaders. We cannot follow the dictates of desire; we cannot simply cleave to the warrior's path, even if that desire is born of loyalty. You have your duty here."

The boy looked as if he would argue.

Serra Diora watched them both as the curtains waited her passage. She had often seen Ser Mareo kai di'Lamberto at a distance; to see him so close was a revelation.

He looked much like Fredero kai el'Sol.

"You should be proud of the trust he places in you," Ser Mareo said, placing an arm upon the boy's shoulder. The difference in the hand that rested upon armor and the face that rested an inch above it told a long tale, and an endless one. "I am. And if we fall in battle, if our enemy succeeds in his goal, I will rest easier knowing that Sarel is in your care."

Gently defeated, Ser Janos hung his head. His beard was not yet a man's; it was too thin for that. But his resolve, untested, was all that she needed to know of Ser Alessandro kai di'Clemente.

Ser Janos knelt at the Tyr'agnate's feet, his knees giving slowly. She saw him swallow his bitter disappointment; he took no comfort in the praise offered him. But he lifted his sword, slowly and awkwardly, from the sheath that bore it, and in silence, he offered it to the Tyr'agnate.

The Tyr accepted the blade, and in turn, offered what was

rarely offered: his blood. The edge of the blade glinted like rubies, like the emblem of the Sword of Knowledge, but although Ser Mareo was no Widan, Diora saw the subtlety of the magic he worked.

"You have not made the trek to Amar, Ser Janaos. When we return, I will call you to Court."

"Tyr'agnate." Gravity remained.

Diora chose that moment to sequester herself in the palanquin.

In the presence of any other Tyr, the boy had just committed a sin against his Tor; no man—no wise man—went above the head of his clan in such a fashion.

But Ser Mareo kai di'Lamberto had chosen to witness what was offered from the heart with heart; he did not call upon the Tor'agar to bear witness to his kai's obvious disobedience.

She liked him, then, and it surprised her.

But she had liked the kai el'Sol as well, and it was his death—and only his death—that had given her the gift she required in order to win the battle that she had chosen.

Avandar Gallais chose to accept the kai Clemente's offer of horse; it was the first time that Jewel had seen him so mounted. The destrier was restive beneath foreign knees, and the robes that Avandar had chosen were not designed to part with ease for such a passage; they were seraf's robes, and serafs did not ride.

But Jewel did; the Winter King bore her aloft, his tines gleaming like new growth in the dawn sky. Purple had given way to pink, and pink to the endless blue of the Lord's regard.

Jewel, in Voyani dress, gripped the stag's antlers. Her hands were shaking.

Jewel?

She shook her head.

ATerafin?

But although she could ignore the question in the Winter

King's secret voice, she could not—quite—ignore Avandar's.

The war, she told him softly. Just that.

You fear it.

Of course I fear it. I'm not an idiot.

His chuckle was not so hidden as his words, and she swung to face him; his horse gave him more of an advantage of height than he already possessed.

After a moment, she said, *I had a dream.*

The laughter fled his face, as anything sane would.

What dream. ATerafin?

You didn't see it?

His frown was *his* frown. In the days after Damar, he had become his old self; there were now whole moments when she could pretend that she was traveling with a merchant caravan, her domicis by her side, her duties to Terafin, and only Terafin.

He didn't condescend to dignify the question with an answer, although his impatience served in its stead.

I've had it before, she said again, but quietly.

When?

In Averalaan. I saw—

Kiriel.

She closed her eyes. She could do that; the Winter King had never let her fall.

And this?

She's on the field, Jewel told him, as if they were in the kitchen in their wing of the Terafin Manse. *And she sits astride a . . . demon. She carries a banner, but it's long and dark; if it has a standard. I can't see it. I'm not sure I want to.*

The demons follow her, Avandar. She looks so unlike the Kiriel I left, I shouldn't recognize her. I wouldn't, if it weren't my *dream. But I know her sword. And I know the man who walks by her side.*

Man?

Demon, she said softly. *He almost killed Angel.*

828   *Michelle West*

ATerafin. Pause. *Jewel. He almost killed you.*

*I try to call her. To call her back. She laughs.
She . . . laughs at me, Avandar.*

Is this a true dream?

I . . . don't know.

His brow rose, changing the line of his face. She loved
that expression.

*But it doesn't matter, does it? Because she's riding at the
head of Allasakar's army. And if she does, we don't have a
hope in Hells of winning.*

Where is she now, Jewel?

Questions. As her eyes were already closed, she couldn't
retreat beneath lids.

He cursed her gift. Or rather, he cursed her inability to direct it, to contain it, to manipulate it as if it were dagger or
sword.

As if it were a talent, he corrected her.

I won't learn that, she snapped, her lips moving noise-
lessly.

It appears that you will not, he replied, his own face
composed and dignified in its stillness. *What are you afraid
of?*

If I learn, she told him, *knowing* the truth was in the
words she was about to say, but unable to hold them back,
people will die.

If you don't, ATerafin, can you say that people won't?

She had no answer to give him.

But she looked to the North and the East, and after a moment, she said, *Kiriel is in the North, at the side of the kai
Leonne.*

But it was not of Kiriel that she thought, although her
thoughts drifted to the North.

Her lips moved slowly around silent syllables; she did
not give them the play of air or breath.

But she wondered what they were doing. Teller. Finch.
Jester. Angel. Carver. Arran.

Tanya Huff

Victory Nelson, Investigator:
Otherworldly Crimes a Specialty

"Smashing entertainment for a wide audience"
—*Romantic Times*

"One series that deserves to continue"
—*Science Fiction Chronicle*

BLOOD PRICE
0-88677-471-3

BLOOD TRAIL
0-88677-502-7

BLOOD LINES
0-88677-530-2

BLOOD PACT
0-88677-582-5

To Order Call: 1-800-788-6262

DAW 20

Tanya Huff

The Finest in Fantasy

SING THE FOUR QUARTERS   0-88677-628-7
FIFTH QUARTER   0-88677-651-1
NO QUARTER   0-88677-698-8
THE QUARTERED SEA   0-88677-839-5

The Keeper's Chronicles
SUMMON THE KEEPER   0-88677-784-4
THE SECOND SUMMONING   0-88677-975-8

Omnibus Editions:
WIZARD OF THE GROVE   0-88677-819-0
(Child of the Grove & The Last Wizard)

OF DARKNESS, LIGHT & FIRE   0-7564-0038-4
(Gate of Darkness, Circle of Light & The Fire's Stone)

To Order Call: 1-800-788-6262

DAW21

C.S. Friedman

The Coldfire Trilogy

"A feast for those who like their fantasies dark, and as emotionally heady as a rich red wine." —*Locus*

Centuries after being stranded on the planet Erna, humans have achieved an uneasy stalemate with the fae, a terrifying natural force with the power to prey upon people's minds. Damien Vryce, the warrior priest, and Gerald Tarrant, the undead sorcerer must join together in an uneasy alliance confront a power that threatens the very essence of the human spirit, in a battle which could cost them not only their lives, but the soul of all mankind.

BLACK SUN RISING	0-88677-527-2
WHEN TRUE NIGHT FALLS	0-88677-615-5
CROWN OF SHADOWS	0-88677-717-8

To Order Call: 1-800-788-6262

DAW 18